PRAISE FOR PAT CONROY'S THE PRINCE OF TIDES

'This is the best novel I've read in two years . . .'
Today

'You wish it would never end'
Vanity Fair

'A moving novel which manages to shock you,
make you cry and laugh'
Daily Mail

'As beautifully descriptive and absorbing
as all his past successes'
Options

'Irresistible'
Independent

'A truly epic story . . . you'll wish there
were another four or five chapters!'
Prima

'Pat Conroy draws all the threads of this superbly
balanced story together'
Sunday Tribune, Ireland

'*The Prince of Tides* is an exquisite book'
Michael Douglas

Pat Conroy

The Prince
of Tides

BANTAM BOOKS
TORONTO • NEW YORK • LONDON • SYDNEY • AUCKLAND

I owe many people for their generosity and support during the writing of this book. My stepfather, Captain John Egan, USN, treated my family and me with great love during the time our mother was dying of leukemia. Turner and Mary Ball let me have the use of their mountain home for long stretches of time during the writing of this book. James Landon and Al Campbell also gave me the key to their mountain home in the Highlands, North Carolina. Judge Alex Sanders, the greatest of South Carolinians, told me many of the stories included in this book as we sat in Joe and Emily Cumming's house at Tate Mountain. Julia Bridges typed the book with gusto. Nan Talese is a splendid editor and a woman of uncommon beauty. And Sara Flynn was superb. Julian Bach is my literary agent and one of the finest men I've ever met. Houghton Mifflin, my publishing company, is family. Barbara Conroy has been a fine lawyer and an exemplary mother to our children. Cliff Graubart of the Old New York Book Shop has been wonderful. Derril Randel has been extraordinarily brave. Thanks also to Dent Acree, Peggy Houghton, and Judge William Sherrill. I've had a lucky life with friendships. I thank all my friends in Atlanta, the ones in Rome, Italy, and all those in between. A hug for you now and I'll get to your names next time out.

THE PRINCE OF TIDES
A BANTAM BOOK 0 553 40484 9

Originally published in Great Britain by Bantam Press, a division of Transworld Publishers Ltd.

PRINTING HISTORY
Bantam Press edition published 1987
Bantam edition published 1987
Bantam edition reprinted 1988 (twice)
Bantam edition reissued 1992

Bantam Books are published by Transworld Publishers Ltd., 61–63 Uxbridge Road, Ealing, London W5 5SA, in Australia by Transworld Publishers (Australia) Pty. Ltd., 15–23 Helles Avenue, Moorebank, NSW 2170, and in New Zealand by Transworld Publishers (N.Z.) Ltd., Cnr. Moselle and Waipareira Avenues, Henderson, Auckland.

Printed and bound in Great Britain by Cox & Wyman Ltd., Reading, Berks.

This book is dedicated with love and gratitude:
to my wife, Lenore Gurewitz Conroy,
who hung the moon;
to my children, Jessica, Melissa,
Megan, and Susannah, Conroys all;
to Gregory and Emily Fleischer;
to my brothers and sisters,
Carol, Michael, Kathleen, James,
Timothy, and Thomas;
to my father,
Colonel Donald Conroy, USMC (Ret.),
still great, still Santini;
and to the memory of my mother, Peg,
the extraordinary woman who built
and inspired this house.

PROLOGUE

My wound is geography. It is also my anchorage, my port of call.

I grew up slowly beside the tides and marshes of Colleton; my arms were tawny and strong from working long days on the shrimp boat in the blazing South Carolina heat. Because I was a Wingo, I worked as soon as I could walk; I could pick a blue crab clean when I was five. I had killed my first deer by the age of seven, and at nine was regularly putting meat on my family's table. I was born and raised on a Carolina sea island and I carried the sunshine of the low-country, inked in dark gold, on my back and shoulders. As a boy I was happy above the channels, navigating a small boat between the sandbars with their quiet nation of oysters exposed on the brown flats at the low watermark. I knew every shrimper by name, and they knew me and sounded their horns when they passed me fishing in the river.

When I was ten I killed a bald eagle for pleasure, for the singularity of the act, despite the divine, exhilarating beauty of its solitary flight over schools of whiting. It was the only thing I had ever killed that I had never seen before. After my father beat me for breaking the law and for killing the last eagle in Colleton County, he made me build a fire, dress the bird, and eat its flesh as tears rolled down my face. Then he turned me in to Sheriff Benson, who locked me in a cell for over an hour. My father took the feathers and made a crude Indian headdress for me to wear to school. He believed in the expiation of sin. I wore the headdress for weeks, until it began to disintegrate feather by feather.

Those feathers trailed me in the hallways of the school as though I were a molting, discredited angel.

"Never kill anything that's rare," my father had said.

"I'm lucky I didn't kill an elephant," I replied.

"You'd have had a mighty square meal if you had," he answered.

My father did not permit crimes against the land. Though I have hunted again, all eagles are safe from me.

It was my mother who taught me the southern way of the spirit in its most delicate and intimate forms. My mother believed in the dreams of flowers and animals. Before we went to bed at night as small children, she would reveal to us in her storytelling voice that salmon dreamed of mountain passes and the brown faces of grizzlies hovering over clear rapids. Copperheads, she would say, dreamed of placing their fangs in the shinbones of hunters. Ospreys slept with their feathered, plummeting dreamselves screaming through deep, slow-motion dives toward herring. There were the brute wings of owls in the nightmares of ermine, the downwind approach of timber wolves in the night stillness of elk.

But we never knew about her dreams, for my mother kept us strangers to her own interior life. We knew that bees dreamed of roses, that roses dreamed of the pale hands of florists, and that spiders dreamed of luna moths adhered to silver webs. As her children, we were the trustees of her dazzling evensongs of the imagination, but we did not know that mothers dreamed.

Each day she would take us into the forest or garden and invent a name for any animal or flower we passed. A monarch butterfly became an "orchid-kissing blacklegs"; a field of daffodils in April turned into a "dance of the butter ladies bonneted." With her attentiveness my mother could turn a walk around the island into a voyage of purest discovery. Her eyes were our keys to the palace of wildness.

My family lived in splendid isolation on Melrose Island in a small white house my grandfather had helped build. The house faced the inland waterway, and the town of Colleton could be seen down the river, its white mansions set like chess pieces above the marsh. Melrose Island was a lozenge-shaped piece of land of twelve hundred acres surrounded on four sides by salt rivers and creeks. The island country where I grew up was a fertile, semitropical archipelago that gradually softened up the ocean for the grand surprise of the continent that followed. Melrose was only one of sixty sea islands in Colleton County. At the eastern edge of the county lay six barrier islands shaped by their daily encounters with the Atlantic. The other sea islands, like Melrose, enscarved by vast expanses of marshland, were the green sanctuaries where brown and white shrimp came to spawn in their given seasons. When they came, my father and other men like him were waiting in their fine and lovely boats.

When I was eight I helped my father build the small wooden bridge that linked our lives to a narrow causeway through the marsh that connected to the much larger St. Anne's Island, which itself was linked to the town of Colleton by a long steel drawbridge across the river. It took five minutes for my father to drive his pickup truck from our house to the wooden bridge; it took him another ten to drive into the town of Colleton.

Before we built the bridge in 1953, my mother would take us to school in Colleton by boat. No matter how bad the weather, she would steer us across the river each morning and be waiting for us at the public dock each afternoon. It would always be a faster trip to Colleton by Boston Whaler than it would ever be by truck. Those years of taking us to school by water turned my mother into one of the finest pilots of small craft I have ever seen, but she rarely entered the boat once the bridge was built. The bridge only connected us with our town; it connected my mother with the world beyond Melrose Island, so inconceivably rich with promise.

Melrose was the one notable possession of my father's family, a passionate but unlucky clan whose decline after the Civil War was quick, certain, and probably inevitable. My great-great-grandfather, Winston Shadrach Wingo, had commanded a battery under Beauregard that fired on Fort Sumter. He died a pauper in the Confederate Soldiers' Home in Charleston and refused to speak to a Yankee, male or female, until the day he died. He had won Melrose Island in a horseshoe game near the end of his life, and that island, uncleared and malarial, passed down through three generations of declining Wingos until it came to my father by default. My grandfather had tired of owning it and my father was the only Wingo willing to pay the state and federal taxes to keep it out of the government's hands. But that horseshoe game would assume celebrated dimensions in our family history and we would always honor Winston Shadrach Wingo as our family's first athlete of note.

I do not know, however, when my mother and father began their long, dispiriting war against each other. Most of their skirmishes were like games of ringolevio, with the souls of their children serving as the ruined captured flags in their campaigns of attrition. Neither considered the potential damage when struggling over something as fragile and unformed as a child's life. I still believe that they both loved us deeply, but, as with many parents, their love proved to be the most lethal thing about them. They were remarkable in so many ways that the gifts they bestowed almost equaled the havoc they so thoughtlessly wreaked.

I was the son of a beautiful, word-struck mother and I longed for her touch many years after she felt no obligation to touch me. But I will praise her for the rest of my life for teaching me to seek out the beauty of nature in all its shapes and fabulous designs. It was my mother who taught me to love the lanterns of night fishermen in the starry darkness and the flights of brown pelicans skimming the curling breakers at dawn. It was she who made me take notice of the perfect coinage of sand dollars, the shapes of flounders inlaid in sand like the silhouettes of ladies in cameos, the foundered wreck near the Colleton Bridge that pulsed with the commerce of otters. She saw the world through a dazzling prism of authentic imagination. Lila Wingo would take the raw material of a daughter and shape her into a poet and a psychotic. With her sons she was gentler, and the results took longer to tally. She preserved for me the multiform appearances of my life as a child, the portraitures and still lifes visible through the blooming window of time. She reigned as the queen of exquisite imagery in the eye of a worshipful son, yet I cannot forgive her for not telling me about the dream that sustained her during my childhood, the one that would cause the ruin of my family and the death of one of us.

* * *

The child of a beautiful woman, I was also a shrimper's son in love with the shape of boats. I grew up a river boy with the smell of the great salt marsh predominant in sleep. In the summers, my brother, my sister, and I worked as apprentice strikers on my father's shrimp boat. Nothing pleased me more than the sight of the shrimping fleet moving out before sunrise to rendezvous with the teeming shoals of shrimp that made their swift dashes through the moon-sweetened tides at first light. My father drank his coffee black as he stood at the wheel of the boat and listened to the heavily accented voices of the other shrimp boat captains keeping each other company. His clothes smelled like shrimp and there was nothing that water or soap or my mother's hands could do to change that. When he worked hard, his smell would change, the sweat cutting into the odor of fish and becoming something different, something wonderful. Standing beside him as a small boy, I would press my nose against my father's shirt and he would smell like some rich, warm acre. If Henry Wingo had not been a violent man, I think he would have made a splendid father.

One bright summer night, when we were very small and the humid air hung like moss over the lowcountry, my sister and brother and I could not sleep. Our mother took us out of the house, Savannah and I with summer colds and Luke with a heat rash, and walked all of us down to the river and out onto the dock.

"I have a surprise for my darlings," our mother said as we watched a porpoise move toward the Atlantic through the still, metallic waters. We sat at the end of the floating dock and stretched our legs, trying to touch the water with our bare feet.

"There's something I want you to see. Something that will help you sleep. Look over there, children," she said, pointing out toward the horizon to the east.

It was growing dark on this long southern evening and suddenly, at the exact point her finger had indicated, the moon lifted a forehead of stunning gold above the horizon, lifted straight out of filigreed, light-intoxicated clouds that lay on the skyline in attendant veils. Behind us, the sun was setting in a simultaneous congruent withdrawal and the river turned to flame in a quiet duel of gold. . . . The new gold of moon astonishing and ascendant, the depleted gold of sunset extinguishing itself in the long westward slide, it was the old dance of days in the Carolina marshes, the breathtaking death of days before the eyes of children, until the sun vanished, its final signature a ribbon of bullion strung across the tops of water oaks. The moon then rose quickly, rose like a bird from the water, from the trees, from the islands, and climbed straight up—gold, then yellow, then pale yellow, pale silver, silver-bright, then something miraculous, immaculate, and beyond silver, a color native only to southern nights.

We children sat transfixed before that moon our mother had called forth from the waters. When the moon had reached its deepest silver, my sister, Savannah, though only three, cried aloud to our mother, to Luke and me, to the river and the moon, "Oh, Mama, do it again!" And I had my earliest memory.

We spent our formative years marveling at the lovely woman who recited the dreams of egrets and herons, who could summon moons, banish suns to the west, then recall a brand-new sun the following morning from far beyond the breakers of the Atlantic. Science was of no interest to Lila Wingo, but nature was a passion.

To describe our growing up in the lowcountry of South Carolina, I would have to take you to the marsh on a spring day, flush the great blue heron from its silent occupation, scatter marsh hens as we sink to our knees in mud, open you an oyster with a pocketknife and feed it to you from the shell and say, "There. That taste. That's the taste of my childhood." I would say, "Breathe deeply," and you would breathe and remember that smell for the rest of your life, the bold, fecund aroma of the tidal marsh, exquisite and sensual, the smell of the South in heat, a smell like new milk, semen, and spilled wine, all perfumed with seawater. My soul grazes like a lamb on the beauty of indrawn tides.

I am a patriot of a singular geography on the planet; I speak of my country religiously; I am proud of its landscape. I walk through the traffic of cities cautiously, always nimble and on the alert, because my heart belongs in the marshlands. The boy in me still carries the memories of those days when I lifted crab pots out of the Colleton River before dawn, when I was shaped by life on the river, part child, part sacristan of tides.

Once while sunning ourselves on a deserted beach near Colleton, Savannah shouted for Luke and me to look out toward the sea. She was screaming and pointing toward a school of pilot whales that had risen out of the sea in a disoriented pack; they surged around us, past us, until forty whales, dark and glistening like cordovan, lay stranded and doomed on the shore.

For hours we walked from back to back of the dying mammals, speaking out to them in the cries of children, urging them to try to return to the sea. We were so small and they were so beautiful. From far off, they looked like the black shoes of giants. We whispered to them, cleared sand from their blowholes, splashed them with seawater, and exhorted them to survive for our sake. They had come from the sea mysteriously, gloriously, and we three children spoke to them, mammals to mammals, in the stunned, grieving canticles of children unfamiliar with willful death. We stayed with them all that day, tried to move them back to the water by pulling at their great fins, until exhaustion and silence crept in with the dark. We stayed with them as they began to die one by one. We stroked their great heads and prayed as the souls of whales lifted out of the great black bodies and moved like frigates through the night and out to sea where they dove toward the light of the world.

Later when we spoke of our childhood, it seemed part elegy, part nightmare. When my sister wrote the books that made her famous and journalists asked what her childhood was like, she would lean back, brush her hair out of her eyes, grow serious, and say, "When I was a child, my brothers and I walked on the backs of dolphins and whales." There were no dolphins, of course, but there were to my sister. That is how she chose to remember it, how she chose to celebrate it, how she chose to put it down.

But there is no magic to nightmares. It has always been difficult for me to face the truth about my childhood because it requires a commitment to explore the lineaments and features of a history I would prefer to forget. For years I did not have to face the demonology of my youth; I made a simple choice not to and found solace in the gentle palmistry of forgetfulness, a refuge in the cold, lordly glooms of the unconscious. But I was drawn back to the history of my family and the failures of my own adult life by a single telephone call.

I wish I had no history to report. I've pretended for so long that my childhood did not happen. I had to keep it tight, up near the chest. I could not let it out. I followed the redoubtable example of my mother. It's an act of will to have a memory or not, and I chose not to have one. Because I needed to love my mother and father in all their flawed, outrageous humanity, I could not afford to address them directly about the felonies committed against all of us. I could not hold them accountable or indict them for crimes they could not help. They, too, had a history—one that I remembered with both tenderness and pain, one that made me forgive their transgressions against their own children. In families there are no crimes beyond forgiveness.

In a mental hospital in New York I visited Savannah after her second suicide attempt. I leaned down to kiss her on both cheeks, European style. Then, staring into her exhausted eyes, I asked her the series of questions I always asked whenever we met after a long separation.

"What was your family life like, Savannah?" I asked, pretending I was conducting an interview.

"Hiroshima," she whispered.

"And what has life been like since you left the warm, abiding bosom of your nurturing, close-knit family?"

"Nagasaki," she said, a bitter smile on her face.

"You're a poet, Savannah," I said, watching her. "Compare your family to a ship."

"The *Titanic*."

"Name the poem, Savannah, you wrote in honor of your family."

" 'The History of Auschwitz.' " And we both laughed.

"Now, here's the important question," I said, leaning down and whispering softly in her ear. "Whom do you love more than anyone in the world?"

Savannah's head lifted up from the pillow and her blue eyes blazed with conviction as she said between cracked, pale lips, "I love my brother, Tom Wingo. My twin. And whom does my brother love more than anyone else in the world?"

I said, holding her hand, "I love Tom the best too."

"Don't answer wrong again, wise-ass," she said weakly.

I looked into her eyes and held her head with my hands, and with my voice breaking and tears rolling down my cheeks, I almost broke apart as I gasped, "I love my sister, the great Savannah Wingo from Colleton, South Carolina."

"Hold me tight, Tom. Hold me tight."

Such were the passwords of our lives.

This has not been an easy century to endure. I entered the scene in the middle of a world war at the fearful dawning of the atomic age. I grew up in South Carolina, a white southern male, well trained and gifted in my hatred of blacks when the civil rights movement caught me outside and undefended along the barricades and proved me to be both wicked and wrong. But I was a thinking boy, a feeling one, sensitive to injustice, and I worked hard to change myself and to play a small, insignificant part in that movement—and soon I was feeling superabundantly proud of myself. Then I found myself marching in an all-white, all-male ROTC program in college and was spit on by peace demonstrators who were offended by my uniform. Eventually I would become one of those demonstrators, but I never spit on anyone who disagreed with me. I thought I would enter my thirties quietly, a contemplative man, a man whose philosophy was humane and unassailable, when the women's liberation movement bushwhacked me on the avenues and I found myself on the other side of the barricades once again. I seem to embody everything that is wrong with the twentieth century.

It was my sister who forced me to confront my century and who finally freed me to face up to the reality of those days beside the river. I had lived life in the shallows for too long and she led me gently toward the deeper waters where all the bones, wreckage, and black hulks awaited my hesitant inspection.

The truth is this: Things happened to my family, extraordinary things. I know families who live out their entire destinies without a single thing of interest happening to them. I have always envied those families. The Wingos were a family that fate tested a thousand times and left defenseless, humiliated, and dishonored. But my family also carried some strengths into the fray, and these strengths let almost all of us survive the descent of the Furies. Unless you believe Savannah; it is her claim that no Wingo survived.

I will tell you my story.

Nothing is missing.

I promise you.

1

It was five o'clock in the afternoon Eastern Standard Time when the telephone rang in my house on Sullivans Island, South Carolina. My wife, Sallie, and I had just sat down for a drink on the porch overlooking Charleston Harbor and the Atlantic. Sallie went in to answer the telephone and I shouted, "Whoever it is, I'm not here."

"It's your mother," Sallie said, returning from the phone.

"Tell her I'm dead," I pleaded. "Please tell her I died last week and you've been too busy to call."

"Please speak to her. She says it's urgent."

"She always says it's urgent. It's never urgent when she says it's urgent."

"I think it's urgent this time. She's crying."

"When Mom cries, it's normal. I can't remember a day when she hasn't been crying."

"She's waiting, Tom."

As I rose to go to the phone, my wife said, "Be nice, Tom. You're never very nice when you talk to your mother."

"I hate my mother, Sallie," I explained. "Why do you try to kill the small pleasures I have in my life?"

"Just listen to Sallie and be very nice."

"If she says she wants to come over tonight, I'm going to divorce you, Sallie. Nothing personal, but it's you who's making me answer the phone."

"Hello, Mother dear," I said cheerfully into the receiver, knowing that my insincere bravado never fooled my mother.

"I've got some very bad news, Tom," my mother said.

"Since when did our family produce anything else, Mom?"

"This is very bad news. Tragic news."

"I can't wait to hear it."

11

"I don't want to tell you on the phone. May I come over?"

"If you want to."

"I want to only if you want me to come."

"You said you wanted to come. I didn't say I wanted you to come."

"Why do you want to hurt me at a time like this?"

"Mom, I don't know what kind of a time it is. You haven't told me what's wrong. I don't want to hurt you. Come on over and we can bare our fangs at each other for a little while."

I hung up the phone and screamed out at the top of my lungs, "Divorce!"

Waiting for my mother, I watched as my three daughters gathered shells on the beach in front of the house. They were ten, nine, and seven, two brown-haired girls divided by one blonde, and their ages and size and beauty always startled me; I could measure my own diminishment with their sunny ripening. You could believe in the birth of goddesses by watching the wind catch their hair and their small brown hands make sweet simultaneous gestures to brush the hair out of their eyes as their laughter broke with the surf. Jennifer called to the other two as she lifted a conch shell up to the light. I stood and walked over to the railing where I saw a neighbor who had stopped to talk to the girls.

"Mr. Brighton," I called, "could you make sure the girls are not smoking dope on the beach again?"

The girls looked up and, waving goodbye to Mr. Brighton, ran through the dunes and sea oats up to the house. They deposited their collection of shells on the table where my drink sat.

"Dad," Jennifer, the oldest, said, "you're always embarrassing us in front of people."

"We found a conch, Dad," Chandler, the youngest, squealed. "He's alive."

"It is alive," I said, turning the shell over. "We can have it for dinner tonight."

"Oh, gross, Dad," Lucy said. "Great meal. Conch."

"No," the smallest girl said. "I'll take it back to the beach and put it in the water. Think how scared that conch is hearing you say you want to eat him."

"Oh, Chandler," said Jennifer. "That's so ridiculous. Conchs don't speak English."

"How do you know, Jennifer?" Lucy challenged. "You don't know everything. You're not the queen of the whole world."

"Yeah," I agreed. "You're not the queen of the whole world."

"I wish I had two brothers," Jennifer said.

"And we wish we had an older brother," Lucy answered in the lovely fury of the blonde.

"Are you going to kill that ugly ol' conch, Dad?" Jennifer asked.

"Chandler will be mad."

"No, I'll take it back down to the beach. I can't take it when Chandler calls me a murderer. Everyone into Daddy's lap."

The three girls halfheartedly arranged their lovely, perfectly shaped behinds on my thighs and knees and I kissed each one of them on the throat and the nape of the neck.

"This is the last year we're going to be able to do this, girls. You're getting huge."

"Huge? I'm certainly not getting *huge*, Dad," Jennifer corrected.

"Call me Daddy."

"Only babies call their fathers Daddy."

"Then I'm not going to call you Daddy either," Chandler said.

"I like being called Daddy. It makes me feel adored. Girls, I want to ask you a question and I want you to answer with brutal honesty. Don't spare Daddy's feelings, just tell me what you think from the heart."

Jennifer rolled her eyes and said, "Oh, Dad, not this game again."

I said, "Who is the greatest human being you've encountered on this earth?"

"Mama," Lucy answered quickly, grinning at her father.

"Almost right," I replied. "Now let's try it again. Think of the most splendid, wonderful person you personally know. The answer should spring to your lips."

"You!" Chandler shouted.

"An angel. A pure, snow-white angel, and so smart.

What do you want, Chandler? Money? Jewels? Furs? Stocks and bonds? Ask anything, darling, and your loving Daddy will get it for you."

"I don't want you to kill the conch."

"Kill the conch! I'm going to send this conch to college, set it up in business."

"Dad," Jennifer said, "we're getting too old for you to tease us like this. You're starting to embarrass us around our friends."

"Like whom?"

"Johnny."

"That gum-snapping, pimple-popping, slack-jawed little cretin?"

"He's my boyfriend," Jennifer said proudly.

"He's a creep, Jennifer," Lucy added.

"He's a lot better than that midget you call a boyfriend," Jennifer shot back.

"I've warned you about boys, girls. They're all disgusting, filthy-minded, savage little reprobates who do nasty things like pee on bushes and pick their noses."

"You were a little boy once," Lucy said.

"Ha! Can you imagine Dad as a little boy?" Jennifer said. "What a laugh."

"I was different. I was a prince. A moonbeam. But I'm not going to interfere with your love life, Jennifer. You know me, I'm not going to be one of those tiresome fathers who're never satisfied with guys his daughters bring home. I'm not going to interfere. It's your choice and your life. You can marry anyone you want to, girls, as soon as y'all finish medical school."

"I don't want to go to medical school," said Lucy. "Do you know that Mama has to put her fingers up people's behinds? I want to be a poet, like Savannah."

"Ah, marriage after your first book of poems is published. I'll compromise. I'm not a hard man."

"I can get married anytime I want to," Lucy said stubbornly. "I won't have to ask your permission. I'll be a grown-up woman."

"That's the spirit, Lucy," I applauded. "Don't listen to a thing your parents say. That's the only rule of life I want you to be sure and follow."

"You don't mean that. You're just talking, Daddy,"

Chandler said, leaning her head back under my chin. "I mean Dad," she corrected herself.

"Remember what I told you. Nobody told me this kind of stuff when I was a kid," I said seriously, "but parents were put on earth for the sole purpose of making their children miserable. It's one of God's most important laws. Now listen to me. Your job is to make me and Mama believe that you're doing and thinking everything we want you to. But you're really not. You're thinking your own thoughts and going out on secret missions. Because Mama and I are screwing you up."

"How are you screwing us up?" Jennifer asked.

"He embarrasses us in front of our friends," Lucy suggested.

"I do not. But I know we're screwing you up a little bit every day. If we knew how we were doing it, we'd stop. We wouldn't do it ever again, because we adore you. But we're parents and we can't help it. It's our job to screw you up. Do you understand?"

"No," they agreed in a simultaneous chorus.

"Good," I said, taking a sip of my drink. "You're not supposed to understand us. We're your enemies. You're supposed to wage guerrilla warfare against us."

"We're not gorillas," Lucy said primly. "We're little girls."

Sallie returned to the porch, wearing an off-white sundress and sandals to match. Her long legs were tanned and pretty.

"Did I interrupt the complete lectures of Dr. Spock?" she said, smiling at the children.

"Dad told us we were gorillas," explained Chandler, removing herself from my lap and mounting her mother's.

"I cleaned up some for your mother," Sallie said, lighting a cigarette.

"You'll die of cancer if you keep smoking that, Mama," Jennifer said. "You'll choke on your own blood. We learned that at school."

"No more school for you," Sallie said, exhaling.

"Why'd you clean up?" I asked.

"Because I hate the way she looks at my house when she comes over. She always looks like she wants to inoculate the children for typhus when she sees the mess in the kitchen."

"She's just jealous that you're a doctor and she peaked out after winning a spelling bee in third grade. So you don't need to clean up everytime she comes over to spread plague. You just need to burn the furniture and spray with disinfectant when she leaves."

"You're a bit hard on your mother, Tom. She's trying to be a good mother again, in her own way," Sallie said, studying Chandler's hair.

Jennifer said, "Why don't you like Grandma, Dad?"

"Who says I don't like Grandma?"

Lucy added, "Yeah, Dad, why do you always scream out 'I'm not here' when she calls on the phone?"

"It's a protective device, sweetheart. Do you know how a blowfish puffs up when there's danger? Well, it's the same thing when Grandma calls. I puff up and shout that I'm not here. It would work great except that your mother always betrays me."

"Why don't you want her to know you're here, Daddy?" Chandler asked.

"Because then I have to talk to her. And when I talk to her it reminds me of being a child and I hated my childhood. I'd rather have been a blowfish."

Lucy asked, "Will we shout 'I'm not here' when you call us when we're all grown up?"

"Of course," I said with more vehemence than I intended. "Because then I'll be making you feel bad by saying, 'Why don't I ever see you, dear?' or 'Have I done something wrong, darling?' or 'My birthday was last Thursday,' or 'I'm having a heart transplant next Tuesday. I'm sure you don't care,' or 'Could you at least come over and dust off the iron lung?' After you grow up and leave me, kids, my only duty in the world will be to make you feel guilty. I'll try to ruin your lives."

"Dad thinks he knows everything," Lucy said to Sallie, and two cooler heads nodded in agreement.

"What's this? Criticism from my own children? My own flesh and blood noticing flaws in my character? I can stand anything but criticism, Lucy."

"All our friends think Dad is crazy, Mama," Jennifer added. "You act like a mom is supposed to act. Dad doesn't act like other dads."

"Here it is. That dreaded moment when my children turn

on me and rip my guts out. If this were Russia, they'd turn me in to the Communist authorities and I'd be in a Siberian salt mine, freezing my ass off."

"He said a bad word, Mama," Lucy said.

"Yes, dear. I heard."

"Grass," I said quickly. "The grass needs cutting."

"The grass always needs cutting when he says that word," Jennifer explained.

"At this very moment my mother is crossing the Shem Creek bridge. No birds sing on the planet when my mother is on her way."

"Just try to be nice, Tom," Sallie said in her maddening professional voice. "Don't let her get under your skin."

I groaned, drinking deeply. "My God, I wonder what she wants. She only comes here when she can ruin my life in some small way. She's a tactician of the ruined life. She could give seminars on the subject. She said she has some bad news. When my family has bad news, it's always something grisly, Biblical, lifted straight out of the Book of Job."

"At least admit your mother's trying to be your friend again."

"I admit it. She is trying," I said wearily. "I liked her better when she wasn't trying, when she was an unrepentant monster."

"What's for dinner tonight, Tom?" Sallie asked, changing the subject. "Something smells wonderful."

"That's fresh bread. I caught flounder off the rocks early this morning, so I stuffed them with crabmeat and shrimp. There's a fresh spinach salad plus sautéed zucchini and shallots."

"Wonderful," she said. "I shouldn't be drinking this. I'm on call tonight."

"I'd rather have fried chicken," Lucy said. "Let's go out to Colonel Sanders."

"Why do you cook anyway, Dad?" Jennifer asked suddenly. "Mr. Brighton laughs when he talks about your cooking dinner for Mama."

"Yeah," Lucy added, "he says it's because Mama makes twice as much money as you do."

"That rotten bastard," Sallie whispered between clenched teeth.

"That's not true," I said. "I do it because Mama makes four or five times more money than I do."

"Remember, girls, it was Daddy who put me through medical school. And don't hurt your father's feelings like that again, Lucy," Sallie warned. "You don't have to repeat everything Mr. Brighton says. Your father and I try to share the household chores."

"All the other mommies I know cook for their family," Jennifer said boldly, considering the bitter look that had entered Sallie's gray eyes. "Except you."

"I told you, Sallie," I said, studying Jennifer's hair. "If you raise children in the South, you produce southerners. And a southerner is one of God's natural fools."

"We're southern and we're not fools," said Sallie.

"Aberrations, dear. It happens once or twice every generation."

"Girls, go on upstairs and wash up. Lila is going to be here soon."

"Why doesn't she like us to call her Grandma?" Lucy asked.

"Because it makes her feel old. Run along now," Sallie said, moving the girls inside the house.

When she returned, Sallie leaned down and brushed her lips on my forehead. "I'm sorry Lucy said that. She's so goddamn conventional."

"It doesn't bother me, Sallie, I swear it doesn't. You know I adore the role of martyrdom—how I blossom in an atmosphere of self-pity. Poor nutless Tom Wingo, polishing the silver while his wife discovers a cure for cancer. Sad Tom Wingo making the perfect soufflé while his wife knocks down a hundred grand a year. We knew this would happen, Sallie. We talked about it."

"I still don't like it worth a shit. I don't trust that male ego strutting around inside you. I know it's got to hurt. It makes me feel guilty as hell because I know the girls don't understand why I'm not there with cookies and milk when they get home from school."

"But they're proud that their mama is a doctor."

"But they don't seem proud that you're a teacher and a coach, Tom."

"Was, Sallie. Past tense. I was fired, remember? I'm not proud of it either, Sallie. So we can't really blame them.

Oh, God, is that my mother's car I hear pulling up in the driveway? May I have three Valiums, Doctor?"

"I needed them for myself, Tom. Remember, I'll have to endure your mother's house inspection before she turns on you," said Sallie.

"Liquor's not helping," I moaned. "Why does liquor fail to numb my senses when I need it most? Should I invite Mom for dinner?"

"Of course, but you know she won't stay."

"Great, then I'll invite her."

"Be nice to your mother, Tom," Sallie said. "She seems so sad and so desperate to be your friend again."

"Friendship and motherhood are not compatible."

"Do you think our kids will think that?"

"No, our kids will only hate their father. Have you noticed they're already sick of my sense of humor and the oldest is only ten years old? I've got to develop some new routines."

"I like your routines, Tom. I think they're funny. That's one of the reasons I married you. I knew we'd spend a great deal of the time laughing."

"Bless you, Doctor. Okay, here's Mom. Could you tie some garlic around my throat and bring me a crucifix?"

"Hush, Tom, she'll hear you."

My mother appeared in the doorway, immaculately dressed and groomed, and her perfume walked out on the porch several moments before she did. My mother always carried herself as if she were approaching the inner chamber of a queen. She was as finely made as a yacht—clean lines, efficient, expensive. She was always far too pretty to be my mother and there was a time in my life when I was mistaken for her husband. I cannot tell you how much my mother loved that time.

"There you are," my mother said. "How are you, dears?"

She kissed both of us, was cheerful, but the bad news lay heavy in her eyes.

"You get more beautiful every time I see you, Sallie. Don't you agree, Tom?"

"I certainly do, Mother. And so do you," I answered, suppressing a groan. My mother could bring inanities tumbling out of me in a loose, ceaseless cascade.

"Well, thank you, Tom. That's so sweet of you to say to your old mother."

"My old mother has the best figure in the state of South Carolina," I replied, counting my second rapid-fire inanity.

"Well, I work hard at it, I can tell you. The menfolk don't know what we girls suffer to retain these girlish figures, do they, Sallie?"

"They certainly don't."

"You've gained weight again, Tom," my mother noticed cheerfully.

"You girls don't know what we menfolk put ourselves through to become fat shits."

"Well, I certainly didn't mean it critically, Tom," my mother said, her voice hurt and sanctimonious. "If you're that sensitive, I won't mention it again. The extra weight is very becoming to you. You always look better when your face is filled out. But I didn't come to fight with you today. I've got some very bad news. May I sit down?"

"Of course, Lila. Let me fix you a drink," said Sallie.

"A gin and tonic, darling. With a squeeze of lime if you have it. Where are the children, Tom? I don't want them to hear."

"Upstairs," I said, looking toward the sunset, waiting.

"Savannah tried to kill herself again."

"Oh my God," Sallie said, stopping outside the door. "When?"

"Last week, evidently. They're not sure. She was in a coma when they found her. She's out of the coma, but . . ."

"But what?" I murmured.

"But she's in one of those silly states she goes into when she wants attention."

"It's called a psychotic interlude, Mother."

"She claims she's a psychotic," my mother snapped back at me. "She's not a true psychotic, I can tell you that."

Before I could answer, Sallie jumped in with a question. "Where is she, Lila?"

"In a psychiatric hospital in New York City. Bellevue or someplace like that. I have it written down at home. A doctor called. A woman doctor like you, Sallie, only a psychiatrist. I'm sure she couldn't make it in any real field of medicine, but each to his own, I always say."

"I almost went into psychiatry," Sallie said.

"Well, it certainly affords a lot of pleasure to see young women doing so well in the professions. I didn't have those kinds of opportunities when I was a girl. Anyway, this woman called to tell me the tragic news."

"How did she try to do it, Mom?" I said, attempting to retain control. I was slipping; I could feel it.

"She slit her wrists again, Tom," my mother said, starting to cry. "Why does she want to do those things to me? Haven't I suffered enough?"

"She did it to herself, Mom."

"I'll get your drink, Lila." Sallie spoke as she moved inside the house.

My mother dried her tears on a handkerchief she pulled out of her purse. Then she said, "The doctor's Jewish, I believe. She has one of those impossible names. Maybe Aaron knows her."

"Aaron's from South Carolina, Mom. Just because he's Jewish doesn't mean he knows every Jew in America."

"But he'd know how to find out about her. To see if she's on the up and up. Aaron's family is very tight."

"If she is a Jew, Aaron's family is certain to have a file on her all right."

"You don't have to be sarcastic with me, Tom. How do you think I feel? How do you think I feel when my children do these terrible things to themselves? It makes me feel like such a failure. You can't imagine how good society people look at me when they find out who I am."

"Are you going to New York?"

"Oh, I can't possibly go, Tom. This is a real hard time for me. We're giving a dinner party Saturday night and it's been planned for months. And the expense. I'm sure she's in good hands and there's nothing we can really do."

"Being there is doing something, Mom. You've never realized that."

"I told the psychiatrist you might go," my mother said, tentative and hopeful.

"Of course I'll go."

"You don't have a job now and it'll be easy for you to arrange."

"My job is looking for a job."

"I think you should have taken that job selling insurance. That's my honest opinion, though you certainly didn't ask my advice."

"How did you know about that?"

"Sallie told me."

"She did?"

"She's very worried about you. We all are, Tom. She can't be expected to support you the rest of your life."

"Did she tell you that, too?"

"No. I'm just telling you what I know. You've got to face facts. You're never going to be able to teach or coach again as long as you live in South Carolina. You need to start afresh, work your way up from the bottom, prove yourself to some employer willing to give you a chance."

"You talk like I've never had a job in my life, Mom," I said, weary and needing to escape my mother's eyes, wanting the sun to set faster, in need of darkness.

"It's been a good long while since you had a job," Mom persisted. "And a woman just doesn't respect a man who doesn't help bring home the bacon; that I can tell you. Sallie's been an angel, but she can't be expected to make all the money while you sit brooding on this porch."

"I've applied for over seventy jobs, Mom."

"My husband can get you a job. He's offered to set you up in business."

"You know I can't take help from your husband. You, at least, understand that."

"I certainly don't understand it," my mother half-shouted at me. "Why should I be expected to understand it? He sees your whole family suffering because you can't get off your fat duff and get a job. He wants to do this to help Sallie and the girls, not to help you. He doesn't want them to suffer any more than they already have. He's willing to help you even though he knows how much you hate him."

"I'm glad he knows how much I hate him," I said.

Sallie returned to the porch with my mother's drink and a fresh one for me. I felt like tossing out the drink and eating the glass.

"Tom was just telling me how much he hates me and everything I stand for."

"Untrue. I merely said, under great provocation, that I hate your husband. You brought the subject up."

"I brought up the subject of your joblessness. It's been over a year, Tom, and that's plenty of time for any man of your abilities to come up with something, anything. Don't you think it's embarrassing for Sallie to be supporting a full-grown man with all his limbs attached?"

"That's enough, Lila," Sallie said angrily. "You've no right to hurt Tom by using me."

"I'm trying to help Tom. Don't you see that, Sallie?"

"No. Not like that. Not ever like that. It's not the way, Lila."

"I have to go to New York tomorrow, Sallie," I said.

"Of course you do," she answered.

"You'll give her my love, Tom, won't you?"

"Of course, Mom."

"I know she's against me as much as you are," she whined.

"We're not against you, Mother."

"Oh yes you are. Do you think I can't feel your contempt for me? Do you think that I don't know how much you hate it that I'm finally happy in my life? You loved it when I was miserable and living with your father."

"We didn't love that, Mom. We had a hideous childhood, which launched us prettily into a hideous adulthood."

"Please stop," Sallie pleaded. "Please stop hurting each other."

"I know what it's like being married to a Wingo male, Sallie. I know what you're going through."

"Mom, you've got to visit more often. I actually experienced a minute or two of happiness before you arrived."

Sallie commanded, "I want this to stop and I want it to stop now. We need to think about how we can help Savannah."

"I've done all I can for Savannah," Mom said. "Whatever she does, she'll blame me."

"Savannah's a sick woman," Sallie said softly. "You know that, Lila."

My mother brightened at this, shifted the drink to her left hand, and leaned forward to talk to Sallie.

"You're a professional, Sallie," she said. "Do you know that I've been reading a lot about psychosis lately? The leading authorities have discovered that it's a chemical imbalance and has nothing at all to do with heredity or environment."

"There's been an awful lot of chemical imbalance in our family, Mother," I said, unable to control my raw, blistery anger.

"Some doctors think it's a lack of salt."

"I've heard something about it, Lila," Sallie agreed kindly.

"Salt!" I cried out. "I'll take Savannah a box of Morton's and let her start spooning it in. If it's just salt she needs, I'll put her on a diet that'll make her look like Lot's wife."

"I'm just quoting what the leading authorities say. If you want to make fun of your mother, feel free, Tom. I guess I'm an easy target, an old woman who sacrificed the best years of her life for her children."

"Mom, why don't you get a job bottling guilt? We could sell it to all American parents who haven't mastered the fine art of making their kids feel like shit all the time. You'd be a shoo-in to win the patent."

"And then maybe you'd finally have a job, son," she said coldly as she rose from her chair. "Call me, please, after you see Savannah. You can reverse the charges."

"Why don't you stay for dinner, Lila? You haven't seen the children yet," said Sallie.

"I'll come visit when Tom's in New York. I want to take the kids up to Pawleys Island for a couple of weeks. If you don't mind, of course."

"That would be lovely."

"Goodbye, son," my mother said. "Take good care of your sister."

"Goodbye, Mother," I answered, and I rose to kiss her on the cheek. "I always have."

After dinner, Sallie and I helped the girls get ready for bed. Then we went for a walk on the beach. We headed toward the lighthouse, walking barefooted in the surf past Fort Moultrie. Sallie took my hand, and I, distracted and troubled, realized how long it had been since I had touched Sallie, since I had approached her as lover or friend or equal. My body had not felt like an instrument of love or passion for such a long time; it had been a winter of deadening seriousness, when all the illusions and bright dreams of my early twenties had withered and died. I did not yet have the interior resources to dream new dreams; I was far too busy mourning the death of the old ones and wondering how I was to survive without them. I was sure I could replace them somehow, but was not sure I could restore their brassy luster or dazzling impress. So, for months, I had not attended to the needs of my wife, had not stroked or touched her until she glowed and moved like a cat beneath my hands; I had not responded when she moved her bare leg against mine or put her hand against my thigh when we lay in solitude through sleepless nights. My body always betrayed me when the mind was restless and suffering. Sallie moved toward me and together we leaned into the summer wind as the waves broke around our feet. Orion the Hunter walked the skies above us, belted and armed, in the star-struck, moonless night.

Sallie said to me, squeezing my hand, "Tom. Talk to me. Tell me everything you're thinking. You're growing so quiet again and I can't seem to reach you at all."

"I'm trying to figure out how I ruined my life," I said to Orion. "I want to know the exact moment it was preordained that I would lead a perfectly miserable life and drag everyone I love down with me."

"You've got something to fight for that's so valuable— something worth the fight. You seem to be giving up, Tom. Your past is hurting us."

"There's the Big Dipper," I said, pointing halfheartedly.

"I don't give a shit about the Big Dipper," Sallie said. "I'm not talking about the Big Dipper and I don't want you to change the subject. You're not even good at changing the subject."

"Why does everything my mother says, every single syllable, every single insincere phoneme, piss me off? Why can't I ignore her, Sallie? Why can't I simply go limp when she comes over. If I just didn't respond to her, she couldn't touch me. I know she loves me with all her heart. But we sit there and say things that wound and damage and destroy. She leaves and we both have blood on our hands. She cries and I drink; then she drinks. You try to intercede and we both ignore you and resent you for even trying. It's like we're in some monstrous passion play where she and I take turns crucifying each other. And it's not her fault and it's not mine."

"She just wants you to find a job and be happy," Sallie said.

"I want that, too. I want it desperately. The truth is I'm having a very rough time finding anyone who wants to hire me. There are dozens of letters I haven't told you about. All very polite. All saying the same thing. All unbearably humiliating."

"You could have taken the insurance job."

"Yes, I could have. But it wasn't an insurance job, Sallie. I would have been an insurance collector, knocking on sharecroppers' shacks on Edisto Island, collecting nickels and dimes from poor blacks who bought insurance so they could have a decent burial."

Sallie squeezed my hand and said, "It would have been a start at something, Tom. It would have been better than sitting around the house clipping recipes. You'd have been doing something to save yourself."

Hurt, I answered, "I've been thinking. I haven't been wasting my time."

"I don't mean this as a criticism, Tom. I really don't, but . . ."

"Every time you use that memorable phrase, Sallie," I interrupted, "you mean it as a bone-crushing criticism, but go ahead. After Mom, I could endure a cavalry charge of Huns and elephants."

"No, this is not critical. I want it to sound loving. You've been so self-pitying, so analytical, and so bitter since what happened to Luke. You've got to forget what happened and go on from here, from this moment. Your life isn't over, Tom. One part of your life is. You've got to find out what the next part is going to be."

For several minutes we walked in silence, in the disturbing solitude that sometimes visits couples at the most incongruous times. It was not a new feeling for me; I had a limitless gift for turning even those sweet souls who loved me best into strangers.

I tried to fight my way back toward Sallie, tried to regain contact. "I haven't figured everything out yet. I can't figure out why I hate myself more than anyone else in the world. It doesn't make sense to me. Even if Mom and Dad were monsters, I should have come out of it with some kind of respect for myself as a survivor, if nothing else. I should have at least come out of it honest, but I'm the most dishonest person I've ever met. I never know exactly how I feel about something. There's always something secret hidden from me."

"You don't need to know the absolute truth. No one does. You only need to know enough to get along."

"No, Sallie," I said, stopping in the water suddenly and turning her toward me, my hands on her shoulders. "That's what I did before. I got along with my part of the truth and it caught up with me. Let's leave South Carolina. Let's get out of here. I'll never get a job in this state again. Too many people know the name Wingo and they don't like what it stands for."

Sallie lowered her eyes and tucked my hands into hers. But she looked directly at me when she said, "I don't want to leave Charleston, Tom. I have a wonderful job and I love our house and our friends. Why do you want to throw even the good things away?"

"Because they aren't so good to me anymore, because I don't believe in my life here anymore."

"But I believe in mine."

"And you make the money," I said, embarrassed at how bitter I sounded, how preening, how male.

"You said that, not me, Tom." •

"I'm sorry. Truly I am. I don't want to go to New York. I don't even want to see Savannah. I'm furious, absolutely furious at her that she tried it again. I'm angry that she's crazy and is allowed to be as crazy as she needs to be. I envy her craziness. But I know she expects me to be there when she starts slicing herself. It's the old dance and I know all the steps."

"Then don't go," Sallie said, slipping away from me again.

"I have to go. You know that. It's the only role I really play well. The hero of the hour. The gallant knight. The jobless Galahad. It's the fatal flaw of all Wingos. Except Mom. She gives dinner parties planned for months and can't be bothered with suicide attempts by her children."

"You blame your parents for so much, Tom. When does it start becoming your own responsibility? When do you take your life into your own hands? When do you start accepting the blame or credit for your own actions?"

"I don't know, Sallie. I can't figure it out. I can't make anything whole out of it. I don't know what it all means."

She turned away from me and resumed walking up the beach again, slightly ahead of me.

"It's hurting us, Tom."

"I know," I admitted, trying to catch up to her. I took her hand and squeezed it, but there was no return pressure. "To my surprise, I'm not a good husband. I once thought I'd be a great one. Charming, sensitive, loving, and attentive to my wife's every need. I'm sorry, Sallie. I haven't been good for you in such a long time. It's a source of great pain. I want to be better. I'm so cold, so secretive. I swear I'll do better once we leave this state."

"I'm not going to leave this state," she said definitively. "I'm perfectly happy living here. This is my home, where I belong."

"What are you saying, Sallie?"

"I'm saying that what makes you happy doesn't necessarily make me happy. I'm saying that I'm thinking things over, too. I'm trying to figure things out, too. I'm trying to figure things out between us. It doesn't seem so good anymore."

"Sallie, this is a bad time to be saying this."

"It hasn't been the same between us since Luke," she said.

"Nothing's been the same," I said.

"There's something you forgot to do about Luke, Tom," she said.

"What was that?" I said.

"You forgot to cry," Sallie said.

I looked up the beach toward the lighthouse. Then back across the harbor at the lights on James Island.

Sallie continued, "There's no statute of limitations on your sadness. It's impenetrable. You've cut me out of your life completely."

"Do you mind if we change the subject?" I asked, and there was a mean edge to my voice.

Sallie said, "The subject is us. The subject is whether you've stopped loving me, Tom."

"I just learned that my sister tried to kill herself," I shouted.

She answered firmly, "No, you just learned that your wife doesn't think you love her anymore."

"What do you want me to say?" I asked, but I felt her urgency, her need to reach an untouchable place in me.

She was close to tears when she said, "The words are easy. Try this: I love you, Sallie, and I don't think I could live for a single day without you."

But there was something in her eyes and voice trying to deliver a far darker message, and I said, "There's something else."

Sallie began to weep gently and there was both despair and betrayal in her voice. "Not something else, Tom," she said, "someone else."

"Jesus Christ," I screamed at the lights of the Isle of Palms. "First Savannah and now this!"

But Sallie said behind me, "This is the first time you've even looked at me in months. I have to say I'm having an affair just so my goddamn husband'll notice I'm alive."

"Oh, Jesus, Sallie. Oh, no, please," I whispered, staggering backward, away from her.

"I was going to tell you when the time was right. I hate to tell you now. But you're leaving tomorrow."

"I won't leave. I can't leave like this."

"I want you to leave, Tom. I want to find out how serious I am about this. If it's real or not. I might even be doing this to hurt you. I'm not sure."

"May I ask you who it is?"

"No. Not yet."

"I promise not to do anything untoward or barbaric. At least until I get back from New York. I'd like to know."

"It's Dr. Cleveland."

"Oh, no!" I screamed. "Not that pompous, intolerable asshole. For christsakes, Sallie, he rides a motorcycle and smokes a meerschaum pipe, a goddamn meerschaum pipe."

"He's better than that second-rate cheerleader you had a fling with," she answered furiously.

"I knew you'd say that. I knew that seductive jackass with the big tits would come back to haunt me for the rest of my life. I'm sorry for that, Sallie. I'm so sorry. I was stupid. Stupid, stupid."

"That hurt me more than you'll ever know."

"I begged you to forgive me, Sallie. I'm begging you now. I did it, and God knows, I've suffered for it and I promised on my knees I'd never do it again."

"You don't have to keep that promise now, Tom. Dr. Cleveland is in love with me, too."

"Well, bully for *Doctor* Cleveland. Has *Doctor* Cleveland told Mrs. Cleveland, that sad, bovine pillar of the community?"

"No, not yet. He's waiting for the right time. Both of us want to make sure. We don't want to hurt people needlessly."

"Grand-spirited people. Let me ask you something, Sallie. When your little beeper goes off at night and you're called off to the hospital for one of those innumerable little emergencies, are you sometimes driving over to inspect the good doctor's meerschaum?"

"That's disgusting, Tom, and you know it."

"I want to know if you both abuse the magic beeper, that holiest, most obnoxious symbol of the doctor as asshole in America."

"Yes!" she shouted at me. "I've done it a couple of times. When there was no other way. And I'd do it again if there was no other way."

I felt an irresistible desire to strike her, felt the ghost of a violent father assume dominion over the blood, felt his surge into power around the heart; my fists clenched, and for a moment I fought with all my strength against the man it was my birthright to be. I controlled myself and sent my father into exile again. I loosened my fists. I breathed and cried, "Is it because I'm getting fat, Sallie? Please tell me it's that. Or because I'm losing my hair? Or maybe it's because I've told you I've got a little dick. You know, I'm one of the few men in America who'll admit he's got a little pecker. I only told you that because you always felt so bad about having small breasts."

"My breasts are not that small."

"Neither is my poor slandered penis."

It surprised me when Sallie laughed. There was something pure in her sense of humor that she could not control even in the most serious moments in her life. Her laughter was intimately related to her generosity and could not be suppressed.

"See, there's hope, Sallie. You still think I'm funny. And I happen to know for a fact that the last time Cleveland laughed was right after Woodrow Wilson was elected president."

"He's only eleven years older than we are."

"Hah! A different generation. I hate old men who ride motorcycles. I hate young men who ride motorcycles."

Sallie sniffed the air defensively. "He's an aficionado. He only collects British motorcycles."

"Please spare me the details. Don't tell me you're leaving me for a guy who collects meerschaum pipes and British motorcycles. I'd feel better if you left me for a tattoo man at the circus, a waterbaby, or a dwarf on a unicycle."

"I didn't say I was leaving you, Tom. I said I was thinking about it. I've found somebody who thinks I'm wonderful."

"You are wonderful," I whined.

"Let's not discuss it any more tonight, Tom. It was hard enough to tell you, and I certainly didn't want to add to your troubles."

"Hah!" I laughed bitterly, kicking a wave. "A mere trifle, my dear."

We said nothing for a long while. Then Sallie said, "I'm going to go back to the house to kiss the girls good night. Do you want to come?"

"I'll come up to kiss them good night later. I'll stay out here a little while. I need to think about everything."

Sallie said to me in a tender voice, "I don't know what happened. I don't know what happened to the fighter I married."

"Yeah, you do," I said. "Luke happened."

She hugged me suddenly, fiercely, and kissed me on the throat, but in the full flower of righteousness, I was both patriot and helot of the male ego; with the patriarchal rectitude of the scorned male, I could not return that kiss or retrieve any value for that moment of grace. Sallie turned unkissed and walked down the beach toward our house.

I began to run down the beach. At first it was controlled, patient, but then I started to push myself, letting it out, until I was sprinting, breaking into a sweat, and gasping for air. If I could hurt the body, I would not notice the coming apart of the soul.

As I ran, I considered the sad decline of flesh. I struggled to increase the speed and remembered how once I was the fastest quarterback in South Carolina. Blond and swift, I would come out of backfields with linemen thundering toward me in slow-footed ecstasy as I turned the corner and stepped toward the amazing noise of crowds, then lowered my head and dazzled myself with instinctive moves that lived in some fast, sweet place within me. But I never wept when I ran in high school games. Now I ran heavily, desperately, away from the wife who had taken a lover because I had failed her as lover, away from the sister too quick with blades, away from the mother who did not understand the awful history of mothers and sons. I was running away from that history, I thought—that bitter, outrageous slice of Americana that was my own failed life—or toward a new phase of that history. I slowed down, sweating, exhausted. I began walking toward the house.

2

It is an art form to hate New York City properly. So far I have always been a featherweight debunker of New York; it takes too much energy and endurance to record the infinite number of ways the city offends me. Were I to list them all, I would fill up a book the size of the Manhattan yellow pages, and that would merely be the prologue. Every time I submit myself to the snubs and indignities of that swaggering city and set myself adrift among the prodigious crowds, a feeling of displacement, profound and enervating, takes me over, killing all the coded cells of my hard-won singularity. The city marks my soul with a most profane, indelible graffiti. There is too much of too much there. On every visit I find myself standing on the piers, watching the splendid Hudson River flooding by and the noise of the city to my back, and I know what no New Yorker I've ever met knows: that this island was once surrounded by deep, extraordinary marshes and estuaries, that an entire complex civilization of a salt marsh lies buried beneath the stone avenues. I do not like cities that dishonor their own marshes.

My sister, Savannah, of course, matches my contempt with her own heroic yet perverse allegiance to New York. Even the muggers, drug addicts, winos, and bag ladies, those wounded, limping souls navigating their cheerless passages through the teeming millions, are a major part of the city's ineffable charm for her. It is these damaged birds of paradise, burnt out and sneaking past the mean alleys, that define the city's most extreme limits for her. She finds beauty in these extremities. She carries in her breast an unshakable fealty to all these damaged veterans who survive New York on the fringes, lawless and without hope, gifted in the black arts. They are the city's theater for her. She has written about them in her poetry; she has learned some of the black arts herself and knows well their ruined acreage.

Savannah knew she wanted to be a New Yorker long before she knew she wanted to write poetry. She was one of those southerners who were aware from an early age that the South could never be more for them than a fragrant prison administered by a collective of loving but treacherous relatives.

At fifteen, she received a subscription to *The New Yorker* as a Christmas present from my grandmother. Each week, she waited breathlessly for her copy of the magazine to arrive, then would sit for hours laughing and giggling over the cartoons. Later, our brother, Luke, and I would stare incredulously at the same cartoons, waiting for the jokes to hit us. Things that had them whooping it up and knee slapping in New York were incomprehensible to me in Colleton, South Carolina. They were impenetrable, a kind of cuneiform of wit, and when I asked Savannah what in the hell she found so funny, she would sigh deeply and dismiss me with some withering phrase she had memorized from a previous cartoon. With Savannah as a sister, fancying herself an exiled Knickerbocker cut off from her native city by the humiliation of her birth in South Carolina, I hated New York long before I ever crossed its glorious rivers.

Savannah left South Carolina and lit out for the boroughs soon after we graduated from Colleton High School. She did it against our parents' wishes, but she had asked for neither their permission nor their approval. She had a life to lead and an elaborate plan by which to live it, and she was seeking no advice from shrimpers or their wives who had chosen a life beside the inland waterway of South Carolina. Instinctively she knew she was a city girl and that she had learned everything about a small town she needed or wanted to know. In New York, she had chosen a city that would require a lifetime of vigilance and study, a city worthy of her gifts.

From the first day, she had loved it all: the pulse, the struggle, the unbridgeable flow of ideas and humanity, the rapture and majesty of the effort to master and tame the fabulous city into something personal and unforbidding. She took to the city on its own terms. She became a collector and archivist of genuine New York experiences. If it originated in New York, if it had the authenticity and stamp of Manhattan approval, then Savannah embraced it with the fervor of a catechist. From the very beginning she was lyrical in her advocacy of New York's essential greatness, which she considered undeniable and beyond discussion. I denied it and discussed it obsessively.

"You've never lived here. You have no right to any opinion at all," Savannah said cheerfully when Luke and I visited her in New York for the first time.

"I've never lived in Peking, either," I replied, "but I bet the city's full of little yellow people."

"It must be the exhaust from all these cars, Savannah," Luke observed, watching the rush-hour traffic move toward the bridges. "It eats away the brain cells. Once the brain cells go, you start liking this shithole."

"You've got to give it a chance, dimwits. Once you catch the New York fever, then nothing is ever good enough. Feel the energy of this city. Just close your eyes and let it take you."

Luke and I both closed our eyes.

"That's not energy," Luke said, "that's noise."

"Your noise," she answered, smiling, "my energy."

In the early days she supported herself by working as a waitress in a vegetarian restaurant in the West Village. She also enrolled at the New School, taking subjects that appealed to her, eschewing those that did not. She lived in a cheap rent-controlled apartment on Grove Street near

Sheridan Square and had decorated it with great charm. There she contended alone with all the mysteries and delicacies of the language and began to write the poems that made her famous in a select circle before she was twenty-five. My parents had put her on the train north with reluctance and apocalyptic prophecies, allowing privately to their sons that Savannah would never last a month in the big city. But she had harmonized herself to the rhythms of New York. "Being in New York is just like living in a *New Yorker* cartoon," she wrote in her first letter, and all of us opened back issues of Savannah's favorite magazine and tried to glean some idea of what her life must be like by translating the inside jokes of the eight million to each other. From the cartoons we supposed that New Yorkers said many clever but arcane things to each other at intimate dinner parties. My father, ignoring the cartoons, studied the advertisements and said aloud to the family, "Who *are* these people anyway?"

When Savannah's first book of poetry was published by Random House in 1972, Luke and I drove to New York to go to the parties and readings attendant to its publication. Savannah and I sat together beneath her hanging plants and beside her pretty desk and she signed a copy of *The Shrimper's Daughter* for me while Luke tried to find a place to park safely through the night. She opened the dedicatory page and watched my face as I read, "To my brother, Tom Wingo, whose love and devotion has made the passage worthwhile. All praise to my fabulous twin." Tears came to my eyes when I read that dedication and I wondered how any poetry at all could come from our childhood.

"Quarterbacks don't cry," she said, hugging me.

"This one does," I answered.

Then she showed me the latest issue of *The New Yorker*, dated March 7, 1972, which carried the title poem of her book on page thirty-seven. We were both screaming madly at each other when Luke returned to the apartment. Then Luke started screaming. He opened the window, crept nimbly out to the fire escape, and shouted to everyone on Grove Street, "My little sister's in *The New Yorker*, you Yankee motherfuckers."

* * *

That night we attended her first major reading, which was given at a deconsecreated Anglican church in the West Village. It was sponsored by Women United to Stamp Out Penises or one of those other maniacal splinter groups Savannah had gravitated toward. Savannah's earliest and dearest friends in the Village belonged to a feminist study group, and they all memorized Virginia Woolf, wore black belts, lifted weights for definition, and cleaned out bars of longshoremen on holiday weekends. "Linemen. Defensive tacklers," Luke whispered as we approached the dimly lit church and saw the grim phalanx of women-warriors fanned out along the rear vestibule, collecting tickets. They looked as if they spent their time translating Sappho and drinking the blood of flies. But these were strange times in the history of the sexes and Savannah had trained both Luke and me to tread lightly among the two-fisted Brown Shirts of the women's liberation movement. Savannah herself was in the middle of a politically militant phase of her own development and there were times her bulky southern brothers were an embarrassment to her. She coached us in how to appear androgynous and benign, and we perfected an obsequious shuffle when we found ourselves surrounded by her more hostile friends. Among this terrifying group, we feigned a state of penislessness that we thought would decrease Savannah's anxiety when we were thrown together with her friends. "All of them have been damaged by *males*," Savannah had explained. "Especially by fathers and brothers. You don't understand how horrible it is to be a woman in America."

Judging from the appearance of the ticket collectors, it must have been dreadful, indeed. But these were private random thoughts and ones we had learned never to express aloud to Savannah, who was known to scream at us if we seemed impervious to her new philosophy or too unregenerately male in our pronunciamentos. Our maleness irradiated unconsciously through Savannah's world and troubled us greatly, because at that time we were too thick and too innocent to understand the nature of our sister's problem with the world of men.

As we entered the church, Luke made a thoughtless mistake when he held the door open for a pretty, scholarly

woman who was entering the church behind us. As southern boys, we were vaccinated with the oily serums of an
instinctive politesse, and it would have been unthinkable
at that time for either of us not to hold a door open for a
lady. The lady reacted to different serums. In a surprisingly
swift move, she grabbed Luke by the throat with one hand,
then stuck two brilliantly sharpened nails beneath his eyeballs.

"You ever do that again, asshole, I'll poke both your
fucking eyeballs out," she said.

Luke answered quietly, respectful of those two menacing
fingers. "I assure you, madam, I will not open a door again
for a single lady in New York City."

"Woman, asshole," the woman hissed. "Woman. Not
lady."

"Woman," Luke corrected himself, and the woman, re-
leasing him, swept triumphantly into the church.

Rubbing his throat, Luke watched her disappear into the
crowd. Then he said in a whisper, "I ain't gonna open the
door for a fucking grizzly bear in this town, Tom. She must
not have known I was a Vietnam vet."

"It didn't look like she gave much of a shit, either, boy."

"But we learned something, Tom. When a door opens,
you just got to kick ass and run on through. That's how
it's done in New York City."

The church was almost full when Savannah walked out
of the vestibule. She was introduced by a supercilious
bearded male who wore a poncho, a beret, and leather-
thonged sandals. According to the program, he was a leading spokesman of the New York School and taught a course
called "Poetry, Revolution, and Orgasm" at Hunter College. I hated him on sight but changed my mind instantly
when his introduction of Savannah proved so heartfelt and
generous. He talked of Savannah's background: her childhood on the island, her father the shrimp boat captain, her
mother the mountain beauty, the family tiger, her grandfather who barbered hair and who sold Bibles on the side,
and her grandmother who visited the Colleton cemetery
and delivered soliloquies to dead relatives. Then he praised
her work: the passionate lyricism of her hymns to nature,
her technical virtuosity, and her celebration of the spirit of
women. All of this, he concluded, was astonishing to dis-

cover in a woman who had spent almost her entire life on
a sea island in the American South. Then, he surrendered
the floor to Savannah.

The applause was sedate and polite except for one single
bone-chilling, foot-stomping rebel yell, which exploded
naturally from Luke as he saw his small sister rise like a
flame in that church, blonde and shy and ethereal, her hair
brushed severely back but moving along her shoulders in
luxuriant waves.

I have always loved my sister's voice. It is clear and light,
a voice without seasons, like bells over a green city or snow-
fall on the roots of orchids. Her voice is a greening thing,
an enemy of storm and dark and winter. She pronounced
each word carefully, as though she was tasting fruit. The
words of her poems were a most private and fragrant orchard.

But, at first, I could not hear her and I could tell she was
aware of her audience, intimidated by it. But slowly, the
language seized her; her language, her poems, and her
voice lifted, steadied, and grew confident. And when it
did, Savannah Wingo took that audience, that West Village
audience, that cultured, jaded, city-hardened New York
audience, by storm. I knew all the poems by heart and my
mouth moved in congruence with hers and I told the stories
of our life as she told them and I felt the supernatural power
of poetry subjugate the crowd as Savannah's voice lifted
up toward the choir loft, lifted up toward the shining battlements of the Empire State Building, toward the stars
above the Hudson, and took us all back to the lowcountry
of South Carolina where this beautiful sister was born to
grief and sadness, and where all these poems, collected in
fragments and images, grew in darkness like sharp pieces
of coral, and awaited the annunciation of the poet, awaited
this night, the collective breath of this audience, as she
shared the poems of the heart by making the language sing
and bleed at the same time.

Halfway through the reading, Savannah looked up and
studied the audience. She sighted Luke and me sitting in
the fifteenth row, conspicuous in our coats and ties. She
smiled and waved and Luke called out, "Hey, Savannah.
Doing good, sweetheart," and the audience laughed.

"My two brothers, Luke and Tom, drove up from South

Carolina to attend this reading and I'd like to dedicate this next poem to them."

The woman who had threatened to put Luke's eyes out at the front door was sitting unnoticed in the pew directly in front of us to the left. We spotted her when Savannah made us rise so the audience could see us. There was some restrained, serviceable applause. Luke put his hands over his head and waved to the crowd, then leaned down to the woman and said, "Thought I was a nothing, didn't you, shithead?"

I pulled him back down into his seat and warned, "Shield your eyes when you insult that woman. Or we'll be investing in Seeing Eye dogs."

Then we returned to Savannah's voice. She read for over an hour and there was a story to it all. A girl had been born to poor parents in South Carolina, had grown up barefooted and brown beside the marshes of Colleton, had learned to measure the seasons by the migration of shrimp and wildfowl and the harvesting of tomatoes, had seized onto the light of her grand, unnamable singularity, had nourished that light, had willed herself to be different, and had felt the language stir in her as she heard the owls moaning in the barn eaves and the buoys chanting in the waterway. Then the world struck back as the world always does and the child, unarmed and sullen, began contending with all the wildness and cruelty of that world. In her last poems, Savannah spoke of her breakdowns, her demons, her insanity. She spoke of them with astonishment and respect and a heartbreaking sadness. But even her demons she invested with inordinate beauty, consecrated them with the dignity of her attention. There were no gargoyles in her work, only defiled angels crying for home. It was all new to New York, but it wasn't new to me and Luke. We were witnesses at the creation. In our house by the river we had watched a poet grow.

As I listened to her read her final poem, I thought of a dream I used to have of Savannah and me in the womb, floating side by side in our mother's inland sea—hearts forming together, fingers moving, the patient blue coloring of four sightless eyes in darkness, the blond hair flowing like underwater grass, the half-formed brains sensing the presence of the other, gathering comfort from that nameless communion which sprang up between us before we were born. In the life before life, in the breathless womb and wordless safety of bloodstreams, I dreamed that something special happened to us, that there was a moment of divine sight known only to twins, of recognition when we turned toward each other in a roll that took weeks and she said, "Hello, Tom," and I, who would grow accustomed to miracles, who would always believe in magic, would cry out, "Hello, Savannah," and then happily, transcendentally, we would await our birth so the lifelong dialogue could begin. I first knew of my sister's light in the darkness. What I didn't know was how much of the darkness she would bring along on the voyage. I believe in the ties of Gemini, the perfect, superhuman connection of twins.

When Savannah finished, there was thunderous applause from that audience who stood and cheered for minutes. I had to talk fast to prevent Luke from racing up to the front of the church and bearing Savannah down the middle aisle on his shoulders. He contented himself with a few ear-splitting rebel yells in praise of his sister. I, secure in my role of the family sentimentalist, bent down between the pews to tie my shoe and dry the tears with my tie.

Later, we were always glad that we had been present on the March evening when Savannah made her triumphant debut in that dog-eat-dog subculture of the New York Poetry World. Much of what is perfectly wonderful about the city of New York was contained in that night, and after dinner at the Coach House, we stayed up late, watching the moon traverse the skyline, fueled by Savannah's triumph, talking and drinking with her friends, exhilarated by how easy and predestined it all seemed, amazed that a girl from South Carolina could deliver a message that could illuminate the hearts of these people born to stone.

If I had left the next day, I might well have come to love the city. But Luke and I lingered and Savannah wanted to show us why she loved the city and why she could never follow us home again. So we shopped at Macy's, went to a Yankees game, took the Circle Line tour, and had a picnic lunch on top of the Empire State Building. She drilled us well in all that was pleasurable and definitive in the New York way of life. But there were other definitions of New

York, dark and unpredictable, that she did not take into account as she force-marched us around Manhattan.

It was on West Twelfth Street in the Village that we received a more treacherous, but no less definitive, view of the city. From far down the street we watched an old woman hobble down the stairs of her brownstone, pausing on each step to wait for her senescent, barely ambulatory French poodle to follow her. There was an imperturbable dignity to the slow descent of both the woman and the dog. The poodle and the lady were of the same general coloring and their walks revealed that they had aged harmoniously by developing the same generous limps. When she reached the sidewalk, she did not see the man appear suddenly behind her and we did not have time to scream out a warning. He was fast and professional and knew exactly what he wanted. He snatched her two gold earrings off her pierced ears, bringing the woman to her knees and tearing the flesh of her ear lobes as she came down hard on the sidewalk. Then he grabbed the gold necklace around her neck and ripped it violently until it broke. The woman began screaming and bleeding from the ears. The man punched her in the face and stopped the screaming. Then, he began walking away from the woman with a studied nonchalance, unhurried and calm. But he had made one serious tactical error. His avenue of escape took him in a direct line toward the Wingo kids of South Carolina.

There were many terrible things about our upbringing in the South, but we were unanimous in how to treat young men who mutilated the ears of old women with poodles. He crossed the street and broke into a run when he saw us move up to challenge him and heard Savannah blowing the hell out of a police whistle. Luke fanned out wide, moving low and fast, as I cut off his line of retreat. I heard a bottle break behind me. The mugger pulled a knife and I heard the small click and saw the flash of the blade as I made my approach.

"I'll cut you, motherfucker," the mugger screamed as he turned and ran straight for me, the knife pushed out before him. I stopped dead in the middle of the street and removed my belt in a single motion, wrapped it around my wrist until a foot of leather and the buckle swung free. He lunged for my throat with the knife, but I stepped back and swung the belt. The buckle snapped against his cheekbone and opened a cut below his eye. He screamed, dropped the knife, looked at me once, then was flattened by the blindside charge of a consensus All-American high school linebacker who smashed into the mugger's spine and drove him face down onto the hood of a Thunderbird. Luke held the man's hair in one hand and punched the back of his head with the other, breaking the man's nose on the crumpling hood of the car. Then the crowd engulfed us, screaming neighbors, gray-haired vigilantes who poked at the man with their weapons and made known their desire to dismember him before the police arrived. Savannah had placed a broken Coke bottle against his jugular and we could hear police sirens in the distance. The old woman, attended to by neighbors, wept softly on her stoop, the poodle licking her bleeding ears.

"Nice city you got here, Savannah," Luke said, giving the mugger another shake. "Nice fucking city."

"It could happen anywhere," Savannah said defensively. "It's still the greatest city in the history of the world."

"Ask that old lady if it's the greatest city in the world."

But New York never quite finishes testing either its devotees or its citizens. On every corner, a thousand facets of that city's infinite variety present themselves in various aspects of the hideous and the sublime. It is a city with too many stories and too many strangers. Throughout that long memorable week, Savannah and I could not stop Luke from helping every wino he encountered. Luke was constitutionally incapable of ignoring these helpless sodden strangers he discovered slumped against doorways, smelling of vomit and wine. He would prop them up, clean them off, lecture them about taking better care of their bodies, then slip a dollar into their pockets, assuring them, Savannah informed him, of a new bottle of wine when they awoke to sunlight and found the miraculous dollar.

"They're perfectly happy," Savannah explained. "A policeman told me that when I first came here and tried to help one of them."

But Luke remained undeterred and continued to offer assistance to every drunk we passed, until one day in a small park on Seventh Avenue, he came upon a young teenage boy, supine on a wooden bench, who did not respond to his soft ministrations at all. When Luke moved him, all of us could see that rigor mortis had set in hours before. There was a hypodermic needle in his coat pocket and a driver's license listing his address as Raleigh, North Carolina.

"He's perfectly happy, Savannah," Luke said as the ambulance crew carried the boy away.

The boy haunted Luke because of his southernness, and he thought it unnatural that any southerner could flourish between the Hudson and East rivers after growing up in the softer, more forgiving zones of the South. A southerner had to change too dramatically to become a New Yorker, Luke thought. He explained his newly conceived theory to Savannah and me over croissants and French coffee at breakfast one morning.

"It's like a trout trying to become a streetcar, Savannah," Luke said, pointing at her with his croissant. "It just wasn't meant to be. You'll see. You may pretend you're a New Yorker, but you're southern to the bone, Savannah. It don't wash out."

"My brother, the redneck philosopher," Savannah said, pouring more coffee.

"I don't mind being a redneck," Luke said. "The only thing wrong with rednecks is that they hate niggers and most everything else. I don't hate anybody. Except New Yorkers. I'm learning to hate eight million of these scumbags because they let kids curl up and die on benches and old men rot in doorways. I can't understand people like that."

"Don't you like my friends, Luke?"

"They're okay, Savannah. Not great, mind you, just okay. I want to be perfectly honest. I see the way they look at Tom and me. I mean, they were actually surprised that we could talk, coming from South Carolina and all. That one critter that introduced you at the reading laughed every time I opened my mouth."

"He loved your southern accent. He told me so later. He said it was like being at the movies."

"No movie. He was talking to Luke Wingo and I could tell that boy never caught a fish in his life except if it was wrapped and frozen in the A & P."

"He's a poet and an intellectual, Luke," Savannah said, growing exasperated. "It's not his job to catch fish."

"And it ain't his job to laugh at those that do. What's wrong with that boy, anyway? He uses his hands funny."

"He's a homosexual, Luke. A lot of my friends are."

"No kidding," Luke said after an uneasy silence. "Is that a guy that does it to other guys?"

"That's right."

"Why didn't you tell me, Savannah?" Luke said, excited. "That makes him a lot more interesting. I heard there were a lot of those guys up here but I never thought I'd get a chance to see one. I'd like to ask him some questions, you know, scientific ones. There's some things I've never understood about all that and he could have told me straight away."

"Thank God," I moaned, "that you didn't tell him, Savannah."

"Luke, that's private," Savannah said.

"Private! He don't give a shit about privacy."

"How do you know, Luke?"

"Because look where he lives. New York Goddamn City. A man who wants privacy would never live here."

"That's what you don't understand, Luke. Someone who really wants privacy will always come to live in New York. You can screw orangutans or parakeets and no one will care at all."

"Well, if I ever start humping parakeets or a loaf of Sunbeam, I want you to help find me an apartment, baby sister. 'Cause you're right, that sure wouldn't go over big back home in Colleton. I just want you to remember where you came from, Savannah. I don't want you to become like these folks."

"I hate where I came from, Luke. That's why I came here to New York, to escape everything in my past. I hated every single thing about my childhood. I love New York because I'm not reminded of Colleton at all. Nothing that I see here, absolutely nothing, reminds me of my childhood."

"Do Luke and I remind you of your childhood?" I asked, suddenly hurt.

"You remind me of the good part of my childhood," she answered fervently.

"Then let's get drunk and eat fatback."

"That doesn't change the past," she answered. "What do you do about the past? Why hasn't it harmed you like it's harmed me?"

"I don't think about it, Savannah," I said. "I pretend it never happened."

"It's over, sweetheart. We survived it. Anyway, we're adults now and we've got the rest of our lives to think about," Luke added.

"Until I figure out the past, I can't bear to think about the rest of my life. It fucked me up, Luke and Tom. I see things. I hear things. All the time. I don't just write that in the poems. I've been seeing a psychiatrist ever since I came to New York."

"What kind of things do you see and hear?" I asked.

"I'll tell you before you go back. I promise I will. I don't want to tell you now."

"It's from eating this kind of shit," Luke said, directing his scorn for the city toward the wilting croissant. "Your constitution just isn't used to it. I had diarrhea the whole time I was in Vietnam from eating all that gook food."

"Please shut up, Luke," I said. "She's talking about mental illness, not diarrhea."

"How do you know mental illness is not some kind of diarrhea of the brain, big man? Something goes haywire and the body has a thousand different ways of letting you know something's wrong. The body's got integrity and you've got to listen to it."

On our last night in New York, I awoke in the middle of the night, hearing a voice coming from Savannah's room. Luke and I were sleeping on the floor in her living room and a streetlamp lit up the room, the light filtered softly through the fog. Listening, I heard my sister's voice, terrified and surreal, speaking to the hidden ones again. I got up, went to her door, and knocked softly. There was no answer and I opened the door and went in.

Savannah was sitting up in bed, addressing something invisible against the opposite wall. She did not appear to see me even when I entered her line of vision. Her lips trembled and saliva spilled out of her mouth, and I listened as she spoke. "No. I will not do what you say. Not even for you. Especially not for you. Not now. Please leave me.

Don't come back. Never again. Stay out of my house. I will
not let you in my house again. There's work to do and I
can't work with your voice in my house."

I walked over to her and touched her on the shoulder.
"Savannah," I said, "what's the matter?"

"They've come back again, Tom. They always come back."

"Who's come back?" I said, getting in bed beside her and
wiping her mouth with a sheet.

"The ones who want to hurt me. I see them, Tom. Can
you see them?"

"Where are they, darling?"

"By the wall. And here, by the window. I see them so
clearly, Tom. You don't seem real to me. But they seem so
real. Can you hear them? Can you hear them screaming at
me? It's going to be bad again, Tom. It's going to be so
bad. I must fight them. I can't write when they visit. And
they stay so long. They hurt me. They won't leave. They
won't listen."

"Who are they, Savannah? Tell me who they are."

"There"—she pointed to the wall—"they're hanging
against the wall. You can't see them, can you?"

"It's just a wall, Savannah. There's nothing there, darling. You're just hallucinating again. It's not real. I promise
you."

"Real. Terribly real. More real than you or me. They
speak to me. They scream at me. Horrible things. Dreadful
things."

"What do they look like? Tell me what they look like so
I can help."

"There," she pointed, and her whole body trembled as
it leaned against mine. "Angels. Lynched. Hanging from
that wall. Dozens of them. Screaming. Blood dripping from
their genitalia. Screaming at me. Talk to me, Tom. Please
talk to me, Tom, and make them stop."

"I'm talking, Savannah. Listen to me. They don't exist
except in your head. They're not there, not in this room,
not in this world. They only live inside you. You've got to
keep telling yourself that. You've got to believe that and
then you can fight them. I know. Remember, I've seen this
before. You can drive them out. Just be patient. It takes
time."

"What happened that day at the house, Tom?"

"Don't think about that, Savannah. Nothing happened. It's your imagination again."

"They're here, Tom. By the door. They're unloosening their belts and screaming. Their faces are skulls. Screaming. And the tiger. Screaming too. I can't take the screaming. Tell me I'm seeing things again, Tom. I need to hear your voice again. They're shitting and moaning and screaming."

"When did you start hearing these things, Savannah?" I said, alarmed. "You used to only see things. Are you sure you're hearing them?"

"The dogs are over here. The black dogs. Black and lean. With human voices. When the black dogs come the others fall silent. The angels grow quiet. The tiger shows respect. The Dobermans rule the dark world, Tom. When they approach, it's the worst. They'll hurt me, Tom."

"Nothing will hurt you, Savannah. I'm here. I won't let anything hurt you. If anything gets near you, I'll kill it. I'm strong enough to kill it and I will. I promise you. Do you hear me? I'm so sorry this happens to you, darling. I'm so sorry. I wish it were me. If it were me, I'd clean this room out of tigers and dogs and angels. I'd destroy everything and make both of us safe."

"You don't know what it's like to have these things come, Tom. It takes so long to get rid of them. It's so hard to fight them. And they always come to hurt me."

"Explain them to me. Please explain what they are and where they come from. I can't help you if I don't understand them, Savannah. I've never had hallucinations. Are they like dreams or nightmares?"

"Worse. Oh, so much worse, Tom. But the same in some way. Except you're awake and know you're awake and know they come because you're sick and helpless and have no power to banish them. They come when they smell your weakness. When they smell your willingness to die and you have to fight them, only there's no strength. There are too many of them. Thousands. Countless. I try to hide it. Especially from you and Luke. I try to pretend they're not here. But they came tonight. When we were walking through the fog. I saw the angels hanging from every lamppost. At first they were silent but as we kept walking, they began moaning and multiplying, until they were hanging and bleeding from every window. They always come to hurt me. I've known they were coming for weeks. I never should have given that reading. It took too much. No strength to give. No strength to fight them with."

"I've got the strength. I've got enough to fight them with. Just tell me how. Tell me how I can help you. I can't see them or hear them. They're not real to me and I don't understand why they're so real to you."

"They're laughing at me for talking to you, Tom. Laughing. All of them. The Doberman is saying, 'He can't help you. No one can. No one can save you from us. No one on earth. No one can touch us. No one believes we're real because we belong only to you. We've come for you again. And will come again. And again. Until you come with us. We want you with us.' "

"Don't listen to them, Savannah. That's your sickness talking. It's not real. That's how the hurt comes to the surface. It comes in these lurid images. But I'm here. You can hear me. You can feel me. Feel my touch. That's real. That's me, Savannah. That voice loves you."

She turned toward me, sweat pouring off her face, her eyes disconsolate and pained. "No, Tom, I can't trust your voice."

"But why?" I asked.

"Because they use all the voices. Remember when I cut myself for the first time?"

"Of course."

"They used the voices that time. The black dogs came. The black dogs filled the room. Glowing in the dark. They snapped at my face with their horrible teeth. All but one. The kind-faced dog. The good dog. He spoke to me, but not in his voice. I like his voice but I didn't that time."

"Whose voice Savannah? I don't understand any of this."

"The good dog spoke and said, 'We want you to kill yourself, Savannah. For the good of the family, because you love us.' He spoke first in Mom's voice."

"But it wasn't Mom."

"I screamed, 'No!' Then I knew it was a trick. Then I heard Dad telling me to kill myself. His voice was sweet and seductive. But that wasn't the worst of all. The good dog leaned close to my ear and close to my throat. And he spoke in the kindest voice of all. 'Kill yourself. Please kill yourself so the family won't suffer anymore. If you love us, take up the razor, Savannah. I'll help you do it. I'll help you.' That's when I slit my wrists the first time, Tom. No one knew about the voices then. I didn't know how to tell anyone in Colleton that I saw and heard things.''

"You're not going to hurt yourself now, Savannah. You won't listen to them this time, will you?"

"No. But I need to be alone to fight them. They'll stay for a long time, but I know how to fight them better now. I promise. Go back to sleep. I'm sorry I woke you."

"No, I'm staying here until they go away."

"I've got to fight them alone, Tom. It's the only way. I know that now. Please get some sleep. I feel better now that I've told you. Thanks for coming in here. I wanted you to."

"I wish I could do something. I don't know how to fight things I can't see or hear."

"I do," she said. "I have to. Good night, Tom. I love you so much."

I kissed her and held her against my chest. I wiped the sweat from her face with my hands and kissed her again.

As I left the room I turned and saw her propped against her pillows, facing the grim population of the room alone.

"Savannah. The voice. The last voice that told you to kill yourself. Whose voice was that? You didn't tell me."

She looked at me, her brother, her twin.

"That was the kindest, most awful voice of all, Tom. It was your voice they used. The voice I love the best."

When I returned to the living room, Luke was awake and listening. He was sitting against the wall, smoking a cigarette, staring at Savannah's door. He motioned to me and I went over and sat down beside him.

"I heard everything, Tom," he whispered, blowing smoke rings at the ferns across the room. "She's crazy as owl shit."

"She comes by it naturally," I whispered, angry at his terminology.

"Why can't she just take your word for it that nothing's there?"

"Because something is there, Luke. That's the whole point."

"Nothing's there. It's just that psychological bullshit again. I think she likes it."

"You've been talking to Mom again."

"It scares me when she's like this. I always want to run. To get away from her. She becomes someone else, someone I don't know, when she starts talking to walls. Then she starts blaming it on the family. On Mom and Dad. If they were so goddamn bad why aren't we seeing dogs on the wall? Why didn't we get hurt the way she did?"

"How do you know we didn't, Luke?"

"You and I aren't crazy, Tom. We're normal. Especially me. You get a little moody sometimes but I think that's because you like to read. People that like to read are always a little fucked up. Let's haul her out of here tomorrow and take her back down to Colleton. I'll put her to work on the shrimp boat. The salt air will clear her head out. So will the hard work. It's hard to be crazy when you're bustin' ass when the shrimp are runnin'. There's no time. Savannah's living proof that writing poetry and reading books causes brain damage."

"And you're living proof that catching shrimp does the same damn thing," I whispered fiercely. "Our sister's a sick woman, Luke. It's like she has cancer of the brain or something horrible like that. Does that help you understand it better? It's that deadly, too."

"Don't get mad at me, Tom. Please don't. I try to understand it in my own way. It's not your way, I know. But I'd feel better if she was near us. She could live with me and I could help her. I really think I could."

"She mentioned that day on the island."

"I heard her. You should have told her it never happened."

"It did."

"Mom told us it never happened."

"Mom also told us that Dad never beat us. She told us we're descendants of southern aristocracy. She told us a million things that weren't true, Luke."

"I don't remember much about that day."

I grabbed my brother's shoulder and pulled him toward me. I whispered brutally in his ear, "I remember everything, Luke. I remember every single detail of that day and every single detail of our whole childhood. I'm a goddamn liar when I tell myself I don't remember those things."

"You swore you would never mention that. We all did. It's best to forget some things. It's best to forget that. I don't want to remember what happened. I don't want to talk about it and I don't want you to talk about it to Savannah. It can't help her and I know she doesn't remember anything about it."

"All right," I said. "But don't you pretend that day never happened. Because that makes me crazy. We've pretended too much in our family, Luke, and hidden far too much. I think we're all going to pay a high price for our inability to face the truth."

"Is that what you think Savannah's in there doing?" Luke said, pointing toward her door. "When she talks to the angels and dogs? When she drools into her sandals? When she checks into the nut house? Is that how you face the truth?"

"No. I just think the truth is leaking out all over her. I don't think she faced it any better than we did, but I don't think her powers of suppression are as strong as ours either."

"She's crazy because she writes."

"She's crazy because of what she has to write about. She writes about a young girl growing up in South Carolina, about what she knows best in the world. What would you have her write about—Zulu teenagers, Eskimo drug addicts?"

"She should write about what won't hurt her, what won't draw out the dogs."

"She has to write about them, Luke. That's where the poetry comes from. Without them, there's no poetry."

"It scares me, Tom. One day she's gonna kill herself."

"She's stronger than we think. And she wants to write lots of poems. That's what will keep her alive. There aren't enough dogs in her head to make her want to stop writing. Let's get some sleep. We've got a long drive ahead of us tomorrow."

"We can't leave her like this."

"We have to leave her like this. This is her life most of the time, Luke."

"I want you to know one thing, Tom. I want you to listen and listen good. I don't understand what's wrong with Savannah. It's not in me to understand it. But I love her every bit as much as you do."

"I know that, Luke. She knows it, too."

Yet I would not sleep anymore on this last remarkable night in New York City. Instead, I thought about how we had all arrived at this point in time, what benedictions and aggrievements each of us had carried from the island and how each of us had an indisputable and unchangeable role in our family's grotesque melodrama. From earliest childhood, Savannah had been chosen to bear the weight of the family's accumulated psychotic energy. Her luminous sensitivity left her open to the violence and disaffection of our household and we used her to store the bitterness of our mordant chronicle. I could see it now: One member of the family, by a process of artificial but deadly selection, is nominated to be the lunatic, and all neurosis, wildness, and displaced suffering settles like dust in the eaves and porches of that tenderest, most vulnerable psyche. Craziness attacks the softest eyes and hamstrings the gentlest flanks. When was Savannah chosen to be the crazy one? I thought. When was the decision made and was it by acclamation and had I, her twin, agreed to the decision? Had I played a part in stringing up the bleeding angels in her room and could I help cut those angels down?

I tried to think of all our roles. Luke had been offered the role of strength and simplicity. He had suffered under the terrible burden of being the least intellectual child. He had made a fetish out of his single-minded sense of justice and constancy. Because he was not gifted in school and because he was the oldest, he was the recipient of my father's sudden furies, the hurt shepherd who drove the flock to safety before he turned to face the storm of my father's wrath alone. It was difficult to mark the damage done to Luke or to tally the sum total of the desolation caused by his place in the family. Because of his enormous strength, there was something untouchable about his presence. He had the soul of a fortress and eyes that had peered at the world from battlements too long. He spoke his gospels and philosophies with his body alone. His injuries were all internal and I wondered if he would ever have to assess the extent of his wounds. I knew he would never understand our sister's running war with the past and the long march of her private, inimitable demons through her daylight hours, nor did I think Savannah could appreciate the magnitude of Luke's dilemma: the undermining responsibilities and duties of inarticulate strength. Luke acted when the heart cried out; the poetry in him was wordless. Luke was neither poet nor psychotic. He was a man of action, and that was the intolerable burden our family presented to him simply because he was born first of all.

And I? What had I become, sleepless and dazzled by the monstrous seraphim prowling before my sister's eyes? What was my role, and did it contain the elements of grandeur or ruin? My designation in the family was normality. I was the balanced child drafted into the ranks for leadership, for coolness under fire, stability. "Solid as a rock," my mother would describe me to her friends, and I thought the description was perfect. I was courteous, bright, popular, and religious. I was the neutral country, the family Switzerland. A symbol of righteousness, I paid homage to the irreproachable figure of the child my parents always wanted. Respectful of the courtesies, I had entered my adulthood timid and eager to please. And while my sister screamed and fought against the black dogs of her underworld and my brother slept like an infant, I stayed up the night and knew that I had passed an important week in my life. I had been married for almost six years, had established my career as teacher and coach, and was living out my life as a mediocre man.

3

It had been nine years since that first visit to New York to witness Savannah's triumphant reading in Greenwich Village. A full three years had passed since Savannah and I, once the inseparable twins, had spoken a word to each other. I could not utter her name without hurting. I could barely think about the past five years without coming apart.

Memory had become both regent and keepsake of night-mare as I again crossed the Fifty-ninth Street Bridge by taxi and came to Manhattan as king's horseman, required by custom to put my sister together again.

Savannah's psychiatrist was one Dr. Lowenstein and she worked out of an elegant brownstone in the East Seventies. Her waiting room was all tweed and leather. The ashtrays were heavy enough to kill squirrels. There were two modern paintings, jangling enough to induce schizophrenia, hanging from opposite walls. They looked like Rorschach ink-blots gone to seed in a field of lilies. I stared at the one hanging behind the receptionist before I opened my mouth.

"Did someone really pay money for that thing?" I asked the proper, no-nonsense black woman behind the desk.

"Three thousand dollars. The art dealer told Dr. Lowenstein he was giving it away," the woman said icily, not looking up.

"Did the artist stick his finger down his throat and puke at the canvas, or do you think he used paint?"

"Do you have an appointment?" she asked.

"Yes, ma'am. I'm supposed to see the doctor at three o'clock."

"Mr. Wingo," she said, checking her schedule and studying my face. "You planning to stay the night? This isn't a hotel."

"I didn't have time to drop my suitcase off at my sister's house. You don't mind if I leave it out here when I see the doctor, do you?"

"Where are you from?" the woman asked me.

For a moment I was going to lie and say I was from Sausalito, California. Everyone loves you if you say you're from California, while everyone is filled with sorrow or loathing if you admit you're from the South. I've known black men who were strongly tempted to fillet me when they heard me drawl out the words "Colleton, South Carolina." I could see it register in their eyes that if they rid the earth of this one sad-eyed cracker they'd be avenging ancestors kidnaped from the veldt centuries ago and brought chained and bleeding into southern ports. Nat Turner lives deep in the eyes of all modern black men.

"South Carolina," I said.

"I'm so sorry," she said, smiling but not looking up.

The music of Bach filled the room, entered my ears. The flowers were fresh on the sideboard at the end of the room; they were purple irises, carefully arranged, and they leaned toward me like the small, delicate heads of birds. I closed my eyes and tried to relax into the music, yield to its seduction. The music slowed my heartbeat and it felt like roses beneath my eyes. My head was aching slightly and I opened my eyes, wondering whether I had packed aspirin in my suitcase. There were books on the sideboard and I rose to inspect them as the Bach concerto ended and Vivaldi spilled into the room. The books were well selected and cared for and some of them were signed by the authors. The inscriptions were personal and I realized many of the writers had sat in this same room, shivering before this unnamed artist's ghastly vision of the world. On the top shelf, I spotted Savannah's second book of poetry, *The Prince of Tides*. I opened it to the dedication page and almost cried when I read the words. But it was good to feel the tears try to break through. It was proof I was still alive inside, down deep, where the hurt lay bound and degraded in the cheap, bitter shell of my manhood. My manhood! How I loathed being a man, with its fierce responsibilities, its tally of ceaseless strength, its passionate and stupid bravado. How I hated strength and duty and steadfastness. How I dreaded seeing my lovely sister with her damaged wrists and tubes running down her nose and the bottles of glucose hanging like glass embryos above her bed. But I knew my role so clearly now, knew the tyranny and the snare of maleness, and I would walk toward my sister as a pillar of strength, a vegetable king striding over the fields of our shared earth, my hands sparkling with the strength of pastures, confident in cycles, singing of her renewal, comforting her with the words of the coach and good news from the king of seasons. Strength was my gift; it was also my act, and I'm sure it's what will end up killing me.

I turned the page to the first poem in the book. I read the poem aloud, accompanied by violins and irises and Vivaldi, trying to catch the tone and spirit of Savannah's inflection, the palpable reverence she brought to the lectern when she read her own work.

I blaze with a deep sullen magic,
smell lust like a heron on fire;
all words I form into castles
then storm them with soldiers of air.

What I seek is not there for asking.
My armies are fit and well trained.
This poet will trust her battalions
to fashion her words into blades.

At dawn I shall ask them for beauty,
for proof that their training went well.
At night I shall beg their forgiveness
as I cut their throats by the hill.

My navies advance through the language,
destroyers ablaze in high seas.
I soften the island for landings.
With words, I enlist a dark army.
My poems are my war with the world.

I blaze with a deep southern magic.
The bombardiers taxi at noon.
There is screaming and grief in the mansions
and the moon is a heron on fire.

Then I turned again to the dedication and read:

Man wonders but God decides
When to kill the Prince of Tides.

When I looked up, Dr. Lowenstein was staring at me
from the door of her office. She was expensively dressed,
and lean. Her eyes were dark and unadorned. In the shadows of that room, with Vivaldi fading in sweet echoes, she
was breathtakingly beautiful, one of those go-to-hell New
York women with the incorruptible carriage of lionesses.
Tall and black-haired, she looked as if she had been air-
brushed with breeding and good taste.

"Who is the Prince of Tides?" she asked without intro-
ducing herself.

"Why don't you ask Savannah?"

"I will when she's able to speak to me. That might be

some time," she answered, smoothing her jacket. "I'm sorry. I'm Dr. Lowenstein. You must be Tom."

"Yes, ma'am," I said, rising and following her into her office.

"Would you like a cup of coffee, Tom?"

"Yes, ma'am, I would," I said nervously.

"Why do you call me ma'am? I believe we're exactly the same age."

"Good home training. And nervousness."

"Why are you nervous? Do you take anything with your coffee?"

"Cream and sugar. I get nervous every time my sister slits her wrists. It's a quirk of mine."

"Have you ever met a psychiatrist before?" she asked, bringing back two cups of coffee from a closet near her desk. Her walk was graceful and assured.

"Yes. I think I've met all of Savannah's doctors at one time or another."

"Has she ever attempted suicide before?"

"Yes. On two other bright and happy occasions."

"Why do you say 'bright and happy'?"

"I was being cynical. I'm sorry. It's a family habit I've fallen prey to."

"Is Savannah cynical?"

"No. She escaped that part of the family horror."

"You sound sorry she escaped your cynicism."

"She tries to kill herself instead, Doctor. I would far prefer her to be cynical. How is Savannah? Where is she? When can I see her? And why are you asking me these questions? You haven't told me about her condition."

"Is the coffee good, Tom?" she asked with complete control.

"Yes. It's fabulous. Now, about Savannah."

"I want you to be patient, Tom. We'll get to the subject of Savannah in a moment," the doctor said in a patronizing voice shaped by far too many advanced degrees. "There are some background questions I need to ask if we're going to help Savannah. And I'm sure we want to help Savannah, don't we?"

"Not if you continue to talk to me in that unbearably supercilious tone, Doctor, as though I were some gaudy chimp you're trying to teach to type. And not until you tell

me where my goddamn sister is," I said, sitting on my
hands to stop their visible trembling. The coffee and the
headache intermingled and the faraway music scratched
along my eardrum like a nail.

Dr. Lowenstein, annealed to hostility in all its multifar-
ious guises, looked at me coolly. "All right, Tom. I will tell
you what I know about Savannah. Then will you help me?"

"I don't know what you want."

"I want to know about her life, everything you know
about it. I want to hear the stories of her childhood. I need
to know where these symptoms first manifested themselves, when she first started demonstrating signs of her
illness. You did know about her mental illness, didn't you,
Tom?"

"Yes, of course," I answered. "Half her poems are about
her madness. She writes about it the way Hemingway wrote
about killing lions. It's the dementia of her art. I'm sick of
Savannah being crazy. I'm tired of all this Sylvia Plath bullshit.
The last time she opened herself up, Doctor, I told her that
I wanted her to finish the job the next time. I wanted her
to swallow the barrel of a shotgun and blow the back of
her head out. But no. She's got this attraction to razor
blades. See? I can't stand looking at her scars, Doctor. I
can't stand seeing her lying in bed with tubes running from
her nose. I'm a good brother, but I don't know what to say
to her after she's slit herself open like she was cleaning a
deer. I'm not good at it, Doctor. And no shrink, no fucking
shrink—and there have been scores of them—has ever
helped Savannah quiet the demons that torture her. Can
you do that, ma'am? Tell me. Can you do it?"

She took a sip of her coffee; her indigenous calm infuriated me as much as it formed a bold-stroked parenthesis
around my lack of control. She replaced her cup into the
saucer, where it clinked into its round groove nicely. "Would
you like another cup of coffee, Tom?" she asked.

"No."

"I don't know if I can help your sister," Dr. Lowenstein
said, turning her professional stare on me once again. "Her
suicide attempt took place over a week ago. She is now in
no danger of dying from her wounds. She almost died the
first night at Bellevue, but the receiving doctor in the emergency room did excellent work, I'm told. She was in a coma

when I first saw her, and we didn't know if she would live. When she came out of it, she started raving and screaming. It was gibberish but, as you might imagine, of a highly poetic and associative quality. I taped it and it might give us some clues about the latest cycle. Yesterday something changed. She ceased to speak. I called a poet I know and she found out your mother's telephone number from Savannah's next-door neighbor. I sent your father a telegram but he didn't respond. Why do you think he didn't?"

"Because you live in New York. Because you're a woman. Because you're a Jew. Because you're a shrink. And besides, it scares him to death every time Savannah has one of her breakdowns."

"So he handles it by refusing to answer a cry for help?"

"If Savannah cried for help, he'd be right here beside her if he could. He divides the world into Wingos, assholes, and asshole Wingos. Savannah is a Wingo."

"And I'm an asshole," she said without emotion.

"You've broken the code," I answered, smiling. "By the way, my father couldn't have received your letter."

"Does your family hate Jews?"

"My family hates everyone. It's nothing personal."

"Did your family use the word *nigger* when you were growing up?"

"Of course, Doctor," I said, wondering what this topic had to do with Savannah. "I grew up in South Carolina."

"But there must have been some educated, enlightened people who refused to use that odious word," the doctor said.

"They weren't Wingos. Except my mother. She claimed that only poor white trash used that word. She prided herself on saying *Negro* with a long 'o.' She thought that put her high in the ranks of humanitarians."

"Do you use the word *nigger* now, Tom?" she asked.

I studied her pretty face to see if she was joking, but these were business hours and the doctor was all seriousness, without time for the small subsidies and occlusions of humor.

"I only use that word when I'm around condescending Yankees like you. Then, Doctor, I can't stop myself from using the word. Nigger. Nigger. Nigger. Nigger. Nigger. Nigger," I said.

"Are you quite finished?" she said, and I was delighted I had offended her upholstered sensibilities.

"Quite."

"I don't allow that word to be used in this office."

"Nigger. Nigger. Nigger. Nigger. Nigger. Nigger," I replied.

She controlled herself with effort and spoke in a tense, coiled voice. "I did not mean to condescend to you, Tom. If you think I did, then please accept my apologies. It just startled me somewhat that the family of the poet Savannah Wingo used that word. It seems hard to believe her family was racist."

"Savannah is who she is today because her family was racist. She reacted against her family. She began writing as an act of outrage that she was born to such a family."

"Are you mad that you were born to such a family?"

"I would be mad no matter what family I was born to. But I'd have chosen the Rockefeller or Carnegie family if I'd had a choice. Being born a Wingo has just made it all the more difficult."

"Explain, please."

"I think life is painful to all human beings. It's especially hard when you're a Wingo. But, of course, I've never been anything but a Wingo, so I'm speaking theoretically."

"What religion did your family practice?" the doctor asked.

"Catholic, for godsakes. Roman Catholic."

"Why did you say 'for godsakes'? There's nothing wrong with being a Catholic."

"You have no idea how weird it is to be raised a Catholic in the Deep South."

"I might have some idea," she replied. "You have no idea how weird it is to be raised Jewish anywhere in the world."

"I've read Philip Roth," I said.

"So what," she answered, and there was real hostility in her voice.

"Oh, nothing. Just a cringing attempt at establishing a fragile bond between us."

"Philip Roth despises both Jews and women and you do not have to be either Jewish or female to see that," she said, delivering her statement as though the subject could be dropped forever.

"That's what Savannah thinks, too," I said, smiling at

the memory of Savannah's vehemence and dogmatism on the same subject.

"What do you think, Tom?"

"Do you really want to know?"

"Yes. Very much."

"Well, with all due respect, I think *both* you and Savannah are full of shit on that subject," I answered.

"With all due respect, why should we entertain the opinion of a white southern male?"

I leaned forward and whispered, "Because, Doctor, when I'm not eating roots and berries, when I'm not screwing mules from the tops of stumps, and when I'm not slaughtering pigs out back at the still, I'm a very smart man."

She smiled and studied her fingernails. In the silence, the hushed music seemed to spill into the room, each note clear and bright, like a waltz coming across a lake.

"In your sister's poetry, Tom," Dr. Lowenstein tried once more, "are you the brother who is the shrimper or are you the coach?" I knew this woman was more than a match for me.

"The coach," I admitted.

"Why did you lower your voice? Are you ashamed of being a coach?"

"I'm ashamed of the way other people feel about coaches. Especially in New York. Especially a shrink. Especially a woman shrink."

"How do you think I feel about coaches in general?" she asked in complete control once more.

"How many coaches do you know in particular?"

"None," she said, smiling. "I don't seem to meet many of them in my circle."

"You wouldn't allow one in your circle if you knew one."

"That's probably true, Tom. Who makes up your crowd in South Carolina?"

"Just other coaches," I said, feeling trapped and constricted in that fragrant room. I could smell her perfume and knew it well but could not recall its name. "We sit around reading the sports section, arm wrestling, and sucking on each other's blood blisters."

"You're a very enigmatic man, Tom. I cannot help your sister if you only answer my questions with jokes or riddles. I need you to trust me. Do you understand?"

"I don't know you, ma'am. I don't speak easily about personal things with people I love, much less with people I've known for only half an hour."

"But this cultural gap between us seems to concern you overmuch."

"I can feel your contempt for me," I said, closing my eyes. The headache surrounded my eyes in a pure netting of pain.

"Contempt?" she said in disbelief, rolling her eyes. "Even if I loathed everything you stood for, I would not feel contempt for you. I need you in order to help your sister—if you'll let me. I'm completely familiar with her work, but I need to know the details of her life so that when she's lucid again I can try to break through this destructive pattern she seems to have been in for as long as anyone can remember. If I can find a few clues in her background perhaps I can help her devise some strategies of survival, so she can pursue her art without such devastating consequences."

"Ah, now I've got it," I said, rising and beginning to pace around the room, disoriented and increasingly out of control, dizzy with the pastels. "You're the heroine in this late-twentieth-century drama. The sensitive and dedicated therapist who saves the feminist poet for the ages, who lays her healing, manicured hands on the artist's gaping wounds and, with the holy words of Sigmund Freud, brings her back from the edge of the abyss. The doctor becomes a small but revered footnote in literary history." I squeezed my head with both hands and began to massage the temples with my fingers.

"Do you have a headache, Tom?" she asked.

"A terrible one, Doctor. Do you have a spot of morphine around?"

"No, but I've got some aspirin. Why didn't you say something?"

"You feel bad complaining about a headache when your sister has slit her wrists."

She had walked to her desk and emptied three aspirins out into her palm. She poured me another cup of coffee and I took the aspirin.

"Do you want to lie down on the couch?"

"No, for godsakes. I was terrified you were going to make

me lie down on the couch when I came in here this afternoon. Like they do it in the movies."

"I try not to do it the way they do in the movies . . . I
don't mean to shock you, Tom, but when I first saw her,
she was covering herself with her own excrement."

"That doesn't shock me."

"Why not?"

"I've seen her covering herself with shit before. It's
shocking the first time. Maybe the second. Then you get
used to it and it becomes part of the scenery."

"Where did you see it the first time?"

"In San Francisco. She was on a reading tour. She got
herself in a genuine loony bin. The most depressing place
I ever saw. I couldn't tell if covering herself with shit was
an act of self-hate or she was just redecorating her room."

"You make jokes about your sister's psychosis. What an
odd man you are!"

"It's the southern way, Doctor."

"The southern way?" she said.

"My mother's immortal phrase. We laugh when the pain
gets too much. We laugh when the pity of human life gets
too . . . pitiful. We laugh when there's nothing else to do."

"When do you weep . . . according to the southern way?"

"After we laugh, Doctor. Always. Always after we laugh."

"I'll meet you at the hospital. Is seven o'clock okay?"

"It's fine. I'm sorry I said some of the things I said today,
Doctor. Thank you for not kicking me out of the office."

"See you tonight. Thank you for coming," she said, then
added in a teasing way, "Coach."

In mental hospitals, no matter how humanistic or enlightened, keys are the manifest credentials of power, the steel
asterisks of freedom and mobility. The march of orderlies
and nurses is accompanied by the alienating cacophony of
singing keys striking against thighs, annotating the passage
of the free. When you find yourself listening to their keys
and owning none, you will come close to understanding
the white terror of the soul that comes with being banished
from all commerce with mankind. I learned the secret of
keys from one of my sister's poems that she wrote at one
sitting after her first internment. She looked upon keys as

the talismans and ciphers of her dilemma, her undeclared war with herself. Whenever she was sick, she would awake to the subtracting noise of keys.

That evening when Dr. Lowenstein took me in to see her, Savannah was crouched in a corner, her arms wrapped around her knees, her head turned away from the door and resting against the wall. The room smelled of excrement and ammonia, the corrupt and familiar bouquet that debases each long hour of the insane, the essential defining fragrance of the mental hospital, American style. She did not move or look up when we entered the room. And I knew this would be one of the bad times.

Dr. Lowenstein approached Savannah and gently touched her shoulder. "Savannah, I have a surprise for you. I've brought your brother, Tom, for a visit."

My sister did not move. Her spirit had been subtracted out of her flesh. There was a mineral stillness to her repose, an immaculate divinity to the black ensemble of her catatonia. The catatonic has always seemed the holiest of the psychotics to me. There is integrity in the vow of silence and something sacred in the renunciation of movement. It is the quietest human drama of the soul undone, the solemn dress rehearsal for death itself. I had seen my sister not move before and I faced her this time as a veteran of her incurable quietude. The first time I had come apart and had hidden my face in my hands. Now, I remembered something she had told me: that deep within her stillness and solitude, her spirit was healing itself in the unreachable places, mining the riches and ores that lay concealed in the most inaccessible passages of her mind. And, she had added, she could not hurt herself when she was not moving, only cleanse herself, only prepare for the day when she reached again for the light. When she reached for that light, I planned to be there.

I took Savannah by the shoulders, kissed her neck, and sat down beside her. I held her tightly and snuggled my face against her hair. I avoided looking at the bandages on her wrists. "Hey, Savannah. How are you, darling?" I said softly. "Everything's going to be all right because the kid is here. I'm so sorry you're feeling bad, but I'm going to be right here until you get well. I saw Dad the other day and he sent his love. No, don't worry, he hasn't changed.

He's still an asshole. Mom couldn't come up to see you this time because she had to wash her pantyhose. Sallie and the kids are fine. Jennifer is starting to grow breasts. She came up to me after her bath the other night, pulled down her towel, and said, 'Look, Daddy, bumps,' then ran giggling and screaming down the hall, with me chasing lewdly behind her. South Carolina hasn't changed much at all. It's still the goddamn cultural center of the world. Even Sullivans Island is starting to get some culture. They cut a ribbon on a new barbecue house out on the highway the other day. I still haven't found a job, but I've been looking hard. I know you've been worried about that. Saw Grandma Wingo at the nursing home in Charleston the other night. It was her birthday. She thought I was the Bishop of Charleston in 1920 and that I was trying to have sex with her. And I saw . . ."

For thirty minutes I talked to my sister, until Dr. Lowenstein interrupted my monologue by touching me on the shoulder and motioning that it was time to make our departure. I stood up. Then I lifted Savannah in my arms and carried her to the bed. She had lost weight and her cheeks were dark and sunken. Her eyes registered nothing; they were two turquoise gems lying inert in a field of off-white. She curled like an embryo when I set her down on her bed. I pulled a brush from my pocket and began stroking her damp, tangled hair. I brushed hard until I could see some of the gold return; I stroked her hair until some of its glorious luster and shine ignited down her back. Then I sang her a song from our childhood.

Take me back to the place where I first saw the light,
To the sweet sunny South take me home,
Where the wild birds sing me to sleep every night.
Oh, why was I tempted to roam?

I stood over her in silence for a moment, then said, "I'll be back to see you tomorrow, Savannah. I know you can hear, and just remember this: We've been here before. And you'll come out of it again. It takes time. Then we'll go singing and dancing and I'll say shitty things about New York and you'll punch my arm and call me a redneck. I'm here, darling. And I'll be here for as long as you need me."

I kissed my twin on the lips and pulled the sheet over her.

When we were outside, in the late spring air, Dr. Lowenstein asked me if I had eaten, and I remembered I had not. She suggested a small French restaurant, Petite Marmite, that she knew well and liked. I instantly thought about the cost, the automatic response of a South Carolina schoolteacher humiliated by years of coolie wages. My joblessness I had forgotten. American teachers are all trained to think poor; we love conferences and book fairs with hospitality suites, expenses paid and banquets of rubbery chicken, sweet French dressing, and unspeakable peas.

"Is it expensive, Doctor? I've paid for some meals in this city where I thought I was sending the chef's kid to private school."

"It's very reasonable by New York standards, I think."

"Wait here. I'll call my bank and see if I can arrange a loan."

"I'll buy, Coach."

"As a completely liberated male, I accept, Doctor."

The maître d' greeted Dr. Lowenstein with an understated intimacy that let you know immediately that she was a regular. He led us to a corner table. The couple at the next table were moaning passionately to each other; their hands were clenched, their eyes orgasmic and engorged with candlelight, and you could tell they wanted to fling themselves across the pure white tablecloth and copulate over the béarnaise sauce. The doctor ordered a bottle of Macon Blanc, then looked briefly at the leather-bound menu.

"Can I have an hors d'oeuvre?" I asked.

"Of course. Have anything you like."

"Can I have all the hors d'oeuvres?"

"No, I want you to eat a well-balanced meal."

"You are Jewish."

"Damn right," she said, smiling. Then, growing serious, she asked, "What did you think about Savannah?"

"It's worse than it's ever been. But I feel a lot better."

"I don't understand."

"I find it much harder to deal with her when she's screaming and hallucinating and out of control. When she's like this it's almost as if she's resting, building up her strength, getting ready to step out into the world again. She'll be coming out of it in a month or two, Doctor. I promise you that."

"Can you make predictions like that?"

"Not really, but this is the pattern I know."

"Why don't you have a job now?"

"I was fired."

"May I ask why?"

"It's part of a long story," I said, "and for now, you cannot ask why."

The sommelier brought the wine to the table and poured some into Dr. Lowenstein's glass. She inhaled it, tasted it, and nodded. I love the small dramas of mealtime, the elegance of ritual. I tasted the wine gratefully and felt it enter my body to begin the night's long siege against the migraine. I knew I should not drink but I wanted to. I was supposed to tell this woman my story in order to help my sister. But I had decided on a different strategy: I would tell her my story to save myself from myself.

"I've got a migraine headache coming on, Doctor. I don't have a job and I have no prospects for getting a job. My wife, who is an internist, is having an affair with a heart specialist. She is thinking about leaving me. I hate my mother and my father, yet in five minutes I'll tell you that I didn't really mean to say that and I love them with all my heart. My brother Luke is a family tragedy. You've heard about Luke but have not yet made the connection with Savannah. Did I mention that my father is in prison? That's why he didn't respond to your telegram. The story of the Wingos is one of humor, grotesquerie, and tragedy. Tragedy predominates. You'll see that Savannah's madness was the only natural response to our family life. And that my response was the unnatural one."

"What was your response?"

"I pretended none of it happened. I have a gift for denial inherited from my mother, and I use it well. My sister calls me the Coach of Unremembrance. But I think I remember a lot more than she does."

"And now?"

"Now I'm in the process of falling apart. That's never been a role reserved for me. My family has always expected me to be the tower of strength, the man with the whistle, the good coach: I've always been the first secretary and star witness to the family melodrama."

"Aren't you being a bit dramatic, Tom?"

"Yes. And now I'll stop and be charming."

As we ordered our meals, she told me about her life, and she grew softer over candlelight. She ate soft-shell crabs encrusted with almonds and I told her about pulling crabs from the Colleton River. I ate salmon napped in a velvet dill sauce and she told me about watching the salmon fishermen in Scotland. There was another bottle of wine and a mushroom salad so fresh it was like tasting the bottom of the forest. The vinaigrette was mottled with basil leaves. The headache was gone now, but I could feel the approach of the migraine in the spine, moving upward, marshaling its forlorn powers slowly, like a train in the mountains. I had raspberries and cream for dessert. When her sorbet arrived, she began questioning me about Savannah again.

"Does the word *Callanwolde* mean anything to you, Tom?" she asked.

"Sure, why?"

"It's one of the things Savannah kept repeating when she first regained consciousness. One of the things she was screaming." She handed me a piece of paper across the table and asked me to read it. "I told you I recorded everything Savannah said in those first few days. I thought it might prove helpful once she's well enough to return to therapy. I culled this paragraph out of a dozen hours of gibberish."

I reached for the wine and read the words.

"Taps for the Prince of Tides. Dogs to my birthday party. Come to live in the white house, the marshes are never safe. Black dog not related to tigers. Daddy get the camera. Daddy get the camera. The dogs are roaming in packs. Three men are coming down the road. Callanwolde. Callanwolde. Out of the woods of Callanwolde and up to house on Rosedale Road. Taps for the Prince of Tides. The brother's mouth is not safe. The marsh is never safe. The shrimp are running, the shrimp are running, the dogs are running. Caesar. Red pins and gardenias. Now. Now. The giant and Coca-Cola. Bring the tiger to the back door. Play Dixie for the seals. A root for the dead men by the crow. Do you hear someone, Mother? The graves are talking again. Someone outside? Someone pretty, Mother. The snow is stolen from the river and someone prettier than me, Mother. How many angels dropped from the womb bloomed into ugliness in springtime? Where is fruit and Grandpa is cross. Stop the boat. Please stop the boat. I'm going to be with you for a very long time. Hurt you. Promise I will hurt you. Hurt the tiger man. Hurt the tiger man. Kill the tiger man. Stop the boat. Where is Agnes Day?"

When I finished reading I said, "Jesus Christ."

Dr. Lowenstein took back the paper and folded it neatly. "Is there anything in this that you recognize as significant?"

"I recognize a lot of it. Everything seems significant."

"What does it mean?"

"She's screaming out her autobiography to you . . . to anyone who is listening . . . to herself."

"Her autobiography? Will you stay in New York and tell me all you know?"

"From beginning to end, Doctor. For as long as you need me."

"Can you start tomorrow at five?"

"Fine," I said. "I've got some terrible things to tell you."

"Thank you for wanting to help Savannah, Tom," she said.

"No," I replied. And, almost strangling, I said, "Help *me*. Help *me*."

It was past midnight when I entered my sister's apartment on Grove Street. Sheridan Square appeared languid and surreal on a moonless night and through it drifted those casteless citizens of the after-midnight city. Each night they crossed each other's paths with no sign of recognition. Always, they moved through the plangent light in a ceremony of surprised nostalgia. Their faces had the glow of some interior, sustained equinox beyond the comprehension of strangers. Nightwalkers, unafraid, I had studied each of them as they passed me by, oblivious of me. I tried to mimic their expressions, so ethereal, unsponsored, and original. But my face is a lousy actor. They knew how to walk in a great city and I did not. Outlander, visitor, I could smell the sea as I entered the lobby of Savannah's apartment, the old familiar scent of the Eastern seaboard roaring up the Avenues.

The antique elevator, the size and shape of a coffin, wheezed and groaned its way to the sixth floor. I set my luggage on the marble floor and tried twelve keys before I discovered the four that slid back the enormous bolts that protected my sister from the world.

Leaving the door open, I walked into Savannah's bedroom and threw my suitcases on the bed. I turned on the lamp by the bed but the bulb was dead. In the darkness, I fumbled around for the wall switch and sent a cut-glass flower vase shattering to the floor, and then I heard a voice screaming at me from the hallway. "Halt! Don't move, asshole. I'm a crack shot, this pistol is loaded, and I take pleasure in shooting criminals in cold blood."

"It's me, Eddie," I shouted from the bedroom. "For godsakes, it's me—Tom."

"Tom?" Eddie Detreville said, puzzled. Then he began to scold. "Tom, you should never break into anyone's apartment in New York without alerting me."

"I didn't break in, Eddie. I have a set of keys."

"That doesn't make you the Lone Ranger, sweetheart. Savannah gives out sets of her keys like they were party favors."

"Why didn't you call me about Savannah, Eddie?" I asked, thinking of the question for the first time.

"Now don't you get cross with me, Tom. I'll not have it. I have strict orders never to call her family about anything unless she dies. Don't you think I wanted to? I was the one who found her. I heard her fall in the bathroom. She'd been gone for months. Months! I didn't even know she was back. I thought she was being murdered by some criminal. I came trembling into this apartment with this loaded gun and found her bleeding on the bathroom floor. It was a total mess and I nearly passed out, as you can imagine. It makes me a nervous wreck just to think about it."

"You were the one who found her? I didn't know that."

"It was a total mess. It took me days to clean up the blood. It was like an abattoir in there."

"You saved her life," I said to Eddie, who stood in the chiaroscuro of the dim light of the hallway.

"Yes. I, too, like thinking of it in those heroic terms."

"You can quit pointing the pistol at me, Eddie," I said.

"Oh, yes. Sorry, Tom," he said, lowering the pistol. "I've been robbed twice this year."

"Why don't you lock your door?"

"My door's got more locks than Shirley Temple's hair, sweetheart. These men are acrobats and stuntmen. One leapt from a fire escape on the next building and landed on my air conditioner. I've greased all my windowsills with Crisco, but these are serious thieves. Serious. I won't even tell you about my insurance premium. It's astronomical. How are you, Tom? I haven't even said hello properly."

I walked to the doorway and embraced Eddie Detreville. He kissed me on the cheek and I returned the kiss, before we walked into the living room. He turned on a lamp and I fell heavily into a soft armchair. The light hurt my eyes and entered my brain with a cruel, stunning voltage.

"Where's Andrew?" I asked with my eyes shut.

"He left me for a younger man, Tom. Called me an old fag. An old, worn-out fag. It wasn't very pleasant. But he calls every once in a while and it looks like we might be friends again. Savannah was an angel when it happened. I practically lived over here."

"I'm sorry," I said, opening my eyes. The light felt as if someone had tossed a tumbler of acid at my retinas. "I liked Andrew. You two were good together. Any other nice boy on the horizon?"

"Ha! Not a one. Unless I can tempt you to cross the line while you're here. Or are you still holding to the ridiculous claim that you're a hopeless hetero?"

"I've become a neuter," I said. "I'm not into sex anymore. I'm into wallowing self-pity."

"Let me make you a drink," he said. "Then I'll begin the slow sensual seduction."

"Make it light, Eddie. The migraine cometh."

"Did you see Savannah?"

"Yeah. It was like talking to a fern."

"She was so out of control for a while. You have no idea. Cuckoo nest time."

"Do you have any pain pills? I left mine back home."

"Pills?" he answered. "I've got uppers, downers, mid-dlers, and in-betweeners. You name it and Dr. Eddie's got it. My medicine cabinet looks like a branch of Bristol-Myers. But it's not good to drink and pill at the same time."

"Since when have I done what's good for me?"

"You look terrible, Tom. I've never seen you look so dreadful. You're hardly even cute anymore."

"Is this how you begin a slow sensual seduction?" I asked, smiling at him. "No wonder you're alone."

"I didn't mean it critically," he said, pouring a drink at the bar beside Savannah's desk. "Yeeesh. Mr. Sensitive. By the way, you didn't tell me how you thought I looked."

He brought me a cognac. I watched him as he crossed the room. Eddie Detreville was elegant, refined, and middle-aged. His sideburns were silver and there were splinters of gray visible in his immaculately combed brown hair. He had the face of a tired king. His skin was soft and slightly exhausted around the mouth and eyes. The whites of his eyes were threaded with red veins. There was a slight yellowing there, as though he were watching you through discolored linen.

"I've told you before, Eddie, and I'll tell you again. You're one of the finest-looking men on the planet."

"You're just saying that because I fished so shamelessly for a compliment. Well, I don't apologize."

"You look good enough to eat," I said.

"Well, well, perhaps we can work something out."

"I didn't mean it that way, Eddie," I said.

"Promises, promises. But you really think I look good? I haven't aged that much, have I?"

"You ask me that every time I s you, Eddie."

"It's important every time I see you. Since you only see me rarely, you're in a perfect position to judge my deterioration. I came across some old pictures of myself the other day, Tom, and I just wept. I was beautiful. Perfectly beautiful when I was a young man. I never turn the lights on in the bathroom when I shave now. I can't bear to study my face in the mirror. It's just too sad. I've started cruising the bars again, Tom. I approached a young man the other night. A lovely child. I wanted to buy him a drink. He said to me, 'Are you shitting me, gramps?' I was perfectly stunned."

"His loss, Eddie," I said.

"I fear getting old far more than I fear dying. But enough

about me. How long do you plan to be in New York this time, Tom?"

"I don't know, Eddie. Savannah's shrink wants me to tell her all the shitty stories about my family so she can put Humpty Dumpty together again. I'd like to just tell her that Mom's wacko, Dad's wacko, all Wingos are wacko, ergo, Savannah is wacko."

"When's the last time you talked to Savannah or heard from her, Tom?"

"It's been over three years," I said, embarrassed by the length of time. "She says that I remind her too much of Luke."

"Tom, I want to tell you something. I don't think Savannah's going to come out of it this time. I think it's gotten to be too much for her. I think it's exhausted her. She's just tired of fighting it."

"Don't say that, Eddie. Say anything else you want to, but I never want to hear you say that again."

"I'm sorry, Tom. It's just something I've felt for a long time."

"Feel it, Eddie. Please don't say it."

"It was stupid of me. I recant every syllable. Let me fix you dinner tomorrow night."

"I'd like that very much. See how I feel in the morning."

After Eddie left, I surveyed the apartment and waited for the migraine to move across my brain like the great shadow of a lunar eclipse. It was still two hours away, but I could feel the high-pressure area building at the base of my skull. Not until it reached the left temple would it bring me to my knees. I took the first pain pill and washed it down with the last swallow of cognac. My eye rested on the photograph Savannah had placed on the wall above her desk. My father had taken it on the deck of his shrimp boat at the beginning of our senior year in high school. Luke and I are smiling at the camera and both of us have our arms draped around Savannah's shoulders. Savannah is laughing and staring up at Luke with pure, uncomplicated affection. The three of us are tanned, young, and, yes, beautiful. Behind us, past the dock and the marsh, small and barely visible, my mother is waving at my father in front of our small white house. If any of us knew what that year would bring, we would not have been smiling. But the photograph stopped time, and those three smiling Wingo children would stand on that boat forever holding one another close in a bond of frail but imperishable love.

I took out my wallet from my back pocket and extracted the folded, crumbling letter Savannah had written to me after I had coached my first football game. I stared at the laughing girl in the picture and wondered when it was, the exact moment, that I had lost her, that I let her fall too far away from me, that I betrayed the laughing girl and let the world have her. The photograph cut into my heart and I began to read the letter aloud.

Dear Coach,

I was thinking about what you can teach your boys, Tom. What language you can use for the love of boys driven by your voice across the grass you mowed yourself. When I saw you and your team win the first game, all the magic of sport came to me silver voiced, like whistles. There are no words to describe how beautiful you looked delivering urgent messages to quarterbacks, signaling for time-outs, pacing the green, unnaturally lit sidelines, loved by your sister for your unimaginable love of play, for the soft gauzy immensity of your love for all the boys and all the games of the world.

But there are some things only sisters can teach the coaches in their lives. Teach them this, Tom, and teach them very well: Teach them the quiet verbs of kindness, to live beyond themselves. Urge them toward excellence, drive them toward gentleness, pull them deep into yourself, pull them upward toward manhood, but softly like an angel arranging clouds. Let your spirit move through them softly, as your spirit moves through me.

I cried last night when I heard your voice above the crowd. I heard you cheering for the clumsy tackle, the slow-footed back, music of your sweet praise. But Tom, my brother, the lion, all golden and hurt: Teach them what you know the best. There is no poem and no letter that can pass your

> one ineffable gift to boys. I want them to take from
> you the knowledge of how to be the gentlest, the
> most perfect brother.   Savannah

When I finished reading the letter, I gazed at the photograph again, then carefully replaced the letter in my wallet.

In the bedroom, I replaced the bulb in the lamp on her bedside table and cleaned up the glass shards of the broken vase. I undressed quickly and threw my clothes on the chair beside the bed. I pulled the covers back and climbed into bed. I closed my eyes, then opened them.

And then the pain summoned me. It came like a pillar of fire behind my eyes. It struck suddenly and hard.

In the perfect stillness, I shut my eyes and lay in the darkness and made a vow to change my life.

4

There are no verdicts to childhood, only consequences, and the bright freight of memory. I speak now of the sun-struck, deeply lived-in days of my past. I am more fabulist than historian, but I will try to give you the insoluble, unedited terror of youth. I betray the integrity of my family's history by turning everything, even sadness, into romance. There is no romance in this story; there is only the story.

Let us begin with a single fact: The island dogs are calling to each other.

It is night. My grandfather listens to them and does not like the sound. In that melody of hounds all the elegiac loneliness of my part of the world is contained. The island dogs are afraid. It is October 4, 1944, ten o'clock in the

evening. The tide is rising and will not be full until 1:49 the
next morning.

My sister is born in the white house by the river. My
mother is not due for a month, but that is of small import
now. Sarah Jenkins, eighty-five, black, and a midwife for
sixty years, is bent over my mother as Savannah is born.
Dr. Bannister, Colleton's only doctor, is dying in Charleston
at this very moment.

Sarah Jenkins is tending to Savannah when she notices
my head making its unexpected appearance. I came as a
surprise, an afterthought.

There is a hurricane moving toward Melrose Island. My
grandfather is strengthening the windowpanes with mask-
ing tape. He goes over and stares down into the cradle at
Luke, who is sleeping. He listens again to the medley of
dogs but he can barely hear them now because of the wind.
The power went out over an hour before and I am delivered
into the world by candlelight.

Sarah Jenkins cleans us thoroughly and attends to our
mother. It has been a messy, difficult birth, and she fears
there might be complications. She was born a slave in a
hut behind the Barnwell Plantation and is the last surviving
slave in Colleton County. Her face is leathery and shining;
her color is café au lait.

"Ah, Sarah," my grandfather said, holding Savannah up
to the lantern light. "A good sign. This is the first girl-child
born to the Wingos in three generations."

"The mama not doin' good."

"Can you help her?"

"All I can. You know that. She needs doctor now."

"The wind's picking up, Sarah."

"Just like it did in the storm of ninety-three. Now that
was a wicked storm. Kill all kinds of poor folks."

"You aren't afraid?"

"Gotta die of somethin'," she said.

"It was good of you to come, Sarah."

"I like bein' with my daughters when their time comes.
Black or white, it no matter. They all my daughters then.
I got a thousand children walkin' around these islands."

"Do you remember delivering me?" my grandfather asked.

"You was a squallin' child."

"Twins," my grandfather said. "What does that mean?"

"Good luck," the black woman said, returning to my mother. "God smiling twice as hard at a troubled world."

In the forest outside the house, the wind began to bear down hard on the trees and the rains gouged the earth with powerful newborn hands. Waves began to crash over the dock. Snakes began to leave their burrows and take to the high branches of trees, sensing flood. A small uprooted palmetto tumbled down the road leading up to the house like a man rolling. No birds sang on the island. Even the insects had battened down.

My grandfather went into the bedroom and found my mother nearly asleep, exhausted, with Sarah Jenkins wiping her face with a cloth.

"You did good, Lila darling. A fine night's work."

"Thanks, Dad," she answered. "The storm?"

"It don't look like much," he lied. "You just get some sleep and let me worry about the storm." He walked back into the living room. From his hip pocket, he withdrew a telegram that my mother had received from the War Department two days before. My father had been shot down during an air raid over Germany and was missing in action. He was presumed dead. He wept bitterly for his son, but then remembered he had his duties and that twins were a sign of luck.

He walked to the kitchen and began to fix a pot of coffee for himself and Sarah. When the coffee was ready, he took a cup to the black woman. Then he felt the wind shouldering against the house and the low-humming of the windows, a song of endangered glass. The water had risen almost to the level of the dock and the tide was still pushing inland, wind-urged and virulent. An osprey's nest torn from the top of a dead tree whipped across the yard like a woman's hat. The river carried it swiftly upstream.

My grandfather took the white Bible he had given my parents as a gift for their wedding and opened it to the glossy pages between the Old Testament and the New. My mother had chosen two names, one for a boy, one for a girl. He took a fountain pen and beneath Luke's name wrote down the name Savannah Constance Wingo. Below that he inscribed my name: Thomas Catlett Wingo.

The storm would be called Bathsheba by the black people of the lowcountry, and she would kill two hundred seventeen people along the South Carolina coast. My grandfather checked his watch. It was almost eleven. He opened to the book of Job and read for an hour. He thought about his son and his wife. My grandmother had left him during the Depression. In his heart, there were times when my grandfather was bitter with the Lord. He read about Job and was comforted. Then he wept again for his only son.

He rose and stared out at the river. There was an otherworldly light, an eerie brightening that had accompanied the storm, but he could not see the river now. He put on his boots, his rain slicker and hat. He took one of the lanterns from the kitchen, checked my mother and Sarah again, and each one of the babies. Then he went out into the storm.

The door almost blew off its hinges when he opened it. It took all his strength to close it. He leaned into the wind and staggered through the yard toward the river. A twig hit his forehead, cutting it like a blade. He shielded his eyes with his hand and listened to the sound of trees breaking in half along the river. When he was twenty-five yards away from the river, he stepped into water up to his knees. Alarmed, blinded by the rain, he knelt down and tasted the water. It was salt.

He prayed to the God of Abraham, to the God who parted the Red Sea, to the God who destroyed the whole world with water; he prayed for strength.

He let the wind carry him back to the house. When he reached the front door he could not open it; the wind had sealed it shut. He ran toward the back door and was knocked to the ground by a limb torn from the oak by my parents' bedroom window. He rose up, dizzy and bleeding from a wound on the back of his head, and crawled on his hands and knees to the back door. The storm felt like a mountain leaning against him. He opened the back door and water poured into the kitchen. For a moment he lay stunned on the kitchen floor. But the waters were rising. He washed the blood from his head in the sink. He moved in the inhuman light of the lantern toward my mother's bedroom. His shadow, huge and portentous, followed him.

Sarah Jenkins was asleep in a chair by my mother's bed. He shook her gently awake.

"The river," he whispered. "It's up, Sarah."

* * *

In Germany, near the town of Dissan, my father, at that very moment, lay hidden in a choir loft, watching a Catholic priest say Mass. The left side of my father's face was paralyzed, his left arm was numb and tingling, and his vision was blurred by his blood. He was studying the priest, who was saying the Common of the Mass in Latin, which my father, in his innocence and pain, thought was German. By observing the priest's gestures, the way he genuflected before a crucifix, his expression as he turned to bless the three bent, misshapen old women who had come to this morning Mass in the middle of the war, the way the priest held the chalice aloft, my father was trying to make a judgment about the man's character. Is this the kind of man who would help me? my father thought. I have killed his people with my bombs, but what does a man of God think of Hitler? What would this man of God do if I asked him to help me? My father had never been in a Catholic church in his entire life. He had never known a Catholic well. He had never seen a priest.

"Agnus Dei qui tollis peccata mundi," he heard the priest say, and the words struck him with their beauty even though they were meaningless to him.

"Agnus Dei." He heard the words again.

My father lowered the pistol he was aiming at the priest's vestments and watched as the three women walked to the rail and received Communion. He thought he saw the priest smile at each of the three women but could not be certain. His head ached. He had never been in such pain, never knew such pain was possible. Before the Mass ended, my father passed out, his head against the stone banisters, his body wedged between the organ and the wall.

The priest's name was Father Günter Kraus, a sixty-year-old native of Munich whose white hair and sharp-nosed, nervous face gave him an odd, inquisitorial appearance. It was a malignant face on a kind man. He had chosen his vocation partly because of what he considered his unredeemable homeliness.

Once he had been the pastor of the third largest congregation in Munich but had quarreled with his bishop over the bishop's collaboration with the Nazis. The bishop had exiled Father Kraus to the Bavarian countryside for his own

good. Several of his colleagues, braver than he, had shel-
tered families of Jews and had died at Dachau. He had once
turned away a family of Jews who sought refuge at his
church. It was a sin he believed no God, no matter how
merciful, could ever forgive. My father had not come to the
church of a brave man. But he had come to the church of
a good one.

After Mass, Father Kraus walked the three women to the
front door and spent ten minutes gossiping with them on
the steps of the church. The altar boy extinguished the
candles, washed out the cruets, then hung his cassock and
surplice in the small closet by the priest's wardrobe. It was
the altar boy who noticed the broken window in the priest's
bathroom. He did not notice the drops of blood on the floor
by the sink. When the altar boy left the church, he told the
priest, who was still at the church door, about the broken
window.

In the distance the priest could see the white-capped
peaks of the Bavarian Alps shining in the sunlight. The
Allies had bombed four German cities the night before.

He locked the front door, checked the level of the holy
water, and walked over to a side altar where he lit a candle
in front of a small marble statue of the Infant of Prague.
He said a prayer for peace. The first drop hit his white
vestment and stained it a deep red. The next drop landed
on his hands folded in prayer. He looked up and a drop
of blood hit him on the face.

When my father regained consciousness, he saw the priest
standing over him, studying him, trying to come to a decision.

"Buenos días, señor," my father said to the German priest.

The priest said nothing in return and my father watched
the tremor in the priest's hands.

"Bonjour, monsieur," my father tried again.

"English?" the priest asked.

"American."

"You cannot stay here."

"There doesn't seem to be a whole lot either one of us
can do about it. It looks like you and me's a team."

"Slowly. Mein English is not good."

"I need your help. Every German in this part of Krautland
is going to be looking for me when they find my plane."

"I cannot help you."

"Why?"

"I am afraid."

"Afraid," my father said. "I've been afraid all night. Are you a Nazi?"

"No, I am a priest. I must report you. I do not wish to, but it would be better. For me. For you. For everybody. They can stop your bleeding."

My father lifted his pistol and pointed it at the priest.

"Bad storm," Sara Jenkins said, rising. "Just like ninety-three."

"We've got to get to the barn and go high," my grandfather said.

"Bad for the babies. Bad for the mama."

"Can't be helped, Sarah," he said. "I'll get you out first."

"What you talkin' about? Sarah old, but Sarah ain't dead. I'll help with the babies, Amos," she said. Sarah Jenkins reserved the right to call even white men by their given names if she had brought them into the world.

My grandfather lifted me from my crib and placed me, still sleeping, into Sarah's arms. She wrapped her shawl around her shoulders and held me tightly to her breasts. He then placed Savannah and Luke on top of a cotton blanket, covered them, then covered them again with his yellow slicker.

Opening the back door, they stepped into the howling bitter rains and ran for the barn. The winds, gusting up to two hundred miles per hour, screamed around them, demonic, and black. Sarah lost her balance or was lifted by the wind and was blown across the back yard, her shawl billowing out around her like a sail. She shielded me as she was thrown into the side of an outbuilding.

My grandfather struggled toward her, caught her with one arm around her waist, and hurt her as he lifted her to her feet. He held her for a moment and they stood there together, mud-splattered and rain-soaked; then they fought their way toward the barn, bearing three screaming infants. Once again he fought the wind as it held a door fast. When he forced it open, the door splintered against the side of the barn.

Inside, he climbed the ladder that disappeared into the

darkness above them. He laid Luke and my sister side by side in a pile of fragrant hay. He sensed the panic of the animals in the barn. He left the hayloft and went back down for me and Sarah.

"Sarah hurt bad," she said. "Can't climb."

He lifted the black woman up in his arms. She was as frail as a child and she moaned as he climbed the ladder, leaving me behind on the floor of the barn. The wind tore through the open door. He propped her up against a bale of hay. She reached for Luke and Savannah and tried to dry them off, but the blankets and her clothes were soaked through. So she unbuttoned her blouse and hugged them close to her bare breasts and let her own warmth flow into them.

When my grandfather materialized in the dark again with me in his arms, she laid me between the others. My grandfather hurried down the ladder and entered into the heart of the storm again. He had no idea how he was going to get my mother up to the loft.

When he entered the house, he saw the water spilling through the front door. He looked out into the darkness and the vision he saw would remain with him for the rest of his life. The river, wild and magisterial, was flowing swiftly, powerfully, against our house. A rowboat, torn from its moorings, lifted in the wind, and as if in a dream, he watched it hurtling out of the blackness, illuminated by the strange light of hurricanes, lifted his hand as if to stop it, and closed his eyes as it crashed through the window on the other side of the room and shattered the dining room table. A piece of splintered glass lodged in his arm. He ran toward my mother's room and he prayed as he ran.

The priest trembled violently when he saw the pistol. He closed his eyes, folded his hands against his chest, and blessed my father in Latin. My father lowered the pistol. The priest opened his eyes.

"I can't shoot anybody dressed up like you, padre," my father said, weakly.

"Are you badly hurt?" the priest asked.

My father laughed, then said, "Badly."

"Come. Later I will report you to them."

Father Kraus helped my father rise to his feet and, bearing my father's weight, walked him to the door near the vestibule leading to the bell tower, which overlooked the village. They struggled up the narrow stairs and my father's blood stained each step as they climbed. When they reached the small room at the top of the stairs, the priest set my father down. The priest removed his ruined, bloody vestments and made a pillow to support my father's head. Then the priest took his chasuble and tore it into long strips, and tied them tightly around my father's head.

"You have lost much blood," the priest said. "I must get water to clean the wound."

My father looked up at the priest and said, "Gesundheit." Speaking the only German word he knew, my father lost consciousness again.

That night when my father awoke, the priest was bent over him, administering the last rites of Extreme Unction. The priest knew that the wounded pilot's temperature had risen sharply and that his injuries were grievous. My father could not see out of his left eye, but he felt the softness of the priest's hands applying the oils of the sacrament.

"Why?" my father said.

"I think you are dying," the priest said. "I will hear your confession. Are you Catholic?"

"Baptist."

"Ah, you have been baptized then, but, I was not sure. I baptized you minutes ago."

"Thanks. I was baptized in the Colleton River."

"Ach. A whole river."

"No, just part of it."

"I baptize you a second time."

"It can't hurt nothing."

"I brought food. Can you eat?"

Years later, my father would describe with undiminishable wonder the taste of that dark German bread, that slab of precious, hoarded butter smeared across that bread, and the red wine the priest gave him from the bottle. The bread in his mouth, the butter, the wine, he would say to his children, and all of us could taste it again with him, the wine spreading like velvet in our mouths, the bread, fragrant as earth, softening and melting on the tongue, the butter coating the roofs of our mouths, the priest holding our hands, the smell of the oils of death on his hands, fear making those soft, veined hands tremble. Outside, in the dark, a German patrol had found the wrecked plane and the countryside was alerted that an American pilot moved among them. There was a reward for his capture and any-one found helping him would be summarily executed.

"They are looking for you," the priest said to my father when the meal was finished. "They came to the village today."

"Did they come to the church?"

"Yes. I told them that if I found you I would kill you with my own two hands. It amused them, coming from a priest. They will return—I am certain—to search for you."

"I'll go as soon as I can travel."

"I wish you had not come."

"It wasn't my idea. I was shot down."

"Ha!" the priest said, "then it was God who brought you here."

"No, sir. I think it was the Nazis."

"I pray to God for you today."

"Thank you."

"I pray to him to make you die," the priest explained. "Then I feel much shame. And I pray for you to live. A priest should only pray for life. It is a great sin. I ask that you would forgive me."

"Gesundheit," my father said, wishing fervently that the priest would sneeze so he could use the word properly. Then he asked the priest, "Where did you learn to speak English?"

"In Berlin at the seminary. I like very much American movies. The cowboys, yes."

"I am a cowboy," my father said.

"Why did you lie to him, Dad?" Luke would ask, always disturbed by this part of the story when it was told and retold to us during our childhood. "There was this nice man scared out of his wits, and you pretending that you were a cowboy."

"Well, Luke," my father would say, considering his ac-tions in the light of his own history, "I figured it this way. I'm half blind, half dead, and every German in the country is hunting my young ass. So here I am with this real nervous priest who happens to like cowboys. So I make a snap decision. I give him a real live cowboy to feed. He wants Tom Mix. I give him Tom Mix."

"You are from California, no?" the priest asked.

"South Carolina."

"This is the West, no?"

"Yes."

As the priest left my father in his hiding place in the bell tower he said, "You sleep now. My name is Günter Kraus."

"Henry Wingo, Günter."

The priest blessed my father in Latin; my father thought it was German.

My father slept as soldiers searched for him in the darkness.

He awoke to Sanctus bells in the amazing light of October. He listened to the voice of Günter Kraus reciting ancient, lovely prayers. His breakfast was on a tray beside him. There was a note on the tray. "Be well," it said. "Eat all your breakfast. It will make you strong. They took an American pilot prisoner last night near Stassen. I think you are safe. Let us pray to God that it is so. Your friend, Father Günter Kraus."

My grandfather shook my mother awake gently. "Lila, I sure do hate to wake you, honey."

"The babies," my mother said dreamily. "My babies are all right?"

"They're fine, honey. Got good lungs. Real good lungs."

"The storm?"

"I've got to move you, honey. The river has come up."

"The babies," she cried out.

"Don't worry. Me and Sarah have them safely in the barn."

"Dad, you took my babies out in this storm?"

"We've got to go, Lila."

"I'm too tired, Dad. Let me sleep."

"I'll carry you, honey. Now, I don't want to hurt you because I know you're sore. You did good tonight, honey. Two fine Wingos. Beautiful kids."

"Henry's dead, Dad. Henry'll never see them," she said, starting to cry.

"Help me, Lila. Help me all you can."

"Henry's dead, Dad. The children won't have a father."

"They won't have a mother if you don't lift up out of that bed," my grandfather said. "He's presumed dead. Presumin' ain't bein'. Henry's a river boy and they're hard to kill."

He reached his hands under her back and lifted her off the bed. He carried her out of the room, hurting her with every step. As he walked through the back door, he stepped into moving water up to his knees. The wind and water almost brought him to the ground. He walked slowly, deliberately, planting his feet solidly before he took each step. The rain was cruel and stinging against his face. He thought of Joseph leading Mary and the child, Jesus, into Egypt during the persecution of Herod. Joseph was a strong man, my grandfather thought, as he struggled through the rising water, and he had faith in God. But he was no stronger than Amos Wingo and there was not a man or a woman alive on the planet with such simple astonishing love of God to sustain him. My mother, clinging to him like a child, moaned as he began climbing the ladder, holding her with a single arm. He was hurting her badly now. When they reached Sarah and the babies, the blanket he had wrapped her in was covered with blood.

It took over an hour to stop my mother from hemorrhaging and he would never in his lifetime understand the nature of that hemorrhage or what his part was, if any, in stopping it. He had torn his shirt from his back and held it tightly between her legs, the blood pumping through his fingers each time her heart beat. Behind him, Sarah tended the three screaming infants the best she could, whimpering with pain each time she had to shift her weight.

My mother grew weaker before his eyes and he was certain she was dying, but he could not even force the thought to consciousness, so aware was he of the rising, ungovernable waters moving through the barn. Below him, he heard the dread of animals and the demonic, cataclysmic howl of the wind as it rushed through the barn. He felt the tension of every nail in the barn as if the wood, suddenly animate, had begun to swell with water running through long dead roots and veins. In the barnwood, he felt the tremor along every grain. The mule began to kick against the stall door when the water reached it, as Amos held that once-white shirt against my mother and pushed hard against the terrible killing flow because he knew of nothing else to do. He saw the small boat he had taken in from the river lift up and move toward the back of the barn.

Two o'clock in the morning, the tide is supposed to be ebbing now, he thought. He could not understand why the water was not receding. Tide was one of the immutable constants of life by the river and he could not fathom why it had chosen this moment to betray itself and his family. Outside, the prodigious winds devastated the trees of the island in a two-hundred-mile-an-hour assault. Oak trees were lifted out of the ground like a child pulling candles out of a birthday cake. Saplings hurtled through the air like leaves. Ah, my grandfather thought, listening to that wind rush through the door of the barn like a train entering a small tunnel, it is the wind holding back the tide. He knew that this storm nullified even the moon's pull and all daily laws were canceled in the horror and majesty of its passage.

The water cannot go back, he thought. It rises against its will.

He lessened the pressure on his shirt and almost wept when he saw that the bleeding had stopped. My mother, in shock, lay unconscious in her own blood. Sarah and the babies lay silent and exhausted. My grandfather searched the loft and found a tarpaulin covered with oil and straw, which he laid over my mother. He covered it with more straw.

Climbing down the ladder, he plunged into the water and swam to the stalls, forcing them open, freeing the animals. He tied his boat to the ladder. In the pandemonium of the escaping livestock, he was almost gored by a cow who swam over him in her desperation to leave the barn.

When he returned to the loft, the three babies were arranged like pale cordwood on Sarah's breast and she held them in her dark arms. He bent down to check if my mother was alive. She was breathing, though her pulse was dim.

He fell down, spent and beaten, listening to the voice of the storm, its whine becoming something almost human to him. He thought of his son, Henry, burnt and twisted beneath the steel sculpture of a downed plane. He imagined the soul of his son, freed of his body, muscular and eager, floating like a young calf, driven by the soft breath of God toward a paradise of light and rest.

"I have given enough, Lord," my grandfather said to the wind. "I will give nothing else."

Exhausted, he fought the urge to sleep, and so fighting, slept.

He awoke to sunshine and birdsong. He looked down and saw the boat resting on the muddy barn floor. I woke up crying. My mother's eyes opened at my cry, and her milk flowed in a reflexive, sympathetic reaction.

Sarah Jenkins was dead and my grandfather had to pry her arms loose from the three white children she had helped save. My first night on earth had ended.

For three weeks my father lived in the bell tower and listened to the life of a German village play out below him. Each night the priest would visit him, change my father's bandages, teach him how to speak German, and bring him news of the war. The priest brought sausages, loaves of bread, great jars of pungent sauerkraut, bottles of wine, and the best beer my father had ever tasted. The first days were very bad for my father because of the pain. But the priest ministered to him with those clumsy, soft hands through one long hard night when my father thought he might die. After that he began to grow stronger.

At first, because of his fear, the priest only came at night. The image of booted Nazis kicking down his door haunted him; and my father's innocent, freckled face, the priest knew well, could bring this image to life. My father's presence had created a moral nightmare for the priest and it tested abundantly the mettle of his character. The priest felt he had been given the soul of a rabbit in times that called for lions. He told my father that after they had passed a week together. My father's coming had required the priest in him to rule over the man.

As my father healed, the priest's evening visitations lengthened. The priest had always found nights very hard. The loneliness of his vocation was unbearable at times. The priest ached for the easy, uncomplicated friendships he witnessed between some of the men in the village.

Arriving after sundown, the priest would often not leave

my father's side until long after midnight. In my father, Günter Kraus had found the perfect friend: captive, injured, and always available.

"Why did you become a priest?" my father asked one night.

"The first war. I was in the trenches of France. I swore to God if he let me live I would become a priest. So."

"Did you ever want to have a family, a wife?"

"I am very ugly," the priest replied simply. "When I was a young man, I could not even speak to a young woman."

"I have a son. His name is Luke."

"Good. That is very good . . . I often wonder what a son of mine should be like. I dream sometimes about the sons and daughters I will never have."

"Have you ever loved a woman?" my father asked.

"Once," the priest answered. "In München. I loved a very pretty woman whose husband was a banker. Nice woman. She liked me very much, I think. But in a friendly way. She was a very good woman but she has many troubles. She came to me to advise her. So, I advise her. Then I start to love her. I feel it inside me. I think she loved me too but in a friendly way. I tell her she must not leave her husband because of God's will. But he beat her. She leaves him and goes to her mother's house in Hamburg. She kiss me on the cheek when she comes to say goodbye. I thought many times of going to Hamburg. I thought I loved her more than I loved God. But I did nothing."

"Why didn't you go to Hamburg and just bang on her door?"

"Because I feared God."

"Look, Günter," my father said, "he'd understand. He made that woman beautiful to you for a reason. He probably put a lot of time into making her. Did she have a nice shape?"

"Please," the priest said, "I am a priest. I do not notice such things."

"Oh, sure."

"She had a good soul. I hope to meet her in the life after life."

"I'm glad you didn't follow that woman up to Hamburg, Günter."

"Because you think it would be a sin?"

"No, because you wouldn't have been here at this church when I needed you."

"Ach. Why did you have to choose my church? This I did not need."

"Well, you sure saved this ol' cowpoke," my father said, turning his head on his pillow and looking straight at the priest. "I want you to visit me when this war is over."

"Ach. This war will never be over. Hitler is crazy. Every day I pray that God will make Hitler a good man. My prayers mean nothing to God."

"You can't make chicken salad out of chickenshit."

"I do not understand."

"Just a saying."

"I pray hard. But Hitler is still Hitler."

There was a full moon over Germany the night my father left the bell tower. The feeling in his left arm had returned slowly, though his face was still partially paralyzed. The priest had brought him clothes for the journey. They ate their last meal together, and my father, touched and grateful, tried to find words to thank the old man, but words failed him, and they ate their meal in almost complete silence.

After the meal, my father studied the route of escape the priest had planned for him, noting where he was most likely to run into Nazi patrols and the exact point where he could enter Switzerland.

"I have brought you a hoe to carry with you, Henry," the priest said.

"For what?"

"If someone sees you, he will just think that you are a farmer. You can sleep in barns when you are tired. Hide yourself well, Henry. I have packed food in this bag, but it will not last. You must go now, Henry."

"You've been so good to me," said my father, overwhelmed with a free-flowing love of this man.

"You needed help, Henry."

"But you didn't have to help me. You did. I don't know how to thank you."

"I am glad you came. It gave me a chance to be a priest. The first time God tested me I did not act like a priest."

"What first time?"

"Long before you came, a family came. They were Jews. The father I knew well. He was a good man, a merchant in the next town. He has three children. All girls. A nice wife, very fat. He comes to me one night and says, 'Father, please hide us from the Nazis.' I refuse to hide the Jews. That is bad enough. But my fear is so great that I turn them in to the Nazis. They die at Dachau. I try to do penance for the Fischer family. I ask God to do something to remove the blood of the Fischers from my hands. But no, even God is not this powerful. Even God cannot forgive this. I cannot escape the eyes of the Fischer family. They gaze at me when I say Mass. They mock my vocation. They know the whole truth about Günter Kraus. So if I had not turned the Fischers over to them, I would not have let you stay, Henry. I could not bear another pair of eyes following me. I fear so many things. I fear so many things."

"I'm sorry about the Fischers, Günter. That means I owe them a debt, too. After the war I'm coming back to see you. Then you and I are going up to Munich to drink beer and chase women."

"Ach. I am a priest. I do not chase women. I pray that God delivers you to your family safely, Henry. I pray for you every day. I will walk with you in my heart. I will miss you, Henry Wingo. You must go now. It is late."

"Before I do, Father, I want to do something."

"Yes, Henry?"

"After the Agnus Dei part of the Mass. You know the part? I hear you saying it every morning to those three women who come to church. After all the bells, you feed them something. I saw it the first morning."

"It is the Eucharist, Henry. I feed them the body and blood of Christ."

"I want you to feed it to me before I leave."

"No, Henry, this is not possible," said the priest. "You have to be a Catholic before I can give you Communion."

"Then I'll become a Catholic," my father said, undeterred. "Make me one right now. Maybe it will bring me luck."

"It is not so easy, Henry. You must study much. There is much to learn before you become a Catholic."

"I'll learn it later, Günter. I promise I will. There's no time now. It's a war. Look, you baptized me, gave me Extreme Unction. Hell, a little Communion won't hurt."

"It is not regular," the priest said, rubbing his chin abstractedly with his hand. "But nothing is regular. First, I must hear your confession."

"Fine. What's that?" my father asked.

"You must tell me all your sins. All that you have done wrong since you were a child."

"I can't, there are too many."

"Then tell me that you are sorry for your sins and that will be enough."

Father Kraus began to say the sonorous prayers of the confessor. He absolved my father from all sin and the moon gleamed whitely like a cleansed soul, its light enfolding them beneath the great bell above Dissan.

They went down the steps that led to the interior of the church. The priest went to the altar, opened the tabernacle with a small key, and brought forth a gold chalice. The priest genuflected before the crucifix. The brutally crucified effigy of Christ gazed down onto the figure of my father, who knelt in the cold darkness of that stone church and prayed for his own deliverance. The priest turned and faced him.

"Henry, you are a Catholic now," the priest said.

"I will try to be a good Catholic, Günter."

"You will have to raise your children as Catholics," he said.

"It will be done," my father said. "Is that the body and blood of Jesus?"

"I must bless it."

"You have to 'Agnus Dei' it?" my father asked.

The priest blessed the host in a dead language, then turned toward the newest Roman Catholic in the world and changed the history of my family's life forever.

The priest knelt beside my father and they prayed together, priest and warrior transfigured by moonlight, by warfare, destiny, and the urgent, mysterious, and ineffable cries and secrets of souls turned inward upon themselves.

When my father rose up, he turned toward Günter Kraus, embraced him, and held the priest tightly in his arms.

"Thank you, Günter," he said. "Thank you so much."

"I wish the Fischers could say the same thing to me, Henry. I am a priest again."

"I'll find you after the war."

"I would like that. Very much I would like that."

My father hesitated, then picked up his hoe and his bag. He stopped and embraced the priest once more.

Günter looked into my father's eyes and said, "For three weeks God sent a son to dwell in my house. I will miss you, Henry Wingo. I will miss you."

And Henry Wingo slipped out the side door of the vestibule, into the moonlight and the countryside of Germany. He looked back and waved to the priest in the doorway. The priest was blessing him. My father turned away, sinless and consecrated, and took the first step toward Switzerland.

For two weeks my father made his way through the hills of Bavaria, following the clear waters of the Lech River, and guiding himself by studying the position of stars and marking his progress as well as he could on the map Father Kraus had supplied him. It amazed him that the stars over Germany were the same as the ones that shone in the Colleton sky. He could look straight up at night and be home; he felt a fraternal, neighborly connection to the arranged light above him.

During the day, he slept in the lofts of barns or curled up in forests. Dogs became his greatest nemeses as he crept past farmhouses at night. He killed two of them in one night with the blade of his hoe and washed their blood off in a clear, mountain-fed stream. The land was lifting as he walked. Once, awakening during the day, he saw the Alps clearly before him and wondered how a stranger could ever find the right valleys and unpatrolled crossings that would carry him to safety. A southerner, he was unfamiliar with snow; a lowcountryman, he knew nothing about the secrets of mountains. He learned as he went along. He was deliberate and cautious.

A farmer's wife discovered him asleep in her barn one day. She was pregnant and had dark black hair and a pretty face that reminded him of my mother. She screamed and ran to get her husband. My father ran through wheat and corn fields and hid himself for the rest of the day in a cave beside a river rushing out of the hills. He did not trust farms after that day, trusted nothing that appeared human. Afterward, he approached farms only to forage food. He milked cows in complete darkness and drank the warm milk from buckets, stole eggs and ate them raw, and plundered orchards and vegetable gardens. He lived for the dark and became impatient in the sunlight. The walk had turned him into a night creature. But then he reached the mountains and it became too dangerous and disorienting to walk at night.

By accident, he found his hoe did protect him, authenticate him. A farmer, plowing on a hilly pasture, spotted my father walking along a country lane just after sunrise. The farmer, far off, waved at him. My father waved back fraternally. It made him bolder and he began walking down obscure, untraveled lanes in broad daylight. Once he was surprised when a large convoy bearing hundreds of German soldiers in open trucks passed by him traveling at great speeds. He waved enthusiastically at the soldiers, smiled broadly. Several of the soldiers, perhaps envying him, waved back. The hoe gave him the right to be there. His labors produced the food that fed the German war machine. He almost began to believe it himself. After he had skirted the German town of Oberammergau, he passed unseen into the heavily patrolled border of Austria.

It was only when he reached the high country that he despaired. For a week he climbed higher and higher. The farms disappeared. He struggled through a beautiful, nightmarish land, past gorges and vertiginous cliffs. He found himself above the tree line, lost and disoriented. The map was useless; the stars lost their meaning. He discovered the treachery of mountains, their false passes and dead ends. He climbed one mountain only to discover he could not descend the other side. He retraced his steps and climbed up toward another peak. Each mountain was different, containing its own surprises and deviations. He was seeing snow for the first time in his life. He ate snow. He ate beetles and grubs. At night he covered himself with the branches of fir trees to keep himself from freezing to death. How can a man freeze to death in October? the Carolinian asked himself. He was in Switzerland for two whole days before he descended, half dead, into a Swiss village named Klosters. He thought he was surrendering to the Austrians.

He came down the mountain and entered the town with his hands raised, listening to the puzzled villagers speaking German to him. That night he ate at the home of the mayor of Klosters.

Three days later, my mother received a telegram from my father saying he was alive and well and had become a Roman Catholic.

My father returned to his squadron and for the rest of the war flew sorties over German territory. When he released his bombs over the blacked-out cities and they exploded into fire beneath him, he would whisper, "Fischer. Fischer. Fischer. Fischer," as the sounds of the explosion reached him. "Fischer" became my father's battle cry as he dove toward the earth, spreading death and fire behind him, a pilot of dazzling, supernatural gifts.

After the war, when my father joined the armies of occupation, he returned to Dissan to thank Günter Kraus and to tell him there were no cowboys in South Carolina. But there was a new priest in Dissan, horse-faced and callow, who took my father to the back of the church to show him Father Kraus's gravestone. Two months after my father was shot down, two British pilots had parachuted to safety somewhere near Dissan. In the ensuing search, the Germans discovered my father's bloody uniform, which the priest had saved as a cherished memento of my father's visit. Under torture, the priest admitted he had once hidden an American pilot and helped him escape to Switzerland. They hung Günter Kraus from the bell tower and his body swung there for a week as a sign to the villagers. In his will, the priest had left all his worldly possessions, meager as they were, to a woman who lived in Hamburg. It was all very strange and sad, the young priest said. Besides, Günter Kraus had never been a very good priest. It was well known in the village.

My father lit a candle at the statue of the Infant of Prague, at the exact spot where his blood once fell on the priest who would save him. He prayed for the repose of Günter Kraus's soul and for the souls of the Fischer family. Then he rose, tears in his eyes, and slapped the young priest across the face and warned him always to speak of Günter Kraus with respect. The young priest ran out of the church. My father took the statue of the Infant of Prague and walked out of the church, carrying it under his arm. He was a Catholic now and he knew Catholics preserved the relics of their saints.

My father's war was over.

Every year on my birthday, my mother would take Savannah, Luke, and me out into the country to visit the small, unkempt Negro cemetery where Sarah Jenkins was buried. The story of Sarah Jenkins was told and retold over and over again until I knew it by heart. On the same day, my father had roses placed on the grave of Günter Kraus. Those two heroic figures were as mythic and immemorial to us as any Caesar could ever be. Yet later, I would wonder if their courage and sacrifice, the selfless, mortal choices that led to their own ruin and to the survival of the house of Wingo was not part of some obscene joke whose punch line would take years to evolve.

When we were old enough, the three Wingo children bought a tombstone for Sarah Jenkins. A year before I married Sallie, I took a short trip to Europe and visited the grave of Günter Kraus. Nothing in Europe, not the paintings in the Louvre nor the stark beauty of the Roman forum, moved me half as much as the sight of that name carved into the gray stone above him. I visited the tower where my father had hidden. I visited Klosters, where my father stayed when he came down out of the mountains. I ate dinner at the mayor's house. I tried to live the whole story over again. Or thought I did. My father did not tell the whole story. There was one part he left out.

When I told this part of my family's history in my next session with Dr. Lowenstein, she listened without interruption.

"What part had he left out?" Dr. Lowenstein asked me.

"He left out one small, insignificant detail," I said. "Do you remember my telling you about the pregnant farmer's wife who discovered him sleeping?"

"The one with the pretty face that reminded him of your mother," she answered.

"I told you that she screamed and ran to get her husband," I said. "That much was true, but my father did not rush out and hide in a cave beside a river. He caught that pretty woman and he strangled her to death in that barn.

Because he was a pilot, he had never seen the faces of the people he killed. The German woman's face was five inches from his own as he crushed the bones of her throat and she died in agony right before his eyes."

"When did you discover that part of the story, Tom?" she asked.

"He told me the night my mother left him," I said. "I think he needed to explain to both me and himself what it was that had turned him into a father to be feared. The German woman was both his secret and his shame. We are a family of well-kept secrets and they all nearly end up killing us."

"The story is fascinating, but I'm not sure it tells me anything about Savannah."

"The tapes, the transcripts," I said. "She mentioned this in the tapes."

"How, Tom?" she asked. "Where? There was nothing about Germany or the storm. Nothing about the priest or the midwife."

"Yes, there was. Or at least I think there was. She mentioned a woman, Agnes Day. I just told you about Agnes Day. Its origin. I told you where Agnes Day came from."

"I'm sorry, Tom. You did not," Dr. Lowenstein said, a puzzled frown on her face.

"When we were children, Doctor, we heard this story over and over again. It was like a bedtime story to us. We couldn't get enough of it. What did Father Kraus look like? Did he have a beard? Where did Sarah Jenkins live? How many people were in the Fischer family? We could actually see Father Kraus saying Mass, or we thought we could. But we'd confuse the story when we were kids. Sarah Jenkins would end up feeding my father in the bell tower. Or Father Kraus would carry my mother through the floodwaters. You know how kids do things to stories. You know how they confuse things and make the story something else."

"But who is Agnes Day?"

"She was a mistake. Savannah made it first. Luke and I picked it up. Savannah screamed it out over the tapes. Agnes Day was the first thing my father heard the priest say."

"I don't remember that, Tom."

"Agnus Dei. In the choir loft. Savannah thought Agnes Day was the woman the priest loved in Hamburg and that he loved her so much he even cried out her name when he was celebrating Mass."

"Wonderful," Dr. Lowenstein said. "Simply wonderful."

5

After the first week, there came to be a shape and character to all those New York summer days—those introspective, confessional days when I spun out the history of my dispirited, sorrow-struck family to Savannah's lovely psychiatrist whose job it was to repair the damage sustained by one member of that family.

The story grew slowly and as it unfolded I began to feel an interior strength flicker into life. I spent the first few days reviewing the tapes that so chillingly recorded the extent of my sister's breakdown. She spoke in hurt fragments of language. I wrote her screams down on paper, studied them, and each day startled myself with some clear vision of memory I had repressed or forgotten. Each of her phrases, no matter how surreal or bizarre, had a foundation in reality, and each memory led to another and another until my head blazed with small intricate geometries of illumination. There were days when I could hardly wait for my five o'clock meetings with Dr. Lowenstein.

But in the unconscious, I began to encounter both wild fruit and vast disciplined vineyards. I tried to censor the superfluous or the commonplace, yet I knew large truths lay hidden in the clovers, sweet grasses, and wild mint. As gleaner of my sister's troubled past, I wanted to leave nothing out but wished to find the one rose that might contain the image of the tiger when found blooming on the trellis.

My enemy was indeterminacy as I sat surrounded by books and plants in my sister's living room. The task I had set for myself that summer was simple enough: I was to embark on a grand tour of self. I would study the events and accidents that had led to the creation of a defensive and mediocre man. I moved slowly through those days. Time pushed through me courteously as I took note of the sun's transit over Manhattan. I tried to place myself in the confluence of things, study my own interior satellites as dispassionately as some astronomer noting the twelve moons attendant to the pearly mass of Jupiter.

The silence of early mornings began to please me. In stillness, I started to keep a journal, making solemn notations in the formal public school handwriting that grew smaller each year, mirroring my own diminishment. At first, I concentrated only on what was essential to Savannah's story, but I kept returning to myself, able to tell the story only through my own eyes. I had no right or credibility to interpret the world through her eyes. The best I could do for my sister would be to tell my own story as honestly as I could. I had lived a singularly uncourageous life, a passive, though surveillant, one, brimming with surfaces of terror. But one strength that I had brought to the task at hand was that I had been present at almost every significant occasion of Savannah's life. My voice would sound a pure noise of witness and I would raise it in a cleansing song.

I had a mission here, a job. I wanted to explain why my sister, my twin, opened her veins, saw hideous visions, and was haunted by a childhood of such conflict and debasement there was small chance of her ever coming to terms with it. And as I would try to explode the levees of memory, I would record the spillage flooding the dry imagined streets of the only town I ever loved. I would tell Dr. Lowenstein of the loss of Colleton and how the death of a town left traceries of whitewash and markings the color of eggshell silvering in memory. If I could summon the courage to tell it all, by speaking without forestallment, by humming the melodies of all those dark anthems that sent us marching so resolutely toward our appointments with a remorseless destiny, I could explain my sister's heartbreaking war with the world.

But first there had to be a time of renewal, time to master a fresh approach to self-scrutiny. I had lost nearly thirty-seven years to the image I carried of myself. I had ambushed myself by believing, to the letter, my parents' definition of me. They had defined me early on, coined me like a word they had translated on some mysterious hieroglyph, and I had spent my life coming to terms with that specious coinage. My parents had succeeded in making me a stranger to myself. They had turned me into the exact image of what they needed at the time, and because there was something essentially complaisant and orthodox in my nature, I allowed them to knead and shape me into the smooth lineaments of their nonpareil child. I adhered to the measurements of their vision. They whistled and I danced like a spaniel in their yard. They wanted a courteous boy and the old southern courtesies flowed out of me in a ceaseless flood. They longed for a stable twin, a pillar of sanity to balance the family structure after they realized Savannah was always going to be their secret shame, their unabsolvable crime. They succeeded not only in making me normal but also in making me dull. But their most iniquitous gift they did not even know they were bestowing. I longed for their approval, their applause, their pure uncomplicated love for me, and I looked for it years after I realized they were not even capable of letting me have it. To love one's children is to love oneself, and this was a state of supererogatory grace denied my parents by birth and circumstance. I needed to reconnect to something I had lost. Somewhere I had lost touch with the kind of man I had the potential of being. I needed to effect a reconciliation with that unborn man and try to coax him gently toward his maturity.

Again and again, I thought of Sallie and our children. I had married the first woman I ever kissed. I thought I had married her because she was pretty, blessed with horse sense and sass, and unlike my mother in any way. But I had married a fine and comely girl, and with brilliance and craft and all instincts of self-preservation jettisoned, I succeeded over the years, through neglect, coldness, and betrayal, in turning her into the exact image of my mother. Because of some endemic flaw in my manhood I could not just have wives or lovers. I required soft enemies humming lullabies of carnage in the playroom, snipers in floral print dresses gunning for me from the bell towers. I was not comfortable with anyone who was not disapproving of me. No matter how ardently I strove to attain their impossibly high standards for me, I could never do anything entirely right and so I grew accustomed to that climate of inevitable failure. I hated my mother, so I got back at her by giving my wife her role. In Sallie, I had formed the woman who would be a subtle, more cunning version of my own mother. Like my mother, my wife had come to feel slightly ashamed of and disappointed in me. The configuration and tenor of my weakness would define the fury of their resurrection; my failure would frame their strength, blossoming, and deliverance.

Though I hated my father, I expressed that hatred eloquently by imitating his life, by becoming more and more ineffectual daily, by ratifying all the cheerless prophecies my mother made for both my father and me. I thought I had succeeded in not becoming a violent man, but even that belief collapsed: My violence was subterranean, unbeheld. It was my silence, my long withdrawals, that I had turned into dangerous things. My viciousness manifested itself in the terrible winter of blue eyes. My wounded stare could bring an ice age into the sunniest, balmiest afternoon. I was about to be thirty-seven years old, and with some aptitude and a little natural ability, I had figured out how to live a perfectly meaningless life, but one that could imperceptibly and inevitably destroy the lives of those around me.

So I looked to this surprise summer of freedom as a last chance to take my full measure as a man, a troubled interregnum before I ventured into the pitfalls and ceremonials of middle age. I wanted, by an act of conscious will, to make it a time of reckoning and, if I was lucky, a time of healing and reconstitution of an eclipsed spirit.

Through the procedure of remembrance, I would try to heal myself, to gather up the strength I would need to manifest as I guided Dr. Lowenstein along the declivities and versants of the past.

I usually awoke with the first light, and after the perfunctory annotation of the night's dreams, I would rise, shower, and dress. Then I would drink a glass of fresh-squeezed orange juice, that first cleansing sting of citrus a

joy to the tongue. I would walk down the back stairway of
the apartment and emerge on Grove Street. At Sheridan
Square, I would buy a copy of *The New York Times* from the
disturbingly anonymous vendor. He was representative of
a whole subspecies of New Yorkers who performed thank-
less yet essential jobs with appearances as unspecified as
subway tokens. Backtracking to Bleecker Street, I would
buy two croissants from a French bakery run by an insou-
ciant Madame from Lyon. As I walked back to the apartment, I would eat one of the croissants. These were admirable
croissants, light and warm as birds, and they broke apart
in crusty leaves while they still contained a slight heat of
the ovens. My hands smelled like good bread as I sat in
the living room chair and opened to the sports section. I
was a lifelong prisoner of the morning sports section and
I memorized its long clean columns of statistics. Because
of its hieratic obsession with numbers, baseball was my
favorite season, each day framed and ennobled by the lucid
numerology of box scores.

With the paper finished and strewn around me, I faced
the terror of summer mornings. Defeat was my theme.

The air-conditioning thermostat in Dr. Lowenstein's office
was always turned down too low. I would come in off those
torrid, filmy streets, begrimed with sweat and dust, and
involuntarily shiver as I entered that suite of well-appointed
offices with their false, unseasonal weather. The outer office
where the receptionist, Mrs. Barber, worked was always a
degree or two warmer than the chill, nearly arctic temperature of the waiting room. Five o'clock sunlight divided her
face into symmetrical slats whenever I entered for my week-
day soliloquies with Dr. Lowenstein.

Mrs. Barber looked up when I came in for one of my
sessions. "Oh, Mr. Wingo," she said, checking her appointment book, "we've got a change of schedule today.
Dr. Lowenstein hoped you wouldn't mind."

"What's up?"

"Emergency. One of her friends called up all upset. Dr.
Lowenstein hoped you'd just wait around and you two
could go out and have a drink somewhere."

"Yeah," I said, "that would be fine. Can I just sit in the

waiting room and catch up on all the back issues of those swank magazines?"

"I'll tell her," Mrs. Barber said. Then, looking at me softly, maternally, she asked, "You doing okay, Carolina?"

"Not really, Mrs. Barber," I said, and my voice trembled with the unsuspected candor of my answer.

"You grin and joke around a lot for someone who isn't doing okay," she said.

"It fools you, doesn't it?"

"Nope," she said, looking at me. "It doesn't fool me for a minute. I've been hanging around people in trouble for a long time. It's always in the eyes. If I can do anything for you, anything at all, you just give me a yell."

"Mrs. Barber, will you stand up for a minute?" I asked, suddenly overwhelmed with a vast, insupportable love of this stranger.

"What for, honey?"

"I want to drop on my knees and kiss your ass. It's a reflex I have these days when anyone is even slightly kind to me."

"You're just worried about your sister."

"No, no, not at all," I said. "She's just a front I use. Whenever I fall completely apart, I use her as my excuse and justification. I blame all my sadness on her and I do it in the lowest, most cowardly way."

"Here," she said, unfastening her purse and casting a furtive glance at the doorway leading to Dr. Lowenstein's inner office. "Whenever I'm having a to-do with my husband or I'm fretting about the children, I go to Dr. Jack for a little relief."

She pulled a half pint of Jack Daniel's out of her purse and poured me a shot in a small paper cup she took from the water cooler.

"Dr. Jack always makes house calls and the boy cures what ails you."

I downed the bourbon in a single swallow and felt its brown glow in my stomach.

"Thanks, Mrs. Barber."

"Don't tell Dr. Lowenstein I gave you that, Carolina."

"My lips are sealed," I promised. "By the way, how are the penguins?"

"What penguins?" she asked suspiciously.

"It's so cold in here I thought the doctor must be raising penguins or that most of her clients must be manic-depressive Eskimos."

"You get out of here, now, Carolina," said Mrs. Barber, issuing me a summary dismissal with a wave of her hand. "Dr. Lowenstein likes it cool in summer and hot in winter. I got to wear sweaters all summer and damn if I don't feel like strutting around this office in a bikini when there's snow piling up outside in February."

"But does she cure a lot of crazy people, then lose them to pneumonia?"

"Get," she commanded, and returned to her typing.

I shivered again as I entered the chilled sanctum where patients awaited Dr. Lowenstein's summons.

I took a stack of *Architectural Digests* from a coffee table and began idly leafing through them, laughing at the thought that any human beings could live and suffer and play in those voluptuous rooms. There was an excessive, overripened sensibility at work in the creation of every house I studied. I turned to a library of an Italian architect so ebullient and rococo that you could tell not a single book had ever been read in those glistening leather chairs that stood artfully arranged in perfect intervals along the walls. Even books had become furniture. The decorator had purloined windows from dismantled estates, lifted paneling from the halls of damaged castles. Nothing was original. Everything was the result of a vision, amalgamations of booty plundered from auction houses—the personal touch surrendered to the stately majesties of overwrought beautification.

"Where are the cat boxes, the playpens, the wastepaper baskets, the ashtrays?" I said aloud, turning the pages and studying the photographs of a restored chateau in the Loire Valley. "Where's the Kleenex, the toilet paper, the Drano, the toothbrushes by the sink?"

Talking back to magazines and newspapers was a much favored hobby of mine: I considered it a calisthenic of mental health. I did not see or hear the woman enter the waiting room and take a seat near the door.

She sat erect in her chair, almost incorporeal in her stillness, grieving and spent. She was one of those classically beautiful women who inspired a wordless awe in me. There is such a thing as too much beauty in a woman and it is often a burden as crippling as homeliness and far more dangerous. It takes much luck and integrity to survive the gift of perfect beauty, and its impermanence is its most cunning betrayal.

She wept without tears and it sounded as though she were strangling. Her face was misshapen from the effort to control her grief, like the ones on those stricken, exhausted Madonnas who hover lovingly over their broken sons in Pietàs all over Europe.

Though I was in the same room, muttering at photographs, she did not look at me or acknowledge my presence.

Ha! A New Yorker, I thought to myself. None of the small talk or little courtesies to ease the embarrassment of this chance encounter.

I returned to the pages of *Architectural Digest* and kept my criticisms to myself. For several minutes I read in silence. When I heard her weeping again, this time there were tears.

Thoughtfully, I considered the tactics of approach. Should I ignore her and mind my own business? But I dismissed that mode of operation as being inconsistent with my nosy, well-meaning character. Should I be professionally considerate, or should I directly ask her what is wrong and whether I can help her in any way?

Because she was beautiful she would think I was making a pass at her no matter what I did or said. That was both the truth and the danger of a beautiful woman in distress, and I did not wish to add to her alarm. So, I thought, I'll use the direct approach and admit to her right away that I'm impotent, that I'm a castrato singing in a Turkish boys' choir, that I'm a homosexual engaged to a longshoreman, that I want to help her, that I cannot bear to see her unhappy like this.

But I say nothing. I do not know how to make overtures of concern in New York. I am a stranger here, unfamiliar with the assizes and codes that govern human behavior in these glorious glass valleys. I decide to tell her that. Otherwise, I think, she will believe I am like all the rest of these alienated people, that I feel nothing more for her than I do when I pass a wino vomiting in a subway station. With utter certainty, I know that if she were homely or plain or even just pretty, I would speak to her immediately, I would offer to get her a handkerchief, to send out for a pizza, buy her a martini, wire her flowers, send her a Hallmark card, or beat up the husband who is abusing her. But I am dazzled by her inexhaustible beauty, rendered speechless by it. Every woman I had ever met who walked through the world appraised and classified by an extraordinary physicality had also received the keys to an unbearable solitude. It was the coefficient of their beauty, the price they had to pay.

I laid the magazine down and without looking at her I said, "Excuse me, ma'am. My name is Tom Wingo, and I'm from South Carolina. Is there anything I can do for you? I feel terrible that you're feeling so bad."

She did not answer. She shook her head angrily and cried even harder. The sound of my voice seemed to upset her.

"I'm very sorry," I whined. "Could I get you a glass of water?"

"I came," she said through tears and gasps, "to see a fucking shrink. I don't need help from one of her fucking patients."

"Ah! A slight misunderstanding, ma'am. I'm not a patient of Dr. Lowenstein's."

"Then why are you waiting around her office? This isn't a bus stop." Then she opened her purse and searched for something and I heard the rattle of keys. "Could you get me a Kleenex, please? I seem to have forgotten mine."

I sprinted toward the door, relieved to be of some service and grateful to be spared the explanation of how I came to be marooned in this office. Mrs. Barber handed me a Kleenex and whispered, "She's in bad shape, Carolina."

Returning to the room, I handed her the tissue. She thanked me and blew her nose. It has always struck me as incongruous that stunning women should have to blow their noses, obscene even, that they too should be saddled with unseemly bodily functions. She dried her tears and in the process smeared the mascara into uneven purple deltas on her cheeks. Extracting a compact from her Gucci bag, she expertly fixed her make-up.

"Thank you," she said, composing herself. "I apologize for being so nasty. I'm having a very difficult time."

"Is it a man?" I asked.

"Isn't it always a man?" she said in a bitter, bereaved voice.

"Do you want me to beat him up?" I asked, picking up a copy of the latest *New Yorker*.

"Of course not," she answered testily. "I love him very much."

"Just offering," I said. "My brother used to do that for my sister and me. If anyone was picking on us at school, Luke would simply ask, 'You want me to beat them up?' We never did, but it always made us feel better."

She smiled at me but the smile dissolved into an affecting grimace. It was a measure of her beauty that the grimace only enhanced her high-cheekboned loveliness.

"I've been going to my shrink for over four years," she said, dabbing at her eyes again, "and I'm not even sure I like the son of a bitch."

"You must have a very good insurance policy," I said.

"My insurance policy doesn't cover mental illness. My insurance policy doesn't even cover physical illness."

"I'm *not* mentally ill," she insisted, fidgeting in her chair. "I'm just very neurotic and I'm always falling in love with assholes."

"Assholes make up a very large percentage of the world. I've tried to figure it out mathematically and I think it's about seventy-three percent and rising."

"In which category do you place yourself?" she asked.

"Oh, me? I'm an asshole. A card-carrying, lifetime member. The only good things about it are I don't have to pay dues and it puts me in a considerable majority."

Her laughter was harsh and unspontaneous. "What do you do for a living?" she asked.

"I'm a high school football coach, or was," I said, ashamed and knowing full well the incredulity of her response.

"No," she said. "I mean really."

"I'm a lawyer," I answered, wanting to end this line of humiliating interrogation as quickly as possible. I always liked the instantaneous admiration it bestowed upon me when I confessed to strangers that I represented a particularly bold and voracious multinational corporation.

"You don't look like a lawyer," she said, suspiciously

looking at my khaki pants and my faded Lacoste shirt with its alligator heraldry only half attached. "You don't dress like one either. Where did you go to law school?"

"Harvard," I answered modestly. "Look, I could tell you all about law school but it would only bore you. The agony of being editor of the *Law Review*. The disappointment I felt when I finished only second in my class."

"I'm sorry I was crying when I came in here," she said, changing the subject back to herself.

"No problem at all," I answered, pleased that she had accepted my credentials.

"I thought you were trying to make a pass at me. That's why I was so rude."

"I don't know how to make a pass at people."

"But you're married," she observed, looking at my wedding ring. "You must have made a pass at the woman who became your wife."

"No, ma'am. She tackled me in a shopping mall and worked my zipper open with her teeth. That's how I knew she wanted to date me. I was shy around girls in my youth."

"I'm just a friend of Dr. Lowenstein's," she said, brushing her luxuriant blonde hair from her eyes with a distracted, indifferent movement of her hand. "I'm not her patient. My goddamn shrink is out of town, goddamn him. Dr. L. lets me use her for emergencies."

"That's nice of her."

"She's a beautiful human being. She's got problems just like everybody else but you're in very capable hands. Oh, shit, I've had a very tough day."

"What's the matter?" I asked.

She looked at me oddly, and said coldly, without malice, I think, "Look, when I need to have a will drawn up, mister, I may give you a ring. But I go to professionals for my personal problems."

"I'm very sorry," I said. "Rest assured that I did not mean to pry."

She wept again, covering her face with her hands.

Dr. Lowenstein came out of her office and said, "Monique, please come in."

When Monique had walked past her, Dr. Lowenstein

said quickly, "I hope you don't mind, Tom. This is a friend in distress. I'll buy you a drink after this."

"It will be a pleasure, Doctor."

So my sister and I began our lives in Colleton as the children of the storm, the twins of Bathsheba. We did not leave Colleton County for the first six years of our lives; those years are unrecallable to me, lost in the coilings and overlays of a memory tight-fisted with the limitlessly prodigal images of a Carolina sea island. Here is how my mother remembered those early years: Her children took the business of growing up seriously and she never left our sides as we took our first steps, tongued those first ill-formed words and sang them to the river, and sprayed each other with hoses as we ran across fragrant summer lawns.

As time passed from solstice to mild solstice in those occluded zones of my early childhood, I played beneath the distracted majesty of my mother's blue-eyed gaze. With her eyes on me I felt as if I were being studied by flowers. It seemed to me that she could not get enough of us; everything we said or thought gave her pleasure. The sound of her laughter followed our barefooted gamboling across the grass. By her own definition, she declared that she was one of those women who adored babies and small children. In six charmed, sun-shot years she poured her heart into the peerless transformational duties of motherhood. It was not easy for her in those early years, and she saw fit to mention the hardships only every single day for the rest of our life together. But we were blond, buoyant children eager to play and to address ourselves to the secrets of the forests and to her astonishing private view of the universe. We did not know then that she was a most unhappy woman. Nor did we know she would never quite forgive us for growing up. But growing up was a misdemeanor compared to our one unforgivable crime: being born in the first place. My mother would not be a quick study. We were born to a house of complication, drama, and pain. We were typical southerners. In every southerner, beneath the veneer of cliché lies a much deeper motherlode of cliché. But even cliché is overlaid with enormous power when a child is involved.

* * *

My father almost always came home after dark. Usually I was in bed when I heard his footsteps on the porch. I began to associate him with darkness. My mother's voice would change and lose its music when he came. She became a different woman the moment he opened the door, and the whole environment of the house would change. I would hear their voices, low and susurrant, speaking over the late dinner, careful not to wake us, as they discussed the events of the day.

Once I heard my mother crying and my father hitting her, but the next morning I saw her kiss him on the lips as he went out to work in the darkness.

There were days when my mother did not speak to us at all, when she would sit on the porch, staring out at the river, at the town of Colleton, her eyes hooded with a melancholy resignation and torpor that even our crying could not banish. Her stillness frightened us. Abstractedly she would run her long fingers through our hair. Tears would flow out of her eyes but her expression would never change. We learned to grieve in silence when these seizures came upon her, gathering around her in a protective blond circle. We could not break through to her; she would not share the hurt. What my mother presented to the world and to her family was some white, impregnable essence, a filigreed and brocaded façade that represented the smallest, least definitive part of her. She was always a little bit more than the sum of her parts because there were essential parts she withheld. I have spent a lifetime studying my mother, and still I am no expert. In some ways she was the perfect mother for me; in other ways, she was the role model for the apocalypse.

I have tried to understand women, and this obsession has left me both enraged and ridiculous. The gulf is too vast and oceanic and treacherous. There is a mountain range between the sexes with no exotic race of Sherpas to translate the enigmas of those deadly slopes that separate us. Since I failed to know my mother, I was denied the gift of knowing the other women who would cross my path.

When my mother was sad or heartsore I would blame myself or feel I had done something unforgivable. A portion of guilt is standard issue for southern boys; our whole lives are convoluted, egregious apologies to our mothers because our fathers have made such flawed husbands. No boy can endure for long the weight and magnitude of his own mother's displaced passion. Yet few boys can resist their mothers' solitary and innocently seductive advances. There is such forbidden sweetness in becoming the chaste and secret lover of the father's woman, such triumph in becoming the demon rival who receives the unbearably tender love of fragile women in the shadows of the father's house. There is nothing more erotic on earth than a boy in love with the shape and touch of his mother. It is the most exquisite, most proscribed lust. It is also the most natural and damaging.

My mother was from the north Georgia mountains. Mountaineers are isolates; islanders are citizens of the world. An islander greets the stranger with a wave; a mountaineer wonders why he came. My mother's face, ethereally lovely, perpetually smiling, was a window on the world, but a window in appearance only. She was masterful at drawing out the slim, wounded biographies of strangers and equally adept at revealing not a single significant or traceable fact about herself. She and my father were oddly matched. Their life together was a thirty-year war. The only prisoners they could take were children. But there were many treaties and lulls, conferences and armistices signed before we could assess the carnage of that war. This was our life, our destiny, our childhood. We lived it the best we could and the island was lovely and kind.

Then, suddenly, we were taken from it, and the period of my life that followed I have retained with almost total recall.

In August 1950, much to his surprise and displeasure, my father was recalled into the service and received orders to report for duty in Korea. My mother decided it was not safe for a woman to live alone with three small children on Melrose Island and accepted my grandmother's invitation to spend that year in Atlanta, where she lived in a house on Rosedale Road. I did not know until that time that I had a grandmother. My parents had never mentioned her name. She rose incarnate into our lives as both mystery and gift.

We bade farewell to Grandpa Wingo in Colleton, locked up the white house, and drove toward Atlanta for our single

year of city life as children. On Rosedale Road, I kissed my
father's mother for the first time as she led us up the narrow
driveway toward her house. She lived with a man named
Papa John Stanopolous. She had deserted my grandfather
and her son during the height of the Depression and headed
for Atlanta to find work. For a year she worked in the
lingerie department of Rich's department store and sent
half her monthly salary back to her family in Colleton. When
her divorce went through, she married Papa John a week
after they met when he got lost in the lingerie department.
She told him she had never been married. I listened with
amazement when my father introduced us to Papa John as
my grandmother's cousins. The story would evolve over
the years but evolve slowly. Our parents did not believe in
telling their children too much; they only told us what they
thought we should know. And by the time we arrived at
the house on Rosedale Road, we had already learned to
hold our tongues and keep our own counsel. My father
introduced me to my grandmother, Tolitha Stanopolous,
and ordered me to call her Cousin Tolitha. An obedient
boy, I did exactly as I was told. When I asked my mother
for an explanation that night, she told me it was none of
my concern and she would explain it when I got older.

When we arrived, Papa John was recovering from the
first of a series of heart attacks that would eventually kill
him. He had a long, haggard face and a fabulous outsized
nose attached to his face like a sheltering of stone. His bald
head was kingly and soft. Childless, he loved us passionately from the first moment we entered that room in which
he would die. He could not kiss us enough. He loved the
taste and smell and sound of children. He called my father
Cousin Henry.

The house was built on a hill in a block of handsome,
unpretentious houses of similar architecture. It was located
in the area of Atlanta known as Virginia-Highlands but my
grandmother insisted that she lived in Druid Hills, a much
tonier address several blocks to the east. The house was
made from a somber red brick, the color of dried blood,
which gave the whole northeastern portion of the city a
certain rusty, sinister patina. My grandmother's house was
composed of sharp spires and angled roofs. From the street
its appearance was both comfortable and slightly wicked.

Inside, the house rambled and spread. Though the rooms were claustrophobic and small, there were many of them, all with bizarre shapes, frightening corners, niches, indentations, and places to hide. It was a house designed to nourish the special fruit of a child's nightmare.

Below the house sat a gruesome, half-finished basement so hideous and fantasy-inducing that not even my mother would enter it after dark. Two walls of concrete, sweating with moisture and rainwater, contended with two walls of red Georgia earth gouged out of the hill, naked and ugly.

The house was almost obscured from the street by four immense oaks whose branches spread over the house like a dark parasol. The trees were so large and thick that the house barely got wet during thunderstorms. But the trees were consistent with both the city and the neighborhood. Atlanta is a place where they built a city and left the forest intact. Possums and raccoons came to our back door at night and my mother would feed them marshmallows. In the spring, the air was censed with the green aroma of freshly cut lawns and as you walked beneath the dogwoods down to Stillwood Avenue, the sky above you was white as a marriage canopy.

It was a time when I was aware of nothing but being a child. But a year is a long, instructive time and the year in Atlanta introduced me to my citizenship in the world. In the first week we were living in the house my grandmother apprehended the three of us children as we headed out the back door with string, a bucket, and a couple of chicken necks to go crabbing. We were on our way to find the sea or the tidal river around Atlanta. It was inconceivable to us that with all the pleasures of Atlanta, it was not possible to go crabbing. We could not imagine or conjure up an islandless world or a street that did not lead to the sea. But the street we would always remember—the one we would try to erase by the simple pleasure of crabbing in a city bereft of oceans—was the one that led to the foot of Stone Mountain.

On the Saturday before my father departed for Korea, he drove us out of Atlanta before dawn, parked the car in darkness, and led us to the footpath that took us to the top of Stone Mountain, where we watched the sun rise out of the eastern sky. It was the first mountain we had ever seen, much less climbed. As we stood on the granite summit with the light coming through Georgia, it seemed as if the whole world had spread out beneath us. Far off we could see the modest skyline of Atlanta framed in sunshine. On the side of the mountain, the half-finished effigies of Robert E. Lee, Jefferson Davis, and Stonewall Jackson were cut into the stone, incomplete horsemen cantering through granite in a timeless ride.

My mother had packed a picnic and she laid out a white tablecloth on the summit of the largest piece of exposed granite in the world. The day was windless and clear and the tablecloth adhered to the rock like a stamp. We children playfully tussled with our father on the mountain that was ours alone. It was on top of Stone Mountain that I received a first lesson on the nature of my father's character and how it would affect my childhood. On that day, I sprang alive and conscious to the dangers of our family.

"Why do you have to go to the wars again, Daddy?" Savannah asked my father, who was lying back with his head flat against the stone, staring up into the blue sky. The veins in his forearms lay thick on his flesh like ropes lying on the deck on a boat.

"I'll be damned if I know this time, angel," he said, lifting her into the air.

Luke said, surveying the terrain, "I want to go back to Colleton. No shrimp here."

"I'll just be gone for a year. Then we'll go back to Colleton."

My mother spread out a feast of ham sandwiches, deviled eggs, and potato salad and was surprised to find a colony of ants advancing in disciplined ranks toward the food.

"I'm gonna miss my babies," my father said, watching her. "I'm going to write you letters every single week and seal each one with a million kisses. Except for you boys. You boys don't want anything to do with kisses, do you?"

"No, Daddy," Luke and I answered simultaneously.

"I'm raising you boys to be fighters. Right! I'm not raising my boys to be lovers," he said, cuffing our heads roughly. "Tell me you won't let your mother turn you into lovers when I'm away. She's too soft on you. Don't let her put you in dresses and take you to teas. I want you boys to promise me something. I want both of you to beat up an

Atlanta boy every single day. I don't want to come back from Korea and find you acting like big-city boys and putting on airs. Okay? Remember, you're country boys and country boys are always fighters."

"No," my mother said firmly but quietly. "My boys are going to be lovers. They're going to be the sweetest boys who ever lived. There's your fighter, Henry." My mother pointed to Savannah.

"Yeah, Daddy," Savannah agreed. "I'm a fighter. I can beat up Tom anytime I want to. And I can almost beat up Luke when he uses only one hand."

"Naw, you're a girl. Girls are always lovers. I don't want you fighting. I want you all soft and sugary, all peaches and cream for your Daddy."

"I don't want to be all soft and sugary," Savannah said.

"You?" I said. "You're not."

Savannah, stronger and quicker than I, surprised me by punching me hard in the stomach. I began crying and ran to my mother, who enfolded me in her arms.

"Savannah, you quit picking on Tom. You're always picking on him," my mother admonished.

"See?" Savannah said, turning to face my father. "I'm a fighter."

"Tom, I'm ashamed of you, boy," my father said, ignoring Savannah, looking beyond her toward me. "Crying when a little girl hits you. That's disgusting. Boys never cry. Never. No matter what."

"He's sensitive, Henry," my mother said, stroking my hair. "So hush."

"Oh, sensitive," my father teased. "Well, I wouldn't want to say anything that might hurt someone so sensitive. Now you'd never catch Luke crying like a baby over something like that. I've whipped Luke with a belt and never saw a tear. He's been a man since the day he was born. Tom, get over here and fight with your sister. Teach her a lesson."

"He better not or I'll hit him again," Savannah said, but I could tell by the sound of her voice that she was sorry for what she had caused.

"No, Henry," my mother said, "that's not the way to do it."

"You raise the girl, Lila," my father growled. "I'll tend to the boys. Get over here, Tom."

I left my mother's arms and crossed five yards of Stone Mountain in a walk that seemed to take forever. I stood facing my father.

"Stop crying, baby boy," he commanded, and I cried all the harder.

"No, Henry," said my mother.

"You better stop crying or I'll give you something to cry about."

"I can't stop," I said between sobs.

"It's my fault, Daddy," Savannah cried out.

My father slapped me across the face, knocking me to the ground.

"I told you to stop crying, little girl," he said, towering over me.

My face was numbed, inflamed where he hit me. I hid my face in the mountain and bawled.

"Don't you touch him again, Henry," I heard my mother say.

"I don't take shit from women, Lila," he said, turning to her. "You're a woman and nothing but a goddamn woman and you keep your goddamn mouth shut when I'm disciplining one of the boys. I don't interfere with you and Savannah because I don't give a shit how you raise her. But it's important to raise a boy up right. Because there's nothing worse on earth than a boy who ain't been brought up right."

I looked up and saw my father shaking my mother, her eyes brimming with tears, with humiliation. I never loved anyone as much as I loved her at that moment. I looked at my father, his back to me, and I felt the creation of hate in one of the soul's dark porches, felt it scream out its birth in a black forbidden ecstasy.

"Let go of Mama," Luke said.

My father, all of us, turned toward Luke's voice, and we saw him holding a small butcher knife he had found in the picnic basket.

"No, Luke, honey, it's all right," my mother said.

"It ain't all right," Luke said, his large eyes blazing with anger. "Let go of Mama and don't hit my brother again."

My father stared at his oldest son, then began laughing. I rose and ran into my mother's arms again as my father's laughter pursued me across the mountain. I would run from that mocking, cheapening laughter for the rest of my life, always away from him, always toward the soft, embracing places.

"What do you plan to do with that knife, boy?" my father said to Luke as he circled him.

"Please stop, Luke," Savannah screamed. "He'll hurt you."

"No, Luke," my mother pleaded. "He didn't hurt Mama. He was just kidding."

"Yeah, Luke. I was just joking around," my father said.

"You weren't joking," Luke said. "You're mean."

"Give me that knife," my father ordered. "Before I tear your ass open with my belt."

"No," Luke said. "Why are you so mean? Why do you have to hurt Mama? Why do you want to beat up a nice little kid like Tom?"

"Put the knife down, Luke," my mother pleaded, leaving me and going between my father and Luke.

My father pushed her away roughly and said, "I don't need a woman to protect me from a seven-year-old kid."

"I was protecting him from you," my mother screamed, and her scream carried off the mountain and fell into the forest below.

"I can take that knife away from you, Luke," my father said, crouching low and starting to move toward his son.

"I know you can," Luke said, the knife glinting in his hand, "but only because I'm little."

My father lunged and caught Luke's wrist and twisted it until the knife fell on stone. Then, slowly, my father removed his belt and began beating Luke's ass and legs with a flashing, brutal movement of his great red-haired arms. My mother, Savannah, and I all huddled together, crying, terrorized, and grieving. Luke looked off the mountain toward Atlanta, endured the beating, the savagery, the humiliation, and did not shed a single tear. Shame and exhaustion, and that alone, made my father quit. He replaced his belt in the loops of his pants and surveyed the scene of the ruined picnic on his last day in America.

Luke turned toward him and with the unbearable dignity that would be his trademark all his life said in a trembling child's voice, "I hope you die in Korea. I'm going to pray that you die."

My father went for his belt again, got it halfway off, then stopped. He looked at Luke. He looked at all of us.

He said, "Hey, everybody. What's all the crying about? Can't anybody in this family take a joke?"

Luke turned away from him and we saw the blood on his pants.

The next day my father left for Korea and disappeared for a year into another war. He woke the three of us early in the morning. He kissed each of us roughly on the cheek. It was the last time my father ever kissed me. Luke could not walk for a week. But I took to the sidewalks of Atlanta fatherless, happy as a spaniel that he was gone.

At night, secretly, in forbidden whispers, I prayed that his plane would be gunned down. My prayers bloomed like antiaircraft fire in the profound sleep of children. In dreams, I saw him coming out of the sky in flames, out of control, dying. These were not nightmares. These were the most pleasant dreams of a six-year-old boy who had suddenly realized he had been born into the house of his enemy.

I have climbed Stone Mountain often since that day. Always, awaiting me at the summit, is a six-year-old boy who dreads the approach of his father; that boy, that incompleted man, lives in the memory of that mountain. I walk up that mountain and discover the invisible cuttings in the granite where I once listened to my father call me a girl. I'll never forget my father's words on that day, or how my face felt after he slapped me, or the sight of the blood on my brother's pants. I did not understand, but I did know that I wanted to model myself after my mother. From that day, I renounced the part of me that was his and hated the fact I was male.

In September school began and Savannah and I entered first grade together, our mother and grandmother walking us to the bus stop on Briarcliff Road. Luke was going into second grade and was put in charge of seeing that we got to school safely and on time. The three of us had notes pinned to our white cotton shirts. My note read, "Hi, I'm Tom Wingo, a first grader. If you find me and I'm lost, please call my mother, Lila, at the following number: BR3-7929. She'll be very worried about me. Thank you, neighbor."

We carried new lunch boxes and wore brand-new saddle shoes. The first-grade teacher was a small, shy nun built like a child herself, who made our entry into the frightening realm of human knowledge as gentle and enriching as any act of love could be. My mother rode the bus with us that first day and told us we were about to learn to read and write, that we were embarking on our first adventure of the mind.

I did not cry until she left me on the playground, slipping away quietly, unnoticed and tentative, when I looked up and saw her on the sidewalk by Courtland Avenue, watching the nun lining up the first graders. I looked around and tried to find Luke, but he was disappearing with the other second graders through a side door.

When I cried, Savannah cried, and we both bolted from the line of suddenly motherless children and ran to our mother, our lunch boxes beating against our knees and thighs. She ran to us and knelt down to receive our charge into her arms. The three of us wept and I held her in the most passionate fury of abandonment and wanted never to be torn away from those arms.

Sister Immaculata approached us from behind and, winking at my mother, led the three of us into her classroom, where fully half the students were crying out for their mothers. Mothers, looking like giants as they moved along the aisles of diminutive desks, consoled each other as they pried their children's arms from around their nylon stockings. There was terribly affecting pain and sorrow loose in that room. Loss and the passage of days showed in the eyes of those gentle women. The nun ushered them from the room one by one.

The nun showed Savannah and me the reading book we would use that year, introduced us to Dick and Jane as though they would be neighbors of ours, and placed us in a special corner to count out apples and oranges the class would have for lunch. My mother looked back at us from the door, then slipped away unseen. Sister Immaculata, with her soft white hands flowing through our hair and over our faces, began the process of creating a home away from home in her classroom. By the end of the day, Savannah had learned the alphabet by heart. I knew it up to the letter D. Savannah sang the ABC's to the class and Sister Immaculata, touched with the wizardry of the fine, unpraised teacher, had given a poet the keys to the English language. In her first book, the poem "Immaculata" would speak of that frail, nervous woman trussed in the black drapery of her order, who made the classroom seem like a part of paradise spared. Years later, when Sister Immaculata was dying at Mercy Hospital in Atlanta, Savannah flew down from New York and read the poem to her and held her hand on the last day of Immaculata's life.

I did not cry again that day until I found a note in my lunch box from my mother. Sister Immaculata read it to me. It said, "I'm so proud of you, Tom. I love you and miss you so much. Mommy." That's all. That's all it had to say and I wept in that good nun's arms. And I prayed the Korean War would last forever.

In the house on Rosedale Road, Papa John Stanopolous lay in the back bedroom, taking his own good time about dying. My mother required absolute silence from us when we were in the house and we learned to speak in whispers, to laugh noiselessly, and to play as quietly as insects when we drifted through the rooms that led to Papa John's door.

Each day when we returned home from school, we would eat cookies and milk in the kitchen and tell what we had learned that day. Savannah always seemed to learn twice as much as either Luke or me. Luke usually recited the latest atrocity committed in the name of Catholic education by the dread Sister Irene, and my mother would frown, disturbed and worried, by Luke's tales of distress. Then she would lead us quietly to the back bedroom and let us visit with Papa John for a half-hour.

Papa John rested with his head propped up on three soft pillows, and it was always dark in his room. His face would materialize out of the half-light and the venetian blinds, half drawn, would divide the room in symmetrical chevrons of light. The room smelled of medicine and cigar smoke.

His flesh was pale and sickly, his chest as hairless and white as a pig's back. There were books and magazines scattered on the night table beside him. He would lean over and turn on the lamp when we entered. We would scramble onto his bed and cover his neck and face with kisses with my mother and grandmother warning us to be careful. They stood watching in soft attendance. But Papa John, his eyes luminous and bright as a retriever's, would wave them off. He would laugh as we crawled over him and tickle us under our arms with his heroic, shadow-casting awning of a nose.

"Be gentle with Papa John, kids," my mother would call out from the doorway. "He's had a heart attack."

"Let the children be, Lila," he would say, caressing us.

"Show us the nickel in your nose, Papa John," Savannah would demand.

With an ostentatious sleight of hand and a few magic words of Greek, he would extract a nickel from his nose and hand it to Savannah.

"Are there any more nickels up there, Papa John?" Luke would shout, peering into his dark spacious nostrils.

"I don't know, Luke," Papa John said sadly. "I blew my nose earlier today and there were nickels shooting out all over this room. But look here. I feel something funny in my ears."

We would search his great hairy ears and find nothing. He would repeat the Greek phrases, wave his hands theatrically, cry "Presto," and pull two nickels from behind his fleshy lobes and place the coins into our eager hands.

At night, before we went to bed, our mother permitted us to return to Papa John's bedroom. Freshly bathed, clean as snow, we arranged ourselves around his pillows like three bright satellites around a new moon. We took turns each night lighting the cigars the doctor had forbidden him to smoke. Then Papa John would lean back, his face framed in a nimbus of fragrant smoke, and tell us a bedtime story.

"Should I tell them about the time I was captured by two hundred Turks, Tolitha?" he asked my grandmother as she stood by the door.

"No, don't scare them before their bedtime," my grandmother answered.

"Please tell us about the turkeys," Luke begged.

"Turks," Papa John corrected. "Not turkeys, Luke."

"They won't sleep a wink if you tell that story, Papa John," my mother said.

"Please, Mama," Savannah said. "We won't sleep a wink if we don't hear about the Turks."

Each night this thin, withered man took us on miraculous, improbable voyages around the globe where he encountered perfidious Turks attacking him in countless, inimical battalions, and each night he would devise ingenious ways to repulse them and return safely between the white sheets of his bed, where he was dying slowly, painfully, and without the companionship or intercession of Agamemnon's soldiers, dying without honor, surrounded not by Turks but by three children as he weakened daily until the stories became as important and essential to him as they were to us. His imagination lit fires in that room in a final shimmering ignition. Papa John had never had children and these stories poured out of him in bright torrents.

Behind us, watching and listening, were our mother and grandmother. I did not know who Papa John was or where he came from or how he was related to me and no one would explain it to any of us children. We had left my grandfather in Colleton and all of us wept as we left him. My mother and father carefully instructed us to call our grandmother by her given name and never under any circumstances reveal that she was my father's mother. Papa John might have been a gifted storyteller, but he had nothing over my grandmother.

At bedtime, there would be one more story. Then my mother would lead us out of his room, into the dimly lit hallway, past the door that led to the dread basement, and up the winding stairs to the large bedroom on the second floor where we, the children, made our home. If a wind was blowing, the branches of the hovering oak trees would scratch the windowpanes. There were three beds set side by side. Savannah had the middle bed, flanked by her two brothers. A small bedside lamp was the only light in the room. We cast enormous, superhuman shadows on those slanted enclosing walls.

Once a week my father would write and my mother would read those letters to us right before we went to sleep. He wrote in a clipped, military prose that read like an order of the day. He described each mission to us as though he were speaking of an errand to buy bread or fill the car up with gas. "I was flying recon with Bill Lundin. We were watching a squad of our grunts winding up some mountain when I spotted something funny going on just above them. I radioed Bill and said, 'Hey, Bill, you see what I see?' I look over and see Bill straining his eyes. Sure enough, ol' Bill sees it too. About halfway up the mountain, there were about three hundred North Korean regulars waiting to ambush these poor grunts. So I get on the radio and I radio down to the grunts and I say, 'Hey, boys, call a halt to your little daytrip.' 'Why?' the guy asks me. 'Because you're walking into the arms of half of North Korea,' I say. He gets my drift. Then Bill and I decide to go down and ruin those nectarines' entire afternoon. I go first and lay a few napalm on their heads. It certainly got their attention. I saw thirty of them trying to wipe flames off their bodies like they were cleaning lint from their coat. But it don't work that way. Then Bill lays a few more eggs and we got us a party going on. I radioed back and a whole squadron lifted off to help us. We chased that battalion for three days. Refueling, then hunting, then refueling and hunting again. Finally we caught what was left of them crossing the Naktong River. Caught them in the open. Turned the river red. It was fun but it didn't do an ounce of good. Folks breed like mink over here and there's plenty more where they come from. Tell the kids I love them very much. Tell them to pray for the old Dad and to watch out for their Mama."

"Who is Papa John, Mama?" Savannah asked my mother one evening.

"He's Tolitha's husband. You know that," she answered.

"But who is he to us? Is he our grandfather?"

"No. Your grandfather Amos lives in Colleton. You know that."

"But Tolitha's our grandmother, isn't she?"

"She's your cousin when we're up here. She doesn't want Papa John to know you're her grandchildren."

"But she's Dad's mother, isn't she?"

"When we're here in this house, she's your father's cousin. Don't ask me to explain. It's too complicated. I don't understand it myself."

"Why isn't she still married to Grandpa Wingo?"

"They haven't been married for years. You'll understand

it later. Don't ask so many questions. It's none of your business. Besides, Papa John treats you as though you're his grandchildren, doesn't he?"

"Yes, Mama," Luke said, "but is he your father, Mama? Where's your mother and father?"

"They died a long time before you were born."

"What were their names?" I asked.

"Thomas and Helen Trent," she answered.

"What were they like?" Savannah asked.

"Very handsome people. They looked like a prince and princess. Everyone said so."

"Were they rich?"

"They were very rich before the Depression. The Depression wiped them out."

"Do you have any pictures of them?"

"No. They were all burned down in the fire that destroyed their house."

"Is that what killed them?"

"Yes. It was a terrible fire," my mother said without emotion, her face drawn and apprehensive. My mother, the beauty. My mother, the liar.

As children, we had but one duty. In the basement, in rows of dusty Mason jars, Papa John kept his collection of black widow spiders, which, as a hobby, he sold to biology teachers, entomologists, zoos, and private collectors around the country. We were given the job of caring for those small malignant spiders, which floated like black cameos in their jars. Twice a week, Luke, Savannah, and I would descend into the moist glooms, switch on the naked exposed bulb, and feed those mute arachnids, any one of which, we were assured by a garrulous Papa John, "could kill us deader than a stone." We had helped feed poultry since we could walk, but these descents required a courage and agitated sense of commitment no chicken ever inspired. When the feeding hour approached, we would gather in Papa John's bedroom, listen to his careful instructions, then descend the wooden staircase to face the minuscule, satanic livestock who watched us in stillness like the approach of flies.

On Saturdays we brought the jars of spiders up to Papa John for his inspection. He would wipe the jars clean of dust with a linen cloth. He eyed the spiders with discrimination. He would question us closely about their feeding habits. He would count the pear-shaped egg sacs and make notations in a small notebook whenever there was a crop of new spiders. Cautiously, he would remove a spider and let it walk back and forth across a dinner plate, turning it with a pair of tweezers when it neared the edge. He would point to the red hourglass delicately tattooed on the female spider's abdomen and say, "There. That's what you look for. That hourglass means 'I kill.' "

"Why do you collect black widows, Papa John?" Savannah asked one day. "Why not goldfish or stamps or something pretty?"

"Because I was a shoe salesman, sweetie," he answered, "a shoe salesman and a damn good one. But being a shoe salesman is the most common thing in the world. I wanted to do something no one else I knew did. Something special. So I became the shoe salesman who raised black widows in his basement. It's an attention getter."

"Do they really eat their husbands?" Luke asked.

"These are very stern women," Papa John answered. "They eat their husbands right after they mate."

"Can they really kill you?" I asked.

"I think they can kill a child fairly easily," he said. "I'm not sure they can kill a full-grown man, though. The guy that got me started in this business had been bitten a couple of times. He said it made him sick enough to think he would die. But he was still walking around."

"How did he get bit?" I asked.

"Black widows are kind of shy except when they're defending their eggs. Then they're a mite aggressive. He liked to let them walk around on his arm," Papa John said, smiling.

Savannah said, "That makes me sick to think about it."

"He sure raised pretty spiders, though," Papa John said, studying his pets.

The care of black widows inspired a patience and concentration rare in young children. We took our responsibilities seriously and studied the life cycle of the spiders with the supercharged zealotry born of caring for creatures who could kill us. My lifelong love of spiders and insects began with my nose pressed close against Mason jars, observing the tedious and horrifying existence of black widows. They hung motionless in webs spun out of their viscera. They lived dangling and still, black in the high wires of their jar-shaped lives. When they moved quickly, it was to kill. Over the months, we watched the females kill and devour the males. We became attuned to the seasons of spiders and time poured out of the red hourglasses in shimmering, ill-formed webs. We watched egg cases exploding into spiders newly minted, scattering like brown and orange seeds across a jar. Our fear of them turned to fascination and advocacy. There was such beauty in the economical structure of spiders; they moved across webs with the secret of lace making and silk screening implied in their loins, aerialists in a quart of Georgia air. They were good at doing what they were born to do.

Behind the house, a large deciduous forest, circumvallated by a low stone fence, stretched all the way to Briarcliff Road. There were "No Trespassing" signs posted along the fence at thousand-foot intervals. Our grandmother informed us in a breathless, conspiratorial voice that "very, very rich people" lived on the property and that under no circumstances were we ever to cross the fence to play in those verboten woods. This was the Candler family, the heirs of Coca-Cola, and whenever my grandmother spoke of them it was as though she were describing a collegial association of some scrupulous peerage. According to my grandmother, the Candlers were the nearest thing Atlanta had to a royal family, and she would not allow us to desecrate their walled baronage.

But we would approach that fence after school each day, that deep-green, perfumed realm forbidden to us, and smell the money coming through the trees. We longed to glimpse a single member of that noble and enchanted family. But we were children and soon we were climbing the fence and taking a few forbidden steps into the forest, then racing back to the safety of the stone wall. The next time we would step off ten paces into the woods before we lost our nerve and returned to our own yard. Slowly, we began to demythologize the outlawed woods. Soon we knew the acreage of that forest better than any Candler ever had. We learned its secrets and boundaries, hid in its groves and arbors, and felt the old thrill of disobedience buoyant in young hearts gallant enough to ignore the strange laws of adults. Surrounded by trees, we hunted squirrels with slingshots, watched from the high branches of trees the lucky Candler children, looking serious and bored, cantering thoroughbreds down forest paths, and spied on the gardener fertilizing banks of azaleas.

And one warm November night, we slipped out of an upstairs bedroom, climbed down the immense oak that ruled our quadrant of the house, and walked through the forest all the way to the Candler mansion itself. Lying on our stomachs, we crawled toward that opulent Tudor mansion through the thick grass and watched, through the silver light of French doors, the great family itself at dinner. Servants were wheeling in food on elaborate dollies. The Candlers, erect and pallid, ate their meal as if they were attending a church service, such was their seriousness, their unruffled ecclesiastical mien.

In awe we watched the meal consumed, the blaze of candelabra lifting off the table like buckheads on fire, the tender light of chandeliers, the lethargy and restrained grandeur of wealth. Lying in a field of freshly mown grass, we attended to every detail of that casual, slowly evolving meal. There was no laughter or conversation from the royal family, and the rich, we assumed, were silent as fish. The servants moved stiffly in penguinesque charades through the room. They measured the pace of the meal, poured wine into half-filled glasses, floated like undertakers from window to window, unaware of our presence. At that very moment, disguised as night creatures, we inhaled the delicious aromas of that meal, watching as secret Candlers, initiates into the extraordinary rites and customs of the Coca-Cola princes. They did not know we owned their forest.

The house was known as Callanwolde.

In the woods of Callanwolde, we found a fitting substitute for the island denied to us by the Korean War. We built a treehouse in one of Callanwolde's extravagant oaks. We resumed our interrupted life as country children in the middle of the South's largest city. Quails called to us at dusk. A family of gray foxes lived beneath an uprooted cottonwood. We would come to the forest to remember who we were, what we had come from, and where we would be returning. Once we had crossed the fence and made our claim on that prohibited acreage, Atlanta became a perfect city.

It was only later that I realized I loved Atlanta because it was the only place on earth I had ever lived without a father. By then, Atlanta had darkened in the imagination. By then, the woods of Callanwolde had become a fearful place. By then, the giant had come into our lives and the children, unafraid of spiders, would learn the harsh lesson that they had much to learn and fear from the world of men.

It was early March and the dogwoods were just beginning to bloom. The whole earth shivered with the green tumult of ripening, sun-soft days, and we were walking through the woods, looking for box turtles. Savannah saw him first. She froze and pointed at something ahead of us.

He was standing beside a tree covered with poison sumac, relieving himself. He was the largest, most powerful man I had ever seen and I had grown up with men of legendary strength who worked around the shrimp docks in Colleton. He grew out of the earth like some fantastic, grotesque tree. His body was thick, marvelous, and colossal. His eyes were blue and vacant. A red beard covered his face, but there was something wrong about him. It was the way he looked at us, far different from the way adults normally studied children, that alerted us to danger. The three of us felt the menace in his disengaged stare. His eyes did not seem connected to anything human. He zipped up his pants and turned toward us. He was almost seven feet tall. We ran.

We made it to the stone fence, clambered over it, and ran screaming into our back yard. When we reached the back porch, we saw him standing at the edge of the woods, observing us. The fence we had to climb over barely came to his waist. My mother came out of the back door when she heard our screams. We pointed toward the man in the woods.

"What do you want, mister?" my mother shouted, taking a few steps toward the man.

She saw the change in his face too; she sensed the demonic, unjoined quality in his eyes.

"You," he said to my mother, and his voice was strangely

high-pitched for such a large man. He did not seem cruel or imbalanced; he simply seemed inhuman.

"What?" my mother asked, frightened by his lack of affect.

"I want you," the giant said, taking his first step toward her.

We ran for the house and as my mother locked the back door I saw him watching her through the kitchen window. I had never seen a man stare at a woman with such primitive lust until I saw that stranger looking at my mother. I had never studied eyes that were born to hate women.

My mother saw him through the window and she walked over and pulled the shade.

"I'll be back," the man said, and we could hear his laughter as my mother dialed the number for the police.

When the police came, he was gone. The police combed the woods and the only thing they found was our treehouse and a single footprint from a size nineteen shoe. My mother spanked us for trespassing on Callanwolde property.

In our minds, I think we children truly believed that we had summoned the visitation of the giant, that he was the manifestation of our willful disobedience, that he had been called out of the netherworld as an instrument of divine, unappeasable justice to punish us for crossing the fence into the taboo frontiers of Callanwolde. We had profaned the lands of the rich, we thought, and God had sent this giant to punish us.

We never entered the Callanwolde property again, but the giant had already exposed the gravity of our sin. He would require expiation. He would bring Callanwolde into our home. He would come as the lordly inquisitor and punish the sins of the Wingo children in a perverse and imaginative way. He would not punish the sinners for their crimes, for he understood well how to punish children most grievously. When he came, he would come for our mother.

Another secret was added to that house of endless intrigue. We could not tell Papa John about the intruder from the forest. "Because he's got such a weak heart, honey," my grandmother explained to me. I thought he should be told immediately, feeling with enormous justification that we needed someone on our side who could slay two hundred

Turks if the giant returned. But my grandmother assured us that she and my mother were big girls and could take care of themselves.

During the next week we were vigilant and cautious, but the days passed without incident and the streets of Atlanta erupted in a white flaming of dogwood. Bees moaned in the ecstasy of clovers and azaleas. My mother wrote a letter to Grandpa Wingo that week, telling him the exact date we would be returning to the island after my father returned stateside. She asked him to hire a black woman to clean up the house for their arrival. She was careful to mention that my grandmother sent him her kindest regards. Then she let each of the children write "I love you, Grandpa" at the bottom of the letter. She addressed the letter to our house on Melrose Island, knowing that he checked our mailbox more frequently than he did his own. Placing the letter in the mailbox on Rosedale Road, she raised the red metal flag to alert the postman as we left for school on Friday morning. It was only when we returned to the island that summer that we learned my grandfather never received that letter. The letter would not be delivered for more than a decade.

On Sunday evening we were watching television in the living room. My mother and grandmother were sitting in brown overstuffed armchairs, watching the *Ed Sullivan Show*. I was sitting on the floor between my mother's legs. Luke was lying on his stomach, watching the screen and trying to finish his math homework. Savannah was sitting in my grandmother's lap. My mother passed me a bowl of hot popcorn. I took a generous handful and spilled two kernels on the rug. I picked them up and ate them. Then I felt the room go dead with fear and heard Savannah say the single, electrifying word: "Callanwolde."

He was standing on the porch in darkness, staring in at us through the glass-paneled door. I do not know how long he had been watching us but there was a quality of vegetable stillness about him, as though he had sprouted like some dissident, renegade vine as we sat there. His eyes were fixed on my mother. He had returned for her and her alone. His flesh was morbidly pale, the color of a tincture

of alabaster, and he filled the doorway like a column up-
holding a ruin.

Placing one enormous hand on the doorknob, he twisted
it violently and we heard the strain of the metal. As my
mother rose she said to my grandmother, "Walk very slowly
into the hallway and call the police, Tolitha."

My mother walked toward the door and faced the
stranger.

"What do you want?" she asked.

"Lila," he replied, and my mother took a step back in
shock when she heard him use her name. His voice was
ill-fitting and still high-pitched. He smiled a hideous smile
at her and turned the knob again.

My mother then saw his penis, exposed and enormous,
rising out of him, the color of pig flesh. Savannah screamed
when she saw it and I saw Luke moving up from the floor.

"The police are coming," my mother said.

Suddenly, the man broke a pane of glass on the door
with a brick and his long arm thrust into the hole. He
reached for the lock on the door. Glass cut him and his
wrist began to bleed. My mother reached for his arm, trying
to keep him from unlocking the door. She grappled with
him briefly but he backhanded her across the chest, knocking her to the floor. Somewhere I could hear Savannah and
Luke screaming but they seemed displaced and faraway,
like voices heard underwater. My whole body lost feeling,
like a Novocained gum. He undid one lock, then struggled
to turn the key that held him away from us. He was twisting
the key, a low animal whine issuing out of him, when Luke
approached him, swinging a fireplace tool. Luke crashed
the poker across the man's wrist. The man shouted in pain
and withdrew his arm. He tried to put his arm through the
window again but Luke was there waiting for him, swinging that poker as hard as any seven-year-old kid on earth.

I heard something behind me, the sound of my grandmother's slippers sliding down the polished floors of the
hallway. I turned and I saw her round the corner with a
small revolver in her hand.

"Duck, Luke," she ordered, and Luke dove to the ground.

Tolitha opened fire on that glass door.

The giant ran when the first shot pierced a windowpane

close to his head. He ran with his penis flopping against his leg. He sprinted off the porch and toward the safety of the Callanwolde woods. We heard the sound of police sirens far off on Ponce de Leon.

My grandmother yelled into the darkness from the porch: "That'll teach you to fuck with a country girl."

"Your language, Tolitha," my mother said, still in shock. "The children."

"The children just watched a guy with his dick in his hand trying to get to their mother. A little language won't hurt 'em much."

When it was over, my mother found me eating popcorn, watching the *Ed Sullivan Show* as though nothing had happened. But for two days I could not speak. Papa John had slept through the entire attack and had not even awakened to the gunfire or the coming of the police. When he wondered at the reason for my silence, my mother said "laryngitis" and my grandmother seconded her lie. They were southern women who felt a responsibility to protect their men from danger and bad news. My silence, my pathetic wordlessness, affirmed their belief in the basic fragility and weakness of men.

For a week the police parked a patrol car on Rosedale Road and a plainclothes detective circled our home several times during the night. My mother could not sleep at night and we would find her hovering over us after midnight, obsessively checking and rechecking the locks on our bedroom windows. Once I awoke and saw her framed in moonlight, staring out toward the forests of Callanwolde. As she stood there, I noticed her body for the first time, observed in guilt and terror its soft, voluptuous features, admired the shape of her full breasts and the curve of her waist as she scanned the moonlit yard for the approach of her enemy.

The word *Callanwolde* changed meaning for us, and, following Savannah's example, we began to refer to the man as Callanwolde. "Did Callanwolde come last night?" we would ask at breakfast. "Have the police caught Callanwolde yet, Mama?" we would ask as she read to us at bedtime. It became a catchall, portmanteau word for everything evil or iniquitous in the world. When Sister Immaculata described the terrors of hell in her sweet voice, she was explaining the boundaries and perimeters of Callan-wolde to me and Savannah. When my father wrote in a letter that his plane had been hit with machine-gun fire and he had fought his plane all the way back to the air base, losing oil pressure and altitude, trailing black smoke, afraid that the plane would explode in midair, we called that dreadful flight a Callanwolde. It was a specific person, a specific place, and a general condition of a world suddenly fearful and a fate uncontrollable.

After two weeks of diligent patrolling, the police assured my mother that the man would never return to the house.

He returned that night.

The phone rang in the house that evening. Again we were watching television and eating popcorn. My mother answered the phone in the hallway and we heard her say hello to Mrs. Fordham, the old woman who lived in the house next door. I saw my mother turn white and watched as she put the receiver down on the side table and say in a drained, uninflected voice, "He's on the roof."

We lifted our eyes slowly to the ceiling and heard the faint sounds of his footsteps walking down the slanted shingles on the roof.

"Don't go upstairs," my mother said. "He might be in the house."

She phoned the police.

For ten minutes we listened to him moving unhurriedly about the roof. He made no attempt to enter an upstairs window. This visit had no meaning, except to establish his credentials in our lives again and to inspire a renewed panic in our hearts. Then the sound of sirens burst far off in the city, hovered over Atlanta like the cry of redemptive angels. We heard his footsteps run across the roof and felt him enter the limbs of the huge oak that grew beside the drive-way. My mother walked to the bank of windows in the music room and saw him as he reached the ground. He paused, looking back, and saw her through the window. He waved at her and smiled. Then he ran in an easy, un-troubled gait toward the dark harboring forest behind us.

The next day the police took bloodhounds through the Callanwolde forest but they lost his scent somewhere along Briarcliff Road.

He did not come again for two months.

* * *

But he was there even when he was not there. He inhabited each alcove and recessed corner of that house. We could not open any door without expecting him to be waiting behind it. We came to fear the approach of night. The nights he did not appear were as spiritually exhausting as the ones when he did. The trees outside the house lost their healthy, luxuriant beauty and became grotesque in our eyes. The woods of Callanwolde became his domain, his safe hermitage, and a region of inexhaustible dread in our imaginations. His face was portrayed subliminally in every window. If we closed our eyes, we saw his image imprinted on our consciousnesses like a face on a veil. He sundered our dreams with his murderous eyes. Terror marked my mother's face; she slept during the day and roamed the house checking locks at night.

With my mother's permission, we moved the forty jars of black widows out of the basement and transported them with great and serious concentration to our upstairs bedroom. None of the children could bear to descend into the terrifying depths of the basement when Callanwolde was threatening the house. The basement also had a door that led to the outdoors and the police had told my grandmother that this provided the easiest entrance into the house. She was as relieved as we were when we arranged the jars of spiders in long rows on an unused bookshelf in the far corner of our bedroom. When Sacred Heart School had a Pet Day, each of us brought a single black widow to school and collectively won the prize for most unusual pet.

At night, with the lamps gleaming brightly, the interior of the house felt like an aquarium and we floated from room to room, feeling Callanwolde's eyes study us from beneath the glooms of oaks. We assumed he was watching and appraising us; we assumed he was omnipresent and was biding his time, awaiting the perfect moment to launch his next sortie against us. Swimming through the electric light of that besieged house, we waited in the charged, breathless atmosphere of our own obsessions. The police checked our house twice a night. They searched the bushes and trees with flashlights. They entered the woods. They would leave and the night would belong to him again.

It was the year that Luke flunked second grade, a fact that humiliated Luke but caused Savannah and me great joy, since the three of us would now be joined happily in the same classroom when we returned to Colleton. It was the year I lost my first tooth, the year Savannah and I got the measles, the year a tornado destroyed three houses in Druid Hills, but in our memories, in the trackless shadows of our subconsciouses, it became the year of Callanwolde.

It was a week before my father's return from Korea. We had all gone into Papa John's room to kiss him good night. He was drawn and wasted and he was forbidden by his doctor to tell us bedtime stories, so we had taken to speaking to him in whispers. We had witnessed his daily diminishment, the leaking out of his fervent vitality, and he taught us a little bit about death each day as he fell further and further away from us. His eyes had already surrendered the light. My grandmother had begun drinking heavily in the evenings.

My mother was feeling safer now that my father's approach was imminent. All of us looked upon my father as the heroic figure, the redeemer, the knight errant who would deliver us from harm's way and the fear of Callanwolde. I no longer prayed for my father to die. I prayed for him to be near me. I prayed for him to save my mother.

That night when she read a chapter of *The Yearling* to us a strong wind moved the trees against the house. We said our prayers together, and she kissed each of us good night. She turned out the light and although we heard her footsteps descend the winding stairs, her perfume lingered in the darkness. I fell asleep listening to the wind in the trees.

Two hours later I awoke and saw his face in the window, staring at me. He put his finger to his lips and bade me to be silent. I heard the knife cutting through the screen like the tearing of cheap silk. I did not move or speak. A paralysis of exquisite, impenetrable terror entered each cell of my body. His eyes transfixed me and I lay as rigid as a bird before the copperhead's approach.

Then Savannah awoke and screamed.

His foot broke through the window in a brutal showering of glass.

Luke rolled off the bed, shouting for my mother.

I did not move.

Savannah grabbed a pair of scissors from her nightstand and when that great arm entered the window and moved along the sill toward the lock, Savannah struck with those scissors and the blade stuck in his forearm. He howled with pain and withdrew his arm. Then he began kicking out the window frame with his foot and pieces of wood and glass splintered and fell into the room.

His head, lionesque and cruel, peered into the room, and he smiled when he saw my mother standing in the hallway looking at him.

My mother, trembling, begged, "Please, go away. Please, go away."

Savannah threw a hairbrush at his face. He laughed. He laughed again when he saw my mother try to control her trembling.

Then the first jar broke against the wall above his head.

Luke threw the next jar straight at Callanwolde's face; it missed and exploded against the windowsill.

Then the man's head disappeared and we saw his huge leg swing into the window, slowly entering as he tried to make himself smaller and squeeze through the opening. Luke opened four jars and emptied them on his trouser leg. Savannah ran to the bookcase and returned with a jar. She hurled the contents at the advancing leg and the jar exploded against the floor. My mother was screaming for my grandmother. The man's other leg slid through the window and he arched his spine, preparing to slide into the room, when the first black widow sent her venom shooting through his bloodstream. It was that enormous howl of pain we would remember most clearly later. In the light of the hallway we saw those huge legs withdraw as a small civilization of spiders found themselves on the loose and alarmed in the folds and creases of his trousers. He felt them moving on him and he rolled down the roof, panicked now, hurting and out of control. We heard his body hit the ground outside the window. He was screaming now, confused, rolling on the ground, beating at his legs and groin with his immense hands. Then, rising, he looked up toward my mother watching him from that destroyed window, screamed again, and ran toward the woods of Callanwolde as if on fire.

We never learned how many spiders bit him. The dogs came the next day and lost his trail by the gas station on Stillwood Avenue. The police alerted every hospital. But no seven-foot giant with a red beard who had been bitten by black widows presented himself for treatment at a Georgia hospital. His disappearance was as mysterious and open-ended as his sudden appearance had been.

My father returned the following weekend and we left the same day for the island. Our mother forbade us to tell our father a single thing about the man who had so shaken our lives. When we asked her why, she explained that our father had just returned from a war and had a right to come back to a happy family. More darkly, she suggested that our father might think that she had done something to invite the attentions of Callanwolde. My father often said to her that no woman was raped who had not asked for it. She told us this matter-of-factly and said there were many things that men could not understand.

Luke, Savannah, and I spent the next three days trying to recapture the missing spiders. We found half a dozen in our bedroom. We found two in the attic and one in one of my old tennis shoes. We never slept in that room again. After we left my grandmother continued to find black widows in different places around the house. When Papa John died, she released all of them deep in the Callanwolde woods. She, nor any of us, ever killed a spider again. The spider became the first of a number of sacred species in our family chronicle.

Many years later while going through some clippings in the Atlanta Public Library, I came upon a photograph and the following news item: "Otis Miller, 31, was arrested in Austell, Georgia, last night for suspicion of having raped and murdered Mrs. Bessie Furman, a local schoolteacher separated from her husband."

I made a photocopy of that story and inked a single word across it: Callanwolde.

6

We passed by healthy palms and fastidious bellhops in the lobby of the Plaza Hotel as we made our way to the Oak Room and took a table in a discreet corner. It was five minutes before the waiter approached us with an imperturbable combination of hauteur and studied indifference. Then he took our orders, imperiously, as though he were issuing stock options. I considered ordering beef jerky or pickled pig's lips but he did not look easily amused. I ordered a martini on the rocks with a twist of lemon, knowing he would bring me my drink bearing the round weight of a blasphemous green olive instead. The word *lemon* is always translated "olive" in a certain category of expensive hotel bars. Dr. Lowenstein ordered a glass of Pouilly Fuissé.

When the drinks came I fished the olive out of the martini and placed it in the ashtray.

"You said olive," the waiter stated as he walked away.

"I always make that mistake," I said.

"Don't you just love New York waiters?" said Dr. Lowenstein.

"I think I prefer Nazi war criminals, but I'm not sure. I've never met a Nazi war criminal." I raised my glass and said, "A toast to you, healer of souls. My God, Doctor, how do you stand being around people in such pain day after dreary day?"

She took a sip of her wine, her lipstick imprinting the glass, then said, "Because I always think I can help them."

"But doesn't it depress you?" I asked. "Doesn't it break you down after a while?"

"Their problems are not my problems. I have enough of my own to worry about."

"Ha!" I laughed. "I bet I'd love to have your problems."

"There you are," she said. "You're absolutely sure you could handle my problems, but you have trouble handling your own. That's the way I feel about my profession. When I leave the office at six o'clock, I leave everything behind me. I don't think once about the patients I saw that day. I've learned to separate my professional life from my private life."

"That sounds so cold and remorseless to me," I said. "I couldn't be a psychiatrist. I'd listen to these stories all day and they'd drive me crazy all night."

"Then you couldn't help anyone. You have to maintain some distance, Tom. Surely, you must have come upon students with emotional problems when you were teaching."

"Yeah, I did, Doc," I said, taking a sip of the martini, wincing when I tasted the salty ghost of the loathed and pungent olive. "And I couldn't stand it; I can take an adult having problems, but it kills me when it's a kid. There was one girl in particular. She was in my sophomore English class, an ugly kid but with a great spirit. Funny as hell. Got terrible grades. Acne. But boys seemed to like her. She had this charm, this incredible joy. She came to school one day with her face all beaten up. Her left eye was swollen shut. Her lip was puffed out to here. She didn't say a word about it, even when the other kids started teasing her. She just joked back at them. I kept her after class and asked her what happened. Her name was Sue Ellen. She started crying as soon as the other kids left the classroom. Her father had beaten her and her mother the night before. Usually, she told me, he would hit them where the bruises wouldn't show. But that night, he'd gone for their faces. So there I was, Doc, in a professional capacity, listening to this great little kid telling me about her father punching her face in. I'm not the type to keep my professional distance."

"What did you do?" she asked.

"I'm not sure it was in the best interest of Sue Ellen, her family, or me, but I did something."

"I hope you did nothing rash."

"Perhaps you'll think so," I said. "You see, the memory of Sue Ellen's face worked on me all day. After practice that night, I drove over to the Isle of Palms and found this tiny little house where Sue Ellen lived. I knocked on the door. Her father answered. I told him I wanted to have a conference with him about Sue Ellen. He told me to go fuck myself. Then I heard Sue Ellen crying somewhere in the house. I pushed him backwards and stepped into the house. She was lying on the couch. She looked up at me and I saw blood coming from her nose. She was embarrassed and said, "Hi, Coach Wingo, what brings you to this neck of the woods?"

"I think you should have gone through proper channels," Dr. Lowenstein interrupted. "Contacted the proper authorities."

"You're right, of course, Doctor. And it's one of the reasons you are rich and respected and I wear sweat shirts when I go to work."

"Then what happened?"

"I kicked him all over that house. I bounced him off walls. I beat his head on the floor. Then I heard a noise. It was like coming out of a dream. The noise was Sue Ellen cheering me on at the top of her voice. The other noise was her mother screaming for me to stop. When he came to, I told him if he ever touched Sue Ellen again, I'd come back and kill him."

"That's the most violent thing I've ever heard, Tom," she said, aghast.

"I take it home with me," I said, glancing down at my drink. "I can never leave it at the office."

"Yet I think there can be a far more helpful response than the one you gave. Are you always that overemotional?"

"Sue Ellen's dead, Dr. Lowenstein," I said, looking into her dark brown eyes.

"How?"

"Like a lot of other girls, she chose a husband like her father. I think I understand it. They start connecting love with pain. They begin searching out men who will hurt them, thinking they are searching for love. Sue Ellen found one of God's losers. He killed her during a domestic quarrel. Took a shotgun to her."

"That's horrible," Dr. Lowenstein gasped. "But you see that your actions didn't do any good at all. That violence does not absolve your own violent acts. What dreadful lives. What hopelessness."

"I wanted to tell your friend Monique about Sue Ellen today. Because I was curious. I had never seen a more beautiful woman than Monique, never in my whole life. I always thought that Sue Ellen had this terrible luck because she wasn't pretty."

"That's not true, Tom, and you know it."

"I'm not sure, Doctor. I'm trying to figure out how it all works. Why does fate select some people to be ugly and unlucky. One is enough to make the world difficult. I wanted to hear Monique's story and compare it with Sue Ellen's to see if she was hurting as badly as she seemed to be."

"Monique's pain is as real to her as Sue Ellen's pain was to her. I'm perfectly sure of that. No one has the patent on human suffering. People hurt in different ways and for different reasons."

"I would make a lousy shrink."

"I agree. I think you'd make a lousy shrink," she answered me, then continued after pausing for a moment. "What did you learn from that incident with Sue Ellen, Tom? What does that story mean to you?"

I thought about it for a moment, tried to conjure the face of a dead girl out of my past, and said, finally, "Nothing."

"Not one thing?" she said, surprised.

"Look, Doctor. I've considered myself in the light of that story for years. It says something about my temper, my sense of right and wrong . . ."

"Do you think you were right to go to her house and beat up her father?"

"No. But nor was I completely wrong."

"Explain that to me, please."

"I don't know if you'll understand. But when I was a little kid and my father would abuse one of his kids or go for my mother, I made a promise that I would never let a man hit his wife or children if I could do anything about it. This has made me a partner to many unpleasant, even hideous, scenes. I have stopped fathers from hitting their children in airports, have broken up brawls between husbands and wives who were total strangers to me, and beat up Sue Ellen's father. Something happens to me that I can't explain. But I think I'm changing."

"Perhaps you're growing up."

"No. I think I no longer care."

"Have you ever hit your wife or your children?" she asked with sudden fervor.

"Why do you ask that, Doctor?"

"Because violent men are usually most violent at home. They are almost always violent around defenseless people."

"And you have decided I am a violent man?"

"You just described a scene where you were violent. You coach a violent sport."

"No," I said, swirling the half-melted ice in my glass. "I am incapable of touching my wife or my children. I promised myself I would not be like my father in any way."

"Has it worked?"

"No," I smiled. "I am like my father in almost every way. Except that one. Chromosomes seem awfully powerful to me."

"Sometimes they don't seem powerful enough to me," Dr. Lowenstein said. She finished her wine and gestured to the waiter. "Do you want another?"

"Sure."

The waiter came and stood above us. He curled his lips as a sign he was ready to accept an order.

"I'd like a martini on the rocks with an olive," I said.

"White wine again," said Dr. Lowenstein.

He returned from the bar quickly. I noted with triumph the yellow sliver of lemon peel winking in the cubes.

Dr. Lowenstein's face softened at the corners and I saw flecks of lilac in her dark eyes as she lifted the wine glass to her lips and said, "I talked to your mother today, Tom."

I lifted my hand in front of my face as if warding off a blow. "Please, Lowenstein, I would consider it an act of mercy if you never reminded me again that I have a mother. She's a leading character in this autopsy of my family and you'll learn that her only job on earth is to spread insanity. She can walk through the produce department of a grocery store and even the Brussels sprouts have schizophrenia when she leaves."

"She sounds wonderful when you tell about her," Dr. Lowenstein said.

"When I was a little kid I thought she was the most wonderful woman in the world," I admitted. "I'm not the first son to be completely wrong about his mother."

"She was very nice on the phone and sounded very concerned," she said.

"A mere front," I answered. "She once read in a textbook that mothers traditionally are supposed to show concern when their daughters slit their wrists. Her phone call is the result of study and strategy, not instinct."

Dr. Lowenstein examined me with her serene but indecipherable eyes, and said, "She told me that you hated her."

"That's not true," I said. "I simply don't believe anything she says. I've watched her for years and I've been absolutely astonished by her power to lie. I keep thinking that she's got to fuck up at least once in her life and tell the truth about something. But my mother is a liar of the first order with oak leaf clusters all over her. She's as adept with small lies as she is with lies that could topple nations."

Lowenstein smiled and said, "That's funny. Your mother told me that you would probably tell a great many lies about her."

"Mom knows I'm going to tell you everything, Doctor," I said. "She knows that I'll tell you things that are too painful for Savannah to remember or for Mom to admit."

"Your mother cried on the phone when she told me how you and Savannah felt about her," said Dr. Lowenstein. "I must admit, she moved me very much, Tom."

"When my mother cries," I warned her, "she could get a job as a crocodile along the river Nile eating the fat natives who beat their clothes against rocks at the water's edge. My mother's tears are simply weapons to be counted when calculating the order of battle."

"She's very proud of her children. She told me how proud she is that Savannah is a poet."

"Did she tell you that she hasn't heard from Savannah in three years?"

"No," Dr. Lowenstein said, "she didn't. But she told me you were the best high school English teacher anyone ever saw. She told me that one of your football teams won the state championship."

"Whenever Mom praises you, you wheel suddenly around, hoping to catch the exact moment when she thrusts the sword in your back," I said, happy that there was gin in the world and that I was drinking a glass of it. "After she told you these wonderful things about me, Doctor, she then breathlessly informed you that I had a nervous breakdown."

"Yes," Dr. Lowenstein said, looking at me with a meticulous tenderness. "That is the exact phrase she used."

"Nervous breakdown," I said. "I've always liked the sound of it. It sounds so reasonable and safe."

"She didn't mention Luke even once," Lowenstein said.

"Of course not. The unspeakable word. We'll come to her silence on the subject of Luke. When I tell these stories, Dr. Lowenstein, observe Luke carefully. None of us suspected it when we were growing up, but Luke was the one living the essential life, the only one that mattered," I said, exhausted by the discussion of my mother.

"Whatever happened, Tom," she said softly, and there was a slightly amorous quality to her voice, "you've come out of it very well."

"I've been an object of pity around my family in South Carolina for a long time now, Lowenstein," I said. "I wasn't going to tell you about my own falling apart. I was going to keep that part of the story secret. Because I wanted to practice becoming a completely new man with you. I've tried to be charming, witty, and I was secretly hoping you would find me somewhat attractive."

Her voice was colder when she answered. "Why do you want to be attractive to me, Tom? I don't see how that could help either your sister or you."

"There's nothing to be alarmed about, Dr. Lowenstein," I groaned. "I did not say what I was trying to say very well. Jesus God, I apologize. I see I've activated every one of the feminist warning flags flapping in your central nervous system. I only wanted you to like me because you're a bright and beautiful woman. I haven't felt attractive in a very long time, Lowenstein."

Again, there was a softening, and I watched her mouth relax as she said, "Neither have I, Tom."

Looking at her, I was astonished to realize that she was speaking a painful truth. There was a large mirror behind the bar and I saw the two of us reflected as languorous images beneath the shining cocktail glasses.

"Do you see yourself in that mirror, Dr. Lowenstein?" I said.

"Yes," she said, turning away from me and looking toward the bar.

"That's not an attractive face, Dr. Lowenstein," I said, rising to leave. "By any measure or by any standard in the world, that is a beautiful face. It's been a pleasure staring at it for the last couple of weeks."

"My husband doesn't find me very attractive," she said. "It's nice of you to say that."

"If your husband does not find you attractive," I said, "he is either a homosexual or an idiot. You look fabulous, Lowenstein, and I think it's high time you got some enjoyment out of the fact. Is it all right if I see Savannah tomorrow morning?"

"You changed the subject," she said.

"I thought you would think I was flirting," I said.

"Were you flirting, Tom?" she asked.

"No," I said. "I was only thinking about starting to flirt, but women laugh when I flirt with them and they find me ridiculous."

"Some of the staff feel that you upset Savannah when you visit," she said.

"That's true," I answered. "The sight of my face fills her with pain. So would the sight of any Wingo."

"They've been adjusting her medication lately," she said. "I think the hallucinations are under control, but her anxiety level has increased recently. Why don't you wait awhile to visit her, Tom," she said. "I'll talk it over with her team."

"I don't tell her things that upset her, Lowenstein," I said, "I promise. I only talk about things that will make her happy. I read poetry to her."

"Has she talked to you at all, Tom?"

"No," I answered. "Does she talk much to you?"

"It's been a slow process," Lowenstein said. "She told me she didn't want you to visit her anymore."

"In those words?" I asked.

"In precisely those words, Tom," said Dr. Lowenstein. "I'm very sorry."

My grandmother, Tolitha Wingo, is now dying in a Charleston nursing home. Her mind, as they say, is wandering a bit, but she still has rare moments of perfect clarity when one can glimpse the full, illuminant personality that her advancing age has veiled with a shroud of senility. The capillaries in her brain seem to be drying up slowly, like the feeder creeks of an endangered river. Time no longer means the same thing to her as it does to us; she no longer measures it out in hours and days. It is a river she walks from its source to its delta. There are moments when she is a child asking her mother for a new doll. In the next eye-blink she is a gardener concerned over her dahlias or a grandmother complaining that her grandchildren never come to see her. On several visits she has mistaken me for her husband, her best friend, my father, or a Rhodesian farmer named Philip who evidently was once her lover. I don't know which part of the river I shall enter when I approach her wheelchair. The last time I saw her, she lifted her arms up to me and said in a quavering voice, "Oh, Daddy. Oh, Daddy. You've come to hold me." I sat her carefully in my lap and felt the terrifying fragility of her bones as she laid her head against my chest and wept like an eight-year-old child being comforted by a father who had been dead for forty years. She weighs eighty-five pounds now. Eventually she will die the way all old people in America die . . . from humiliation, incontinence, boredom, and neglect.

There are times she does recognize me, when her mind is sharp and frisky and we spend the day laughing and reminiscing. But when I rise to leave, her eyes register both fear and betrayal. She clutches my hand in a hard, blue-veined grip and pleads, "Take me home with you, Tom. I refuse to die among strangers. Please, Tom. I know you understand that, at least." My departures kill her a little bit more each time. She breaks my heart. I love her as much as I love anyone in the world, yet I do not allow her to live with me. I lack the courage to feed her, to clean up her shit, to ease her pain, to assuage the abysmal depths of her loneliness and exile. Because I'm an American, I let her die by degrees, isolated and abandoned by her family. She often asks me to murder her as an act of kindness and charity. I barely have the courage to visit her. At the front desk of the nursing home, I spend a great deal of my time arguing with the doctors and nurses. I scream at them and tell them that an extraordinary woman is living among them, a woman worthy of their consideration and tenderness. I complain about their coldness and unprofessionalism. I claim that they treat old people like meat carcasses hanging on steel hooks in freezers. There is one nurse, a black woman in her fifties named Wilhelmina Jones, who works there and receives the brunt of my frustrated tirades. She once told me, "If she's such an extraordinary woman, Mr. Wingo, why did her family put her in this hellhole to rot away? Tolitha ain't meat and we don't treat her as such. The poor chile just got old and she didn't walk in here by herself. She was dragged in here by you, against her will."

Wilhelmina Jones has my number. I am the architect of my grandmother's final days on earth, and because of a singular absence of nerve and grace, I have helped to make them squalid, unbearable, and despairing. Whenever I kiss her, my kisses mask the artifice of the traitor. When I brought her to the nursing home, I told her we were going for a long ride in the country. I did not lie . . . The ride has not yet ended.

When Papa John Stanopolous died late in 1951, Tolitha buried him properly in Oak Lawn Cemetery in Atlanta, sold the house on Rosedale Road, then set out on an extravagant odyssey that would take her around the world three times in three years. So deeply did she associate her grief over losing Papa John with the city of Atlanta that she never returned there, even for a visit. She was the kind of woman who knew instinctively that extreme happiness could not be duplicated; she knew how to shut a door properly on the past.

Tolitha traveled by ship, always first class, and in those years of relentless footloose travel managed to visit forty-seven countries. She sent back hundreds of postcards elucidating those travels, and those postcards, written in her barely legible scrawl, became the first travel literature any of us ever read. In their right-hand corners, they bore the most luminous, wonderful stamps, miniature aquarelles and landscapes from obscure countries or grand replicas of world-class art from the European ones. The African nations celebrated the fabulous sunshine over rain forests and the breadth of savannahs; their stamps sang with bright fruit, parrots preening in mango trees, mandrills scowling with fierce rainbow faces, elephants fording deep rivers, and a processional of gazelles crossing the plains below Mount Kilimanjaro. Without knowing it, she transformed us into passionate philatelists as we struggled to decipher those hasty travelogues she wrote during storms along the horse latitudes, as she navigated the sea lanes of the world. Whenever she wrote letters she included a handful of coins from all the countries she had entered. Those coins, solid and exotic, were our introduction to the idle joys of numismatics. We stored those coins in a grape jelly jar and would spread them out on the dining room table and match each coin with its country by placing it on a map of the world my father had bought to monitor Tolitha's wanderings. Using a pale yellow crayon we colored in each country on the map once she had set foot inside its borders. We grew fluent in the invocation of mysterious place names: Zanzibar, the Belgian Congo, Mozambique, Singapore, Goa, Cambodia. Those names tasted like smoke in our mouths; they reverberated with bell echoes of the primitive and the obscure. As children we considered Tolitha brave, prodigal, and lucky. On the day that Savannah, Luke, and I were confirmed by the Bishop of Charleston, a white rhinoceros struck my grandmother's jeep on the plains of Kenya. During the week we entered third grade, Tolitha wrote about the stoning to death of an adulteress in Saudi Arabia. She took enormous risks and told about all of them in exhilarated detail. Far up the Amazon, she watched a school of piranha reduce a tapir to bones in several horror-filled minutes. The tapir's screams echoed off the walls of an impenetrable jungle until the fish reached the animal's tongue. The tongue was like dessert, she added wickedly, in one of those chilling, exquisite details that enlivened her prose the more experienced her eye became as she slowly circumnavigated the earth. At the Folies-Bergère, she wrote that she saw more teats on stage than she'd ever seen on a milk farm. From Rome, she sent us a postcard picturing the macabre arrangement of monks' skulls stacked like artillery ordnance in a side altar at the Capuchin catacombs. She sent boxes of seashells she had collected on the East African coast, a shrunken head she had purchased "for a song" from a reformed headhunter with bad teeth in Brazil. One Christmas she bought my father a salt-cured tongue of a water buffalo. She purchased and mailed a flute used by cobra charmers, a piece of the true cross she had bought from a one-eyed Arab, a camel's tooth, the fangs of a bushmaster, and a loincloth she had bought directly off the genitalia of a savage (which my mother promptly burned, saying we had enough germs in South Carolina without worrying about African germs). Tolitha took a child's delight in the bizarre, the surreal, the definitively unique.

Bragging, she admitted she had contracted diarrhea in twenty-one countries. To my grandmother, a severe case of diarrhea was some sort of traveler's badge of merit, signifying a willingness to forsake the merely picturesque for the wilder backwaters of the world. In Syria, she consumed a bowl full of sheep's eyeballs, which she reported tasted exactly like one would imagine sheep's eyeballs to taste. She was more adventurer than connoisseur but made careful entries about her diet. In various parts of the world she dined on caiman's tail, the poisonous flesh of blowfish (which made her fingers numb), shark fillets, ostrich eggs, chocolate-covered locusts, elvers pickled in brine (for years I thought she had eaten elves, tiny people preserved like dill pickles), antelope liver, goat genitals, and boiled python. After studying her diet, one did not wonder long over her recurrent bouts of diarrhea; one only wondered how she kept herself from vomiting during every meal.

For three unstoppable years her task was endless voyage, the discovery of uncommon things in uncommon places, the study of herself in the text and footnotes of alien geographies. Later, she admitted that she wanted to build up a reserve of scintillant memories for the old age she felt was fast approaching. She traveled to be amazed, transformed into a woman she was not born to be. Not by intent but by example, she became the first philosopher of travel our family produced. By rambling about, Tolitha discovered that there were things to be learned on the tangents and the extremities. She honored the margins; the wild side made all the difference. At the summer solstice of 1954, an amiable band of Sherpas led my grandmother on a two-week trek through the Himalayas where at dawn one morning on the brutally cold rooftop of the world, she watched sunlight disclose the snowy flanks of Mount Everest. A month later she saw a migration of sea snakes in the South China Sea and was on her way home.

She arrived in Colleton somewhat exhausted and threadbare. Very significantly, she also came into our town penniless. My mother would do the figures out loud in a bit of obsessive calculation of assets lost and moaned that Tolitha had gone through more than a hundred thousand dollars. But if she had surprised her family and her town by satisfying some innate lust to travel, she shocked them all when it came to settling down again. Unknown to any of us, she had reopened diplomatic channels with my grandfather, rekindled whatever amity or affection the Depression had extinguished, and wrote him engaging, sisterly letters throughout her peregrinations. Whether out of a sense of privacy or tact, he never mentioned those letters to anyone; my grandfather Wingo was the only one in our town who was not stunned when our grandmother arrived back in Colleton after an absence of more than twenty years and went directly to his house on Barnwell Street, unpacked her clothes, and placed them in the same chest of drawers she had abandoned so long ago. "Even a sea bird's got to rest sometime" was the only thing she offered as explanation to anyone. Ten trunks full of the most marvelous and useless exotica followed her to Colleton, and her house overflowed with much of the eccentric memorabilia of the planet that had struck her fancy. My grandfather's living room, which had been so quintessentially southern, filled up with African masks and art, ceramic elephants from Thailand, and trinkets from every bazaar she had plundered in Asia. Each item had a story behind it, a country, a specific set of adventures, and she could retrace her steps by letting her eyes circle the room. Her secret, we would discover, was that once you have traveled, the voyage never ends, but is played out over and over again in the quietest chambers, that the mind can never break off from the journey.

My father's family reconstituted itself when he was thirty-four years old.

My mother took inexhaustible pleasure in demeaning the life and times of my grandmother. There was not a woman alive whom my mother did not consider a rival, and my grandmother's return to the fold after her romp about the continents brought forth torrents of my mother's self-righteous denunciations. "I don't see how a mother could ever leave her children during a depression," she would snort privately. "Men abandon their families all the time, not a *mother*. A true *mother*. Your grandmother committed a crime against nature, against all natural law, and I've never heard her once mention it or drop to her knees to beg your father's forgiveness. And don't think it didn't hurt your father. Don't you think it didn't affect him. No, you can trace all his problems back to that day he woke up and found that he no longer had a mama to feed and care for him. That's why he's mentally ill. That's why he acts like a beast sometimes. Then Tolitha went and squandered a future on her own follies instead of investing it in a savings account. She came back to this town without a dime. If I was Amos, I'd have kicked her out on her ear. But men are more sentimental than women. Mark my words."

She revealed these misgivings only to her children. When she was with Tolitha, my mother praised her independence, her courage, and her complete nonchalance about the attitude of the town toward her. Tolitha gave not a shit about the public opinion of Colleton. She was the only woman I knew when I was growing up who had ever been divorced. In many ways, she was the first modern woman that Colleton had produced. She offered no explanations and no apologies for her actions. After her return there were rumors of other marriages on the road, alliances with lonely men on ships, affairs of both convenience and the heart, but Tolitha said nothing. She simply returned to my grandfather's house and began living with him again as his wife. Amos still bored her with the rapture of his religious convictions. But there was something ineffable between them, something comfortable, something friendly. My grandfather was delighted to have her back. He had never looked at another woman. He was one of those rare men who are capable of being fully in love only once in their lives. I think my grandmother could have loved a hundred men. As I grew older and got to know her, I think she probably did. She was irresistible to men and a threat to every woman who crossed her path. Her allure was offbeat, indefinable, and original.

Now, I think she came back because she had done everything she wanted to do; I also believe that she came back to save her grandchildren from the fury of her son and the emotional coldness of her daughter-in-law. Whatever, she provided a voice, a conscience, a court of appeals we could fall back on during a crisis. She understood the nature of sin and knew that its most volatile form was the kind that did not recognize itself. Like many men and women who make egregious and irretrievable mistakes with their own children, she would redeem herself by becoming the perfect grandmother. Tolitha never scolded us, disciplined us, disapproved, or made her love conditional on our behavior in any way. She simply adored us in all the manifestations, both troubling and endearing, of our childhood. From her mistakes, she had codified an unadulterated ethic: Love was not a bridesmaid of despair; love did not have to hurt. Armed with such potent knowledge, she returned quietly to the life she had abandoned. Whenever my father hit us, my mother would say, "He only did it because he loves you." Whenever my mother struck us with her hairbrush, her broom, her hands, she did it in the name and under the sign of love. Such love as we got hovered beneath the sign of Mars, a frayed refugee of some debased and ruined zodiac. But my grandmother brought back from her journeys a revolutionary doctrine: Love has no weapons; it has no fists. Love does not bruise, nor does it draw blood. At first, the three of us drew back when she tried to hug us, to take us on her lap. Tolitha stroked our hair and faces. She kissed us until we purred like cats. She praised us in songs of her own making. She told us we were beautiful. She told us we were extraordinary and would do great things.

Her return strengthened the already formidable Wingo matriarchy. The Wingo line produced strong men, but none of us were a match for the Wingo women. In their eyes we could elicit the czar's metallic glint, the tyrant's cold assumptions. When Tolitha returned, a duel of power began that would not end until my mother drove with me to place

my grandmother in the nursing home in Charleston twenty-
five years later.

The man she returned to, Amos Wingo, was one of the
strangest men I've ever met and certainly one of the finest.
Any study of my grandfather becomes a meditation on saintliness. His whole life was one long hymn of praise to the Lord,
one long, boring hymn of praise. Prayer was his single hobby;
the great God, Triune, his only subject. To analyze my
grandmother's wilder, more secular biography, you must
have some compassion for the impossibility of living out a life
with a man committed to saintliness. Saints make wonderful grandfathers but lousy husbands. Years later, my grandmother revealed that when Amos made love to her he kept
moaning, "Thank you, Jesus. Thank you, Jesus," as he
writhed within her. She claimed it took her mind off what she
was doing when he invited Jesus between the sheets.

When we were very small, my grandfather walked the
three of us down to the dock on Melrose Island and told
us the history of his spiritual life. As he soaked his long,
thin feet in the Colleton River, it did not surprise me one
single bit when Grandpa Wingo revealed the secret that
God himself had appeared to the young Amos Wingo and
instructed him to live a life according to the Word. God
often honored my grandfather with these chatty, arbitrary
visitations throughout his entire life. Amos would write
long letters to the editor of the *Colleton Gazette*, spelling out
in exact detail where each vision had occurred and a word-
for-word disquisition on what exactly the Creator had on
his mind. From these letters (which Savannah carefully preserved) you could deduce that God spoke without much
thought for the codes of spelling or grammar and an uncanny fondness for southern vernacular. "God talks like a
redneck," Luke said after reading one of these epistles. In
fact, God spoke in a voice unnervingly similar to my grandfather's, and those desultory letters to his townsmen were
both the bane and secret glory of my childhood. But Amos
himself admitted it was hard to lead a normal life when
God was constantly interrupting him with spectacular and
time-consuming interviews.

Savannah was the first to ask the question, "What does
God look like, Grandpa?"

"Well, Savannah," my grandfather answered, "he's a right pretty-looking fellow. There's always a lot of light around him, so I can't see him too good, but his features are regular and his hair is darker than you might suspect. It's kind of long, too, and I've thought maybe I should ask to cut his hair. I wouldn't charge him a cent. Just trim it up a little bit. Shape it around the sides."

Savannah was the first person who ever said aloud that Grandpa Wingo was crazy.

But it was a sweet, uncomplicated craziness if that is what it was. During the height of the Depression, God appeared to him on a daily basis and his family had to live on what they could fish out of the river and that alone. He quit his job as a barber and quit selling Bibles, believing that the Depression was a celestial sign that the Second Coming of Christ was at hand. He took to preaching on street corners, screaming out bizarre psalms of faith and perdition to anyone within earshot, sometimes lapsing into the terrifying, arcane grammars of the unknown tongue that manifested itself like some tortured epilepsy of the soul.

Grandpa Wingo was also something of a wanderer, "gypsy blooded," my grandmother called it, but she said it cynically, because she felt that Amos did not put that much imagination into his travels. He just liked the feeling of being on the road, and it did not matter much to him where he was going. The summons would strike him without warning and he would leave Colleton straightaway and on foot, drifting around the South for months at a time, selling Bibles and cutting hair. Even in repose he had a distracting nervous mannerism—his right leg would shake and jiggle as if there were an engine idling beneath his knee. That vibrating leg was always a reminder that he could be gone the next day, heading south for Florida or west for Mississippi, to spread the word of the Gospel and to sprinkle talcum on freshly barbered necks. He deposited the Lord's word like pollen on the stamens and pistils of every human soul he drifted upon in his errant, unpremeditated ministry.

Along the back roads of the rural South, he carried one suitcase filled with his clothing and his barbering tools and another, larger one, brimming with Bibles of all shapes and sizes. The least expensive Bibles were small, black, and utilitarian, the size of children's shoes. But their print was small

THE PRINCE OF TIDES 155

and could induce myopia if read too fervently in bad light. He considered it his duty to push the showier lines. The Cadillac of Bibles was one of dyed, milky white Naugahyde with gold tassels to use as page markers. It was sumptuously illustrated by the Biblical paintings of "The Great Masters." But the crowning glory of this radiant volume was that the spoken words of Jesus of Nazareth were printed in vivid red ink. These most expensive Bibles were invariably snatched up by the poorest families, who purchased them on a generous time-payment plan. In my grandfather's wake, poor Christians would often have to make the difficult choice between paying the monthly tariff for their flashy white Bible or putting food on their table. The memory of my grandfather's pious and God-struck presence must have made the choice more disruptive than it should have been. Not making a payment on a Bible my grandfather equated with grievous, unspeakable sin, but he would never bring himself to repossess a Bible once he had filled out for free the family chronology in the middle of the book. He believed that no family could feel truly secure or American until they were all named up in a decent Bible where Jesus spoke in red. Though it sometimes strained his relationship with the company that supplied him with Bibles, he refused to take the Word of God from a poor man's house. The Bible company had to send other men in my grandfather's footsteps to repossess the Bibles or collect the money due. But Grandpa Wingo sold more white Bibles than any other salesman and that was where the real money was made.

As a salesman of Bibles, my grandfather became something of a legend in the small-town South. He would hit a mill village or a crossroads town and start going door to door. If a family was not in need of a Bible, then someone in that family was probably in need of a haircut. He would cut a whole family of hair at a group rate. He loved the feel of human hair between his fingers and had an abiding affection for bald men. He spoke of the life of Christ above the razor's hum and the dense clouds of talcum as he brushed the falling hair from the necks of squirming boys and girls. When he retired, the Bible company bestowed upon him a set of gold-plated hair clippers and a certificate of gratitude that legitimized a fact we'd suspected all along: Amos Wingo had sold more Bibles than anyone in the history of the company who had gone door to door. In its final testimonial and in a last stunning moment of poetry, the company referred to him as "Amos Wingo—The King of the Red-Letter Bible."

But as a traveling salesman whose territory covered five southern states, my grandfather often left my father in the lackadaisical, inconstant care of maids, cousins, maiden aunts, or whomever Amos could rustle up to care for his son. For very different reasons, neither of my grandparents ever got around to the fundamental business of raising their only child. There was something unsponsored, even unreconcilable, about my father's quarrel with the world. His childhood had been a sanctioned debacle of neglect, and my grandparents were the pale, unindictable executors of my father's violations against his own children.

My grandparents were like two mismatched children and their house retained some flavor of both sanctuary and kindergarten for me. When they spoke to each other it was with the deepest civility. There were no real conversations between them; no light, bantering moments, no hints of flirtation, no exchange of gossip. They never seemed to be living together, even after my grandmother's return. Nothing human interfered with their unexamined affection for each other. I studied their relationship with something approaching awe because I could not figure out what made it work. I felt love between these two people but it was a love without flame or passion. There were also no rancors or fevers, no risings or ebbings of the spirit to chart, just a marriage without weather, a stillness, a resignation, just windless days in the Gulf Stream of their quiet aging. Their uncomplicated joy in each other's company made our own parents' marriage appear obscene. It had merely taken them half a lifetime of separation to grow perfect for each other.

I looked to them for some explanation of my father and I could find nothing. He was not present in their eyes. Their merger had produced something completely new and unseen. I never heard Tolitha or Amos raise their voice. They never spanked us and were almost apologetic when they corrected us in the slightest way. Yet they had created the man who fathered me, who beat me, who beat my mother, who beat my brother and sister, and I could find no explanation or clue in my grandparents' house. Their very decency, their inviolate calm, disturbed me. I could not look to these people to discover where I came from: There was something missing, broken, unanswered. Somehow these two gentle souls had produced a violent son who in turn had produced me. I lived in a house where the shrimper was feared. It was never said aloud. My mother forbade us to tell anyone outside the family that my father hit any of us. She put the highest premium on what she called "family loyalty" and would tolerate no behavior that struck her as betrayal or sedition. We were not allowed to criticize our father or to complain about his treatment of us. He knocked my brother Luke unconscious three times before Luke was ten. Luke was always his first target, the face he turned to always. My mother was usually hit when she tried to intervene on Luke's behalf. Savannah and I were struck when we tried to pull him off our mother. A cycle was born, accidental and deadly.

I lived out my childhood thinking my father would one day kill me.

But I dwelt in a world where nothing was explained to children except the supremacy of the concept of loyalty.

I learned from my mother that loyalty was the pretty face one wore when you based your whole life on a series of egregious lies.

We divided years into the number of times our father hit us. Though the beatings were bad enough, it was the irrationality of my father's nature that was even worse. We never knew what would set him off; we could never predict the sea changes of the soul that would set the beast loose in our house. There were no patterns to adhere to, no strategies to improvise, and except for our grandmother, no impartial tribunal to which we could appeal for amnesty. Our childhood was spent waiting for him to attack.

In 1955, he put me to the floor three times. In 1956, he felled me five times. He loved me even more in 1957. His ardor increased in 1958. Each year he loved me more as I cringed my way toward manhood.

Since the year in Atlanta, I had prayed for God to destroy him. "Kill him. Kill him, please, Lord," I would whisper on my knees. My prayers buried him up to his neck in the marsh flats as I prayed to the moon to make the ocean surge over him, watched the crabs swarm over his face, going for his eyes. I learned to kill with my prayers, learned to hate when I should have been praising God. I had no control over how I prayed. When I turned my mind to God, the poisons streamed out of me. With hands folded, I sang of pillage and slaughter inside the city wall, and my rosary became a garrote. These were introspective, dangerous years for me. Whenever I killed a deer, it was my father's face beneath the rack of horns; it was my father's heart I cut out and held aloft to the trees; it was my father's body I strung up and emptied of viscera. I turned myself into something heinous, a crime against nature.

When my grandmother returned I slowly realized that she was someone my father feared, and thus attached myself to the destiny of the woman who had the courage to leave her family during the Depression and had never apologized to anyone for doing so. This gentle woman and my gentle grandfather had created a man who was dangerous to children. My mother taught us that it was the highest form of loyalty to cover our wounds and smile at the blood we saw in our mirrors. She taught me to hate the words *family loyalty* more than any two words in the language.

If your parents disapprove of you and are cunning with their disapproval, there will never come a new dawn when you can become convinced of your own value. There is no fixing a damaged childhood. The best you can hope for is to make the sucker float.

7

It was not until my second week in the city that I developed the first unmistakable symptoms of the New York willies. I always felt an ineluctable guilt when I was just taking it easy in New York when all those grand museums, libraries, plays, concerts, and that whole vast infinitude of cultural opportunities beckoned me with promises of enrichment. I began to have trouble sleeping and felt as if I should be reading the complete works of Proust or learning a foreign language or rolling out my own pasta or taking a course at the New School on the history of film. The city always stimulated some long-dormant gland of self-improvement when I crossed her rivers. I would never feel good enough for New York, but I would always feel better if I was at least taking steps to measure up to her eminent standards.

When I couldn't sleep, when the noise of postmidnight traffic proved too dissonant or the past rose up like a pillaged city in the displaced instancy of dreaming, I would rise out of my sister's bed and dress in the darkness. On my first morning in New York, I had tried to jog to Brooklyn but had only made it to the Bowery, where I stepped over the recumbent shapes of malodorous bums who slept in the vestibules of fifty lamp shops on a street overripe with sconces and chandeliers. The next day I ran in the other direction and in the darkness surprised myself by entering the flower district when the trucks were unloading their fragrant cargoes of orchids and lilies and roses. It was like running along the wrist of a beautiful woman who had anointed her veins with cologne. I had smelled many New Yorks but never the one governed by the sweet monarchy of a thousand slain gardens. At its best, New York was a city of accidental epiphanies and I vowed that I would open myself to many such moments as I made my way around the city that summer.

I composed a list of things I would do before I returned to South Carolina: I would run six miles in under fifty minutes; I would find ten great books in my sister's library that I hadn't read and read them; I would increase my vocabulary; I would learn to make a *beurre blanc* without having it separate on me; I would eat a meal at Lutèce, the Four Seasons, La Grenouille, La Côte Basque, and La Tulipe; I would watch the Mets play the Atlanta Braves and the Yankees play the Boston Red Sox; I would attend three plays and see five foreign movies; I would write in my journal every day and write home to my family three days a week; I would do fifty push-ups and sit-ups when I woke up in the morning; I would tell Dr. Lowenstein all the stories of my family that would help her keep my sister alive.

During the summer I would add to the list from time to time. My task was simple: By illuminating the mordant, unglossed chronicles of the past, I wanted to rediscover that spry, finger-popping, ambitious boy I had been when I grew up on a Carolina sea island and could name every creature that spilled onto the decks of my father's shrimp boat when I loosened the teeming nets. With luck, I wished to return to my native land in superlative shape. My physical condition embarrassed me greatly, but I was a coach of uncommon skills and I understood how to rectify the situation. I knew how to make my body pay for years of cordial neglect.

It had been a week since I had last visited Savannah when I brought up the subject of my rescinded visitation privileges with Dr. Lowenstein. She had scheduled me late on a Tuesday afternoon but she seemed distracted and brittle during our session together. When she checked her watch three times in the last ten minutes of our hour, I could barely contain my aggravation.

It was nearly seven o'clock when she rose from her chair, signaling the end of our time together for another day. She motioned for me to stay for a moment and walked to her desk to use the telephone.

"Hello, darling," she said lightly. "So sorry I couldn't call you before now. I've been tied up. Will you be able to make dinner?"

Exhaustion had turned her face delicate, undefended. She was a woman in the middle of aging extraordinarily well. Except for the delicate suturing around the eyes and mouth—laugh lines that seemed more like a concordance than a quarrel with time—she could have been mistaken for a teenager. She wore her black hair swept to one side and she had developed a nervous, though lovely, gesture of sweeping that luxurious hair away from her eyes as she spoke.

"I'm sorry your rehearsal is going so badly, darling," she said. "Yes, of course, I understand. Bernard will be home tomorrow evening for supper. He'll be disappointed if you're not there. All right. I'll talk to you later. Goodbye."

Turning, she revealed a look of hurt or disappointment on her face, but she recovered quickly, smiled at me, and began to check her appointment book to see when she could next fit me into her schedule.

"When can I see my sister?" I asked. "I came up to New York because I thought it would do her some good to know she had family in the neighborhood. I think I have a right to see Savannah."

Dr. Lowenstein did not look up but said, "I have a cancellation tomorrow at two. Can you make it then, Tom?"

"You're ignoring my question, Lowenstein," I said. "I think I can do Savannah some good. I think she needs to know that I'm still around and that I'm up here to try to help her."

"I'm very sorry, Tom," said Dr. Lowenstein. "I already told you that her team noticed that your visits upset Savannah enormously. And, as you know, Savannah herself asked that your visits be curtailed for a while."

"Did she explain why?" I asked.

"Yes, Tom," Lowenstein said, meeting my gaze, "she did."

"Do you mind telling me, Lowenstein?"

"Savannah is my patient, Tom," Lowenstein explained. "And what she tells me as my patient is confidential. I'd like you to trust me and trust her team . . ."

"Would you quit calling the rest of those assholes 'her team,' Lowenstein? It sounds like you've got her trying out for the New York Giants."

"What would you like me to call them, Tom?" she said. "I'll call them anything that you desire."

"Call them 'those assholes at Bellevue.' Team, my ass. There's the psychiatrist who sees her once a week and puts enough drugs in her to anesthetize a blue whale. Then there's that feckless resident with the red hair, and that randy frontline of weightlifting, humorless nurses, and didn't I meet a grinning activity therapist who'll encourage Savannah to make potholders? The team! The fucking team! Who else is in on this all-American team? Oh, yes. The orderlies. Those muggers whose IQs are identical to the freezing point of water on the centigrade scale. Those paroled criminals hired for peanuts to beat up on crazy people. Why don't you get her out of that place, Lowenstein, and into some posh country club where middle-class fruitcakes go to improve their Ping-Pong?"

"Because Savannah is still a danger to herself and others," Lowenstein said, sitting down in her chair again. "She'll stay in Bellevue until she's no longer a threat to herself, until she's stabilized sufficiently . . ."

"You mean drugged sufficiently, Lowenstein," I said, my voice louder than I meant it to be. "You mean when she's so chock-full of Thorazine or Stelazine or Artane or Trilafon or whatever goddamn drug-of-the-month is in vogue at this minute. Stabilized! My sister's not a goddamn gyroscope, Lowenstein. She's a poet and she can't write poetry when her bloodstream's got more drugs than white blood cells floating in her brain."

"How many poems do you think Savannah will write if she succeeds in killing herself, Tom?" Lowenstein asked angrily.

"Unfair question, Lowenstein," I said, lowering my head.

"Wrong, Tom," she said. "A very fair and very relevant question, I would say. You see, Tom, when I first saw Savannah after she slit her wrists, I was very grateful to 'those assholes at Bellevue' because whatever therapy I had used with Savannah had not worked. Savannah has picked up your same fear and distrust of drugs and would not allow me to prescribe the very medicine that could have prevented her suicide attempt. I'm grateful she's now in a hospital where they force her to take drugs if she refuses to cooperate. Because I want Savannah to make it out of this alive, Tom. I don't care if it takes drugs or voodoo or Extreme Unction or reading the tarot cards—I want her alive."

"You have no right to keep me away from my sister, Lowenstein," I said.

"The hell I don't," she answered.

"Then, why am I up here, Lowenstein," I said. "What's the point? Why do I sit around decoding a tape you made when Savannah was in her most lunatic phase, when she was elected generalissimo of the cuckoo's nest? I don't even know for sure what Savannah meant when she was screaming out all that gibberish. I know what some of it suggests to me, but I don't know if it means the same thing to her. I feel like it's me you have in therapy. How can my vision of my ghastly childhood possibly help Savannah? It was horrible being a boy in that family. Being a girl is unimaginable. Let her tell you all those stories and let me go home to fry catfish where I belong."

"You're not my patient, Tom," Lowenstein said softly. "I'm trying desperately to help your sister. You concern me only because of the light you can shed on her past. Her situation is still desperate. I've never seen such a quality of despair with any patient before. I need you to continue to help me with Savannah. We don't even have to like each other, Tom. That's not what's important. We want your sister to have a life."

"How much are you getting paid, Dr. Lowenstein?" I asked.

"The money is inconsequential to me. I'm doing this for the sake of art."

"Oh, sure!" I laughed. "A psychiatrist oblivious to money is like a sumo wrestler oblivious to body fat."

"You can laugh at me, Tom, and I don't give a damn if you do or not," she said. "You may even have superior insights into my motives and think that this is some ego trip where I can reconstruct the psyche of the poet and make it whole again. I wish from the bottom of my heart to perform that service."

"And Savannah, cured by the magic laying on of hands, would write endless poems extolling the miraculous powers of the shrink who exorcised the demons who possessed her frail soul," I said.

"You're right, Tom," she said. "It would cast no small amount of credit on me if I could save her, if I can provide her the resources that will enable her to write again. But there's one thing you don't understand about me. I loved your sister's poetry long before I ever knew I would be her doctor. I loved it and still do. Just read her poems, Tom . . ."

"What?" I shouted, lifting out of my chair and moving angrily toward Lowenstein. "Just read my sister's poetry? I said I was a coach, Doctor, not an orangutan. And you must have forgotten that other minor detail in my pitiful curriculum vitae. I'm an English teacher, Lowenstein, a wonderful English teacher with astonishing, outsized gifts for making slack-jawed southern morons fall in love with the language they were born to damage. I was reading Savannah's poetry long before you were having dialogues with hopeless neurotics, my friend."

"Excuse me, Tom," she said. "I apologize. I don't think of you reading it because of the subject matter. Her poems are so personally written for and about women."

"They are not." I sighed wearily. "Goddamn it. They are not. Why is everyone in this fucking city so stupid? Why does everyone say the exact same thing about her poetry? It cheapens her work. It cheapens any writer's work."

"You don't think it's written mostly for women?" she asked.

"No, it's written for people. Men and women who feel passionately. It's meant to edify, even to amaze, but it does not require a certain politics to understand or enjoy. What is extraordinary about her poetry is not her politics. That's what is commonplace and trivial about her poetry. That's what weakens her poetry and sometimes makes it banal and predictable. There are a million pissed-off women in this city who have the same politics. But only Savannah can take the language and make it soar like a bird or sing like some wounded angel."

"You could hardly be expected to understand a feminist viewpoint," Dr. Lowenstein said sharply.

I looked up at her suddenly and something about her look struck me as overupholstered and studied to a fault.

"Ask me if I'm a feminist, Doctor," I said.

She laughed and said, sarcastically, "Are you a feminist, Tom?"

"Yes," I said.

"Yes?" she said. Then she started laughing, the first genuine laughter I think I had heard issue from the game and steadfast Dr. Lowenstein.

"Why are you laughing?" I asked.

"Because that was the last answer I was expecting you to give."

"White southern male and all that."

"Yes," she answered seriously, "white southern male and all that."

"Kiss my ass," I said coldly.

"I knew you were a chauvinist," she answered.

"Savannah taught me to say that, Doctor. Your feminist patient. She told me not to take any shit from feminists or racists or Third Worlders or obscurantists or lion tamers or one-armed jugglers—if I thought they were wrong, to trust my instincts and call them anything I wanted to."

"That's wonderful, Tom," she said. "Very advanced, for a coach."

"What's your first name, Doctor?" I asked, studying her. "I've been up here for almost three weeks now and I don't even know your first name."

"That's not important. My patients don't call me by my first name."

"I'm not your goddamn patient. My sister is. I'm her Cro-Magnon brother and I'd like to call you by your first name. I don't know a soul in this city except for a few of Savannah's friends and I'm suddenly feeling very alone and I'm even forbidden to visit my own sister when I feel she needs me to be near her more than anything in the world. You're calling me Tom and I'd like to call you by your given name."

"I'd prefer to keep our relationship professional," she answered, and I felt trapped in the sterile airlessness of that room, overwhelmed by a surfeit of pastels and understated good taste. "Even though you're not my patient, you have come here because you're trying to help me with one of my patients. I would like you to call me Doctor because I'm most comfortable with that form of address in these surroundings. And it scares me to let a man like you get too close, Tom. I want to keep it all professional."

"Fine, Doctor," I said, exasperated and bone-tired of it all. "I'll agree to that. But I want you to quit calling me Tom. I want you to call me by my professional title."

"What's that?" she asked.

"I want you to call me Coach."

"The feminist coach."

"Yes, the feminist coach."

"Is there a part of you that hates women, Tom?" she asked, leaning toward me. "Really hates them?"

"Yes," I answered, matching the dark intensity of her stare.

"Do you have any idea why you hate women?" she asked, again the unruffled professional, dauntless in her role.

"Yes, I know exactly why I hate women. I was raised by a woman. Now ask me the next question. The next logical question."

"I'm afraid I don't understand."

"Ask me if I hate men, New York feminist doctor," I said. "Ask me if I hate fucking men."

"Do you hate men?" she asked.

"Yes," I replied. "I hate men because I was raised by a man."

For a moment we held each other in the tensile embrace of a mutual transfiguring hostility. I was trembling all over now and a great sadness had bivouacked in my heart again. I burned with the despair that slips up on the powerless and the disinherited. Something in me was dying in this room, but there was nothing I could do about it.

"My name is Susan," she said quietly.

"Thank you, Doctor," I almost gasped in my gratitude toward her. "I won't use your name. I just needed to know it."

I saw the softening around her eyes as we both began the voluntary withdrawal from the field of conflict. Her temper was quick but so was her willingness to draw back without inflicting any further wounds. There was a grace and a scrupulous integrity in the manner she salvaged something essential from our dangerous tournament of wills. She had allowed me a small, inconsequential victory and it was her voluntary compliance that made it important to me.

"Thank you, Lowenstein," I said. "You handled that situation beautifully. I don't mind making an ass out of myself, but I hate making a *male* ass out of myself."

"Why did you stay in the South, Tom?" she asked after a few moments.

"I should have left it," I answered, "but I lacked the courage. Because my childhood wasn't right, I thought if I stayed in the South I could fix that childhood by making my adult life wonderful. I traveled some but nothing was right. I could never trust a place enough to take me in. So, like an asshole, I stayed in South Carolina. It wasn't so much a failure of nerve as it was a failure of imagination."

"And?" she asked.

"And each year, I lose a little bit more of what made me special as a kid. I don't think as much or question as much. I dare nothing. I put nothing on the line. Even my passions are now frayed and pathetic. Once I dreamed I'd be a great man, Lowenstein. Now, the best I can hope for is that I can fight my way back to being a mediocre man."

"It sounds like a desperate life."

"No," I disagreed, "I think it sounds like an ordinary one. Look, I've kept you here late. Is it possible I could take you to dinner to make up for my inexcusable behavior?"

"My husband was supposed to meet me for dinner, but his rehearsal session went badly," she said.

"There's a place I took Savannah and Luke when her first book came out."

"Where's that?" she asked.

"The Coach House," I said.

She laughed and said, "The Coach House? Was that intentional?"

"No, it wasn't," I admitted. "Savannah thought it was a hoot and had to explain the rather overobvious pun to me, but I read an article that said it was a quintessential New York restaurant."

"I should be getting home," she said. "My son is arriving home from school tomorrow."

"Never refuse free food and liquor, Lowenstein," I said. "It's bad luck and bad taste."

"All right," she said. "The hell with it. This is the fourth time in two weeks I've been stood up by my husband. But you have to promise me one thing, Tom."

"Anything, Lowenstein."

"You'll have to tell me again during dinner that you think I'm beautiful. You'd be amazed, Tom, how many times I've thought of that since you said those words at the Plaza."

I offered her my arm. "Will the beautiful Susan Lowenstein accompany Coach Wingo to a quintessential New York restaurant?"

"Yes," she said, "the beautiful Susan Lowenstein would be happy to."

Until 1953 my family were the only Catholics in the town of Colleton. My father's wartime conversion, the one radical

act of the spirit in his lifetime, was a perilous and invigor-
ating voyage on weedy, doctrinal seas. My mother accepted
her own conversion without a word of protest. Like him,
she looked upon his deliverance in Germany as incontro-
vertible proof that God was alive and dabbling still in the
quotidian affairs of humankind. And such was the nature
of my mother's naiveté that she thought her conversion to
Catholicism would mean an automatic rise in her social
prestige. She would learn, slowly and painfully, that there
is nothing stranger or more alien in the American South
than a Roman Catholic.

My parents came to their roaring faith with their ignorance shining and intact. They knew nothing of that immense, intricate architecture which supported the See of
Rome. They learned their theology piecemeal, a tenet at a
time, and like most converts brought a scrupulous obstin-
acy to their efforts to become the first practicing papists
along their stretch of the Atlantic seaboard. But though they
feasted on that succulent corpus of dogma whole hog, they
remained hard-shell Baptists masquerading under the veils
and gauderies of an overripe theology. Their souls were
like summering fields, accustomed to indigenous crops,
suddenly required to produce amazing and unnatural veg-
etation. But their consciousness of the Church's rules and
more obscure codicils was always sketchy at best.

For years, my mother would read to us from the Bible
every night after dinner, her pretty voice skipping in breathless arpeggios up and down the scales of the King James
Version. It was not until I was ten that my mother learned
her new church proscribed the reading of that singing work
of post-Elizabethan prose and demanded the study of the
more pedestrian verses of the Douay-Rheims Version. She
was ignorant of the laws of imprimatur, but she adjusted
quickly, and the last phase of our youth resonates with the
ponderous, workmanlike phraseology of the Catholic Bible.
Even my mother's voice, like water running, could not coax
authentic rhythms from the Douay Version. It always
sounded a bit off, like a mistuned guitar. But what we
sacrificed in poetry we made up for by the knowledge that
we had corrected a theological error. My mother even claimed
that she far preferred the Douay-Rheims Version and knew

it was the real thing the first time she opened its pages randomly and began to read from Deuteronomy.

Such was their innocence that my parents seemed to be the only Catholics in America who took the doctrine of the Pope on birth control seriously. Despite the estrangement of their marriage, they managed a healthy and, I imagine, vigorous sex life—if the number of my mother's pregnancies is an indication of anything. Later, I would find out that they diligently used the rhythm method, checking the calendar every night, discussing whether they would partake of sex (their language of sex would always remain chaste and obscure). There were probably more children born of the rhythm method in the 1950s than were sired by random sex. Savannah, far more advanced in the arcane knowledge of such things than her brothers, later dubbed my mother Our Lady of the Menses. The nickname did not amuse my mother when she discovered it, but it had accuracy and style.

For four straight years, from 1952 to 1956, my mother was pregnant. She carried each child full term and each child was stillborn. We buried those sightless, wordless half-children beneath the grove of oaks at the rear of our house, fashioning crude wooden crosses and carving their names in the wood as my mother wept in her bed. My father never participated in these small ceremonies of grief, nor did he ever mention out loud any emotion he might have felt over the loss of these children. He would baptize them perfunctorily under tap water from the kitchen sink, then freeze them in plastic bags until my mother was well enough to return from the hospital.

"This one is Rose Aster," he said in the summer of 1956 as we watched silently from the kitchen table. "She wouldn't be much good on a shrimp boat anyhow, I suppose."

"I'm good on a shrimp boat, Daddy," Savannah said, her eyes fixed sadly on the dead child.

"You aren't worth a damn on a shrimp boat, Savannah," he answered. "All you can do is head shrimp." Then he baptized the frail-boned Rose Aster in the Name of the Father, the Son, and the Holy Ghost, doing so in a flat, atonal voice purged of both sadness and pity, as though he were saying grace before a meal. He walked out to the back porch,

placed the tiny girl in a clear plastic bag, and laid her on
top of the boxes of frozen shrimp and fish in the freezer.

"I didn't get a chance to say hello to my sister, Daddy,"
said Savannah, following him to the back porch.

He opened the top of the freezer and said, "Now's your
chance. Say hi. Say anything. It doesn't matter, girl. Rose
Aster isn't nothin' but dead meat. There's nothing there.
Do you hear me? She's like five pounds of dead shrimp.
There's nothing to say hello to or goodbye to. Just some-
thing to plant in the ground when your mother gets home."

When my father left for the shrimp boat the next morning, I lay awake in my bed hearing some small, unidentified
animal yelping in the darkness. I couldn't tell if a wildcat
had crawled beneath the house to have her kittens or what
the sound was. Leaving my bed, I got dressed without
waking Luke. I walked out into the living room and heard
the noise coming from Savannah's bedroom. Before I
knocked, I listened to my sister's violently suppressed
weeping, that murderous coming apart of the soul that
would become both the recessional and the trademark of
her madness. I entered her room quietly, fearfully, and
found her clutching something tightly to her chest. There
was such anguish in her cries that I almost did not disturb
her, but there was a scoured, raw quality about Savannah's
pathetic sorrowing that I could never walk away from. I
turned her over and in a kind of daze or seizure of brotherly
pity, I pried her arms loose from the cold, still body of Rose
Aster.

"Let me hold her, Tom," Savannah cried out. "She was
going to be our sister and no one ever stopped a moment
to love her. I just wanted to talk to her for a minute. She's
got to know the whole world isn't like them."

"It's not right, Savannah," I whispered. "There's nothing
you can tell her. Mom and Dad would both beat you if they
knew you took her out of the freezer. Besides, you might
spoil her before we bury her."

"There is something I can tell her," Savannah said,
snatching the small form back from me and pressing her
close to her chest again. "There's a lot I could tell her. I
just told her we'd have taken good care of her. We wouldn't
have let them hurt her in any way. We'd have protected
her from them. Tell her that, Tom. She needs to know that."

"Savannah, you can't talk like that. God hears everything. It's a sin to talk like that against your parents."

"She's the fourth one that's died, Tom. That's some kind of sign from God, don't you think? I think these poor little creatures are choosing not to live. I think they hear what goes on in this house and are just saying, 'No, sir, this surely ain't for me.' They don't know that you, me, and Luke are good."

"Mama says we're bad," I said. "She says it every day. She says we get worse each year. Dad said the reason she loses the babies is because we're so bad and don't give her any peace of mind."

"She blames everything on us. But you know what I think, Tom? I think these little kids like Rose Aster are the lucky ones. I think they're smarter than we were. They know that Mom and Dad are mean. They probably just feel that their time is coming and they just probably commit suicide in Mom's belly. I wish you and I had been that smart."

"Let me take Rose Aster back to the freezer, Savannah. I think it's a mortal sin to take a baby out of the freezer."

"I'm just comforting her, Tom. She never even got to see the pretty world."

"She's in heaven now. Dad baptized her."

"What are the names of the other ones? I always forget."

"There's David Tucker. Robert Middleton. Ruth Frances. And now Rose Aster."

"We would've had a big family if they'd all lived."

"But they didn't, Savannah. They're all in heaven taking good care of us. That's what Mom says."

"They aren't doing a very damn good job at it," she said with astonishing bitterness.

"The sun's gonna be up soon, Savannah. The house is gonna smell like Rose Aster and we're gonna be in a heap of trouble."

"I slept with her all night. She's got such pretty hands and feet . . . the tiniest little fingers and toes you've ever seen. I thought all night how wonderful it would be to have a little sister. I'd have killed Mom and Dad if they tried to hurt her."

"Mom and Dad would have loved her," I said, troubled, "just like they love us."

Savannah laughed out loud, then said, "Mom and Dad don't love us, Tom. Haven't you figured that out by now?"

"That's a terrible thing to say. Don't even think such a thing. Of course they love us. We're their children."

"They hate us, Tom," she said, her eyes forlorn and wise in the pale light. "It's easy enough to see."

She held the small corpse up in her hands and kissed it tenderly on its small hairless head.

"That's why Rose Aster here is one of the lucky ones. I was crying because I envied her. I wish I could be with her and the others."

I took the pale blue body from my sister's arms, gently, and carried it to the back porch. The sun was starting to rise as I wrapped my baby sister again in plastic and laid her down once more among the fish and shrimp.

When I returned I heard Savannah talking to herself in a voice I didn't recognize, but I did not disturb her again. Instead, I started the fire in the stove and laid six pieces of bacon in the iron frying pan. It was my morning to cook breakfast and our mother would be returning from the hospital that afternoon.

We buried Rose Aster in unconsecrated ground late that day before my father returned from the river. My grandparents had driven my mother home from the hospital and she was lying in bed when we got home from school. She had refused to let my grandparents stay with her, saying she needed some time to be alone.

Luke and I dug the grave and Savannah wrapped the twice-frozen corpse in a clean white blanket my mother had brought from the hospital. My mother stayed in her room until Luke went up to the house to get her. She leaned heavily on him as she came out to the back yard for the ceremony; she walked as though each step was hazardous and excruciatingly painful. She sat down in a kitchen chair Savannah had brought from the house. Her face, bereaved and anemic, was as long-suffering as any Byzantine Madonna, distraught beneath a cross, awaiting the death of her transfigured child. Grief had changed her mouth into a thin, bitter horizon. She had not spoken a word to us since we had come home; nor had she allowed us to tell her how sorry we were. When she was seated, she nodded for Luke and me to begin the burial.

Savannah had laid Rose Aster in the small wooden box we had built for the interment. The box was not much longer than an oversized bird house, and the infant herself looked like some defeathered, unevolved species of bird. We nailed the box shut and I brought the small coffin and laid it on my mother's lap. She wept as she stared at the box. Then she lifted the box slightly and covered it with kisses. She raised her eyes skyward and screamed out suddenly in helplessness and anger. "No, I do not forgive you, Lord. This is not allowed. It's simply not allowed. I've now buried four of them under this tree and I will not give you another. Do you hear me, Lord? I'm no longer interested in your Holy Will. Don't you dare to take another child of mine. Don't you dare."

Then she lowered her eyes and said, "Bring your sister, boys. And all of you pray with me. We have given the heavens another angel. Be gone to the arms of the Lord, Rose Aster. Watch over the family that would have loved and protected you and kept you safe from harm. You'll be one of God's small angels now. Keep watch over this house with your brothers and sisters. There are four Wingo angels now and that should be enough to watch over any house. If it's not, then God help us all. But that decision is plainly the Lord's and not mine. His wish upon the earth is a mystery to those of us who worship him. Oh God. Oh God. Oh God, damn you."

Though we could say the Confiteor in Latin, believed in transubstantiation and the transmigration of souls, there was in all of us something strange and unassimilated that made us respond to ecstasy and madness more than simple catechismic piety. The Catholic soul is Mediterranean and baroque and does not flourish or root easily in the inhospitable soil of the American South.

"The least you can do is pray for your sister. Get on your knees. I'll call you in for supper."

"Storm is coming, Mama," I heard Luke say.

"You won't even pray for your sister's soul," my mother said in a haggard, exhausted voice.

We fell to our knees, bowed our heads, and closed our

eyes as my mother limped back toward the house. The wind lifted the moss in the trees and dark clouds scudded angrily out of the north. I prayed hard for the small soul of Rose Aster. I saw that soul as something light and fragrant as a biscuit. Her soul rose up out of that grave into rain and thunder over the island. Sudden rungs of lightning pulled her upward. Thunder praised that smallest, most fragile relic of our desperate lives. The rain fell heavily and we looked toward the house, waiting for our mother to call for us.

I heard Savannah say again, "You're the lucky one, Rose Aster. You're lucky not to have to live with them."

"If lightning hits this tree, she'll be burying the whole lot of us," Luke said.

"We gotta pray," I said.

"If God wanted us to pray in the rain, he wouldn't have us build no churches," Luke said.

"They're both crazy," Savannah said, her hands still folded on her chest. "They're both crazy, Lord, and you got to help us make it out of here."

"Savannah, shut up. God doesn't want to hear that," I said.

"He may not want to hear it, but I'm gonna say it. He put us here with 'em so he must know they're nuts."

"They're not nuts, Savannah. They're our parents and we love them."

"I've watched the way other people act, Tom. I've studied it. No one acts like they do. They're just plain odd."

"Yeah, who ever heard of praying for a dead baby in a rainstorm?" Luke said.

"We want Rose Aster to go to heaven," I argued.

"Shoot," Savannah said. "Tell me one good reason why Rose Aster isn't in heaven right now? What kind of God would send Rose Aster to hell?"

"That's none of our business," I said piously.

"The devil it's not. Why are we out here half-drowning if it's none of our business? The poor little child just got born dead, baptized in a sink and deep-frozen with a hundred pounds of shrimp and Spanish mackerel, and I want you to tell me what that poor creature could have done to deserve hellfire, Tom Wingo."

"It's God's business. It's none of ours at all."

"My sister! My business! Especially when I've got to pray for her in the middle of a storm," Savannah said, her hair darkened and tangled with rainwater.

I began shivering and the storm worsened. Wiping the water from my eyes, I turned toward the house, wondering if it was possible that my mother simply did not know it was raining. I could barely see the house through the rain, so I turned again to the small, forlorn grave.

"Why is Mom always pregnant?" I asked for no particular reason and expected no particular response.

With her hands folded in a mimicry of prayer, Savannah sighed and said in an exaggerated tone, "Because she and Dad are always having sexual intercourse."

"Quit talking nasty," Luke warned as he prayed. He was the only one who could keep his mind on the repose of my sister's soul.

"They do?" I said. This was the first time I had encountered that fancy and peculiar phrase.

"Yes, they do," Savannah said definitively. "And it makes me sick to my stomach. Luke knows all about it," Savannah said. "He's just shy and doesn't want to talk about it."

"I ain't shy. I'm praying like Mom told both of you to do."

"You and Tom got to quit saying *ain't*, Luke. You and Tom sound like rednecks."

"We are rednecks and so are you," Luke answered.

"Speak for yourself," Savannah said. "Mom told me secretly that we descend from the very highest southern aristocracy."

"Oh sure," Luke said.

"I'm certainly not a redneck," said Savannah, shifting her knees on the wet, displaced soil. "Mom says I've got a certain amount of refinement."

"Yeah," I said, giggling. "You sure had a lot of refinement last night when you were sleeping next to Rose Aster."

"What?" Luke said.

Savannah looked at me through the rain with a baffled, noncommittal glare, as though she had missed the punch line of a joke. "What are you talking about, Tom?"

"I'm talking about finding you all wrapped up with a dead baby you got out of the freezer sometime last night."

"I didn't do that, Tom," she said seriously, shrugging

her shoulders at an appalled Luke. "Why would anybody do such a strange thing? Nothing gives me the creeps more than a dead baby."

"I saw you, Savannah," I said. "I took her back to the freezer."

"You must have been dreaming, boy," said Luke.

"How can you dream something like that?" I asked. "Tell him, Savannah. Tell Luke it wasn't a dream."

"It sounds like a nightmare to me, Tom," she said. "I don't know what you're talking about."

I was about to answer when we heard my father's truck coming down the dirt road toward the house. All of us bowed our heads and began to pray deeply and reverently again for the newly anointed Wingo angel. He pulled the truck up behind us and we could hear the windshield wipers slapping the rain from side to side. For a minute or two he watched us in mute and uncomprehending astonishment before he said, "Have you lost your goddamn minds, idiots?"

"Mama told us to pray for Rose Aster," Luke explained. "So that's what we're doing, Daddy. We buried her today."

"We'll be plantin' the three of you under that same tree if you don't get out of this rain. It isn't enough that they're all born dead; she tries to kill the ones that live, too. Get your butts into the house."

"Mom'll get mad if we go in too soon," I said.

"How long you been kneeling out here in the storm?"

" 'Bout an hour, I reckon," Luke said.

"Jesus Aloysius Christ. When it comes to religion, don't listen to your mother. She used to pick up rattlers when she was a kid to prove that she loved God. I baptized Rose Aster. She's in a hell of a lot better shape than any of us right now. Now move your butts into that house and I'll handle your mother. She's going through what they call post-departum depression. It happens to women after they lose a kid. You all be especially sweet to your mama for the next few weeks. Bring her flowers. Make her feel special."

"Did you bring her any flowers, Dad?" asked Savannah.

"I almost did. At least I thought about it," he answered, driving the truck to the barn.

As we rose from our knees, drenched and shivering,

Savannah said, "What a sweet guy. His baby dies and he doesn't bring his own wife flowers."

"At least he thought about it," Luke said.

"Yeah," I added. "He almost did."

We walked into the house suppressing a forbidden and dissident laughter, the ill-made humor of children who were developing the dark wit of the luckless, the black laughter of subjugation. It was that laughter which ended our hour of prayer over the small body of my sister, that preserving laughter which sustained us as we walked toward the house and our parents and away from that small garden of sleeping Wingos. My mother would plant roses above each grave and those roses would grow luxuriously, splendidly, stealing all the color and beauty from the rich hearts of infants. She called them "the garden angels" and they spoke their narratives in roses each spring.

That night, my mother had not left her bedroom and we had all made peanut butter and jelly sandwiches for dinner. The three children had prepared what we considered an elegant meal of fried shrimp and corn on the cob, and brought it on a tray to our mother's bedside with a bouquet of wildflowers. But she could not stop crying and only ate one of the shrimp and did not touch the corn. My father sat in the front room and read back issues of *Southern Fisherman*—thumbing through them angrily, looking back occasionally toward the room where his wife lay crying, his eyes glistening in the electric light as though they had been softened with Vaseline. He was one of those men incapable of making the smallest gestures of tenderness. His emotions were like some perilous mountain range obscured beneath clouds. When I thought of his soul, tried to visualize what was real and essential to my father, I saw only an endless acreage of ice.

"Tom," he said, catching me staring at him. "Go in and tell your mother to quit boo-hooing. It's not the end of the world."

"She's feeling bad on account of the baby," I said.

"I know why she's feeling bad. But she's just crying over spilt milk now. Get on in there. It's you kids' job to make your mother feel better."

I tiptoed into my mother's bedroom. She was lying on

her back, tears rolling down her cheeks, crying easily and softly. Afraid to approach her, I stood by the door, unsure of what to do next. She was staring at me with the most bereaved, inconsolable face I had ever seen. There was such defeat and hopelessness in her eyes.

"Daddy wants to know if you need anything, Mama," I whispered.

"I heard what he said," she said, sobbing. "Come here, Tom. Lie down beside me."

I climbed into bed beside her and she laid her head against my shoulder and cried hard, digging her nails into my arm. Her tears wet my face and I lay there paralyzed by such sudden and passionate intimacy. Her body pressed against me and I felt her breasts, still heavy with the milk she could not use, press hard against me. She kissed my neck and mouth, pulled down my shirt, and covered my chest with her kisses. I did not move but was keenly alert for noises in the main room.

"I've only got you, Tom," she whispered fiercely in my ear. "I don't have anyone else. It's going to be all up to you."

"You've got all of us, Mama," I said quietly.

"No. You don't understand. I've got nothing. When you marry nothing, you have nothing. Do you know how the people of this town look at us?"

"They like us fine, Mama. People like you a lot. Dad's a good shrimper."

"They think we're shit, Tom. You know that word, don't you? Your father uses it all the time. They think we're river shit. Low class. We've got to show them, Tom. You've got to be the one. Luke can't do it because Luke's stupid. Savannah can't do it because she's only a girl."

"Luke's not stupid, Mama."

"He might as well be retarded as far as school's concerned, Tom. The doctor thinks it was the forceps they had to use when he was born. It's up to you and me to show this town the stuff we're made out of."

"What stuff, Mama?"

"That we're better than anyone in this town."

"That's right, Mama. We are."

"But we've got to show them. I wanted to fill this house with children. I wanted eight or nine kids that I'd raise smart and proud and given enough time we'd take this town over. I'm going to marry off Savannah to the richest boy in town. I don't know what I'll do with Luke. Maybe a sheriff's deputy. But you, you, Tom, are my hope for the future."

"I'll do good, Mama. I promise you."

"Promise me you won't be anything like your father."

"I promise, Mama."

"Say it. Say it to me."

"I promise not to be anything like my father."

"Promise me you'll be the best in everything."

"I'll be the best in everything, Mama."

"The very best."

"I'll be the very best."

"I'm not going to die in a house like this, Tom. I promise you that. No one knows this yet, except me. But I'm an amazing woman. You're the first one I've told. Do you believe that?"

"Yes, ma'am," I said.

"I'm going to prove it to everybody, even to your father."

"Yes, ma'am."

"You won't ever let anybody harm me, will you, Tom? No matter what I do, I can depend on you, can't I?"

"Yes, ma'am," I said again, and her eyes transfixed me with both their gauntness and their burning intensity.

"You're the only one I can trust," she whispered. "I'm so isolated out here on the island. So alone. But there is something wrong with your father. He's going to hurt us."

"But why?"

"He's a sick man, Tom. He's very sick."

"Then we should tell someone."

"No. We must be loyal. Family loyalty is the most important thing. We have to wait for the right time. We must pray for him. We must pray that his good qualities defeat his bad qualities."

"I'll pray. I promise I'll pray. Can I go back to the living room now?"

"Yes, Tom. Thanks for coming in here. I needed to tell you this. Something else, darling. Something important. Very important. I love you more than any of them. More than all of them put together. And I know you feel the same about me."

"But Luke and Savannah love you just . . ."

"No," she said harshly, pulling me close to her again. "Savannah's a hateful child. She's been that way since she was born. Not good. Disobedient. Luke's dumb as a goat. You're the only one I care for. That'll be our secret, Tom. You and Mama can share a secret, can't we?"

"Yes, ma'am," I said, moving toward the door. "If you want anything, Mama, please call me and I'll get it for you."

"I know you will, darling. I've always known that since the night you were born."

I stumbled out of that room carrying a terrible, inadmissible weight and could hardly bear the puzzled gazes of my brother and sister as I came out of my mother's bedroom. I was shaken by both the monstrousness and the nakedness of my mother's confession to me and wondered what relationship it had to the loss of her child. She had imprisoned me with the bitterness and honesty of her testimony; by taking me into her confidence, she made me an unwilling co-conspirator in her undeclared war against Luke and Savannah. She bound me in an unsolvable dilemma: By agreeing to become her most trusted confederate I was also giving my consent to the betrayal of the two people I loved best on earth. Yet her rawness, the urgency of her approach, the imprint of her lips on my throat and chest—all of it was forbidden in the way I understood the order and proper alignment of the world, yet it was seductive to be chosen by our mother on the day she was half crazed over the loss of a child. I took this selection to be emblematic, honorable, and proof that I was something special and extraordinary. By the scandal of her revelations she ensured the inviolability of my oath of secrecy. My father would not have believed a word of what I said if I had confessed every syllable of what my mother had told me in that room. Nor could I ever bear to hurt my brother and sister by revealing the context of my mother's passionate dismissal of them as allies. She was looking for lieutenants, not relatives, and though her method was unclear to me, I understood that my mother, who until that time I had thought of only as a mother, had some plan of attack of indefinite shape and structure, which she planned to initiate at some future time. Before, I had thought of her as only beautiful and unapproachable, but now I became aware of something dissatisfied, even cunning, behind the prettiest blue eyes I would ever see. I left her room less of a child. I walked toward the rest of my family with my heart troubled with adult terror. My mother had tired of her solitude and martyrdom in that house on the river. From that night on, I began a long study of this woman I had underestimated for so long. I revised my assessment of her almost daily. I learned to fear the things she left unsaid. She was born in my consciousness that night, and for the first time in my young life I felt alive and fully cognizant.

Many years later, I told Luke and Savannah what my mother had revealed to me in her bedroom that night. I expected outrage from them when confronted by the knowledge of my mother's secret pact, when she enlisted me as an agent in her unformulated agenda against both her family and Colleton. But, no, there was no anger at her whispered perfidy, only profound amusement. Both Luke and Savannah roared with laughter when I imparted this information that had caused me such great shame and guilt. My mother might have been new to conspiracy but she mastered its tricks and stratagems with a felicity that indicated she carried a natural affinity for it. In that same week that Rose Aster was buried, my mother took both Savannah and Luke aside, isolated them as she had done me, and took them into the strictest confidence. She told them the exact same thing she told me, that she could trust only them, that the others were unreliable, and that she required of them an intimate oath of allegiance, a solemn affirmation that they would stand beside her through any test or skirmish or storm. She told them (as we compared notes) that I was frightened, unsteady, and could not be trusted in a crisis. She enlisted Savannah because Savannah was a woman and understood intuitively the difficulty and unfairness of a woman's situation. Luke was strong, unshakable, the perfect soldier—she needed him as intercessor and champion. All of us were seduced by the naked avowal of her need for us. There was no room for refusal, no possibility of disclosure. Her faith in us left us awestruck. By dividing us, she left herself in control, impregnable, the softest enigma in our lives.

But by the time I traded notes with Luke and Savannah

my mother had already proven herself the most formidable woman who had ever walked the streets of Colleton.

It was still raining when we went to bed that night. My father put out the lights in the house and smoked a pipe on the screened-in porch before he retired. He seemed uncomfortable with us when my mother was not orchestrating the tenor of household life. Several times during the evening, he had yelled at us when something minor and insignificant had irritated him. My father was an easy read. When there was real danger you knew instinctively to avoid him; he had a genuine gift for tyranny but no coherent strategies. He was both brutal and ineffectual as a man who would always be a stranger in his own house. As his children, we were treated as some species of migrant worker who happened to be passing through. My father was the only person I ever knew who looked upon childhood as a dishonorable vocation one grew out of as quickly as possible. He would have been lovable for his fecklessness and his blustering eccentricities if he had not been born a violent and unpredictable man. I think my father loved us, but there has never been a more awkward or deviant love. He considered a slap to the face a valentine delivered. As a child he had felt neglected and abandoned and neither of his parents had ever laid a hand on him. He never noticed us except to scold us; he never touched us unless in anger. At night, surrounded by his family, my father looked trapped, and he taught me a great deal about the self-made loneliness of mankind. I began my life by being taken prisoner in my father's house; I would begin my manhood by walking over him on my way out the door.

When Savannah asked me into her room for a talk that same night, the rain was making sweet music on the copper roof as it fell. I sat on the floor by her bed and we watched the sheet lightning flashing over the islands to the north.

"Tom," she whispered, "if I ask you something seriously, will you answer me?"

"Sure."

"You can't laugh or tease me. This is too important."

"Okay."

"Did you really find me in bed with Rose Aster this morning?"

"Of course I did," I said, irritated. "And then you lied about it to Luke."

"I didn't lie about it, Tom," she said, and her face was worried in the dark. "I don't remember it at all."

"She was in your arms when I found you. Dad would have killed you if he had found her."

"I thought you were crazy when you told us that out in the yard," she said.

"Ha! Who's the crazy one?"

"I didn't believe you until I got into bed tonight."

"What changed your mind?" I asked.

"There's a wet spot in the bed."

"She was in the freezer. She was kind of melted when I got here."

"Tom, I don't remember that at all. It's frightening."

"It doesn't make any difference, Savannah. I won't tell anyone."

"Tom, there's a lot I don't remember after it's happened. Then I have to pretend I remember everything. It gets confusing."

"What else?"

"Do you remember that time in Atlanta when we were on Stone Mountain and I hit you?"

"Sure. You were a jerk that day."

"I don't remember anything about it. That whole day is blank to me, like it never happened. And the giant. When he came into our room and Luke and I threw all those jars of spiders . . ."

"I know, and I just lay there in bed doing nothing."

"I don't remember a single thing about that night. I only know it happened when I hear people say it happened."

"Are you serious?"

"Tom, I need you to remember things for me. I can't sometimes. There are too many days that disappear from me and it frightens me more than anything in the world. I tried to talk to Mama about it but she just laughed and said I wasn't concentrating."

"Sure. I'll be glad to tell you, Savannah. Only you can't

call me a liar and make fun of me every time I tell you
something that's happened. Luke looked at me like I was
a plain fool when I told about you and Rose Aster today."

"Tom, I didn't believe you until I felt this wet spot in the
bed. And my nightgown was damp, too. Why would I do
such a thing?"

"Because you were sad about the baby and thought she
might be lonely. You didn't mean anything harmful. You
care about things, Savannah. Mom says you're oversensi-
tive because you're a girl and that it's going to cost you a
lot of grief in your life."

"Something's wrong with me, Tom," she said, holding
my hand and looking out toward the storm of the river.
"There's something awful wrong with me."

"No there's not," I said. "You're wonderful. You're my
twin. We're exactly alike."

"No! No! Tom. You've got to be the twin that remembers.
I'll do everything else, I promise. But you've got to tell me
the stories. I'm starting to keep a journal. You tell me the
stories and I'll write them down."

So Savannah began to write, filling a small school notebook with the jottings and chiselings of her daily life. There
was nothing insurrect or minatory in these early writings.
They were fresh and childish. She recorded conversations
she had with favored dolls and imaginary playmates. Even
then, her interior life was far more important to her than
her external one.

It was the year my mother made us learn the prayer to
our guardian angels. All our religion we learned by rote,
and prayer was no exception. It was the same year we
memorized the Act of Contrition and the Act of Hope. Yet
our mother could never explain to our satisfaction just who
these guardian angels were. They sat nameless on our right
shoulders, whispering to us whenever we were stumbling
blindly toward actions that would offend God. Assigned
to us at birth, they would not forsake their posts just above
our shoulder blades until we died. They monitored our sins
like scrupulous accountants. On our left shoulders an am-
bassador of Satan acted in maleficent counterbalance to our
guardian angel. This devil, a black articulate seraph, tried
to lead us toward the succulents of perdition.

The duality led to much theological confusion. But Savannah welcomed two invisible companions into her life. She called the good angel Aretha; the dark angel was called Norton.

But she had misheard my mother's pronunciation of the word *guardian* and when she wrote down the dialogues between Aretha and Norton, she described them as her "garden angels." There were many "garden angels" surrounding our house, hovering like the souls of azaleas above us. There were unborn Wingo children simmering beneath the thorns of roses. The garden angels were under a divine obligation to love and protect our house. They said vespers in the trees and watched over us, not because God required it, but because they cherished us and could not help it. She even recruited Norton as a foot soldier in that silent army of occupation which patrolled the winds above the river. Even a dark angel was susceptible to Savannah's enthusiastic overtures. Savannah never believed that Norton was an agent of Satan; she claimed he was just Presbyterian.

Yet the garden angels did not intervene when my mother burned my sister's notebook in the wood stove after Savannah recorded a fight between my mother and father word for word. In a rage, my mother burned a year's work one page at a time as Savannah wept and begged her to stop. The words of a child became smoke above the island. Sentences took wing and fell in black fragments upon the river. My mother screamed that Savannah was never to write another word about her family again.

The next week I found Savannah kneeling in an exposed sandbar in the river at the lowest tide. She was writing furiously in the sand with her index finger. I watched from the shore for half an hour. When she had finished, the tide was turning and the water began to cover her words.

She stood and looked back toward the house and saw me watching her.

"My journal," she cried out happily.

There was something orderly and refined about the Coach House that made it seem like home territory. A carriage house always retains a secret memory of the business of feeding well-bred, exhausted horses. Its proportions are

graceful, never ostentatious, and I have yet to see a carriage
house fail to make a charming residence or restaurant. The
Coach House, at 110 Waverly Place, was the nonpareil of
the breed. Its very shape was pleasant to my soul; the place
exuded seriousness about food, and all the waiters looked
competent enough to curry a thoroughbred if they burst
from the kitchen and found themselves transported back
to the days when hansoms glided across the cobblestones
of Greenwich Village. It was the only restaurant in New
York I had found without Savannah's guidance, and Luke
and I had taken her there for dinner on the publication day
of *The Shrimper's Daughter*. The Coach House had served
us a splendid meal as Luke and I toasted our sister again
and again and had her sign copies of her book both to our
waiter and to Leon Lianides, the owner. Before we left, Mr.
Lianides sent us each a glass of cognac, courtesy of the
house. In memory, that evening carried weightlessly all the
grandeur of celebration, all the rich courses of a feast we
considered timeless, and all the love that flowed without
effort when the three of us locked arms in our perfect,
extravagant affection for each other. I carried that evening
with me, flawless and exhilarating, and I brought it forth
often during years of sadness, suffering, and waste, brought
it out of darkness with the happy taste of champagne on
my tongue and laughter in my eyes, brought it out when
my life fell apart around me and my brother was gone from
the river and my sister could not trust herself around knives;
it was the last happy ending that the three of us would
ever have together.

It was raining when I arrived at the Coach House at 9:30
to meet Susan Lowenstein for dinner. The maître d' led me
to a comfortable table upstairs, placed remotely beneath
several folk paintings aging well on the red brick walls. I
ordered a Manhattan, honoring the island on which I sat,
and only when I tasted the ghastly concoction did I remember why I had never developed a fondness for that
particular cocktail. The waiter understood perfectly and
brought me a dry martini to cleanse my palate.

Alone, I watched the mannerisms of the other diners as
they ordered their meals and spoke to one another in the
inscrutable and melancholy light of candles. I felt an intimate connection to myself as I drank alone in all the com-

plex validation a stranger could summon when a city began to allow him access into its rarest and most tantalizing obscurities. A good restaurant freed me from the desolate narrowness, the definitive thinness of experience, that is both the vainglory and the dead giveaway of a provincial man. Above the perfect napery, I could purchase my own place in the city for the night and compose a meal that I would remember with unstinted pleasure for the rest of my life. Drinking my martini, I thought of all the exquisite meals being prepared at that very moment in Manhattan. By coming to the Coach House I had connected myself to the largess and sublimity of a city's grand cuisine. Though I lifted my voice often in an endless baleful serenade against New York, there were times when the food and wine of that bewildering, insuperable city could make me the happiest man on earth. Susan Lowenstein approached the table unseen as I studied a sculpturally impeccable list of appetizers. I smelled her perfume, which entered into a modest agreement with the fresh flowers on the table, before I looked up and saw her face.

She possessed one of those faces that was different every time you saw it. Though lovely in all its forms, it never seemed to belong to one person but to an entire nation of beautiful women. She could change her hair and change the way the world perceived her at the same time. Her beauty was uncapturable and vague, and I would bet that she did not photograph well. She wore a white, low-cut dress and it was the first time I had noticed the superb figure of my sister's psychiatrist. Her black hair was piled high, long gold earrings dangled against her cheekbones, and she wore a thick gold necklace on her throat.

"Lowenstein, you look dangerous tonight," I said.

She laughed, pleased, and said, "I bought this dress as a present for myself last year. I've never quite had the courage to wear it. My husband thinks I look too virginal in white."

I studied her with generous appreciation and said, "You do not look virginal in white, Lowenstein."

"What's good to eat here, Tom?" she said, but she was smiling at the compliment. "I'm utterly famished."

"Everything is good here, Lowenstein," I said as the waiter brought us a bottle of cold Chablis I had ordered brought to the table when my guest arrived. "They're famous for their black bean soup, but I prefer their lobster bisque. They poach their channel bass to perfection. They are flawless with their presentation and preparation of red meat of any kind. The appetizers are terrific, especially the smoked trout with horseradish sauce. Desserts are simply ambrosial here."

"How do you know so much about food?" she asked.

"Two reasons," I said as I lifted my glass to hers. "My mother was a terrific southern cook who thought she could improve her social status if she learned about French cuisine. Her social status remained precarious but her sauces were terrific. When Sallie went to medical school, I was forced to learn to cook. I surprised myself by loving it."

"If I couldn't afford to hire a cook," she said, "my family would perish from malnutrition. The kitchen has always seemed like a slave galley to me. This wine is lovely."

"That's because it's very expensive, Lowenstein. I'm charging this meal on my American Express card and the bill will be sent to my house in South Carolina and paid for by my wife."

"Have you heard from your wife since you've been in New York?" Dr. Lowenstein asked.

"No," I said. "I've talked to my children several times on the phone, but she's never been at home."

"Do you miss her?" she said, and I saw my wine glass reflecting off the gold at her throat.

"No, Lowenstein," I said. "I've been a lousy husband for a long couple of years now and I'm just grateful to be away from her and the kids awhile so I can try to put myself together in some form recognizable as a man."

"Every time you say something personal, Tom," she said, "it seems as though you're putting more distance between us. There are times you seem very open, but it's a false openness."

"I'm an American male, Lowenstein," I said, smiling. "It's not my job to be open."

"What exactly is the American male's job?" she asked.

"To be maddening. To be unreadable, controlling, bullheaded, and insensitive," I said.

"You'd be amazed at the different points of view I hear expressed by my male and female patients," she said. "It's as though they were speaking of citizens from entirely different countries."

"There's only one crime a woman cannot be forgiven for," I said. "No husband will ever forgive her for marrying him. The American male is a quivering mass of insecurities. If a woman makes the mistake of loving him, he will make her suffer terribly for her utter lack of taste. I don't think men can ever forgive women for loving them to the exclusion of all others."

"Didn't you tell me that Sallie was having an affair, Tom?" she said.

"Yes," I said, "and it's funny. I've noticed my wife for the first time in over a year. Only when she stopped loving me did I realize how much I loved her."

"Have you told your wife you love her?" she asked, drinking her wine.

"I'm a husband, Lowenstein," I said. "Of course I haven't told my wife I love her."

"Why do you joke when I'm asking you a serious question, Tom?" she asked. "You always divert serious questions with your humor."

"I find it painful to even think about Sallie," I said. "When I talk about her I can barely breathe. Laughter is the only strategy that has ever worked at all for me when my world was falling apart."

"I would think tears would be far more effective than humor," she said.

"With me," I said, "tears seem to spring only from cheap moments. I cry when I watch the Olympics, when I hear the national anthem, at all weddings and graduations."

"But you're talking about sentimentality," she interrupted. "I was speaking of grief and sorrow."

"Southerners don't look at sentimentality as a flaw of character, Lowenstein. A southerner can be moved to tears by almost any absurdity. It binds them to other southerners and makes them ridiculous to anyone born in the Northeast. I think it's more a matter of weather than of temperament. The language of grief is an impoverished one in the South. Sorrow is admired only if it's done in silence."

She leaned across the table and said, "Savannah's language of grief is certainly not impoverished, Tom. Her poems resonate with a terribly powerful anguish that she articulates brilliantly. And there's not one drop of sentimentality in her poems, yet she's southern too."

"But she's in the wacko ward, Doc," I said. "And I'm drinking Chablis with her shrink at the Coach House. She's paid a dear price for her lack of sentimentality."

I was grateful when the waiter arrived to take our orders. I could see I had angered Susan Lowenstein with my unseemly remark about my sister's institutionalization. Yet there was something unsettling about her ingrained curiosity about the South that could produce both a suicidal poet of magisterial gifts and a coach on the downslide who was that poet's twin brother. There were times when she studied me with such withering intensity that she looked like a geologist hoping to find a trace of gold in the luster of gneiss. Also, I had the unsettling intuition that Dr. Lowenstein was withholding something from me about Savannah's condition. The revoking of my visiting privileges appeared odd to me and somehow inevitable, as if Savannah had preordained my exclusion from her company long before she entered the hospital. Whenever I told Dr. Lowenstein some memory of my family, I always expected her to say, "That's exactly how Savannah remembered it," or "That's very helpful in light of what Savannah told me, Tom." It was like screaming into the mouth of an echoless cave that I was forbidden to enter. My duty was to dance to the music of my interrogation, my interpretation of those wounded screams of my sister. I would receive no corroboration in return, no applause for my honesty, and no censure for my lies. I would simply receive the next question from Susan Lowenstein and go on from there. I had somehow become the repository of memory in a family where memory had entered a fatal concubinage with suffering. I was the only witness available to explain why my sister's madness was only a natural response to an indiscriminate curriculum of ruin.

Turning my attention to the menu, I ordered, to start with, a pair of soft-shelled crabs sautéed in butter and lemon juice and sauced with a *beurre blanc* studded with capers. Lowenstein had ordered the smoked trout as an appetizer and the poached sea bass for an entrée. There was not a single entrée on the menu that did not appeal to me, but I finally settled on sweetbreads in a wine and morel sauce.

"Sweetbreads?" Dr. Lowenstein inquired with a raised eyebrow.

"Part of our family chronicle," I said. "It was referred to obliquely on the tapes. My mother introduced them one mealtime and they caused a bit of friction between my parents."

"You speak of your mother with half awe and half contempt," she said. "It confuses me."

"I think it shows a proper balance when speaking of my mother," I responded. "She's a remarkable and beautiful woman who spent her whole life searching for who she really was. With her murderous skills, she should have gotten a job sharpening guillotines. Otherwise she was simply wasting her talents."

"Does Savannah share your exaggerated view of your mother's powers?" she asked. Again I felt constricted as Dr. Lowenstein tried to break new ground with each question.

"You should know the answer to that question better than I do," I said as the waiter approached with our appetizers. "She's your patient and I'm sure she's got very strong feelings on the subject."

"Tom," Dr. Lowenstein said, "Savannah was my patient for only two months before her suicide attempt. There are some things I can't tell you about our time together in those two short months, but I'll try to tell you sometime. I'll need Savannah's permission and she's in no condition to grant it right now."

"So you really don't know Savannah at all, do you, Lowenstein?" I said.

"No, Tom, I really don't know her," she answered. "But I'm learning amazing things all the time. And I know that my instinct to ask you to stay in New York was absolutely correct."

"Savannah could tell you these stories much better than I could," I said.

"But could she suggest such wonderful food at restaurants?" Lowenstein answered as she took a bite of smoked trout moistened with horseradish sauce.

"No, Savannah is one of those anorexic New York women who exist on salads, tofu, and diet drinks," I said. "She'll eat nothing that contains a nest of unsightly calories or a streak of animal fat. Eating with Savannah is an ascetic experience rather than a voluptuary one."

"She and I once compared diets," Lowenstein said. "She could skip two meals a day with no problem. I've bought every diet book published in America for the last ten years, but . . ."

"Why, Lowenstein?" I asked as I chewed a buttery claw of a soft-shelled crab.

"My husband thinks I'm too fat," she said, and there was real pain in that admission.

I smiled and continued eating my crab as the waiter returned and poured us both another glass of wine.

"Why are you smiling, Tom?"

I looked across at her and said, "Your husband's wrong again. It's not virginal and it's not fat, Lowenstein, and it's a crying shame that neither you nor your husband is deriving much pleasure from the fact."

She changed the subject and began talking about her childhood, but she had received the compliment and it pleased her. She talked about her mother's coldness, a reserve so innate and measureless that Susan Lowenstein could never remember a single time in her life when she had won her mother's unsparing approval. Instead she had lived for the praise of her father, which was precious but extortionate. He was the kind of father who could never condone his daughter's unsanctioned sexuality. She was his favorite child until she reached puberty; then he abandoned her for a younger brother. Though both her parents were proud that she had gone to medical school, they were both appalled when she decided to study psychiatry. But she had thought that her own failed and needy childhood would help her understand those patients who would come to her with their own desolate childhoods shining in their eyes. She thought she brought a gift of compassion for those exhausted souls who had not received a just portion from the people who raised them. If compassion and therapy did not work, she could always send her patients to the local pharmacy for drugs. As a psychiatrist, she felt like an all-powerful father, but one who would always forgive his daughter for the crime of becoming a woman. It was the power of psychiatry that both frightened and engaged her, the irresistible seriousness of her connection with her patients, the delicacy of each alliance, and the responsibility to enter each of these tenuous affiliations with humility and good faith.

As we talked and ate our dinner, I began to see once more a loosening in the features of Susan Lowenstein, a slow abandonment of that resolute professionalism she wore in her office. When she spoke of her patients, her voice grew supple and loving, and I imagined it would be a wonderful thing indeed to be driven to your knees in New York and to find yourself ministered to by her warm, forgiving gaze. The arch professionalism was a frontispiece erected to ward off the discomposed superiority of men like me and her father. When she spoke of that father who had worshiped then abandoned her, Susan sounded as though he were unique to her own experience. Yet something in her voice, something that sang with all the undertones of a hard-earned wisdom, knew that her father's story was the oldest and most dispiriting story in the world. It made me think of all the women in my life—my mother, sister, wife, and daughters—and how I could make a strong case that I had betrayed each of them by a strategic collapse of my own love when they needed it the most. I could not hear about Susan's father without cringing at the thought of the harm I had caused the women of my own family. In happy times, love poured out of me like bright honey from a stolen hive. But in times of hurt and loss I withdrew into a self-made enclosure of impenetrable solitude, and the women who tried to touch me there—all of them—drew back in utter horror as I wounded them again and again for daring to love me when I knew my love was all corruption. I was one of those men who killed their women slowly. My love was a form of gangrene withering the soft tissues of the soul. I had a sister who had tried to kill herself and who did not wish to see me, a wife who had found a man who loved her, daughters who did not know a thing about me, and a mother who knew far too much. "Change it all," I said to myself as I sat listening to Susan Lowenstein while she relaxed under the influence of the wine and the sedate ambiance of the Coach House. "Change everything about yourself and change it absolutely."

My main course arrived and it was superb. The sweetbreads were rich and tender and the morels tasted like pieces of truffled earth turned into dark, smoky flesh. I heard Susan moan with admiration as she tasted the bass, whose white glistening flesh fell off its bones in tender segments. My mouth was a happy place and I thanked God for the scrupulosities of gifted cooks and the inexhaustible beauty of women as I watched Susan eating her dinner and drinking a wine that had been aged for us and us alone in the generous and ancient fields of France. I ordered another bottle of wine in honor of those glorious fields.

Susan told me that she had a dream the night before last in which we had met by accident in a snowstorm. To escape the storm we had gone to Rockefeller Center and took an elevator ride to the top. Then we watched the city turn white while having a drink in the Rainbow Room and then danced a slow dance when the storm turned wild and we could no longer see the city through the snow.

"What a great dream, Lowenstein," I said. "I can never remember a single detail about my dreams. They can wake me up and I know they must be horrible, but I can't recall a single image."

"Then you're missing a wonderful and important part of your life, Tom," she said. "I've always thought that dreams were both the love letters and the hate mail of the subconscious. It's just a form of discipline to remember your dreams."

"I can do without the hate mail," I said. "I have stacks of that stuff that I write to myself."

"But isn't it rather amazing that you were in one of my dreams," she said, "when I've only known you for such a short time?"

"I'm delighted that you didn't present it as a nightmare," I said.

"I can assure you it wasn't a nightmare," she said, laughing. "By the way, Tom, do you like concerts?"

"Sure," I answered. "Except when they play modern music. Modern music always sounds like trout farting in salt water to me. Of course, Savannah loves modern music."

"Why do you think she's so open to modern culture and you seem so closed to it? I must admit, Tom, that it irritates me every time you don your mantle of cultural yahoo intimidated by the big city. You're too smart a man to play that role very effectively."

"I'm sorry, Lowenstein," I said. "No one finds my role of New York debunker and cultural redneck more tiring than I do myself. I just wish it wasn't a cliché to hate New York, that it was a startling new doctrine originated by Tom Wingo."

"Anytime I hear someone like you say they hate New York, I automatically think they're anti-Semitic," she said.

"Please explain the connection between anti-Semitism and not liking New York, Lowenstein. I'm from Colleton, South Carolina, and at times these distinctions confuse me."

"There are more Jews in New York than there are in Israel," she said.

"There are probably more Albanians here than in Albania and more Haitians here than in Haiti and more Irishmen here than in Ireland, Lowenstein. There might even be more southerners here than there are in Georgia; I have no idea. I don't like New York because I find it huge and impersonal. Are you always so paranoid?"

"Yes," she said. "I've always found paranoia to be a perfectly defensible position."

"Now you understand how I feel about being southern when I come to New York," I said. "What did you think about the South, Lowenstein, before you met me and Savannah?"

"The same thing I think about it now, Tom," she said. "I think it's the most backward, reactionary, and dangerous part of the country."

"But do you like it, Lowenstein?" I asked.

She laughed and it was a fine laugh, but I continued, "Why is it that there are times in history when it's all right to hate Jews or Americans or blacks or gypsies. There's always a group deserving of contempt in every generation. You're even suspect if you don't hate them. I was taught to hate Communists when I was growing up. I never sighted one, but I hated the sons of bitches. I hated blacks when I was growing up because it was a religious belief in my part of the world to consider them inferior to whites. It's been interesting to come to New York, Lowenstein, and to be hated because I am a white southerner. It's rather bracing and refreshing, but odd. It makes me understand your theory of paranoia."

"The reason I asked you if you like concerts, Tom, is because my husband is giving one next month," she said. "I got you a ticket and I hope you'll come as my guest."

"I'd love to come," I said, "if you promise he won't play anything modern."

"I think the program is mostly baroque."

"What's his name?" I asked.

"Herbert Woodruff," she said.

"*The* Herbert Woodruff?" I said, surprised.

"The one and only," she said.

"You're married to Herbert Woodruff! Goddamn, Lowenstein. You sack out with someone world famous every night."

"Not every night, I'm afraid. Herbert's on tour over half the year. He's in great demand. Especially in Europe."

"We've got his records," I said. "At least a couple of them. Sallie and I get drunk and listen to them. That's wonderful. I'll have to call Sallie and brag. Is he Jewish, Doc?"

"No," she answered. "Why do you ask?"

"I thought Jews were like Catholics," I said. "When I didn't marry a Catholic, my father acted like I got caught peeing in the altar cruets."

"My father is the most assimilated Jew I've ever known," Dr. Lowenstein said seriously. "We never went to temple, never celebrated Passover, and put up a Christmas tree every December. I never knew how seriously he took his religion until I married a Christian. I thought he was going to sit shiva for me on my wedding day."

"What's shiva?"

"Prayers for the dead," she answered.

"But he must be proud that his son-in-law is world famous."

"I wouldn't know, Tom," she said. "He's never forgiven me. He's never even met his grandson."

"That explains a lot to me, Lowenstein," I said. "I thought you were a Presbyterian who had converted to Judaism.

Why didn't you take your husband's last name when you married?"

"I chose not to," she said, effectively shutting down that line of conversation.

"How old is your son?" I asked, changing the subject.

"That's what I wanted to talk to you about, Tom. That's why I'm glad we could have dinner tonight."

"About your son?" I asked, puzzled.

"I have a son who is very interested in athletics," she said.

"You're kidding."

"Why do you say it like that?" she asked, unable to mask the irritation in her voice.

"It just surprised me," I said. "I doubt if he got much encouragement from home."

"It shocked his father. Bernard attends Phillips Exeter. He was a freshman there this year. We received a copy of the yearbook recently and his father found a picture of Bernard on the freshman football team. We have never allowed him to play contact sports because of what it might do to his hands. You see, we want Bernard to concentrate on his violin lessons. That's why we worry about his hands."

"Ha," I could not help hooting. "A surprise jock in the family."

She smiled. "It's not funny. The most distressing part about this whole affair is that Bernard lied to us. Or at least he simply did not tell us. He was also on the junior varsity basketball team. He evidently is quite competent."

"Why don't you just let him play ball and take music lessons too?"

"My husband wants Bernard to be a total musician."

"Is he any good at it?"

"Yes, he's good at it. It's just that he's not a genius at it, Tom. You can imagine the difficulty in following in Herbert Woodruff's footsteps. I always thought we should have him play a different instrument from his father. Then the comparisons wouldn't have been so threatening to Bernard. Herbert won an international competition when he was only nineteen."

"You see a lot of that as a coach. I can't tell you the

number of boys who come out for a team because their father is trying to relive his youth through his kid. It's sad when it doesn't work out."

"For the fathers or the sons?" she asked with aggrieved earnestness.

"The sons," I said. "Fuck the fathers. They should know better."

"I don't think it's that way with Herbert at all," she replied. "I just think that no other instrument exists in his imagination. He loves the violin so much he just can't imagine someone not sharing that love. Especially someone related to him. Especially his only son."

"How do they get along with each other?" I asked. Her face darkened and something passed across her eyes. She chose her words carefully and I could feel their weight and gravity as she spoke them.

"Bernard respects his father a great deal. He's very proud of him and what his father has accomplished."

"Do they pal around? Go to ball games? Play catch in the park? Wrestle in the living room? That kind of thing."

She laughed but it was a taut and nervous laughter. In discussing her child, I was touching something essential in her.

"I can't imagine Herbert wrestling on the living room floor. He's a very fastidious and serious man. Besides, he could do damage to his hands, and his hands are his life."

"But is he fun, Doc?" I asked. "That's what I think I'm asking."

She thought for a long moment, then said simply, "No, I wouldn't describe Herbert as fun. Not for a teenage boy anyhow. I think Bernard will appreciate Herbert far more after he becomes an adult."

"What's Bernard like?"

Once more I saw a shutting down near the eyes, some internal hatch-battening in the face of this interrogation about her family. It occurred to me that this psychiatrist would rather listen to the griefs of others in her office than speak of her own pressing and worrying concerns. Her face was pale as she leaned her head back and rested it against the brick wall behind her. She looked like one of those

long-necked elegant women you see in profile against a
background of dark agate in cameos.

"Bernard is difficult to describe," she said with a long
sigh. "He's an attractive boy who thinks he's ugly. He's
very tall, much taller than his father. He has enormous feet
and black curly hair. He doesn't speak much, especially to
adults. He's a mediocre student. We had to pull every string
imaginable to get him into Exeter. We've had him tested,
and he's done brilliantly, but he's lazy and I think he enjoys
hurting his parents by making poor grades. What else can
I say, Tom? The adolescent years are tough on everyone."

"Is he fucked up?" I asked.

"No," she said sharply. "He is not fucked up. He's a
perfectly normal teenage boy whose parents are both
professional people. Herbert and I probably made a mistake
by not being around him more during his formative years.
I admit that and take full responsibility."

"Why are you telling me this, Lowenstein?" I asked.

"I thought, Tom," she said, leaning forward across the
table, "that since you seem to have so much free time on
your hands, you could coach Bernard a couple of times a
week."

"My first job offer in many a moon."

"Would you do it?" she asked.

"Have you talked to Bernard about it?"

"Why should I do that?" she asked.

"He may not want a coach, and besides, it's polite to
ask. Why don't you get Herbert to go out to Central Park
and throw batting practice to Bernard, maybe even hustle
up a pickup game."

"Herbert loathes athletics, Tom," she said, giggling at
the thought. "In fact, it would infuriate him to know I
wanted a coach for his son. But Bernard told me he was
going to play sports next year no matter what we thought
about it. Also, I think you'd be good for Bernard, Tom, and
I think he'd like you, because you're the kind of father he's
always dreamed of having. An athlete, funny, irreverent.
And I'll bet money you can't play the violin."

"You've never heard my recording. Wingo playing the
shit out of the old masters. You stereotyped me again,
Doctor."

"And I saw you stereotyping me," she said edgily.

"No, I didn't."

"Yes, you did, Tom. Admit it. You were thinking to yourself, old Dr. Lowenstein, psychiatrist and healer of the mentally ill, cannot raise a happy son."

"Yeah," I admitted, "I did think that. There must be a reason why shrinks can't raise kids. It's a cliché, I know, but it is a problem, isn't it?"

"Not in this case," she declared firmly. "Bernard is just shy. He'll grow out of all these problems. I think why psychiatrists do have trouble with their children—and not all of them do, let me assure you—is that they know far too much about the damaging consequences of a bad childhood. Too much knowledge paralyzes them and makes them afraid to take even the smallest false step. What begins as too much caring sometimes ends in neglect. Now, what about your remuneration?"

"Money?" I said. "Don't worry about the money."

"No, I insist we keep this on an entirely professional basis. What is your schedule of fees?"

"My schedule of fees. You've got to be kidding."

"Look, I insist we do this on a strictly professional basis. What do you charge an hour?"

She had taken a notebook from her purse and was making a notation with a thin Dupont fountain pen.

"How much do you make an hour?" I asked.

"I hardly see the connection," she said, looking up from the notebook.

"The connection is this, Doctor. Since you want to do this in a strictly professional manner, I want to oblige you. I don't know what people make in New York City. I need some figures to work with."

"I charge seventy-five dollars an hour," she said.

"Fine." I grinned. "I'll take it."

"I certainly didn't agree to pay you that."

"Look, Doc, because you're a friend of the family, you get a cut-rate deal. Sixty bucks an hour and don't even bother to thank me."

"I hardly think that *coaching* for an hour is comparable to an hour of psychiatric therapy," she said, and her voice was even, but I did not like the belittling emphasis she put on the word *coaching*.

"Oh really? Why not? What's the difference?"

"You have no idea the cost of going to medical school."

"Yes, I do. I sent my wife through medical school."

"What was your top salary as a coach?"

"I made seventeen thousand dollars one year, before taxes," I answered.

"How much does that amount to an hour?" she asked.

"Well, let's take three hundred sixty-five days. I teach and coach for nine months. Then I would coach baseball in the summer. That's about forty-six bucks a day, I think. Let's divide that by a ten-hour day."

She wrote the figures down in her notebook, then looked up and announced, "That's four dollars and sixty cents an hour. I'll pay five dollars an hour."

"How generous," I said.

"That's the highest pay you've ever received."

"Oh, the humiliation," I moaned, looking about the restaurant. "The utter and constant humiliation. A coach going one on one with a shrink and losing in overtime by seventy big buckeroos."

"Then it's a deal," she said, snapping her notebook shut.

"No," I said. "Now that I've been slaughtered on this field of battle, I want to gain some measure of self-respect from this debacle. I'd like to coach Bernard for free, Doctor. Once again I've been annihilated when I tried to equate coaching with a real way of making a living. Tell him we'll start the day after tomorrow. Now let's order a fabulous dessert."

"I've eaten far too much already."

"Don't worry about gaining weight, Lowenstein," I said. "We'll rustle up a mugger right after dinner and let him chase you all the way to Central Park. It's a perfect way to burn off calories after a New York meal."

"Which reminds me," she said. "Remember when you met Monique at my office? Why did you tell her that you were a corporate lawyer? She mentioned that to me when she was in my office."

"She didn't believe me when I said I was a coach," I said. "Also, she was beautiful and I wanted to impress her. Also, I was lonely at the time and I wanted to keep talking to her."

"Do you think she's beautiful?"

"I thought she was the most beautiful woman I'd ever seen," I said.

"It's very strange, Tom. That's the second time she's come to my office hysterical and out of control. She's having a ghastly affair with an investment banker who works for Salomon Brothers—at least that's what she tells me."

"Her shrink's out of town," I said. "Is there anyone in this city who doesn't go to a psychiatrist, or do they make those folks all move to New Jersey?"

"She plays the flute in my husband's ensemble," Dr. Lowenstein said. "You'll see her again next month."

"Ah, shit. She'll ask me about my law practice," I said. "Let me get you a glass of cognac, Susan. You're right, we can skip dessert."

When the cognac came, we toasted each other again and the taste of cognac took me spinning into the past, when I last had sat in this restaurant with my brother and sister. While drinking the cognac that the owner of the Coach House had given us for free, Savannah had pulled out four new poems she was working on and read them aloud to Luke and me. She was planning to write an autobiography in a long cycle of poems and she read to us about the white porpoise of Colleton, my grandfather's annual walk on Good Friday, and the first football game of Benji Washington. Her language was lush and fiery and she pulled bright images from her life like peaches from a fragrant orchard. When spoken, her poems were like a gift of fruit, and on that night we had perfumed the fruit with cognac.

"What are you thinking about, Tom?" Susan asked.

"I was thinking about the time I was here with Luke and Savannah," I said. "We were all so happy then."

"What happened?"

"Nature abhors a vacuum, but it abhors perfect happiness even more," I said. "Susan, do you remember my mentioning my nervous breakdown?"

"Of course," she said softly.

"It wasn't a breakdown," I said. "It was a sadness so overwhelming that I could barely move or speak. I didn't think it was mental illness then; I don't think it now. For two years, I managed to function even though I carried this sorrow around in my heart. I had suffered a terrible loss and I was simply inconsolable. I coached three sports and

I taught English five classes a day and my work held me together. Then I could no longer bear the weight of this sadness. I was teaching one day and reading "Fern Hill" by Dylan Thomas to one of my classes; I became so moved by the poem that it brought tears to my eyes. The poem is beautiful and it moves me every time I read it, but this time was different. I couldn't stop crying. My class was distraught. I was distraught, but I couldn't help myself."

"And you didn't consider this a breakdown of sorts, Tom?" she said, softly.

"No," I said. "I thought it was a normal response to great sadness. It was abnormal to have carried the weight of that sadness around so long without crying. A week later I was walking on the beach when I passed a man who looked like my brother and I fell apart again. I sat on the rocks overlooking Charleston Harbor and shook with my own sobbing for over an hour. Then I thought there was something I was supposed to be doing. I had forgotten something important, but didn't know what. Sallie found me on the beach that night shivering in the cold."

"What had you forgotten?"

"A game. I forgot that my team had a game that night. I forgot that my own team that I had coached and drilled and disciplined had a game."

"That was when they fired you?"

"Yes, that was when they fired me," I said. "So I stayed at home and refused to get help from anyone. I let the sadness take me and it took me hard. After a month, my wife and my mother had me sign some papers and they took me to the tenth floor of the Medical College and I had a couple of shock treatments."

"You don't have to tell me any of this, Tom," she said.

"Since I'm going to be coaching Bernard, I thought you should know you were getting damaged merchandise."

"Are you a good coach?" she asked.

"I'm a terrific coach, Susan," I answered.

"Then I'm very lucky that you've come into my life at this very moment," she said. "Thanks for telling me all that. I'm glad you told me here instead of at the office. I think you and I are going to be good friends."

"There's something you're not telling me about Savannah, isn't there?"

"There's a lot I'm not telling you about Savannah," she said. "There's a lot I'm not telling you about a lot of things. When I just mentioned Monique, it nearly killed me when you told me you thought she was so beautiful."

"Why?"

"I think she's having an affair with my husband."

"Why do you think that?"

"Because I know my husband very well," she said. "I can't figure out why she keeps coming to me for help, whether it's cruelty or just curiosity. She always makes me swear not to tell Herbert she's been to see me."

"I'm sorry, Susan," I said. "Maybe it's your imagination."

"I don't think so."

"Well, Lowenstein, I've met both you and Monique. Monique is lovely but she's got a lousy personality and she's a little on the mean side. Since you wore that terrific dress tonight, I could not fail to notice that you're walking around in a world-class body. You're a little serious for my taste, but I love being with you. Monique can't hold a candle to you, darling," I said.

"Not darling, Tom," she smiled. "Remember, I'm a feminist."

"Monique can't hold a candle to you, feminist," I said.

"Thanks, Coach," she said.

"Do you want to go dancing at the Rainbow Room?"

"Not tonight, Tom," she said. "But ask me again this summer."

"Will you promise to wear that dress?" I asked.

"I've got to get home," she said. "Fast."

"You're perfectly safe, Lowenstein. I've had electroshock therapy," I said, rising from the table. "C'mon. I'll pay the bill and hail you one of the city's hideous, but colorful, cab drivers."

"I've had a wonderful evening," Susan Lowenstein said as I opened the cab door on Waverly Place in a light rain. She kissed me on the lips, softly, just once, and I watched the cab disappear into the rain and the night.

8

Within weeks of her surprise return, my grandmother went to purchase her own coffin from Winthrop Ogletree, and we learned that she enjoyed visiting the Colleton cemetery to speak to the dead. Like most southerners, Tolitha had fashioned a small and personal art form out of ancestor worship, and the authentic intimacy of cemeteries made her happy. She looked upon death as a dark and undiscoverable longitude encircling the secret geography of the earth. The subject of her own death filled her with pleasant reveries of journeys both imminent and surprising.

Because my grandmother did not attend church regularly or openly profess a belief in God, it gave her license to embrace more exotic prescriptives of the spirit, more vivid distillations and tonics to add character to her view of the world. She maintained an innocent trust in horoscopes and planned her days around the proud alignment of stars and the obscure cues and insinuations of the zodiac. With ceaseless curiosity, she sought the advice of fortunetellers, believed in the shining powers of crystal balls, the cryptic allusions in the pattern of tea leaves, the marching orders she received from carefully shuffled tarot cards, and anything else that seemed suspect and revolutionary in a southern town. A gypsy in Marseilles had read Tolitha's palm, studied her abbreviated, bifurcated life line, and made a prediction that Tolitha would not live past her sixtieth birthday. Tolitha had just turned fifty-six when she hit Colleton to make her peace with the world. Each day she consulted the *I Ching*, which my grandfather considered a satanic text, at best. She believed in every divagation and acknowledgment of the Ouija board—no matter how entangled in obscurity. Her faith was a catechism of undigested verities. She consorted with psychics, witch doctors, and prognosticators. All were weathermen of her bouncy, untroubled soul. Tolitha was the most Christian woman I have ever known.

But she took the gypsy's death sentence with a stoical and bemused gravity, and she began to prepare for her own demise as though it were a voyage to a fabulous country whose borders had long been closed to tourists. When it came time to purchase her casket and to make the final arrangements for her interment, she insisted that her grandchildren accompany her. Always the teacher, Tolitha wanted us to learn not to fear death. She spoke about the impending purchase of her coffin with gaiety and acted as though she were about to confirm a hotel reservation at the end of a most arduous journey.

"It's simply the last stage of life. The most interesting stage, I imagine," she said as we walked along the Street of Tides, passing by the storefronts and saying how-de-do to neighbors and strangers alike.

"But you're in perfect health, Tolitha," Luke said, looking up at her in the sunlight. "I heard Dad say you're going to be peeing on all of our graves."

"Your father is a vulgarian, Luke. Please do not imitate the speech of shrimpers," my grandmother answered, walking straight ahead, proud as a mast. "No, I will not survive my sixtieth year. This was not just a gypsy who read my palm. This was the *queen* of the gypsies. I only seek opinions from specialists. I've never been to a GP in my life."

"Mama told us it was a sin to get your future told by a gypsy," said Savannah, holding my grandmother's hand.

"Your mother has only been in two states in her whole life," Tolitha sniffed. "She doesn't have my world view."

"Did the gypsy say what you're gonna die of?" I asked, studying her, worried that she would drop dead on the street.

"Heart failure," my grandmother announced proudly, as though she had just given the name of a much favored child. "I'll drop like a stone."

"Are you going to be buried like a Zen Buddhist?" Savannah asked.

"It's too impractical," Tolitha said, nodding sweetly to Jason Fordham, who ran the hardware store. "I wanted your grandfather to take me up to Atlanta and lay me out naked on Stone Mountain and let the vultures devour my earthly flesh, but he was horrified. That's how they do it in India. I wasn't sure they had enough vultures in Georgia to really do the trick."

"That's the most terrible thing I ever heard of, Tolitha," said Luke, looking at her with true admiration.

"I hate doing things the common way, children. But what can I do? Each society has got its own customs."

"You're not afraid of dying, are you, Tolitha?" I asked.

"We all got to turn up our toes someday, Tom," she replied. "I'm just lucky enough to be able to plan for my time so it won't come as such a shock to my family. I want everything to be ready."

"What kind of coffin do you expect to buy, Tolitha?" Savannah asked.

"A pine box. Nothing fancy for me. I want the worms to get at me as soon as possible. Let's face it, that's how they make their living, and I've never been against the way a man makes his living."

"How do worms eat you? They don't have any teeth," Luke asked as we passed Wayne Fender's barbershop.

"They have to wait for the earth to soften you up some," Tolitha explained, and her voice rose to a higher pitch. Such grisly detail excited and animated my grandmother. "See, the undertaker drains all your blood out of you so you're dry as a corncob. Then they fill you up with embalming fluid so you won't rot too fast."

"Why don't they leave the blood in there?" Savannah asked, her eyes wide with horror.

"Because you spoil too fast with the blood in."

"But they stick you in the ground and you're s'posed to spoil in there," I said.

"They don't want you to stink up your funeral. You kids ever smelled a corpse that's going bad?"

"What does it smell like, Tolitha?" Luke asked.

"It smells like a hundred pounds of shrimp which has done turned."

"That bad?"

"Worse. It sickens me just to think about it."

We came to the intersection of Baitery Road and the Street of Tides and to one of Colleton's two traffic lights. Out in the harbor, sailboats canted into the wind, their sails papery and overwhelmed with sunlight. A fifty-foot yacht made the turn in the river and signaled the bridge tender with four throaty barks of the horn. Mr. Fruit, sporting a baseball cap and white gloves, was directing traffic at the intersection. We waited for him to grant us permission to cross the street. It did not matter to Mr. Fruit if the light was red or green. Mr. Fruit relied on intuition and his own internal sense of balance and symmetry to get the traffic through his corner of the world.

Fantastic, bizarre, and vigilant, he was a tall, lanky black man of indeterminate age who seemed to consider the town of Colleton his personal responsibility. I don't know to this day if Mr. Fruit was retarded or deluded or some harmless sweet-faced lunatic given free rein to drift about his native town spreading the joy of an inarticulate gospel to his neighbors. I don't know his real name or who his family was or where he spent the night. I know he was indigenous and that no one questioned his right to direct the traffic on the Street of Tides.

There was a time when a new deputy tried to teach Mr. Fruit about the difference between a red and a green light, but Mr. Fruit had resisted all efforts to reorder what he had been doing perfectly well for many years. He not only monitored the comings and goings of the town, his presence softened the ingrained evil that flourished along the invisible margins of the town's consciousness. Any community can be judged in its humanity or corruption by how it manages to accommodate the Mr. Fruits of the world. Colleton simply adjusted itself to Mr. Fruit's harmonies and ordinations. He did whatever he felt was needed and he did it with style. "That's the southern way," my grandmother said. "That's the nice way."

"Hey, babe," he cried out when he saw us, and "Hey, babe," we cried back. He wore a silver whistle around his neck and a beatific, inerasable smile on his face. He tooted his whistle and waved his long arms in graceful exaggerated swoops. He pivoted and danced toward the lone approaching car, his left hand at a right angle to his bony wrist. The car stopped and Mr. Fruit motioned for us to cross the street, blowing on his whistle in perfect synchronization with my grandmother's footsteps. Mr. Fruit was born to direct traffic. He also led all parades in Colleton, no matter how solemn or festive the occasion. Those were his two functions in the life of the town and he performed them very well. My grandfather would always tell us that Mr. Fruit had done as well with what he had as any man my grandfather had ever met.

The town of Colleton had a population of ten thousand backwater souls when I was born, and each passing year it lost a small percentage of this population. The town was built on the land of the Yemassee Indians, and it was considered a mark of eminence that there was not a single Yemassee remaining on earth. *Yemassee* was a word that shimmered with the dark luster of extinction. The last battle between the settlers and the natives had been fought on our island, on the northern end of Melrose. Colleton's militia had surprised the tribe by attacking at night, slaughtering as many as they could in their sleep; then, using dogs, they drove the survivors through the forests, driving them like deer, until at dawn they had pushed them down to the sandy flats by the river. They herded the Yemassee into the river and cut them down with swords and muskets, sparing neither women nor children. I once found a small skull when I was searching for arrowheads with Luke and Savannah. A musket ball rattled in the brainpan and dropped out of the mouth when I lifted it out of the underbrush.

As we passed the row of stunning white mansions along the Street of Tides, we walked by the house where the most threatening dream of our time was in the process of being born. We waved to Reese Newbury, who was standing on his porch, looking out toward the river. He was Colleton's most powerful man. He was a brilliant attorney, owned the only bank and vast acreage throughout the county, and was chairman of the city council. In that salute, we were acknowledging our future, our town's most amazing dreamer; we were waving guilelessly and smilingly at the fall of the House of Wingo.

* * *

The undertaker, Winthrop Ogletree, was waiting in the foyer of the large, rambling Victorian house at the end of the Street of Tides where he practiced his trade. He was dressed in a dark suit and his hands were folded against his stomach in an attitude of enforced piety. He was tall and thin and had a complexion like goat cheese left on the table too long. The funeral parlor smelled like dead flowers and unanswered prayers. When he wished us a good day, his voice was reptilian and unctuous and you knew he was only truly comfortable in the presence of the dead. He looked as if he had died two or three times himself in order to appreciate better the subtleties of his vocation. Winthrop Ogletree had the face of an unlucky vampire who never received an adequate portion of blood.

"I'll get right to the point, Winthrop," my grandmother said officiously. "I'll be dying sometime after my sixtieth birthday and I don't want to be a burden on my family. I'm going to pick out the cheapest coffin you carry in this boneyard and I don't want no high-pressure salesmanship trying to get me to buy some million-dollar box."

Mr. Ogletree looked both hurt and offended but answered in a mollifying voice. "Oh, Tolitha, Tolitha, Tolitha. I'm here only to serve your best interests. It would never occur to me to try to talk anyone into anything. I am here only to answer your questions and to be of service. But Tolitha, I wasn't aware that you were ill. You look like you could live to be a thousand."

"I can't think of a more horrible fate," she answered, peering into a room off to her right where a corpse was laid out in an open casket. "Is that Johnny Grindley?"

"Yes, he passed to his reward yesterday morning."

"You work fast, Winthrop."

"I do my best, Tolitha," Mr. Ogletree said humbly, bowing his head. "He lived a good Christian life and it's a privilege to be able to give him a dignified sendoff."

"Johnny was the meanest son of a bitch that ever wore shoelaces, Winthrop," my grandmother said, walking to the casket and peering down on Johnny Grindley's waxen, inhuman face.

The three of us crowded around the coffin, studying the features of the corpse.

"He looks like he just nodded off for a nap, doesn't he?" Mr. Ogletree said proudly.

"Naw, he looks dead as a stump," my grandmother answered.

"On the contrary, Tolitha," Mr. Ogletree said, offended. "I think he looks as though he could rise up and whistle a John Philip Sousa march. Notice the animation in his face. The slight hint of a smile. You have no idea how hard it is to put a smile on a cancer victim's face. Oh, I mean, anyone can put a fake smile on a corpse's face. But it's an artist who can make that smile seem natural."

"I don't want no smile on my face when I kick, Winthrop," Tolitha ordered. "You better write that down. I don't want to be grinning like a chessy cat while folks go peeking over the side. And I want you to use my own personal make-up. Not that cheap crap you use."

"I use the finest cosmetics that money can buy, Tolitha," he said, straightening up to his full height.

"I want to be lovely in death," said Tolitha, ignoring him.

"I shall make you splendid," he said, bowing his head in modesty again.

"Poor Johnny Grindley," Tolitha said, staring with a strange tenderness at the body. "Do you know, kids, I remember the day that Johnny was born in his mama's house over on Huger Street. I was eight years old and I remember it clear as if it happened fifteen minutes ago. That's the only strange part of life. I still feel like an eight-year-old girl trapped in an old body. Johnny was as ugly as a muskrat from the day he was born."

"He had a full life," Mr. Ogletree intoned, his voice as serious as D-flat major on an organ.

"He didn't do one interesting thing his whole life, Winthrop," said Tolitha. "Now show me the room where you keep the models."

"I've got one that has 'you' written all over it, Tolitha," said Mr. Ogletree as he led us up the winding staircase. We passed beside a nondenominational chapel to our right and entered a room filled with a variety of caskets of all shapes and sizes. Mr. Ogletree walked directly to a mahogany casket in the center of the room, tapped it affectionately with his hand, and declared, "There's no use looking any further, Tolitha. This is the only proper casket for a lady of your stature in the community."

"Where's a pine box?" Tolitha asked, her eyes sweeping the room. "I don't want to be a burden on my family."

"That's no problem. We have a generous time-payment plan. You just pay a few dollars a month and by the time you go for your final reward, it won't cost your family a cent."

Tolitha studied the casket with a shrewd eye for a long minute. She ran her hand along the embroidered silk that lined the inside of the casket. I walked over to a casket that had a picture of Christ and the Apostles gathered for the Last Supper emblazoned in silk on the bottom of the lid.

"That's a mighty fine one you're looking at, Tom," Mr. Ogletree said. "You'll notice that Judas is not pictured. It's a fine thing to be buried with Jesus and his closest followers but the manufacturers wisely decided that Judas should have no place in a good Christian's final home."

"It looks mighty nice to me," I said.

"Tacky," Savannah whispered.

"I like the 'Praying Hands' coffin better," Luke said from across the room.

"Methodists seem to prefer that one, Luke," said a pleased Mr. Ogletree. "But it's actually nondenominational. Those could be Buddhist or Moslem hands in prayer. Do you understand my point? But I don't think Tolitha would care for a picture decorating her final resting place. She's always had the elegance of simplicity, if you'll permit me to offer a compliment, Tolitha."

"No compliment needed, Winthrop," my grandmother said. "How much is this model you first showed me?"

"Usually it runs for about a thousand dollars," he said, his voice lowering as though in prayer. "But because you're a friend of the family, I'll let it go for eight hundred twenty-five dollars and sixteen cents plus tax."

"I'll think about it, Winthrop," she said. "Now, could you leave me with my grandchildren for a while and let us mull this over? This seems like an important decision and I want to discuss it with them privately."

"Of course, I understand perfectly. I was going to suggest it myself. I'll be downstairs in my office, Tolitha. Just drop by there on your way out. If nothing satisfies you here,

I've got a special mail-order catalogue that lists every resting place made in the United States."

"What's the cheapest job you've got here on the floor?"

Winthrop Ogletree snorted as though trying to blow something unclean from his nostrils and walked stiff-backed to an unlit corner of the room where he touched, with only a hint of repugnance, a small, unprepossessing casket the color of a gun barrel. "This pitiful thing goes for two hundred dollars, Tolitha, but I could never let a woman of your stature in the community be buried in such a thing. Only unidentified drifters and the lower sort of Negro are buried in these. No, you wouldn't want to embarrass your family by being seen in this thing."

He looked at my grandmother as though she had suggested that he bury her up to her neck in chickenshit. Bowing deeply, he left us to confer in private.

When we heard his footsteps on the stairway, my grandmother said, "It makes me sick to think that ghoul is going to see me buck naked when I'm dead."

"How disgusting, Tolitha," said Savannah. "We won't allow it. We won't even let him peek."

"He has to get you naked when he cuts open your veins to drain the blood. I guess it won't make that much difference to me then. I just wish it could be someone besides Winthrop Ogletree. You could add a little vinegar to his voice and pour it on a Caesar salad. If you're drawing a level breath, it depresses him for days. Here, someone hold this."

She pulled a small Brownie camera out of her purse and handed it to Luke. "What's this for, Tolitha?" Luke asked.

My grandmother moved a straight-backed chair over to the first casket Winthrop Ogletree had suggested. She carefully removed her shoes and climbed nimbly on top of it. We watched. I did not speak. Tolitha climbed into the casket as though she were installing herself in the berth of a first-class railroad car. Lying down, she adjusted herself by twisting her body back and forth. She wiggled her toes and tried to stretch out. Then she closed her eyes and lay perfectly still.

"I don't like the way these box springs feel," she said at last, her eyes still tightly closed.

"It's not a mattress, Tolitha," Savannah said. "It's not supposed to feel like a hotel bed."

"How in the hell do *you* know how it's supposed to feel?" Tolitha asked. "Look, I'm paying quite a bit of money for this thing. At least they can make me comfortable. Besides, I'll be in it for quite a spell."

"Hurry up and get out of there, Tolitha," I begged, running to the window, "before someone spots you and we all get in trouble."

"How do I look?" my grandmother asked, nonplused.

"What do you mean how do you look?" Savannah answered. "You look great."

"I mean how do I look in the coffin?" she said, her eyes still unopened. "Does this dress go with this color or shall I wear that purple one I wore in Hong Kong last Easter?"

"We weren't in Hong Kong last Easter," Luke said.

"That's right. Well, I think this one is a lot more dignified. I hate for people to look frivolous when they've died. Take a few snapshots of me, Luke."

"I can't do that, Tolitha. It's not right."

"Look, I'm not going to buy this contraption until I see how I look in it. You wouldn't expect me to buy a dress without trying it on, would you?"

Luke took a few pictures, shrugging his shoulders at us as he advanced the film and shot from different angles.

"Mrs. Blankenship's coming up the walk, Tolitha," I said in a half-scream. "Please get out of there."

"Who cares what that old bitch thinks. She and I were in school together. She wasn't worth a damn then and she's not worth a damn now. Now listen to me, children. I want my hair done up right when my time comes. I want Nellie Rae Baskins to do my hair and *not*, I repeat *not*, Wilma Hotchkiss, who should only be allowed to sweep up hair and not to touch it. Tell Nellie Rae I want my hair done up in one of those new highfalutin French styles I've been reading about lately. Something a little flashy. I want to give the gossips something to wag their tongues about even after I'm gone. And also . . . Is anyone taking notes? Someone should be taking this down. You kids will never remember all this . . . I'd like my hair dyed red."

"Red!" Savannah cried out, surprised. "You'll look silly as a redhead, Tolitha. It won't look natural."

Tolitha, her eyes still tightly shut, her head resting comfortably on the satin pillow, said calmly, "I was a redhead when I was a girl. I had beautiful red hair, not that sickening brassy color of that Tolliver girl who lives on Burnchurch Road. I saved a locket of my hair from when I was fifteen, so they can match it. Nellie Rae's a good colorist. Wilma couldn't color an Easter egg without messing it up. Besides, Savannah, who wants to be a natural-looking stiff? For godsakes, I'm just trying to put a little pizzazz in my funeral."

"A funeral is not supposed to have pizzazz," Savannah argued. "Now please get out of there before Mr. Ogletree comes back."

"How is my mouth?" Tolitha asked. "I want my mouth just like this, I think. Take another snapshot with that, Luke. Remember, I don't want that jackass Ogletree putting a big grin on my face. He's famous for that. You know, happy to be up here with Jesus and all that crap. I want to look serious and dignified, like a dowager queen."

"What's a dowager queen?" I asked.

"I don't know exactly, Tom, but it sounds like something I'd like to be. I'll look it up in the Webster's when I get home. Hand me my compact out of my purse, Savannah honey. I want to check my make-up."

Savannah reached into the giant purse and fished out a small gold compact, which she handed to our recumbent grandmother. Tolitha snapped it open and studied her face in the small round mirror. She dabbed some powder on her nose and cheeks, then, satisfied with the result, snapped the compact shut, handed it to Savannah, and closed her eyes again.

"Perfect. My make-up is just perfect. This is exactly how I want it. Take another snapshot, Luke. This is exactly the shade of lipstick I want used. Ogletree uses stuff that they paint fire engines with. He should only be allowed to paint niggers . . ."

"Someone's coming," I howled, pointing toward the door. "Please, Tolitha. Please get out of the coffin."

"You're not a bit attractive when you're hysterical, Tom."

"You shouldn't use the word *nigger*, Tolitha," Savannah scolded. "It's not kind."

"You're right, princess. I won't do it again."

"Someone is coming, Tolitha," Luke said, whispering into Tolitha's ear. "Please get out."

"Hee hee hee," my grandmother giggled. "This'll be great. A trial run."

Ruby Blankenship swept into the room, regal and inquisitive, her gray hair brushed severely back on her head, her eyes set like raisins in the sagging pastry of her flesh. She was a huge, grandly proportioned woman who struck immediate terror in the hearts of children. In Colleton she was thought of as "a presence," and she stood in the doorway eyeing us with that peculiar overpowering intensity that older people who loathe children have developed to the point of art. Part of her fame in town was her insatiable curiosity about the health of her fellow citizens. She was a ubiquitous denizen of both the hospital and the funeral home. She had to be physically restrained at fires. She had a police radio in both her home and her car and could be found probing the wreckage at even the most grisly of accidents.

"What are you Wingo children doing here?" she demanded, sweeping into the room. "Nothing has happened in your family for years."

Before we could answer, she spotted Tolitha lying peacefully with her hands folded across her stomach.

"It must have been sudden. I haven't heard a word about it," Mrs. Blankenship said.

Ignoring us, she briskly crossed the room and stood beside the casket, scrutinizing my grandmother.

"Look at that stupid grin poor Ogletree put on her face," she said, motioning to Luke with a bony, discolored index finger. "This whole town goes down grinning. He did a good job otherwise. Don't she look natural, kids? She almost looks alive."

"Yes, ma'am," Luke said.

"What did she die of?"

"I'm not rightly sure, ma'am," Luke answered, and there was real misery in his voice as he looked to us for assistance. Savannah and I both shook our heads, indicating that we were not touching this one. Savannah walked to the window and looked out toward the river. Her shoulders were shaking and she was approaching hysteria. I was far too mortified to appreciate the hilariousness of the situation.

"What do you mean you don't know?" Mrs. Blankenship demanded. "Was it her heart? Or some kind of cancer she picked up in Africa? Or her liver. I bet it was her liver. She was a very heavy drinker. I bet none of you know that. She left your grandfather in the middle of the Depression. I remember the very day she took off. I took a casserole over to your granddaddy's house. I reckon she's got some explaining to do to God Almighty. When's the funeral?"

"I don't rightly know, ma'am," Luke said.

"You don't know when your own grandmother's being buried?" Mrs. Blankenship asked.

"No, ma'am," Luke said.

"When did it happen?"

"Please, ma'am, I'm too upset to talk about it," Luke said, suddenly putting his hands over his face and his shoulders, which were shaking with suppressed laughter.

"Don't be upset, young man," Mrs. Blankenship said kindly. "Death is natural and the black horseman is going to come for all of us one day to ride us back up to the Judgment seat. The best thing we can do is be ready when the summons comes. I know you're upset because you probably think your grandmother's smoking in hell this very second. But that was her choice. She chose to live a life of sin and this can be an example to all of us to try to live better lives here on earth. Here's a piece of Juicy Fruit for all of you," she said, removing an open package of gum from her pocketbook and expertly sliding out three yellow-wrapped pieces.

"Chewing gum helps you not to cry and it freshens your breath. I've noticed today that young children have hideous breath. Do you know why? Because their mothers don't teach them to brush their tongues. I know, you think I'm crazy. But my mother taught me it was necessary to brush my tongue as strenuously as I brushed my teeth."

As she handed a stick of gum to Luke, my grandmother stopped her by reaching out and grabbing hold of her wrist. Tolitha, sitting erect out of the casket, then took the piece of gum, unwrapped it, put it in her mouth, and lay back down in her casket, slowly chewing the gum.

There was a moment of absolute silence in that room before Ruby Blankenship screamed and bolted for the door. We heard her footsteps taking the stairs three at a time.

Tolitha hopped nimbly out of the casket, vaulting over the sides with two hands. She slipped her shoes back on her feet and with a demonic smile, she whispered, "I know the back way out."

Downstairs, Mrs. Blankenship was hysterical and we could hear her trying to explain to Winthrop Ogletree what she had just witnessed, but she was too unnerved to weave together a coherent narrative. We followed our grandmother down a narrow set of back stairs and through the small, bricked-in garden at the back of the mortuary. When we were safely out of view, the four of us threw ourselves down onto a patch of grass and screamed with laughter until our stomachs ached. Tolitha laughed with her feet straight up in the air and her underpants showing. Savannah and I rolled in each other's arms, trying to stifle our laughter by pressing our mouths against each other's shoulders. Only Luke's laugh was soundless, but he shook like a wet puppy on the ground.

But it was Tolitha's laugh that overwhelmed the street. She had a head-turning, musical laugh like a bell coming apart in her throat. Her laughter was a titanic, passionate thing that seemed to pass up like a wave from her toes to her mouth.

Between paroxysms we heard her beg, "Please stop me from laughing. Please stop me."

When I could answer her finally, I said, "Why, Tolitha?"

She laughed some more, helpless, undone, then said, gasping, "I always pee in my pants when I laugh this hard."

This was enough to stem my laughter but it made Luke and Savannah laugh all the harder.

"Please, Tolitha. Don't pee in your pants. You're my grandmother," I said, but the dignity and quality of pleading in my voice set her off again. Her thin legs danced above her head like a wounded insect. Her little white underpants shone in the sunlight.

"Put your legs down, Tolitha. I can see your thingama-jig," I begged.

"I'm going to pee. I'm going to pee. Oh, God, I can't help it," Tolitha screamed ecstatically as she rose to her feet, still laughing.

She ran behind an azalea bush, pulled off her panties,

and laughed uncontrollably with tears streaming down her face as she urinated loudly on the azalea.

"Oh, Lord," I cried, "our grandma's watering the plants in the middle of town."

"Hush, boy," she said when she regained control of her breath. "You hush and hand me back my step-ins."

She put her underpants back on, then stepped out from behind the azalea bush, her rapturous femininity and regal mien restored again. From the mortuary, we could still hear Ruby Blankenship's screams as they boomed through those vast Victorian hallways.

Then we regrouped and arm in arm we made our way back down the Street of Tides, letting Mr. Fruit signal us across the street once more.

9

In springtime my mother would wear gardenias in her hair. When she came into our room to kiss us good night, a flower would blaze like a piece of white jewelry stolen from a king's greenhouse. When the gardenias had exhausted themselves on the bush and the bruised flowers lay on the ground, haunting the air with their sweet decay, we knew the roses would not be far behind. We could annotate the spring and summer days by noticing the movable garden set daily in our mother's hair. To see a woman lift her arms and place a flower in her curls is still an act of indescribable delicacy and beauty to me. In that sensual gesture, I have placed all the sadness and pity of lost mothers. And it was from this innocent and charming habit that I learned my first unforgettable lesson about the disfiguring cruelty of class in my own southern town. There would be many more, but none of them hurt as much as the first one; none of them do I remember with such authentic clarity.

My mother always wore her gardenias when she shopped in Colleton. Though she seldom bought much, she loved the rituals and courtesies of small-town shopping, the pleasantries exchanged over counters, the cheerful gossip of shopkeepers, and all the streets alive with the commerce of neighbors. She dressed carefully on those days when she went downtown. Walking down the Street of Tides, Lila Wingo was the prettiest woman in Colleton and she knew it. It was a joy to watch her walk, to see the eyes of men attendant and respectful as she approached. The eyes of women registered something else when my mother passed. I watched the women of Colleton withhold approval as my mother made her way past storefronts, pausing briefly to admire her reflection in the window and to note the stir she made in her lovely passage. She moved with a flawless coherence of instinct but she moved with beauty alone. With a gardenia in her hair and her makeup artfully applied, she entered Sarah Poston's dress shop in May of 1955. She said "Good morning" to Isabel Newbury and Tina Blanchard, who were looking at dresses for the annual spring ball of the Colleton League. Mrs. Newbury and Mrs. Blanchard returned her greeting politely. My mother took a dress she could not afford from the rack and went to the dressing room in the back of the store to try it on. Luke and I were looking at fishing rods in Fordham's Hardware. As she stood in the dressing room, she heard Isabel Newbury say to her friend, "I shouldn't be surprised if Lila attended galas with a rose hanging out of her mouth, snapping her fingers like a flamenco dancer. Her instinct for acts of questionable taste is unerring. I'd like to pull those flowers out of her hair and teach her how to do her nails."

Savannah was in the booth with my mother when those words were spoken. Isabel Newbury had not seen them walk back to the dressing room. My mother smiled and put her fingers to her lips. Then she turned back to look at herself in the mirror. She reached up and took the gardenia from her hair and tossed it into the wastepaper basket. Then she studied her nails. They stayed in that dressing room for an hour as my mother pretended to be making up her mind about buying that dress she could never afford. And from that day on we never saw her adorn her glorious hair with a single blossom, nor was she ever in our long childhood invited to a single gala. I missed those gardenias and those times she would pass me in the house and I would catch the sweet-smelling passage of her, that irresistible tunic of perfume she carried with her, attractive to bees and worshipful sons. I cannot smell a gardenia today without thinking of my mother the way I did when I was a boy, and I cannot think of a woman's fingernails without hating Isabel Newbury for stealing the flowers from my mother's hair.

There are two kinds of Wingos: There is the forgiving Wingo, exemplified by my grandfather, who spent his life absolving his neighbors of all sins and trespasses against him. And there is the other kind of Wingo, who holds onto a grudge for a century or more. This portion of the family, by far the majority, had a heroic and merciless racial memory of all hurt and injustice. To cross these Wingos one year would ensure drawing the attention of an avenging Wingo generations later. These Wingos passed their grievances through their children and these feuds and germinating vendettas entered our bloodstreams like bruised heirlooms. I hold membership in the ranks of the second kind of Wingo.

Behind the wheel of his shrimp boat my father would instruct us in this part of our legacy. He would say, "If you can't beat up an enemy at school, wait twenty years and beat up his wife and kid."

"Always take the high road, huh, Dad?" Savannah would answer, repeating one of my mother's oft-quoted clichés.

"People got to get the picture, Savannah," he answered. "If they don't get the picture, then sometimes you got to paint roses on the end of their noses."

"Mama doesn't allow us to fight," I said.

"Ha," my father roared. "Your mother! That broad is the real killer in the family. She'll cut your heart out and eat it before your eyes if you're not careful."

He said it with total admiration.

* * *

It was a year after that fateful shopping expedition that the subject of gardenias came up again. I was walking from the school cafeteria to my locker when I saw Todd Newbury and three of his friends pointing at my feet. Todd was the only child of Isabel and Reese Newbury and he moved in that self-conscious manner so common among only children. Everything about him seemed overindulged and fussed over. He stood in the middle of a squirrelly though articulate group of boys. Dicky Dickson and Farley Bledsoe were the sons of bankers, both employed by Reese Newbury. Marvin Grant was the son of the lawyer who represented the bank. I had known them my whole life.

"Nice shoes, Wingo," Todd said as I walked by them, and the others laughed.

I looked down and saw the same tennis shoes I had put on in the morning. They were neither new nor old; they were simply broken in well.

"Glad you like 'em, Todd," I said, and the other three boys laughed even harder.

"It looks like you stole 'em off a dead nigger's feet," said Todd. "I can smell 'em from here. Don't you have a pair of loafers?"

"Yeah," I answered, "but they're at home."

"You saving 'em for spring plowing?" he asked me. "Admit it. You've never had a pair of loafers in your life."

"My daddy says your family doesn't have enough money to buy a hambone to make shit soup out of," Farley Bledsoe said. "So how are they going to afford a pair of Bass Weejuns, Wingo?"

"They're at home, Farley," I answered. "I'm not allowed to wear them at school."

"You're a liar, Wingo," Todd said. "I've never known a river rat who wasn't a complete liar in my whole life. I heard my mama say the other day that a Wingo was the lowest form of white man on the face of this earth, and I tend to agree with my mama."

He took a five-dollar bill out of his wallet and threw it on the floor in front of me.

"Here, Wingo. This won't buy you a new pair of loafers, but you already got a pair at home, don't you, liar? Just get a new pair of sneakers so I don't have to go around smelling your stinking feet."

I knelt down and picked up the five-dollar bill and held it out to Todd Newbury, saying, "No thanks, Todd. Just put this back in your billfold. I don't need your money."

"I'm just trying to be a good Christian, Wingo. I just want to help clothe the poor."

"Please put it back, Todd. Put it in your wallet. I'm asking you nicely."

"Not after you touched it, river shit. It's got your germs on it now," Todd said, his bravado matched by the laughter of his pals.

"If you don't put it back in your wallet, Todd, I'm going to make you eat it," I said, and by the reaction of Todd Newbury I knew for the first time in my life that I was big.

"You can't lick four of us, Wingo," Todd said confidently.

"Yes, I can," I disagreed.

I hit Todd, silenced him with three strong blows to the face, each one of them drawing blood. He slid down a wall and sat crying, looking at his friends with a wounded disbelief.

"Get him. He hurt me," he cried out, but the other three boys moved away from us.

"Eat the money, Todd," I said, "or I'll hit you again."

"You can't make me, river shit," he shouted, and I hit him again. He was swallowing the money when a teacher grabbed me from behind and escorted me to the principal's office.

There was pandemonium loose in the hallways as the news of the fight spread through the student body. Todd's blood stained my white T-shirt and I stood facing the principal, Mr. Carlton Roe, with the proof of my guilt embossed on my chest.

Mr. Roe was a lean blond man who had been a college athlete. He was normally good-humored but had a volatile temper when aroused. He was one of those rare educators whose whole life revolved around his school, and he did not tolerate fisticuffs in the hallway. I had never been in trouble with the principal in my life.

"Okay, Tom," he said easily when the teacher had gone. "Tell me what happened."

"Todd said something about my shoes," I said, my eyes resting on the floor.

"So you beat him up."

"No, sir. He called my family river shit. He gave me five bucks and told me to go buy a new pair of shoes."

"Then you hit him."

"Yes, sir. Then I hit him."

There was a noise by the doorway and Todd Newbury stormed into the room, holding a bloody handkerchief to his lip.

"You better whip him good, Mr. Roe. I mean whip him within an inch of his life. I just called my daddy and he's thinking of calling the cops."

"What happened, Todd?" Mr. Roe asked. "And I don't remember inviting you into my office."

"I was standing by my locker, minding my own business, when this kid jumped me from behind. I got three witnesses who'll back me up."

"What did you say to Tom?" Mr. Roe asked, his brown eyes expressionless.

"I didn't say one word to him. Why would I talk to him? I hope you like it in reform school, Wingo."

The phone in the office rang and Mr. Roe lifted the receiver, keeping his eyes on Todd. It was the superintendent of schools calling, and I heard Mr. Roe say, "Yes, Mr. Aimar, I'm aware of the situation. I have both boys in my office right now. No. If Mr. Newbury wishes to see me, he can come to my office. This is school business and there's no need for me to go to his office to talk about this. Yes, sir. I'll handle it. Thanks for calling."

"You'll learn not to mess with a Newbury," Todd said to me. "I'll guarantee you that."

"Shut up, Todd," Mr. Roe said.

"You better not talk to me like that, Mr. Roe. My father won't like it one little bit."

"I told you to shut up, Todd," he repeated. "Now you run along to your next class and I'll take care of Mr. Wingo."

"Are you going to paddle him good?" Todd asked, pressing his handkerchief to his mouth.

"Yes, I'm going to paddle him good," Mr. Roe said, lifting a wooden paddle from the top of his desk. Todd smiled at me and left the room.

Mr. Roe walked over to me, brandishing the paddle. He stood me up and made me lean down and grab my ankles with my hands. He drew back on the paddle like he was going to break me in half. Then he tapped me lightly, lovingly, on the behind, as gently as a bishop slapping the cheeks of a confirmed child.

"If you ever get into a fight in my school again, Tom, I'm going to take all the skin off your ass, and that's a promise. And if you ever fight Todd Newbury again and don't do a better job of shutting his mouth, I'm going to whip you to within an inch of your life. Do you understand me?"

"Yes, sir," I said.

"Now, I'm going to hit the paddle on this geography book. Every time I do, you give out a yelp. Make it convincing. Because I'm going to tell Reese Newbury that I tore your butt up."

He struck the book hard with his paddle and I yelled. It was in Mr. Roe's office that day that I decided to become a schoolteacher.

My mother was waiting for me when I got home from school that day. I had seen her mad before, but I had never seen her so completely out of control. She began slapping my face as soon as I entered the back door. Luke and Savannah were both trying to pull her off me.

"You want to fight someone, you little low-class bastard," she screamed, striking me again and again as I retreated to a neutral corner between the stove and refrigerator, "then you can fight with me. If you want to be like all the rest of them, then I'll treat you like all the rest of them. Shame me and your family, will you? Act like trash when I've taught you better?"

"I'm sorry, Mama," I cried, covering my face with my arms.

"Get off him," Savannah yelled, trying to pin my mother's arms. "He already got a whipping from the principal."

"Not like the one he's gonna get from me."

"Stop it, Mama," Luke demanded. "You stop it right now. He was right to punch that Newbury boy."

"What will people think if I let my children grow up to be ruffians? Nice children will never bother with you again."

"Newbury insulted our family, Mama," Luke explained. "That's why Tom hit him. I'd have hit him too."

"What did he say about our family?" my mother said, poising her hand in mid swing.

"He called us low class," I said, lowering my guard.

She slapped me hard across the face and I put up my guard again.

"And then you proved him right, you stupid cracker. My poor stupid, low-rent son. Ignoring him would have been the best thing to do. It would have proven you the better man . . . the better trained and better raised. You'd have been the perfect gentleman I've tried to make out of you."

"Oh, Mother," Savannah said, "you sound like the president of the Daughters of the Confederacy again."

"I'm the one who has to walk the streets of this town trying to hold my head up proud. Now everyone will know I've raised ruffians instead of decent young men."

"Do you want that snotty little Newbury running down your family?" asked Savannah.

"People have a right to their opinions," my mother said, crying out of frustration. "I believe in the Fourth Amendment or whatever that amendment is. It's a guaranteed right of all Americans and what he thinks should not concern us at all. We should walk tall and show them we're too fine and proud to care about their opinions."

"I care about their opinions," I said.

She slapped me again and screamed, "Then you better care about my opinion a lot more because I'm going to teach you how to act in this world or I'm going to half kill you trying. I won't have you acting like your father. I won't have it, do you hear?"

"You're acting like our father," Savannah said, and the house grew deadly still as my mother turned to face her only daughter.

"I'm acting in the only way I know how to act, Savannah. I'm hitting Tom because I know what my son is in danger of becoming. I know the danger for all of you. If I don't train you well, if I don't drive you, push you to the absolute limits, then this stinking mean town and this stinking mean world will eat you alive. Don't you think I've learned from our own failures? Look at me. What am I? Nothing. Nothing at all. A shrimper's wife without a dime, living in a tiny house on an island. Don't you think I know what they think about me and how they look at me? But I will not let them win."

"You care too much, Mama," Savannah said. "You're trying too hard to be something you're not."

"I forbid you to solve your problems with your fists. That's your father's influence."

"Tom was just letting everyone know a simple fact, Mama," Luke said. "It's an easy thing to make fun of a Wingo, but it ain't such a smart thing. It's okay for people to think all Wingos are trashy, but it's not such a good thing to air those opinions."

"Fighting just proves their point. Gentlemen don't fight."

"Tom was defending *your* honor, Mama. He knows the way people think about us is important to you. Dad doesn't care. Neither do we," Luke explained.

"I care," I said.

"If you care," my mother said, turning to face me again, "then you'll go with me to the Newbury house and apologize to Todd man to man. And apologize to his mother. She called me today and said the most horrendous things about us."

"So that's why you're so mad," Savannah said. "That's why you tried to beat Tom to death. Because of Isabel Newbury."

"I won't apologize to him, Mama," I said. "There's nothing you can do to make me apologize to that jerk, nothing in the whole world."

The Newbury house was set beneath an enfolding grove of water oaks on a small knoll along the Street of Tides. It was centered among a distinguished group of eleven pristine mansions that had housed the plantation aristocracy before the War Between the States ended forever the system which sustained that aristocracy. Before the war, a secret parliament of secessionists had met in the house to discuss the creation of the Confederacy. Isabel Newbury's great-grandfather, Robert Letellier, had presided over that meeting and had later perished in an artillery exchange during the Battle of Tulafinny. During the Civil War, Colleton fell into Union hands after the naval engagement of Port Royal Sound, and the Union army had requisitioned the house

for a hospital. Wounded soldiers had carved their names
on the marble mantelpieces and wooden floors as they waited
their turns for amputations. The house owed its remarka-
bility to that tormented, still visible roll of injured men, the
graffiti of unanesthetized soldiers awaiting their moment
beneath the knives of surgeons in a strange, inhospitable
land. Pain and history had coalesced behind the fanlit doorway of the Newbury house, and it was this litany of anonymous men desecrating the grain of both marble and
woodwork which imparted a sense of distinction and immortality to the house where Todd Newbury spent his
childhood.

As we passed through the front yard and approached
the front door, my mother gave me final, whispered instructions in the gentle art of groveling before a lady.

"You just tell her how sorry you are and how you'd do
anything if it never had happened in the first place. You
tell her that you couldn't even sleep last night you felt so
bad about what you did."

"I slept like a baby," I said. "I never thought about it
once."

"Hush now. I'm telling you what to say. So you just look
and listen. If you're real nice she might let you see those
poor Yankee boys' names carved all over her fireplace. That's
what happens when you let Yankee boys into a fine home.
They just carved it up because they weren't brought up
right. You'd never hear of a southern boy doing that."

We walked up the front steps of the house and my mother
tapped the gleaming brass marker against the oaken door.
It sounded like an anchor drumming against a submerged
hull. I stood in the sunlight on the verandah, clearing my
throat, fidgeting with my belt, and shifting my weight from
foot to foot. I had been more uncomfortable in my life, I
was sure, but I could not have told you when. I heard the
light footsteps approaching the door. Isabel Newbury stood
before us in the doorway.

Isabel Newbury had the most soul-chilling presence I
have ever encountered. Her lips were thin and colorless
and her mouth registered a most articulate narrative of unspoken disapproval. Her nose, sharp and well made, was
her one perfectly wrought feature, and it twitched prettily
as she stood in the gloom of her house as though the smell

of me was repugnant to her. Her hair was blonde, but with help.

But it was the cold aquamarine glitter of her eyes enclosed in a harsh fretwork of lines that arrowed out toward her temples which drew my most breathless attention; they were like the rays of the sun in a child's drawing. There were three deep wrinkles in her forehead, evenly spaced, which moved in harmony when she frowned. Every wound and grievance of her life had signed its name on her face, offered proof of its passage like those Yankee soldiers afraid to surrender to surgeons. She was a year younger than my mother and it was the first time I ever realized that human beings age differently. My mother's generous beauty deepened every year and I had thought this true for all women. Standing there, mute and ashamed, I knew instinctively and for all time why Isabel Newbury disliked my mother, and it had nothing at all to do with her being a Wingo. Time had marked her early and cruelly with all the bend sinisters and cinquefoils of its inerasable heraldry. There was an aura of sickliness about her, the kind of decay that begins in the heart and works its way out to the eyes.

"Yes?" she said at last.

"My son has something to tell you, Isabel," my mother said. Her voice was hopeful and repentant, as though it were she who had hurt Todd Newbury.

"Yes, ma'am, Mrs. Newbury," I said. "I surely am sorry about what happened yesterday and I want to apologize to Todd and to you and Mr. Newbury. The whole thing was my fault and I take full responsibility for whatever happened."

"He's been worried sick about it, Isabel," my mother said. "That I can vouch for. He didn't get a moment's rest last night. In fact, he woke me up in the middle of the night to tell me he was going to come over here today and say how sorry he was for everything."

"How moving," the woman answered.

"Is Todd here, Mrs. Newbury? I'd like to speak to him if I could," I said.

"I'm not sure he wants to speak to you. Wait here, please. I'll ask him."

She closed the door and my mother and I stood on the verandah facing each other nervously.

"Isn't this a lovely view," my mother said finally, walking over to one of the banisters and looking at the bay through palmetto fronds. "I've always dreamed of living in one of these houses. When your daddy first brought me to Colleton he promised he'd buy me one of these mansions when he hit it big." Then she paused and said, "There aren't enough shrimp in this part of the world to buy one of these houses."

"Nice of her to ask us in, Mom," I said furiously.

"Oh, that. That's nothing. We probably surprised her so that she forgot her manners momentarily."

"She did it on purpose."

"Wouldn't you like to sit out here at night in one of these wicker chairs, drink iced tea, and wave at the whole town passing by?"

"I want to go home," I said.

"Not until you apologize to Todd. I'm still so ashamed of you for doing what you did."

The door opened again and Mrs. Newbury, severe and spectral in the shadows, stepped forth into the light. My mother and I turned to face her.

"My son has nothing to say to you, boy," she said, and the way she said "boy" was not endearing. "He wants you to get off our property."

"If Tom could just see your son, Isabel. Just for a sec. I'm sure they could part as friends."

"Friends! I wouldn't allow Todd to make friends with a boy like this."

"But Isabel," my mother continued, "you and I are friends. We've known each other for such a long time. Why, I was just telling Henry the other day about something I heard you say at a PTA meeting and we both laughed so about it."

"We know each other, Lila. This is a small town. I know everyone but not everyone is my friend. I do want to tell you that if this bully ever touches my Todd again I'm going to call the law. Good day. You do know the way out, don't you?"

"Yes," I heard my mother say, and I heard her voice stiffen. "We know our way out since we were never invited in. Goodbye, Isabel, and thank you for your time."

I followed Mom off the porch and down the stairs and could hear her muttering unintelligible oaths to herself. She walked at a brisk pace down the sidewalk between two islands of immaculately trimmed caterpillar grass. She was a natural ambler and any increase in velocity was an accurate gauge of her displeasure. When she took a left toward town, she almost knocked Reese Newbury into the street.

"Whoa, Lila," he said, "I didn't hear the fire bell."

"Oh, hello, Reese," she said, flustered.

"What brings you to these parts?" he asked, his mood darkening as he spotted me coming up behind my mother.

"Our boys got into a little tiff yesterday, Reese. You probably heard about it."

"Yes, I certainly did," Mr. Newbury said, studying me grimly.

"Well, I brought Tom here to apologize. He wanted to and I thought your son deserved an apology."

"That's mighty nice of you, Lila," he said, his eyes softening as they returned to my mother. But I had caught the hint of fury in their steely glint. "Boys get into these kinds of scrapes sometimes. That's what makes them worth a damn. It makes them boys."

"I don't tolerate that kind of behavior, Reese. I simply won't have it in my sons. I whaled the tar out of Tom last night when the principal called."

He looked at me again, a long appraising look as though he were seeing me for the first time in his life, as though I suddenly had become worthy enough to merit his attention.

"It takes a big man to apologize, son," he said. "I'm sure no good at it myself."

"Neither is your son," I said.

"What do you mean?"

"He wouldn't come down to accept my apology," I said. "He told us to get off your property."

"Follow me, please," he said, and he turned down his walk and skipped up his stairs, taking them two at a time.

He disappeared into the house without waiting for us. We hesitated on the landing, then took a few tentative steps into the vestibule, where we awaited our summons. There was an Oriental rug running the length of the foyer to the curved mahogany stairway in the back of the house.

My mother pointed to it and said, "Oriental. It comes from the Orient."

Motioning to a chandelier overhead, she whispered, "English. Made in England. I remember it from the Spring Tour."

"Why isn't our house on the Spring Tour," I whispered back, trying to make a joke.

"Because we live in a dump," my mother said quietly.

"Why are we whispering?"

"Because when you're guests in Reese Newbury's house, it's correct behavior to be reserved."

"Is that what we are? Guests in his house?"

"Of course. How gracious of him to invite us."

We heard the back door slam and saw Mr. Newbury enter the foyer from the rear of the house.

"Isabel had to go out to do some shopping, Lila. She said to make yourself at home. Why don't you have a little nip of something from the bar while I take young Tom up here to see my son."

He led my mother by the arm through the living room and into a sumptuous paneled den where the leather chairs gleamed and made the room smell like a tannery.

"What'll it be, Lila?" he said, smiling at my mother. "What will be your pleasure, ma'am?"

"I think a little wine would do just fine, Reese. What a lovely room."

He poured my mother a glass of wine and led her to a seat by the fireplace.

"Please make yourself comfortable and we'll be back in a jiffy," Mr. Newbury said, his voice thick enough to be squeezed from a tube. "We menfolk are gonna have a little powwow in my study upstairs."

"I can't tell you how much I appreciate this, Reese," my mother said. "It's so kind of you to take an interest."

"I like a boy with spunk. I've been known to have a little spunk too, haven't I?" he said, laughing. "Come along, Tom."

I followed him up the stairs and saw the white fleshy legs above his socks. He was amply but softly built.

We came to his study, which was lined with leather volumes along one wall. He sat me in a chair facing his desk and went to get his son. I studied the titles of the books:

THE PRINCE OF TIDES

The Works of Thackeray, The Works of Dickens, The Works of Charles Lamb and *Shakespeare.* I did not look up when Todd came into the room with his father. Mr. Newbury sat Todd in the chair next to mine, then walked around the desk and took a seat in his own oversized chair. He lifted a cigar out of a humidor and circumcised one end of it with his teeth, then lit it with a gold lighter he took from his coat pocket.

"Now you've got something to say to my son, I believe," he said to me.

When I looked at Todd I was shocked by the puffiness of his face. His lips were swollen and there was an ugly bruise under his right eye, and I understood why he had not wanted to face me.

"Todd," I said, "I wanted to come by to apologize. I'm awfully sorry for what I did and it'll never happen again. I was hoping we could shake hands and be friends."

"I wouldn't shake your hand for anything," Todd said, staring at his father.

"Why did you hit my son, Wingo?" Mr. Newbury said, blowing a blue plume of smoke toward me.

Todd jumped in and said, "He and his brother ambushed me in the schoolyard, Dad. I was just walking by minding my own business when his brother jumped me from behind and this one started hitting me in the face."

"Why didn't your brother come to apologize too?" Mr. Newbury asked. "I never liked two against one."

"Why do you want to lie about it, Todd?" I said incredulously. "You know Luke wasn't anywhere near when all that happened. Besides, Luke wouldn't have needed me. He could eat you alive, boy, and you know it."

"Are you telling me the truth, son?" Mr. Newbury asked Todd.

"If you want to believe that piece of trash instead of me, Dad, just go ahead. Be my guest. See if I care."

"He called my family trash yesterday, Mr. Newbury," I said, looking directly at the man.

"Did you say something about his family?"

Todd looked wildly about the room, then said, "I simply told him the facts of life. I was kidding around with him."

"Did you call his family trash?"

"I said something like that. I don't remember exactly."

Turning his inquisitional gaze on me, Mr. Newbury continued, "And you took offense and with your brother's help beat up my son."

"My brother had nothing to do with it."

"Wingo, you're such a goddamn liar," Todd said, rising out of his chair.

"Mr. Newbury," I said, appealing to his father, "I don't need my brother's help to fight Todd. He's weak as water."

He spoke to Todd while staring at me. "Why did you call his family trash, son?"

"Because they are trash. Wingos have always been like white niggers in this town," Todd said, screaming at me.

"That's why your son gets hit, Mr. Newbury," I said angrily. "He doesn't know how to keep his mouth shut."

"He doesn't have to keep his mouth shut here, Tom," Mr. Newbury said. "This is his house."

"And I don't like you stinking up my house," Todd said.

"Keep your voice down, son. Mrs. Wingo is downstairs," Mr. Newbury cautioned his son. Then he said to me, "What do you think about your family, Tom? I'm interested. Very interested indeed."

"I'm proud of my family."

"But why?" he said. "What are you proud of? Your mother's a fine woman. A little rough around the edges maybe, but she tries real hard. But what else? Your grandfather is soft in the head. Your grandma could be called a whore except she managed to coax a couple of drifters to the altar. Your daddy's been a failure at every single thing he's tried. I even knew your great-granddaddy and he was nothing but a harmless drunk who used to beat his wife until she was half dead. I don't see why you should get so mad at Todd for just speaking the truth. Why don't you just go ahead and admit that your family's shit? It takes a real man to face up to reality. A real man to face facts."

I looked at him in an absolute stunned silence and he smiled at me behind his cigar.

"Even if you can't admit it, Tom, I want you to know something. If you ever touch my son again, I mean lay a single finger on him, you're going to be crabmeat somewhere in the river. My wife wanted to call the sheriff on you but that's not the way I like to operate. I do things my own way. In my own time. I'll get you back and you won't ever know it's me that got you. Except you will. You'll be smart enough to figure it out. Because I want you to learn something from this experience. A Wingo doesn't dare touch a Newbury. It's law in this town. You didn't know it before, but you know it now. Do you understand me, Tom?"

"Yes, sir," I said.

"That's good, son. Now, Todd, I want you to shake hands with Tom."

"I don't want to shake hands with him."

"Get up, boy. I told you to shake hands with him," his father ordered. "But before you shake hands I want you to slap his face and slap it hard."

Todd looked at his father in absolute disbelief and I saw he was about to cry. There were two boys in that room about to cry.

"I can't do that, Daddy. He'll get me at school."

"He'll never touch you again. I promise you that."

"I can't, Daddy. Please. I just can't hit someone in the face."

"You just slap him, Todd. Look in the mirror and see what he did to you. Get mad, son. Look how he humiliated you. Then go slap his ugly face. A Newbury doesn't let somebody like that get away with it. He's sitting there, son, and he wants you to hit him. He came here today so you could even things up between you. He's crawling because he knows it isn't smart to have the Newburys hating him."

"I'm not going to. I'm not going to do it, Daddy. Why do you always have to make things so much worse? Why do you have to always do it?"

Mr. Newbury rose from his chair and put out his cigar in an ashtray. He walked around his desk past his son and stood facing me. I dropped my head and concentrated on watching the pattern in the rug.

"Look up, Tom," he said.

I looked up and he slapped me once, hard, across the face.

I began crying and I heard Todd crying, too. Then Mr. Newbury looked down and whispered to me; "Don't ever tell anyone I did that, Tom. I did it for your own good. If you ever tell a soul, I'll run your family clean out of this town. And please, son, don't ever be stupid enough to pick on a Newbury again. Now, you two boys shake hands and become friends. I really want you to be friends. Stay up here until you calm down. Then wash your face, Tom, and come downstairs. I'll be talking to your pretty mother."

Crying, Todd Newbury and I shook hands as his father left the room.

I knew I had to go down and face my mother's interrogation about the meeting. My humiliation was pure and complete, but I did not want her to share in it. In a primitive way, I thought I had discovered the secret of the way powerful men attain and uphold their status in the world. I walked to a bathroom off the study, dried my tears, and washed my face. I let the water run for a long time and carefully pissed all over the bathroom floor, thinking: Tom Wingo, unrepentantly low class to the bitter end. When I emerged, Todd was still weeping, his head thrown back against the leather chair, the tears streaming down his plump cheeks.

"Please don't tell anyone, Tom. I beg you, please don't tell anyone at school. They all hate me enough as it is."

"If you didn't act like a jerk, no one would hate you, Todd," I said.

"Yeah, they would. Because he's my father. Everyone hates him. Don't you see I couldn't stop him from doing that?"

"I know that. It wasn't your fault."

"He does things like that all the time. It's what I have to live with."

"Why did you tell him Luke helped me?"

"Because I had to. He could understand me getting beat up by two guys. But he would have made me fight you at school again if he knew it was just you. He's scary when he gets mad."

"So's my father."

"But your father doesn't hate you. My father's hated me since the day I was born."

"Why?"

"Because I'm not handsome. Because I'm not strong. Because I'm nothing like him."

"I'd be glad I was nothing like him."

"He's the most prominent man in South Carolina," Todd said defensively.

"So what? You yourself said no one likes him."

"He says you can control men if they fear you."

"Then he gets to sit all alone in this big house, slapping

kids who tangle with his kid. I'm real happy you're rich and powerful and come from an old family, Todd. But I wouldn't want to be you for nothing."

"I shouldn't have said that about your family, Tom."

"No," I agreed, "you shouldn't have."

"They're not all that trashy. There are dozens of trashier families in Colleton. Hundreds even."

"Thanks tons, fat shit," I said, angry again.

"I didn't mean it that way. It came out all wrong. I meant to say you can come over any time you want. I've got a stamp collection and a pool table. We could do things after school."

"I don't want to come to this house ever again."

"I could show you where the poor Yankees scratched out their names."

"I don't care if you could show me where General Sherman took a shit; I ain't hanging around this house."

"Maybe I could come out to your place sometime."

"You don't even know where I live."

"I do too. You live out on Melrose Island," he said. He rose and went to a huge map of the county, a navigational chart that enumerated the depths of all the rivers and creeks with small numbers.

I looked at the map and studied the outline of our island, an irregular diamond of green surrounded by a blue border of water.

"Why is there a red pin on our island?" I asked. The whole map was studded with an irregular phalanx of these pins.

"Oh, that. Dad places red pins on all the places he plans to buy. The green pins represent all the property he owns."

"He owns the whole damn county," I said. "Why does he want our land?"

"Land is his hobby. He says land is money."

"That's one piece of land he'll never own. I promise you that much."

"He'll get it if he wants it bad enough," Todd said simply. "He always does."

"Come out there if you want, Todd. I can't stop you."

"You don't really want me to, though, do you?"

"No, not really. I need to go get my mother now."

"Do you know what I can't figure out, Tom? I can't figure out why the kids at school like you so much better than they like me."

"That's an easy one, Todd. No secret to that. I'm a lot nicer guy than you are. I say hello to people without worrying about what their daddies do for a living. You've never been able to do that. You don't say hello to anybody."

"I don't feel comfortable saying hello to just anybody."

"That's fine. But then don't get upset when everyone thinks you're an asshole."

"I'll walk you downstairs."

My mother was sitting in the den, giggling at everything Mr. Newbury said. She was sitting with her legs crossed prettily, sipping a glass of wine. Mr. Newbury was convivial and charming as he punctuated his stories with solemn, precise gestures. While I waited for him to finish one of his stories, I took time to memorize his features. He belonged to the same blue-eyed stock of his wife, but his were flecked with green; they changed color or seemed to when they caught the sunlight pouring into the room from the back yard. His hands were small, pudgy, and uncalloused. All his movements were lethargic, as though he had a layer of silk insulating his central nervous system. His voice was deep and glutinous. Speaking, his words poured out of him in rotund, pontifical essays of self-praise. My mother, of course, was charmed down to her toes.

"And so I told the governor, Lila, I said, 'Fritz, you know there's no use talking about this over drinks. Come down to Colleton next week and we'll meet in my office and get this straightened out.' He was here on Monday morning with his hat in his hand. Now I have all the respect in the world for our governor—in fact, I was on his campaign committee—but my philosophy is that business is business."

"I couldn't agree with you more, Reese," my mother said enthusiastically. "I never thought that friendship should interfere with a business matter."

Mr. Newbury looked up and saw Todd and me standing in the doorway. He waved us into the room. Before he could speak, I heard my mother gasp when she saw Todd's face for the first time.

"Oh, Todd. Your face, darling," she said, coming out of her chair and touching his face solicitously. "Oh, I'm so sorry about all this. I hope Tom told you that I whipped him good last night. Oh, Todd, you poor darling."

"It's all right, Mrs. Wingo. I deserved it," Todd said, to my infinite relief.

"Did you boys have a good talk?" Mr. Newbury asked sternly.

"Yes, sir," I answered.

"If you ever have any problems, Lila," Mr. Newbury said, rising out of his chair and escorting us to the front door, "please don't hesitate to call on me. After all, that's what neighbors are for."

At the front door, Mr. Newbury put his arm around my shoulder and walked me down the steps. He squeezed my left shoulder very hard, a warning.

"It takes a real man to say he's sorry, Tom. I appreciate your coming over to clear the air. I won't say a word about it to anyone. And I know you won't, either. It was worth the whole day just to get to know you a little better. I've always taken an interest in the young folks. They're the future. Yep, the future of this whole town."

"Goodbye, Tom. I enjoyed the talk," Todd said, standing behind his father.

"Goodbye, Todd."

"Toodly-doo, Reese. Bye, Todd, honey," my mother said.

When we walked half a block down the street, my mother, tipsy from both the wine and her half-hour of being entertained in the Newbury house, said, "I've always said to everyone who'd listen, the most successful men are always the nicest men."

"Tom, why did you tell me that story?" Dr. Lowenstein asked. I had been talking for almost an hour in her office. "It doesn't seem to have anything to do with Savannah. It sheds a lot of light on why you became the man you did, but how does it fit in with her story? She wasn't even present when Mr. Newbury struck you."

"Savannah was the only one I told that story to. I didn't tell Dad or Luke because I thought they might have caught Newbury out on the street and broken his legs. So I told her that night and we sat up late trying to figure out what it all meant."

"But it did not affect her directly. I mean, she empathized with you, I'm sure. She felt the same hurt and humiliation, but it doesn't seem to have had any direct impact on her life."

"In a way that story is essential to her history, Doctor. You can't see it now, but I'm getting to it. I'm talking as fast as I can. I'm trying to eliminate the parts that only affect me, but all of it seems related now. Pieces are starting to fit together in my mind like they never did before."

"But you're not making it clear to me. You've got to tell me what the connections are as soon as you see them. I understand that your mother's paranoia about her social standing had a profound effect on Savannah. You've made that abundantly clear. But was Savannah ever connected to the Newburys in any way?"

"Did my mother ever write to you?"

"Yes, right after we first spoke on the phone."

"Do you have that letter?"

She went to a file cabinet by the desk and came back with a letter. I recognized my mother's handwriting on the envelope.

"Here it is. It was a very nice supportive letter."

"My mother writes wonderful letters. She's a good writer. Savannah's gift did not come out of a vacuum. Did you notice the return address?"

"It's from Charleston," she said, picking up the envelope.

"What else do you notice?"

"No!" she said, stunned.

"Yes," I said.

10

In Central Park, I watched a polar bear suffering in mute dignity on a sweltering day in late June. Behind me, the immense gathering of buildings along Central Park South cast mile-long shadows that eclipsed most sunlight from the zoo but did little to ease the bear's discomfort. A pigeon floating in the air currents between the Sherry-Netherland hotel and the zoo did not see the hawk flare its wings and plummet two hundred feet with its talons extended. The hawk broke the pigeon's back and small feathers fell on top of the baboon's cage. The pigeon, like me, probably thought that citizenship in New York City at least made you safe from hawks, but New York never forfeited its rights of surprise. When I walked through the zoo, I always expected to see extraordinary animals staring at me from the grim interiors of their cells—animals worthy of the city, unicorns sharpening their spiraled horns against weathered bars or dragons setting fire to pages from the *Daily News* as the sheets blew along the walkway. Instead, fallow deer shyly pawed the baked ground and ocelots scratched Manhattan fleas from their shining coats.

From the zoo, I walked straight across the park for my rendezvous with Susan Lowenstein's son. I kept looking up for another hawk, but only saw those ranks of great buildings huddled along the edges of the park all around me.

Bernard Woodruff stood waiting for me beneath a young oak tree near his parents' apartment on Central Park West. As I approached him I noticed that he had inherited his mother's vivid, pretty face except for a statelier, more prominent nose. He was taller than I had expected and his hands were long and graceful. In repose his fingers almost reached his knees. He had a magnificent crown of black hair that framed his thin face in a curled, abundant wreath. But his demeanor worried me immediately. His face was a cove of stifled insolence. I saw that flare of adolescent underlip, the insubordinate bravado and vulnerable sneer that young boys in their powerlessness sometimes assume will mask their own fear of exposure. Bernard faced me as a tough guy, Manhattan boy weathered in the war zones, street kid. Before we spoke, this old coach, veteran of a generation of boys, saw the nocturnal light moving beyond the horizons of his dark eyes and heard the distant thunder of his small but consequential war with the world.

"Hi, Bernard," I shouted to warn him of my approach. "I'm Tom Wingo."

He did not say a word but lifted his gaze and studied me with bored, suspicious eyes.

"Yeah, I thought it was you," he said when I neared him.

"How are you doing?" I said, extending my hand.

"I'm okay," he answered, staring out beyond the traffic. He ignored my hand.

"Looks like a nice day to toss a football around, doesn't it?" I asked.

"It's okay," he said in a hostile voice that told me Bernard was not going to make this initial encounter an easy one.

"Been waiting long here?"

"Long enough," he said to the traffic more than to me.

"I got lost," I admitted. "I always get lost in Central Park. It's always bigger than I remember it."

"No one asked you to come here," he said, glancing at me briefly.

"Wrong, tiger," I said, lowering my voice and tiring of his slouching insolence. "Your mother did."

"She's always making me do things I don't want to do."

"That right?" I said.

"Yeah," he answered. "That's right."

"You don't want me to coach you."

"Hey, you get the picture fast, don't you?" Bernard said. "Besides, I got a coach at school already."

"You play in any games last year?" I asked, and I could tell he heard the doubt in my voice.

"I was only a freshman."

"You play in any games last year?" I repeated the question.

"No. Where do you coach, anyway?"

"In South Carolina."

"Hey." He laughed. "Real big time."

"No, not big time, Bernard," I said, my voice nearly freezing in my throat. "But let me assure you of one thing. I've coached teams who could take any Phillips Exeter team in history and drive them into the Atlantic Ocean."

"How do you know?" he asked contemptuously.

"Because I don't coach little rich kids who get sent to boarding school because their parents can't stand to have them around the house."

"So what?" he said.

I could tell I had touched a sensitive area in his life. But I had no intention of letting up on Bernard. "And none of my kids play the violin, Bernard. They eat kids who play the violin."

"Yeah," he answered, "and I bet none of them are forced to play the violin, either."

"And I'm not going to force you to learn some football from me. I don't like wasting my time with snotty-nosed, wise-assed kids. I coach kids who like the game. I don't coach kids whose mothers make them."

"My mother didn't even know I played football last year."

"You didn't play football last year, Bernard," I said, amazed by the boy's refusal to make eye contact. "You already told me you didn't get into any of the games."

"You don't understand!" he whined. "I was behind the other guys. I'd never gone to a school that had a football team before."

"What position do you play?" I asked.

"Quarterback."

"I played quarterback," I answered.

"So what?" he said, his sneer disfiguring the entire right side of his face. "I came here to tell you I don't need you."

I lateralled him the football and he handled the ball nicely. I ran out ten yards and then said to him, "Throw me a pass." He threw a wobbling though accurate pass. He had a nice arc on the ball, a soft touch. I took the ball, and without saying a word, I turned and began walking out of Central Park. I knew his eyes were on me.

"Hey, where are you going?" he asked.

"Home," I said without looking back. I heard him jogging up behind me.

"Why?"

"Because you're not worth a shit, kid," I said meanly. "Go practice your violin and make your parents happy. Also, I can't stand your attitude. And if I can't stand it, how are you ever going to lead a team? How are you ever going to transform your whiny, self-pitying ass into a quarterback?"

"Look," he said, "that was the first pass I've thrown in six months."

My present mood did not include charity or forgiveness and I answered, "It looked like the first pass you ever threw in your life."

"Throw it back and I'll try it again," he said, and his voice changed for the first time and I stopped and faced him.

"First we talk."

"What do you want to talk about?" he asked.

"Your mouth, for one thing."

"What do you want me to do about it?"

"Shut it, kid," I said coldly. "Now, Bernard. I don't care if you like me or not, my friend. And I'm not sure whether I'm going to coach you or not. But when I talk to you I want you to look me straight in the eyes. That's it. It won't hurt a thing. The next time I put out my hand to shake and you pretend you don't see it, I'm going to break every bone in your hand. Then when you talk to me I want you to speak to me with respect and kindness. Now . . . I want you to tell me why you're pissed off at the world. I won't tell your mother a word of what you say. I promise you that. But you're a nasty son of a bitch and I'd like to help you figure out why."

He was breathing hard, trembling, unnerved.

"Go fuck yourself, buddy," he said in a voice that forecast tears.

"I already fucked myself when I agreed to have something to do with you."

"There's nothing wrong with me," he said, controlling his voice with difficulty.

"That's where you're wrong, Bernard," I said, going for the kill, hating myself as my voice grew colder and meaner. "You're one of the unhappiest kids I've ever met in my life. And there's something I know about you and I've only seen you for five minutes. You don't have a friend in the goddamn world, boy. Lonely up there at Phillips Exeter in the winter, is it, Bernard? Do they pick on you, Bernard? Do they tease you? I know they exclude you, but do they also make your life a living nightmare, Bernard? Do they slap you around, Bernard? You see, I know boys real well and I know how they treat misfits. What's the name of your friend, Bernard? Tell me his name."

He started crying, tried to hold it back but the tears flooded out of his eyes like the floodwater over a levee. His shoulders shook and he sobbed loudly, lifting his hands to his face. The tears streamed out between his fingers and fell on the grass.

Then he looked up and stared at his wet hands. "I'm crying," he said, surprised. "You made me cry."

"I bullied you, Bernard," I said. "I was hoping you would cry so I could see if there was something human down there."

"Is that how you coach?" he asked bitterly.

"With a kid like you," I said, "yeah. That's how I coach."

"I don't like it."

"I don't give a shit, kid."

"My mother said you were nice," said Bernard. "She lied."

"I'm real nice to nice people. I'm real nice to people who like me."

"I'm going to tell her what you said to me," he threatened. "How you treated me, everything."

"My knees are suddenly jelly, kid."

"She thinks adults should treat children as if they were adults."

"Is that right?"

"That's right. She's not going to like this one little bit, I can tell you that," Bernard said, still unable to control his breathing.

"Let's go see her, then," I said. "Right now, Bernard."

"She's working. She's seeing patients now."

"So what," I insisted. "We'll catch her during one of her ten-minute breaks. Then you can tell her everything I said. Then I'll explain why."

"She doesn't like to have her time wasted when she's working."

"Neither do I, kid. And you've just wasted a pile of it."

"You call this work?" he said, sneering again.

"I call this hard labor, Bernard," I said, my voice rising again. "Cruel and unusual punishment. Torture. I hate hanging around kids like you."

"Well, who's asking you to?" he said, offended.

"Your mother. So let's go to her office and get this settled."

"No. It'll just get me in trouble."

"No, Bernard," I said, unable to control the mockery. "She'll just talk to you as though you were an adult."

"Yeah, well, I'll tell my father and get both of you in trouble."

"You can't get me in trouble, Bernard."

"Oh, yeah?" he said, pointing his finger at me. "Do you know who my father is? Do you?"

"No. Who is he?"

"He's Herbert Woodruff."

"Same last name, huh?" I said, tiring of Bernard rapidly.

"Do you know who he is?" Bernard shouted at me. "He's one of the most famous violin players in the world."

"I've always been scared shitless of violin players," I said.

"He knows some really powerful people. Really powerful people, mister," Bernard said, and his voice was so unhinged and pathetic that I thought he would cry again.

"Is it hard, Bernard?" I said wearily. "Is it hard being an asshole? I've always wanted to ask that question every time I've met one, but I've never really gotten the chance."

He threw his hands up in the air in an odd, inappropriate gesture and said, "So that's what you think of me, huh? You don't know me. You can't know a person after talking to them for only fifteen minutes."

"Wrong again, Bernard. There are times when you can know all you ever want to know about a person in thirty seconds."

He turned as if to walk away from me, then stopped, and his breathing came hard again. "I'd rather you not talk to my mother," he said quietly.

"All right," I answered.

"You mean you won't?" he said, turning around to face me again.

"No. That's a reasonable request and you made it nicely. I like to reward nice behavior."

"What will you tell her when you see her?"

"That you're a prince of a guy who very naturally decided he wanted to work on his violin playing instead of being coached in football."

He diverted his eyes to the ground again and began kicking at the dirt with his gym shoe.

"I didn't play football last year."

"Your mama said your daddy spotted you in a team picture."

"I was the equipment manager. I went out for the team and didn't make it. The coach asked us to tackle people the first day. I never tackled anyone in my whole life. They all laughed at me."

"Do you remember who laughed at you?"

"Of course, but why?" he asked.

"Because, if you let me coach you, Bernard, we'll take the smiles off those boys' faces . . . I'll teach you to tackle so hard they'll think they were hit by a Buick when you take them down. But why did you tell your daddy you were on the team?"

"Because I wanted him to think I was on the team."

"Why, Bernard?"

"I don't know," Bernard said. "Because I knew he'd hate the thought of it. He hates sports. It makes him furious that I'm interested."

"You're not interested, Bernard. You've spent the afternoon proving that to me."

"You don't like me very much, do you?" he said in a half plea, half whine.

"Bernard," I said, "I don't like you at all. I don't like the way you treated me. I don't like your attitude. You're a mean, unhappy bastard and I don't know if football can help you or not. Because the only good thing about football, Bernard, the only good thing at all, is that it can be a lot of fun to play. That's it. Otherwise, it's a stupid, useless game. You don't look like you've ever had any fun in your whole life. But more important for me is that coaching you doesn't look like it would be any fun for me, Bernard. Because I like it. I take it seriously. Football is a joyous thing for me and I don't want you to ruin it for me."

"My father made me practice the violin two hours a day," he said strongly.

"Bernard, I'd much rather be able to play the violin than play football. I promise you that. If I could play the violin, I'd bring the birds out of the trees I'd play that son of a bitch so pretty."

"Do you play any instrument?" he asked.

"No. Do you know what I can do? I can still pass a football forty yards in the air. It makes me a real hit at dinner parties. Well, look, Bernard, I've got to be going. It was nice meeting you. I'm sorry we didn't hit it off better. I like your mother a lot. I won't tell her anything about what happened. That's a promise."

I walked away from this disconsolate, sullen kid and headed across the park toward Fifth Avenue. I walked for twenty yards, carrying the football in my right hand and loving the feel of it, the laces biting into the joints of my fingers. Bernard did not say goodbye, said nothing—until I heard him call out behind me.

"Coach Wingo."

I had not been called Coach for so long it both surprised me and moved me. When I turned I saw his hands half raised in a melancholy, supplicating gesture. His voice trembled, rose, and broke as he fought to get the words out, as he sought to connect.

"Teach me," he said, and the tears were coming again. "Teach me, please. I want them to stop laughing."

I turned and walked back to him, striding toward him as something new and unknown in Bernard Woodruff's life. I returned to him as his mentor, his coach.

"We'll make them bleed," I said to the boy. "First they'll laugh. Then they'll bleed. I promise you. Now you've got to promise me some things."

"What?" he asked suspiciously.

"You got to shut up, Bernard," I said. "Your mouth pisses me off."

"Yeah," he said, gasping. "Okay, okay."

" 'Yes, sir' is the correct way to answer me now, Bernard," I said. "There are certain courtesies and forms we are going to follow. When we meet here on this field, you may call me Coach or sir, whichever you prefer. You'll never be late under any circumstances. You'll do whatever I tell you to do and you'll do it with enthusiasm. I'm putting you on a weight program immediately. I'm going to run your ass off every day. I won't be interested in your home life, your music lessons, your sex life, your pimples, or anything else. I'm not going to become your buddy or try to impress you. I'm going to teach you how to look and act like a football player. I'm going to teach you how to block, tackle, punt, run, and pass, and I'm going to teach you well. You've got good size, real good size. I'm going to make you strong, Bernard. I'm going to make you tougher than you ever thought you could be. Because the guy you're going to be blocking and tackling is going to be me, Bernard."

"But you're a lot bigger than me."

"Shut up, Bernard," I said.

"Yes, sir," he answered.

"And, Bernard, after I run you till you drop, make you lift weights until you can't move, make you do push-ups until you're breathing pure grass, and make you tackle me until your arms cramp, something's gonna happen that's never happened in your shitty life."

"What's that, sir?" he said.

"You're gonna love my ass, Bernard," I said.

11

My mother never quite finished the task of creating herself; she was always a work in progress. She rarely told a story about her childhood that was not a lie and she practiced the study of her own history with the reckless, renegade eye of the fabulist. Never daunted by something as inconvenient as truth, she made her lies an essential part of her children's identities.

In a thousand days of my childhood, she offered a thousand different mothers for my inspection. As a child, I never got a clear sighting of her; as a male, I never received a clear signal from her. I became a lifelong geographer of my mother's character but I could never resolve the irregularities along the antipodes or in the torrid zones. She could smile one moment and make me think of the shy commerce of angels; the next moment the same smile could suggest a hermitage for morays and an asylum for terrorists. She was always too much woman for me.

In her secret self she legislated a whole series of untested laws of behavior that became her own freemasonry of cunning and design. There was not a single person in Colleton who did not underestimate the powers of Lila Wingo, including herself. It would take me thirty years to realize that the woman who raised me was a warrior of inalienable talents. Discussing her variety of gifts, her children later devised a list of occupations in which our mother would have excelled. She could have prospered, we decided, as a princess in an obscure Himalayan country, an assassin of minor cabinet officials, a fire-eater, the wife of the chairman of AT&T, or a belly dancer who brought the heads of saints to kings. When I once asked Luke if he thought our mother was pretty, he reminded me that her beauty had been powerful enough to lure a homicidal giant out of the woods in Atlanta, beautiful enough to inspire the demonic obsession of Callanwolde.

"Did that prove that she was beautiful?" I had asked.

"It proved it to me," he had said.

Her childhood in the mountains of Georgia had been hideous. Her father, a drunkard with an evil temper, had died of cirrhosis of the liver on her twelfth birthday. Her mother worked the night shift in a textile mill and died of brown lung when Lila was sixteen. After her mother's death, my mother took a bus to Atlanta, got a room at the Imperial Hotel, and was hired by Davison's department store as a trainee. Two months later she met my father and made a child's mistake by falling in love with the merry, fast-talking pilot from South Carolina. My father presented himself as a great land owner from the lowcountry who was a gentleman truck farmer with interests in the "fisheries industries." He never told her he was a shrimper until they arrived on Melrose Island.

But my mother had already begun the process of revising her own life. She told people in Colleton that her father had been a successful banker in Dahlonega, Georgia, ruined by the Depression. By a simple effort of will, her austere mother—whose photograph featured a flat, tortured face as nondescript as a cutlet—was transformed into a refined grande dame with entrée into the finest elements of society. "The finest elements," my mother would repeat breathlessly years later. Her voice conjured up a distilled, privileged subculture floating over golf greens, languidly sitting beside aquamarine pools, with the silky murmuring of gentlemen in the endless twilight and sherbets served by white-gloved hands. Though we descended from shrimp and textiles, we began to construct an inaccurate image of ourselves based on our dreamy mother's glass palace of lies. Savannah was the first poet our family produced, but Lila Wingo was certainly the first to practice the craft of fiction.

As her children, she looked upon us inconsistently as both her co-conspirators and her enemies. She was the only mother I ever met who held her children responsible for her unfortunate choice of a husband. She looked upon our births as crimes we committed against her. Yet it was extraordinarily rare for her to complain about her fate. She could not bring herself to admit, except during rare outbursts of candor, that anything was unpleasant. She possessed a heroic glossary of optimistic phrases. In public, she overdid happiness. She was militantly cheerful. Once we reached school age, she volunteered for every charitable function in Colleton. In the town, she slowly became known as someone you could depend on in a pinch. People outside the family considered her sweet, beautiful, industrious, and much too good for my father. Lila Wingo was all those things and a field marshal to boot.

From my father I inherited a sense of humor, a capacity for hard work, physical strength, a dangerous temper, a love of the sea, and an attraction to failure.

From my mother I received far darker and more valuable gifts: a love of language, the ability to lie without remorse, a killer instinct, a passion to teach, madness, and the romance of fanaticism.

Luke, Savannah, and I inherited all these tendencies in a deadly and varied mosaic of genes. In an outcry of pure bitterness my mother would later sum it all up by saying, "Luke, the fanatic. Tom, the failure. Savannah, the lunatic."

By then, my mother had laid waste to the town and family that had failed to appreciate the fearful resonance of her shame at being only a shrimper's wife.

When I was growing up my heart was full of sorrow for my mother and unspoken rage against my father. It need not have been. Henry Wingo just wasn't in her league. While my father had his temper, his enormous strength, his hapless ideas of sudden wealth, and his fists, my mother had a plan. She proved to all of us that nothing is as powerful or unconquerable as a simple dream slow in the dawning. She wanted to be a woman to be reckoned with, a woman of remarkable parts. In Colleton, her position in town was set, but she refused to accept this painful social reality. In 1957 she somehow managed to get herself nominated to the Colleton League, and a deadly business was born.

The Colleton League. It had been founded in 1842 by Isabel Newbury's great-grandmother. In its charter, the stated purpose of the League was to initiate good works and worthwhile projects among all citizens of Colleton. The women of the League would be drawn from the finest families and include, at all times, the most remarkable women living within the borders of Colleton County. It was this final proviso that endowed my mother with the sanguine expectation that she would one day find herself inducted into full membership. What began as an aspiration turned soon to an unappeasable hunger. My mother's nomination for the Colleton League was unanimously rejected by the membership committee and Isabel Newbury had said in a withering summation that eventually reached my mother's ears, "Lila Wingo is definitely not League material."

Not League material. How this delicate, summary phrasing must have devastated my mother when she heard it. There is little discretion or protocol to these bloodless autos-da-fé of small-town southern life. Mom played her part well and never complained; she merely went about her task of convincing League members that she would be an asset to their club. It was not until 1959 that she saw her first real chance to convince the ladies of the Colleton League of her worth.

In April of that year, the League announced in a full-page ad in the weekly paper that it was inviting all the women of the town to submit recipes for possible inclusion in a cookbook containing the best recipes in the lowcountry. My mother viewed this as a splendid opportunity to impress the members of the cookbook committee, which included a healthy percentage of her most articulate detractors, with her culinary skills. She went to her closet and pulled out all the back issues of *Gourmet* magazine. Tolitha had given my mother a subscription to *Gourmet* in 1957, and it was this magazine which provided my mother with her entry into the world of cuisine. It was this magazine which also made my mother one of the finest cooks ever to boil water in a Carolina kitchen.

She did not just read *Gourmet* magazine; she studied it exhaustively. She had always been a superior southern cook, one who could work a personalized magic with biscuits, a handful of beans, and a freshly killed fryer. She could even make grease taste good. But through her careful readings of *Gourmet*, she made the observation that the preparation of food was one eloquent signature of social class. Once she made the connection that there was a higher palisade of cuisine than the southern one, she initiated another one of her long projects of obsessional self-improvement that further alienated her from my father and endeared her to us. Henry Wingo was a meat and potatoes man and considered my mother's béarnaise sauce a French plot to ruin a perfectly good steak.

"For christsakes, Lila, it's got wine in it," my father said one night after my mother had prepared coq au vin. "You don't pour wine over chicken. You pour it down your throat."

"This is just an experiment, Henry. I don't know whether I should submit a whole bunch of recipes or just one. How does it taste?"

"It tastes like a drunk chicken," he answered.

"It tastes great, Mama," Luke said, and the battle lines were drawn.

For several heady months my mother pored over her limp, butter-softened copies of *Gourmet* magazine, taking assiduous notes in her sensual handwriting and using the evening meal for improvisation and experiment. She studied her own vast recipe collection and began making subtle emendations and improvements, borrowing ingredients from one recipe to empower the body or consistency of another. She arrived slowly at the idea that she would devise her own recipe, something arresting and original that issued out of her own imagination and her acute, if limited, knowledge of food and its properties. The four burners of the stove worked overtime and the kitchen sweltered as the blue flames simmered the brown and white stocks, which she then transformed into bright velvety sauces that clung to knives like oil-based paint. All April and May, the stock-pots exuded the fragrance of the crushed bones and marrow of cattle and fowl, seasoned with the crispate herbs and vegetables from her own luxuriant garden. The smells coalesced into a dark perfume that felt like a layer of silk on the tongue. My nose grew kingly at the approach of my home. There would be the redolent brown stocks the color of tanned leather, the light and chipper white stocks, and the fish stocks brimming with the poached heads of trout smelling like an edible serving of marsh.

In June we would return home from a day on the shrimp boat exhausted, sunburnt, and famished. As we left the truck, the smell of my mother's labors would assault my nostrils, and my mouth, dry and salty, would come alive like the birth of a stream; the path to my home was a concourse of smells for which there was no adequate glossary. In the kitchen, my mother would be lathered in her own sweat, singing a mountain song, happy in the vainglory of her art. I have never eaten so well before or since. I would grow three inches that summer and put on ten pounds of hard boyflesh. I owed it all to the melancholy fact that my mother was not a member of the Colleton League.

It was in late June that my mother had labored mightily on what she called "her big surprise of the summer." She had worked out an arrangement with the butcher at the Piggly-Wiggly and he had begun to save her the cuts and organs he normally discarded as unfit for human consumption. The Wingo family became the first citizens of Colleton ever to eat sweetbreads prepared from a recipe in *Gourmet* magazine.

Dad seated himself at the head of the table. Luke and I showered, changed clothes, and joined him. Savannah brought the sweetbreads from the kitchen and with a huge grin on her face began spooning them onto Dad's plate. Dad stared morosely and began jabbing at them with his fork. My mother entered the room and took her place at the other end of the table. By the look on his face, my father appeared to be trying to derive secrets from the entrails of a sacrificial beast. Mom was radiant and there were fresh roses on the table.

"What in the hell are these things, Lila?" my father asked.

"These are sweetbreads cooked in cream and white wine," she answered proudly. "It's a very special Sauce Français Wingo."

"It looks like Calcutta pussy to me," my father said.

"How dare you speak like that in front of my children at the dinner table," she said, and her voice was hurt. "This is not a shrimp boat and I'll not have language like that used at my table. Besides, you haven't even tried the sweetbreads, so you don't know if you like them or not."

"This isn't bread, Lila. I don't care what your little Frog cookbook tells you. I been eating bread my whole life and this ain't even close. It ain't corn bread or spoon bread or loaf bread or biscuits."

"Simpleton! I married a dyed-in-the-wool simpleton," my mother said angrily. "These are the thymus glands of a cow, dear."

"Honey," he said, "I don't want to be eating cow nuts when I could be eating T-bone. That's not too much to ask. I've been eating this kind of crap for three months now and I'm getting sick of it."

"These are cow balls, Mama?" Luke asked, turning a sweetbread over in his plate.

"Of course not, and you watch your language too, Luke Wingo. The thymus lies elsewhere in the cow."

"Where?" I asked.

"I'm not sure," my mother said. "But far, far away from the animal's genitalia. Of that, I am reasonably sure."

"Why can't a man have a little red meat at the end of a day?" my father asked, laying down his fork. "That's all I ask. Even a fried fish or a mess of shrimp and gravy. We eat meat a nigger wouldn't touch. Or a dog. Where's Joop? Come here, boy. Come here, Joop."

Joop was sleeping in his chair and he raised his amiable gray-flecked head in the last summer he would be alive and jumped heavily to the floor. He approached my father cautiously, his eyes milky with cataracts, trembling from the effect of the heartworms that would kill him.

"Come here, Joop. Come on over here," my father yelled impatiently. "Goddamn it, dog, get your black ass over here."

"You can tell Joop's smart," Savannah said. "He's always hated Dad's guts."

Joop stopped five feet away from my father and awaited further developments. Dad was the only human being on earth that Joop did not unreservedly adore.

"Hey, Joop, you dimwit hound, eat a plate of sweetbreads, pal."

My father set his plate on the floor and Joop approached the sweetbreads slowly. He sniffed them scornfully, licked off a bit of cream, then turned and went back to his chair.

"I spent all day preparing this meal," my mother said.

"See that," my father said, crowing. "See the living proof. I'm supposed to eat food a dog won't touch. I get up at five in the morning, bust my ass catching a shrimp or two, work like a dock nigger from morning till night, then come home and eat food the dumbest dog in the world won't touch."

"Try to look at it as an adventure in food, dear. Just an adventure. I want the children to experience all different kinds of food. I'm trying to broaden their horizons. This is a classic French dish. A classic. I found it in *Gourmet*," she explained in a wounded, defeated voice.

"French!" my father yelled. "Am I French? I hate the goddamn French. You ever hear the way they talk? Jesus Christ, Lila, it's like they've got twenty pounds of Cheddar cheese stuffed up their behinds. I'm an American, Lila. A simple, shit-kicking American out trying to make a buck. I like American food—steaks, potatoes, shrimp, okra, corn, that kind of shit. I don't like snails or caviar or frog livers or dragonfly balls or any of that other crap the French jack off about. I don't want an adventure in food, honey. I just want to eat. I don't mean to hurt your feelings."

Luke had begun eating his sweetbreads with exaggerated relish.

"I think this food is great, Mom," he said. "In fact, I think this is the best food I've ever tasted."

I took a small, cautious bite and was surprised to find the taste agreeable.

"Fab, Mom," I said. "Really fabulous."

"Great stuff, Mom," Savannah agreed. "Relax, Dad, and I'll fry you up a wahoo in a couple of minutes."

"The stupid dog wouldn't eat it," my father said, feeling the pressure of the family's gathering solidarity against him.

"He won't eat nothin' unless it comes out of a can," Luke explained.

"Anything," Mother corrected, smiling again. "Grammar should be stressed until it becomes a habit."

"Why don't you give Dad a can of Alpo?" Savannah suggested.

"Let him fight it out with Joop," I said.

At that moment, if my mother had served us horse turds in white wine we would have praised their texture and delicacy. It was part of a complex unwritten system of ethics that caused us to rally thoughtlessly around our mother whenever our father sallied forth on these gratuitous expeditions against her spirit. No matter how valid his point, Henry Wingo could never shake his image as the archetype of the swaggering bully. It both isolated and enraged him, yet it was a fixed destiny. His eyes took it all in, his children gaily savoring those fresh glands as an act of defiance against the man of the house.

"Well," he said, "you've succeeded in turning all of my children against me, Lila. I guess I'm the big heavy in all this."

"Just be polite, Dad," Luke said gently. "Mom worked hard on this meal."

"Hey, big mouth. I work hard so your mother can put this shit on the table. I'm the breadwinner in this mouthy family, not the goddamn sweetbread winner. If I want to gripe, then I've earned the right to gripe."

"Say it nicely, Dad," Savannah said in an even but imperiled voice. "You can be so nice when you're not being a bully."

"Shut up," Dad said.

"I have a right to my opinion," she answered, eating her meal. "This is America and I'm an American citizen. You've no right to tell me to shut up."

"I said 'shut up,' " he repeated.

"Big man. Big brave man," my mother taunted with a perfectly ill-timed interjection.

"You go cook me some decent food, Lila," Dad ordered. "Right now. I've been working all day and I've got a right to some food."

"Relax, Dad," Luke said, his voice pained and conciliatory.

My father slapped Luke hard across the mouth. Luke stared at my father in surprise, then bent his head down toward his plate.

"Now, get me some meat," my father said. "Any kind of meat will do. I've got to teach this family to have a little respect for a working-man."

"Are you all right, Luke?" my mother asked.

"Yes, ma'am," he answered, "I'm fine."

"There's some leftover hash. And some rice. I'll heat it, Henry," she said.

"I'll help you, Mama," Savannah said.

I slid back my chair from the table and said, "Me too."

Only Luke remained in the dining room with my father.

I sought refuge in the kitchen, for long experience had taught me to retreat from my father's angle of attack when he erupted.

"Could you chop an onion, Tom?" my mother asked.

"Sure."

"And, Savannah, could you heat the rice, honey? It's in a covered dish way back in the Frigidaire."

"I'm so sorry, Mama," Savannah said, opening the refrigerator door.

"Sorry?" she said. "There's nothing to be sorry for. This is the life I chose. The life I deserve."

She was searching through the canned goods in the pantry and emerged carrying a can of dog food. She ignored our glances of disbelief, opened the can, then began sautéing the onions in the butter.

"Chop another onion, please, Tom," she asked as the smell of cooked onions began to fill the kitchen. "And peel me a couple of cloves of garlic."

When the onions and garlic had turned transparent in the butter, my mother spooned the Alpo into the frying pan and began vigorously to combine the ingredients. She salted and peppered the meat, dashed it with Worcestershire sauce and Tabasco, and added a cup of tomato sauce. She threw a handful of chopped chives into the pan, then added the day-old rice and brought it to a hot sizzle. Arranging the concoction prettily on a clean plate, she garnished it with chopped scallions and fresh parsley. She carried it proudly into the dining room and placed it with a triumphant flourish before my father.

Joop awoke once more, dropped heavily to the floor, and approached my father.

"See, the dumb dog knows what's good to eat."

My father took a bread dish and spooned a small portion out for Joop and set it on the floor. Joop ate it quickly, then returned to his chair, snorting with pleasure.

"The king's taster," Savannah said as she resumed her meal.

His authority restored, my father tasted the hash and pronounced it to his satisfaction. "Now, this is food, Lila. Simple food, but good. I'm a simple man and I'm not ashamed of it. But I know what's good and what's good for you. This is a fitting meal and I thank you for going to the trouble."

"Think nothing of it, darling. It was my pleasure," my mother answered acidly.

"I hate it the way we always fight at mealtimes," Luke said. "It always feels like I'm getting ready to land on Normandy Beach when I sit down to this table."

Savannah said, "It's one of the pleasures of family life, Luke. You ought to be used to it by now. You eat a few peas for strength, then you get punched in the mouth."

"That'll be quite enough out of you, young lady," my mother warned.

"It's character-building, Luke," my father said, innocently shoveling in a forkful of Alpo and speaking with a full mouth. "I wish my father had whipped my butt when I screwed up instead of making me read ten pages out of the Bible."

"The Bible helped make your father the booming success he is today," my mother said bitterly.

"I'm sorry I'm not a heart surgeon or a white-shirt banker, Lila," my father said, "but it's about time you quit being ashamed of me being a shrimper."

"I'm just ashamed that you're not even the best shrimper. There are ten men on the river, half of them colored, who catch more shrimp than you do."

"But they ain't got the business ideas I got. Their brains ain't bustin' with ideas to make money."

"You've lost more money than some men ever made."

"That's because my ideas have always been ahead of their time, Lila. Even you have to admit that. I got more pizzazz

than the average Joe. I just need to borrow a little capital
and take a bow from Lady Luck."

"You're a natural-born loser and you smell like shrimp,"
my mother said cruelly.

"I shrimp for a living," my father said, and his voice was
tired. "The smell comes with the territory."

"If you'd rub a little garlic across your chest, you'd smell
just like shrimp scampi," she said.

"I love the smell of fresh shrimp," Luke said.

"Thanks, Luke," my father said.

"Ha!" my mother said to Luke. "How would you like to
go to bed with a two-hundred-twenty-pound shrimp?"

"See what I mean," Luke said. "Everything becomes a
fight."

"It's hard to think of Dad as a shrimp," Savannah said,
looking at my father who was sadly finishing up his plate
of Alpo.

"Why don't we talk and laugh and tell about the day's
activities like the families on TV do? Those fathers always
wear coats and ties to dinner, Dad," Luke said.

"Can you see me trying to set nets in a storm wearing a
coat and tie, Luke? Besides, those aren't real fathers. They're
Hollywood fruitcakes."

"But they're always happy at dinner," Luke insisted.

"You'd be happy too if you had a couple of million smacks
socked away in the old safety deposit box," Dad said, finishing his meal with an animal belch of pure satisfaction.
"Now, that hit the old spoteroo, Lila. Just remember, you're
cooking for an American, not a Frog."

"I could deep-fat-fry rocks and you'd gulp them down
like a black-bottom hog, Henry. But I'm also trying to ed-
ucate these children in the ways of the world. And I'm
trying to improve myself at the same time. I'm looking for
the right recipe, the one that will impress those members
of the Colleton League who've been voting me down. So
I'm going to experiment with food until I come up with
something so original that it'll make all of them realize I'd
be an asset to their organization."

Dad looked directly at my mother and said the words
that had never been said around our table: "Honey, they
ain't never gonna let you in no Colleton League. Don't you
know that by now? They have a Colleton League just so

they can keep people like you out of it. You can cook all the food in France and Italy and cook the living hell out of it and they still aren't going to let you in. It's better that you hear it from me than from them. It's just the plain facts you've got to be facing."

"Don't even bother to send them a recipe, Mom," I said. "Please, Mom, Dad's right."

Savannah said softly, "Mom, why are you even trying to help those ladies in the Colleton League out by sending them a recipe? All they do is hurt your feelings."

"Your feelings can be hurt only if you allow people to hurt them," she said proudly. "I know that I'm just as good as every one of those women, and deep down inside they know it too. In my own quiet way, I contribute to this town as much as any of them. But Rome wasn't built in a day. They've had advantages I've never had. But I make full use of the resources at hand. I'll get in the League some day. There's no doubt about that."

"But why do you want to join, Mama?" Savannah asked. "I wouldn't want to be in a club that didn't want me."

"They want me," she said. "They just don't know it yet."

My father rose from the table and said, "You don't have a Chinaman's chance in hell to get in the Colleton League, Lila. And it's because of me, darling, not you."

"Yes, I know, Henry," my mother said, disregarding his rare note of grace. "You're certainly not what I'd call an asset."

For the rest of the summer she concentrated on working with materials native to the lowcountry. Her powers of concentration were astonishing and heroic. She cooked chicken ten different ways and each variation seemed like the creation of a new bird beneath my mother's attentive hands. Whenever Dad complained, he finished the meal with Alpo and rice, but even that entrée improved with time. She did magic things with pork and changed the way I looked at the flesh of pigs forever. If she had published her recipe for pit barbecue, it would have altered the quality of life in the South as we knew it. But barbecue was indissolubly linked to her past and she eliminated it from contention as too simple and pedestrian. We had family arguments over which recipe should be chosen to send to the ladies of the Colleton League. She fixed a shrimp mousse that I thought was the finest thing I had ever put in my mouth. Savannah favored a bouillabaisse my mother had concocted from a day's catch on the shrimp boat. My father remained loyal to her fried chicken. It was as happy a summer as my family would ever have. Even when Joop died, there was a sweetness to his passing, an easiness in the way we cried, a quiet beauty to his burial. We found him dead on his chair and we decorated the box we made for him with photographs of Joop and all of us together, from the time Joop was a puppy to the last year of his life. He had always been with us and he represented the best part of us, the part that could love without recompense or expectation. We buried him by our stillborn brothers and sisters and we buried him with two cans of Alpo to help him along the journey and to let anyone know who disturbed his bones that Joop was a dog tenderly cared for by a family who loved him well.

The day after we buried Joop, Luke caught a twelve-pound Spanish mackerel off the dock before Sunday dinner. Mom stuffed it with shrimp, mussels, and scallops and baked it with wine, heavy cream, and a handful of herbs she selected at random. When we ate it, the white flesh fell lightly from the bones and the shellfish exploded with the perfectly married flavors of the vineyard, the dairy, and the sea. Two hours before we ate it, the mackerel had been feeding in the Colleton River. Luke had found a whole shrimp in its belly, eaten moments before the fish struck the bait on Luke's hook. Luke cleaned the single shrimp and Mom added it to the stuffing for luck.

"This is it," I said. "This has got to be the one."

"I don't know," my father said. "I like fried fish just fine."

"You couldn't get this good of a meal in a really fine restaurant," Luke said.

"How would you know, Luke?" Savannah teased. "You've never been to a really fine restaurant, except one that served yellow grits."

"It's a little too much," my mother said, chewing slowly. "Too heavy and too much. And a little too commonplace in some ways. I read today that simplicity is the key to elegance in anything. But I think a thing can be too simple."

"Yeah, take Dad for instance," Savannah said.

"Ha!" my father said brightly. "Simplicity, huh! That must mean I'm one of the most elegant sons of bitches in the lowcountry."

"No," my mother answered, "I'm sure that's not what it means."

"Did you find any more good recipes today, Mom?" I asked.

"I found one for a Neapolitan soup that includes parts of a pig's lung, heart, and windpipe. I decided not to make it."

"Good," Dad said, with a mouthful of mackerel. "It makes me want to puke just to hear you describe it."

"How repulsive," Savannah said.

"I bet it's good," my mother replied. "It's the idea of it that's disgusting. I bet the first person ever to eat a snail felt a small twinge of revulsion."

"I bet he puked," Dad said.

At the beginning of August she announced in quiet triumph that she had finally discovered the perfect recipe. She had thawed eight wild ducks that Luke had killed the previous winter. The stock she made from the discarded duck bones and parts was dark as chocolate and its flavor was wild and sun-charged but slightly overpowering. She cut the wildness with a little red wine and a dash of cognac. She then sat down for an hour and thought about everything she knew about the flavor of wild duck. She cooked the ducks slowly with turnips and onions and tart apples and scuppernong grapes from the arbor. She considered the mysteries of balance and proportion in a perfect meal. When we sat down to dinner, we could sense her apprehension. She was worried about the grapes. She had consulted no cookbooks; she had cast off into the unknown without her copies of *Gourmet* to guide her. Using only what she found in her larder, she was on her own.

I was worried about the turnips but my mother assured me that wild duck was the only meat she knew of capable of holding its integrity against a turnip. That bothered me not at all; I simply hated turnips. But the fruit cut the bitterness of the turnips and the turnips played their role flawlessly by diminishing the cloying sweetness of the grapes.

The meat was the color of wild roses and even my father ceased his nightly lament on the joys of fried food and ate with silent gusto. It was my mother's own creation, it was marvelous, and we stood and gave her a standing ovation after the meal was finished. It was her seventh standing ovation of the summer.

Mom curtsied and blew us kisses and her eyes shone with a pleasure rare in our house. In an uncommon display of affection, she went around the table and kissed each of us. She even kissed my father, and the two of them began to waltz toward the living room as my mother giggled and hummed a melody remembered from the sweet days of their courtship in Atlanta. My mother looked comfortable and natural in my father's arms and for the first time I noticed how handsome they were together. It was a summer of extravagant, almost elegiac, happiness for all of us. In the kitchen my mother performed like some inspired magus above the stove and my father was filling up the hold of his boat with shrimp. Our home began to feel like a home was supposed to feel, the anchorage I had been longing for my whole life. The summer was sun-darkened and glad. My parents were handsome and I ate like a king after I worked all day gathering shrimp from the sea.

After supper, she was smiling to herself as she addressed the envelope to the cookbook committee. The doors of the house were open and a cool wind from the river swept through the rooms. I watched my mother lick a stamp and place it in the corner of the envelope. Then I saw Savannah watching her sadly. Savannah looked up at me. Our eyes met briefly in that blinding prescience and telepathy sometimes granted to twins. We could feel our mother setting herself up as a victim once again and were helpless to do anything about it.

The answer came within a week. We knew there had been an answer because there were no smells coming from the kitchen when we drove up to the house that night. The house was empty and Luke and I went out into the back yard and found Savannah comforting our mother, who had gone to the grape arbor to weep alone when the letter had come. Savannah handed the letter to me and Luke.

Dear Mrs. Wingo,

The committee and I wish to thank you from the bottom of our hearts for submitting your "old family recipe" for Canard Sauvage de Casa de Wingo. Unfortunately, all of us agree that we want our cookbook to represent the very best of regional cuisine and do not have the space to include the more exotic foreign offerings of our town's finest cooks. Thank you so much for your thoughtfulness and time.

Sincerely,
Isabel Newbury

P.S. Lila, you simply must tell me what cookbook you copied that recipe out of. It sounds absolutely divine.

I exploded and said, "Tell her you copied it out of *A Guide to Poisonous Mushrooms in America*, and you'll be glad to serve it at her next tea."

"That does it," Luke said. "I'm going to beat the shit out of her son."

"Please, please," my mother said through her tears. "There's no need to be vulgar and her son has nothing to do with it. It's nothing, really. I'm sure they only want certain names and certain families in the book. I'm just glad I had an opportunity to be considered. It was honor enough just to be able to send in a recipe. And I won't let a little thing like this bother me. I have too much pride to let them see me hurt. Did y'all notice anything funny about the title of my dish? I worried that the title might be a little too-too."

"I don't even understand the title," Luke said, still perusing the letter. "I thought you'd fixed duck."

"I thought the French made it sound more elegant," said Mom, drying her tears.

"It's a perfect name for a wonderful dish," Savannah said.

Mom said, "I think they'd adore it if they just gave it a chance, don't you, dear?"

"It would be very hard for them to taste the meal where I was going to put it, Mama," my sister said.

"She's gonna stick it up their fat asses, Mama," Luke explained cheerfully.

"Maybe they know my children are vulgar," my mother said, rising from the bench where she sat. "Maybe they think if I can't control my own children, I don't deserve to be in the League."

Luke went over and lifted her off her feet. He kissed her gently on the cheeks. She looked like a mannequin in a children's store in his arms.

"Mama," he said, holding her up, "I'm so sorry they hurt you. I can't stand to see you crying. If they ever hurt you again, I'll break into one of their meetings and kick all their asses. I'll make them eat wild duck with turnips and grapes until they start flying south for the winter."

"It's just a club, Luke," my mother said, straightening her dress as he set her gingerly on the grass. "I swear you children get more riled up about it than I do. I'm just trying to get a little bit ahead so you children have a few more advantages than I had. I was crying because I thought I'd messed up the name of my dish. Something isn't quite right about it. I wasn't sure until Isabel Newbury wrote the entire name of the recipe in her note. As if it were a big joke. As if she had gotten a big laugh over the name. *Casa* is the French word for house, isn't it, children?"

"Yes," we answered simultaneously, even though not one of us knew the French word for French.

That night we lay awake in the dark listening to the winds roaring out of the north and the waves crashing into the sea wall along the river. Beneath the tremendous sound of wind and water we could hear Mom crying in her room and the murmur of my father's rough, ineffectual voice trying to comfort her. After dinner, she had discovered that the French word she should have used was *chez*. She could bear almost any humiliation except one that demonstrated the immense deficiencies of her education.

"Could anyone please tell me why Mom wants to get in the Colleton League so bad?" I asked.

"She doesn't like who she is," Savannah answered.

"Where did she get these ideas?" Luke asked. "That's what I can't figure out. Where did they come from?"

"She just picked them up along the way," Savannah explained.

"Hell," Luke said, "she's going to be president of the Garden Club next year. You'd think that would make her happy."

"Anyone can belong to the Garden Club," said Savannah. "All you have to be is white and able to bury a seed. No, Mom has to have what she can't get. That's the only thing that's ever meant anything to her."

Then the bad season came upon my family, the deadly season when the river betrayed us and all the other Carolinians who made their living from the sea. It began in January, six months after the duck, and we could tell it was a cold like we had never known before. We awoke for the first time in our lives to snow, four inches of it, that covered the island and froze the black water pond in the center of the island. The marsh was white along the fringes and the rabbits and field mice, foraging for grain, were easy targets for the hawks. The sky was bitter and gray and the temperature hung around ten degrees Fahrenheit during the day for an entire week. The pipes froze, then burst, and the house went without water for two weeks. The power lines leading to the island were dropped by an icy limb, plunging us into darkness. We lived in the soft glow of kerosene lanterns. We built great fires and my mother melted snow from our shoes on the wood stove when we came in from gathering wood. There was a sense of gaiety and an atmosphere of some surprising and illicit festival in our house, and the schools were closed for five days. There was not a single snow-removing vehicle in the whole state, nor was there a sled in all of Colleton County. We had our first snowball fight in the front yard and built our first snowman.

An old arthritic black man, Clem Robinson, died of exposure not three miles from our house. Before the snow could melt for good, an ice storm covered the lowcountry and we learned the deeper treachery of ice. At night, we could hear the disconsolate sounds of trees breaking under the weight of their glistening unnatural burden. Limbs broke with a terrifying violence, like the snapping of healthy bones. We did not know that trees could die beneath a lens of chilling ice. We did not know they could die aloud in sharp, enfilading reports that made the forest resonate with the ghostly firepower of a season up in arms. In the Atlantic, the temperature of the water began to drop below forty-five degrees Fahrenheit and the shrimp my father had a rendezvous to catch the following spring began to die. They perished in countless billions and news of their decimation would go unreported until the shrimpers of Carolina all came up with empty nets in March. The shrimp did not return to the inlets and creeks in the innumerable, teeming shoals. They seemed to come singly or in pairs and the gravid females, flooding the marshes with their eggs, carried with them the awesome responsibility of the preservation of the species as they urged themselves toward the spawning creeks. It was the year that the bank repossessed seventeen shrimp boats and sold them at auction. In two weeks of relentless, backbreaking shrimping from daylight to darkness, my father's boat pulled up only forty pounds of shrimp. The sea was barren. The fish and sea birds behaved strangely. There was insufficiency and famine in the tides. For the first time in modern memory, shrimp became a rare and prized delicacy on Colleton tables.

In May, my father missed the first payment on the shrimp boat and the next day he headed south toward Georgia waters. But there, too, the nets came up with catches so meager that he never caught enough shrimp to cover the expense of fuel. He continued south, talking to other shrimpers, listening to rumors of fabulous catches in the Florida Keys and the Gulf. In Saint Augustine, the authorities caught him sweeping a river channel that had been closed to shrimpers because of the freeze. It was both a gamble and an act of desperation and they impounded his shrimp boat and fined him five hundred dollars. He took a job as an auto mechanic in a transmission shop on Highway 17. It would take him six months to pay the fine and get his boat back to Carolina waters. He called my mother and said it was up to us to keep up the payments on the boat.

Luke, Savannah, and I began a ritual of rising at five in the morning and setting a string of crab pots in the river. We would empty the traps of blue crabs, spilling them into a large barrel centered in the boat and baiting the traps with fresh mullet and trash fish. We began with twenty traps and by summer's end we were pulling out fifty along twenty miles of river and creek. Because we were new on the river, we had to respect the rights of the commercial crabbers and set out pots in remote channels far from Colleton proper. We ranged far and wide throughout the county, leaving the wire traps as the signature of our passing. Tying white floats to a rope, we would haul the baited traps into the advancing or withdrawing tides. You could follow us from float to float over the wildest, most desolate stretches of our county. At first we worked slowly and our movements were inexpert and wasteful. But we grew into our task, learned the rhythms of the work, and developed an expertise based on our initial mistakes. In the first month, it took us ten minutes to empty a trap of crabs and to bait it again for the next tide. But in the second month, the same operation took us less than two minutes per trap. It was a matter of perfecting the technique of crabbing. We refined our movements; we learned grace and the economy of precise gestures; we learned that crabbing, like everything else, had its own native beauty, its own properties of dance. We broke even the first month because all our profits went into buying new traps. In the second month, we paid the note on our father's shrimp boat. The older crabbers watched our progress as we brought our catch to be weighed. In the beginning, we were the object of their derision and jokes. By August, we were initiates into their brotherhood. They would gather around to admire Savannah's rough and calloused hands. They gave sound advice. They taught us the mysteries of their rugged craft. Then, after we had mastered the essentials, they praised us by their silence. We were born to the river and they expected us to be good at what we were born to do.

But no matter how we labored on the waters, we could not assuage our mother's fears. There was not enough money to pay the bills. In September the electricity was turned off on the island. My mother's face was vulnerable and worried beneath the soft light of kerosene. Then, she could not pay for the insurance on the shrimp boat. The phone was disconnected. I was teased at school for wearing pants far too short for my size. My mother tried to get a job in every store in Colleton, but there were no openings. Each night after school, I wandered into the creeks and threw the cast net for our dinner. We hunted deer out of season, killing even does and fawns to put meat on our table. We were made desperate by our mother's silent but explicit terror. She would not let us tell anyone, not even our grandparents, of the seriousness of our dilemma. The frissons of her unalterable pride made her incapable of asking her neighbors for help. Her withdrawal from the town was aboriginal and primitive. She could not pay her bills at the grocery store or the hardware store so she simply quit going to town. She turned inward. Her silences became prolonged and troublesome. She worked her garden with a compulsive rage. A tentativeness settled over our house. We waited for our luck to change. The shrimp returned to the river and the nets were swollen again with huge catches of white shrimp. But our father was still trying to earn enough money to ransom his dry-docked boat in Florida.

On the day before Thanksgiving, we heard a car coming across the causeway on the other side of the island and ten minutes later it pulled up in our yard and four immaculately dressed women approached our house. I opened the door to Bettina Potts, Martha Randall, Thelma Wright, and Isabel Newbury, the four officers of the Colleton League, and Mrs. Newbury asked if she could speak to my mother.

My mother came to the door and something died in her eyes the moment she saw them. She dried her hands on her apron and asked them to come inside the house.

"We can't stay long, Lila. We have three other turkeys to deliver by dark," Isabel Newbury said sweetly.

"I don't understand," my mother said as the four ladies seated themselves uncomfortably around the living room, their eyes glancing about the room.

"You must have heard that one of the functions of the League is to distribute turkeys at Thanksgiving to less fortunate families in the county, Lila. We wanted to make sure that you and your family did not go without during the holiday season," said Bettina Potts.

"There must be some mistake, Bettina. My family is doing just fine."

"Could you put on a light in here, Lila?" Mrs. Newbury said. "It's rather difficult to see in this gloom."

"I thank you for thinking of us, ladies," my mother said, controlling her temper with difficulty, "but there are many families in the county who are in need of your charity far more than this one."

"Please don't think of this as charity, Lila," Thelma Wright said. "Think of it as a gesture of good will among friends who are worried about you."

"Please, don't do this to me," I heard my mother say. "Please, I beg of you."

"Think of your children and their Thanksgiving, Lila," Mrs. Potts said. "Don't just think of yourself."

Then I heard Luke's voice speak and it quivered with a murderous rage. He came roaring out of the kitchen, saying, "Get out of my mother's house."

"What a rude young man," Martha Randall said as Savannah and I emerged from the bedroom we had retreated to.

"I can't see your children's faces in this light, Lila," Isabel Newbury said again. "Please switch on a lamp for us."

"My son asked you to leave, Isabel."

"We will as soon as we give you the turkey," Bettina Potts insisted.

"Then leave it out in the yard when you go. I'll send one of the boys out for it later," my mother said, regaining her composure with some difficulty.

"You made this very hard for us, Lila," Mrs. Randall said.

"Not as hard as you made it for me, Martha," my mother answered as the women got up to leave.

They left the frozen turkey on the grass and we listened as their car pulled out of the yard.

There were tears of rage in her eyes as my mother walked to the gun rack in the living room and took down her shotgun. She grabbed a handful of shells, loaded the gun, and placed the other shells in the pocket of her apron. She went out into the yard and stood staring at the turkey she had been granted as an act of charity and debasement by the Colleton League.

"They were waiting for this to happen. They were biding their time and waiting," she said as she put that shotgun to her shoulder. The first shot bounced the turkey across the lawn; the second dismembered it into a thousand pieces.

"I want you to remember this one, children. This is what they're all like. Every one of them."

She lowered her gun and walked back into the house.
I do not remember Thanksgiving dinner that year.

In late December, after my father had returned from Florida, a loggerhead turtle washed up on the marsh near our
dock. The turtle was already dead when we found it. Dad
ordered that Luke and I remove it before it began to de-
compose and stink up the yard. At breakfast that morning,
Savannah had read to us from the social columns that Reese
and Isabel Newbury and their son, Todd, were in Barbados
for their annual winter vacation. It was Luke who made
the connection between the turtle and Barbados. Luke and
I lifted the loggerhead and put it into the Boston Whaler,
and that night before we went to sleep, Luke revealed his
plan to me and Savannah.

We awoke at three in the morning and slipped out of the
house through our bedroom window. Soundlessly, we made
our way down to the dock, and Luke did not start the motor
until we had drifted a quarter of a mile from our house.
He turned the boat into the main channel and he headed
for the lights of Colleton across the river. He opened up
the throttle and we flew through a light, choppy sea on a
full tide. We were laughing as we passed under the bridge,
but grew silent as we approached the landing at the end
of the Street of Tides. Luke cut the motor and we drifted
a hundred feet up to the shore where I jumped out and
tied the boat to the community dock. We lifted the turtle
out of the boat, and stopping often to rest, we moved through
the dark abandoned streets of our town toward the Newbury house. We passed beneath the oaks that formed the
green canopy along the most distinguished row of houses
between Savannah and Charleston. Dogs barked far off in
the town. I cut my hand on one of the barnacles that had
adhered to the loggerhead's back. The air was cold and
Christmas tree lights winked in some of the windows.

When we reached the Newbury house, we set the turtle
down in the back yard and Luke went around to try the
windows. He shinnied up one of the columns and found
a bathroom window open on the second floor. Savannah
and I heard the back door open and saw Luke motion to
us. We lifted the turtle again and moved as quickly as we
could up the back stairs. We went directly to the master

bedroom, where Luke had thoughtfully pulled back the covers on the immense four-poster bed of Reese and Isabel Newbury. We laid the turtle between the sheets and propped its head on a pillow, then covered it with the blankets. Savannah twisted the valve on the radiator full blast. Luke found one of Mrs. Newbury's sleeping bonnets and placed it rakishly on the turtle's great head. The room smelled like the hold of a shrimp boat. The loggerhead had already started to turn. We were back in our beds when our mother called us to breakfast.

The Newburys could not live in their home for six months after they returned from their annual trip to Barbados, nor did they ever go to Barbados again. The turtle's decomposition had been ghastly and hideous in the extreme heat of the bedroom. The four-poster bed and the mattresses were burned. For a month, no maid could enter the room without vomiting. Reese Newbury promised a thousand dollars to anyone who could provide information leading to the conviction of the person who had left the turtle in his bed. There was an editorial in the *Colleton Gazette* denouncing the crime. I have never seen my mother happier than when she was reading that editorial.

On her next birthday, Savannah bought my mother a copy of the Colleton League cookbook. It was a gift from the three of us. I could see the old look of hurt and disappointment in my mother's eyes as she held the book in her hands. The gift troubled her and I could tell she was wondering if we were making fun of her.

"Open it to the back page, Mama," Savannah said. "Luke, Tom, and I wrote you a recipe."

On the last page, Savannah had written out the entire recipe for Canard Sauvage Chez Wingo. On the facing page was a recipe of our own invention:

LOGGERHEAD TURTLE CHEZ NEWBURY

Take one loggerhead turtle, preferably ripe. Choose a dark night and take the turtle across the river when your parents are sleeping. Be careful that no one sees you. Find an open window. Unlock the back door. Place the turtle on a four-poster bed and turn the heat on high. Simmer the turtle until done, usually two weeks. Serve with toast points and a strong red wine. Wish your mother Happy Birthday. Tell her you love her. Remember the turkey.

> Love,
> Savannah, Luke, and Tom

I will always believe that recipe was my sister's first authentic poem. At first, my mother scolded us, screamed out that she was raising us to be decent, law-abiding citizens and not cat burglars, threatened to talk to Reese Newbury and collect the thousand-dollar reward, told us that we had to turn ourselves in to the sheriff, that once again we had disgraced the family and would make her the laughingstock of Colleton. She stopped scolding us and read the recipe again. Then she giggled like a schoolgirl and could not help herself. She grabbed the three of us together and hugged us in a rare physical embrace. Then she whispered, and there was both fury and exaltation in that whisper, "My kids are something. Lila Wingo may be nothing, but by God, her kids are hell."

12

In the dead center of a troubled adolescence, Bernard Woodruff made the game of football a pleasure to coach. He was one of those unconfident, hurting boys who needed just a brief opening to win the admiration of his peers. He lusted to be an athlete, and no matter how hard I drove him, he learned to ask for more. Part of his training was to master the hard curriculum of endearing himself to coaches and winning their respect with his unquenchable enthusiasm. Coaches were simple creatures, I told Bernard, who wanted all their boys to behave like rabid animals on the field and perfect gentlemen in the school hallways. On the field, coaches prized the willed aura of fearlessness; off the field they rewarded the quiet virtue of courtesy. Coaches wanted you to hurt the man carrying the football, but help carry him from the field, then write him a get-well letter in the hospital with all the grammar correct. If you are not a great athlete, pretend you are, I instructed Bernard. The great athletes do not need to be actors, but the rest of us do, I said during the first week I met with Bernard as I showed him how to carry himself and to think like an athlete.

I instructed him in the fundamentals of the game, took him from the very beginning and, working slowly, proceeded to teach the boy everything I knew about football. On the first day we began with the three-point stance and worked on firing out low from that stance for an hour. I showed him how to throw a football properly, how to cock the arm, how many steps to retreat into the protection of the pocket, how to step toward the receiver when passing, and how to cover the ball when the pass protection broke down. I began the long process of teaching Bernard how to play every position on the field, offensive and defensive. My sister still refused to see me and I had plenty of time on my hands. It felt good to coach again and it pleased me to discover that Bernard had good foot speed, could throw a nice pass, and needed a coach as badly as I needed a team.

I taught him how to run a pass pattern against a quicker defensive back and how to pass block against a charging defensive lineman. We took things slowly, by the number, and we repeated them daily until Bernard's movements on the field seemed instinctual instead of learned.

Each morning he met me at eight; he was always there waiting when I jogged into the park from the Village. We ended our practice sessions in a series of wind sprints where I would race Bernard in the forty-yard dash. On the first day, we ran ten dashes and I won six of them. On Friday of the same week, Bernard won seven of them. After practice I would buy him a Coke and send him home to shower before he began his violin lessons. As his coach, I was making him obedient to a cold and wearying discipline.

Because of his desire, he found, to his happy surprise, that he loved it. At the end of the first week, Bernard began to think of himself as a football player. I had transformed him into something he was never supposed to be. He returned the favor by making me feel like a coach again. His mouth still bothered me and he asked too many questions. It took him far too long to learn the basics of the game. But he kept trying and he burned with a love of the sport. He thrilled me and made me understand again the mystery of why I loved to teach boys the rudiments of a game I had played as a child. If a boy came to me in good faith and wanted to learn the game of football, I could make him better than he ever thought he could be. I could light a fire in that boy and other boys would hate to see him on the same field. Already, I could tell that there were boys from Phillips Exeter now asleep in Newport and Westchester who would hurt in the coming autumn because Bernard Woodruff spent his summer learning the fine points of his game in Central Park.

For ten days I worked hard to get Bernard and myself into shape. Then I went to talk to his mother about buying her son a uniform.

Now, whenever I went to Susan Lowenstein's office, I would try to decide which of her features she had given to her son. Bernard had inherited his mother's long legs, her full lips, those dark expressive eyes, and a complexion as smooth as new fruit. Except for a constant scowl, he was an exceptionally handsome boy. Our first drill each morning was to have Bernard practice smiling at me. He acted as though smiling was an unendurable calisthenic; it was the only part of our sessions together he hated.

I was entering my fourth week in New York and Sallie had not called or written me once. I was making elaborate plans to paint Savannah's apartment, and I had filled up one of my journals and started on another. Each week I would write Savannah a letter at Bellevue and stick it in a package with the other mail she received at her apartment. In the morning, I exercised and coached Bernard; in the late afternoon I walked uptown to his mother's office and continued to relate my sister's screams on the tapes to her life as a child. I read wonderful books from my sister's library of three thousand books. I was putting my damaged life in order. For the first time in a year, I started to have dreams of teaching again. I was in a classroom and the subject was Tolstoy and I was telling a class composed of all those students who had ever loved me as a teacher that the reason Tolstoy was great was because he was passionate. Why was it, I wondered, that I was most passionate talking about books I had loved? In the dream it was easy. Those books honored me; those books changed me. Alone, the greatest writers would sit with me and, in their own voices, tell me everything there was to know about the world. When I woke from the dream, I realized that I had no classroom to enter whenever a new book took possession of me. I needed students to complete myself. I began to write letters of application to all the high schools in Charleston again. As a teacher, I had been a happy man. Now, I was only a diminished one.

After I had told Susan about my mother's fruitless effort to get selected for the Colleton League, she had glanced at her watch.

"I believe our time's up for today, Tom," she said, then paused. "Do you know what strikes me as the strangest detail in that whole story?" she asked. "The fact that your family had a subscription to *Gourmet* magazine."

"You've always got to remember that my grandmother took off on that three-year world cruise and picked up a lot of strange notions," I said. "It was far stranger to me when she got Savannah a subscription to *The New Yorker*. Who would have ever thought that Savannah would one day spend much of her adult life in some of New York's most notorious wacko wards."

"You've been writing letters to Savannah, Tom," Susan said.

"That's right, Lowenstein," I said, angry at her admonishing tone. "You see, she's my sister and we have a long tradition in my family of writing letters when we want to tell someone that we love them and wish them well."

"The letters are upsetting her," she said. "She received one from your mother yesterday. They had to sedate her."

"That's understandable," I said. "Guilt just leaks off on your fingers when you read one of my mother's letters. My letters, on the other hand, are models of decorum. I've had long experience in not offending the sensibilities of lunatics, even when they're related to me."

"Savannah is not a lunatic, Tom. She's a very disturbed woman."

"That was meant to be a joke, Lowenstein."

"It wasn't funny."

"I admit, it wasn't world-class humor, Lowenstein, but Jesus Christ, it's difficult to be funny with someone who's had her sense of humor surgically removed."

"Most things don't amuse me," she said. "I can't help that."

"Yes you can, Susan," I disagreed. "Since we have found ourselves sitting together every day, you could take this opportunity to improve your personality."

"And you, Tom Wingo of South Carolina, think that you could improve my personality?" she answered, her voice crackling with irony.

"Notice that I choose to ignore the slur on my home state and stick to the point. See, Lowenstein, I'm a very funny man. There are times when I tell a joke or come roaring out with some startling and hilarious bon mot that you could respond to with something as simple as a smile. I'm not asking for a horse laugh. Otherwise, I consider you to be a perfect human being."

"Bernard tells me that you make him practice smiling every day, Tom," she said, and she smiled.

"Why are you smiling now?" I asked.

"Because he complains about it," she said. "Because it makes him feel like an idiot grinning twenty-five times before you let him near a football."

"He's handsome when he smiles," I said. "He's got the face of a killer mugger when he wears that scowl."

"Would you like me to smile twenty-five times before we begin our sessions together?" she asked, teasing me.

"You look great when you smile, Lowenstein," I said.

"How do I look when I don't smile?" she asked.

"Absolutely sensational," I said. "But I'd love for you and Bernard to enjoy yourselves a little more. By the way, Susan, could you invite me to your house for dinner some night when Herbert's out of town?"

"Why?" she said, and I could tell she thought my presumption troubling.

"Because Herbert doesn't know about his son the quarterback. Nor, I presume, do you want him to know."

"He's giving a concert in Boston tomorrow night. Could you come then?"

"Let me cook a fabulous meal," I said. "We'll eat like royalty."

"Could I ask you a question, Tom?" she said.

"About the meal?"

"No, about my son," she said. "Is he gifted in football at all?"

"Yes," I said. "To my great surprise. Bernard isn't bad at all."

"Why are you so surprised?" she asked.

"Because he didn't grow up in Bear Bryant's household, did he?" I said.

"Who is Bear Bryant?" she asked.

"This is a joke, isn't it, Lowenstein?" I said in amazement. "You're setting me up for something. No, I apologize. Where I come from, not knowing Bear Bryant would be like your husband not knowing Yehudi Menuhin. He's a football coach."

"What is a line of scrimmage?" she asked.

"Why on earth would you want to know, Susan?"

"Because Bernard thinks I'm the village idiot when I try to talk to him about his new interest in football," she said. "Bernard talks about nothing but football now, about strange things like flare-out patterns, power plays, screen passes, buttonhooks. It's as if he's suddenly gone to some foreign country."

"You're getting the lingo down good, Doctor," I said.

"Is it necessary for him to lift weights, Tom?" she asked.

"Yeah," I said. "It's all part of the discipline, Susan."

"How do you find Bernard, Tom; and I'd like an honest answer," she said. Her voice was raw and edgy.

"How honest?"

"As honest as you can be without making me angry with you," she said, and I thought she was going to smile, but she did not.

"He's a nice boy, Susan," I said.

"A little more honest than that, Tom," she said. "Surely you know I'm tougher than that."

"He's unhappy, Susan," I said, her face in shadow now. "He seems miserably unhappy for reasons unknown to me. His misery touches me in some way, perhaps because it matches mine, perhaps because I can see a way out of it for Bernard where I can see no escape for me at all."

"He told me what you said to him the first day," she said. "I was furious with you, Tom. He told me that you made him cry twice."

"He was disrespectful," I said. "I don't know how to coach a boy who doesn't show me simple decency. I demanded that he be courteous. It won't cause permanent damage, I promise."

"He was in therapy for three years, Tom," she said in a whisper.

"It didn't quite work, Doctor," I said. "Something is wrong. Bernard's got neglect written all over him. He's never been approved of in his whole life. It hurts him to breathe sometimes."

"I know," she said. "I thought it might do him some good to go off to school. I thought it might give him a chance to make some friends. Do you know that he's never spent the night away from home with a friend? He's been a difficult child since the day he was born. He was never cuddly and sweet like other babies I saw in the park. There's something in Bernard that I've never touched in my whole life. Some lonely place."

"Does the loneliness come from you or from Herbert?" I asked.

"The loneliness comes from me," she said.

"Football is a game where you can't feel lonely," I said. "Maybe that's why Bernard is attracted to it. I know you're upset about his playing football, but it touches a chord of beauty in your son. And it's his game alone. He chose it without the consent of his parents. When I tell you that I think Bernard's unhappy I'm not lying to you. But the kid is happier than a pig in shit when I'm running him through drills or sending him out for long passes."

"Tom," she said, "I've never watched a football game in my whole life."

"You haven't missed a fucking thing, Lowenstein," I said.

"And I never plan to see one in the future," she added.

"You want to bet?" I said. "I bet you and Herb go up to Phillips Exeter to watch Bernard play next year."

She groaned loudly and said, "Will this be before my divorce or after?"

I reached down and took her purse from the bookcase behind her desk and set it in the middle of the room. Motioning for Susan to rise, I placed her on one side of the purse and I lined up directly opposite.

"All right, Susan," I said, pointing to the purse and going down into a three-point stance. "This purse is the football. You're the defensive team and I'm the offensive team. I'm trying to take this football and put it inside your goal line behind you. You are trying to stop me. Your team always has to line up on that side of the ball until the ball is moved by my team. My team always has to line up on this side of the ball until the ball is snapped."

"Tom, this is unbearably tedious," she said, but she was laughing.

"Don't interrupt the coach again, Lowenstein," I said, "or you'll be running laps around the reservoir in Central Park. Wherever the ball is on the field is known as the line of scrimmage. Do you understand?"

"I didn't understand a single thing you said," she replied.

"Lowenstein, it's un-American not to know what a line of scrimmage is," I said.

"Maybe your coaching is a little rusty," she said.

"It might be," I said, "but there are still some things I know. Watch Bernard's eyes tomorrow night after the big surprise."

"What's the surprise?" she asked.

"It's a holy night to any athlete," I said. "Tomorrow night I issue uniforms to the boys who've made the team. Bernard's made the varsity. Do you want me to bring you a book explaining a little about football, Susan?"

"Please don't," she said, stepping toward me as I rose. She touched me lightly on the arm.

"Offsides," I said, and I felt a desire stir in me like some nearly extinct beast shaking off the effects of a long and troubled hibernation.

13

My life did not really begin until I summoned the power to forgive my father for making my childhood a long march of terror. Larceny is not a difficult crime to condone unless your childhood was the item stolen. Without equivocation, I will tell you he was a terrible and destructive father. Yet it will always remain one of life's most ineluctable mysteries that I would one day come to feel an abiding compassion for the man and a frayed, nervous love. His fists were the argosies of his rule and empowerment. But his eyes were the eyes of my father, and something in those eyes always loved me even when his hands could not. He brought no natural talent to the dilemma of loving his family properly. He had developed none of the soft gifts of fatherhood. We mistook his love songs for battle hymns. His attempts at reconciliation were mistaken for brief and insincere cease-fires in a ferocious war of attrition. He lacked all finesse and tenderness; he had mined all harbors, all approaches to his heart. Only when the world brought him to his knees could I reach up and touch my father's face without him bloodying mine. By the time I was eighteen I knew everything there was to know about a police state, and it was only when I left his house that the long state of siege was ended.

When my first child, Jennifer, was born, Savannah flew down from New York to help Sallie when she came home from the hospital. We toasted Jennifer's health with cognac, and Savannah asked me in a voice tinged with an ineffable sadness, "Do you love Dad, Tom?"

It took me several moments to reply and then I said,

"Yes. I do. I do love the asshole. Do you love him, Savannah?"

She also took her time in answering, then said, "Yes, Tom. It's the strangest thing. I love him, too, and I don't have the vaguest idea why."

"Maybe it's brain damage," I suggested.

"Maybe it's just the realization that he couldn't help who he was. By loving him, we're just being who we are and we can't help it either," she said.

"Naw, I just think it's brain damage," I said.

A large, florid man, Henry Wingo seemed to fill up every room he entered with a superabundance of energy. He considered himself a self-made man and the salt of the good southern earth. He lacked all those incommunicable, limpid depths that introspection might provide. Recklessly, he came at the world full throttle, manic and exuberant, leaning into the almost unbreachable gales whipped up in the turbulence of his passage. He was more a force of nature than he ever was a father and there were always hurricane warnings registering on the Beaufort scale when he entered the home of my childhood.

But because there was no established system to calibrate my own secret hatred of the man, I learned the strategies of silence and truancy. I took lessons from my mother in rearguard actions and learned the deadly art of the sniper by examining my father privately with the insurrect, unforgiving eyes of a damaged child. I studied him through the cross hairs of a telescopic sight I leveled at his heart. What I know of human love I took first from my parents; with them, love was a deprivation and a withering. My childhood was one of disorder, peril, and small craft warnings.

Failure seemed only to stimulate my father. My sister called it "the Sadim touch." When she coined the phrase, I don't remember, but it must have been in high school, when she cheerfully embraced profanity as a way to make her opinions and ideas understood more clearly. When shrimping season was over each fall, Dad turned his full attention to other, more creative, ways to earn his family's bread. His brain teemed with unworkable projects to make fast, easy money. Plans, blueprints, and schemes leaked out of him in incessant floods and he promised all his children we would be millionaires when we left high school. He grounded his whole life on the premise that his ideas, brilliant and unconventional, would lead all of us to unimaginable riches and honor. He also brought a gift to American enterprise shared by very few others: He never learned a single thing from his mistakes. Each failure, and there were dozens of them, only served to convince him that his time was approaching and that his apprenticeship in the harsh milieu of commerce was nearing its end. All he lacked was luck, he told us again and again.

But behind the wheel of his shrimp boat, with the dawn spilling its fine oils across the waters and the winches groaning beneath the weight of the nets, my father was the perfect master of his environment. His time on the river had left its mark and he would always look ten years older than his actual age. Each year his wind-tortured face would sag a bit around the edges and the Carolina sun at nigh noon would loosen and flense the pouches beneath the eyes. His skin was hard and leathery and it looked as though you could strike a kitchen match on the stubble of his chin. His hands were rough and his palms were glazed with layers of calluses the color of vellum. He was a hard-working and respected shrimper, but his talents were not amphibious; they did not follow him up onto dry land. Very early on, my father became obsessed with getting off the river. Shrimping was always a "temporary" situation with him. Neither of my parents could ever admit that shrimping was a beautiful way of life. They kept aloof from the shrimping fraternity and cut themselves off from any of those natural alliances so common among peers. Of course, the shrimpers and their wives were far too common for my mother's speciously cultivated and unattenuated tastes. My parents had no close friends. Together, they spent their whole lives waiting for their luck to change, as though luck were some fabulous tide that would one day flood and consecrate the marshes of our island, christening us in the iridescent ointments of a charmed destiny. It was an article of faith to Henry Wingo that he was a businessman of genius. Never has a man's basic assumption about himself been so heartbreakingly wrong or caused him or his family so much prolonged and unnecessary grief.

When my father was away from the river, he could take marvelous ideas and execute them disastrously, with seemingly little effort on his part. Some of his schemes could have worked, almost everyone admitted that: He invented and built machines to head shrimp, to clean crabs, to eviscerate fish, and all of them worked a little bit. There were no complete failures nor any resounding successes, just a lot of funny-looking machines cluttering up the small workshop he built behind the house.

And yet it was on the river that my father's most fabulous and misconceived ideas were spun out in an endless free association of language as he guided his boat through the shallow channels in morning darkness. He would sit behind the wheel, listening to the hum of the diesel, steering through the unmarked channels that led to the main river. The marsh was a huge but invisible presence, and he would conduct long monologues in the gloomy alcove of the wheel house in that sweet time of morning before the birds awoke with the sun coming up out of the Atlantic. Rare among shrimpers, he took his three children with him as often as he could wrest control of us from our mother, and I think he took us to cut the edge of the solitude of the shrimper's life.

On summer mornings, in the starry darkness, my father would wake us gently and we would dress soundlessly and leave the house with our footfalls printed softly in the dewy yard. In the back of the pickup, we would listen to the early-morning radio as our father moved down the dirt road that led to the wooden bridge on the opposite side of the island. We breathed in the marsh air as the disc jockey issued the weather report and told of small-craft warnings from Cape Hatteras to Saint Augustine, gave the wind direction and its speed, and told all shrimpers for a hundred miles the exact figures they would need to know. Each morning I felt that infusion of strength granted to the early riser as my father drove the five miles to the shrimp docks. Lester Whitehead, the striker who had worked for my father for fifteen years, would be filling the hold with five hundred pounds of ice as my father's truck pulled into sight. The nets hung from the uplifted outriggers like dark chasubles. Walking down the long gangway from the parking lot to the dock, we could smell diesel fuel, coffee brewing in the galleys, and the overpowering aroma of fresh seafood. We passed the giant scales silvering beneath the cheap light where the black women who could head shrimp faster than the eye could see would be awaiting us when we returned with the day's catch. That sharp perfume of fresh fish and shrimp always made the walk to the boat seem as if I were under water, breathing immaculate salt tides through the pores of my skin. As the children of a shrimper, we were just one more form of marine life in the lowcountry.

When my father gave the word and we heard the engine burst into sudden life, we would untie the boat and leap aboard as he headed out toward the sounds and channels of our island-dappled watery realm. On our right we would pass the sleeping town of Colleton, the mansions and stores along the Street of Tides, and my father would sound the horn to signal the bridge tender to open the bridge for the lordly passage of the *Miss Lila* on its way out to sea. My father's boat was a fifty-eight-foot beauty with an incredibly shallow draft for such a large boat. He made his three children memorize at an early age the essential numbers of his boat before he would confer official status on us as members of the crew. Shrimping always involves a tireless worship of numerology and when shrimpers discuss their boats they toss arcane figures back and forth that define the capabilities of their respective crafts. My father's main engine was a 6-DAMR-844 Buda manufactured by the Allis-Chalmers Company, Boston. It developed 188 horsepower at 2100 rpm. His reduction gear was a 3.88:1 Capitol. The brass shaft turned a 44-by-36-inch four-blade Federal propeller. The main bilge pump was a 1¼-inch Jabsco. In the deckhouse was a 42-inch Marty's wheel, a Ritchie compass, a Marmac throttle and clutch controls, and a Metal Marine automatic pilot. There was a Bendix DR16 depth recorder and a Pearce Simpson Atlantic 70 radio. On deck, the *Miss Lila* carried a Stroudsburg 515½ T-hoist, Wickwire cable, and Wall Manila rope. The anchor was a 65-pound Danforth and the horn was a 32-volt Spartan. In the language of shrimpers there were other brand names that imparted specific information: Oil City Brass blocks, Surrette Marine batteries, Dodge pillow blocks, Timken bearings, and a hundred others. Like all jobs, shrimping required its own idiom of precise communication. For me this language was as com-

forting as mother's milk and served as the background music of the part of my childhood spent afloat.

It all meant that my father's boat, if properly handled,
could catch one hell of a lot of shrimp.

In starlight we would gather around him on a thousand
brilliant mornings. When we were small, he would take
one of us into his lap and let us steer the boat and he would
correct our errors by exerting a gentle pressure on the wheel.

"I think we ought to be a little starboard, honey," he
would whisper to Savannah.

"You might want to remember that sandbar coming off
Gander's Point, Tom. That's it. That's the program."

But mostly he would talk to himself, about business,
politics, dreams, and disillusions. Because we were silent
children and mistrustful of the man he became when he
returned to land, we learned much about our father by
listening to his voice as he spoke to darkness and to rivers
and to the lights of other shrimp boats moving out for their
grand appointment with the swarming shoals of shrimp.
His voice in the morning was inexhaustible as we made
our slow passage toward the barrier islands. Each day of
his life in season was a duplication of the day before; tomorrow would always be an encore of today's labor; yesterday would always be a rehearsal for a thousand future
days, an elaboration on proven habits of excellence.

"Okay, kids," he said on one of those long mornings,
"this is the captain speaking. The captain and chief officer
of the *Miss Lila*, a fifty-eight-foot shrimping vessel licensed
by the state of South Carolina to ply the waters from the
Grand Strand to Daufuskie Island, and today we're heading
due east of the lighthouse off Gatch's Island and will set
our nets in fifteen feet of water one-half mile to the starboard of the wreck of the *Windward Mary*. Yesterday we
hauled up two hundred pounds of white shrimp in the
thirty-fifty range. What do I mean by thirty-fifty shrimp,
Savannah?"

"That means that there were between thirty and fifty
shrimp in each pound, Daddy."

"That's my girl. The winds will be out of the north at
eight miles an hour and small-craft warnings are in effect
as far south as Brunswick, Georgia, and as far north as
Wilmington, Delaware. The stock market fell five points in

moderate trading yesterday because investors are worried
about whatever it is investors worry about. Reese Newbury
bought two hundred acres of farmland from Clovis Bishop
yesterday for five hundred dollars an acre, which, in the
way I figure, makes Melrose Island worth about half a million smacks at the going rate. The son of a bitch offered
me twenty-five grand for the whole island last year and I
told him it was an insult. Damn right, I did. He thinks ol'
Henry Wingo don't know the value of property in this
county. I've got the best piece of land in this state and I
know it. So does your mother. I'm so far ahead of Newbury
and those other assholes, it's practically a crime. I got plans
for our island, kids. Big plans. Long-range plans that I'll
put into effect as soon as I get a little working capital to
play with. Don't tell your mother yet, but I'm thinking of
setting up a little chinchilla farm near the house. They got
bozos all over this country getting rich off chinchilla and
I'm not one to let a sure thing get away. I figure you little
boogers could take turns feeding the little critters while I
make the deals with the big-time furriers in New York and
then laugh my way to the bank. What do you think? Smart,
huh? Damn right. I was thinking about a mink ranch but
chinchillas are a lot more cost-efficient. I've done my homework. Yes, sir, if you don't do your homework, you can't
dance with the big boys. Your mother laughs at me, kids,
and I'll admit, I've made a few mistakes, but they were
mistakes of timing. The ideas themselves were absolutely
first class. You kids stick with me. I'm so far ahead of the
average Joe it's almost criminal. Ideas are always percolat-
ing in the old noggin. I'm burning up with schemes. Sometimes I wake up in the middle of the night just to write
them down. Hey, you kids love the circus?"

"We've never been to the circus," Luke said.

"Hey, that's first on the old agenda. A must. Next time
one gets near Charleston or Savannah, we'll load up the
pickup and get a front-row seat. You've just seen these
little half-assed fairs that play the small towns, but we'll fix
that. I like the Barnum and Bailey Circus. The goddamn
real McCoy. Don't breathe a word about this plan to anybody. If I ever get a little nest egg stashed away, I'm going
to set it up myself. I'm sick of assholes using my ideas to
become millionaires. Watch it now, Luke. There's the buoy

up ahead. When you pass it, head across the river at a forty-five-degree angle right toward the North Star. Good boy. You're a natural, son. There's a rock pile up ahead where ol' man Winn gutted his boat a couple of years go. I once pulled two hundred pounds out of this creek on a full tide. But it's not usually a productive creek. I've never figured out why one creek would yield more shrimp than another from year to year, but that's just the way it is. Shrimp are funny. They've got their natural preferences just like folks."

He was in the middle of a lifelong soliloquy, a loosely organized high-octave monologue addressed to no one in particular. There was such fluency and eloquence in these morning valedictories that I imagined him declaiming away even when his children were absent from the wheel house. These were his private discourses and musings with the universe and he thought no more of the presence of his mute, attentive children than he did of the stars in the belt of Orion. In the boat, as he talked, we might as well have been landscape, still life, inanimate listeners. From the galley below, the rising aromas of breakfast came to us, and these pillows of smells would cut through my father's voice. As Lester Whitehead cooked, the smell of coffee, bacon, and biscuits enfolded the boat in invisible trailing sleeves of the most cutting aromas. As we passed close to the entrance of the main sound, we set the tables for breakfast in the dreams of sleepers who slept near the river with their windows open. The engine murmured below us and a music played through the vibrating timbers of the boat's wood frame and the river was panther-colored before dawn and it sang to the town in soft canticles of those tides that bore us gloriously out toward the breakers beyond the most beautiful sea islands in the world. Here my father was most comfortable and relaxed. Only on the river were we safe to visit with him. He never hit us once when we were on the shrimp boat. There, we were workers, brothers of the nets, and he treated us with the dignity he accorded to all mariners who make their living on the water.

Yet nothing my father could accomplish as a shrimper would ever have value to my mother. In my mother's eyes, my father was vulnerable, helpless, and shrill. He tried hard to remake himself in the image of the man he thought she

wanted him to be. He hungered for my mother's unqual-
ified respect. His efforts were self-defeating and pathetic,
but he could not help himself. Their marriage was dissonant
and harsh. His success as a shrimper financed his disastrous
business schemes. The bankers laughed behind his back.
He became a joke in town. His children heard the jokes at
school; his wife heard them on the streets of Colleton.

But on the river, Henry Wingo was in harmony with the
planet and the shrimp seemed to come to his nets singing
with pleasure. He pulled up tons of shrimp each season
and kept careful and meticulous records of his catch. By
consulting his log book, he could tell you where he caught
each and every pound of shrimp he ever lifted out of Colleton waters, the depth of the tides at the time, the con-
ditions of the weather. "The whole banana," he called it.
The river was the dark text my father had memorized for
joy. I could trust the man when there was water beneath
him and shrimp filling up his billowing nets. But it was on
the same water that he concocted the schemes that kept
him dangling precariously on the high wire between ruin
and his dreams of sudden wealth.

"Next year, I'm thinking about planting watermelons,"
he said one night at dinner.

"No, please no, Henry," my mother said. "If you plant
watermelons, then Colleton will find itself covered by a
blizzard or a flood or a plague of locusts. Please don't plant
anything, Henry. Think of another way to lose all of our
money. You're the only person I know who couldn't grow
kudzu."

"You're right, Lila. As usual, you're absolutely right. I'm
much more of a technocrat than I am a farmer. I'm more
comfortable working with sound business or economic
principles than I am with agriculture. I think I knew that
all along but I saw all these other big shots making money
growing tomatoes and I thought I'd jump on the bandwagon."

"Don't jump on any more bandwagons, Henry. Let's
invest any extra money in blue chip stocks, like South Carolina Electric and Gas."

"I bought a Bell and Howell movie camera in Charleston
today, Lila."

"For God's sake why, Henry?"

"The future is film," my father answered, his eyes gleaming.

As my mother began screaming, my father calmly pulled out his new hand-held camera, plugged a cord into an outlet, turned on the spotlight, and recorded her entire diatribe for the amusement of posterity. Through the years, he operated the camera relentlessly. He filmed weddings, christenings, and family reunions. In the local paper, he advertised under the preposterous logo of "Wingo's Professional Cinematics." He would lose less money in his movie business than in any of the others. Looking through the aperture of his movie camera, my father was a perfectly happy and perfectly ridiculous man.

My father did not lack the courage of his convictions and it was Savannah who remarked that this peculiarity of his ungovernable temperament was his greatest flaw.

So he continued a brilliant career on the river diminished by his passionate and futile attraction to free enterprise. There were other failed projects we did not learn about until long after we were adults. He was a silent partner in a putt-putt golf course in Myrtle Beach that folded after one season. He invested in a taco stand run by a genuine Mexican who spoke in flawed, imperfect English and could not make tacos. My parents had appalling fights over money and how it was spent. My mother mocked him, screamed at him, scolded him, cajoled and pleaded with him, all to no avail. He was not susceptible to her inclination for restraint or moderation. Her arguments always took the form of a cautionary tale, and when that failed, she would scream out a terrifying summation of the apocalypse that would ensue if he continued to waste their money indiscriminately. Their storms and eruptions disfigured whatever tranquillity was natural to our home. Since their arguments were so common, we did not see the exact moment when my mother's umbrage and cross-grained wrath turned into a deadly hatred of my father. But the cycle of her impotent rage began early and there were years of fruitless interchange before my mother entered the field of fire with her own bitter reprisals. Henry Wingo believed that women should never discuss business. There were two types of

southern men: those who listened to their wives and those
who did not; my father had a black belt degree in turning
a deaf ear to my mother.

If you grow up in the house of a man who both loves and
mistreats you, and who does not grasp the paradox of his
behavior, you become, out of self-defense, a tenacious student of his habits, a weatherman of his temperament. I
made summaries of my father's most conspicuous flaws
and figured out early that he was both opéra bouffe and
blunt instrument. If he had not been cruel, I think his children would have adored Henry Wingo, and that sense of
adoration would have been boundless and accommodating
to all the strange geodesics of his fortune. But early in my
life he had installed himself as a cheapshot emperor in a
house where women and children were wise to be afraid.
His approach was always heavy and inconscient. He employed a scorched-earth policy in the raising of his children
and the taming of a strong-willed wife.

In an early poem, Savannah called him "the liege of storm,
the thane of winds" and when she came to New York, she
always claimed, smiling, that she and her brothers had been
fathered by a blitzkrieg. He avoided all that was lovely. He
feared delicacy as though it were a corruption that would
undermine all the fundamental scruples he held sacred.

All he lacked was brains, my mother said, through tears.

"The Sadim touch," Savannah whispered to me behind
closed doors one Christmas after my mother discovered
that my father had three thousand boxes of unsold Christmas cards left, which he had bought on consignment. He
had sold only seventy-five boxes going door to door in
Charleston.

"It's the complete opposite of the Midas touch," Savannah said. "Everything Dad touches turns to shit."

"He didn't even tell Mom that he bought thousands of
Easter cards, too," Luke said. "I found them in the barn."

"He always loses a pile of money," Savannah said.

"Did you see the Christmas cards he was selling?" Luke
asked from his bed.

"No."

"Jesus, Mary, Joseph, the shepherds, the wise men, the
angels, everybody—they were all colored people."

"What?"

"That's right. Dad was only selling them to Negro families. He heard they were selling like hotcakes up North, so he thought he'd jump on the bandwagon down here."

"Poor Dad," I said. "What a dimwit."

"It gives you a lot of confidence knowing his blood is running through your veins," Savannah said. "How humiliating!"

"Has he ever made money on anything?"

"Shrimping," Luke said. "He's the best shrimper that ever lived. It's too bad that's not enough for the both of them."

"If he did, there wouldn't be any such thing as the Sadim touch," Savannah said.

"You can make fun of him all you want, Savannah," Luke said, "but always remember that our father turns to Midas when he puts his nets into the water."

I believe my parents' marriage might have endured out of sheer habit if my father had not bought the gas station and we had not gone to the traveling circus that made a stop near Colleton for the first time in history. I think their life together would have been redeemable, if not ecstatic, if my father could have learned to control the impulses that led him to such excessive and futile gestures. And he made his most flamboyant decisions without allowing my mother the common courtesy of her advice. He treated his business ventures as though they were covert actions, the work of an intelligence officer cut off from communication with his home office, operating freestyle in a hostile environment. Each deal was to be the restoration of his lost honor and lost capital. He never forfeited the faith in his ability to regenerate his dreams through the successful conclusion of one of his extraordinary improvisations. With my father, business was both his contagion and his asylum; it was an incurable illness, a form of gambling and self-destruction. I think that if someone had handed him a million dollars, he could have devised a thousand imaginative ways to squander every penny of it. It was not his fatal flaw—no, he had at least a dozen of these—but it was certainly one of his most dramatic, and the one that kept his family in a precarious situation. His faith in himself was endemic and incorrigible. To protect herself and us, my mother became cunning in handling money and secretive in handling him. They undermined the entire superstructure of their vulnerable love through a lifetime of evasion and subterfuge. Both of them became adept at killing off the best qualities of the other. In some ways, there was something classic and quintessentially American in their marriage. They began as lovers and ended up as the most dangerous and unutterable of enemies. As lovers, they begat children; as enemies, they created damaged, endangered children.

Like all of his pronouncements, my father waited until dinnertime to announce the fact that he had purchased the defunct Esso station near the Colleton Bridge. He believed implicitly in my mother's good manners at mealtime.

"I've got some great news," my father said, but his voice was charged with uncertainty, a rare vulnerability. "Especially for the boys."

"How exciting for the girl," Savannah said, quietly eating her soup.

"What is it, Daddy?" Luke asked. "Did you buy me a new catcher's mitt?"

"Naw. Your old one's just fine. We were tougher when I played ball. We didn't whine for a new glove every year."

"Luke's hand can't fit in the glove anymore, Dad," I said. "Neither can mine. He's had that glove since Little League."

"I bought us a little business today," he said, averting his eyes from my mother. "I've always believed the key to success was diversification. After that lousy season with the shrimp, I figured we needed a little nest egg to fall back on in times of emergency."

"What is it this time, Henry?" my mother said, controlling herself with effort. "What have you done to us this time and when will you ever learn? When will you have enough? We don't have a nickel in our savings account, so how could you even think about buying anything?"

"Banks are there to lend credit, honey. That's their job."

"But they lend money to people who have money. That's their real job," she retorted. "What did you use for collateral, Henry? You didn't mortgage the shrimp boat again?"

"No," he admitted, "I haven't quite finished paying off that last mortgage. I had to be a little creative to pull off this deal. Creative financing, they call it."

"Who calls it that?"

"The big boys. That's who calls it that."

"Since we're practically paupers, it must have been damn creative, Henry," my mother said, her mouth a thin line across her face like a knife-cut on a piece of fruit. "You didn't mortgage the island, did you, Henry? Tell me you didn't mortgage the only real thing we've got. Tell me you didn't mortgage our future and the future of our children. Even you aren't that stupid, Henry."

"I didn't mortgage *all* the island," he said, "just forty acres of it near the bridge. It's so marshy over there you couldn't raise swamp cabbage. I think I took them pretty good if you ask me. And I thought it was time to branch out into other fields. I can even get my fuel for my shrimp boat now that I run my own service station."

"How are you going to drive your shrimp boat to the pumps across three hundred yards of marsh grass?" my mother said furiously. "I can't stand this, Henry. I simply can't tolerate this. The kids will be off to college soon."

"College?" my father said. "I never went to college. Let them get out and work for it if they want college so bad."

"Our children are going to college. We've been paying up on those insurance policies since they were babies and I'm giving that to them at least. They're going to have a chance we didn't have, Henry. I'm not going to let them get trapped like we did. We discussed this when we were first married, and you agreed with me a hundred percent."

"I had to cash in those insurance policies," my father said. "They wanted some hard cash down on the gas station. But I'm gonna make enough money to buy them a college if that's what they really want."

"You sold your children's education for a gas station, Henry Wingo?" my mother asked, and her shock was genuine. "You sold their land and their future so you could pump gas and check oil?"

"The boys can work there during the summers. I got Lanny Whittington to promise that he'll run the station. We're employing people now, Lila. The boys can take over the station one day."

"You think I want Tom and Luke making their living pumping gas?"

"I don't mind pumping gas, Mama," Luke said.

"I've got bigger plans for you than that, Luke. For all of you," she said.

"She only wants her precious boys to pump high-test gasoline," my father sneered. "Besides, there's no use jawing about it. Wingo Esso has its grand opening a week from Tuesday. It's going to be a real extravaganza. Balloons, free Cokes, ribbons, fireworks. I've even hired a clown from that traveling circus to entertain the children."

"You don't need to hire a clown, Henry. You already got one who owns the gas station."

"You've always lacked vision, Lila," my father said, stung. "Who knows what I'd have accomplished if I'd married a woman who believed in me."

"I know, Henry. I know very well. Not a goddamn thing," my mother said, getting up from the table and walking quickly to her bedroom, slamming the door behind her.

When she was gone, my father looked around at us and said, "Isn't there anyone who's going to congratulate me? This is a big moment in the Wingo family's history."

"Congratulations, Dad," Savannah said, raising her glass of milk for a toast.

"This is the big one," my father said. "This is the chance I've been waiting for. Don't be upset by your mother. She's really happy about the whole thing. She's always had trouble expressing her real feelings."

Savannah said, "She didn't seem to have much trouble expressing her real feelings this time, Daddy. She thinks you're going to lose your shirt again."

"No, wrong. This time I can smell the ol' jackpot. Henry Wingo's number is coming up. You wait. This gas station is going to take off and your mother's going to be wearing ermine and having strings of real pearls hanging down to her ankles. She doesn't understand that you got to take risks. I'm the risk taker in the family. I'm like a riverboat gambler. I take chances the average Joe would never dream of taking."

The Esso station my father had bought was located directly across the street from Ferguson's Gulf station, the most successful service station in Colleton County, by far. Three men before my father had tried to make a go of the gas station on that corner but had failed. There was no logical reason why people would pull into the Gulf station instead of the Esso station except for some mysterious concept known as location. In all small towns, there is such a thing as a good corner and a bad one, and it has more to do with metaphysics than with geography. One corner of a street simply welcomes a gas station more than another. My father purchased the corner station that did not feel right. He believed his flair and showmanship would ensure his success where others before him had failed so dismally.

He did have a singular talent for extravaganza and he opened Wingo Esso with enough fanfare to bring half the town to his corner of the world. He talked the band director into marching the high school band straight down the Street of Tides at high noon, led by baton-twirling majorettes and Mr. Fruit shimmying and shaking out his own wild improvised dance, keeping time with his whistle, throwing his head straight back into sunlight, then jackknifing forward until his nose nearly touched his shoelaces. When the band made the turn into the gas station, my father released three hundred helium-filled balloons, which rose straight up into the air and hovered over the town like lost flowers. He handed out lollipops and bubble gum to the kids. Roman candles exploded on the roof, showering sparks to the ground. The circus clown showed up late and my father was both surprised and delighted that he was a midget. The clown was drunk and broke a dozen Coke bottles trying to juggle them on the back of our pickup truck. The mayor of Colleton, Boogie Weiters, at the ribbon-cutting ceremony, made a rather impassioned speech on the importance of attracting new industry to Colleton County. The drunk clown shouted that that should be easy since Colleton County had never attracted any old industry. The crowd applauded the clown, who responded with a spectacular handstand on the cab of the pickup. The Volunteer Fire Department arrived with their new fire truck and received a whole tank of gas free of charge because Henry Wingo wanted them to know how much he appreciated the fine job they were doing protecting the property of Colleton. A reporter from the *Colleton Gazette* interviewed my father and took his picture with the clown sitting on his shoulder. The high school band played a medley of patriotic songs and my father raised an American flag on top of the gas station when they played "The Star-Spangled

Banner." Toward the end of the day, the flag was set afire
by an errant Roman candle and was extinguished by the
members of the Volunteer Fire Department.

That night we celebrated the successful opening-day ceremonies of Wingo Esso by going to the circus. Even though
my mother had refused to attend either the opening-day
festivities or the circus, I had never seen my father's mood
so effervescent or irrepressible. If he had been a nimble
man, I'm sure he would have backflipped his way onto the
circus grounds. There was a new buoyancy and cockiness
to his walk and he high-stepped it among the crowd that
moved to the rhythms of the carnival music. Outside the
circus tent, he pitched baseballs at weighted tenpins until
he won my mother a teddy bear. He applauded as Luke
and I sank free throws with a cheap basketball at a tilted
steel rim.

We entered the freak show and watched in amazement
as the bearded lady spit tobacco juice into a Dr. Pepper
bottle. Luke shook hands with the hundred-year-old baby
and we listened to Siamese twins sing "What a Friend We
Have in Jesus." We cheered as Altus Rossiter, the town
bully, was knocked unconscious by a kangaroo wearing
boxing gloves.

The owner of the circus, Smitty Smith, came up to talk
with my father. They had met at the shrimp dock the morning the circus arrived in Colleton and Smitty had bought
every fish my father caught that day to feed the five seals
that Smitty had described as the backbone of the circus. He
had claimed to have the best seal act in the Southeast and
the worst tiger and elephant show in the world. The elephant was too old, Smitty had explained, and the tiger was
too young. There was nothing lower than a one-clown circus, my father had said after the midget had passed out in
the back of the pickup truck that afternoon, but we saw
him working the crowd at the entrance to the main tent,
and though he seemed wobbly, he was performing a pass-
able handstand.

We pulled our father away and took seats high in the
bleachers on the top row. A woman dressed in a gold-
sequined outfit rode an elephant around the ring. The elephant was wrinkled with great age and when he went
down on his knees to make his bow, he had to be helped

to his feet again by the woman, the clown, and Smitty. The elephant looked weary and threadbare to the point of extinction. The clown juggled two balls in the air and Savannah said that *she* could juggle two balls.

"I wonder how much he'd take for the elephant?" I heard my father say. "He'd be great for the gas station."

"Yeah, he could pump high-test with his trunk," said Luke.

The spotlight centered on Smitty, who, dressed in a top hat and a garish red tuxedo, spoke into a scratchy microphone. The echoes made it sound as if four men were exhorting the crowd; his words overlapped like waves.

"Ladies and gentlemen, I will now enter the cage of the great Bengal tiger, Caesar, who was taken from his home in India after he killed three rajahs and thirteen villagers. Thirteen very slow villagers. Caesar is a new addition to my circus family and is rather jumpy in front of crowds. We must ask for absolute silence during the next act. Caesar mauled our former animal trainer outside of Aiken, South Carolina, and I have been forced to step in because, as you know, ladies and gentlemen, the show must go on."

The elephant may have been old and the kangaroo a little seedy, but the tiger was a young, magnificent animal. It watched Smitty as the ringmaster entered the large cage armed with a whip and a chair. Everything about the tiger implied menace. It lacked the humility of a circus animal, that quality of appeasement and cringing servitude that comes from years of bondage and performance under the glaring lights. The tiger's gaze was a study in wildness. Smitty snapped his whip above the tiger's ear and commanded that the tiger circle the ring. The tiger did not move but stared at Smitty with a concentration that unnerved the crowd. The whip sang again and Smitty's voice rose once more above the hum of the crowd. The tiger left his perch and circled the cage reluctantly, snarling with discontent. Smitty threw his hat near the tiger and shouted "Fetch" to the tiger. The tiger pounced on the hat, hurled it into the air, and cut it into pieces with his claws before it could hit the earth. The whip caught the tiger on the shoulder and Smitty drove the beast into a corner and bent down angrily to study what was left of his hat, which now looked like the remnants of a blown-out retread. You could tell Smitty

was not taking the loss of his top hat well. The performance
became secondary to the shimmering, palpable hatred between the tiger and the ringmaster.

Smitty lit a ring of fire and, lashing the tiger again and
again, made the tiger leap through the burning hoop, its
shining coat iridescent against the flames. The audience
cheered. Smitty, lathered with perspiration, then approached Caesar with his chair, his whip exploding above
the tiger's yellow eyes, and shouted another command; but
Caesar moved directly toward Smitty, slashing the air with
his claws fully extended. Smitty withdrew and the cat sent
him on a headlong dizzying retreat across the ring, and the
sweeps of the forepaws caused tremors of awe in the exhilarated crowd. Smitty was running backward with only
the chair between him and certain decapitation. Two roust-
abouts rushed up to the cage with long poles and stopped
the tiger's furious attack, allowing Smitty to make his escape through the cage door. Caesar took one of the poles
in his jaws and snapped it in half, then retreated with
dignity to the center of the cage and sat on his haunches
in the most kingly repose. In frustration, Smitty lashed the
cage with his whip and the crowd rose to its feet to applaud
the untamable cat. Caesar rolled and stretched voluptu-
ously in folds of black and gold. Then he lifted his eyes
when he heard the seals barking as they were moved into
the center ring. The lights shifted and the tiger disappeared
into the night.

The seals were snappy, enthusiastic, and seemed to be
born entertainers as they bounced into the lights balancing
great yellow balls on their shining ebony noses. Smitty had
recovered his composure and he directed the performance
like a man pulling silk through a loom. After each trick, he
flung them a fish, which they caught and consumed in a
single fluid motion. Their heads were cunning, angelic, and
sleek. Brightly, they applauded themselves with their front
flippers.

"Those are my fish those seals are eating, kids. My fish.
I think they ought to make an announcement," said my
father.

The five seals were named Sambone, Helen of Troy, Ne-
buchadnezzar, Cleopatra, and Nashua, but Sambone was
clearly the star of their frivolous satiny performance. They

moved like otters who had mated with dolphins, and there
was an ungainly grace to their spirited antics. The five of
them sent one ball spinning from black nose to black nose,
bouncing it high in the air and sending it aloft until it fell
expertly on the nose of another seal who executed the same
precise moves and sailed the ball high into the lights again.
When Cleopatra finally misjudged the ball and it went sailing into the darkness, she sulked when she was not rewarded with a fish. Then the seals had a bowling match
and a baseball game before Sambone mounted a small platform and began playing "Dixie" on a row of horns. The
other seals barked along in harmony and the crowd joined
in the song. We had only got to "Look away, look away,"
when we heard a loud roar from Caesar in his cage in the
darkened downstage ring. As the song ended, the spotlight
moved away from the seals and we saw the tiger with his
face pressed against the bars swinging his powerful forelegs
outside the cage, roaring out his hatred for the seals. Sambone took no notice and began again his cacophonous rendition of "Dixie." Still working the seals, Smitty moved out
of the center ring and moved Caesar out of the limelight
by whipping his ferocious head until he went snarling back
in retreat.

"He either hates seals or those horns hurt his ears," my
father said.

"Maybe he just hates 'Dixie,' " Savannah said.

For the grand finale the seals spread out in a wide circle
and began to toss the ball again, and this time they hurled
the ball twenty feet in the air, each seal trying to toss the
ball higher and higher, the circle widening each time. Each
time it seemed like the ball had strayed too far from the
perimeter, a seal would make a running spectacular catch
and then, taking a moment to control the ball, would launch
it anew in a towering parabola toward the other side of the
ring. Once again it was Cleopatra who made the error of
judgment that ended the act. Nashua sent the ball in a
towering arc that almost touched the trapeze hanging from
the roof supports; Cleopatra could not quite reach the ball
and it veered off her nose into the dark. Sambone, who
played the game with the passion of a center fielder, pursued the ball into the darkness and Smitty blew his whistle
for the seals to assemble for the final bow.

Through the applause we heard the death screams of Sambone. The lights swung to the downstage ring and caught the moment when the tiger lifted the seal against the bars and bit Sambone's head off. Smitty was there, illuminated in ghastly shadow, whipping the tiger. Children were running from their seats and the entire crowd groaned when the tiger put Sambone to the ground and, with one great swipe of its claws, eviscerated the seal. Sambone's intestines flowed out of his body in a glistening flood and the tiger's jaws were bright red with blood. In hysteria and revulsion, the crowd ran for the exits and mothers hid their children's eyes with their hands. The tiger began eating the seal before three hundred schoolchildren.

That was the night my father bought the tiger.

I thought my mother would take her shotgun down from the gun case and kill both my father and Caesar when we arrived home towing the tiger's cage behind our pickup. Caesar was still gnawing on the half-eaten seal when my mother began screaming at Dad. She was not so much angry as she was homicidal. Smitty was going to kill Caesar himself after the show when my father intervened and offered to take the tiger off Smitty's hands. Someone had forgotten to feed the tiger before the performance and my father had pleaded for the tiger's life by suggesting he had only done the natural thing. My father wrote Smitty a check for two hundred dollars and got him to throw in the whip, the cage, and the ring of fire in the deal. Sambone had been the heart and soul of the animal act, the only one of the seals who could play "Dixie" on the horns. The other seals, Smitty explained hysterically, could only toss balls and eat mullet. When the clown had teased Smitty about his prowess as an animal trainer, Smitty hung the midget on a coatrack in his trailer. The clown's profanity added a touch of unreality to the purchase of Caesar. As we stood outside in the darkness, we watched the tiger devour the entrails of the seal he had forced through the bars of his cage. Luke speculated that Sambone was the first seal in history ever devoured by a tiger.

"Seals don't worry much about tigers in the wild," Luke explained as we watched the tiger while Dad was haggling over the price with Smitty. "It's just not one of their big problems."

"I wonder if a message goes out to all the seals in the world," Savannah mused. "When you play 'Dixie' on the horns, look out for tigers. Isn't that how evolution is supposed to work?"

"I'd look out for anything that big," I said in awe. "What in God's name does Dad want with a Bengal tiger?"

"We haven't had a house pet since Joop died," Savannah said. "You know how sentimental Dad is."

"You did it again, Henry," my mother said, inspecting the tiger at a distance. "We'll be the laughingstock of Colleton once again. I want that tiger gone by sunrise. I don't want word to get out again that I married the biggest fool in South Carolina."

"I can't just set the bastard loose, Lila. He's liable to eat one of those nice families while they're heehawing at us Wingos. He killed that seal he's chewing on in there. That's how come I got him so cheap."

"I guess I couldn't expect you to pass up a golden opportunity like that, could I now, Henry?"

"It's an advertising gimmick," my father said proudly, "for my gas station. I thought of it almost as soon as I heard that seal screaming. It hit me, bang, a brainstorm: This will draw the customers in."

"Dad's going to teach the tiger how to play 'Dixie' on the horns," Savannah said.

"Nope, he's gonna throw a live seal to the tiger every night and let the customers bet on who wins," Luke said, doubling over with laughter.

"I may throw my mouthy children to the tiger if they don't shut their yaps and have some respect for their father. I'm in a real good mood, so I don't want anyone pissing me off. Got it? I can teach you something about the way the modern world works if you'll just listen. We just bought an Esso station, right?"

"Right," Luke said.

"Esso advertises all over the world, right? Follow me so far? They spend millions of dollars advertising their products so grinning butthooks will drive their cars into an Esso station when they could just as easily fill up with Shell or Texaco or Gulf. Still with me?"

"Yes, sir."

"Okay, nectarines. What is their advertisement right now, this very minute?" he said, his voice rising in excitement. "Playing on every television and radio in the free world. Making people buy Esso instead of that other crap. Bringing droves of paying customers up to the Esso pumps begging for the right kind of gas because they've been brainwashed by a brilliant advertising campaign. Get it? Get it?"

"Oh, no," Savannah said, nearly hysterical. "I got it. I got it."

"Well, what is it, Savannah?" my mother asked impatiently.

"When you buy Esso, Mama," she said, "you put a tiger in your tank."

"Damn right," my father exploded. "And who's the only goddamn Esso station owner in the country who's got him a real tiger sitting beside the pumps? Wingo Esso. That's who. Henry Goddamn Genius Wingo, that's who."

Henry Goddamn Genius Wingo kept his gas station running for six months, and he was proven right about the tiger. He set the tiger's cage up on the corner next to the bridge and motorists could watch the tiger pace and growl as they got their car serviced. Children begged their parents to take them to see the tiger even if there was no need to buy gas. Caesar held children in the same high esteem as he held seals and there was some initial worry about Caesar making his lunch of the preschoolers of the town, but the tiger inspired a rare vigilance among the mothers of Colleton. Languor and ferocity were the tiger's two prevailing moods, but the appearance of children always stimulated Caesar to interludes of extraordinary wildness. He would lunge out of his cage, claws extended and swinging, sending the children and their parents surging backward, squealing and having a marvelous time. My father thought Caesar acted like a rabid dog but noted that he outweighed any rabid dog by four hundred or more pounds.

Feeding Caesar was a problem my father happily assigned to his sons. I had never entertained a single prejudice against a tiger until I realized that Caesar would as soon eat me as he would a chicken neck. Nor was it a simple thing to approach Caesar's cage during feeding time. From the beginning, Caesar and I had a simple, straightforward relationship, one built on a solid foundation of mutual loathing. Caesar would come to love Luke and even allow him to scratch his back through the bars, but the relationship would evolve slowly and did not apply during the first months of Wingo Esso. Luke would signal for me to approach the front of the cage, where I would speak to the tiger in a soothing voice as he tried to behead me with those fabulous claws. While I was risking my life, Luke would sneak around to the back of the cage and slide a hubcap, brimming with chicken necks and dry cat food, through the bars. Caesar would hear Luke, disengage from my side of the cage, and with the quickest, most unpredictable movement I had yet witnessed in the animal kingdom would be trying to impale Luke with one of those violent swings as Luke fell away from the bars and landed on his back.

"You've got to keep him busy, Tom," Luke would say.

"What do you want me to do? Let him chew on my fist?"

"Whistle 'Dixie,' " Luke said, brushing gravel from his back. "Do anything."

"I don't want him relating me to a seal in any way."

Luke would stand near the cage and watch Caesar crack chicken necks as if he were melting butter on his tongue.

"This is the prince of the animal kingdom," he said, "the most beautiful animal in the world."

"Why couldn't Esso have a different advertising campaign, Luke?" I complained. "You know, something like 'Put a guppy in your tank' or 'Put a hamster in your tank.' "

"Because they just aren't interesting animals, Tom. Not like Caesar. He doesn't give of himself lightly. I like that. I really like that. He makes you earn it all."

Ferguson's Gulf station started the first full-fledged gas war in Colleton's history. Ferguson lowered the price of gasoline a nickel a gallon and my father had little choice but to follow suit. In vain, he did everything to keep his station open, but it was rumored that Ferguson had picked up a powerful sponsor. When the bank finally repossessed our station, the price for a gallon of gasoline had fallen from thirty cents a gallon to a dime. Dad tried to include the tiger as a disposable asset, but the bank refused. Once again there were terrible arguments, sad, interminable arguments, in the house of Wingo. Dad had managed to pay

back the mortgage against the island land but lost everything else. Again we were in desperate financial straits and
again he made us solvent by having his best year as a
shrimper. Soon after the loss of the gas station, Reese Newbury drove out to the island in his Cadillac and offered to
buy the island for fifty thousand dollars with no questions
asked. My father refused. A week later my father discovered it was Reese Newbury who had been the silent financial partner who ensured the success of Ferguson's Gulf
during the gasoline war.

"He thought he could get my island," my father said.
"He ruined my business because he wanted the island."

So my father went back to the river and my mother grew
more silent and more embittered and the Wingos ended
up as the only family in Colleton County with a tiger who
could jump through a burning ring as a pet.

Throughout my childhood I would find myself studying
my parents when they were reposed and peaceful in their
home. Secretly, I would try to figure out what made it work,
what sinister or benevolent forces kept their militant alliance intact, what tender or explosive elements lay beneath
the surface of their strange and incandescent love for each
other. For I could always feel the fury of some higher love
shimmering between them, even in their worst and most
dangerous moments. It was something I could only feel,
never touch. I could not figure out what my mother saw
in my father or why she remained as both ruler and prisoner
in his house. Their signals were always mixed and confused
and I could never sound the depths of their always volatile
relationship. It was clear my father adored my mother, but
it was not clear to me why a man should feel compelled to
abuse what he loved the most. My mother often seemed
to despise everything my father stood for, but there were
moments of strange complicity when I would see a look
pass between them so charged with passion and awareness
of the other that I would blush for having accidentally shared
it. I wondered how I would come to love a woman, and
with both pleasure and terror, I would think that somewhere in the world there was some laughing, singing girl
who would one day become my wife. In my mind, I could
see her dancing and playing and flirting in preparation for

that day of awe and wonder when we would meet and in mutual ecstasy declare, "I shall live with you forever." How much of my father would I bring to that singing girl's life? How much of my mother? And how many days would it take before I, Tom Wingo, child of storm, would silence her laughter and song for all time? How long would it take for me to end the dance of that laughing girl who would not know the doubts and imperfections I brought to the task of loving a woman? I loved the image of this girl long before I ever met her and wanted to warn her to beware the day when I would come into her life. Somewhere in America she was waiting out her childhood innocent of her destiny. She did not know that she was on a collision course with a boy so damaged and bewildered he would spend his whole life trying to figure out how love was supposed to feel, how it manifested itself between two people, and how it could be practiced without rage and sorrow and blood. I was thirteen years old when I decided that this wonderful girl deserved much better and I would warn her long before I interfered with her lovely passage and transfiguring dance.

During these meditations on the nature of love, I held fast to one story of my parents that my father told again and again as he moved his boat in darkness out toward the Atlantic breakers. It was the story of their first meeting in Atlanta, when my father was a young lieutenant visiting the town for the first time on leave and my mother was selling children's clothing in Davison's department store on Peachtree. There was always rapture on his face and pleasure in my father's voice when he told of their chance encounter. He was a stranger in town and wanted to meet some city girls and a barber had told him that the prettiest girls in the South could be found walking on Peachtree Street. He was wearing his uniform and felt handsome as only young men about to go to war can feel. He spotted my mother coming out of Davison's when she got off work and he said he had never seen a more beautiful girl in his life. She was carrying a shopping bag and a red purse and she crossed the street through traffic to get to the bus stop. He followed her, trying to figure out how to approach her, how to speak to her, how to ask her name. He was shy with girls, but he was afraid the bus would come and she would disappear from his life forever, before he had the chance to praise her beauty or hear the sound of her name. Boldly, he introduced himself and told her that he was a pilot in the Army Air Corps and in Atlanta on furlough and he would appreciate it highly if she could show him around her city. She ignored him and looked down Peachtree for the bus. Desperate, he told her that she seemed unpatriotic, that he would be off to the war in a year or two, that he would most likely be killed but that he could accept his fate if she would just let him take her to dinner. He told jokes and tried to make her laugh. He told her he was Errol Flynn's younger brother, that his father owned Davison's, that he wished it was raining so he could throw his coat over a mud puddle and let her step across it. The bus approached from the south and he could not stop talking. Like any properly raised southern girl, my mother continued to ignore him, but my father noticed that she was amused. From his back pocket, he pulled out a letter from his mother and pretended it was a letter of recommendation from Franklin D. Roosevelt, testifying that Lieutenant Henry Wingo was a man of sterling character who could be trusted by any American young woman, especially the prettiest woman ever seen on Peachtree Street in the history of Atlanta. My mother blushed and stepped up onto the bus and paid her fare without looking back. Walking down the aisle, she took a seat by an open window. My father stood outside the bus below that window and begged her to give him her phone number. She smiled and considered it. The bus began to pull away from the curb and my father raced alongside it. As the bus shifted into second gear, my father, sprinting as fast as he ever ran in his life, fell behind and lost the image of my mother's face framed in the window. He kept running, even though the bus was almost past him when he saw my mother's head sticking out the window and he heard her cry out the first words she ever directed to him, "Macon three-seven, two, eight, four."

When my father would tell that story, Savannah would always whisper, "Tell him the wrong number, Mama. Please tell him the wrong number." Or she would say, "Forget the number, Dad. Just forget it."

But he remembered. Henry Wingo remembered as he steered his boat through tides.

* * *

The tiger in the back yard became a source of embarrassment to my mother and a source of constant joy to Luke. To my mother, Caesar was symbolic of my father's clumsiest and most ill-managed folly, the living heraldry of defeat recumbent among a pile of bones. But Luke discovered a natural and artless affinity for tigers and he began a slow apprenticeship designed to gain both Caesar's trust and his affection. It was Luke's theory that Smitty had abused Caesar and that the tiger, like any animal, would respond to a soft laying on of hands and a long strategic season of kindness. Luke was the only one who fed Caesar and it took more than two months before Luke could approach the cage without Caesar trying to pull him through the bars. Then, there came the day when I found Luke scratching the tiger's back with a garden rake. The tiger was purring in ecstasy and I watched, stricken, as Luke reached inside the cage and scratched the tiger's great golden head with his hand.

Three months after we brought the tiger home, Savannah woke me up during a rainstorm and whispered, "You ain't gonna believe this one."

"It's two o'clock in the morning, Savannah," I said irritably. "Juries don't even convict people who kill their sisters after being woke up at two o'clock in the morning."

"Luke is with Caesar."

"I don't care if he's with the three Magi. I want to go back to sleep."

"He's got the tiger out of the cage. In the barn."

We went out the window and silently made our way to the barn. Slowly we peered through the slight crack in the barn door and in the lantern light saw Luke with a chain and a whip, sending Caesar in controlled circles around the barn. Luke then lit rags soaked in kerosene and called for the tiger to go through the burning ring. "Now, Caesar," he said, and the tiger flowed through the ring like sunshine through a glass window. Caesar made another turn around the barn and came roaring back in that same fluid motion, going through that burning circle in a celebration of strength and speed. Luke then cracked the whip three times in succession and the tiger walked to the open door of his cage and jumped inside. Luke rewarded him

with venison steaks and nuzzled his head against Caesar's
when the steaks were devoured.

"He's crazy," I whispered to Savannah.

"No," she said, "that's your brother Luke. And he's magnificent."

14

I grew up loathing Good Fridays. It was a seasonal aver-
sion that had little to do with theology but everything
to do with the rites of worship and the odd slant my grandfather brought to his overenthusiastic commemoration of
Christ's passion.

Good Friday was the day when Amos Wingo each year
walked to the shed behind his house in Colleton proper
and dusted off the ninety-pound wooden cross he had made
in a violent seizure of religious extravagance when he was
a boy of fourteen. From noon to three on that commemo-
rative day he would walk up and down the length of the
Street of Tides to remind the backsliding, sinful citizenry
of my hometown of the unimaginable suffering of Jesus
Christ on that melancholy hill above Jerusalem so long ago.
It was the summit and the Grand Guignol of my grandfather's liturgical year; it embodied characteristics of both
the saints and the asylum. There was always a lunatic beauty
to his walk.

I would have preferred that my grandfather celebrated
Good Friday in a quieter, more contemplative fashion. It
embarrassed me deeply to watch his gaunt, angular body
bent under the weight of the cross, trudging through the
congested traffic, stopping at intersections, oblivious to the
admixture of scorn and awe of his townsmen, sweat dis-
coloring his costume, and his lips moving continuously in

the inaudible worship of his Creator. He was a figure of majesty to some, a perfect jackass to others. Each year the sheriff would issue a ticket for obstructing traffic and each year the parishoners of the Baptist church would take up a special collection to pay the fine. Through the years, his offbeat spiritual trek of remembrance had become something of a venerated annual phenomenon and had begun to attract a sizable ingathering of pilgrims and tourists who collected along the Street of Tides to pray and read the Bible as Grandpa Wingo huffed and puffed his way through his solemn reenactment of the single walk that changed the history of the Western soul. Each year the *Colleton Gazette* published a photograph of his walk the week following Easter Sunday.

When we were children, both Savannah and I would beg him to take his act to Charleston or Columbia, cities we considered to be far more gaudy and reprehensible in the eyes of the Lord than small, mild Colleton could ever be. My grandmother expressed her own mortification by retreating to her bedroom with a full bottle of Beefeater gin and a collection of back issues of *Police Gazette* that she had commandeered from Fender's barbershop. When the walk was completed at three, so was the bottle, and my grandmother would be comatose until late the next morning. When she awoke to her memorial headache, she would find my grandfather on his knees, praying for her sweet, boozy soul.

During the entire Easter vigil, Amos would watch over the recumbent, motionless body of his wife, who had elaborated her own ritual as an act of self-defense to protest the ceremony of observance he insisted on performing. There was a bizarre euphony in the counterbalance of their spirits. On Sunday morning, sickened by her debauch but having made her annual point, my grandmother, as she put it, "rose from the goddamn dead" in time to accompany my grandfather to Easter Sunday services. It was her only church appearance of the year and, in its own way, became as traditional in the spiritual life of the town as my grandfather's walk.

In my junior year, on the Wednesday before Easter, I walked to my grandfather's house after school with Savannah. We stopped by Long's Pharmacy for a cherry Coke and took it out by the river and drank it sitting on the sea wall, watching the fiddler crabs wave their claws in the mud below us.

"Good Friday is coming up again," I said to my sister. "I hate that day."

She grinned and punched me on the arm, saying, "It's good for a family to face total humiliation once a year. It's character-building to have a whole town laugh at your grandfather, then laugh at you."

"I wouldn't mind it if I didn't have to be there," I answered, my eyes fixed on the hypnotic movement of the crabs beneath us. They were like quarters scattered randomly across the mud. "Dad's putting you on the lemonade stand this year. He's going to film the major highlights of the walk again."

"Oh, grotesque," she said. "He's filmed it for the past five years. He's got five years of film to prove to any court that grandpa's a lunatic."

"Dad says it's for the family archives and that we'll thank him one day for making a record of our childhood."

"Oh, sure," she said. "That's all I want. A photographic history of Auschwitz. Of course, you think this is a normal family."

"I don't know if it's a normal family or not," I said. "It's the only family I've ever lived in."

"It's a nut-house factory. Mark my words."

My grandfather's house in Colleton was a simple one-story frame house, painted white with red trim, built on a half acre of land beside the Colleton River. When we entered the house we found our grandmother in the kitchen watching my grandfather work on his cross in the back yard.

"There he is," she said in a weary, exasperated voice, nodding toward the back yard as she saw us enter. "Your grandpa. My husband. The village idiot. He's been working on his prop all day."

"What's he doing to it, Tolitha?" I asked, calling her by her given name according to her own desires.

"A wheel," Savannah said, laughing as she ran to the window.

"He said folks won't mind a sixty-year-old man putting a wheel on his cross. He said that Jesus was only thirty-three when he took a walk up that hill, so no one should expect a sixty-year-old man to do much better. He gets softer in the head each year. I'm going to have to put him in a home soon. No question about it. The highway patrol was out here again this week trying to get him to hand in his driver's license. They say he's a danger on the road every time he takes his Ford for a spin."

"Why did you marry him, Tolitha?" Savannah asked. "It seems ridiculous that two people so different in every way could live together."

My grandmother looked out toward the yard again, the window reflected off her glasses in a trapezoid of light, repeating in glass what she saw from the window. The question had taken her by surprise and I realized Savannah had asked one of those forbidden questions, one with daunting implications, whose mystery predated our own birth.

"Let me get you some iced tea," Tolitha said finally. "He'll dawdle in here in a while and I don't get a chance to visit with you so much now that you're grown and out spoonin' and such."

She poured three huge glasses of tea, then floated mint leaves above the chipped ice. When she sat on her stool, she adjusted her eyeglasses over her nose.

"I knew your grandpa was a Christian man when I first met him. That's because everybody in town was Christian then. I was a Christian, too, only I was fourteen when we got married, too young to know anything one way or the other. It wasn't until later that I realized he was a fanatic. He kind of hid it from me when we were courting because he was so riled up and eager to get at me."

"Tolitha," I said, totally embarrassed.

"You're such a child sometimes, Tom," Savannah said. "You act like you were snake-bit every time the subject of sex comes up."

My grandmother laughed and continued. "I stirred him up good when I was a girl-child, and I never heard nothing much about Jesus when I had him beneath the sheets in those early years."

"Tolitha, please, for God's sake," I begged. "We don't want to hear all that."

"Yes, we do," Savannah disagreed. "It's fascinating."

"Who but a weirdo like you wants to hear a play-by-play description of sex between their grandparents?"

"Then, as the years passed, he got tired of me as all men do and he started praying to our Lord on what you might call a twenty-four-hour basis until he got kind of soft in the head about it. Never made a decent living in his life. Just cut hair, sold a few Bibles, and ran his mouth about heaven and hell and everything in between."

"But he's such a good man," I interjected.

She turned and gazed out the window at my grandfather. There was no ardor in her gaze, but there was softness and an abiding affection. He was still hunched over his cross, attaching a rubber tricycle wheel to its base. "People ask me all the time what it's like being married to a saint. Boring, I tell them. Better to marry a devil. I've tasted a little bit of heaven in my life and a little bit of hell and I'll take hell every time. But what you say is true, Tom. He is a mighty fine man."

"Why did you leave him during the Depression?" Savannah asked, encouraged by her openness, the guileless spillage of old secrets. "Dad won't even talk about it."

"I guess you're old enough to know," she said, turning toward us, her voice suddenly despondent, almost dreamy. "In the middle of the Depression, he quit his job and started preaching the Lord's word down in front of Baitery's Pharmacy. That paid even less money than barbering. He got it into his head that the Depression was a sign that the world was going to end. It was easy to think that. A lot of boys got the same idea about that time. We were starving or close to it. I didn't cotton too much to starving. I told Amos I was leaving him. Of course, he didn't believe me because folks didn't divorce in those days. I told him to take care of your father or I'd come back and kill him, and I hitched a ride and headed for Atlanta. I got a job at Rich's department store the same week. After a while, I met Papa John and married him a couple of days later."

"That's horrible, Tolitha," I said. "That's the worst thing I ever heard."

"That's the saint out in the back yard, Tom," she said, her eyes narrowing behind the glasses, her eyebrows touching like two slightly mismatched caterpillars. "The woman is here in the kitchen. I'm not proud of everything I did, but I'll tell you everything I did."

"No wonder Dad's so screwed up," I said, whistling.

"Shut up, Tom. You're such a traditionalist," Savannah said archly. "You don't understand a thing about survival."

"I did the best I could under the circumstances. Seemed like the whole world went a little crazy around that time and I didn't get no exemption."

"Go on," I said, "before Grandpa gets in here."

"Don't worry about Grandpa. He'll be playing with that cross until dinnertime. Well, it was hardest on your father. I'll admit that. He was only eleven or so when I brought him up to Atlanta, and he hadn't seen me in maybe five years. He hardly even knew me and couldn't understand either why I had left or why he had to call me Tolitha and not Mama. He used to cry out in his sleep, 'Mama, Mama, Mama,' and Papa John used to hear it and it liked to break his sweet heart. He would go in and sing Greek songs to your daddy until he went back to sleep. Your daddy didn't know no Tolitha and didn't want to know her. I'd do it differently now. Honestly, I would. But now isn't then. And there's no returning to then."

"It's hard to see Dad as a tragic figure," Savannah said. "Especially a tragic child. I can't even imagine him as a little kid."

"Did you have other husbands, Tolitha?" I asked.

"Ha," she laughed. "Your mother's been talking again."

"No," I said quickly, "I've just heard rumors around town."

"After Papa John died I was half crazy with grief. I took the money he left me, and it was a fair sum, I mean to tell you, and lit out for all these places I heard about. Hong Kong, Africa, India. I went around the world, traveling by ship. First class from port to port. And I had this problem. Everybody's always loved me. Especially men. I'm just that kind of person. Men just love to buzz around me like there was a sweet smell coming from me. I just sat there and watched 'em line up trying to make me laugh or buy me a couple of drinks. I married a couple of those old boys. The longest lasted about six months. That marriage lasted exactly the time it took to sail from Madagascar to Capetown. He wanted me to do unmentionable, filthy things to him."

"What unmentionable, filthy things?" Savannah asked breathlessly, leaning toward my grandmother.

"No. No. Don't ask her that," I pleaded. "Don't ask her."

"Why?" Savannah asked me.

"Because she'll tell us, Savannah. She'll tell us and it will be something horrible and embarrassing."

"He wanted me to suck the area where his legs met," my grandmother explained, rather primly for her, I had to admit. She always told you a bit more than you ever wanted to hear.

"How disgusting," Savannah said.

"He had animal appetites," Tolitha said. "It was a nightmare."

"Why did you come back to Grandpa?" I asked, wanting to steer the conversation from animal appetites.

She turned her gaze toward me and lifted her glass of tea to her lips. For a moment I thought she wasn't going to answer, or couldn't.

"I got tired, Tom. Real tired. And I was starting to get old, to look old, to feel old. I knew Amos would always be here by the river and always be waiting for me. I knew I could light down here and he would never say a word to me. He'd just be thankful I came back. Your Daddy's the same way about Lila. He's only been interested in a single woman his whole life. Just like his father. It just goes to show you that it's easier for blood to carry a fanatic down to a new generation than whatever it was that made everyone love me."

"But everyone loves Grandpa, too," I said, suddenly feeling sorry for the man in the background.

"They love him because he's a fanatic, Tom. Because he picks up that cross each year. But I say who needs a saint? I'd rather have a drink and a couple of laughs."

"But you love Grandpa, don't you, Tolitha?" I insisted.

"Love." She turned the word over in her mouth like a flavorless lozenge. "Yes, I suppose I do love him. You have to love what you can always come back to, what's home waiting for you. I was thinking about time the other day. Not love, but time, and they're related somehow but I'm not smart enough to know how exactly. I was married to your grandfather and to Papa John for about the same amount of time. But when I look back at my life it seems I was married to Papa

John for a few days. That's how happy I was. Seems like I was married to your grandpa for a thousand years."

"This is an adult conversation," Savannah announced proudly. "I've been waiting for a long time to have a truly adult conversation."

"Your parents are just trying to protect you from things they don't think children should know, Savannah. They don't approve of the life I've led. But since it's an adult conversation, I don't think they need to know anything about it."

"I'd never tell," Savannah said. "But Tom can be such a child sometimes."

I ignored Savannah and asked Tolitha, "Do you think Dad ever got over being left when he was a little boy?"

"Do you mean do I think he's forgiven me, Tom?" she said. "I think so. In family matters you can get over anything. That's one thing you'll learn as an adult. There's a lot you have to learn which is a lot worse than that. You'd never think of forgiving a friend for some of the things your parents did to you. But with friends it's different. Friends aren't the roll of the dice."

"I need to help Grandpa fix up his cross," I said.

"Yeah, and I need to get to the liquor store," Tolitha said.

"You plan to get liquored up again on Good Friday?" I asked.

"Tom, you are so rude," Savannah said.

Tolitha laughed and said, "That's the only civilized response to his walk I can think of. It also reminds him that he doesn't own me and never will. It's my way of telling him how ridiculous the whole thing is. Of course, he talked it over with God a few days ago and got the go-ahead, so there's no talking sense into him."

"He's just being a good Christian. That's what he told me," I said. "He said if the world was acting right, the whole town of Colleton would be out there with crosses walking with him."

"Then they'd lock the whole town up. No, Tom. I'm not saying anything against being a good Christian. Believe me. I want you to be a good Christian man; just don't take it so goddamn seriously."

"Are you a good Christian, Tolitha?" asked Savannah. "Do you think you're going to heaven?"

"I've never done one thing in my life that makes me deserve to burn in hell for all eternity. Any god that does that isn't deserving of the name. I've tried hard to live an interesting life and I don't see any harm that comes from that."

"Don't you think Grandpa's led an interesting life, too?" I said.

"Tom, you ask the silliest questions," Savannah scolded.

"Remember, Tom, whenever you consider what makes up an interesting life, think of this. When your grandpa was cutting hair and your mom and dad were picking crabs and heading shrimp, I was coming through the Khyber Pass, riding into Afghanistan disguised as an Afghan warrior. I'm probably the only person you'll meet who's ever done that."

"But you're back here, Tolitha. What good did it do you if you have to end up back here in Colleton? Back where you started?" I asked.

"It means that I ran out of money," she said. "It means I failed to do what I set out to do."

"I think you're the only success our family has produced, Tolitha," Savannah said. "I really do. You're the only reason I know I can escape from all this."

"You got Tolitha written all over you, Savannah. You have ever since you were a little girl. But play it smarter than me. I had the wildness in me. I didn't have the smarts. It was harder for women back then. Much harder. But try to get out if you can. Colleton's a sweet poison, but poison nonetheless. Once it gets into a soul it can never wash out. It's funny. But all the places I saw in Europe, Africa, and Asia, some were so beautiful it would make you cry. But none of them was more beautiful than Colleton and that's the truth. None of them could make me forget the marsh and the river right out yonder. The smell of this place rides in the bones wherever you go. I don't know if that's a good or a bad thing."

She rose and lit the fire in the stove. The afternoon was still and the air was cool and silken in the late afternoon. A barge, laden with a cargo of timber, urged upriver, and we saw my grandfather wave at the bargemen. The barge answered with a deep-throated salute from its horn and simultaneously the bridge across the river began its slow, ponderous division in the middle.

"Go out and talk to your grandpa, kids," she said. "I'll get us a little dinner, but first, why don't you go gather a couple of dozen oysters from the river and I'll fix 'em up while we're waiting for the chicken to bake."

We walked out into the back yard and into the very different world of Grandpa Wingo. He was lifting up the cross now and, laying it on his shoulder and walking it across the grass, testing the new wheel. The wheel squeaked slightly as it rolled across the grass.

"Hello, children," he said, smiling when he saw us. "I can't quite get the squeak out of this wheel."

"Hello, Grandpa," we said, and both of us ran to kiss him beneath the cross.

"How do you think the cross looks, children?" he asked, worriedly. "Be honest now. Don't be afraid to hurt your grandpa's feelings. Do you think the wheel looks all right?"

"It looks fine, Grandpa," Savannah said, "but I've never seen a cross with a wheel on it before."

"I was in bed for a week last year after the last walk," he explained. "I thought the wheel would make it easier, but I'm worried that folks'll get the wrong impression."

"They'll understand, Grandpa," I said.

"The cross got rained on this winter, and it's starting to rot in the center beam. I may have to build a new one for next year. Maybe a lighter model if I can find the right kind of wood."

"Why don't you retire, Grandpa?" Savannah said. "Let a younger man in the church take over."

"I've thought a lot about that, child," he said. "I've always hoped Luke or Tom would take over after I'm gone. That's what I pray to the good Lord for. It'd be nice to keep it in the family, don't you think?"

"I'm sure Tom would love to do it," Savannah offered graciously. "In fact, I've been praying to the good Lord for the same thing."

I pinched Savannah on the back of the arm and said, "Tolitha wants us to go across the river and pick some oysters, Grandpa. You want to go with us?"

"I'd be mighty pleased to go, children. Tom, could you

just walk this cross over to the garage? I've got to find out where this squeak is coming from."

"He'd be glad to," Savannah said. "It'll also give him a little practice for when he takes over the job."

I took the cross from my grandfather and laid it over my right shoulder and began moving it quickly across the yard. I could hear my grandmother hooting at me from the kitchen.

"Just a minute, child," my grandfather said. "I see where that squeak is coming from."

He bent down and applied oil to the wheel from a rusted can.

"I think that might do it. Try it again."

I resumed my surly walk, trying to ignore Savannah's grinning face and the chuckling image of my grandmother framed in the kitchen window. My grandfather, of course, was oblivious to all occasions of mirth and humiliation.

"I think that cross looks good on him, don't you, child?" my grandfather said to Savannah.

"I think it looks divine, Grandpa," Savannah agreed. "That boy was born to carry that cross."

"It's heavy," I said miserably.

"You ought to carry it without the wheel. It's a man's work. But when I think of the Lord's suffering and all he went through for me," Grandpa said.

"Yeah, Tom. Quit complaining. Think of what the Lord went through for you," Savannah chided.

"Just walk it this way one more time, child," said my grandfather. "I want to make sure I got that squeak."

After returning the cross to the garage, the three of us loaded into Grandpa's small green boat. He hand-cranked the motor and I gathered in the ropes and we headed across the Colleton River toward the oyster bank near the *Hardeville* wreck on St. Stephen's Island. The *Hardeville* was an old paddlewheel ferry that had sunk during the same hurricane when Savannah and I were born. Its great wheel lay buried in the mud and from a distance it looked like a half-made clock. Thousands of oysters clustered around the base of the hull and at full tide it was one of the most productive, bountiful fishing holes in the county. A family of otters lived in the brown encrusted hull of the ship, and had ever since I could remember. Tradition made those otters sacrosanct and inviolable and no hunter had ever attempted to trap them. Two otter pups were pursuing each other between the ribs of the foundered ship when my grandfather killed the motor and we slid into the flats exposed by the receding tide.

"Wasn't it nice of Jesus to place these oysters so near to the house? He knows how much I enjoy them," my grandfather said as Savannah and I leaned over the side of the boat and began dislodging oysters from the bank. We pulled up a dozen large singles the size of a man's hand, then a cluster of ten smaller oysters, which we broke apart with a hammer in the front of the boat.

I got onto the mud, sank to my knees. I made my way carefully across the bank, selecting the largest singles and throwing them back into the boat.

"Oysters always look to me like they're praying," Grandpa said. "Two hands folded together, offering thanks."

They were also sharp and ominous and I walked unsteadily, gingerly, as if I were dancing across a field of blades. I could feel the shells of dead oysters slice the rubber of my tennis shoes as I handled the tongs and brought the oysters up into the dying light.

When we had gathered forty oysters, I climbed over the sides of the boat and kicked us off into the river again. Grandpa couldn't get the motor started right away and we floated like an oak leaf through waters of soft pearl as otters flashed around us in brilliant circles. Their swift wakes agitated the water into a deeper pearl as Grandpa jerked the starter rope again and again, sweat forming on his brow. In the wreck an adult otter with a silver face climbed onto one of the ship's lower ribs with a trout still quivering between its jaws. The otter stood on its haunches and studied the fish between its paws, then began devouring it like a man eating an ear of corn. Savannah was the first one to see the Snow.

"Snow," she cried aloud, rising and nearly capsizing the boat. I steadied the boat with both hands, shifting my weight back and forth until we settled into the tide again. Grandpa quit trying to start the motor and looked downstream in the direction where Savannah's finger pointed. Then, two hundred yards away, we saw the white porpoise break through the waves as she made her way toward us.

I was ten when I first saw the white porpoise known as

Carolina Snow following our shrimp boat as we returned
to the dock after a day dragging the beaches along Spauld-
ing Point. It was the only white porpoise ever sighted along
the Atlantic seaboard in the memories of the shrimping
brotherhood, and some said the only white porpoise ever
to inhabit the earth. Throughout Colleton County, with its
endless miles of salt rivers and tidal creeks, the sighting of
the Snow was always cause for wonder. She was never
seen with other porpoises, and some shrimpers, like my
father, surmised that porpoises, like humans, were not kind
to their freaks and that the Snow was sentenced by her
remarkable whiteness to wander the green waters of Colleton, exiled and solitary. That first day, she followed us
almost all the way to the bridge before she turned back
toward the sea. Snow lent to the county a sense of spe-
cialness, and all who saw her remembered the first moment
for the rest of their lives. It was like being touched by a
recognition that the sea would never forfeit its power to
create and astonish.

Through the years, the Snow had become a symbol of
luck in the town. Colleton would prosper and flourish as
long as the Snow honored these waters with her visitations.
There were times when she disappeared for long periods
and then suddenly would return to the waters of the Carolina sea islands. Even the paper noticed her comings and
goings. Her entrance into the main channel and her slow,
sensual passage through the town would bring the entire
citizenry to the river's banks. Commerce would cease and
collectively the people of the town would stop what they
were doing to acknowledge her return. She visited the main
river rarely, and because of its rarity, her appearance was
a precious town-stopping thing. She approached us always
as a symbol, monarch, and gift; she approached us always
alone, banished, and the people on the shore, calling her
by name, shouting out in greeting, acknowledging her divine white passage, formed the only family she would ever
know.

Grandpa started the motor and headed the small boat
out toward the channel. The Snow rose out of the river
ahead of us, her back lilying in the dimming light.

"She's going our way," Grandpa said, steering the boat
toward her. "Now if that ain't proof of a living God then

nothing is. You'd think he'd be satisfied with just a plain porpoise. That's as beautiful as any creature on earth. But no, he's still up there dreaming up things even more beautiful to please man's eye."

"I've never seen her this close," Savannah said. "She's pure white, like a tablecloth."

But it was not a pure white we were seeing when she surfaced twenty yards from us. Faint ores of colors shimmered across her back as she cut through the water, a brief silvering of her fins, evanescent color that could not be sustained. You knew she could never be the same color twice.

We watched her as she circled the boat, saw her beneath us, and she flowed like milk through water. Rising, she hung suspended, concolorous with peaches and high-risen moons, then down as milk again.

These are the quicksilver moments of my childhood I cannot recapture entirely. Irresistible and emblematic, I can recall them only in fragments and shivers of the heart. There is a river, the town, my grandfather steering a boat through the channel, my sister fixed in that suspended rapture she would later translate into her strongest poems, the metallic perfume of harvested oysters, the belling voices of children on the shore . . . When the white porpoise comes there is all this and transfiguration too. In dreams, the porpoise remains in memory's waters, a pale divinity who nourishes the fire and deepest cold of all the black waters of my history. There were many things wrong with my childhood but the river was not one of them, nor can the inestimable riches it imparted be traded or sold.

As we passed under the bridge I looked back and saw the shadows of people who had gathered to watch the Snow's passage. Their heads appeared in clusters above the bridge's cement railing, at intervals, like the beads of a damaged rosary. I heard the voice of a small girl begging the Snow to return beneath the bridge. Men and women began assembling on the floating docks, which bobbed in the moving tide; they were all pointing toward the last spot the porpoise had surfaced.

When the white porpoise came, it was for my grandfather like seeing the white smile of God coming up at him from below.

"Thank you, God," my grandfather said behind us in one of those unrehearsed prayers that burst naturally from him when he was deeply moved by the external world. "Thank you so much for this."

I turned. My sister turned. And that good man smiled at us.

Later, long after my grandfather was dead, I would regret that I could never be the kind of man that he was. Though I adored him as a child and found myself attracted to the safe protectorate of his soft, uncritical maleness, I never wholly appreciated him. I did not know how to cherish sanctity; I had no way of honoring, of giving small voice to the praise of such natural innocence, such generous simplicity. Now I know that a part of me would like to have traveled the world as he traveled it, a jester of burning faith, a fool and a forest prince brimming with the love of God. I would like to have walked his southern world, thanking God for oysters and porpoises, praising God for birdsong and sheet lightning, and seeing God reflected in pools of creekwater and the eyes of stray cats. I would like to have talked to yard dogs and tanagers as if they were my friends and fellow travelers along the sun-tortured highways, intoxicated with a love of God, swollen with charity like a rainbow, in the thoughtless mingling of its hues, connecting two distant fields in its glorious arc. I would like to have seen the world with eyes incapable of anything but wonder, and with a tongue fluent only in praise.

As the white porpoise began moving upriver in all the cut-off solitude of the outsider, I related to the aloneness of the creature. But my grandfather—ah! I always knew what my grandfather felt when he saw the Snow moving upriver. He watched the porpoise disappear, following the deep water around a dogleg in the channel, flashing once more before moving behind a green isthmus of land where the river goes to the right.

Luke was standing on the dock waiting for us. With the sun to the west of him, he gazed at us facelessly, a remote chiaroscuro, a pillar of light and shadow. When Grandpa cut the motor, Luke guided the boat along the dock with his foot and caught the rope I threw to him.

"Did you see Snow?" he asked.

"She was frisky as a dog," my grandfather answered.

"Tolitha invited us all for dinner."

"We've got enough oysters," I said.

"Dad brought over five pounds of shrimp. Tolitha is going to fry them up."

"You looked like a giant standing on the dock when we were out on the river, Luke," Savannah said. "I swear if I don't think you're still growing."

"I am, baby sister. And I don't want no midgets scrambling up my beanstalk."

I began gathering the oysters and threw them up on the dock where Luke put them in a washtub. We tied up the boat and walked up to the house through the grass.

Savannah, Luke, and I stayed out on the back porch and opened the oysters. We placed them in a bowl my grandmother passed out the kitchen door. I opened a large single and sucked it out of its shell, held it for a moment in my mouth, tasted its liquor on my tongue, inhaled its perfume, and let it slide down my throat. Nothing is more perfect to me than the freshness and bouquet of a raw oyster. It is the taste of the ocean barely made flesh. We could hear the voices of my mother and grandmother in the kitchen, the timeless serious voices of women preparing food for their families. Venus, a nugget of mild silver, rose in the east. The cicadas began their lunatic parliament in the trees. Someone turned on the television in the house.

"I talked with Coach Sams today," Luke said, snapping an oyster open with one graceful flick of his wrist. "He told me the colored boy's really coming to school."

"Who is it?" Savannah asked.

"Benji Washington. The undertaker's kid."

"I've seen him around," Savannah said.

"He's a nigger," I said.

"Don't say that word, Tom," Savannah said, glaring at me. "I don't like it. I don't like it one little bit."

"I can say anything I want," I retorted. "I don't have to ask your permission to say anything I please. He's just gonna cause trouble and ruin our senior year."

"It's a nasty, disgusting word," she said, "and it makes you sound mean when you use it."

"He doesn't mean anything by it, Savannah," Luke said softly in the darkness. "Tom always tries to be tougher than he really is."

"He's a nigger. What's wrong with me calling him a nigger," I said, tougher than ever.

"Because kind people don't use that word, you son of a bitch," she said.

"Well, well," I said angrily. "I guess real kind people use 'son of a bitch' as a term of endearment."

"It's suppertime," Luke said forlornly. "I guess it's time for another fight. Jesus Christ, you two. Just drop it. I'm sorry I brought the subject up."

"Don't you say that word, Tom. I'm warning you," Savannah said.

"I didn't see the exact moment you turned into a beauty queen for the NAACP."

"Let's just shuck oysters and listen to frogs," Luke entreated. "I hate it when you two fight like this."

"You don't say that word around me, Tom. I'm warning you. I hate that word and I hate people who use it."

"Dad uses it all the time," I said.

"He has an excuse. He's an idiot. You're not."

"I'm not ashamed of being southern, Savannah," I said. "Like some people I know who read *The New Yorker* every week."

"You ought to be ashamed of being that kind of southerner. That kind of low-rent scum."

"Excuse me, your royal highness."

"Hush up, you two," Luke said, looking toward the kitchen window. My grandmother's biscuits anointed the night air. "Mom doesn't allow us to say that word, Tom, and you know it."

"You don't have the right to think like the worst part of the South thinks. I won't allow that kind of ugliness in you. I'll slap it out of you if I have to," Savannah said.

"I can beat the shit out of you, Savannah," I said, looking up at her defiantly, "and you know it."

"That's right, rough guy. You can," she sneered, "but if you lay a finger on me, Big Luke over there will break you in half. And you're weaker than water compared to Luke."

I looked at my brother, who was smiling at both of us. He nodded his head.

"That's right, Tom. I can't let you go around hurting my little sugar-peeps," he said.

"Hey, Luke. Admit it. She started this fight, didn't she? I just innocently mumbled something about the niggers."

"Yep!" he agreed. "She started it and she's winning it too, little brother," he smiled.

"You're prejudiced," I said.

"I'm just big," Luke replied.

"A prince," Savannah said, hugging Luke and kissing him on the lips. "My redneck linebacking prince."

"No physical stuff, Savannah," he said, blushing. "The ol' bod is off limits."

"Just supposing I hit Savannah," I said. "Now this is only theoretical. Just supposing I tapped her on the cheek in self-defense, Luke. You wouldn't do anything to me, would you? I mean you love me just as much as you love Savannah, don't you?"

"I love you so much it hurts me," Luke said, snapping open an oyster. "You know that, Tom. But if you ever touch Savannah, I'll break your ass. It'll hurt me a lot worse than it'll hurt you, but I'll break every bone in your body."

"I'm not afraid of you, Luke," I said.

"Yes, you are, Tom," he said lightly. "It's nothing to be ashamed of. I'm a lot stronger than you."

"Do you remember when Mom read us *The Diary of Anne Frank*, Tom?" Savannah asked.

"Of course."

"Remember how you cried when the book ended?"

"That's got nothing to do with what we're talking about. There wasn't a single nigger in all of Amsterdam, I'm sure."

"But the Nazis, Tom. There were Nazis that used the word *Jew* the same way you're using the word *nigger*."

"Give me a break, Savannah."

"And when Benji Washington comes through that school door on the first day of school next year I want you to remember Anne Frank."

"Jesus Christ. Let me just shuck oysters in peace."

"She's just whipped your ass, boy. I always love to listen to you two fight. You start out like you're gonna take on the world, Tom. When it ends up, you can't say a word."

"I just don't enjoy arguing very much," I said. "That's the major difference between Savannah and me."

"That's not the major difference between us, Tom," Savannah said, rising and going to the back door.

"What is the main difference, then?" I said, turning toward her.

"You really want to know? Not worrying about your feelings?"

"You can't hurt my feelings. I know everything you think anyway. We're twins, remember?"

"You don't know this."

"Then tell me."

"I'm a lot smarter than you, Tom Wingo."

She disappeared into the kitchen and left Luke and me to shuck the remaining oysters in the darkness. My brother's laughter rumbled off the porch.

"Whipped your ass, boy. Just whipped your poor country ass."

"I got in a couple of good lines."

"Not one. Not a single one."

"Anne Frank doesn't have shit to do with it."

"She sure made it sound like she did."

At noon on Good Friday, my grandfather lifted the wooden cross and laid it upon his right shoulder. He was dressed in a white choir robe and he was wearing a pair of sandals he had bought at a K Mart in Charleston. Luke made last-minute adjustments on the wheel with a set of pliers.

Mr. Fruit directed traffic and waited for my grandfather to signal that the walk was about to begin. Since Mr. Fruit directed traffic and led all parades, he always had to perform double duty on Good Friday. For reasons known only to him, Mr. Fruit considered my grandfather's walk a parade. A small parade, and not much fun, but a parade nonetheless.

Mr. Fruit put the whistle to his lips and my grandfather nodded his head. Mr. Fruit blew the whistle and strutted up the Street of Tides, high-stepping it like a drum major, his knees pumping as high as his chin. My grandfather followed ten yards behind. I heard a couple of people laugh when they saw the wheel. Up by Baitery's Pharmacy, I watched my father filming the first part of the walk.

About halfway down the street, my grandfather fell for the first time. It was a spectacular fall and he hit the street hard, with the cross falling on him. He loved the falls best of anything in the three-hour walk. They always surprised the crowd, and besides, he was a good faller. My father was zooming in when my grandfather fell and it was evident that the two of them had worked out a system of signals whenever the highlights of the walk were coming up. Amos was also a good staggerer, and his knees buckled under him when he tried to rise. My grandfather knew nothing about the theater of the absurd, but he managed to invent it for himself year after year.

After the first hour, the wheel broke and had to be discarded. Sheriff Lucas appeared at the traffic light by the bridge and wrote out the annual citation for obstruction of traffic. Mr. Fruit stopped marching and directed cars through the intersection as some of the crowd booed the sheriff. Mr. Kupcinet, a deacon at Grandpa's church, read aloud from the Bible about the walk of Jesus through the streets of Jerusalem, his crucifixion on Calvary flanked by two thieves, the darkness over the city, the great cry of agony *Eli, Eli lama sabachthani* ("My God, my God, why hast thou forsaken me?"), and the centurion saying again as he would say for all the centuries that would pass, "Truly this is the Son of God."

And my grandfather would walk back and forth between stores that sold shoes and real estate and lingerie, sweat pouring from his face but his eyes serene, knowing he was serving his God as best as he knew how. Savannah and I sold lemonade in front of Sarah Poston's dress shop and Luke had the job of stopping my grandfather in the middle of his walk and forcing a Dixie cup of vinegar between Amos's lips. Then Luke played the part of Simon of Cyrene and helped bear the weight of the cross for one whole transit of the street. By the third hour, my grandfather would be staggering for real. When he fell the last time, he could not rise to his feet until Luke reached him and lifted the cross off his body. There was blood in a thin strip along the shoulder of the choir robe. He rose, smiled, and thanked Luke, promising to cut my brother's hair later on in the day. Then he continued down the street, lurching and weaving from side to side.

I did not know then and do not know now what to make of my grandfather's awesome love of the Word of God. As a teenager I found his walk humiliating. But Savannah would write about his walk in poems of uncommon beauty. She would celebrate the "shy Oberammergau of the itinerant barber."

And when Amos Wingo's walk ended that day and we caught him as he fell and carried him to the lemonade stand, where we rubbed his face with ice and made him drink a cup of lemonade, I had a feeling that sainthood was the most frightening and incurable disease on earth.

He was trembling and delirious as we laid him out on the sidewalk. People pressed forward to get Grandpa to sign their Bibles and my father filmed his collapse.

Luke and I got him to his feet, and with his arms around our shoulders, we bore his weight and carried him home, with Luke saying the whole way: "You're so beautiful, Grandpa. You're so beautiful."

15

The doorman who guarded the entrance to Dr. Lowenstein's building watched my approach with mistrustful eyes. He observed me as though he knew I harbored criminal intentions, but it was his job to see the world in those terms. A powerful man, dressed in gaudily antiquated livery, he took my name with grave formality and called upstairs. The lobby was filled with cracked leather furniture, giving it the air of the dreary elegance of a men's club whose membership had almost voted to admit women.

The doorman nodded toward the elevator and went back to reading the *New York Post*. Though I was carrying two huge shopping bags, I managed to press the correct button on the elevator, which lifted me with a shudder of straining cables and moved upward so slowly it felt as if it were rising through seawater.

Bernard was waiting for me at his front door.

"Good evening, Bernard," I said.

"Hello, Coach," he answered. "What do you have in the bags?"

"Dinner and some other stuff," I said, coming into the entrance hall.

I whistled as I looked around. "Jesus Christ, what a house. This looks like a wing of the Met."

The foyer was decorated with velvet-covered chairs, cloisonné vases, sidetables, a small Waterford chandelier, and two grim eighteenth-century portraits. I could see a grand piano in the living room and a portrait of Herbert Woodruff playing the violin.

"I hate it," Bernard said.

"No wonder she doesn't let you lift weights in the house," I said.

"She changed the rule last night. Now I can lift weights when my father's not at home. But only in my bedroom. I've got to keep my weights under the bed so he doesn't see them."

"If he wants to," I said, looking at the portrait over the fireplace, "I could put him on a weight program and you could lift together."

He was a handsome and fine-boned man with a thin mouth that suggested either refinement or cruelty.

"My father?" Bernard said.

"Okay, let's get moving, Bernard. Let me take this food to the kitchen; then show me your bedroom. I want to get you decked out before your mother gets home."

Bernard's bedroom was on the opposite side of the apartment and was decorated as tastefully and expensively as any of the other rooms we passed. It had none of the garish trappings of a boy's room, no posters of sports heroes or rock stars, no clutter or excess. I ripped open the bag and said to Bernard, "Okay, Tiger. We is going to do the whole thing. Whip your clothes off."

"For what, Coach?" he asked.

"Because I like watching guys get naked," I answered.

"I can't do that," he said, deeply embarrassed.

"Do I have to teach you to get undressed, Bernard?" I said. "That's not in my contract."

"Are you gay, Coach?" he asked in a nervous voice. "I mean, it's okay. It doesn't bother me or anything. If you are, I mean. I believe in people doing whatever it is they want to do."

I did not answer but lifted a beautiful set of Wilson shoulder pads out of its wrapping.

"Those are for me?" he asked.

"No," I said. "But I wanted you to try them on before I gave them to your mother."

"Why would my mother want them, Coach?" he asked as I put them over his head and began to lace them up.

"Bernard, let's work on your sense of humor instead of your passing. Let me take two hours each day and try to teach you what a joke is."

"I'm sorry I asked if you were gay, Coach. Hey, you understand. I was a little confused and us here alone and everything."

"Right, Bernard. Now get out of those clothes, boy. I got a meal to cook. But first I'm going to show you how a football player gets dressed."

Susan Lowenstein was late. I was sitting in a wing-backed chair in her living room, looking across Central Park as the sun began to pull back from the Hudson River behind me. I could smell the leg of lamb roasting in the oven, filling the house with a brown perfume. I could see my own pale reflection in the picture window and the baroque light of chandeliers dreamily illuminating the rooms behind me. In the falling light, the window became both mirror and fabulous portrait of a darkening city. The huge buildings of the lower city turned sapphire and rose in the descendent retreat of sunlight, then began to answer back with their own interior light. The city was laid out before me in a forest of transfigured architecture, devotional and splendid. The sun, exhausted, caught one building whole in its last sight and imparted the hues of a coral reef in a thousand grateful windows, then slid down that building from window to window, losing itself halfway down as the whole city rose like a firebird into the singing night. The city shook off the last foils of sunset and in a thrown-back, overreaching ecstasy transformed itself into an amazing candelabrum of asymmetrical light. From where I sat, in complete darkness now, the city looked as if it were formed from glass votive candles, lightning, and glowing embers. In the beauty of those rising geometrics and fabulous metamorphosed shapes, it seemed to enlarge the sunset, improve upon it.

"I'm so sorry I'm late," Susan Lowenstein said, coming through the front door. "There was a problem with a patient at the hospital. Did you find the liquor cabinet?"

"I was waiting for you."

"The lamb smells divine," she said. Then, looking out on her city, she exulted, "Now tell me that's not one of the most beautiful sights you've ever seen in your life. I want to hear you rail against New York when you're looking at the best she can do."

"It's stunning," I admitted. "I just don't get to see this that often."

"I see it every night and I still find it absolutely astonishing."

"This is a hell of a place to watch the other side of a sunset," I said admiringly. "You and your husband have exquisite taste, Lowenstein, and an awful lot of money."

"Mother," a voice called from behind us.

We both turned and saw Bernard in full football gear walk softly into the living room in his sweat socks. In his hands he was carrying his new shoes with their gleaming cleats. In the strange light he looked enormous, misshapen, reborn to something he was never meant to be.

"Coach Wingo got this for me today. A whole uniform."

"My God" was the only thing the stunned Susan Lowenstein could get out.

"Hey, don't you like it, Mother? C'mon, Mom. Tell me I don't look good. Everything fits except the helmet, and Coach Wingo said he could fix it."

"Dr. Lowenstein," I said, "I'd like to introduce you to your son, Killer Bernard. They call him the Mississippi Gambler because he always goes for the long bomb on fourth and one, deep in his own territory."

"Your father will divorce me if he ever sees you like this," she said. "You must swear you'll never let him see you in this uniform, Bernard."

"But how do you like it, Mother? How do you think I look?"

"I think you look deformed," she said, laughing.

"Okay, Bernard," I said. "Go dress for dinner. We eat like kings in forty-five minutes. You lifted weights today?"

"No, sir," Bernard said, still flooded with anger at his
mother and breathing hard again.

"Try to press seventy-five pounds. I think you're about
ready for it."

"Yes, sir."

"And when you come out for dinner, my name is Tom.
I don't like being called sir when I eat dinner."

"You look very different, Bernard," his mother said. "I
didn't mean to hurt your feelings at all. It'll just take me a
little while to grow accustomed to you looking so fierce."

"So you think I look fierce, huh?" Bernard said happily.

"Son, you look positively bestial."

"Thanks, Mom," Bernard said, sprinting across Oriental
carpeting back to his room.

"Compliments take the oddest form sometimes. Let me
fix us both a drink," she said.

Dinner was a subdued affair, unsullied at first. Bernard
mostly talked about football, his favorite teams and players.
His mother kept looking at him as though she were discovering a new child at her table. She asked several questions about the game, revealing an ignorance so astonishing
that she reduced me to wordlessness when I tried to reply
to her.

I noticed that mother and son were nervous around each
other and seemed glad to have a dinner companion to de-
fuse the tension between them. This tension stimulated the
gland of entertainment in me and I found myself in the role
of master of revels, the evening fool, with cards in my
sleeves and a ready joke for every interval of silence. I hated
myself in this role, yet I was incapable of refusing the performance. Nothing made me more edgy or neurotic than
the silent hostility of people who loved each other. So I
spent the evening cracking jokes, carving the lamb with
the flair of a surgeon, serving the wine like a sommelier
trained in burlesque, tossing the salad wildly. By the time
I brought in the *crème brûlée* and espresso I was exhausted,
worn down by my own theatrics. And as we ate dessert
the old silences between mother and son took control again
and I heard the deadly tinkling of silverware against the
small glass bowls.

"Why'd you learn to cook, Coach?" Bernard finally
asked.

THE PRINCE OF TIDES   335

"When my wife went to medical school, I had to. So I bought a good cookbook and for three months I performed unspeakable acts upon wonderful cuts of meat. I made bread that birds wouldn't touch. But I learned that if I could read, I could cook. I surprised myself by liking it."

"Didn't your wife ever cook?" he asked.

"She was a great cook but she didn't have time to when she was in medical school. She didn't even have time to be married. It hasn't changed that much since she became a doctor and we had kids."

"So your kids didn't see their mother when they were little either?" he said, looking at his mother.

"Sallie wasn't around much for a while, Bernard," I said quickly. "But she never would have been happy with just an apron and a stove. She was too bright and ambitious and she loves being a doctor. It makes her a better mother."

"How many of the meals do you cook now?"

"I cook all of them, Bernard," I said. "I lost my job more than a year ago."

"You mean you're not even a real coach?" Bernard said, and I detected a note of betrayal in his voice. "My mother didn't even hire me a real coach?"

Dr. Lowenstein said in a thin-lipped, barely controlled voice, "That will be quite enough from you, young man."

"Why aren't you coaching now?" Bernard demanded.

"I was fired from my coaching job," I said, taking a sip of my coffee.

"Why?" he asked again.

"It's a long story, Bernard. One I don't usually tell to kids."

"False pretenses," he said to his mother. "He's coaching me under false pretenses."

"You apologize to Tom immediately, Bernard," his mother said.

"Why should I apologize? He's been pretending he's a coach and now I find out he's not. He's the one that owes me an apology."

"Then I apologize, Bernard," I said, poking at my dessert with a spoon. "I didn't realize you required an employed coach for your purposes."

"Adults just kill me. They really do. I hope I'm never an adult."

"You probably won't be, Bernard," I said. "You might have peaked out as a teenager."

"At least I don't lie about what I am," he answered.

"Lest we forget, Bernard, you told your parents you were on the football team at school. You were not. It's a small lie but it helps us define our terms," I said.

"Why do you always have to do this, Bernard?" the doctor asked, and she was close to tears. "Why do you lash out at anyone who tries to get close to you or tries to help you?"

"I'm your kid, Mother. Not one of your patients. You don't have to give me any of that shrink talk. Why don't you just try to talk to me?"

"I don't know how to talk to you, Bernard."

"I do, Bernard," I said as the boy turned furiously on me, breathing hard, sweat forming on his upper lip.

"You do, what?" he asked.

"I know how to talk to you," I said. "Your mother doesn't but I do. Because I understand you, Bernard. You're hating yourself for ruining this evening but you couldn't help yourself. It was the only way you could hurt your mother and you had to do it. That's fine. That's between you two. But I'm still your coach, Bernard. And tomorrow morning you're going to meet me in that same field and this time you're going to be wearing full battle array."

"Why should I let you coach me? You just admitted you were a fake."

"You'll find out if I'm a fake or not, Bernard," I said, facing this sad, unformed man. "And I'll find out tomorrow if you're a fake or not."

"What do you mean?"

"Tomorrow I find out if you're afraid to hit or not. That's the real test. If you can take a hit or dish one out. Tomorrow, for the first time in your life, Bernard, you play a contact sport."

"Oh, yeah, and who am I gonna hit? Some tree or bush or wino walking through the park?"

"Me," I said. "You're going to try to tackle me, Bernard. And then I'm going to try to tackle you."

"But you're a lot bigger than me."

"You don't have anything to worry about from me, Bernard," I said coldly. "You see, I'm nothing but a fake."

"Oh, real fair."

"Are you afraid when I say I'm going to tackle you?"

"No," he said defiantly. "Not at all."

"Do you know why you're not afraid, Bernard?"

"No."

"Well, I'll tell you. Because you've never played football, Bernard. If you had, then you'd know that you should be afraid. But I also know you want to play football, Bernard. For whatever screwed-up reason, you want that more than anything in the world, don't you?"

"I guess so," he said.

"If you learn to tackle me, Bernard," I said, "and you learn to take it when I tackle you, then you'll make your team next year. I promise you that."

"Tom, I think you're too large to tackle Bernard."

"Oh, Mother, please," he pleaded with his mother. "You don't know the first thing about football."

"So help me clear the table, Bernard," I said, rising and stacking the dessert dishes. "Then go to bed and get rested up for tomorrow."

"I don't have to clear the plates," he said. "We've got a maid for that."

"Son," I said to Bernard, "please don't talk back to me again. And please don't ever again run a number on me and your mother like you ran tonight. Now grab a few plates and hustle your ass into the kitchen with them."

"Tom, this *is* Bernard's house, and the maid is coming tomorrow."

"Shut up, Lowenstein. Please shut up," I said, exasperated, walking toward the kitchen.

When I said good night to Bernard, I returned to the living room and felt the immense solitude of that harmonious, obsessively orderly room. Everything was expensive yet nothing was personal. Even Herbert's portrait looked like some idealistic impression of the man instead of the man himself. In it, he was playing his violin, and though one could not judge the tenor and depth of the man from the rendition, one could feel the rapture of his art. I saw that the sliding glass door to the terrace was open and it was there that I found Dr. Lowenstein. She had poured both of us a glass of cognac. I sat down and inhaled the perfume of the Hennessey; it flowered in my brain like a rose. I took the first sip and felt it slide down my throat, half silk, half fire.

"Well," Dr. Lowenstein said, "did you enjoy the Bernard and Susan show?"

"Do you have these performances often?"

"No," she said. "Generally, we try to ignore each other. But the edge is always there. Even our politeness is murderous. My stomach is usually tied in knots whenever we have dinner together alone. I find it hard, Tom, to be hated by the only child I'll ever have."

"What's it like when Herbert's here?" I asked.

"He fears his father and rarely makes a scene the way he did tonight," she said reflectively. "Of course, Herbert does not allow conversation at dinner."

"Excuse me?" I said, looking at her.

She smiled and took a long sip of cognac. "A family secret. A family ceremony. Herbert likes to relax completely at the dinner table. He listens to classical music during dinner as a way to decompress after a day's work. I used to fight him about it but I've gradually become accustomed to it. It even relieves me since Bernard has entered this new aggressive stage."

"I hope you will forget that I told you to shut up in front of your son," I said to her dark silhouette. "That was my obsession in the kitchen. That I would finish the dishes and that you would tell me to get the hell out of your house and never come back after I dried the silverware."

"Why did you tell me to shut up?"

"I had just re-established some control over Bernard and I didn't want you to break that hard-won spell because you could not stand to see someone hurt your son."

"He's very vulnerable. I saw the expression on his face when you spoke so roughly to him. He's very easily hurt."

"So are we, Doctor. But it was open season on the both of us for ten minutes. I didn't like it one teensy-weensy bit."

"He's just as spoiled as his father. I think what bothered Bernard the most was that he saw right away that you and I are friends. That would bother Herbert too. Herbert has always made it a practice to despise any new friend I made on my own when I was not with him. He used to treat my friends contemptuously, so badly, in fact, that I quit inviting them to dinner, quit seeing them socially at all. Herbert, of course, has gathered a fascinating, glittering set of friends around him who have become my good friends too. But the lesson was clear. Herbert has to be the one who discovered them and brought them to the inner circle. Does that sound strange to you, Tom?"

"No," I answered. "It sounds like a marriage."

"Do you do that to Sallie?"

I cupped my hands behind my head and looked straight up into the stars of Manhattan, dim as buttons above the free-flung light of the city.

"I guess I do," I said. "I've loathed some of the doctors and their wives she's dragged home to dinner over the years. If I hear a doctor talk about income tax or socialized medicine in England one more time in my life, I will ritually destroy myself before their very eyes. But then I've brought home some of my friends from the coaching profession who would spend every evening writing out plays on paper napkins and talking about the time they scored 'the big one' in high school, and I've watched Sallie's eyes glaze over in utter boredom. So we've gathered a set of friends that survived the mutual cut. There's one high school coach, whom Sallie adores. There are two doctors I thought were terrific guys. Of course, one of those terrific guys is now Sallie's lover, so I may try to change the system when I get home. I'm beginning to like the sound of Herbert's system."

"Is Sallie's lover a friend of yours?"

"He was. I liked the son of a bitch and even though I acted like I was annoyed that Sallie would choose such an asshole for a fling, I could understand it perfectly well. He's very handsome. He's successful, bright, and funny. He collects British motorcycles and smokes meerschaum pipes, two flaws I homed in on when Sallie told me about it, but I couldn't be too hard on her."

"Why not?"

"Because I understand why Sallie would prefer him over me. Jack Cleveland is the kind of man I could have been if I had stayed on course. He's the kind of man I had the potential to become."

"When did you stop?"

"I think it began when I chose the absolutely wrong

parents. I know, you don't think children have a choice in the matter. I'm not sure. I have an intuitive feeling that I chose to be born into that particular family. Then you spend your life making a series of false assumptions and wrong moves. You set yourself up for catastrophe. You find yourself in danger and peril because of the choices you've made. Then you discover that fate is also busily working to set you up, to lead you into regions that no one should be required to enter. When you realize all this, you are thirty-five years old and the worst is behind you. No, that's not true. The worst is ahead of you because now you know the horror of the past. Now you know you have to live the memory of your fate and your history for the rest of your life. It is the Great Sadness and you know that it's your destiny."

"Do you think Savannah has it?"

"She got dealt the royal flush," I said. "Look where she is now, Doctor. She's in a nut house with scars all over her body, barking at dogs that only she can see. I'm her feckless brother trying to tell you stories that will illuminate her past and make you put Humpty Dumpty back together again. And yet most of the time, Doctor, when I think about the past, I come to these blank spaces, black holes of memory. I don't know how to enter those dark regions. I can tell you most of the stories behind those pained fragments you recorded on tape. I can usually explain where they come from. But what about the things she forgot, what about her blank spaces? I've got this feeling that there is so much more to say."

"Would you be afraid to tell me these things, Tom?" she asked, and I could not see her face. I only saw the spires of the city behind her rising in great pillars of light.

"Doctor, I'll tell you anything. What I'm trying to say is that I don't know if I can tell you enough."

"You've been extremely helpful so far, Tom. I promise you that. You've already cleared up some things that have puzzled me about Savannah."

"What's wrong with Savannah?" I asked, leaning toward her.

"How often have you seen her in the last three years, Tom?"

"Rarely," I said, then admitted, "Never."

"Why is that?"

"She said it depressed her too much to be around the family. Even me."

"I'm so glad you came up here this summer, though, Tom," she said.

She rose with the burning lights of the city behind her and came over to get my glass.

"Let me replenish these."

I watched her as she disappeared inside the apartment and saw the moment she glanced at her husband's portrait, then, just as quickly, averted her eyes. I felt then, for the first time, the sadness of this controlled, cautious woman who was playing such a crucial and necessary part in my life during this melancholy summer. I considered her role of listener, of advocate, of healer—her rising up each morning and dressing in her room, knowing she would walk out and face the pain and suffering of that part of the race who had come to her by accident or by referral. Yet I wondered if the lessons she gleaned from her patients could ever be applied successfully to her own life. Did her mastery of the tenets of Freud ensure her own happiness? I knew it didn't, but why did her masked, expressionless face move me so much whenever she was unaware of my studying her. That face, lovely and moon-shaped, seemed to reflect every grotesque story she had ever heard, all the testimonies of injured histories. In her house, her solitude seemed to deepen. She was far more relaxed in her office, protected by the fortress of her pedigrees, and there, among strangers, she had no responsibility for the grisly stories that had brought her patients to the end of their tethers. But in this house, her own failures and sorrows moved with her in phantom legions. She and her son approached each other like councilors of enemy nations. The power of her husband's presence manifested itself everywhere, the consequences of his fame. I had no clear image of Herbert Woodruff from anything that either his wife or his son had said about him. They both emphasized that he was a genius; they both feared his disaffection and reprisals but could not understand what shape his formidable disapproval might take. He listened to classical music at mealtime instead of conversing with the family, but after hearing Bernard and his mother in full battle cry, I could under-

stand the inclination. Why had Dr. Lowenstein told me
about her suspicion that her husband was having an affair
with that stunning, aggrieved woman I had met in her
office?

Sex, the old leveler and destroyer, spreading its wicked,
glorious seeds even into the houses of culture and privilege
—and who knew what monstrous hybrids or what deadly
orchids would blossom in these hushed salons. The flowers of my own garden, a southern variety all stunted and
unoriginal, were hideous enough. I thought I would never
think about sex again once I had gotten married or, more
precisely, would think about it in connection only with my
wife. But marriage had merely been an initiation into a
frightening world of fantasy, frightening because of its furious ignition, its secret betrayals, its uncontrollable desire
for all the lovely women of the world. I walked through
this world burning with the love of strange women and
I could not help it. In my mind, I slept with a thousand
women. In my wife's arms, I made love to shapely women
who had never spoken my name. I lived and loved and
suffered in a world that had no reality but did exist in some
wild kingdom near the eyes. Goat, satyr, and beast roared
and howled within the porches of the ear. I loathed this
part of me; I trembled when I heard the lewd snickering
of other men admitting to the same fevers. I equated fucking with power and hated the part of me where that flawed
and dangerous truth dwelt. I longed for constancy, for purity, for absolution. I brought one murderous gift to sex.
All the women who loved me, who took me to their breast,
who felt me inside them, moving in them, whispering their
name, crying out to them in darkness, all of them I betrayed by turning them slowly and by degrees from lovers
into friends. Beginning as lovers, I turned them all into
sisters and bequeathed to them the gift of Savannah's eyes.
Once inside a woman, to my horror, I heard my mother's
voice, and though my lover would be calling out "yes yes
yes," it was not as powerful a cry as my mother's cold
"no." I took my mother to bed with me every night of my
life and I could not help it.

These thoughts came unannounced, unbidden. Sex, I
thought, as I watched Susan Lowenstein walk toward the

terrace holding the two brandy snifters, the central issue of my conflicted, unsuccessful manhood.

She handed me my glass, slipped out of her shoes, and sat down in a wicker chair.

She sat quietly for a while before she spoke. "Tom, do you remember how we talked about what a closed man you are?"

I shifted in my chair and looked at my watch. "Please, Lowenstein, remember my age-old contempt for psychotherapists. You're off duty now."

"I'm sorry. But I was just thinking as I was pouring the drinks, that as you tell me story after story about your family, Savannah is emerging slowly. And Luke. And your father. But I still don't know or understand your mother at all. And you, Tom, remain the vaguest of all. You reveal almost nothing of yourself in these stories."

"I suppose that's because I'm never sure of who I am. I've never been just one person. I've always tried to be someone else, live someone else's life. I can be other people far too easily. I know what it's like to be Bernard, Doctor. That's why it affects me so when I see him suffering. I find it easy to be Savannah. I feel it when the dogs are on her. I want to take her sickness and lay it on my own soul. I don't find it easy to be me because this strange gentleman is unknown to me. Now that nauseating revelation should satisfy even the most scrupulous therapist."

"Can you be me, Tom?" she asked. "Do you know what it's like to be me?"

"No," I said uneasily, taking a sip of cognac. "I have no idea what it's like to be you."

"You're lying, Tom," she said with conviction. "I think you're very perceptive about me."

"I see you in your office and I run my mouth for an hour. Or we've had some drinks. We've now had dinner three times. But there hasn't been enough time to get any clear picture of you. I thought you had it made. You're beautiful, you're a doctor, you're married to a famous musician, you're rich, you live like a queen. Bernard, of course, has made the picture a bit cloudy, but overall, you're way up there in the top one percent of the world's brawling masses."

"You're still lying," she said in the darkness.

"You're a very sad woman, Doctor," I said. "I don't understand why and I'm deeply sorry. If I could help you, I would. But I'm a coach, not a priest or a doctor."

"Now you're not lying. And I thank you for it. I think you're the first friend I've made in a long time."

"Well, I appreciate what you're doing for Savannah. I really do," I said, feeling dreadfully uncomfortable.

"Have you been lonely?"

"Lowenstein, you are speaking to the prince of solitude, as Savannah referred to me in one of her poems. This city exacerbates loneliness in me the same way that water makes Alka-Seltzer fizz."

"Loneliness is killing me lately," she said, and I could feel her eyes upon me.

"I don't know what to say."

"I'm very attracted to you, Tom. No, don't leave just yet. Please listen to me."

"Don't tell me, Doctor," I said, rising to go. "I can't even think about this now. I've considered myself incapable of love for so long that the mere thought of it terrifies me. Let's be friends. Good friends. I'd be a terrible addition to your romantic life. I'm a walking *Hindenburg*. Pure disaster no matter how you look at it. I'm trying to figure out how to save a marriage that I don't have much chance of saving. I can't even consider falling in love with someone as beautiful as you are and as different from me. It's too dangerous.

"I have to go now, but I thank you for telling me that. I've needed someone to tell me that since I've come to New York. It's good to feel attractive and wanted again."

"I'm not very good at this, am I, Tom?" she said, smiling.

"No," I said. "You're terrific at it, Lowenstein. You've been terrific about everything."

I left her on the terrace as she looked out again at the lights of the city.

16

It was almost summer when the strangers arrived by boat in Colleton and began their long, inexorable pursuit of the white porpoise. My mother was baking bread and the suffusion of that exquisite fragrance of the loaves and roses turned our house into a vial of the most harmonious seasonal incense. She took the bread fresh from the oven, then slathered it with butter and honey. We took it steaming in our hands down to the dock to eat, the buttery honey running through our fingers. We attracted the ornery attention of every yellow jacket in our yard, and it took nerve to let them walk on our hands, gorging themselves on the drippings from our bread. They turned our hands into gardens and orchards and hives. My mother brought the lid of a mayonnaise jar full of sugar water down to the dock to appease the yellow jackets and let us eat in peace.

We had almost finished the bread when we saw the boat, *The Amberjack*, bearing Florida registry, move through the channels of the Colleton River. No gulls followed the boat, so we were certain it was not a fishing vessel. It lacked the clean, luxurious lines of a yacht, yet there was a visible crew of six men whose sun-stained burnt-amber color announced them as veteran mariners. We would learn the same day that it was the first boat ever to enter South Carolina waters whose function was to keep fish alive.

The crew of *The Amberjack* were not secretive about their mission and their business in these waters was known all over Colleton late that afternoon. Captain Otto Blair told a reporter from the *Gazette* that the Miami Seaquarium had received a letter from a Colleton citizen, who wished to remain anonymous, that an albino porpoise frequented the waters around Colleton. Captain Blair and his crew planned to capture the porpoise, then transport it back to Miami, where it would be both a tourist attraction and a subject for scientific inquiry. The crew of *The Amberjack* had come to Colleton in the interest of science, as marine biologists, inspired by a report that the rarest creature in the seven seas was a daily sight to the people of the lowcountry.

They may have known all there was to know about porpoises and their habits, but they had badly misjudged the character of the people they would find in the lower part of South Carolina. The citizens of Colleton were about to give them lessons free of charge. A collective shiver of rage passed invisibly through Colleton; the town was watchful and alarmed. The plot to steal Carolina Snow was an aberrant, unspeakable act to us. By accident, they had brought the rare savor of solidarity to our shores. They would feel the full weight of our dissent.

To them the white porpoise was a curiosity of science; to us she was the disclosure of the unutterable beauty and generosity of God among us, the proof of magic, and the ecstasy of art.

The white porpoise was something worthy to fight for.

The Amberjack, mimicking the habits of the shrimpers, moved out early the next morning, but it did not sight the porpoise that day and it set no nets. The men returned to the shrimp dock grim-lipped and eager for rumors about recent sightings of the Snow. They were met with silence.

After the third day, Luke and I met their boat and listened to the crew talk about the long fruitless days on the river, trying to sight the white porpoise. Already, they were feeling the eloquent heft of the town's censure and they seemed eager to talk to Luke and me, to extract any information about the porpoise they could from us.

Captain Blair brought Luke and me on board *The Amberjack* and showed us the holding tank on the main deck where specimens were kept alive until they could reach the aquariums in Miami. He showed us the half mile of nets that they would use to encircle the porpoise. A man's hand could pass easily through the meshing of their nets. The captain was a cordial middle-aged man and the sun had burned deep lines in his face, like tread marks. In a soft, barely discernible voice he told us how they trained a porpoise to eat dead fish after a capture. A porpoise would fast for two weeks or more before it would deign to feed on prey it would ignore in the wild. The greatest danger in the capture of a porpoise was that the animal would become entangled in the nets and drown. Hunting dolphins required a swift and skilled crew to ensure that drowning did not occur. He then showed us the foam rubber mattresses they laid the porpoises on once they got them on board.

"Why don't you just throw them in the pool, Captain?" I asked.

"We do usually, but sometimes we've got sharks in the pool and sometimes a porpoise will hurt himself thrashing around in a pool that small. Often it's better to just lie 'em down on these mattresses and keep splashing 'em with seawater so their skin won't dry out. We move 'em from side to side to keep their circulation right and that's about all there is to it."

"How long can they live out of the water?" Luke asked.

"I don't rightly know, son," the captain answered. "The longest I ever kept one out of the water was five days, but he made it back to Miami just fine. They're hardy creatures. When's the last time you boys spotted Moby in these waters?"

"Moby?" Luke said. "Her name is Snow. Carolina Snow."

"That's what they've named her down at Miami, boys. Moby Porpoise. Some guy in the publicity department came up with that one."

"That's the dumbest name I've ever heard," Luke said.

"It'll bring the tourists running, son," Captain Blair answered.

"Speaking of tourists, a whole boatful spotted the Snow yesterday morning in Charleston Harbor as they were heading out for Fort Sumter," said Luke.

"Are you sure, son?" the captain asked, and one of the crewmen leapt to his feet to hear the rest of the conversation.

"I didn't see it," Luke said, "but I heard it on the radio."

The Amberjack left for Charleston Harbor the next day, cruising the Ashley and the Cooper rivers looking for signs of the white porpoise. For three days they searched the waters around Wappoo Creek and the Elliott Cut before

they realized that my brother Luke was a liar. They had
also taught my brother how to keep a porpoise alive if the
need ever arose.

The call to arms between *The Amberjack* crew and the town
did not begin in earnest until the evening in June when the
crew tried to capture the white porpoise in full view of the
town. They had sighted the Snow in Colleton Sound, in
water much too deep to set their nets for a successful capture. All day, they had followed the porpoise, remaining
a discreet distance behind her, stalking her with infinite
patience until she began moving into the shallower rivers
and creeks.

Just as the crew tracked the porpoise, the shrimpers of
the town kept issuing reports on the position of *The Amberjack* on their short-wave radios. Whenever the boat
changed course, the eyes of the shrimp fleet noted and
remarked upon the shift of position, and the airwaves filled
up with the voices of shrimpers passing messages from
boat to boat, from boat to town. The shrimpers' wives,
monitoring their own radios, then got on the telephone to
spread the news. *The Amberjack* could not move through
county waters without its exact bearings being reported to
a regiment of secret listeners.

"*Amberjack* turning into Yemassee Creek," we heard one
day through the static of the radio my mother kept above
the kitchen sink. "Don't look like they found any Snow
today."

"Miami Beach just left Yemassee Creek and appears to
be settin' to poke around the Harper Dogleg up by Goat
Island."

The town carefully listened to these frequent intelligence
reports of the shrimpers. For a week the white porpoise
did not appear, and when she did it was one of the shrimpers who alerted the town.

"This is Captain Willard Plunkett and Miami Beach has
got the Snow in sight. They are pursuing her up the Colleton River and the crew is preparing the nets on deck. It
looks like Snow is heading for a visit to town."

Word passed through the town in the old quicksilvering
of rumor, and the prefigured power of that rumor lured

the whole town to the river's edge. People kept their eyes on the river and talked quietly. The sheriff pulled into the parking lot behind the bank and monitored the shrimpers' reports. The eyes of the town were fixed on the bend in the Colleton River where *The Amberjack* would make its appearance. That bend was a mile from the point where the river joined three of its sister rivers and bloomed into a sound.

For twenty minutes we waited for *The Amberjack* to make the turn, and when it did a collective groan rose up in the throats of us all. The boat was riding high above the marsh on an incoming tide. One of the crewmen stood on the foredeck with a pair of binoculars trained on the water in front of the boat. He stood perfectly still, rapt and statuesque, his complete immersion a testament to the passion he brought to his task.

Luke, Savannah, and I watched from the bridge, along with several hundred of our neighbors who had gathered to witness the moment of capture of the town's living symbol of good luck. The town was only curious until we saw Carolina Snow make her own luxurious appearance as she rounded the last curve of the river and began her silken, fabulous promenade through the town. She silvered as the sunlight caught her pale fin buttering through the crest of a small wave. In her movement through town she achieved a fragile sublimity, so unaware was she of her vulnerability. Burnished by perfect light, she dazzled us again with her complete and ambient beauty. Her dorsal fin broke the surface again like a white chevron a hundred yards nearer the bridge, and to our surprise, the town cheered spontaneously and the apotheosis of the white porpoise was fully achieved. The ensign of Colleton's wrath unfurled in the secret winds and our status as passive observers changed imperceptibly as a battle cry, unknown to any of us, formed on our lips. All the mottoes and passwords of engagement appeared like fiery graffiti on the armorial bearings of the town's unconscious. The porpoise disappeared again, then rose up, arcing toward the applause that greeted her sounding. She was mysterious and lunar. Her color was a delicate alchemy of lily and mother-of-pearl. The porpoise passed argentine beneath the sun-struck waters. Then we looked

up and saw *The Amberjack* gaining ground on the Snow and
the crew getting the nets into a small boat they were going
to lower into the water.

The town needed a warrior and I was surprised to find
him standing beside me.

Traffic jammed the bridge as drivers simply parked their
cars and went to the bridge's railing to watch the capture
of the porpoise. A truck loaded down with tomatoes from
one of Reese Newbury's farms was stuck on the bridge and
the driver was leaning on his horn in vain, trying to get
the other drivers back into their cars.

I heard Luke whisper to himself, "No. It just ain't right,"
and he left my side and mounted the back of the truck and
began to toss crates of tomatoes down among the crowd. I
thought Luke had gone crazy, but suddenly I understood,
and Savannah and I bashed a crate of tomatoes open and began to pass them along the railing. The driver got out and
screamed for Luke to stop, but Luke ignored him and continued passing the wooden crates down to the outstretched
arms of his friends and neighbors. The driver's voice grew
more and more frantic as people began taking tire tools from
their trunks and splitting the crates wide open. The sheriff's
car moved out of the parking lot and headed out toward the
Charleston highway on the opposite side of town.

When *The Amberjack* neared the bridge, two hundred tomatoes hit the deck in a green fusillade that put the man
with the binoculars to his knees. The tomatoes were hard
and green and one of the other crewmen working on the
nets was holding his nose near the aft of the boat, blood
leaking through his fingers. The second salvo of tomatoes
followed soon afterward and the crew scrambled, dazed
and insensible, toward the safety of the hold and cabin. A
tire tool cracked against a lifeboat and the crowd roared its
approval. Boxes of tomatoes were passed down the line,
the driver still screaming and not a single soul listening to
his pleadings.

The Amberjack disappeared beneath the bridge and two
hundred people crossed to the other side in a delirious,
headlong rush. When the boat reappeared we showered it
with tomatoes again, like archers on high ground pouring
arrows on an ill-deployed infantry. Savannah was throwing
hard and with accuracy, finding her own good rhythm, her

own style. She was screaming with pure pleasure. Luke threw a whole crate of tomatoes and it smashed on the rear deck, sending ruined tomatoes skittering like marbles toward the battened-down hold.

The Amberjack pulled out of range of all but the strongest arms when the porpoise, in a thoughtless gesture of self-preservation, reversed her course and turned back toward the town, passing the boat trailing her on its starboard side. She returned to our applause and our advocacy. We watched her move beneath the waters below the bridge, grizzling the bright waves like some abstract dream of ivory. When the boat made its long, hesitant turn in the river, even more crates of tomatoes were passed through the mob. By this time, even the truck driver had surrendered to whatever mass hysteria had possessed the rest of us and he stood with his arm cocked, holding a tomato, anticipating with the rest of us The Amberjack's imminent return. The boat started back for the bridge, then turned abruptly away from us and moved north on the Colleton River as Carolina Snow, the only white porpoise on our planet, moved back toward the Atlantic.

The next day the town council passed a resolution enfranchising Carolina Snow as a citizen of Colleton County and making it a felony for anyone to remove her from county waters. At the same time, the South Carolina state legislature passed a similar law rendering it a felony for anyone to remove genus Phocaena or genus Tursiops from the waters of Colleton County. In less than twenty-four hours, Colleton County became the only place in the world where it was a crime to capture a porpoise.

Captain Blair went straight to the sheriff's office when he reached the shrimp dock that night and demanded that Sheriff Lucas arrest everyone who had thrown a tomato at The Amberjack. Unfortunately, Captain Blair could not provide the sheriff with a single name of even one of the miscreants, and the sheriff, after making several phone calls, could produce four witnesses who would swear in a court of law that no one had been on the bridge when The Amberjack passed beneath it.

"Then how did I get a hundred pounds of tomatoes on the deck of my boat?" the captain had asked.

And in a laconic reply that was well received in each Colleton household, the sheriff had answered, "It's tomato season, Captain. Those damn things will grow anywhere."

But the men from Miami quickly recovered their will and developed a new plan for the capture of the porpoise. They kept out of sight of the town and did not enter the main channel of the Colleton River again. They began to haunt the outer territorial limits of the county, waiting for that perfect moment when the Snow would wander out of county waters and beyond the protection of those newly contracted laws. But *The Amberjack* was shadowed by boats from the South Carolina Game and Fish Commission and by a small flotilla of recreational boats commanded by the women and children of the town. Whenever *The Amberjack* picked up the trail of the porpoise, the small crafts would maneuver themselves between the porpoise and the pursuing vessel and slow their motors. *The Amberjack* would try to weave between the boats, but these women and children of Colleton had handled small boats all their lives. They would interfere with the Florida boat's progress until the white porpoise slipped away in the enfolding tides of Colleton Sound.

Each day Luke, Savannah, and I would take our boat and ride up the inland waterway to join the flotilla of resistance. Luke would move the boat in front of *The Amberjack*'s bow, ignoring the warning horn, and slow the Whaler by imperceptible degrees. No matter how skillfully Captain Blair maneuvered his boat, he could not pass Luke. Savannah and I had our fishing gear rigged and we trolled for Spanish mackerel as Luke navigated between *The Amberjack* and the white porpoise. Often, the crew would come out to the bow of the ship to threaten and taunt us.

"Hey, kids, get out of our goddamn way before we get pissed off," one crewman yelled.

"Just fishing, mister," Luke would shoot back.

"What're you fishing for?" The man sneered in exasperation.

"We hear there's a white porpoise in these waters," said Luke, slowing the motor with a delicate movement of his wrist.

"Is that right, smartass? Well, you're not doing such a good job catching it."

"We're doing as good as you are, mister," Luke answered pleasantly.

"If this were Florida, we'd run right over you."

"It ain't Florida, mister. Or haven't you noticed?" Luke said.

"Hicks," the man screamed.

Luke pulled back the throttle and we slowed almost to a crawl. We could hear the big engines of *The Amberjack* throttling down behind us as the bow of the boat loomed over us.

"He called us hicks," Luke said.

"Me, a hick?" Savannah said.

"That hurts my feelings," I said.

Up ahead, the white porpoise turned into Langford Creek, the alabaster shine in her fin disappearing behind a green flange of marsh. There were three boats waiting at the mouth of the creek ready to intercept *The Amberjack* if it managed to get past Luke.

After thirty days of delay and obstruction, *The Amberjack* left the southern boundaries of Colleton waters and returned to its home base of Miami without the white porpoise. Captain Blair gave a final embittered interview to the *Gazette*, listing the many obstacles the citizens of Colleton had erected to disrupt the mission of *The Amberjack*. Such deterrence, he said, could not be allowed to frustrate the integrity of scientific investigation. But on their last day, he and his crew had taken sniper fire from Freeman's Island and he, as captain, had made the irrevocable decision to discontinue the hunt. The shrimp fleet observed *The Amberjack* as it passed the last barrier islands, maneuvered through the breakers, then turned south, angling toward the open seas.

But *The Amberjack* did not go to Miami. It traveled south for forty miles, then turned into the mouth of the Savannah River, putting in to the shrimp dock at Thunderbolt. There it remained for a week to resupply and to let the passions in Colleton County cool, still monitoring the short-wave radio, following the travels of the white porpoise by listening to the Colleton shrimpers give accurate reports of her soundings. After a week *The Amberjack* left the harbor in

Savannah in the middle of the night and turned north out beyond the three-mile limit. They cruised confidently out of sight of the shore-bound shrimp trawlers. They were waiting for one signal to come over the radio.

They had been offshore for three days when they heard the words they had been waiting for.

"There's a submerged log I just netted in Zajac Creek, shrimpers. You boys be careful if you're over this way. Out."

"There's no shrimp in Zajac Creek anyhow, Captain," a voice of another shrimp boat captain answered. "You a long way from home, ain't you, Captain Henry? Out."

"I'll catch the shrimp wherever I can find them, Captain. Out," my father answered, watching Carolina Snow moving a school of fish toward a sandbar.

Zajac Creek was not in Colleton County and *The Amberjack* turned west and came at full throttle toward the creek, the crew preparing the nets as the shoreline of South Carolina filled the eyes of Captain Blair for the last time. A shrimper from Charleston witnessed the capture of the white porpoise at 1130 hours that morning, saw Carolina Snow panic and charge the encircling nets, saw when she entangled herself, and admired the swiftness and skill of the crew as they got their ropes around her, held her head above the water to keep her from drowning, and maneuvered her into one of the motorboats.

By the time the word reached Colleton, *The Amberjack* was well outside the three-mile limit again, set on a southerly course that would take them into Miami in fifty-eight hours. The bells of the church were rung in protest, an articulation of our impotence and fury. It was as if the river had been deconsecrated, purged of all the entitlements of magic.

"Submerged log" was the code phrase my father had worked out with Captain Blair and the crew of *The Amberjack*. He had agreed to fish the boundary waters at the edge of the county until he sighted the white porpoise moving into the territorial waters of Gibbes County to the north. My father was the anonymous Colletonian who had written the Miami Seaquarium informing them of the presence of an albino porpoise in our county. Two weeks after the abduction of Snow and a week after her picture appeared in the *Colleton Gazette* being lowered into her aquarium tank in her new Miami home, my father received a letter of gratitude from Captain Blair and a check for a thousand dollars as a reward for his assistance.

"I'm ashamed of what you did, Henry," my mother said, barely able to control her temper as my father waved the check in front of us.

"I earned a thousand big ones, Lila, and it was the easiest money I ever made in my life. I wish every porpoise I passed was an albino so I could spend all my time eating chocolate and buying banks."

"If anybody in this town had any guts, they'd go to Miami and set that animal free. You'd better not let anyone in town hear that you're responsible, Henry. Folks are still steaming mad about that porpoise."

"How could you sell our porpoise, Daddy?" Savannah asked.

"Look, sweetie, that porpoise is gonna be in fat city, chowing down on gourmet mackerel and jumping through hoops to make kids happy. Snow doesn't have to worry about a shark the rest of her life. She's retired in Miami. You got to look at it in a positive light."

"I think you've committed a sin that not even God can forgive, Daddy," Luke said darkly.

"You do?" My father sneered. "Hey, I never saw 'Property of Colleton' tattooed on her back. I just wrote the Seaquarium that Colleton had a natural phenomenon that could lure in the crowds and they rewarded me for being on my toes."

"They couldn't have found him if you hadn't radioed every time you spotted him in the river," I said.

"I was their liaison officer in the area. Look, it's not that great a shrimping season. This thousand bucks is going to put food on the table and clothes on your back. This could pay for a whole year of college for one of you kids."

"I wouldn't eat a bite of food you bought with that money," Luke said. "And I wouldn't wear a pair of Jockey shorts you bought with it either."

"I've been watching the Snow for more than five years

now," my mother said. "You once punished Tom for killing a bald eagle, Henry. There's a lot more eagles in the world than white porpoises."

"I didn't kill the porpoise, Lila. I delivered it to a safe harbor where it will be free of all fear. I look upon myself as the hero of this affair."

"You sold Snow into captivity," my mother said.

"They're going to make her a circus porpoise," Savannah added.

"You betrayed yourself and your sources," Luke said. "If it was a businessman, I could understand. Some low-life creepy Jaycee with shiny hair. But a shrimper, Dad. A shrimper selling Snow for money."

"I sell shrimp for money, Luke," my father shouted.

"Not the same," Luke said. "You don't sell what you can't replace."

"I saw twenty porpoises in the river today."

"And I promise you, Daddy, not one of them was white. None of them was special," Luke said.

"Our family is the reason they captured the Snow," said Savannah. "It's like being the daughter of Judas Iscariot, only I bet I'd have liked Judas a lot better."

"You shouldn't have done what you did, Henry," my mother said. "It'll bring bad luck."

"I couldn't have had any worse luck than I've had," my father answered. "Anyway, it's done. There's nothing anyone can do about it now."

"I can do something about it," said Luke.

Three weeks later, in the languorous starry dark, when my parents were asleep and we could hear the soft chaos of my father's snoring, Luke whispered a plan to us. It should not have surprised us, but years later, Savannah and I would talk and wonder about the exact hour when our older brother turned from a passionate, idealistic boy into a man of action. Both of us were terrified and exhilarated by the boldness of his proposal, but neither of us wanted any part of it. But Luke continued to urge us quietly until we found ourselves imprisoned by the magnetic originality of his gentle eloquence. His decision was already made and he spent half the night enlisting us as recruits in his first real dance on the wild side. Ever since the night we watched him facing the tiger alone in the barn, we had known Luke was brave, but now we were faced with the probability that Luke was also reckless.

Three mornings later, after Luke had made exhaustive preparations, we were on Highway 17, thundering south, with Luke stepping hard on the accelerator, and the radio turned up high. Ray Charles was singing "Hit the Road, Jack" and we were singing it along with him. We were drinking beer iced down in a cooler and had the radio tuned to the Big Ape in Jacksonville as we shot across the Eugene Talmadge Memorial Bridge in Savannah. We slowed up at the toll gate and Luke handed the old man who was doling out tickets a dollar for a round tripper.

"You gonna do a little shopping in Savannah, kids?" the old man asked.

"No, sir," Luke replied, "we're on our way to Florida to steal us a porpoise."

On that bizarre and headlong flight to Florida my senses blazed like five brilliant fires behind my eyes. I felt as if I could point at a palm tree and it would burst into flame. I was electric, charged, ecstatic, and terror-stricken. Each song that came on the radio sounded as though it were sung expressly for my pleasure. Though I have an execrable singing voice, I thought my singing was terrific as we stayed on the coastal highway and burned down the oak-lined Georgia roads with Luke changing gears only when we slowed down for towns. Speed was in Luke's blood and we crossed the Florida state line two hours after we had left Melrose Island, and we didn't even stop for a glass of free orange juice at the welcome station.

The city of Jacksonville slowed us up some, but the St. Johns River was a grand thing and the first river we had ever seen that flowed north. Once we hit Highway A1A we were blistering the asphalt again and the tires sang against the macadam and the ocean appeared in intervals to our left. As the warm wind rushed into the cab, we felt that the sea was racing south with us, aware of our mission, yes, aware and approving and partisan.

We rode south with larcenous hearts and the sensibilities of outlaws, feeding off one another's bewildered energy. I turned and saw Luke laughing at some remark that Savan-

nah had made and I felt the flow of her long hair against
my cheek and the sweet smell of that hair, and I filled up
with a perfect, ineffable love of my brother and sister, a
love so vivid and powerful I could taste it on my tongue
and feel its glorious heat burn deeply in my chest. Leaning
over, I kissed Savannah on the neck and I squeezed Luke's
shoulder with my left hand. He reached up and squeezed
my hand, then surprised me by taking my hand and bringing it to his lips in a gesture of surpassing tenderness. I
leaned back and let the smell of the state of Florida flood
my senses in the watery light of Sunday.

After ten hours of hard driving and two stops for gas, the
city of Miami rose out of the sea as we drove past the sign
for the Hialeah racetrack. Coconut palms rattled in the warm
breezes and the scent of gardens overwhelmed by bougainvillea cologned the broad avenues. We had never been
to Florida in our lives and suddenly we were cruising the
streets of Miami looking for a place to set our tents beneath
the lime and avocado trees.

"What do we do now, Luke?" I asked. "We can't just
walk up and say, 'Hello, we've driven down here to steal
your white porpoise. Do you mind packing her bags?'"

"We look around," Luke answered. "We put our heads
together. I got a preliminary plan. But we got to be prepared. First we case the joint. There's got to be a night
watchman, some yo-yo who makes sure little kids don't
sneak in at night to try and catch Flipper with a cane pole."

"What will we do about the night watchman?" Savannah
asked.

"I don't want to have to kill him," said Luke evenly.
"How about you two?"

"Are you crazy, Luke?" I said. "Are you out of your
goddamn tree?"

"That's just a contingency plan."

"No, it's not, Luke," said Savannah. "If that's a contingency plan, then we're not part of it."

"I was only joking. They've got a killer whale locked up
in this place. We can check him out tomorrow too."

"We aren't rescuing the killer whale, Luke," Savannah said.
"I know that sound in your voice and the killer whale is out."

"Maybe we can set every fish in the whole goddamn place free," Luke said. "I mean, have a real breakout."

"Why do they call them killer whales?" I asked.

"I think they love to kick ass," Luke explained.

We took the causeway that led out toward Key Biscayne and passed the Seaquarium on our right. Luke slowed the truck as we drove through the parking lot, observing the single light that shone from a security man's office. He came to the window and looked out, his face framed by a corona of electric light, making him featureless and absurd. An eight-foot fence, topped with barbed wire, protected the compound from intruders. Luke gunned the engine and we scissored out of the parking lot, spitting gravel behind us. We knew we were going by the zoo when we passed a place on the road that smelled like Caesar's cage magnified a hundred times. An elephant trumpeted somewhere in the darkness and Luke answered him with a trumpeting of his own.

"That didn't sound like an elephant, Luke," Savannah said.

"I thought it was pretty good," Luke said. "What do you think it sounded like?"

"An oyster farting through Crisco," she answered.

Luke roared and put his arm around Savannah and hugged her to his chest. That night we slept on a bench at Key Biscayne and the sun was high when we arose the next morning, gathered our belongings, and headed for a visit to the Seaquarium.

We paid our admission fees and walked through the turnstiles. For the first half-hour we circumnavigated the park, following the parabola made by the large Cyclone fence and its ugly toupee of barbed wire. Beside a cluster of palms contiguous to the parking lot, Luke stopped and said, "I'll back the truck up to these trees and I'll cut a hole right through here."

"What if they catch us, Luke?" I asked.

"We're just high school kids from Colleton who came down to rescue Snow on a dare from our classmates. We act like total hicks and pretend the coolest thing we ever did was spit watermelon seeds at sheets hanging in our mama's back yard."

"The guard at the gate was wearing a gun, Luke," Savannah said.

"I know, honey, but no guard is going to shoot at us."

"How do you know?" she asked.

"Because Tolitha gave me a whole bottle of sleeping pills. You know, the ones she calls her little red devils."

"Do we just tell him to say 'ah' and pop a pill in his mouth?" I said, fearing that Luke's master plan would prove a bit leaky in its execution.

"I haven't figured that out yet, little brother," Luke said. "I just found me the place where I'm going to cut the hole."

"How we gonna get Snow out of the water?" I asked.

"Same way. Sleeping pills," he answered.

"That'll be easy," I said. "We'll just jump in the water, swim our asses off until we catch a porpoise that it took experts a month to catch when they had all the equipment in the world, and then slip a few sleeping pills between her lips. Great plan, Luke."

"More than a few pills, Tom. We've got to make damn sure that the Snow is completely tranquilized."

"This will be the first porpoise in history to die of a drug overdose," Savannah said.

"No, I figure the Snow weighs about four hundred pounds. Tolitha weighs a hundred pounds. She takes one pill every night. We'll give Snow four or five of the babies."

"Who ever heard of a porpoise taking sleeping pills, Luke?" Savannah said. "Tom's right."

"I haven't either," Luke admitted. "But I've heard of a porpoise eating fish. And if that fish just happens to be chock-full of sleeping pills, then it's my theory that porpoise will be ready for rock-a-bye-baby time."

I asked, "Do porpoises sleep, Luke?"

"I don't know," he answered. "We're going to find out a lot about porpoises on this little expedition, Tom."

"What if it doesn't work, Luke?" Savannah asked.

Luke shrugged his shoulders and said, "No harm in that, Savannah. At least we'll know we tried to do something. And ain't we had some fun so far? All those people in Colleton crying about losing their porpoise and you, me, and Tom down here in Miami planning the jailbreak. We'll tell our kids about it. If we manage to get Snow out of here, there'll be parades and confetti and riding in convertibles.

We'll brag about it until the day we die. But first, you got to see it. Neither of you see it yet. Now that's real important. Here, I'll help you. Close your eyes . . ."

Savannah and I closed our eyes and listened to our brother's voice. "Okay. Tom and I have the porpoise in the water. We move her over to the place where Savannah is waiting with the stretcher. We get ropes around the Snow and very gently we roll her out of the water and tie her to the stretcher. The guard is asleep because we drugged his Pepsi a couple of hours before. See it? Can you visualize it? We get the porpoise in the pickup and we're off. And here's the important thing. Listen to this. We're standing in the boat landing in Colleton and we take the Snow and we untie the ropes and we set her free in the river where she was born and where she belongs. Can you see it? Can you see it all, Tom and Savannah?"

His voice was hypnotic, transported, and we both opened our eyes at the same time and we nodded toward each other. Both of us could see it.

We continued our long walk around the perimeter of the park and saw *The Amberjack* tied up at its berth at the south end of the Seaquarium. There was no sign of the crew around, but we avoided any approach to the boat. Turning toward the porpoise house, we crossed a wooden bridge suspended high over a deep clear moat where huge sharks moved sluggishly in an endless circle. The sharks swam at twenty-yard intervals and there was very little room or inclination for them to pass one another. We watched a hammerhead and a young mako make their torpid passage beneath us as the crowd watched with breathless wonder. So monotonous was the movement of their great tails, so proscribed was their freedom for improvisation or movement, that they seemed purged of all their ferocious grandeur. Beneath the gazes of tourists, they looked as docile and harmless as black mollies.

The crowd was large and good-natured and we followed a processional of Bermuda shorts and rubber-soled thongs toward the amphitheater where the killer whale, Dreadnought, would perform at noon. From our brief encounter, Florida seemed to be a place where amiable crowds met to display white shapeless arms and acres of sun-starved hairless legs. The sun had parched the grass to the palest of greens and automatic sprinkler systems worked the infields off the gravel paths and ruby-throated hummingbirds droned among the lilies. As we neared the amphitheater, we passed a sign that read, "Visit Moby Porpoise at feeding time."

"I think we will," Luke said.

We listened to the tourists talking about the white porpoise as they filed into the rows of seats that ringed a vast two-million-gallon tank aquarium. When we were all seated, a well-made blond boy with coppery shoulders walked out onto a wooden peninsula jutting out over the water and waved to the crowd. A woman announcer presented the history of Dreadnought, the killer whale who had been captured in a pod of twelve whales near Queen Charlotte Strait off Vancouver Island and flown to Miami by special flight. The Seaquarium had paid sixty thousand dollars for the purchase of Dreadnought and it had taken a year to train the killer whale. The whale could not be incorporated into the porpoise show because porpoise was a favorite food of *Orcinus orca*.

As she spoke, a gate opened invisibly underwater and the passage of something awesome roiled the opaque depths below.

The tanned boy peered into the water, seeing something rising up toward him. His platform was twenty feet above the surface and you could study the intensity of his concentration by counting the lines on his forehead as he leaned forward holding a Spanish mackerel by the tail. The boy made a circling gesture with his hand and in obedience the water was suddenly runnelled with waves spun outward from the center of the aquarium. Then the whale went to the bottom of the tank, maintaining his speed and momentum, and came out of that water like a building launched from below and took the proffered fish daintily, like a girl accepting a mint. Then the whale fell back down in a long arc. His shadow blocked the sun for a moment and when he hit the surface of the aquarium it was as if a tree had toppled into the sea from a high ridge.

Then a massive wave, in answer, broke over the railing and drenched the crowd with seawater from row one to row twenty-three. You watched Dreadnought do his act and bathed at the same time, the salt water running out of your hair, smelling of the essence of whale.

As he made the circuit around his pool again, urging himself toward his moment of piebald beauty in the Florida sun, lifting out toward the heavy-scented odors of citrus and bougainvillea, we could glimpse his white-bottomed streaking image in the water and the amazing iridescences on his black head; he was the color of a good pair of saddle shoes. His dorsal fin was set like a black pyramid on his back and moved through the water like a blade hissing through nylon. His lines were clean and supple; his teeth were set in his grim mouth, each one the size of a table lamp. I had never seen such contained and implied power. Dreadnought leapt again and rang a bell that was suspended over the water. He opened his mouth and let the blond boy brush the whale's teeth with a janitor's broom. For his finale, Dreadnought came blasting out of the water, his flukes gleaming and shedding gallons of seawater, and the whale grasped a rope with his teeth and ran our American flag to the top of a flagpole high above the aquarium. Whenever the whale reached the apogee of one of his agile leaps, the crowd cheered, then braced itself for his graceful, streamlined plunge back into the water, when again we would be covered by a prodigious wave.

"Now that's an animal," Luke said.

"Can you imagine being hunted by a killer whale?" Savannah said.

Luke said to her, "If that thing's after you, Savannah, there's only one thing you can do. Submit. You'd have to submit to your fate."

"I'd love to see a whale like that in Colleton," I said, laughing.

"This is how they should execute criminals," Luke said suddenly. "Give them a bathing suit, stick a few mackerel in their jockstraps, and let them try to swim across this pool. If they made it they would go free. If they didn't, they'd really cut down on the food bill at Seaquarium."

"Real humane, Luke," said Savannah.

"I mean the really mean criminals. You know, the mass murderers. Hitler. Baby killers. The real creeps on the planet. I don't mean jaywalkers and shit."

"What a hideous death," I said, watching the whale leap through a ring of fire and douse the flames with the backwash of his landing.

"Naw, they could make it part of the act. Get Dad to run it. The killer whale jumps up and rings the bell, so as a reward, he gets to eat a criminal."

Dreadnought's last colossal free fall covered us with a final wave and we joined the hundreds of drenched tourists moving out toward the porpoise house.

After the killer whale, the porpoises looked diminutive and inconsequential and their act, though far more spunky and accomplished than the whale's, seemed trifling after Dreadnought's pièce de résistance. Their tricks were dazzlers, all right, they just weren't whales. But they were sure a happy, supererogatory tribe as they left the water like artillery shells leaping twenty feet in the air, their bodies jade-colored and smooth. Their heads were creased with perpetual harlequin smiles that lent sincerity to their high-spirited performances. They played baseball games, bowled, danced on their tails the full length of their aquarium, threw balls through hoops, and took lit cigarettes out of their trainer's mouth in a vain attempt to get him to give up smoking.

We found Carolina Snow in her own small enclosed pool, cut off from the companionship of the other porpoises. A large and curious crowd surrounded her enclosure and she swam from side to side, looking disoriented and faintly bored. She had not yet learned a single trick but was certainly earning her keep as an item of curiosity. The announcer described the capture of the white porpoise and made it sound like the most dangerous, exotic venture since the discovery of the Northwest Passage. At three o'clock we watched a keeper bring a bucket of fish to feed the Snow. He threw a blue runner at the opposite end of the pool from where Snow was swimming. She turned and in a movement of surprising delicacy accelerated across the pool and took the fish from the top of the water. We listened as the tourists tried to describe her color. We, her liberators, listened with pride as we heard strangers speak of her pale luminous beauty.

We watched the feeding and noticed that the man kept alternating where he threw the fish and that it was all part of an elaborate design for the training of the Snow. Once he got her in one rhythm of going from side to side in the pool, he reversed the procedure and brought her closer and closer until she lifted out of the water and took the last fish from his hand. The keeper was patient and skillful and the crowd applauded when Snow came out of the water. It was like watching a priest administering the Eucharist to a young girl in a Communion veil when he put the blue runner in Snow's open mouth.

"We got to get to a fish market, Tom," Luke whispered. "Savannah, you try to make contact with the night watchman before closing time. It don't close until eight."

"I've always wanted to play the wicked seductress," she said.

"You aren't seducing anyone. You're just going to make friends with him. Then put the son of a bitch to sleep."

In Coconut Grove we bought half a dozen whitings and a bucket of Kentucky Fried Chicken. When we returned to the Seaquarium it was a half-hour before closing time and we found Savannah talking with the night watchman, who had just arrived at the security office for duty.

"Brothers," Savannah said, "I have met the nicest man."

"Is she bothering you, mister?" Luke said. "She's only free on a daily pass from the nut house."

"Bothering me? It's not often I get to talk to such a pretty girl. I'm the one who's usually here when everybody's gone home."

"Mr. Beavers is from New York City."

"You want some fried chicken?" Luke offered.

"Don't mind if I do," Mr. Beavers said, pulling out a drumstick.

"How about a Pepsi?"

"I'm strictly a coffee man. Hey, it's getting close to closing time. I got to run you kids out of here. This job gets lonely. That's its only drawback."

He sounded a loud foghorn that was followed immediately by a recorded announcement asking that all visitors leave the grounds of the Seaquarium at once and giving the opening time for the next day. Mr. Beavers went outside his office door and blew his own whistle, walking between the killer whale amphitheater and the porpoise house. Savannah refreshed his coffee from the pot he had already brewed on his desk, snapped open the contents of two sleeping pills, and stirred the coffee until the powder dissolved completely.

Luke and I followed Mr. Beavers around the park as he good-humoredly urged the tourists to go home and return the next day. He stopped at the holding tank where the Snow was moving restlessly from one side to the other.

"She's an aberration of nature," he said. "But a beautiful aberration."

As he turned, he spotted a teenager throwing a Popsicle wrapper on the ground. "My good young man," he said, "littering is a crime against the maker of this green earth."

As he walked toward the boy, Luke dropped the whiting into the water of Carolina Snow's aquarium. The Snow passed it twice before she downed it.

"How many pills did you put in that fish?" I whispered.

"Enough to kill you or me," he answered.

Mr. Beavers was sipping his coffee as we waved goodbye to him. I whispered to Savannah as we walked to the pickup, "Nice work, Mata Hari."

Luke came walking up behind us and said, "I'm hot. How 'bout let's go swimming in Key Biscayne."

"What time are we coming back for the Snow," I asked.

"I figure about midnight," he said.

We watched the moon rise like a pale watermark against the eastern sky. We swam until the sun began to set in an Atlantic so different from the ocean that broke against our part of the eastern seaboard that it did not seem possible that they were related in any way. The Florida ocean was clear-eyed and aquamarine and I had never been able to see my own feet as I walked chest-deep in the sea.

"This water don't seem right," Luke said, expressing exactly what I felt.

The sea has always been feminine to me but Florida had softened its hard edges and tamed the azury depths with clarity. The mystery of Florida deepened on the shore as we ate mangoes for the first time. The fruit tasted foreign but indigenous, like sunlight a tree had changed through patience. We were strangers to a sea you could trust, whose tides were imperceptible and gentle, whose cologne-colored waters were translucent and calm below the palm trees. The moon laid a filament of silver across the water for a hundred miles before it nested in the braids of Savannah's hair. Luke stood up and fished his watch out from his jeans pocket.

"If we get caught tonight, Tom and Savannah, just let me do the talking. I got you into this and it's my responsibility to get you out if we hit trouble. Now let's pray that Mr. Beavers is counting sheep."

Through the window of his small office we could see Mr. Beavers with his head on his desk, sleeping soundly. Luke backed the pickup into a grove of trees by the Cyclone fence and, working quickly, cut a large hole in the fence using his wire cutters. Entering the fence, we made our way through the shadows passing over the moat of sharks where we could hear the creatures moving through the water below us in their endless circuit, their horrible punishment for having been born sharks. We were running by the amphitheater when we heard the sound of the killer whale's implosion of breath.

"Wait a minute," Luke said, removing a fish from the bag he had brought for Snow in case she wanted a snack on the ride north.

"No, Luke," I said, alarmed. "We don't have time for no foolishness."

But Luke was running up the stairs into the amphitheater and Savannah and I had no choice but to follow him. In the moonlight we watched him as he climbed the platform and we saw the great fin break the water below him. Then Luke moved to the edge of the platform, and mimicking the gestures of the blond trainer we had witnessed earlier in the day, he made a circular movement with his arm and we saw Dreadnought dive deep into his tank and heard the punished waters slapping against the sides of the aquarium as the invisible whale gathered speed beneath my brother. Luke put the whiting in his right hand and leaned far out over the water.

The whale exploded out from below and took the whiting from Luke's hand without so much as grazing his fingers. Then the lordly fall from space carried the whale over on his side, exposing his brilliant white underbelly, and he washed twenty-three rows of bleachers as he entered the water again in a fabulous wave.

"Stupid, stupid, stupid," I whispered as Luke joined us again.

"Wonderful, wonderful, wonderful," Savannah said, exhilarated.

We ran to *The Amberjack* and went to the storage bin on deck where the crew kept the equipment we knew we would need. Luke pulled out the ropes and the stretcher. He threw the foam rubber mattresses to Savannah. She took them and raced back to the truck to lay them out neatly on the flatbed. Luke and I hurried to the porpoise house and Luke again used his wire cutters to enter the area where the Snow was kept.

We reached her just in time. She was almost motionless in shallow water and I think she would have drowned if we had waited another hour. When we entered the water, she was so drugged that she did not even move. We caught her beneath the head and stomach and moved her over to the side of the pool where we had placed the stretcher. She was so white my hand looked brown against her head. She made a tender, human sound as we floated her across the pool. Savannah returned and the three of us girded the stretcher beneath her in the water and bound her with the ropes in three places.

Again, we passed through the shadows of palms and citrus trees, Luke and I bearing the stretcher like medics in a war zone, keeping low and moving fast. We passed through the opening in the ruined fence and untied the Snow gently and rolled her onto the mattresses. Savannah and I splashed her with the Key Biscayne water we had gathered in buckets and in our beer cooler. Luke closed the tailgate, and running to the cab, he started the motor and eased out of the parking lot and moved down the causeway toward the lights of Miami. I think we were the nearest to getting caught in those first two minutes, because going down that nearly deserted highway, the three Wingo kids from South Carolina were screaming, screaming, screaming.

Soon we had left Miami forever and Luke had his foot pressed against the accelerator almost to the floorboard, and the warm air streamed through our hair as every mile brought us closer to the border of Georgia. Snow's breathing was ragged at first, like the tearing of paper, and once or twice when it seemed as though she had stopped breathing I blew air into her blowhole. She answered me with a breath of her own but the effect of the pills did not seem to wear off until we stopped for gas at Daytona Beach. Then she rallied and was perky for the rest of the trip.

After we got gas, Luke drove the truck out onto the beach and Savannah and I leapt out and filled up the buckets and cooler with fresh seawater, then hopped back in as Luke spun through the sand and made it to the highway again.

"We're doing it. We're doing it," he screamed out the back window to us. "We got five more hours and we'll be home free."

We doused the porpoise with salt water and massaged her from head to tail to keep her circulation going and spoke to her with those phrases of endearment kids normally reserve for dogs. She was supple and pliable and her flesh was satiny to the touch. We sang lullabies to her, recited children's poems and nursery rhymes, and whispered that we were taking her home and she would never have to eat dead fish again. When we crossed into Georgia, Savannah and I danced around the flatbed and Luke had to slow down because he thought we might dance ourselves right out of the truck.

It was right outside of Midway, Georgia, that a highway patrolman pulled Luke over for going about forty miles over the speed limit. Luke said through the back window, "Cover Snow's head with one of those mattresses. I'll handle this."

The sun had already risen and the patrolman was young and slim as a blade. He had that maddening arrogance of the rookie. But Luke bounded out of that truck just bubbling over about something.

"Officer," I heard him say as Savannah and I got Snow's head covered. "I'm so sorry. Honest I am. But I was so excited about catching this here shark and I just had to get it back so my daddy could see it while it was still alive."

The patrolman came over to the truck and whistled as he looked in.

"He's a big 'un," the patrolman said. "But that's no cause for you speeding like that, son."

"You don't understand, Officer," Luke said. "This here is a world record. I caught him with a rod and reel. It's a white shark. They're the real man-eaters. I caught this one near the jetty off Saint Simons Island."

"What'd you catch him with?"

"I caught him with a live shrimp, if you can believe such a thing. They caught a white shark in Florida last year and found a man's boot and shinbone in his stomach."

"I got to give you a ticket, son."

"I expect that, sir. I was speeding I was so excited. You ever catch a fish this big?"

"I'm from Marietta. I once caught a twelve-pound bass in Lake Lanier."

"Then you know exactly how I feel, sir. Look, let me show you his teeth. He's got teeth like razor blades. My poor brother and sister are half dead from trying to hold this rascal down. Let the officer have a look, Tom."

"I don't cotton to seeing no shark, son. Just you run along now and slow it down a bit. I guess you got a right to be excited. That bass I caught, that was the biggest one taken out of Lake Lanier that whole day. My cat ate it before I could show it to my daddy."

"Thank you so much, sir. You sure you don't want to see its teeth? He's got a powerful mouthful."

"I'd sure rather be driving than sitting on that dang thing," the patrolman said to me and Savannah as he walked back to his car.

My mother was hanging out wash when we came blitzing down the dirt road and Luke made a few triumphant doughnuts on the lawn and we slid to a stop. My mother ran to the truck and did a little softshoe of triumph around the lawn, her arms raised in the air. Luke backed up the truck to the sea wall and we rolled the porpoise back onto the stretcher. Mama kicked off her shoes and the four of us stepped into the high tide and moved out toward deeper water. We held Snow in our arms and walked her into deeper water, letting her get used to the river again. We let her float by herself but she seemed unbalanced and unsure of herself. Luke held her head above the water until I felt her powerful tail flip me off her and she began to swim slowly and unsteadily away from us. For fifteen minutes she looked like a dying animal and it was painful to watch her suffer. We stood on the dock praying for her, my mother leading us through a rosary without beads. The Snow floundered; she seemed to have trouble breathing;

her sense of balance and timing were not functioning. Then it changed before our eyes. Instinct returned and she dove and the old sense of rhythm and grace returned in the easy fluency of that dive. She sounded after a long minute and was two hundred yards further out in the river.

"She's made it," Luke yelled, and we gathered together, holding on to each other. I was exhausted, sweaty, famished, but I had never felt so wonderful in my life.

Up she rose again and, turning, she passed us standing on the dock.

We cheered and screamed and wept. And we danced a new dance on our floating dock on the most beautiful island in the world on the finest, the very finest, day of Tom Wingo's life.

17

On the day that Benji Washington integrated Colleton High School, television crews from Charleston and Columbia recorded the exact moment his parents let him out of their lime-green Chevrolet and he began his solemn walk toward the five hundred white students who silently watched his approach. The atmosphere of the school that day was estranged, dangerous, and tense. The halls were magnetized like sea air before a hurricane. Hatred prowled the rooms and alcoves. The word *nigger* appeared in angry, hastily applied graffiti in whichever room the black boy had a class until the teachers, nervous and unstrung, would enter and expunge the word from sight with birdlike skitterings of the erasers. In each class, he chose the last seat by the window and spent much of the first day staring impassively toward the river. The seats around him were empty, a forbidden zone that no white student would or

could enter. Rumors circulated and annealed in the boys'
lavatory, where the tough kids smoked illegally between
classes. I heard one boy say he had shoved the nigger in
the cafeteria line; another claimed to have jabbed him with
a fork. He had not responded to either provocation. It was
as if he had no emotions, that he had been trained not to
feel. Plans to get him behind the gymnasium alone were
whispered along the breezeway. Chains and clubs appeared in the lockers down the main hall. There was a
rumor of a gun. I heard Oscar Woodhead, left tackle on
the football team, swear he was going to kill the nigger
before the school year was out. You could see switchblades
outlined against the buttocks of swaggering boys with slicked-
back hair. I had never been so afraid in my life.

My plan was a simple one, as my plans always were. I
was going to ignore the fact of Benji Washington's existence, go my own way, and cheerfully navigate through
the tainted electorate of that aroused high school population as well as I could. I could talk nigger talk with the best
of them, and had a glossary of a thousand nigger jokes on
file to entertain my contemporaries should my loyalty to
the tribe ever be questioned. But my racism issued forth
from my passionate need to conform rather than from any
serious credo or system of belief. I could hate with ardor
but only if I was perfectly sure that my hatred echoed the
sentiments of the majority. I was without moral courage of
any kind and it suited me well. Unfortunately, my twin did
not share these secret troves of superficiality.

I did not know that Benji Washington was in my sixth-
period English class until I saw that sullen mob who had
shadowed him all day gathered outside the door. I looked
around for the teacher but he was nowhere in sight. I made
my way through the crowd like a sheriff parting a lynch
mob in a bad Western.

I saw the black kid staring out the window, sitting in that
final forlorn seat. Oscar Woodhead was sitting in the windowsill, whispering something to him. I took a front-row
seat and pretended to write something in a notebook. I
could hear Oscar saying, "You're an ugly nigger. Did you
hear me, boy? You're an ugly fucking nigger. But that's
natural, I guess. Because all niggers are ugly, ain't they,
boy?"

I did not see Savannah come into the room and did not know she had entered until I heard her voice behind me. "Hello, Benji," she said in her most perfect cheerleaderly voice. "I'm Savannah Wingo. Welcome to Colleton High School."

She extended her hand.

Washington, who without question was the most stunned inhabitant of that room, shook her hand reluctantly.

"She touched it," Lizzie Thompson squealed near the doorway.

"If you have any trouble, let me know about it, Benji," Savannah said. "If you need any help, just holler. These folks aren't as bad as they seem now. They'll get used to you being around in a couple of days. Is this seat taken?"

I put my head down on my desk and moaned inaudibly.

"There hasn't been a seat taken around me all day," Benji answered, looking out to the river again.

"There is now," she said, placing her books on top of the desk next to him.

"She's sitting next to a nigger," Oscar said loudly. "I ain't believing that."

Then Savannah called from the back of the room. "Hey, Tom. Bring your books back here. Yoo-hoo, Tom. I see you. It's me, Savannah. Your loving sister. Get your ass over here."

Furiously, knowing there was no use arguing with Savannah in front of a roomful of people, I obeyed and brought my books to the back of the room as the entire class watched.

"Hmmmmph!" Oscar snorted. "I wouldn't let no girl talk to me like that."

"No girl would want to talk to you, Oscar," Savannah shot back. "Because you're stupid and because you got more pimples than the river's got shrimp."

"You don't mind talking to black niggers, though, huh, Savannah?" Oscar cried out.

"Why don't you go down to the guidance department and try to break into double figures on an IQ test, creep," she said, rising out of her seat.

"I don't mind, Savannah," Benji said softly. "I knew it would be like this."

"Nigger, you don't know what it's going to be like yet," Oscar said.

"Why don't you get a job selling zits to young teenagers, Oscar," said Savannah, approaching him with her fists clenched.

"You nigger-loving bitch."

My cue and I entered that arena cautiously, filled with dread and praying for the arrival of Mr. Thorpe, a notorious late-arriver from the teachers' lounge.

"Don't talk to my sister like that, Oscar," I said weakly, sounding like a postoperative eunuch.

"What're you going to do about it, Wingo?" Oscar muttered at me, grateful to have a male antagonist at last.

"Tell my brother Luke," I said.

"You ain't big enough to fight your own battles?" he asked.

"I'm not as big as you are, Oscar. You'd beat me up if we had a fight. Then Luke would come hunting for you and rearrange your face anyway. I'm just skipping the step where I get beat up."

"Tell your big-mouthed sister to shut up," Oscar ordered.

"Shut up, Savannah," I said.

"Kiss my ass, Tom," she replied sweetly.

"I told her, Oscar."

"We don't like our white girls talking to niggers," he said.

"I'll talk to anyone I please, Oscar, darling."

"You know you can't tell Savannah anything," I said to Oscar.

"Come over here, Tom," Savannah said.

"I'm busy talking to my good friend Oscar," I said, smiling at Oscar.

"Come over here, Tom," she repeated.

I walked, without enthusiasm, toward her and shook hands with Benji Washington.

"He touched it on the hand," Lizzie Thompson wailed near the door. "I'd rather die than touch a nigger."

"You'd rather die than have a thought, Lizzie," Savannah said to her. Then she turned to me. "Pull that seat up next to Benji, Tom. That's where you're going to sit."

"I'm sitting up front, Savannah. You're not going to tell me where I have to sit. And I'm not going to take crap from every redneck in this school just because you read Anne Frank when you were a kid."

"Pull up that seat, Tom," she whispered smugly. "I'm not fooling."

"I'm not sitting next to Benji, Savannah. And you can embarrass me all you want."

"Are you going out for football, Benji?" she asked, turning from me.

"Yes," he said.

"We're going to kill you on that field, boy," Oscar said.

"Where's the goddamn teacher?" I said, looking at the door.

"You won't kill him, Oscar," Savannah sneered. "You may be strong, but I've heard Tom say you're complete chickenshit on the football field."

"Did you say that, Wingo?"

"No, of course not, Oscar," I lied. Oscar was one of those overweight hoodlums who could not transfer their violent antisocial behavior well to the realm of sport. Southern schools were filled with street brawlers and knife fighters who could not block or tackle.

"Tom will look out for you at practice," Savannah said. "Won't you, Tom?"

"I'll be too busy looking out for myself," I said.

Savannah grabbed my wrists and dug her nails in deep, drawing blood in four places. "Yes, you will, brother."

And then it happened—Oscar threw down the gauntlet. "She's a twat, Wingo. Your sister is a nigger-loving twat."

"Take that back, Woodhead."

"Will not, Wingo, and if you want to do anything about it I'll meet you behind the band room after school."

"He'll be there," Savannah said, "and he'll kick the shit out of you, Oscar."

"Savannah!" I said.

"There won't be enough left of you to feed a fiddler crab," she continued. "Hey, Lizzie, run out and call the hospital. Tell them Oscar's gonna need emergency surgery on his face this afternoon."

"He's no fighter. I can tell he's scared shitless," Oscar said, appraising me correctly.

"He and Luke became karate masters this summer. And I mean black belt masters. He breaks boards in half with his hands, Oscar. Take a good look at those hands. They're registered officially. That's why he doesn't want to fight. He goes to jail if he touches you with those hands."

I raised my deadly hands and studied them thoughtfully, as though I were appraising two dueling pistols.

"Is that like judo?" Oscar asked suspiciously.

"Judo maims," Savannah said. "Karate kills. He learned it from a karate master in Savannah this summer. An *Oriental* karate master."

"Niggers and chinks. Do the Wingos ever hang around white folks anymore? See you behind the band room, Wingo. Bring your registered hands with you."

There was a huge celebratory crowd gathered behind the band room when I arrived with my registered hands that afternoon. I was concentrating on breathing and thinking how much I enjoyed it and how much I would miss it after Oscar killed me. When I made my cringing appearance, a sudden cheer broke through the crowd and I saw Savannah, leading the other nine cheerleaders, racing toward me. They surrounded me and I walked toward Oscar with ten pompoms fluttering around my head as they broke into the Colleton High victory song.

Fight, fight, fight for Colleton,
May victory make us bold.
We'll fight all night with all our might,
We'll fight for the green and gold.

A look of the coldest, most brutal fury had settled in Oscar's eyes. He was surrounded by a covey of shrimpers' sons, boys I had known my whole life, whose sleeves were rolled up high on their arms and who stood watching me in a betrayed, lipless circle of solidarity. Luke was standing in front of Oscar. I walked toward Luke, the pompoms moving with me like a sea of restless chrysanthemums. I had hoped to be massacred in the presence of only a few skinny river boys and had not counted on Savannah turning my assassination into a pep rally.

I heard Luke say: "I hear you called my sister a twat, Woodhead."

"She was talking to the nigger, Luke," Oscar answered, looking over Luke's shoulder toward me.

"She don't need your permission to talk to anyone. Now apologize to my sister, Woodhead."

"I know what you're trying to do, Luke," Oscar said, and I noticed how gingerly and deferential he was toward Luke. "You're trying to pick a fight with me so your little pansy brother doesn't have to fight me."

"No. Tom's gonna whip you himself. If for some reason you hurt my little brother, then you will have to fight me, and that's gonna ruin your whole afternoon, Woodhead. I want you to apologize to my little sister for calling her a twat."

"I'm sorry I called you a nigger-loving twat, Savannah," he called out above the crowd. The pompoms stilled and the river boys laughed nervously.

"I want a nice apology, Woodhead. A sincere apology. If it doesn't sound sincere, I'm gonna tear your head off."

"I'm sorry I said that, Savannah," Oscar said in a chastened voice. "I really am."

"That didn't sound so sincere to me, Luke," I said. My voice was a pitiful thing.

"You just don't want to fight," Oscar said.

"Do you want me to fight him, Tom?" Luke asked, staring into Oscar's eyes.

"Well, I can always wait my turn," I said.

"It's your fight, Wingo," Artie Florence, one of the shrimpers' kids, said to me.

"Let me talk to Tom for a minute," Luke said. "Then he'll cut your butt."

Luke walked me away from the others with his arm around my right shoulder as Savannah led the cheerleaders through their routines, warming up the crowd.

"Tom," Luke said, "do you know how fast you are?"

"You want me to run away?" I said incredulously.

"No, I mean your hands. Do you know how fast your hands are?"

"What do you mean?"

"He can't hit you unless you make a mistake. He's strong but he's slow. You keep away from him. Dance around. Have fun. Don't get near him. Pop him when you see an opening, then get the hell out of there. When you can, punch his arms."

"His arms?"

"Yeah. When his arms tire, they'll drop. He'll have trouble lifting them. When you see that, move in."

"I'm scared, Luke."

"Everyone is always scared in a fight. He's scared too."

"He ain't half as scared as I am. Where's Earl Fucking Warren now that I need him?"

"You're too fast to lose to him. Don't let him charge you and get you onto the ground. He'll pin your arms and start beating your face in."

"Oh, God. Can I punch Savannah just once before the fight starts? She's the one who got me into this. Why do I have to come from the only family in Colleton that loves niggers?"

"Do that later. Punch Woodhead for the time being. Keep away from him. He swings wild."

The crowd pulled back to give us room as I stepped forward on the grass to face Oscar Woodhead. I was going to get beat up because of the 1954 Supreme Court decision, because of integration, because of Benji Washington, and because of my big-mouthed sister. Oscar, smiling, put up his fists and moved toward me. His first punch caught me off guard. It was a roundhouse right that almost connected to my jaw, and I lost my balance. He came after me, throwing punch after ferocious punch, an animal wail rising out of him as he stalked me across the grass.

"Dance," Luke commanded.

I moved to his left, away from his terrible right hand. One punch glanced off my head. I blocked another with my arm. I circled and moved away from him. For three minutes I moved and dodged and could see his mounting frustration as he pursued me. Then, unconsciously, I began to watch him. Following his body closely, watching his eyes, I knew when he was going to throw a punch. Conversely, he had no idea when I would throw one, since I had not even attempted an ineffectual jab thus far.

"Stand still and fight, you chickenshit," he said, panting.

I stood still and he charged. When he charged, he changed sports and entered a province I understood and excelled in far more than he. Linemen on opposing teams had been moving toward me in disciplined sweeps for three years. I dodged out of his way, and as he passed me, I stunned myself by delivering a solid punch to his ear. His momentum brought him to the ground and the crowd exploded and the cheerleaders, led by an exultant Savannah, broke into the Colleton fight song again.

But Oscar was back on his feet in an instant, furious, and he stalked me again. I could hear him breathing hard and could feel his need to end the fight quickly. I dodged six more punches, or, more accurately, I simply moved out of their way, circling and backpedaling. Then I began punching his arms, hard jabs against his wrists and biceps. I moved in suddenly and the movement toward him surprised him and he moved back. He swung another wild, fruitless salvo at my face and I retreated into the noise of the crowd as I kept working on his arms.

Then he settled down and tried to maneuver me against the schoolhouse wall. He began to select his punches with greater care. He hit me with a jab above the eye that numbed the right side of my face.

"Dance," Luke shouted, and I faked left, moved to the right, and as I moved I came in with a right hand that caught him on the side of the face and I saw him stumble backward and his hands come down from his face.

"Now," Luke commanded.

I moved toward him and started hitting him with left jabs. He tried to pull his arms up to protect his face, but he could not lift or control them and they dropped down to his chest and the blood began to run out of his lips and nose. The person who was hitting him was me but it did not feel like me, had no relationship to me at all, though I felt the movement of my left hand, its steadiness as it damaged the flesh before it. Then Luke stepped into my field of vision and stopped the fight.

I dropped to my knees and wept from sheer relief, from fear, and from the numbing pain over my left eye.

"You did good, baby brother," Luke whispered.

"I'm never gonna do that again," I said, tears flooding out of my eyes. "I hated it. I absolutely hated it. Tell Oscar I'm sorry."

"You can tell him later. We've got to get to practice. I told you you were fast."

Savannah rattled a frayed pompom in my face and said, "What is the matter for godsakes, Tom? You won the fight."

"I've known Oscar since I was a baby."

"He was a creep even then," Savannah said.

"I didn't like it," I said and then felt suddenly embarrassed when I realized sixty people were watching me cry.

"Quarterbacks don't cry," Luke said. "C'mon, we've got to get to practice."

The first practice ended that day, as it always did with Coach Sams, with forty-yard wind sprints. The guards and centers went first, bursting out of the end zone in clumsy gaits and running toward the coach, who blew the whistle downfield. Then the tackles lined up and I watched as Luke easily outsprinted his large, ill-made tribe.

I lined up with the backs and found myself beside Benji Washington.

"I hear you're fast," I said. "I was the fastest man on the team last year."

"Was," he said.

The whistle blew and I took off running downfield. I had gotten a good start and pulled out ahead, hearing the cleats plowing the earth behind me. I was running as fast as I could, with all the confidence of a boy who has been the fastest kid in his class since the first day of first grade, when Benji Washington passed me on my left and won the sprint going away by five yards.

In the next sprint of the backs, I ran with all the confidence of one who knows he's only the second-fastest boy in his class. I saw Coach Sams check his stopwatch again. Last year he had been the most vociferous and intransigent member of the staff against integration. His stopwatch was broadening his social horizons. Benji was running the forty-yard dash in 4.6 seconds. My best time was 4.9, and that was with hurricane winds behind me. The whistle sounded across the field again and once more I sprinted toward the coach and once more saw Benji pass me with extraordinary effortless grace as he flew past the hash marks toward the coach.

"That coon can fly," I heard one of the backs say, but it was a statement more of admiration than of malice.

We ran ten sprints and Benji won ten of them. I finished second in ten of them. By the time Coach Sams blew the whistle and the team raced toward the locker room, the tenor and complexion of our season had changed. We were going to have a good football team just with the veterans returning from last year's team. But now, we had added the South's fastest human being to the backfield and I was thinking of the state championship.

18

It is September of 1961 on Melrose Island in the most deeply lived-in year of our lives. The shrimp are running well and my father's boat approaches the docks each evening with its bins brimming with fish and shrimp. It is his finest season since 1956 and my father's buoyant, high-stepping gaiety pays wordless homage to the sea's generosity. The price of shrimp is holding at a dollar a pound and he acts like a rich man when he checks the groaning scales at the shrimp dock. At night, he talks about owning a fleet of shrimp boats. He tells my mother that he saw Reese Newbury at the bank and that Reese had told a group of men that Henry Wingo was married to the prettiest woman in Colleton County. My mother blushes, pleased, and says that she's just a middle-aged woman who does the best she can with what God gave her.

Savannah emerges from her bedroom dressed in her cheerleader costume for the first game. She cannot quite hide her pleasure. She creates a field of vibrancy and disturbance with her pale beauty. Her off-beat prettiness impinges softly as we turn to watch her entry. Our applause lies in the margins of our silence, the delicacy of our awe. She has unfolded before us, a secret ripening, and as she stands in the living room awaiting our approval, she spins in a slow circle, lovely in the places where a woman is lovely, her complexion immaculate as first fruit, her hair brushed and shining and blonde as a palomino's mane.

Luke rises from his chair and begins clapping his hands
and I rise, joining him, and together we begin to cheer.
She lifts her arms and approaches us, thinking we are making fun of her, but stops when she realizes we are praising
her. Her eyes fill up with tears. She is the girl of dreams
but she had never dared dream that she would one day be
beautiful. There is a perfect economy of feeling between
us. Again, I am overwhelmed with the love of my sister
and brother, and of their love for me. My mother looks up
from the stove and knows she is not part of this moment.
My father does not know enough to want to be a part of
it. It is the beginning of a long and uncanny season in the
house of Wingo. There will be honor and decency and the
testing of the qualities of our humanity, or the lack of them.
There will be a single hour of horror that will change our
lives forever. There will be carnage and murder and ruin.
When it is over, we will all think that we have survived
the worst day of our lives, endured the most grisly scenario
the world could have prepared for us. We will be wrong.
But it begins with my sister spinning in a charming pir-
ouette for her brothers. It begins with a moment of ingenuous beauty. In three hours we will play our first football
game and it is September again on Melrose Island.

My father was the first to make the connection between
the Colleton High Tigers and the Bengal tiger who roared
outside our house each night. He rented Caesar out to the
school's Booster Club at ten dollars a game, a paltry sum
that barely covered the price of chicken necks for a week,
but the deal encouraged my father to think that he could
turn Caesar into a money-making operation.

"How about it, kids?" he said before we left for the game.
"I could rent Caesar out at birthday parties. Halloween
parties. I could take pictures of Caesar eating a piece of
birthday cake. Or a picture of a kid riding Caesar on his
birthday. We could build a saddle."

"Caesar doesn't eat cake," Luke said.

"He likes kids, though. We could take pictures of Caesar
eating a kid at his last birthday party. Then we could take
pictures of the hysterical mother trying to pull the tiger off
her only child. Then we could take pictures of Caesar devouring the mother," I said.

"The nicest thing we could do to Caesar would be to put

him to sleep," my mother said. The whole subject of Caesar infuriated her. "We can barely afford a goldfish, much less a tiger."

"Ha! Caesar got ten bucks a game out of the Booster Club, didn't he? Six home games times ten and that's an extra sixty dollars of pure profit. You add that to the twenty-five bucks I'm paid to film the game and you got real money rolling in."

"Why don't you ride Caesar, Dad?" I suggested.

"I'm the idea man," Dad said, offended at the thought. "Besides, I'd break that poor creature's back. I ain't built like no jockey. You know, come to think of it, Savannah's the lightest member of the family."

"Forget it, Dad," Savannah said. "I'll ride the elephant. Let Tom ride the tiger."

"What elephant?" Mom asked.

"I'm sure Dad will buy an elephant soon," Savannah explained. "You know, for Republican fund raisers. That kind of thing."

"I still think we should have Caesar put away," my mother said. "It's the most humane thing we could do."

"We're not killing Caesar," Luke said.

"I'll think of something else," my father promised. "The birthday racket isn't that good an idea. It's about time to leave for the game. I've got to go hook Caesar's cage up to the pickup."

"I'll ride with the kids," my mother stated.

"Why?"

"Because I still have some dignity left. I will not go to every game dragging a tiger behind me. We're enough of a laughingstock in this town as it is."

"It's just to help school spirit, Lila," my father said. "It's to help the boys beat North Charleston."

"Do you remember when we played them when we were freshmen, Tom?" Luke asked.

"Remember?" I said. "They beat us seventy-two to zero."

"At the end of the game their band started playing 'The Tennessee Waltz' and all their players were waltzing with each other when we huddled up."

"You ready, Captain?" I asked.

"I'm ready, Captain," he answered. "I want to be the one waltzing when this game is over."

"And I'll be cheering my little fanny off, boys," Savannah said, punching Luke on the shoulder, "in the inferior role granted to women all over the world."

The team, forty of us, fully dressed, moved through the long corridor that led from the locker room to the conference room. Our spikes dragged along the cement and we sounded like the approach of bison crossing a plain of flint. Hanging bulbs illuminated our white jerseys; huge shadows cast by the strange light danced off the wall as we walked in the superhuman unearthly disguise of our violent sport.

We entered the conference room and sat down unhurriedly in folding chairs. Outside, we could hear the crowd humming in the long dusk. The pep band played a medley of fight songs. Then we heard Caesar roar, and with Luke leading the cheers, we roared back. Then the coach began to speak.

"Tonight I'm gonna learn and the town's gonna learn who my hitters are. All you've proved so far is that you know how to put on pads and get dates to the sock hop after the game, but until I see you in action, I won't know if you're hitters or not. Real hitters. Now a real hitter is a headhunter who puts his head in the chest of his opponent and ain't happy if his opponent is still breathing after the play. A real hitter doesn't know what fear is except when he sees it in the eyes of a ball carrier he's about to split in half. A real hitter loves pain, loves the screaming and the sweating and the brawling and the hatred of life down in the trenches. He likes to be at the spot where the blood flows and the teeth get kicked out. That's what this sport's all about, men. It's war, pure and simple. Now tonight, you go out there and kick butt all over that field. If something moves, hit it. If something breathes, hit it. And if something has tits, fuck it."

There was some laughter in the room but not much. This was the fourth year in a row Coach Sams had delivered the exact same pre-game speech and even the obligatory joke was the same. He always talked about football as if he were in the hysterical final stages of rabies.

"Now do I have me some hitters?" he screamed, veins throbbing along his temple.

"Yes, sir," we screamed back.

"Do I have some fucking hitters?"

"Yes, sir."

"Do I have me some goddamn headhunters?"

"Yes, sir."

"Am I going to see blood?"

"Yes, sir."

"Am I going to see their guts hanging off your helmets?"

"Yes, sir."

"Am I going to hear their bones breaking all over the field?"

"Yes, sir," we happy hitters cried aloud.

"Let us pray," he said.

He led the team in the recitation of the Lord's Prayer.

Then he turned the floor over to Luke and he left the room and waited for the team outside.

Luke rose, massive in his pads. He surveyed the room. At two hundred forty pounds, Luke was one of the largest men in Colleton County and certainly the strongest. His presence soothed; his calmness made us calm.

"You young kids on the team," Luke began, "don't worry too much about Coach Sams. He just likes to talk it up. It doesn't mean all that much. And he forgot to tell you something. Forgot to tell all of us something. The reason we play this game is to have fun. That's the long and short of it. We go out to have a good time, to block and tackle and run the best we can, and to work together as a team. I want to talk about the team in a very specific way. We should have talked about it since the season began. We need to talk about Benji."

There was a stirring of discontent through the room and everyone looked around to find the black boy. He was sitting alone in the last chair in the room. He faced the eyes of his teammates with the same silent, resolute dignity with which he navigated the halls of the school. He looked impassively at Luke.

"Now none of us wanted Benji to come to our school. But he did. We didn't want him to come out for our team, either. But he did. At practice we went after him with everything we had. We gang-tackled him, punched him, beat up on him, tried to hurt him—anything we could to make him quit. I did it, too. He took everything we dished out.

And now, I want you to know, Benji, that you're a member of this football team, and I'm proud that you're on it. I think you've made it a hell of a lot better team than it would have been, and I'll beat the shit out of anyone here tonight who thinks any different. Benji, come on up here and sit in the front row."

Benji hesitated and I could hear the room breathing again. He got up and walked down the center aisle with every eye of every boy riveted upon him, his eyes never leaving Luke's.

"Now tonight, North Charleston is going to go after Benji. They're gonna call you nigger and every other thing, Benji, and there's nothing we can do to stop it. But I want all the rest of you to know that Benji ain't no nigger when we go out that door. Benji's a teammate. And there ain't no word more beautiful to me than teammate. He ain't no nigger now and he ain't gonna be one for the rest of the year. He's a Tiger from Colleton High just like the rest of us. And if they get on him, we get on them. That's the way I see it. And Benji, I hope I didn't embarrass you by all this, but I don't see how it can't be said. I had to get it out. Does anyone disagree with me?"

There was the sound of the band, the crowd, the nervous tapping of cleats on the floor, but no voices of dissent.

"Tom, do you have anything to say to the team?"

I rose, turned to my teammates, and said in a breathless, excited voice: "Let's win."

I carry with me always the memories of my time as an athlete and those life-changing, exultant nights when I took to the measured fields and tested my strength and swiftness and character against that of other boys. I lived for the subsidies and praise of ingathered crowds, the rousing music of bands, the pixilation of cheerleaders high-kicking to the rhythm of drums, chanting out the urgent banalities of the sport with both eroticism and religious conviction. The sight of the opposing team, black-helmeted and serious, sent a shiver of delectating pleasure down my spine. I listened to the happy cadences of their vigorous warming-up like a blind man leaning toward a window full of birds. Games, games, games, I sang, as my brother and I led our team in calisthenics. On this green field of Colleton, I would taste immortality for the first and last time in my life. I could smell the salt air coming off the river, the piquant tang of that endless acreage of familiar tides spiced with a hint of crops mellowing on sea islands. My senses deepened, ignited, and I was fully alive, like something not quite human staring into the eyes of God on the first day of Eden. I could feel the breath of God running like light through my bloodstream. I shouted, I exhorted my teammates, I danced in the lean, honed grandeur of being a boy, gifted in his chosen game, as the referee's whistle pierced the air and Luke and I walked to the center of the field for the toss of the coin. The referee flipped a silver dollar high in the air and Luke called "heads" and heads it was. We elected to receive.

And on this night, I raised my fist in a gesture of concordance with Benji Washington as he and I took our positions as deep backs and awaited the opening kickoff from the North Charleston High Blue Devils. I watched their kicker approach the ball, saw their team break and flow and the ball spinning high through the lights, and heard myself yell, "You take it, Benji."

He caught it in the end zone and sprinted to the thirty-five before he was hit and hit hard by two North Charleston players. He vanished beneath a pile of blue jerseys. The North Charleston team, unhinged, frenzied, out of control, leapt to their feet, screaming at Benji. Five hundred fans from North Charleston had traveled south for the game, and a chant of "nigger, nigger, nigger" rose up from the visitors' side of the field.

"We're going to kill you, nigger," their safety, number twenty-eight, shouted at Benji, who rose from the ground slowly.

They rushed up to Benji and followed him almost to the huddle in a profane, violent pack.

"Nigger. Nigger. Fucking nigger," they screamed at him.

They were still screaming when I called the first play of the season. My teammates were shaken. Benji was in a state of shock.

As we lined up, the North Charleston line went down

in tandem, screaming, "Kill the nigger." As I bent down over the center, their safety yelled at me, "Give me the goddamn coon."

I lifted up, pointed my finger at the safety, and shouted pleasantly, "Fuck you, cocksucker."

The whistle blew and the head linesman signaled a fifteen-yard penalty against us for unsportsmanlike conduct. He said the words *unsportsmanlike conduct* with a nasal drawl that made him sound like an off-duty Klansman. I would find no Supreme Court justices among the referees of rural South Carolina.

"Hey, ref," I said, "how about making them stop yelling at number forty-four?"

"I don't hear them yelling at anyone," the referee said.

"Then you must not have heard me say 'Fuck you, cocksucker' to that zit-faced back."

The whistle blew a second time and the referee marked off half the distance to the goal line. So far, my brilliant quarterbacking had lost us twenty-five yards and I had yet to receive a snap from center.

"Shut up and play ball," the referee ordered.

"Come and get it, nigger," their safety yelled across to Benji. "I'm gonna kick your nuts in, nigger. Gonna kill us a nigger tonight. Gonna eat nigger meat."

The North Charleston crowd maintained the cry of "nigger" and it grew louder. The Colleton fans were silent and watchful. I saw Benji's parents sitting alone at the top of the bleachers. His mother's face had turned away from the field. His father watched stoically and I knew where Benji's impassive, regal bearing originated.

I called time out.

My teammates were cringing in the huddle, like those scurvy hounds who live off garbage at county landfill projects. I, ever the prescient quarterback, recognized that my team had not quite jelled. Their lethargy matched my rising fury. I wanted to eat a goal post or beat their faces in. From down field, along the track, I saw the cage where Caesar slept, kindly untutored in the malevolence of the language.

I knelt and spoke to my team: "Okay, men. It's me, the quarterback. The fucking golden boy. Ol' Tom Wingo is going to give a pep talk."

"Nigger, nigger, nigger." The cry echoed off the schoolhouse wall as the citizens of Colleton watched in eerie silence.

"Now I want you to loosen up. Benji, I know this is tough on you. It's tough on all of us. It's scary. But before we show them that you're the fastest black-assed bastard in the world, we're going to take care of a little business. Now you guys are acting dead. I want a little life. I want some noise."

A small cheer, which would not do, rose up from the team.

"Luke," I said, taking my huge brother by the shoulder pads and slapping the side of his helmet with an open palm. "Luke, make Caesar roar."

"What?"

"Make Caesar roar," I ordered again.

Luke walked away from the huddle toward the North Charleston team and looked at the cage, which was parked in darkness. He walked almost to the line of scrimmage, looked far down the field, and screamed out over the noise of the chant to the Wingo family tiger, who, bored by lights and football, slept amidst fish bones and the remnants of chicken necks until he heard the powerful strained voice of the human being he loved best, calling, "Roar, Caesar, roar."

Caesar came to his cage's bars, not as pet, not as joke, not as mascot, but as Bengal tiger, and he roared out a greeting of affirmation and constancy to the largest right tackle in the state.

Luke answered him with a human affectionate roar of his own.

Caesar roared again and it crossed that football field like a plane, drowning out the puny chant of "nigger," dwarfing the voice of crowds, crossed the fifty-yard line, swept into our ears, broke through the parking lot, hit the brick wall off the gymnasium, and echoed back as if a second great cat had been born behind us. Caesar answered his own echo and I shouted at my teammates, "Now, motherfuckers, gutless shits, babies. Answer back. Answer Caesar."

Together, my teammates roared like tigers at the tiger. Again and again, they roared, and Caesar, no rookie under the lights, who had been born to perform and preserved the instinct for the center ring, responded with that magnificent feral voice that had originated in the steaming forests of India. Caesar, whose parents had awakened Hindu tribes at night and stirred the adrenaline of elephants, delivered a message to the soul of my team. Then the Colleton crowd ignited, remembering the spirit of the game, and the tiger moved through their ranks and the field trembled with their roaring.

I raced to the sidelines and shouted at Mr. Chappel, the band director, to strike up "Dixie." When that band broke into "Dixie," Caesar went wild. I watched the North Charleston team stare at the full-grown Bengal tiger snarling, crazed, attacking the bars of his cage, his forelegs swinging outside the bars, claws fully extended: a study in the limits of wildness. Luke charged up to me furiously.

"Why did you do that, Tom?" he said. "You know that song upsets Caesar."

"He's looking for one of those fucking seals," I said, swollen with pride. "Enjoy this, Luke. This is the greatest time-out in the history of football."

I walked toward the North Charleston team, who watched transfixed as their fans grew silent and baffled.

"Hey, boys," I yelled above the din, "piss me off again and I'm gonna let that tiger loose on the field."

The whistle blew and we were penalized for delaying the game.

Then we huddled and something magic had happened. In the eyes of my teammates I saw that sacred gleam of oneness, of solidarity, of brotherhood, which is the most glorious thing in the kingdom of sport. It lives in the heart but is secreted through the eyes. I saw the coming together, the making of the team.

"Nigger, nigger. Roar, roar." The sounds enveloped us.

I said, "The first offensive play of the season for the Colleton Tigers is this: Quarterback sneak. Only no one block for me. While those jerks are creaming my ass I want every single person on this team except Benji to go after that creep of a safety. I'm just going to run around a little in the backfield and give you time to get him."

"Nigger, nigger. Roar, roar," said the crowds.

When I received the snap, I did a small inelegant softshoe toward a slight opening off left guard when five hundred pounds of boyflesh and leather hit me at the same time and drove me into the ground, my face crushed into the grass and lime of our own five-yard line. The whistle blew and when I got up I could see their safety lying on his back, clutching his face and knee. Our team was assessed another fifteen-yard penalty for unnecessary roughness and the referee walked off half the distance of the goal line. I had skillfully engineered this retreat, which left us thirty-two yards behind our original scrimmage line. But I watched with pleasure as they carried the safety out of the game, bleeding, as Luke happily described it, from every orifice in his body.

"The nigger's gonna pay for that," one of their linebackers shouted.

In the huddle, I knelt and said, "Good boys. Good boys. I like it when you listen to Uncle Tom. Now, on the next play we're gonna try to score a touchdown."

"Here comes Benji," Luke crowed.

"Not yet," I said. "The master strategist ain't using Benji yet. But he'll be the decoy. I'm sending you right up the middle, Benji. I'm going to tell them you're getting the ball and gonna show them the hole you'll be coming through."

"Jesus," Benji said.

"That's stupid, Tom," Luke said.

"But I ain't gonna give you the ball. I'm bootlegging it around left end. Get me some blockers down field. On two. Break."

As I approached the line, before I put my hands beneath Milledge Morris's redolent behind, I walked toward that monotonous chant of "nigger" again. I said aloud to the whole North Charleston team: "You want the nigger? I'm gonna send him through this hole right here." I pointed to the hole between the center and left guard. "And none of you have the nuts to stop him."

I watched their linebacker shift and the defensive backs shift a few steps toward the hole as the cadence rolled off my tongue.

"Set, fourteen, thirty-five, two."

I came up with the ball held low, heard the helmets and pads of the linemen break out behind me, crouched low and stuck the ball into Benji's stomach as he shot past, watched him drive toward the hole, then pulled the ball slickly out as he disappeared into the arms of the white South.

With the ball on my hip, I looked back, pretending to slow up as I saw the pile of blue jerseys pulling Benji to the earth. Then I hit the corner and shot down those sidelines right past those North Charleston fans who suddenly remembered there were white boys on the Colleton team, too. At the twenty, Luke joined me and we both ran with our eye on the defensive back with a talent for not believing liars. He moved to cut me off at the sidelines and I faked to my right as if I were reversing my field. He slowed and straightened and Luke half killed him with a cross-body block as I leapt over both of them without breaking stride and moved into the clear at our own twenty-five-yard line.

I have kept my father's film of that game and have watched that ninety-seven-yard dash up the sidelines a hundred times and will watch it a hundred times again before I die. I watch the boy I once was and marvel at his speed as I observe his progress in the grainy, surreal image of the film and run my hand though thinning hair. I try to recapture that moment when I ran toward the end zone, entering into my own territory, now pursued vainly by frantic boys in blue jerseys. The crowd took possession of me at the fifty-yard line; I felt it in my legs, that dreaming hum of human voices urging me toward speed, toward the highest thresholds of those ecstatic running days. I ran as a Colleton boy who had brought his town to its feet, and there is nothing happier on earth than a running boy, nothing so innocent or untouched. I was gifted and young, uncatchable as I sprinted down the sidelines followed by a referee I left in the dust. Swift and dazzling through the light I ran, past the eyes of my screaming father, who followed my progress through a glass aperture, past my twin sister leaping and twisting on the sidelines, cherishing the moment because she cherished me, past my mother, whose beauty could not disguise her shame at who she was and what she had come from. But at this moment—mythic and elegiac—she was the mother of Tom Wingo and had given the world those legs and that speed as a gift, and I crossed the forty and in the next second the thirty, sprinting past my life as a boy toward the end zone. But as I watch this film, I often think that the boy did not know what he was really running toward, that it was not the end zone which awaited him. Somewhere in that ten-second dash the running boy turned to metaphor and the older man could see it where the boy could not. He would be good at running, always good at it, and he would always run away from the things that hurt him, from the people who loved him, and from the friends empowered to save him. But where do we run when there are no crowds, no lights, no end zones? Where does a man run? the coach said, studying the films of himself as a boy. Where can a man run when he has lost the excuse of games? Where can a man run or where can he hide when he looks behind him and sees that he is only pursued by himself?

I crossed the end zone and threw the ball fifty feet straight into the air. I threw myself down and kissed the grass. I ran to Caesar's cage and rattled the bars. "Cheer, you yellow son of a bitch." Imperially, he ignored me.

Then Luke caught me up in his arms, lifted me off the ground, and spun me around and around. Luke and I, at last, had our waltz.

We kicked off and I knew from the way we swarmed all over the ball carrier that this was our night. On their first play from scrimmage, Luke met their fullback head on and drove him back five yards into the grass. The whole right side of the line was in on the tackle when they tried a power sweep around the end. Luke blitzed and threw the quarterback for a seven-yard loss on the third down. Our whole team was on fire and we pounded each other on the shoulder pads and helmets, embraced each other after every play, and screamed encouragement to the lineman who made the first hit. There were unquenchable titanic fires loose on that field, a sense of recognition and payoff and destiny.

The punter kicked a fifty-yard punt that went out of bounds on the fifty-yard line.

Now I planned to set Benji loose. When I was scoring the touchdown Benji was at the bottom of the pile getting his eyes thumbed, his leg bit, and his dander up.

"Benji, we're going to teach these poor crackers about the merits of Brown versus the Board of Education. Tackle slot right on four. Break."

I always felt a bit sorry for the kid who played across the line from Luke. At the beginning of the game he would be a nice strapping healthy kid, and at game's end he would be a paraplegic for at least a day. With Luke's remarkable size and grace it was no accident that he discovered a natural affinity for tigers.

As I approached the line, the word *nigger* had disappeared for a time from the vocabulary of the North Charleston Blue Devils.

I handed off to Benji Washington, the first time a white boy had ever handed the ball to a black boy in my part of the world. He broke off tackle (Luke had done something like eat the boy in front of him), spun off a linebacker who cracked into him, shot off the end who tried to arm-tackle him, then in a series of astonishing moves of such swiftness and deception, he danced into their backfield, wiggling, frenetic, untouchable, and cut suddenly against the flow, reversing his field; then dashing past the right defensive back to the sidelines, then cutting hard, he raced the whole North Charleston team for the end zone. Three players had shots at him but all three misjudged his speed. As we slow-footed boys followed him to the goal line, we had scored our second touchdown in less than two minutes. I could feel the ambivalence of the Colleton crowd, and for a moment, there was nothing but polite stunned applause. This was a white crowd, southern to the very bone, mired in all the inhumane traditions of our time, and something in them wanted Benji to fail, even if it meant the team had to fail. Some of them probably even wanted Benji to die. But somewhere in that seven-second dash, resistance to integration weakened just a tiny bit in Colleton. And every time Benji Washington carried the ball that night, the southerners' awesome love of sport won out over the bruised history that had brought the fastest human being in the American South into our backfield.

When the team surrounded Benji, half killing him with their punches and slaps, he said to Luke, "God, these white boys are slow."

"Naw," Luke answered, "you were just scared they'd catch you."

I learned that night that with Benji Washington in the

backfield I was a much better quarterback than I was meant to be. I sent him through the line or around end thirty times that night. I watched him break up the middle for five, sweep end for twenty-five, slant off tackle for eleven. In the third quarter, I sprinted to my right on an option play, watched the defensive end overcommit himself as I faked a lateral to Benji. I darted through the hole over left tackle and angled toward the sideline until I was hit by the outside linebacker. As I fell, I flipped the ball to Benji who caught it and in a straight pure celebration of speed raced down the sidelines for eighty yards, untouched by human hands.

In the fourth quarter North Charleston rallied for two touchdowns, but they were hard-earned, furiously contested scores. Both times they scored on long grueling marches down field and both times their fullback broke over from the one-yard line after being repulsed twice before. With the clock winding down and with us leading 42-14, our band played "The Tennessee Waltz" and as North Charleston broke for their huddle, they found us dancing helmet to helmet at the line of scrimmage with the crowd singing the words in the bleachers.

Then the whistle blew, ending the game, and our town was on us. They burst onto the field and we walked back to the locker room crushed and pummeled by a thousand students and fans. Savannah found me and kissed me on the lips, laughing when I blushed. Luke tackled me from behind and wrestled me on the grass. Three North Charleston linemen fought their way through the crowd and shook Benji's hand. Their middle linebacker apologized for calling him a nigger. Caesar began roaring again and was joined by the crowd. My father filmed it all. My mother jumped up into Luke's arms and he carried her like a bride all the way to the locker room, her arms wrapped around his neck, telling him how wonderful she thought he was, how proud she was.

In the locker room, the team threw Coach Sams into the showers fully clothed. Oscar Woodhead and Chuck Richards picked up Benji and carried him almost reverently to the shower room, where he was baptized in the ritual waters of victory. Luke and I were lifted and carried, too, until the whole team, ecstatic and triumphant, stood dripping and screaming on the tiles as photographers snapped pictures and our fathers lit cigarettes and discussed the game outside the locker room.

After I showered I sat on the long wooden bench beside my brother, dressing without speed, feeling the sweet, postgame ache creep into my body like a slow-moving drug. I put on my shirt and had difficulty lifting my left arm to the top button. My teammates were putting on their suits and the room was aromatic with steam and sweat and after-shave lotion. Jeff Galloway, the left end, came up to me, brushing his dark hair straight back.

"You going to the dance, Tom?" he asked.

"We'll probably drop by for a while."

"You're not going dressed like that, are you?" he asked, looking at my shirt.

"No, my real clothes are hanging out in Caesar's cage, Jeff," I answered. "Of course I'm going in these clothes."

"You guys have got the worst sense of style I've ever seen. Why don't you wise up and buy a couple of Gant shirts. And you're the only two guys at the school who don't wear Weejuns. Man, everyone on the team's got Wee-juns."

"I don't like Weejuns," Luke said.

"Yeah, I bet you like those shit-kicking tennis shoes a lot better," he said, laughing as I laced up my shoes. "What kind of shirt is that you're wearing, Tom?"

He pulled back my collar and read the label.

"Belk's." He sneered in disbelief. "A Belk's polo shirt. Jesus Christ. That's embarrassing. I'm nominating you two for Best Dressed in the Senior Superlatives. You've worn the same pair of khakis for two straight weeks, Tom."

"No, I haven't," I protested. "I've got two pairs of khakis. I alternate them."

"That's pitiful. That's just plain pitiful. Not at all cool. Not fitting the image at all."

"You don't like our clothes, Jeff?" Luke asked.

"There's nothing to like, Luke. You guys obviously don't care how you look. Practically all the guys dress up after the game. We not only play good football. We set the trends in the school. We walk down the hall together and all the girls and all the geeks in the band say, 'Here comes the team, man, here comes the fuckin' team and they're looking good. Hell, Benji knows how to dress and he's just a . . ."

"A nigger," Luke concluded his sentence for him. "He's gone now. Don't worry, he just won the damn game for us, but you can go back to calling him a nigger again."

"Benji's colored," Jeff corrected himself. "He's just a colored boy who's been colored all his life and he dresses like a prince compared to you two guys. Belk's, man, I mean that's actually embarrassing that the co-captains go buy their vines at Belk's department store."

"Where do you buy your clothes, Jeff?" Luke asked. "London-fucking England?"

"No, man. Me and some of the boys ride up to Charleston and spend all day shopping at Berlin's and Krawcheck's. Men's stores. Stores that specialize, man. Not Belk's. You don't shop at a store that generalizes, man. Anyone can tell you that. I mean, they got enough alligator belts hung up in the rack at Berlin's that they could start their own gator farm. You ought to go up and just look around at those shops. You need to start developing taste."

"I'm glad I don't have the same taste as you, Jeff," Luke said, closing his locker door. "You don't have to wear our clothes, so keep your mouth off 'em."

"Hey, this comes under the heading of friendly advice," he said. "I got to look at your clothes, so I got a right to my opinion. Agreed? You know Coach made it a rule that we should all wear sport coats to school on the days of games. Don't you love it? Three-piece suits in the morning, sweating in the trenches during the game, shower, throw on a little English Leather, then killing the girls with those three-piece suits at the dances. I got this three-piece at Krawcheck's for under a hundred bucks."

"It looks like shit," Luke said, pausing a moment to notice Jeff's light blue suit.

"Ha, it's the best suit they got for the price. I guess those tacky khakis are a lot better."

"I like khakis," Luke said sourly.

"See you style setters at the dance. You probably won't see me, boys. I'll be surrounded by a couple of hundred broads trying to get their hands on my threads. Great game, though, you two," Jeff said as he left the locker room.

We could hear the dance band playing rock and roll in the school cafeteria. I shut my locker and snapped the combination lock in place. Luke did the same.

"You want to go to the dance, Luke?"

"Do you?"

"Not particularly."

"Me neither. Especially now that I think everyone's gonna be staring at me, thinking 'There's that poor bastard wearing a Belk's polo shirt.' "

"I don't mind that," I said. "I can't dance."

"Neither can I," he said.

Coach Sams stuck his head around the corner and said, "Lights out, men. Hey, Tom and Luke, I thought you'd be up at the dance. You guys might get raped after the game you played tonight."

"We were just going, Coach," I said.

"Hey, where are your sport coats?" Coach Sams said. "I told everyone to dress up for the game. You're my captains for christsakes."

"Forgot, Coach," Luke said. "We were too excited about the game."

"Hey, uh," the coach said, punching Luke in the arm. "Hey, uh. Some game. Hey, uh."

"Hey, uh," we repeated.

"Hey, uh. Hey, uh. Hey, uh," he said, grinning at us both. "Hey, uh, some game."

We walked with him to the back door of the locker room and watched him throw the switch that extinguished the lights on the field.

Luke and I walked toward the music.

When I try to recall my mother's voice as a child, it is lifted in a grave euphorious lament of our economic situation; I hear her chansons and plainsongs of her ineradicable belief that we lived out our days in the most hideous poverty. I could not tell you then if we were poor or not. I am not sure if my mother was miserly or frugal. But I do know that I would rather have asked to suckle her right breast than ask her for ten dollars. The subject of money caused a new woman to be born in her soul; it also diminished her in her children's eyes. It was not because she didn't have it; it was because of how she made us feel when we asked for it. And I always suspected there was more of it around than she claimed. I always feared that she simply loved it more than she loved me. But I never knew.

The lack of a sport coat began to obsess me and the morning following the North Charleston game I went to her after breakfast and said, "Mom, can I talk to you?"

"Of course, Tom," she said as she hung up the wash in the back yard. I started hanging wash beside her. "I want you always to feel free to talk to me."

"Can I do some jobs around the house?"

"You've already got your jobs assigned."

"I mean, to make a little extra money."

"I don't get paid for all the work I do around the house, Tom," she said. "Think about it. If I got paid for cooking and cleaning and keeping everyone's clothes in nice shape, there wouldn't be enough money left over for food, now would there? But I wouldn't think of taking money for my work. I do it because I love my family."

"I love my family, too," I said.

"You know we're having some difficulty, don't you?" she said in a whisper, one of those binding asides, intimate and conspiratorial, which made you a member of my mother's most earnest thoughts. "Even though the shrimp are running good, your father's buying the gas station and the tiger has put us into a very bad situation. I don't like to tell you this because I know that you worry so much about me. But we could go bankrupt at any time. I try to tell your father. But what can I do?"

"I need to buy a sport coat."

"That's ridiculous," she said, her mouth full of clothespins. "You don't need a sport coat."

"Yes, I do," I answered, feeling as though I had just asked for a sailing yacht. "Coach Sams wants us to wear sport coats on the days of games. It's a rule. Luke and I were the only ones on the team who weren't dressed in sport coats yesterday at school."

"Well, that's a ridiculous rule and one that we won't follow. You know about last year's bad shrimping season, Tom. You know how much your father lost in his gas station venture. You know all of this and yet you don't mind making me feel bad about having to refuse you. What you don't know is how I'm struggling just to keep our heads above water. Now it's not that we can't afford sport coats, it's a matter of priorities. Your father would go through the roof if he heard you asked for a sport coat now. It's selfish of you to even think about it. Frankly, I'm surprised at you and more than a little disappointed."

"All the other guys have sport coats. We could buy them second-hand somewhere."

"You're not all the other guys. You're Tom Wingo and you stand head and shoulders above all the rest. Those other boys may dress nicer, but my sons are the captains of the team."

"How come Savannah always has nice clothes and Luke and I always have to dress like we were going to work on the shrimp boat?"

"Because Savannah's a girl and it's important for a young girl to put her best foot forward. And I don't feel the least bit guilty that I sacrifice to dress my daughter appropriately. I'm surprised that you resent it and don't understand why it's necessary."

"Why is it necessary? Tell me that, Mom."

"If she's going to marry a proper young gentleman, she'll need to dress with distinction. Gentlemen from fine families wouldn't think of courting a girl who didn't know how to dress. Clothes are the first thing that attract a man to a woman. Well, maybe not the first, but one of the first."

"What's the first thing a girl looks for in a young man, Mom?"

"Certainly not his clothes," she sneered. "Clothes mean nothing on a man until he's out in business or joins a law firm. A young girl looks at a man's character, his prospects, his family, and his ambition."

"Is that what you looked for when you married Dad?"

"I thought I was marrying a different man. I was stupid and sold myself far too cheaply. I don't want Savannah to make the same mistake I did."

"You don't think a girl will mind how my clothes look?"

"Of course not, unless she's mindless and shallow and no account."

"Then why should a man care about a woman's clothes?"

"Because men are much different from women, much more shallow by nature."

"Do you really believe that's true, Mom?"

"I know that's true. I've lived a lot longer than you."

"Will you give me some money to put down?"

"I won't give you a dime. I want you to learn to work for everything you get. Everything you really want. You'll cherish that coat when you've sweated blood to get it. Earn that coat, Tom. You'll respect yourself more if everything's not handed out to you on a silver platter."

"I've never been handed anything on a silver platter."

"That's right, Tom. And you never will. Not by me, anyhow. I know you think I'm being cheap."

"I do, Mama. I can't help it."

"It doesn't bother me at all. Because I know something that you don't. I know that all the boys on the team will look back on this year and they won't even be able to remember what color their sport coats were."

"So what?"

"They won't know the value of things. But you, Tom, when you look back to this year, you'll always remember the sport coat you didn't own. You'll be able to see it, feel it, even smell it."

"I don't get the point, Mama."

"You'll appreciate a sport coat when you finally own one. And you'll always remember your mama when you wear one. You'll always remember that I refused to buy you one and you'll have to ask yourself why."

"I'm asking you that now."

"I'm teaching you to treasure what you can't possess, what is just beyond your reach."

"How stupid."

"It might be stupid, Tom. But you're sure gonna love your first sport coat. And that's a promise."

"Mom, this is the best shrimping season since 1956. We've got the money."

"Not for sport coats, Tom. I'm saving the money for your father's next stupid investment. If it wasn't for him, you could have everything you want. We all could."

19

In Savannah's apartment, I began to look for clues that might give me some insight into the secret life she had been leading before she slit her wrists. Her absence allowed me the guilty leisure to earn a voyeur's intimacy with her daily existence. Signs of neglect were vivid reminders of her slippage toward the inner frontiers of her madness. I found unopened mail, including a stack of letters from my mother, my father, and me. Her can opener didn't work. She had two bottles of cayenne on her shelf, but no marjoram or rosemary. In her bedroom, I found a pair of Nike running shoes that she had never worn. Her bathroom lacked aspirin and toothpaste. When I had arrived, there was a single can of tuna fish in the pantry and the freezer had not been defrosted for years. Obsessive about cleanliness her whole life, Savannah had let layers of dust accumulate on the shelves. It was the apartment of someone who wanted to die.

But the apartment had mysteries to reveal if I was only patient enough to receive them. I trained myself to be patient and vigilant for any hint that might shed light on the syntax of her madness.

On the Sunday afternoon of my sixth week in New York, I read all of Savannah's poems over and over again, both the published ones and those I discovered. I searched for clues, for secrets superimposed in her lush iambics. Though I knew the central events and traumas of my sister's life, I felt that I was missing something essential in her story, that she had created some desperate and provisional life in the three years away from me to which I was denied access.

When Savannah was a child she developed a habit of concealing her gifts. They were never under the tree on Christmas morning, but she would provide us with elaborate maps to help in the search for our presents. She had once hidden an opal ring for my mother, a ring she had bought with the help of my grandmother, but had hidden it too well in the black-water swamp near the center of the island. She had placed the ring in the nest of a painted bunting, framing it among stems and moss in the hollow of a tree. But her written directives were fuzzy and unsure and she could never lead my mother to that nest. Opals would always remind Savannah of stolen Christmases. After she lost the ring, Savannah went back to being a gift-giver of a more traditional sort.

Later, Savannah would write about that lost ring and describe it as the perfect, the most immaculate, gift. A perfect gift, she wrote, is always hidden too well, but never hidden from the poet. In what became a key to the understanding of her small canon of work, she called the poet "the mistress of owls." When the poet closed her eyes the wingspan of the great horned owl cast a tawny shadow over the green immense forests. The owl returned to the forsaken nests of migrating buntings, entered the perfect circle in the heart of cypress, and found the misplaced opal, the color of buttermilk tinted with the inks of crushed violets. The she-owl, taloned queen of ungovernable instinct, took the ring in a cruel beak berimmed with the blood of stunned rabbits and flew through a lacery of fabulous dreams, through air voluted and perfumed with language, and delivered the lost ring to the poet, again and again, poem after poem. Nothing was ever lost to Savannah; she transformed everything into mysterious sensuous gardens of language. She retained her love of games in her poetry, hiding her gifts behind a trellis of words, making bouquets out of her losses and nightmares. There were no dark poems in Savannah's work, only beautiful fruit surrounded by flowers that could put the taster forever to sleep on thorns dusted with cyanide—even her roses came with their assassins. All her poems had their puzzles, their misdirections, their feints and pivots. She never stated a thing directly. She could not break a lifelong habit of hiding her gifts. Even when she wrote about her madness, she made it attractive, an inferno spoiled by paradise, a desert strewn with breadfruit and mangoes. She could write about a killing sunlight and come triumphantly out of it, proud of her tan. Her weakness as a poet was singular and profound: She could walk along the rim of Alps, her motherland, but she could not trim the wings that would set her sailing toward the high currents. The ring was always returned to her when she should have reported it lost. Even her screams were muted, softened to pale harmony, like the imprisoned hum of the sea in conch shells. She feigned to hear music in those shells but I know she didn't. She heard the wolves, all the black notes, all the satanic madrigals. But they were so pretty when she wrote them down with the help of her ghostly owl and her dreams of opal. She sang of water lilies floating like the souls of swans on the pools in the enclosed yards of lunatic asylums. My sister had fallen in love with the grandeur of madness. Her last poems, which I found scattered about her apartment in secret places, were obituaries of exquisite loveliness. A nostalgia for her own death had made her work grotesque.

While staying in her apartment I paid her rent and her bills and collected her mail. With the help of her neighbor, Eddie Detreville, I painted the apartment in a warm tan, the color of flax. I arranged her vast library according to subject. Her library would have been valuable to a bibliophile except she treated her books execrably. I would rarely open a volume that she had not desecrated by underlining her favorite sections with a ball-point pen. Once I had told her that I would rather see a museum bombed than a book underlined, but she dismissed my argument as mere sentimentality. She marked her books so that stunning images and ideas would not be lost to her. There was a fruitful exchange between her reading and writing. She had developed the appealing habit of collecting books on subjects she knew nothing about. I found one book, heavily underlined, on the life cycle of ferns, and one called *The Sign Language of the Plains Indians*. There were six books on various aspects of meteorology, three books on sexual deviation in the nineteenth century, a book on the care and feeding of piranhas, a *Mariner's Dictionary*, and a long treatise on the butterflies of Georgia. She had once written a poem about the butterflies that came to my mother's garden on Melrose Island and through the notes in the book's margins I discovered how my sister picked up a working knowledge of swallowtails, hairstreaks, and coppers. She used her books well and no fact was too obscure to escape her passionate scrutiny. If she needed a ladybug in her poetry, she would buy ten books on entomology to find the absolutely correct ladybug. She created mysterious worlds with the priceless information she gleaned from long-neglected books. Because she ruined those books in her passage, I could follow the history of her reading by noting which books were marked and which were perfectly clean. It was an authentic way, I thought, to learn about my sister, browsing through her library and taking notes on the subjects she had annotated or underlined. It was also a breach of trust, but I was trying to bridge a distance of three years in which not a single word had passed between us.

I began my summer by reading all the works of the poets who were Savannah's friends and who had inscribed copies of their books to her. From the tone of these bright yet formal inscriptions, I could tell that most of them had admired Savannah's work but did not know her well at all. Most of these poets were living out their American lives in proud obscurity, and after reading their work, I understood why. They were all troubadours of the microscopic epiphany. They wrote about calyxes and pomegranates but their theme was meaninglessness. Nothing had ever made Savannah happier than when I admitted that I didn't understand one of her poems. She took this as a sure sign that she had been faithful to her gift. After reading her friends, I thought that all modern poets should be immunized against abstruseness. But the lines she underlined had a dark, incongruous beauty and I wrote them all down in a notebook of my own as I tried to construct my sister's life from her journeys into her own books.

From her poems I found out that Savannah was bidding farewell to the South as a subject. I could still find glimmerings of her past, but my sister was succeeding in turning herself into what she had always most wanted to be—a New York poet. I came across a series of subway poems that gave a snowy, decorous symmetry to the nightmare of the post-midnight city. There were Hudson River poems and Brooklyn poems. She no longer signed every poem as soon as she had finished working on it. She left her poems in anonymous piles throughout her apartment. Only the buffed, untouchable sorcery of her talent remained to mark the work as indisputably hers. In the last years, her poetry had grown stronger, more melancholy, and more beautiful still. But something was puzzling and unclear to me, and I would have remained troubled if I had not found the blue and white memory book beneath the Bible on her night table. In a green diamond centered in a white stripe, I read the words "Seth Low J.H.S." I unzipped a rusty zipper and turned to the first page. There was a photograph of an eighth-grade girl named Renata Halpern. The name was vaguely familiar, but I could not place it exactly. Her face was pretty, self-conscious, but a pair of unfortunate glasses disfigured her appearance. The smile was unnatural, institutional, and I could almost see the dimwitted photographer grimacing the word "cheese," revealing his unpleasant mouthful of teeth. Her teachers, she recorded on the following page, were Mrs. Satin, Mrs. Carlson, and Mrs. Travers. Renata Halpern had graduated from Seth Low on June 24, 1960. She was not a class officer but Sidney Rosen was the greatly honored president of her class. Sidney had signed her memory book, "To Renata, dated till butter flies, Take the local, take the express, don't get off, till you reach success." Renata's best friend, Shelly, who was blessed with a handwriting like folded silk, wrote, "To Renata, dated 4 ever, Twinkle twinkle little star, Powderpuff and cold cream jar, Eyebrow pencil—lipstick too, will make a beauty out of you. Congratulations to Seth Low's 'Queen of Hearts.' "

How wonderful, I thought, that my new friend, Renata Halpern, was once Queen of Hearts at Seth Low Junior High School, but I wondered how her life had intersected with Savannah's. My sister had a whole shelf full of discarded yearbooks that she had collected from used bookshops around the city. She loved to steal intimate glimpses into the lives of perfect strangers. But the name reverberated and I was certain I had seen it before.

I walked back into the living room and searched the jackets of all her friends who were poets. Then I saw the stack of mail my sister had received in the last week and I remembered that I had seen the name in that stack.

The *Kenyon Review* had sent a copy of its latest issue to a Renata Halpern and had sent it to Savannah's address. I had thought when I first checked the mail that I should just steal the magazine, but I was afraid I might offend some pal of Savannah's who was using her apartment to receive mail. I opened the brown envelope and found a letter from the editor of the *Kenyon Review* addressed to Renata stuck between the pages of the magazine.

Dear Ms. Halpern,
    I want to tell you again how proud I am that the *Kenyon Review* has the honor of publishing your first poem. Also, I want to emphasize that we would like to see any work that you should like to show us in the future. We want to publish as much as we can before one of the "biggies" steals you away from us. I trust your work is going well.
                                Sincerely,
                                Roger Murrell

P.S. Mazel tov on the publication of your children's book.

I scanned the contents page of the *Kenyon Review* and turned to page thirty-two, where I began to read a poem by Renata Halpern. I had read eight lines when I realized the poem was written by my sister.

Coats are the plenary music I make with my
    dreaming hands,
but only the hunter knows the true hazard of fur.
He takes the tiger's many-pillared coat and buries his
    face
in the starshine and strength of a thousand Bengali
    nights.
This pelt is a perfect text of creation, the attar of a
    sacred wildness.
The soft rind of its beauty turns gold on the bodies
    of vain women.
The ermine proves the playfulness of God

when he conjures up his milky dreams of plumage
  and snow,
but the tiger's coat is a wedding song to the
  eminence of blades.

Daughter, take all the words of blood and lavender
  and time.
Bring them shining and clear into the light.
Search them carefully for flaws.
Know that the tiger puzzles over the cunning of
  well-placed traps
as his nostrils fill with the incense of death.
He watches unafraid as strangers approach him with
  knives.
How lordly and solemn is the woman who will wear
  his coat.

With my own hands I fashion the prodigal coats
and send them out as love letters from Sigmund
  Halpern
to those slim, amatory women who honor my craft
each time they move in the peerless lust of furs.
For you, I have chosen my best work, daughter,
the furrier's only poem.
This gift is the scripture I have lifted from the mink's
  spine
as I sought to praise the longitudes of your cautious
  shape.

My skins are the new trustees of your comeliness.
Before the poet dreams of coats, she must master the
  blazonry of fur
and learn to make art from the blood of brothers and
  tigers.

When I finished reading the poem, I told myself that it
could all be explained, that a simple solution existed and,
in time, would present itself to me. As far as I knew, my
sister knew little about Jews and nothing of furriers. Yet I
was certain that Savannah had written the poem. The tiger
was the dead giveaway, not to mention the inimitable, un-
fakable rhythms of her poetry. I reopened Renata's memory

book and looked at the first pages again. It did not take long to find it. Mother's occupation: housewife; father's occupation: furrier.

I knew I was touching something essential in the life of my sister, but I did not know exactly what it meant. It had to do with my sister's fierce rejection of her history in South Carolina. The furrier had redirected the poet's voice back to the island and her childhood, and its images were clear and thrilling to me. She was approaching the story none of us could tell, but indirection weakened her art; hers was not deceitful art but it was both circumambient and oblique. It suggested a subject but did not meet it head on. If you're going to write about the tiger, Savannah, then write about *the* fucking tiger, I thought. And do not hide behind a furrier's craft, Savannah. Refuse to cover your poems in lush pelts and the choice skins of wintering animals broken in the jaws of cruel traps. A furrier warms; a poet simmers in her own exquisite elixirs. A furrier sews a coat from matched brook mink and leopard skins; a poet resurrects the mink and sets a fish wriggling in its mouth; she returns the leopard to the veldt, filling his nostrils with the smell of rutting baboons. You are hiding behind fur and finely sewn coats, Savannah. You are making the terror warm, making it beautiful by enfolding it softly in ermine, merino, and chinchilla when it should stand naked and raw in the cold.

But you approach it, dear sister, you are coming to it and I am coming to it with you.

I turned back to the *Kenyon Review* editor's postscript and read it again carefully: "Mazel tov on the publication of your children's book." Was he talking about the real Renata Halpern's children's book or had my sister taken up the writing of children's books under the same pseudonym she used to publish her poems? For an hour I carefully checked every bookcase in the apartment, searching for a children's book written by Renata Halpern. I failed to turn up a single children's book in her entire library and I wondered how Savannah had planned to write in that form. Frustrated, I was about to abandon the search when I remembered that the *Kenyon Review* always ran small autobiographical sketches of its authors in the back of the magazine. I turned quickly to the back pages and under "H" I read the brief description of Renata Halpern.

> Renata Halpern lives in Brooklyn, New York, and works in the library of Brooklyn College. The poem in this issue is her first published poem. Her children's book, *The Southern Way*, was published by Random House last year. She is currently at work on a collection of poems.

When the salesman handed me the book in the children's section of the Scribner Book Store, I trembled only slightly. There was no photograph of the author on the back jacket, and the illustration on the front pictured three young girls on a dock, feeding seagulls. Behind the three girls, far off against a horizon of trees, was a small white house identical to the one in which I grew up. Even the placement of the barn was the same and the odd number of windows across the front of the house.

I opened the book, read the first page, and knew, beyond any doubt, that the prose was written by Savannah.

That I had stumbled on something invaluable and essential I had no doubt, but the discovery left me far more baffled than enlightened. Savannah's merger with Renata seemed to be another form of evasion to me, one more way to circumnavigate the island instead of gathering the materials for a landing craft to storm ashore. I went directly to Eddie Detreville's apartment and knocked loudly at the door.

When Eddie answered he said, "Dinner's at eight, sweetheart. You're only four hours early. But do come in."

"Okay, Eddie," I said as I entered his apartment and fell heavily on his Victorian couch. "You've been holding back on me."

"Indeed," he said sardonically. "Let me fix you a drink and then you can tell me the secrets Uncle Eddie is withholding. How about a martini?"

"Who is Renata, Eddie?" I asked as he made the drink

at the bar. "And why haven't you told me about her before?"

"There's a very good reason why I haven't told you about her before," he answered with maddening equanimity. "I have never heard of any creature named Renata."

"You're lying, Eddie. She's a friend of Savannah's whose name Savannah feels free to use in signing her own work."

"Then please introduce her to me. I'd love to meet her. Here's your drink, Tom. I suggest you take a good hard swallow, let the alcohol enter the bloodstream, then explain why you're so mad at me."

"Because there's no way you could not know Renata. I mean, she must have come up to visit Savannah. They must hang out together a lot and I'm sure Savannah would have told you about this wonderful new friend of hers. She wouldn't take on a new name without there being some powerful connection."

"Savannah and I find it unnecessary to visit each other's boudoirs, Tom. For reasons that even you can understand."

I opened the Seth Low memory book to the photograph of Renata and asked, "Have you ever seen this woman, Eddie? At the mailbox, or waiting for the elevator?"

He studied the photograph for a few minutes, then shook his head and said, "No, I've never seen her before in my life. Cute, though. A shame she's female."

"This photo was taken over twenty years ago. Think hard, Eddie. The face would be older now. Maybe she has gray hair by now. Wrinkles."

"I've never seen anyone who looks like that, Tom."

"What about this book?" I said, handing him the children's book. "I think Savannah wrote this book. Has Savannah ever showed you this book?"

"I don't read many children's books, Tom," he said. "You may not have noticed, but I'm forty-two years old. I must look younger in this dim light. Thank the Lord for rheostats."

"So you're claiming that your best friend, Savannah, did not ever show you this book?"

"Yes, Sherlock. That's what I'm claiming."

"I don't believe you, Eddie. I simply don't believe you."

"And I'm not the least bit interested whether you believe me or not. Why would I lie to you, Tom?"

"To protect my sister."

"Protect her from what, darling?"

"You know, maybe she's having a lesbian relationship with Renata and you think I couldn't handle that kind of information."

"Tom," he said, "I would be charmed, perfectly charmed, if she was having a lesbian relationship, and I wouldn't care one bit if you could handle that information or not. But please do me the honor of believing me when I tell you I know nothing of Renata or this book."

"I don't know. I just thought you could explain this whole weird thing to me. I'm so used to Savannah being fucked up, Eddie, that it scares the hell out of me when I get some inkling that she might be even more fucked up than I ever thought possible."

"These last years have been horrible for her. She hasn't even wanted to see me much in that time, Tom. Frankly, we haven't had that much to do with each other. Only when my fickle lover took off in search of younger bodies. Then she was a princess. She's always wonderful when a friend is in a crisis."

"So are you, Eddie. I'll be back at eight. What's for dinner?"

"There are two lobsters shivering and depressed in my refrigerator. I will be forced to murder them; then, I will force you to eat what I have slain."

"Bless you, Eddie. And I'm sorry I yelled at you."

"It added piquancy to an otherwise boring day," he said.

In Savannah's apartment, I picked up the receiver of the phone and dialed information. When the operator answered, I said, "I would like the number of a Halpern family who resides, or used to, at Twenty-four-oh-three Sixty-fifth Street in Brooklyn."

"You got a first name?" the operator asked.

"I'm sorry, I don't. This is an old grade school friend. I don't even know if she still lives there."

"I have a Sigmund Halpern at that address. The number is 2-3-2–7-3-2-1."

I dialed the number. On the fourth ring, a woman answered.

"Hello. Is this Mrs. Halpern?"

"It could be. Then again, it couldn't be," she answered in a suspicious Eastern European accent. "So, who's calling?"

"Mrs. Halpern, this is Sidney Rosen. I don't know if you remember me, but I was president of Renata's junior high school class."

"Of course, I remember you, Sidney. Renata used to talk about nothing but Sidney Rosen. She had quite a thing about you, but, as you know, she was so shy."

"I'm calling to ask how Renata is, Mrs. Halpern. I'm looking up some of the old gang in the neighborhood and I always was curious about what happened to Renata."

There was no answer, none at all.

"Mrs. Halpern, are you there?"

She was crying and it took several moments before she could form the words. "You haven't heard then, Sidney?"

"Heard what, Mrs. Halpern?"

"Sidney, she's dead. Two years ago, Renata killed herself by jumping in front of a subway train in the East Village. She had been so depressed. We tried everything to help her, but nothing worked. Our hearts are broken."

"She was a wonderful girl, Mrs. Halpern. I'm so sorry."

"Thank you so much. She looked up to you, Sidney."

"Please tell Mr. Halpern how sorry I am."

"I will. It was so kind of you to call. It would have pleased Renata so much. You're the only one from her class that's ever called. That's enough."

"Goodbye, Mrs. Halpern. And good luck to you. I'm so sorry. Renata was such a sweet girl."

"But so sad, Sidney, so very sad."

I hung up the phone and instantly called Susan Lowenstein's number. After three rings, Susan answered herself.

"Dr. Lowenstein," I said, "we're not talking about my family tomorrow."

"Why, Tom. What's wrong?"

"Tomorrow you're going to tell me all about the Queen of Hearts, Renata Halpern."

"We'll talk about it," she said.

I hung up the phone and opened the children's book once again. This time I read slowly and took scrupulous notes.

The Southern Way

BY R. HALPERN

On an island off the coast of South Carolina a black-haired mother lived alone with her three brown-haired daughters. The mother's name was Blaise McKissick, and she was beautiful in that quiet way that pleases children when they are very small. Blaise had passed this gift generously to her three daughters and their faces looked like three different varieties of the same flower.

Blaise's husband, Gregory, was lost at sea during a storm at the beginning of June. He had gone off to the Gulf Stream to fish for albacore and dolphin and had simply not returned. When he failed to come home, Blaise alerted the Coast Guard and her townsmen put off in a much smaller boat in search of her husband. For two weeks every boat in the county searched the Atlantic, with all its coves and bays and inlets, hoping to find some trace of Gregory McKissick or his craft. Each night, the three girls awaited their mother at the dock, awaited her in sunlight and in rain, watching her emerge out of the mists that arose in the cooling air.

After the fourteenth day with no sign and no reason for hope, the search was abandoned and Gregory was declared dead. They had a funeral service, and as was the custom among the fishermen of the village, they buried Gregory McKissick in an empty coffin beneath the oak tree near the white house. The whole town turned out for the funeral. Small towns have good hearts.

But after the funeral, the townsmen, their wives and

414

children, went back to their lives and their homes. The white house on the island was silent, where once it had been a house of laughter. Each night the girls would watch as their mother went out to visit the grave. The air around the grave smelled like their mother's dressing table where she kept crystal vials and mysterious scents. She would always sit at that table before she went to visit her husband. Her passage through the house was always fragrant and sad. But more troubling to her daughters was the fact that their mother had stopped speaking after her husband's death. When they talked to her, she smiled and tried to speak, but could not.

Soon they became accustomed to silence, and they grieved for their father in the same way. When they did talk to one another, it was always in whispers. They felt the sound of their voices reminded their mother of when their father was alive. They did not wish to add to her sadness. The days passed and they passed wordlessly.

The three girls were as different from one another as it was possible to be. Rose McKissick was the oldest, the prettiest, and the most talkative. The silence of the house troubled her the most, but so did the death of her father. She had known him the longest and had been his special favorite, since she had been born first. It was not easy for her to stop talking about anything that came into her mind. She wanted to talk about her father, to fix in her mind exactly where heaven was and what her father would be doing there and if anyone thought he had had time to talk to God and what they would talk about. But there was no one to ask and it made her afraid. She was twelve and her breasts were beginning to grow and she wanted to discuss this astonishing fact with her mother. She wanted to understand what it meant. She also wanted to ask her mother why it was so easy to forget her father's face. Already, Rose was finding it difficult remembering it exactly as it was. Sometimes, when she slept, she could see it clearly. He would be laughing and holding her, telling her one of his silly jokes and tickling her ribs. Behind him she could see storm clouds moving toward them and she knew one of those clouds contained the terrible cutlery of light that would kill her father. Dark clouds were enemies of the McKissick children now and Rose lived in a house that feared storms.

But for her, particularly, it was difficult to learn to be happy in a house of silence.

Lindsay McKissick had never had any trouble being quiet. She had received this gift at birth and had nurtured it wisely through her ten years. Like her mother, she measured every word before she spoke. It was not even a habit. As she explained it after thinking about it for a long time, "That's just the kind of girl I am." Besides, she said, "Who can talk when Rose is around anyhow?" Even when she was an infant she hadn't cried often. She had a serenity that both troubled and attracted adults. Grownups always suspected that she was judging them and finding them ridiculous. They were usually right. She found adults both too large and too loud. She was perfectly happy being a child and taking her time about things. She worried that she had taken too much time with her father and that he had died without knowing how much she loved him. This knowledge troubled her and helped make a naturally quiet girl even more withdrawn and introspective. She would lie in the hammock in the front yard and stare out at the river. Her blue eyes looked fierce and seemed to burn with the fury of pure water or wildflowers in storm. But there was no fury there. Only the love of a father she would never see again, a father who did not know her and never would.

Sharon McKissick was eight years old and felt the full weight of being the youngest. She thought that no one in her family ever took her seriously because she was so small and fragile. Everyone had called her "Baby" McKissick until she was six and reminded everyone that she had a name and it was Sharon. No one had taken the time to explain her father's death to her because they thought she was too little to understand. On the day of her father's funeral, her mother had come to her room and in a trembling voice told her that her father had gone to sleep. She had made her mother cry by answering, "For how long?" So she had been afraid to ask any more questions. She had watched the grass grow over her father's grave. At first it was a few blades coming out of the earth, then one day, it was all green, like a pretty bedspread covering the place where he was sleeping. She could see her father's grave from her window and it bothered her at night that he might be lonely. When the wind would rise off the river, she would climb from her bed and gaze out the window toward his grave. In moonlight, she could see it, though it seemed to have nothing to do with her father. She tried to imagine angels gathering around his tombstone, helping him survive the solitude of the windswept night. But nothing helped and she vowed to herself if she ever had an eight-year-old, that child would know everything there was about life, death, and everything in between. She would show them all when she was nine. At nine, they would listen to her and she certainly had some things to say.

The island was called Yemassee after the tribe of Indians who lived there before the white men came and took it away. Before he died, Gregory McKissick would tell his daughters the stories of the phantom tribe who still roamed the forests at night. You could still hear the chief cry out when the owl hooted in the trees. The women gossiped when the cicadas screamed in the forest surrounding the house. The Indian children rode on the backs of the deer who wandered the island in silent herds. But there were no Indians on the island, only arrowheads, which would surface each spring when their father plowed the rich acres in the center of the island. They were like prayers tossed up for the dead. Each of the girls had her own private collection of arrowheads, tokens of extinction gathered by pale-faced girls. But their father told them that the tribes had survived in the lowcountry of South Carolina because of words. Some of the Indian's language survived, in fragments, in symmetrical forms, like arrowheads, like razor-sharp poems. "Yemassee," their father said. "Yemassee and Kiawah. Combahee," he whispered. "Combahee and Edisto and Wando and Yemassee." The girls grew up on the island fluent in arrowheads and the lost words of tribes.

Each of the girls thought about their father when they studied their personal collections of arrowheads. The tribes were extinct, but so was their father. He had left no arrowheads for them to remember him by. If only they were quiet enough, they would hear his voice again. He would come as an owl or a mockingbird or a hawk. They would hear him again. They would see him. They were sure. They knew. Shamans had worked magic on these islands, their father had told them. They would look for their father riding on the backs of deer or sitting on the backs of the great green dolphins who played in the streaming tides beside their island.

They believed in magic, these girls, and they found it. Each of them, alone, in her own time, in her own way, in her own world, found it. Because they were watchful and silent.

Rose found it one day as she was patching a bird's wing in her animal hospital. She had founded her hospital when she discovered the puppies of a wild dog who was killed one night, run over by her father's truck. She had taken the puppies, fed them with an eyedropper, and raised them to be proper house pets with good manners. When they were old enough, she placed them in proper homes with people who knew how to appreciate well-trained dogs. That was only the beginning. She found that the whole kingdom of nature seemed to require her services. Baby squirrels and birds were constantly falling out of their nests. Hunters, shooting out of season, would kill mother possums and raccoons, leaving the babies to starve to death in the hidden places. Something always led her to these trees and stumps where the orphans awaited the return of their parents. She would walk in the forest and hear voices calling to her, "A little further, Rose. A little to the left, Rose. Near the pond, Rose." She would follow these voices. She could not help it. She knew how it felt to be abandoned. She discovered she possessed a gift to cure, to soothe the fright of small creatures, to comfort the wounded. None of this surprised her. What did surprise her was that she could speak to all of them when they were in her care. She saw a fox in the river, wounded, pursued by hounds, swimming toward Yemassee Island. The fox's blood stained the water and trailed behind him like a banner. The hounds were almost on him when the fox looked up and saw Rose watching from the shore.

"Help me," the fox said.

There was a strange murmuring in her throat, something inhuman and unnatural. "Stop," Rose commanded the hounds.

The dogs looked up startled. "This is our job."

"Not today. Return to your master."

"It is Rose," said one of the hounds.

"The girl. The brown-haired girl. The one who saved us when our mother was killed."

"Ah. Rose," the second hound said.

"Thank you, Rose," the third one said. "Care for the fox. It is good you came."

"Why do you hunt?"

"It is our nature, Rose," the first hound explained as the three hounds turned and swam back to the opposite shore.

The fox struggled to the land and collapsed at Rose's feet. She carried him to the barn, cleaned his wound, and nursed him through the night. He was the fiftieth animal that had come to her. He told her about the life of a fox. Rose found it very interesting. She was lonely and sad in her house, but never in the barn.

In the house without words, Lindsay listened for the song of the fields. She cared for the beef cattle that roamed the lovely pasturage on the south side of the island. She rode in the bed of her mother's pickup truck and threw off bales of hay in thirty-yard intervals each time her mother came to a stop. The herd moved around the truck, their white faces serene and comely—all except the face of the great bull, Intrepid, who would watch her from a distance, appraising her with dark wild eyes. Intrepid was muscular and dangerous, but Lindsay returned his stare. He was the lord of these fields, she knew, but she wanted him to know that he had nothing to fear from her. She loved the herd, her eyes said. You are one of them, his eyes said back. I cannot help what I am, her stare replied. Nor can I, said his.

She wandered the pastures alone, playing with the young calves, naming them pretty names that tickled her ear. There was Petunia and Casper, Beelzebub and Jerusalem Artichoke, Rumpelstiltskin and Washington, D.C. Always she kept her distance from Intrepid, who had once almost killed a trespasser on a farm near Charleston. She would always lock the gate to his pasture and walk among the cows and calves unafraid and welcome. Whenever a cow delivered a calf, she would wait in the field beside her, whispering to the mother, and, when necessary, helping with the birth. She admired the resignation of these

huge patient beasts. They made good mothers and ordered their lives simply. But Lindsay was attracted to the
kingly presence of Intrepid. Like her own father, he was
silent. Only his eyes spoke. Until the night the magic
changed her life.

She was asleep and the rain sang against the tin roof.
She was dreaming of herself as a calf limping into sunlight
on the first day of her life. Her own mother was a cow with
a pretty white face and her own father was watching her,
a softer, more kindly Intrepid. She heard a voice, which
did not surprise her. What surprised her was her response,
a lovely murmurous sound rising like smoke from her dream,
and her voice rose up in her room in the secret language
of herds.

"You must come," a deep voice said. "There is need."

"Who asks me?"

"The herd king. You must hurry."

She opened her eyes and saw the huge fierce head of
Intrepid through her window, his awesome features blurred
by the rain. His cold eyes met hers. She got up out of bed
and walked to the window. She opened it and the rain was
warm against her face. She climbed through the window
and onto the back of Intrepid. She wrapped her arms around
his neck and held onto his fur with her fingers. Then she
held on tightly as the great bull thundered out of the yard
and down the dirt road toward the pastures. She felt his
enormous strength in the darkness. As she rode beneath
the gloom of oaks, the wet moss hung down and touched
her like the secret laundry of forest angels. The earth moved
away from her and she saw the road from between his
great horns curve away from the swamp. She dug her feet
against his flanks and her flesh moved with his and she
felt horns flowering from her own hair, felt herself becoming part bull, part hooved and dangerous, part lord of the
south pastures. Lindsay ran with Intrepid and for one miraculous mile she ran as Intrepid. When he came to the
pasture, he slowed. Then he stopped by the three giant
palmetto trees that formed the eastern boundary of the
pasture. The young cow, Margarita, was giving birth to her
first calf. She was early and something was wrong. Intrepid
knelt and Lindsay hopped off and ran toward Margarita.
It was a breech birth and she could see the calf's legs pro-

truding from his mother at an odd angle and she felt the desperation of the cow's struggle. Lindsay seized the calf's legs and began to pull the calf gently toward her. For over an hour she tried to coax the calf from the mother. Her hair was wet and she could feel the silent presence of Intrepid behind her. She could smell his power as he watched. Though she did not know what she was doing, she felt something slip into place finally, something correct itself. A small female rested on the grass, exhausted but alive. Margarita licked the calf with her great silver tongue and the rain fell. Lindsay named the new calf Bathsheba and nuzzled her face against it.

Intrepid knelt again and Lindsay rose up on his back again, swinging up on his right horn like a maypole. She rode back to her house in triumph and all the cows applauded as she left the pasture, honored her with their soft mooing. The great bull was silent as he ran down the road again but Lindsay did not care. She put her nose against him and inhaled his wet strength. She licked the rainwater from his neck and returned to her home a changeling, something new and wild and beautiful. She climbed back through her bedroom window, dried herself carefully, and said nothing to her family.

The power had come to her and she would not abuse it. To speak of it would be to betray it. But that was easy in a house of silence, a house without words.

The next day Lindsay was walking toward the pasture down the same road she had ridden the night before. She could see the great hoofprints of Intrepid where they had plunged into the soft earth. She had made a circle of flowers to put around Margarita's neck. But when she passed by the swamp, she heard a rough, eerie cry, a sound she had never heard on the island. Then she felt that strange aura return and a sound issued out of her own throat in reply. This time she was not surprised, but trusting. She felt a connection to wilderness that made her feel invulnerable. She felt alive and open to all things.

A frightening sound came from her throat, a demonic grunting that startled her. But it was an answer to the smoky voice that had called her.

"Please," the voice called, and she plunged into the part of the woods her father had forbidden the girls to enter.

She kept to the firm ground, leapt over water, avoided the soft uncertain ground. The heads of water moccasins lifted out of the water like small black periscopes as she passed. They did not speak to her; they were not part of her magic.

In the center of the swamp she heard a violent thrashing and she rounded a cypress tree and found the old wild boar, Dreadnought, up to his shoulders in quicksand. Her father had hunted Dreadnought for years and never even seen him. Each time the boar struggled, the earth took him deeper and softer into itself. It was like the rescue of the calf's struggle to be born. Dreadnought's tusks shone fiercely in the sunlight. His eyes were yellow and the black hair on his back was raised like a line of pine trees on a bare mountain ridge. Lindsay grabbed a dead branch of a sycamore tree, and lying on her belly, she began to advance over the soft ground until she felt herself slipping into the unsteady earth. She balanced her weight and moved forward again, thrusting the branch toward Dreadnought.

"Please." The word came to her again.

She edged forward slowly until the branch reached the boar's snout. He grabbed it with his savage teeth. She inched backward.

"Be patient," she ordered. "Float like it was water."

The wild boar relaxed his muscles and the hair on his back flattened. He floated up in the killing mud and he felt the tiny pressure of a ten-year-old girl in his gums. She was patient and moved him only a few inches at a time. Behind her all the wild pigs on the island had gathered to watch the death of their king. Lindsay pulled when she could and rested when it was necessary. Her body hurt but there are duties in the service of magic. At last, Dreadnought put a hoof on a fallen log and his great body quivered as he pulled himself out of the muck and bellowed out his relief and deliverance to the forest. He stepped gingerly along the log and did not take a step without carefully testing the land before him. Lucifer, the fifteen-foot alligator, moved through the shallow water and watched the boar as he reached dry land.

"Too late, Lucifer," the boar cried out.

"There will be another time, Dreadnought. I ate one of your sons last week."

"And I've eaten the eggs of a thousand of your sons."

Then Dreadnought turned toward Lindsay. A flick of his tusk could lay her open from head to foot. Surrounded by boars, she was almost losing her belief in magic. But the boar comforted her with these words before he left with his fierce black tribe.

"I owe you, daughter. Thank you for my life."

And the wild hogs melted like shade into the forest and all the snakes of the island trembled and hid at their approach. Lindsay tried to speak to the alligator, Lucifer, but he sank beneath the black water without a ripple thirty feet from where she stood. "So I can't talk to alligators," she thought. "Big deal." But it was the first time she knew her gift was limited.

The silence of the house bothered Sharon, the youngest child, most of all. She wanted to talk about her father, to tell her favorite stories about him. It would be easier for her to remember him if her mother and sisters would reveal what they loved most about him. When she was nine they would listen to her. She was certain of that.

She was also the kind of girl who kept her eyes on the ground or lifted them up to gaze into the sky. She cared very little for what was in between. Often, she would bump into trees as she was walking along looking up at ducks winging north or south along the southern flyway. The freedom of birds was attractive to her and she considered it an oversight on God's part that he had not fitted Adam and Eve with wings. Each sunset she would walk out to the end of the dock, loaded down with bread and scraps to feed the seagulls. She would throw pieces of bread high in the air and the gulls would catch them on the fly. She would be surrounded by the frantic beating of wings and the impatient cries of gulls. Hundreds of birds waited for her every night. Her mother and sisters would watch her nervously from their screened-in porch. Often she would disappear from sight in a flurry of wings and feathers. But all birds made Sharon happy.

So did bugs. Her mother kept bees and she was the only one of the girls who would help Blaise when she gathered the honey from the hives. To Sharon, a bee was a perfect creature. Not only could it fly, but it had this wonderful

job, to visit flowers and gardens all day and then return to
chat with all its friends and to make honey at night. But
once she noticed bees, she started to study and admire their
neighbors. Her room teemed with small boxes of insects,
astonishing beetles, praying mantises, grasshoppers who
spit tobacco juice on her hands, a whole colony of ants
behind glass, butterflies. She loved the wonderful economy
of insects. They couldn't do much, but they could do what
they did very well. Her hobby had earned the contempt of
her sisters.

"Yuk, bugs!" Rose had once said upon entering Sharon's
room.

"Anyone, just anyone, can like a dog or a cow," Sharon
had answered. "It takes a real person to like a bug."

Her sister had laughed.

It happened when Sharon was walking through the woods
near her house, looking for new ant colonies. She was carrying a bag full of chocolate chip cookies. Whenever she
found a colony, she would place a single cookie near the
anthill and watch with pleasure as the worker ants stumbled on this bonanza and sent one ant back with this juicy
piece of gossip. Then ants would spill joyously out of the
hill, dismantle the cookie crumb by crumb, and take all the
crumbs back under the earth. She had found two new ant-
hills this day and was looking for another when she heard
a small voice call her name.

She looked in the direction where the voice had come.
She saw a wasp entangled in the huge silvery web of a
garden spider. The garden spider was moving toward the
wasp, sliding easily down the web like a seaman coming
down rigging. The wasp cried out again and it twisted
desperately in the web. Sharon felt strange words forming on her tongue. But they were not words. They were
secret sounds and it scared her when she heard herself
speak out in a language never spoken by humans on earth.
"Stop."

The spider stopped with one of his black legs mounting
the wasp's abdomen.

"It is the way," the spider said.

"Not this time," Sharon answered.

She took a hairpin and cut the wasp free. The web, as
intricate as lace, fell in tatters between the tree. She could

hear the wasp singing a love song to her as he flew above the trees.

"I'm sorry," Sharon said to the spider.

"It's not right," the spider said grumpily. "This is my role."

Sharon hunted through the leaves and found a dead grasshopper, which she placed in the high part of the web. The web quivered like a harp when she touched it.

"I'm sorry I broke your web. I could not let you do that. It is too terrible."

"Have you ever seen a wasp kill?" the spider replied.

"Yes," she admitted.

"It is no prettier. But it is the way."

"I wish I could help fix your web."

"You can. Now you can."

Sharon felt a trembling in her hands, a power born. The blood of her hands filled up with silk. She reached for the damaged web and lines of silver began to flow from beneath her fingernails. She could not do it at first. She would loop when she should have gone in a straight line. But the spider was patient and soon she had woven a lovely web and it hung like a fisherman's net between two trees. Then she talked with the spider about his lonely work; there was a lizard living beneath an oak stump nearby who had almost eaten him twice. Sharon suggested he move nearer her house so they could visit more frequently. He agreed and walked the length of her arm to her shoulder. As she walked the spider back toward her house, she heard the colonies of ants singing beneath the earth, praising her and her chocolate chip cookies. Wasps flew up and kissed her lips, tickling her nose with their wings. She had never been so happy.

She found the spider a new home without lizards. He was placed between two camellia bushes and together they wove a web even more beautiful than the last. She said goodbye to him when she saw the sun was setting. She heard the cries of the gulls at the end of the dock.

The seagulls were waiting for her, hovering in the air currents above the river like a hundred kites extending from strings of varying lengths. She left the house carrying a shopping bag full of scraps her mother had saved for her. Running, she heard the voices of crickets and beetles in the grass telling her to watch her step. She could hardly even walk to the dock without endangering some small creature.

When she reached the end of the dock, she threw a whole handful of torn bread into the air. Each piece was caught before it hit the water. Again she tossed bread into the air and again the air was full of bread and wings. She was not surprised that she could understand what the gulls were saying to one another. They were quarrelsome, testy, and arguing that some birds were getting more bread than others. High overhead an osprey hovered above the river, waiting for a fish. A small mullet flashed on the surface and she heard the osprey scream, "Now," as he dove toward the water. He rose up with the fish quivering in his claws.

There was a strange gull watching her. He was larger than the other gulls, black-backed and surly, an ocean-flier, and he hung above the river, appraising her. She called hello to him but there was no reply. When she was finished feeding the birds, she wished all of them good night. The black-backed gull flew to the end of the dock and blocked her way. The fatigue of long travel was in the gull's eyes.

"What do you want?" Sharon asked.

"Your father is alive."

"How do you know?"

"I have seen him," said the tired gull.

"Is he in danger?"

"He is in great danger."

"Return, gull. Please, help him."

Wearily, the gull flapped his great wings, lifted into the air, and turned south. Sharon watched until the bird disappeared. The crickets sang in the grass and Sharon understood every word.

She returned to the house and found her mother at the stove, cooking dinner. The smell of onions turning gold in butter filled the house. She wanted to tell her mother what the gull had said but did not know how to explain her gift. But she was happy knowing her father was alive. She helped her sisters set the table. The radio was playing in the kitchen. Blaise kept the radio on all day, just in case there was news of her husband. But there was no news of importance to her. The price for pork was falling. The rains had hurt the tomato crop. And three men had escaped from the state correctional institute in Columbia after killing a guard. They were thought to be heading in the direction of North Carolina.

It was late in the afternoon the next day. The forest was quiet and the three men studied the house from the woods. Each of them had a face that had forgotten how to smile. They studied the movement of the three girls and the woman as they moved in and out of the house. They saw not a trace of a man. They began to move unseen toward the house. But they were seen. The spider watched their approach from his place between the camellia bushes. A wild pig, daughter of Dreadnought, noticed their approach. A gull watched their every movement. A wasp moved in the trees above them. A puppy in the barn, barely able to walk, newly found by Rose, sniffed the air and wondered about the smell. It was the smell of evil come to quiet places. The three men moved toward the house.

They broke into the house through three separate doors and they broke in violently, leaving no room for escape.

Rose screamed when she saw their faces and their pistols. All three girls ran to the chair where their mother was sitting reading a book.

The short man ran to the gun rack and took the three shotguns from the rack and threw boxes of ammunition into a paper sack. The fat man moved toward the kitchen and began filling a trash bag full of canned food. The large man trained his pistol on Blaise and her daughters. He could not take his eyes off Blaise.

"What do you want?" Blaise asked, and the girls could hear the terror in her voice.

"C'mon," the short man shouted from the kitchen. "We got to keep moving."

Still staring at Blaise, the man said, "Before we kill them, I want to take the woman to the back room."

"We ain't got time," the fat man whined.

The large man moved toward Blaise, grabbed her roughly by the wrist, and pulled her toward him. Rose attacked the man, suddenly and furiously. She ran at him, her hand formed into a claw, and she ripped his cheek with her fingernails, drawing blood. He slapped her hard in the face and she went down on her knees. Tears filled her eyes but she put her head on the floor and a strange voice came from her throat in waves of anger and terror. It was an inhuman voice and the men laughed when they heard it.

But the puppy in the barn did not laugh. She had been brought there that morning by Rose. The puppy had been abandoned on the schoolhouse steps and Rose had found her and brought her home. The puppy moved out of the barn and down toward the river. She stumbled once over her floppy ears and her outsized feet. Panting, she reached the dock and paused to catch her breath. Looking out to the river, she lifted her voice in a high-pitched cry for help. Her whelps carried across the river but there was no response. She tried again. Still nothing. But the fox that Rose had once saved from the dogs heard the puppy. The fox began to sing near his lair. A farm dog from across the river picked it up and passed the message from farm to farm until it reached the town. Rose kept screaming on the floor, certain that no one had heard her.

But at that very moment all the dogs of the town had begun to stir in that vast green county. They began to dig holes under fences that restrained them, escape from kennels, break through the windows of their master's houses, all of them. The highways of the county were clogged by the movement of dogs migrating overland. At the pound where the doomed ones awaited their execution, a stray dog bit a hole through a wire fence and fifty dogs who would be dead in a week joined the fierce sprint to the island. They were a lean, united pack and a hunger possessed them. An evil man had mistreated Rose, so new to womanhood, the lover of dogs, the one who had taken the time to learn their language. The pack moved swiftly. It shared a mission.

Lindsay, seeing her sister weeping on the floor, picked up an ashtray and flung it at the tall man. She lowered her head and charged into his legs. "I won't let you hurt my mother," she screamed. The large man lifted her face and slapped it hard, sending her spinning across the room, blood spilling out of her nose. But Lindsay did not cry as the men expected. Instead, they heard her scream out in a tongue of pure anguish, a language of astonishment and fury that they did not understand. There was no delicacy to her quivering voice—it was a language of horns and hooves and tusks. She called out to the cattle feeding near the old rice fields and to the great hogs, wild and black, who grazed in the center of the island.

Near the house, the calf, Bathsheba, that Lindsay had helped bring into the world, had strayed far away from her mother. The calf was new to this language herself and knew only a few words of that secret speech which held all the mysteries of the new world of pastures and grass. But she knew that something was terribly wrong in the white house and she raced on thin, unsteady legs down the main road that cut through the center of the island. She ran swiftly until she broke out of the forest and saw the herd grazing and ran directly up to the bull, Intrepid, who grazed alone, away from the herd.

The bull appraised her sullenly. "What do you mean by this, daughter? Get back to your mother."

"Girl," the calf said, out of breath.

"Girl? What girl? You?" the bull answered, stamping his foot in the grass.

"The blue-eyed girl."

"You mean our girl. Lindsay. She of the herd."

"Yes. The girl of the herd."

"What about her? Speak well and quickly."

"Help."

"Help what, daughter? Help whom? Help when?"

"The girl says help. The girl said that she needed the herd."

There was a sound of distress in the herd and Intrepid looked up in time to see the boar, Dreadnought, moving swiftly toward the calf. The bull moved between the boar and the herd and lowered his horns in warning.

"Swine," the bull said.

The old hog stopped, hideous and cruel, despised by the cows. Behind him, coming out of the trees, his tribe appeared, their tusks shining like lances in the sunlight.

"What's this I hear? What about the girl?"

"She's our girl. She belongs to the herd," the bull said.

"She loves the swine," Dreadnought insisted.

"She loves the cattle," the bull said fiercely.

"Both," said the calf, Bathsheba. "That is what the girl said. She loves both. She said help."

Then the language of the swine and the cattle commingled and the hooved animals began to move in awful sym-

metry toward the house on the river. Dreadnought and
Intrepid marched at the head of their formidable regiment.
Ahead, they could hear the baying of dogs swarming onto
the bridge that led to the island.

Blaise looked to her daughter Lindsay, bleeding on the
floor. She glanced at the three armed men and smelled their
evil in the room like some debased flower. Outside she saw
the river peacefully flowing as it always had.

She said to the men, "I'll go into the room with all of
you if you'll leave my daughters alone. If you won't harm
us."

"You ain't got a choice, lady," the big man said, grabbing
her by the blouse and tearing it at the shoulder. Then the
small girl, Sharon, advanced toward the man.

"You leave my house," she said as she moved forward,
but she began stuttering in a fabulous, newly learned language unintelligible to the humans in the room.

The garden spider moved like a dancer up his gleaming
web, mounted a windowsill of the house, and peered into
the living room. He heard Sharon's words, then turned to
sound the alarm. He felt his web tremble beneath him and
he saw the yellow wings of a monarch butterfly fluttering
against the invisible netting. He moved toward the butterfly
in the terrifying ancient approach of spiders and the butterfly sang her deathsong into the air. The spider touched
the butterfly with his black legs, and gently set the monarch
free. The butterfly rose, dazzled and puzzled, into the air.

"Send the alarm, monarch. The girl is in trouble."

The butterfly flew high above the island and began to
hum the forest melody of distress. She heard the spider
screaming from his web a cry of alarm. The ants heard. The
cicadas heard. A million bees left their hives and the business of flowers and flew toward the house. Wasps droned
like fighter planes through the trees. A gull heard the warning of the monarch and took up the cry of birds and the
air around the island darkened with the angry wings of sea
birds.

The swine, the cattle, and the dogs were all racing full
speed toward the house and all noticed that the leaves were
alive with movement, that the trees streamed with insects,
that the forest floor swarmed with a countless flow of in-

sects, that the little ones were flowing like a river toward the house. The forest moved; the earth moved.

The big man pushed Blaise roughly toward the back of the house. The three girls screamed for him to stop. The men laughed at them. They laughed hard. They laughed until they heard the noise outside. It began as a low, eerie hum but rose in pitch and frenzy. The men glanced at one another, puzzled by the strange noise. It sounded like the dawn of creation when all the creatures of the world were trying out their new voices for the first time. All the fear and glory of Eden burst into a song of vengeance around the house by the river. Swift deer mounted by the ghosts of Indian boys patrolled the river's edge. The sky was black with wings. The grass was covered with insects of every hue. The herd bellowed. The swine thundered. Birds screamed.

The men in the house froze.

The girls continued to speak in their new tongues.

"Kill them" was the translation of all three. "Kill them."

The big man, holding his pistol aloft, crept to the window and looked out. He looked out and screamed. The scream was easily translatable. He screamed out of fear. The other two men joined him and their screams echoed his.

"They are mine," thundered Intrepid, the bull.

"Let us have them," commanded Dreadnought, the boar.

"The bees and the wasps will make short work of them," a small voice buzzed.

"The dogs will rip them apart," a hound said.

"The birds will feed them to the fishes," an old gull cried, hovering.

What the men saw from the window was the whole kingdom of nature rising out of the light to meet them. They did not see the silent army of fire ants streaming through the cracks of doors, moving up their pants legs, across their shirts. They did not see the spiders dropping like parachutists from the ceiling into their hair, or the wasps adhering like clothespins to the back of their shirts.

They were transfixed by the nearness of their own deaths. The air filled up with the dreadful language of beasts, the beating of wings, the stamping of hooves, the rattle of horns, the rustle of insects, the anger of hives, the arrival of straggling hounds. In the last moments they were permitted to understand, to translate, but not to react. There is no mercy in the forest. That is not the way.

The garden spider moved up the big man's shirt, climbing along his spine. When he reached the neck, he chose a soft place beneath the ear. He bade farewell to Sharon and sent his venom shooting into the man's bloodstream. The man screamed and killed the spider with a single blow, but then all the wasps, noting the signal, drilled into flesh and the ants set the men on fire. They staggered around the room, beating at their bodies. They rushed for the front door, toward the amazing noise, opened it, and stumbled into the hooves and fangs and wings and jaws.

Blaise and her daughters sat on the sofa and listened to the cries of the three men. Blaise would not let her daughters near the windows. Because they were human, they felt pity for the men. But there was nothing they could do now except refuse to watch. After a while the screaming stopped. Then the island was silent again.

When Blaise looked out the window, she saw only grass and water and sky. There was not a single trace of the men, not a piece of clothing, a sliver of bone, or a lock of hair.

That evening they buried the spider in the family cemetery for pets. They prayed for his soul and that his webs would spin out for thousands of miles, connecting planets and stars, and that angels would sleep in his silk and that his weavings would always please God.

Two days later, Gregory McKissick's boat drifted onto Cumberland Island in Georgia. When he returned to his house he told the story of floating for weeks at sea. He would have died, he said, except for a single black-backed gull who always dropped fish into his boat from the sky.

After his return, the house became complete again. The girls grew older and gradually lost their gift. They never spoke about the day the three men came. Rose continued to care for lost dogs her whole life. Lindsay never lost her affection for cattle and swine. Sharon retained her love of birds and insects all her days. They loved nature and they loved their family. They heard their mother singing again. All of them led good lives.

It was their way.

20

Whenever I am angry, my displeasure is written in code on my mouth in a thin-lipped, downturned crescent. I have perfect control of the rest of my face but my mouth is the renegade that broadcasts my vexation and wrath to the outside world. Friends who have mastered the art of reading my mouth can chart the emotional weather of my soul with uncanny accuracy. Because of it I can never take either comrades or enemies by surprise, no matter how vital the enterprise between us. They can decide for themselves to retreat or advance against me. In anger, my mouth is a hideous thing.

But even when I was not incensed, I was no match for Susan Lowenstein's impenetrable composure. She could accommodate my anger by a strategic withdrawal into the snows of her impeccable breeding. Whenever I attacked her, she drew back into the vast and confident reaches of her intelligence. She could wither me with her brown eyes that served as rose windows illuminating memories of some prehistoric ice age. When I lost control, those eyes made me feel like an aberration of nature, a hurricane approaching a battened-down coastal town. When calm, I felt that I could face Dr. Lowenstein as an equal; when aroused, I knew she could make me feel like a perfect southern asshole.

My mouth twisted in a torque of exquisite displeasure as I confronted Dr. Lowenstein and threw the children's book across the coffee table toward the therapist.

"Okay, Lowenstein," I said, taking my seat, "let's cut out all the formal little courtesies like 'Did you have a nice

weekend?' and get directly to the point. Who the fuck is
Renata and what does she have to do with my sister?"

"Did you have a nice weekend, Tom?" she asked.

"I'm going to report you to the proper authorities, Lowenstein, and get your license suspended. You have no right
to hide anything about my sister from me."

"I see," she said.

"So spit it out, Doctor. Give it to me straight and you
might be able to salvage your endangered career."

"Tom," she said, "you must know how much I like you
on normal occasions. But I find you rather repulsive whenever you feel threatened or insecure."

"I feel threatened and insecure twenty-four hours of every
day, Doctor. But that's not the point. I just want to know
who Renata is. Renata is the key, isn't she? If I understand
about Renata, then I'll understand why I've been staying
in New York this summer. You've known about Renata the
whole time, haven't you, Susan? You've known about her
all the time and you've chosen not to tell me."

"Savannah chose not to tell you, Tom," Dr. Lowenstein
said. "I was merely acceding to her wishes."

"But it would help me to understand what's wrong with
Savannah, wouldn't it, Susan? Do you deny that?"

"It might help you to understand, Tom. I'm not sure."

"Then you owe me an explanation, Lowenstein."

"Savannah can tell you herself when the time is right.
She specifically made me promise that I would not talk to
you about Renata."

"But that was before I knew that Renata had some connection with my sister. And, I mean, Dr. Lowenstein, we
are talking about a bizarre connection. Savannah's now
writing books and poems and publishing them under Renata's name."

"Who told you about the children's book, Tom?"

I ignored her question and said, "I called Renata's house
in Brooklyn and found out that Renata had hit the tracks
and gone one-on-one with an incoming train two years ago.
Renata's mother described the suicide to me. That leads to
several conclusions. Either Renata faked a suicide and loves
torturing her nice Brooklyn mama or something rather odd
is going on in my sister's head."

"Have you read the children's book?" Dr. Lowenstein asked.

"Of course I read the book."

"What do you think?"

"What the hell do you think I think?" I said. "It's about my goddamn family."

"How do you know?"

"Because I'm not an idiot. Because I can read and because I can see a thousand things in that story that Savannah and only Savannah could know. I can understand why Savannah used a pen name for this story, Susan—my mother would flip her gourd if she ever read this thing. Savannah wouldn't have to commit suicide. My mother would rip her pancreas out with her teeth. Now who is Renata? I want to know what her relationship to Savannah is. Are they lovers? You can tell me. Savannah's had female lovers before. I've met them and broken pita bread with them and served them bean sprout sandwiches and fed them soup with potato-peel base. She's been attracted to the wimpiest males and females on the continent. I don't care who she's screwing. But I demand some explanation. You haven't let me see Savannah in weeks. Why? There's got to be a reason. Is Renata the one who hurt Savannah? If she is, I'll find her and kick the shit out of her."

"You'd hit a woman," she asked. "How surprising."

"If she was hurting my sister, I'd punch her fucking guts out."

"Renata was a friend of Savannah's. That's all I'm going to tell you."

"No shit. Look, I don't deserve this from you. I've done everything you've asked. I've told you every story I can remember about my family and I . . ."

"You're lying, Tom," she said evenly.

"What do you mean I'm lying?"

"You haven't told me all the stories. You haven't told me all the ones that really count. You've given me the history of your family as you would like to remember and preserve it. Grandpa was a real character and Grandma was a real eccentric. Dad was a little odd and he'd whip us when he got drunk but Mom was a princess and held us all together with her love."

"I haven't gotten to the end of the story, Susan," I said. "I'm trying to put it all into a context. You handed me a bunch of tapes with Savannah screaming out gibberish the first day I met you. Some of it is meaningless to me. I am trying to put it in order, but I can't tell you the ending unless you understand the origins."

"You're even lying about the beginnings."

"How do you know? One thing I'm perfectly sure of is that I know what happened to my family a lot better than you do."

"Perhaps you just know one version of it better and that's all. It's an instructive version and it's been helpful. But the things you leave out, Tom, are every bit as important as the things you leave in. Talk to me less about the Huck Finns you and your brother were and tell me a little more about the girl who spent her life setting the table. It's that girl I want to know about, Tom."

"She's talking," I said. "Savannah's talking and you're not letting me see her."

"You know Savannah made the decision not to see you, Tom. But your stories about your childhood have been exceptionally helpful to her. They've helped her remember things she repressed long ago."

"She hasn't heard a single one of the stories I've told about our childhood."

"Yes, she has. I've taped them all and played parts of them to her when I see her at the hospital."

"Watergate!" I screamed, rising, and began pacing the length of the room. "Get Judge Sirica on the phone. I want those tapes erased, Lowenstein, or used to light your charcoals the next time you barbecue steaks on the terrace."

"I often tape sessions, Tom. There's nothing unusual about it and you told me you'd do anything to help your sister. I took you at your word. So please sit down and quit trying to bully me."

"I'm not trying to bully you. I'm thinking about beating you up."

"Sit down, Tom," Dr. Lowenstein said, "and let's settle our differences calmly."

I sat down heavily in the soft chair and stared once more at Susan Lowenstein's unruffled countenance.

"It's that self-pitying male ego I fear the most when you finally do get to see Savannah again, Tom."

"I'm a completely defeated male, Doctor," I said edgily. "You have nothing to worry about. I've been neutered by life and circumstances."

"Not a chance. I've never seen a male yet who wasn't completely ruled by the necessity of being male at any cost. And you're one of the worst I've ever seen."

"You don't know anything about men," I said.

She laughed and said, "Tell me everything you know. We've got ten minutes."

"What a lousy thing to say. It's not as easy being a man as you seem to think."

"Oh, I've heard this sad song before, Tom. Half my male patients try to enlist my sympathy by humming the bars to this tragic lament. My husband uses the same exhausted strategy, not knowing I hear it fifty times a week. Now you'll start telling me about the old agony of command, won't you, Tom? It's lonely at the top, little girl. The awesome responsibility of the head of the household. I've heard all this before."

"Lowenstein," I said, "there's only one thing difficult about being a male. It's something the modern woman doesn't understand. Certainly Savannah and her radical feminist friends didn't understand it. All her friends used to scream at Luke and me when we'd come up to New York to visit Savannah. I think my sister thought it was good for her poor redneck brothers to be screamed at about the evils of wearing a penis in the modern world. Radical feminists! God preserve me. Because of Savannah, I've been screamed at by radical feminists more than any southern man alive. They believe that they can scream at you at will for forty-eight-hour intervals, then expect you to be so grateful for the lessons that you'll gladly stick your dick into a blender and punch the frappe button."

"When I first met you, Tom, you told me you were a feminist."

"I am a feminist," I said. "I am one of those feckless, sad-sack males who learned how to whip up a soufflé and make a perfect béarnaise sauce while his wife opened cadavers and comforted cancer patients. I say this knowing that a man who calls himself a feminist is the most ridiculous figure of our silly times. When I say it to my men friends, they chuckle and tell me the latest pussy joke. When I say it to most southern women, they look at me with utter contempt and say how much they enjoy being women and having car doors opened for them. When I say it to feminists, they are the most vicious of all. Feminists take it as an unctuous, patronizing gesture coming from some hairy spy planted by the enemy camp. But I *am* a goddamn feminist, Lowenstein. I'm Tom Wingo, feminist, conservationist, white liberal, pacifist, agnostic, and because of all these things I can't take myself seriously at all and neither can anyone else. I'm thinking about applying for lifetime membership as a redneck so I can get back some small measure of self-respect."

"I think you're still a redneck, Tom. Despite all your protestations."

"No, a redneck has integrity."

"You were about to tell me something about being a man. What was it?" Dr. Lowenstein asked.

"You'll just laugh at me," I whined.

"Probably," she admitted.

"There's only one thing difficult about being a man, Doctor. Only one thing. They don't teach us how to love. It's a secret they keep from us. We spend our whole lives trying to get someone to teach us how to do it and we never find out how. The only people we can ever love are other men because we understand the loneliness engendered by this thing denied. When a woman loves us we're overpowered by it, filled with dread, helpless and chastened before it. Why women don't understand us is that we can never return their love in full measure. We have nothing to return. We were never granted the gift."

"When men talk about the agony of being men," she said, "they can never quite get away from the recurrent theme of self-pity."

"And when women talk about being women, they can never quite get away from the recurrent theme of blaming men."

"It's not easy being a woman in this society."

"Boo-hoo. Let me tell you something, Lowenstein. Being a man sucks. I'm so sick of being strong, supportive, wise, and kingly that I may puke if I have to pretend I'm any of those things again."

"I haven't seen much evidence that you're any of those things, Tom," said the imperturbable Dr. Lowenstein. "Most often I don't know what you are or what you represent or what you stand for. There are times you're one of the sweetest men I've ever met. But there are other times, always unpredictable, when you become bitter and cornered. Now, you tell me you can't feel love. Other times you claim to love everybody in sight. You've declared your love for your sister over and over again, then you get furious at me when I'm trying to do everything in my power to help your sister. I can't trust you completely, Tom, because I don't know who you are. If I tell you about Savannah, I don't know if you can handle it. So what I think I'm asking, Tom, is that you start acting like a man. I want you to act strong and wise and responsible and calm. I need it and so does Savannah."

"I began this discussion, Doctor," I whispered, "by merely asking about the relationship between Renata and my sister. I considered this a fair question. By some twist of rhetoric you have succeeded in putting me on the defensive and making me look like a horse's ass in the process."

"You began this discussion by storming into this room and throwing that book across the table at me. You screamed at me and I don't get paid to have people scream at me."

I covered my eyes and could feel her level gaze on my hands, steady and judgmental. I dropped my hands and met her brown gaze. Her beauty, dark and carnal and disturbing, stirred me as it always did.

"I would like to see Savannah, Doctor. You've got no right to keep us apart. None in the world."

"I'm her doctor, Tom, and I'd keep you away from her for the rest of her life if I thought it would help her. And I think it just might."

"What are you talking about?"

"Savannah believes, and I'm beginning to see her point, that she may have to break off all relations with her family if she is to survive."

"That's the worst thing she could do, Doctor," I said.

"I'm just not sure of that."

"I'm her twin, Doctor," I said acidly. "You're nothing

but her fucking shrink. Now who is Renata? I would like
to know and think I've earned the right to know."

"Renata was a very special friend of Savannah's," Dr.
Lowenstein began. "She was very fragile, very sensitive,
and very angry. She was a lesbian, a radical feminist, and
she was Jewish. I'm afraid she didn't like men very much
. . ."

"Jesus Christ," I moaned. "She sounds like half the assholes Savannah pals around with up here."

"Shut up, Tom, or I won't continue."

"Excuse me. That was uncalled for."

"Savannah had a psychotic episode a little over two years
ago. Renata nursed her through it. They had met in a poetry
workshop that Savannah taught at the New School. When
Savannah had her breakdown, Renata wouldn't let Savannah go to a mental hospital and pledged to Savannah that
she'd see her through the whole thing. Savannah was much
the same way she was when you saw her in the hospital,
Tom. But Renata got her through the bad part. According
to Savannah, Renata was like having her own personal
guardian angel. Three weeks after Savannah was able to
return to her own apartment, Renata threw herself in front
of the train."

"Why?" I asked.

"Who knows why? The same reason anyone attempts
suicide. Life has become unbearable and there seems to be
only one way out. Like Savannah, Renata had a history of
suicide attempts. After Renata's death, Savannah went into
another long decline. She began walking the streets, disoriented and out of control. She'd wake up in strange doorways, having spent the night out in the city. She would
have no memory of these long fugue states. She would
recover slightly, go back to her apartment, and try to write.
Nothing would come. She would try to remember her childhood, Tom, and nothing would come back to her. She could
only have nightmares about her childhood. One night, she
dreamed of three men coming to your island. She knew
the dream was important, essential. She knew that something like that had happened but she could not recall enough
details. The children's story came directly out of the dream.

"Savannah then decided to sign Renata's name to the
children's book as an act of homage to Renata's memory.

She sent it out to a different agent to see if she could get it published. Then Savannah came up with what she thought was the grand idea of her life, the one that would save her."

"I tremble to hear what this is," I said.

"She decided to become Renata Halpern, Tom," Susan Lowenstein said, leaning slightly toward me.

"Pardon me," I said.

"She decided to become Renata," she repeated.

"Back up, Doctor. I'm missing something."

"When Savannah first came to see me as a patient, Tom, she told me her name was Renata Halpern."

"Did you know she was really Savannah Wingo?" I asked.

"No. How would I have known that?"

"You've got her books out there in the waiting room."

"I've got Saul Bellow's books out there too, but I wouldn't know him if he entered my office and told me he was George Bates."

"Oh, God," I said, "my soul is queasy. When, pray tell, did you find out that Savannah was Renata or Renata was Savannah or Savannah was Saul Bellow or whatever you found out?"

"It's hard to fool me about being Jewish."

"She told you she was Jewish?" I asked.

"She told me she was Renata Halpern. When she described her parents to me, she told me they were both Holocaust survivors. She even remembered the numbers tattooed on their arms. She said her father worked as a furrier in the garment district."

"I don't understand any of this. Don't people usually come into therapy for help? I mean, why would she come to you pretending she was someone else? Why would she refuse to try to get help based on her own history instead of getting help for one she made up?"

"I think she wanted to try out her new identity to see if she had her story absolutely right. Also, I think she was in deep trouble no matter who she claimed to be. She was coming apart at the seams, Tom, and it really didn't make any difference who she said she was. She was in desperate trouble as either Renata or Savannah. Calling herself Renata was only part of the disturbance."

"When did she tell you she wasn't Renata?"

"I started asking her a series of questions about her past she couldn't answer. I asked her what shul she attended and she didn't know what a shul was. I asked her the name of her temple and her childhood rabbi. She told me her mother kept a kosher kitchen but did not know what I meant when I asked her if she ever ate food that was trayf. She knew very few words of Yiddish even though she claimed her parents were from a shtetl in Galicia. Eventually, I told her I didn't believe her story and that if I was going to help her I had to know the truth. I also told her that she didn't look Jewish to me."

"You're a racist, Lowenstein," I said. "I knew it the minute I set eyes on you."

"Your sister has a classic shiksa face," she answered, smiling.

"Is that an unforgivable insult?"

"No, it's simply an undeniable fact."

"What did she do after you confronted her?"

"She got up and walked out of my office without saying goodbye. She missed her next appointment, but she called to cancel it. The next time we met she told me that she once was called Savannah Wingo, but was planning on assuming a new identity, moving out to the West Coast, and living out the rest of her life as Renata Halpern. She was never going to get in touch with any member of her family again. As long as she lived. It was too painful to see any of them, she said. She could not bear the memories any longer and she was losing what memories she had. She refused to continue being surrounded by so much pain. She had been inconsolable for long enough. As Renata Halpern, she thought she had a chance to live a reasonable life. As Savannah Wingo, she thought she would be dead within a year."

"Jesus Christ," I said, and I closed my eyes and tried to think of us as children, blond and lean in the Carolina sun. A vision of the river appeared before me: marsh birds fished in the estuaries and we three children swam in the green river, full-tided and still as linen. There was one ritual we developed when we were very small that we revealed to not another living soul. Whenever we were hurting or damaged or sad, whenever our parents had punished or beaten us, the three of us would go to the end of the floating dock, dive into the sun-sweet water, then swim out ten yards into the channel and form a circle together by holding hands. We floated together, our hands clasped in a perfect unbreakable circle. I held Savannah's hand and I held Luke's. All of us touched, bound in a ring of flesh and blood and water. Luke would give a signal and all of us would inhale and sink to the bottom of the river, our hands still tightly joined. We would remain on the bottom until one of us squeezed the hands of the others and we would rise together and break the surface in an explosion of sunlight and breath. But on the bottom I would open my eyes to the salt and shadow and see the dim figures of my brother and sister floating like embryos beside me. I could feel the dazzling connection between us, a triangle of wordless, uplifted love as we rose, our pulses touching, toward the light and terror of our lives. Diving down, we knew the safety and silence of that motherless, fatherless world; only when our lungs betrayed us did we rise up toward the wreckage. The safe places could only be visited; they could only grant a momentary intuition of sanctuary. The moment always came when we had to return to our real life to face the wounds and grief indigenous to our home by the river.

At this very moment, in Dr. Lowenstein's office, I wanted to seek the asylum of slow currents, deep places, river bottoms. I would like to have taken my sister, hugged her to my chest, and sunk to the bottom of an azure sea to hold her close to me. A new man, I would hurt or destroy anything that moved in to harm her. I could always take down a large ordnance of the finest, most cutting weaponry to defend her when I thought or dreamed about Savannah. But in real life, I could not even shield the soft veins of her wrists from her own interior wars.

"I told Savannah," Dr. Lowenstein said, "that I would try to help her in any way I could. But I had to know what she was running away from in her past or I could not help her. Unless she resolved the problems of Savannah Wingo, I didn't think Renata Halpern had a chance."

"Why would you help someone become another person?" I asked. "I mean, what are the ethics of this, or if

not ethics, what are the therapeutic statistics you're relying
on? How in the world do you know that this is best for
Savannah? What if you're wrong, Lowenstein?"

"I've never known of another case like this, so I'm not
relying on any set body of professional literature. Nor did
I agree to help Savannah become Renata Halpern. I simply
told her I would try to help her become the most fully
integrated person she could become. She had to make the
difficult choices. I would help her make those choices right
for her."

"You have no right to do that to Savannah, Dr. Lowenstein. You have no right to help turn her into someone
who will never see her family again. I can't reconcile myself
to a kind of therapy that will turn my southern sister into
a Jewish writer. It's not therapy you're practicing now. It's
black magic, witchcraft, all the dark arts combined. If Savannah wants to become Renata Halpern, then that's simply one manifestation of her madness."

"It might be one manifestation of her health. I simply
don't know."

I was suddenly exhausted, depleted down to the very
center of the soul, and I rested my head on the back of the
chair, closing my eyes and trying to clear my mind. I struggled to marshal some reasonable arguments to use against
Susan Lowenstein, but I was feeling far too eclipsed and
alienated to be reasonable.

Finally, I summoned the strength to say, "This, Lowenstein, is the reason I loathe the century I was born in.
Why did I have to be born in the century of Sigmund Freud?
I despise his mumbo jumbo, his fanatical adherents, his
arcane incantations to the psyche, his dreamy unprovable
theories, his endless categorizations of all things human. I
would like to make an announcement, and I'd like to make
it after great thought and deliberation. Fuck Sigmund Freud.
Fuck his mother, his father, his children, and his grandparents. Fuck his dog, his cat, his parakeet, and all the
animals at the zoo in Vienna. Fuck his books, his ideas, his
theories, his daydreams, his dirty fantasies, and the chair
he sat in. Fuck this century year by year, day by day, hour
by hour, and take everything in this miserable hundred-
year abortion of time and flush it down Sigmund Freud's
fragrant commode. Last, but not least, fuck you, Lowen-

stein, fuck Savannah, fuck Renata Halpern, and fuck anyone else my sister might wish to become in the future. As soon as I can move, I'm going to leave your well-appointed office, pack my meager belongings, and order one of those unspeakable, scrofulous cab drivers to take me to La Guardia. Ol' Tom's going home to where his wife is in love with a heart specialist. And as terrible as that is, it at least makes sense to me, whereas nothing about Savannah and Renata does."

"Have you quite finished, Tom?" she asked.

"No. As soon as I can think of something truly insulting to say to you, I'm going to launch into another long speech."

"I may have been wrong not to tell you everything from the beginning. That was my decision. You see, I was warned about you, Tom. Savannah knows you very well. She understands that though you pretend to be helpful, you're deeply ashamed of her problems, that you fear them, that you would do almost anything to be rid of them, to deny them, to cast them out into the darkness. Yet she also knows you have a strong sense of family and duty. My job was to balance these two counterweights. If I could have done this without you, so help me God, I would have. I've dreaded the day you'd find out about this—I've dreaded your self-righteousness and anger."

"How do you expect me to react?" I asked. "What if I had done the same thing to Bernard? What if I had taken this morbidly unhappy child and instead of coaching him, I taught him a way to get out of his miserable family life? Change your name, Bernard. Come with me to South Carolina. We'll get you on the football team and set you up with a nice family who'll let you start all over again."

"It's not the same thing and you know it. My son did not try to kill himself."

"Give him time, Lowenstein," I said. "Just give him a little time."

"You son of a bitch," she said, and I did not see her pick up the *American Heritage Dictionary* on her coffee table and, with remarkable accuracy, hurl it in my direction.

It hit me squarely on the nose, bounced off my lap, and lay open on the floor. It was opened to page 764, and in shock, I looked down and saw the heading "load displacement." Then I saw my own blood obscuring the entry describing the Russian mathematician Nikolai Ivanovich Lobachevski. As I lifted my hand to my nose, the blood pulsed through my fingers.

"Oh, my God," she said in horror at her own loss of control. She gave me her handkerchief. "Does it hurt?"

"Yes," I said. "I find it agonizing."

"I have some Valium," she said, opening her purse.

I roared laughing but it made the blood rush faster and I stopped. "Do you think I can stop the bleeding by sticking two Valiums up my nostrils? It's lucky for the world you didn't try to become a medical doctor."

"It might help calm you."

"I'm not agitated, Lowenstein," I said. "I'm bleeding. You injured me. I see a big malpractice suit coming out of this."

"You took me to the limits of my endurance," she said. "I've never had a violent moment in my whole life."

"Now you've had one. That was a good throw."

"It's still bleeding."

"That's because you almost took my nose off," I said, laying my head on the back of the chair. "If you'll just quietly close the door behind you, on your way out, Doctor, I'll just good-naturedly bleed to death."

"I think you should see a doctor," she said.

"I'm with a doctor."

"You know what I mean."

"Why don't you go down to the mental hospital and rustle me up a catatonic. I'll just press him up against my nose for an hour or two. Look, Doc, relax. I've had nosebleeds before. This too will pass."

"I'm very sorry, Tom. I'm deeply embarrassed," she said.

"I'll never forgive you," I said, and the silliness of this scene had brought me again to the point of giggling. "Holy God, what a day. I get dropped by a dictionary and I find out my sister is practicing to be a Brooklyn Jew. Jesus Christ!"

"When you stop bleeding, Tom, please let me take you to lunch."

"It's going to be expensive, Lowenstein," I said. "No hot dog at Nathan's today. No cheese pizza. I can see it now.

Lutèce or La Côte Basque or the Four Seasons. Everything I order will come to the table on fire. You're going to spend money, Lowenstein. Plenty of money."

"At lunch, I want us to talk seriously and reasonably, Tom," Dr. Lowenstein said. "I need to explain further about Savannah and Renata and me . . ."

She could not go on. My laughter stopped her cold.

When I walked through the doors of Lutèce, I felt that I was moving in my own half-dreamt fugue state, so giddy and lightheaded was I after the nosebleed and the unraveling of the mystery of Renata. Madame Soltner greeted Susan by name and they conversed in colloquial French for a minute as I marveled again how easily Susan managed the customs and fluid courtesies of her charmed and civilized life. She was effortlessly poised and unstintingly correct, like a brilliant creature trained in all the plenary arts one could cultivate with access to the proper circles and an abundance of clean folding money. She was the first person I had met in New York who was not atomized and made ridiculous by the roaring, plenipotentiary authority of the city. Indigenous to the avenues, her gestures were economical and sure. To me, her confidence was an exorbitant gift, but then, I had only met immigrants to New York. Susan Lowenstein was the first incumbent of the great island I had known, my first Manhattanite. I had learned there was a sublayer of passion beneath those cool lawns of her exterior, and my throbbing nose was testament to this.

We were led to a good table with Madame Soltner casting only a single troubled glance at the tissue I had wadded up my left nostril. I thought of the high probability that she had escorted very few customers into the hushed interiors of Lutèce suffering from nosebleeds. Excusing myself, I went to the men's room to remove the ghastly Kleenex; then, having satisfied myself that I was no longer hemorrhaging, I washed my face and returned to the main salon. My nose had swollen like a fat nugget of puff pastry. I was not handsome but I was hungry.

A waiter, who looked as if he had been cornstarched in arrogance, took our orders for drinks. I leaned across the immaculate napery and whispered, "When the drinks come, you won't be embarrassed if I just soak my nose in mine for a minute or two? The alcohol will disinfect the wound."

She lit a cigarette and blew a plume of smoke my way. "At least you're joking about it. I still can't believe I threw a book at you. You can be very exasperating at times, Tom."

"I'm a perfect jerk at times. I said something unforgivable about Bernard and I fully deserved to have a dictionary flatten my schnozz. I owe you the apology."

"My failure to be a good mother for Bernard is a constant torture, Tom," she said.

"You're not a bad mother. Bernard is a teenager. Teenagers are, by definition, not fit for human society. It's their job to act like assholes and make their parents miserable."

The waiter brought the menus and I studed mine with both thoroughness and anxiety. This was the first time I had ever dined within earshot of a world-class chef and I did not want to squander my opportunity by a thoughtless and unimaginative order. Carefully, I questioned Susan Lowenstein about every meal she had ever eaten at Lutèce and I admitted that she would ruin my entire meal if I ordered something simply grand, only to be eclipsed by her order of something ambrosial and otherworldly. Finally, she offered to order my complete meal and I sat back as she asked the waiter to bring me the duck mousse studded with juniper berries as a first course. For my next course, she chose a *soupe de poisson au crabe* and with a wink guaranteed its sublimity. My brain reeled happily as she listed a choice of entrées she described as flawless. Again she noted my hesitation, my choking in the clutch, and she directed the waiter to have Chef Soltner prepare the *râble de lapin*.

"Rabbit!" I said in surprise. "This is described as a gastronomic temple, Lowenstein, by all the hotshot food magazines, and you're going to humiliate me by ordering me a bunny rabbit?"

"It will be the best meal you've ever eaten," she said confidently. "Trust me on this one."

"Do you mind if I tell the waiter I'm the food critic for *The New York Times*?" I asked. "I'd like to put real pressure on André to do some serious overachieving in the kitchen back there."

"I'd rather you didn't, Tom. Let me order us some wine and then I'd like to talk a little bit about Savannah."

"Could I have the waiter remove every item on the table that might be flung in my direction? Or would you allow me to wear a catcher's mask?"

"Tom, do your friends and family sometimes find your joking a bit excessive?" she asked.

"Yes, they all find it repulsive. I'll be dull for the rest of the meal, Doctor, I promise."

The wine arrived at the table, a Château Margaux. My duck mousse materialized simultaneously. I tasted the wine and it was so robust and appealing that I could feel my mouth singing with pleasure when I brought the glass from my lips. The aftertaste held like a chord on my tongue; my mouth felt like a field of flowers. The mousse made me happy to be alive.

"My God, Lowenstein. This mousse is fabulous," I moaned. "I can feel battalions of calories marching toward my bloodstream. I'd like to get a job gaining weight in this restaurant."

"Savannah has repressed a great deal of her childhood, Tom," Dr. Lowenstein said.

"What does that have to do with duck mousse?" I answered.

"She has whole periods of her life she has blanked out. She calls them her white intervals. They seem to coincide with those times when her hallucinations are out of control. They seem to exist outside of time or space or reason."

"She's always had trouble remembering things," I said.

"She told me it had always been a problem with her when she was growing up, but an unmentionable one. Her terrible secret. She said she had always felt different, unsafe, and alone because of it. She became a prisoner of lost time, unremembered days. Lately, she was disturbed because her poetry was suffering. She felt that her madness was overtaking her, coming at her in overwhelming forces. The thing she feared most is that she would enter one of these periods in which there was no memory and never return to herself."

As she spoke, I watched Susan Lowenstein's face soften imperceptibly, a transformation caused by her passion for her profession. It was one of the few times I felt the zeal she carried into her office, the spirit she invoked in her role

as sojourner among wounded, disabused souls. Her voice
was animated as she recalled those first months when Savannah would come to her office to speak of her life, her
youth, her work, but always there were incredible blank
spots, diffusions of memory and impasses that brought her
again and again to frustration and dead ends. Something
was at work, deep in Savannah's subconscious, that was
censoring out her youth entirely. Whenever she turned to
her childhood, she could recall only disconnected fragments, all of them attached to a vague and debilitating sense
of terror. There were times that whenever she conjured up
a solitary image of that childhood—a marsh bird in languorous flight, the starting up of the shrimp boat's engine,
her mother's voice in the kitchen—she would enter into a
realm of darkness, into timelessness, into a life that was
not her own. It had been like this for two years and by an
effort of will she trained herself to concentrate only on her
life in New York. Her cycle of poems "Considering Manhattan" was completed in one feverish three-month period
when she felt her powers return, felt the old welcome weight
of the language and saw herself once more as the center of
the world, sending out love songs and requiems.

It was the writing of the children's book that had sent
her reeling back into the weightless harmonics of her madness. When the story had come to her in the nightmare,
she transcribed it in an eight-hour burst of unbroken cre-
ativity exactly as she had dreamed it. As she wrote it, she
realized she was describing one of these lost interludes in
her life. She could feel missing elements in the story and
they were far more powerful than the ones she had included. The three men struck a particularly mordant chord
in her and their approach to the house caused something
to sound in her, far off, like a bell of some deconsecrated
church ringing in the wind. She studied the story as though
it were a lost sacred text that held inscrutable allusions to
the mysteries of her own life. She read the story over and
over again, convinced it was a parable or outline for something with far graver implications. Something had happened to her, but for the story she wrote she could come
up with only one missing element: the statue of the Infant
of Prague her father had brought back from World War II
that sat on a table by the front door. She did not know the

role the statue had played in the story but she knew it should be there. After Renata killed herself that statue made a hideous appearance in those hallucinations which always came to her in periods of suffering. The Infant of Prague joined forces with the chorus of voices within her, linked up with the black dogs of suicide and the angels of negation. Again, these apparitions chanted the withering litany she had heard since childhood, taunting her with her worthlessness, regaling her with murderous hymns and chants, calling for her death. She began to see the dogs hanging on meat hooks from her apartment wall, their bodies twisted in agony. Hundreds of these crucified dogs screamed out, their voices sibilant and intertwined, for her to kill herself. "They're not real. They're not real," Savannah had repeated to herself, but her voice was drowned out in the demonic howling of the impaled accusatory dogs. She would rise up from her living room chair and walk into her bathroom to escape the gathering of dogs. There she found the menstruating angels hanging from the shower rod and the ceiling, with their necks broken, moaning with exquisite suffering. Their voices, delicate and soft, asked her to come home with them, to the safe place with long vistas, to the corridors of endless sleep, to the long night of silence, of voicelessness, where the angels were whole, immaculate, and kind. They lifted their arms toward her in a gesture of solidarity and possessiveness. Their eye sockets were black holes flowing with pus. Above them, she saw the small feet of the Infant of Prague, lynched from the ceiling, his face disfigured and bruised, speaking to her in her mother's voice, demanding that she maintain her silence. Whenever she took out her razor blades and began to count them, she could hear the pleasure of the dogs twisting on the hooks, the ecstasy of those disfigured angels with their fluted, encircling voices. Each night, she counted razor blades and listened to that sullied nation clamoring out the laws of storm, murmuring a compline of suicide.

"I only saw Savannah for a couple of months before her suicide attempt, Tom," Susan Lowenstein said. "I didn't fully realize the danger of her trying to hurt herself. The therapy was so exhilarating. A therapist should not feel that kind of exhilaration. You need to remain calm, aloof, and professional. But Savannah was a poet who spoke to me and dazzled me with words and images. I made a mistake, Tom. I wanted to be known as the therapist who made it possible for a poet to write again. I made a terrible blunder of arrogance."

"It wasn't arrogance, Susan," I said as my knife cut into the rabbit on my plate. "It just got too weird for you, just like it's gotten too weird for me."

"I don't understand."

"Let's take my experience," I said. "I hear about my sister cutting her wrists up here on happy Manhattan isle. I come dashing up here to play my ritual role of savior, twentieth-century Christ figure, a role I can play, by the way, in my sleep, marching in a band, or with my hands tied behind my back. Because it makes me feel needed. It makes me feel superior. The golden twin mounts his steed to ride to the rescue of his lovely sister, poet, crazy person, unsuccessful suicide."

"What if I'd told you on that first day that Savannah was thinking of simply disappearing from New York and going to a strange city to live out her life as Renata Halpern?" she asked.

"I'd have laughed my ass off," I admitted.

"Of course you would have," she said. "You made no secret of your contempt for therapy the first day we met."

"I grew up in a lucky town, Doc," I said. "We didn't even know what a psychiatrist was."

"Ah, yes," she said. "A very lucky town. From your description of Colleton, it sounds as though the whole town was suffering from some collective psychosis."

"Well, it no longer suffers from anything." I turned my attention to the rabbit before continuing. "You still haven't explained to me why Savannah can't tell you the same stories I have."

"I tried to tell you, Tom, but you were either not listening or you didn't believe the explanation. There are great blank spaces in her memory, vast areas of repression that sometimes span years at a time. It was Savannah who once told me that you could tell the stories. You've always told me about the strange closeness you and Savannah had as twins. I discounted it at first because I thought you were part of her problem. But you've led me to believe otherwise."

"Thanks."

"You served a valuable function for Savannah when you were growing up, Tom. You and Luke protected her from the world, and especially her world. Even though she was different from the very beginning, her brothers gave her the appearance of normality. You both led her way through a very difficult childhood. And you, Tom, performed a critical role. She began the process of blocking memories very early in her life; the process of subtracting out the killing memories. I would call it repression but I know how much it disturbs you when I resort to Freudian terminology. So she assigned you a job very early on. You became Savannah's memory, her window to the past. You could always tell her what had happened, where she had been, and what she had said when she surfaced from one of her dark periods."

"If she had no memory," I asked, "how could she have been a poet?"

"Because she has genius and her poetry comes from the pain of being human and the pain of surviving as a woman in our society."

"When do you think she first started relegating the duty of memory to me?"

"She remembers far more about your early childhood than you do, Tom. She remembers your mother's brutality when you were very small."

"Bullshit. Mom wasn't perfect, but she wasn't brutal either. She's mixing up Mom with Dad," I said, chewing slowly.

"How do you know?"

"Because I was there, Lowenstein," I snapped back. "An eyewitness, you might say."

"But did you notice when you began to tell me this chronicle that you started with your birth during the storm, an event you could not have remembered. You simply recited a family myth that had been recounted to you, which is perfectly natural, Tom. Then you skipped six years to your first year of school in Atlanta. What happened in those first six years?"

"We were babies. We puked, we shat, we drank mother's milk, we grew up. How am I supposed to remember all that?"

"Savannah remembers it. She remembers too much of it."

"All bullshit, Doc. Total bullshit," I said, but I could only come up with a single image for that time in my life, the moon rising in the east, called forth by my mother.

"It could be, but it certainly has the ring of truth to this old shrink."

"Don't talk shrink talk to me. Please, Lowenstein. You've got to let me out of this city with my utter loathing of your profession intact."

"Tom, your hatred of therapy is perfectly all right with me," she said coolly. "You've made that absolutely clear. This doesn't bother me at all anymore. In fact, I'm beginning to find you rather charming and stupid on the subject."

"Look, let's discuss this later," I said, gesturing around the room. "This is Lutèce, Susan. I've always wanted to eat in Lutèce. I've read about it. It's described as a gastronomic paradise in *The New York Times*. I like to sit in gastronomic paradises and moan over the food. This wine is the best-tasting liquid that has ever rolled around my mouth. The ambiance is wonderful. Understated elegance. Of course, I would prefer overstated elegance because my background is redneck and has not evolved enough socially to prefer the understated variety. But it's nice. It's real nice. Now when you eat at Lutèce for the first and last time in your life you want to talk about art, poetry, cuisine, maybe a little philosophy. It breaks the spell a bit when you start talking about Savannah seeing angels with pus dripping out of their eye sockets. Do you see what I mean? This is a gastronomic paradise and my nose hurts and I need time to absorb all this. See, until three hours ago I thought Savannah was just plain wacko Savannah. This is very, very hard to take in, Lowenstein. Look at it from my point of view. This morning you introduced me to my twin sister, whom I have known rather well for thirty-six years. Only we have a surprise for Tommy. This isn't really your sister, Tom, this is Renata Halpern. But wait, Tom, you southern dope, that's not all. She plans to move away and never see you for the rest of your life. So when I get a little miffed that I was kept in the dark for so long, her highly trained, consummately professional therapist bounces a dictionary off my sniffer and I lose a pint of blood. This meal is your act of contrition for shedding my precious blood and I now want to shift the conversation to reviewing the latest film or Book-of-the-Month Club alternate selection."

"Let's talk about her children's story," she suggested.

"Ah! The Rosetta stone. Savannah tried to write about evil, but she couldn't do it. She made it beautiful. She betrayed herself and her gift by making it lovely."

"It's fiction, Tom. It's a story."

"It shouldn't be fiction. It should have been written as cold fact. Savannah is good enough to write that story so it could shake up the whole world. It didn't deserve to be prettied up and read to kids at bedtime. It should have brought grown men and women to their knees, trembling with pity and rage. Savannah was not true to the integrity of the story. It's a crime to present that story as artful and ending happily. One should weep after reading that story. Tomorrow, I'll tell you that story. There won't be any chatty spiders or cute dogs or inarticulate calves stuttering out messages to the King of the Bulls or any of that horseshit."

"An artist isn't required to tell the truth, Tom."

"The hell she's not."

"You know what I mean. Artists tell the truth in their own way."

"Or they lie in their own way. And I promise you that Savannah is lying in that story."

"Maybe she told all the truth she could tell."

"Bullshit, good Doctor. I always knew she was going to write about it someday. My mother, I know, has lived in constant fear that Savannah was going to put it down on paper. But none of us has ever mentioned out loud what happened that day on the island. When I started reading her book, I thought she was going to get it out in the open at last. Then I saw the moment she lost her courage. It was when those children had a magic gift. We didn't have magic to protect us."

"Tom," Dr. Lowenstein said, "she told enough truth in her writing that it took her to the point of trying to kill herself."

"You're right," I said. "But will you tell her something for me? Tell her that if she decides to become Renata Halpern, I'll visit her in San Francisco, or Hong Kong, or anywhere she decides to live and never give anyone a clue that I'm her brother. I'll just be some friend from the South she met at a poetry reading or an art opening. The worst thing for me would be if she just disappeared. I couldn't stand that. I simply could not bear it, and no one understands why any better than Savannah. I want her to live. I want her to be happy. I can love her if I don't see her. I can love her no matter what she does."

"I'll tell her, Tom. And, Tom, I promise you this. If you keep helping me, I'm going to give you your sister back. She's working to save herself. She's working so hard."

Susan Lowenstein reached across the table and took my hand in hers. She put my hand to her lips and bit the flesh on the top of my hand and that is what I remember most from my meal at Lutèce.

21

The same night as the lunch at Lutèce I telephoned my mother's house in Charleston. It took only two shots of bourbon before I could dial the grisly combination of numbers that would call forth her voice from the present and send me spinning out of control into the past. On the phone it took my mother only a minute or two before she rallied her wits and got down to the serious business of ruining my life.

I had spent the rest of the afternoon reading case histories of various psychotics that Dr. Lowenstein had lent me. All were hurt, grieving souls, damaged hideously in their childhoods, who had created elaborate palisades to defend themselves against the unbearable infringements of their lives. Here was a marketplace of hallucinations and pain. All of them had been lucky enough to be born into the warm embrace of monstrous families. A spirit of wearying self-congratulation ennobled the text and commentaries of the reporting psychiatrists. The doctors all seemed to be wonderful, miracle-working shrinks who took those subdivided souls and made them all fit to plant Bermuda grass in the suburbs again. This was a literature of triumph and affirmation, an orgy of yea-saying that left me bilious. But I got the point Lowenstein was trying to make. No matter how shocking Savannah's condition appeared to me, there was reason to hope. If Savannah was lucky and Lowenstein was good and all the cards were placed on the table at last, my sister might walk away from this one and leave all the grim demonology of her life on the road behind her.

I took another shot of the bourbon as I heard the phone ring in Charleston.

"Hello," my mother said.

"Hi, Mom," I answered. "This is Tom."

"Oh, Tom, darling. How is Savannah?"

"Savannah's just fine, Mom. I think everything is going to be all right."

"I've just been reading that there have been some amazing breakthroughs in the treatment of mental illness. I've cut out some articles that I want you to be sure to give to Savannah's psychiatrist."

"I will, Mom."

"And I want you to stand over her and make sure she reads them thoroughly. Can I call Savannah yet?"

"I think maybe soon, Mom. I'm not sure."

"Well, what have you been doing up there all summer? I frankly think you're neglecting your wife and children."

"Yes, I'm sure you're right, Mom. But I'll be coming home soon . . . Mom, the reason that I'm calling is to tell you that I'm going to tell the shrink about what happened on the island that day."

"Nothing happened on *that* day," my mother said clearly, calmly. "We made a promise, Tom. And I expect you to live by that promise."

"It was a stupid promise, Mom. I know it's one of the things that's bothering Savannah and I think that it might help her and help her doctor if I tell everything. It will all be confidential. It's all past history."

"I don't want to hear you even mention it."

"Mom, I knew you'd try to make me feel bad about this. I didn't have to call and tell you this. I could have just told Dr. Lowenstein. But I think it might help all of us, you included, if we aired this."

"No," she screamed. "You cannot talk about it. It almost ruined our lives."

"It did ruin a part of our lives, Mom. I haven't even been able to say out loud what happened that day. Sallie doesn't know about it. Luke never spoke of it. Savannah doesn't even remember it. It's just sitting inside all of us, ugly and hideous, and it's about time to spit it out."

"I forbid you to do it."

"Mom, I am going to do it."

There was silence and I knew she was gathering her forces. "Tom," she said, and I heard the old, fretted menace creep into her voice and braced myself for the assault. "I hate to have to be the one to tell you this, son, but Sallie is having a rather indiscreet affair with another doctor at the hospital. It's the talk of Charleston."

"Mom, I know you loved being the one to tell me that, and I thank you for that delectable tidbit, but Sallie already told me about the affair. What can I tell you? We're a modern couple. We like hot tubs, Chinese food, foreign movies, and screwing strangers. That's Sallie's business, Mom. Not yours."

"And what you're about to reveal is my business," my mother said. "If you tell Savannah about it, Tom, then sooner or later she'll write about it."

"So that's what you're worried about."

"No," she said. "I'm worried that it will open horrible new wounds, Tom. I've forgotten all about it. I don't think about it at all. And you promised never to speak of that day again."

"It can't do any harm."

"It would do me a great deal of harm. I could lose everything I have. I could lose my husband if he found out. And if I were you, Tom, I'd have more pride. You'll have to tell what happened to you that day."

"I'll tell it, Mom. Well, I've enjoyed our little chat. How are the kids? Have you seen them recently?"

"They seem to be doing fine, as well as can be expected for three adorable children who've been abandoned by both their parents. Do you want me to talk to Sallie and tell her how repulsed I am by her behavior?"

"God, no, please don't, Mother. That would be the worst possible thing you could do. Just let the affair run its course. I haven't been a fabulous husband in the past couple of years."

"You're the spitting image of your father."

"I know, Mom, and the translation of that is I'm a worthless shit, but I would appreciate it greatly if you would say nothing to Sallie."

"Well, now," my mother said. "Maybe we can make a deal. I'll keep quiet down on this end if you'll keep quiet up on that end."

"Mom, I'm doing this to help Savannah. I know you don't believe that. I know you think I'm only doing it to hurt you, but it's not true."

"I don't know what to believe when it comes from my children. I've been hurt by my children so many times that I don't ever trust it when they're nice to me. I keep wondering what they're after and how they're going to betray me. If I had known how all of you were going to turn out, I would have murdered you in your sleep when you were babies."

"Considering our childhood, that sounds like an act of mercy," I said, feeling the blood rushing to my temples, trying to hold my tongue, failing . . . "Mom, this is getting out of hand. So let's stop it before we start really drawing blood. I only called because I felt I owed you a kind of explanation. It happened almost twenty years ago. It does not reflect on any of us. It was an act of God."

"The Devil, I would say, dear," she said. "Only I would advise you to go along as though it never happened. It would be much better for Savannah. You know how morbid she is. And I know it would be better for you and me."

"Where did you get that theory of yours, Mom?" I asked. "Where did you come up with the idea that if you simply pretended something didn't happen, then it lost its power over you."

"It's just common sense. If I were you, Tom, I wouldn't

dwell so much on the past. I would look to the future. That's what I'd do. I never look back. Do you know I've not thought of your father a single time in the last two years?"

"You were married to him for over thirty years, Mom," I said. "Surely he appears as Count Dracula in nightmares or something."

"Not a single time," she assured me. "When I say good-bye to something in my past, then I just shut the door and never think of it again."

"How about Luke, Mom?"

"What?" she said.

"Do you ever think about Luke?" I said again, regretting my words, and their unadorned cruelty, as soon as they left my mouth and made their way through the humming wires to Charleston.

"You're a mean man, Tom," my mother said, her voice breaking as she gently placed the receiver down.

I considered calling her back but there was too much undigested history scintillating between us. My recovery of my mother's good will would be an arduous process and would require a delicacy and tact I could not muster over the phone. It had been a long time since my mother and I had faced each other as friends; it had been years since she could utter a single word without my interpreting it as a cunning strategy to leave me helpless before one of her soft and perfumed assaults on the soul. There was an uneasy honor, even adoration, in my hatred of her. Because I failed to understand her, I would face all the women of the world as strangers and adversaries. Because I did not understand her fierce treacherous love for me, I would never be able to accept a woman's love without a sense of profound dread. Love would always come to me disguised in beauty, disfigured by softness. The world can do worse than make an enemy of your mother, but not much.

I dialed the telephone again. It rang four times and I heard Sallie answer at the other end.

"Hi, Sallie," I said. "It's Tom."

"Hello, Tom," she said in a sisterly tone. "We got your letter today and all the girls sat down at the kitchen table to write you."

"Wonderful. Sallie, my mother just threatened to call you

to express her high moral outrage. She found out about you and your doctor somehow."

"You didn't tell her, did you, Tom? Oh, Jesus Christ. That's all I need."

"No, of course not."

"Did you tell her it was just a vicious rumor and you were positive that my virtue was impeccable?"

"No," I said, "I wish I'd thought of that. I just acted like we were two aging swingers screwing like minks in the suburbs. I told her I knew all about it."

"How did she react?"

"She was in a kind of mild ecstasy that her son had been reduced to the status of a grinning cuckold. Then she threatened to call you and make moral judgments. I thought I'd better warn you. She claims everybody in Charleston knows about the affair."

Sallie said nothing.

"Have you come to any decisions, yet?" I asked, leaning my head back on my sister's favorite chair. "I mean, about us. About you. About him. About the end of the fucking world as I know it."

"Tom, quit it."

"Has he told his wife yet, Sallie?" I said. "That's the big moment—when he tells his wife."

"He's thinking of telling her next week."

"Then I should come home."

"I'm afraid that won't be convenient, Tom."

"Then you can move out of the house and into the Francis Marion Hotel. Look, Sallie, I want you to be there. I want you to be my wife. I want to woo you, fuck on the beach, on the kitchen table, on the tops of automobiles, hanging from the Cooper River Bridge. I'll tap dance, cover your whole body with whipped cream and lick it off slowly. I'll do anything you want. I promise. I've figured a lot of things out up here and one of them is that I love you and I'm going to fight to keep you."

"I don't know, Tom," she said.

"You don't know," I shouted.

"Tom, that sounds wonderful. But it would be nice if you could say it without all the cleverness and all the jokes. You know, I don't believe you've ever told me you loved me without making a joke out of it."

"That's not true, Sallie, and you know it. I have told you
I loved you at night with great sheepishness and embarrassment. I've done it any number of times."

"Jack tells me that all the time, Tom. He's never sheepish
and he's never embarrassed. He says it simply and sweetly
and sincerely."

"It's so difficult to talk over the phone. Give all the girls
a hug for me."

"Call early tomorrow so they can speak to you."

"I will. Take care of yourself, Sallie. Please take your time
about this. Think about it hard."

"I rarely think of anything else, Tom."

"Goodbye, Sallie."

When I hung up the phone I said, "I love you, Sallie."
I said it simply and sweetly and sincerely into the darkness
of that empty room, without all the cleverness, without the
jokes.

22

On graduation night, my mother presented two large
boxes to Luke and me as we were dressing for the
ceremony. She gave Savannah a small gift elegantly wrapped.

"If I were rich, there'd be three Cadillacs parked out on
the lawn," my mother said, and her voice was teary and
nostalgic. "And I'd just hand over the three keys."

"Speaking of being rich, I had a brilliant idea the other
day . . ." my father said, but was cut dead by a withering
glance from my mother.

Savannah opened her gift first and drew out a gold-plated
fountain pen, which she held up to the light.

"That's to write your first book with. In New York City,"
my mother said.

Savannah hugged my mother fiercely and said, "Thanks so much, Mama. It's beautiful."

"It was way too expensive. But I got it on sale. I figured you'd have to write prettier poems if you used a prettier pen."

"I'll write beautiful poems with it, Mama. I promise," said Savannah.

"Write one about the Big Dad," my father said. "A really great poem requires a really great subject. Like me."

"What a silly idea, Henry," my mother said.

"I'm sure I'll write lots of poems about you," Savannah said, smiling at us.

"Open your presents," my mother commanded Luke and me.

Together, Luke and I unwrapped our gifts. I opened mine first and saw the navy blue sport coat my mother had made. Luke pulled an identical though much larger sport coat from his box. We tried them on and they fit perfectly. For months, my mother had sat by her sewing machine while we were at school, preparing for this moment. I walked to my mother's room and looked at myself in her full-length mirror. For the first time in my life, I appeared handsome to myself.

She drifted up behind me, surreal, quiet as a movement of clouds, and whispered, "I told you once that you'd always remember your first sport coat."

"How do I look?"

"If I was young enough, I'd have a go at you myself," she said.

"Mama," I said, blushing, "don't talk dirty."

"I'm just speaking the truth. You're better looking than your father ever was on the best day of his life."

"I heard that," my father cried out from the living room. "And it's a goddamn lie."

The graduation was held in the gymnasium and the seniors filed through the front entry two by two to the sound of "Pomp and Circumstance." When Savannah's name was announced as the valedictorian, my mother, grandfather, and grandmother rose to their feet and cheered loudly as Savannah walked to the podium to deliver her valedictory address. My father stood near the podium and filmed her entire speech for posterity. She began her speech with the line, "We were raised by the music of rivers, artless and unself-conscious, and we have spent our childhood days beside these waters, seduced by the charms of the loveliest town in the Carolina lowcountry." Her speech was impressionistic and burned with a series of indelible images common to us all. It was the poet going public for the first time, cocky with the majesty of words that she used like a peacock fanning his gorgeous tail feathers for the sheer joy of ostentation. Savannah had a genius for the final act and. the farewell gesture. She bid adieu to the world we were leaving behind and she did it in Savannah's way: inimitably, memorially.

The superintendent of schools, Morgan Randel, handed out our diplomas one by one and wished us luck in the world. There was modest applause from the sweating crowd for each of us, but a murmur began moving through the bleachers as Benji Washington walked toward Mr. Randel to receive his diploma. The senior class did not murmur but rose collectively to its feet and gave Benji a standing ovation as he solemnly took his diploma and, with that same unbearably lonely dignity, crossed the stage and returned to his seat. He was surprised and embarrassed by the fuss and I turned and saw his mother pressing her face against her husband's shoulder in heartfelt relief that her son's long ordeal was over. It is history we are applauding, I thought, as I cheered for Benji Washington, history and change and a courage so superhuman that I would never see its like again, never feel its flame burning so brightly in subjugation to an ideal. The applause rose as he neared his seat and I thought about how many Benji Washingtons there were tonight in the South, black sons and daughters of lordly image, who have tested their resources in the bitter milieus of white kids trained from birth to love Jesus and to hate niggers with all their hearts.

To music again we marched out into the June heat. I was sweating profusely because I had insisted on wearing my new sport coat beneath my graduation gown.

It is midnight after graduation and we are sitting on the wooden bridge that connects our island and our lives to the continental United States. The moon quivers on the water of an in-breathing tide, a pale disc nickling in the current. Above us, the stars are in the middle of their perfect transit through the night and constellations are reborn in the luminous mirror of tides below us. On either side of us, the marsh accepts the approach of the tides with a vegetable pleasure, an old smell of lust and renewal. In the lowcountry, the smell of the marshlands is offensive to visitors, but is the fragrant essence of the planet to the native born. Our nostrils quiver with the incense of home, the keen pastille of our mother country. Palmettos close ranks at the head of each peninsula and the creek divides into smaller creeks like a vein flowering into capillaries. A stingray swims just below the surface like a bird in night-mare. The wind lifts off the island, a messenger bearing the odor of moonsage and honeysuckle and jasmine. In an instant the smell of the night changes, recedes, deepens, then recedes again. It is sharp as vinaigrette, singular as bay rum.

Savannah sits in the middle of her two brothers, lovely in the economy of her fragile lines. My arm is around my sister's shoulders and I hold Luke's massive neck in my hand, just barely. Luke takes a drink of Wild Turkey and passes it down the line to us. Luke has bought the bourbon not because it is expensive but because he associates it with hunting turkeys on cold winter mornings.

"It's over now," Savannah said. "What did it all mean?"

"It was just something we had to go through before they let us go," Luke suggested.

Softened by the bourbon, I said, "It wasn't that bad. I bet we look back on this as the best time of our lives."

"It was dreadful," said Savannah.

"Oh, c'mon. Look at the bright side. You always dwell on the bad stuff," I said, passing the bottle to Savannah. "A sky can be perfectly blue and you start yelling about a hurricane."

"I'm a realist," she said, elbowing me in the stomach. "And you're just a poor, dumb jock. You're the only person I know who actually enjoyed high school."

"I guess that makes me a terrible person, right?" I answered.

"I'll never trust anyone who liked high school," Savannah continued, ignoring me. "I'll never trust anyone who looks like they even tolerated high school. I'll refuse to even talk to anyone who looks like they played high school football."

"I played high school football," I said, hurt by her sweeping dismissal.

"I rest my case," she said, throwing her head back and laughing.

"I don't understand your hatred of high school, Savannah," I said. "You did so well. You were valedictorian, cheerleader, secretary of the senior class, and you were voted best personality."

"Best personality!" she screamed out toward the marsh, high on the bourbon. "I sure had a lot of competition for that title. I was one of the few people in that high school with any personality at all."

"I have a wonderful personality," I said.

"You throw touchdown passes," Savannah said. "You don't light up the world with personality."

"Yeah, Tom," Luke teased, "you don't have personality for shit."

"Who is that big hulk sitting on your left, Savannah?" I said, squeezing Luke's neck. "He's too big to be a human being and too dumb to be a hippopotamus. Now tell me that wasn't a terrific line. Tell me that we're not dealing with a world-class personality."

"I'd like to be a hippopotamus," Luke said. "Just sitting down there on the bottom of rivers, kicking ass on occasion."

"Why don't you try to find out who you are in college, Tom?" she asked. "Why don't you take some time to find out who inhabits that soul beneath the shoulder pads."

"I know exactly who I am. I'm Tom Wingo, southern born and southern made, and I'm an ordinary guy who's going to live an ordinary life. I'm going to marry an ordinary woman and have ordinary kids. Even though I am related to this goofball family and have a brother who wouldn't mind being a hippo."

"You're so shallow you're going to marry the first girl with big tits who comes along," she said.

"Sounds good to me," Luke said, taking a swallow of the bourbon.

"What about you, Luke?" said Savannah. "What's in it for you?"

"In what?"

"In life," said Savannah. "This is our graduation night and we're required to talk about our future and make plans and plot out our destinies."

"I'm going to be a shrimp boat captain like Dad," Luke said. "Dad's going to the bank at the end of the summer and help me finance my own shrimp boat."

"He's got a great credit rating at the bank," I said. "I bet they wouldn't let him finance a cast net and a cane pole."

"He needs to clean up some debts before we go to the bank."

"You could be more, Luke," said Savannah. "You could be so much more. You listened to them and believed everything they said about you."

"Why don't you call up the coaches at Clemson or Carolina and tell them you've decided to play football for them, Luke," I said. "Those guys would cream in their Fruit of the Looms if you'd play ball."

"You know I can't get passing grades in college," Luke said to us. "I wouldn't have passed in high school if you two hadn't cheated for me. I don't need college to remind me that I'm stupid."

"You're not stupid, Luke," she said. "That's the lie they fed you and the one you swallowed whole."

"I appreciate your saying that, Savannah. But let's face it. God forgot to pack the brains along with the muscle. I finished second from the bottom in our class academically. Only Viryn Grant finished lower than me."

"I was working in the guidance department at the end of the year, helping Mr. Lopatka record grades in our permanent records and when he went out to lunch I found out what all of our IQs are," Savannah said.

"No kidding," I said. "That's top-secret information."

"Well, I saw them. And it was real interesting. Especially about Luke. Do you know that you have a higher IQ than Tom, Luke?"

"What?" I said, highly offended.

"Whoopee," Luke screamed, flushing a marsh hen from

its nest in the high grasses. "Pass the bourbon to Tom. This is going to ruin his whole graduation."

"Why should it ruin his graduation?" Savannah asked. "Everyone knows an IQ doesn't mean anything."

"What was yours, Savannah?" I asked.

"Mine was one forty, which puts me up there with the geniuses," she said. "I assume this comes as no surprise to my worshipful brother."

"What was mine?" Luke asked, and I could not bear the triumph in his voice.

"Yours was one nineteen, Luke. Tom scored one fifteen."

"I'm your twin," I shouted. "I'm your goddamn twin. I demand a recount."

"I always thought Tom was a little slow," Luke said, grinning.

"Kiss my fat fanny, Luke," I said, infuriated and worried. "I thought twins automatically had the same IQs."

"Not even identical twins have the same IQ, Tom," said Savannah, enjoying herself. "But you really got the short end of the stick."

"Imagine that. I'm smarter than you, Tom," Luke said. "I'll drink to that."

"But I use what I've got a lot better," I said.

"Yeah, you sure do, little brother. You've done right well with that shabby little IQ of yours," Luke replied, and he and Savannah fell back on the bridge, laughing.

"Well, I've decided to be a football coach," I said, reaching for the bourbon, "so I don't need to have a world-class brain."

"You won't need a brain at all," Savannah said. "What a waste, Tom."

"Why do you say that?"

"I'd like to take a team of assassins and kill all the coaches in the world. We'd go around and torture every male and female above the age of twenty-one we found wearing a sweat shirt and a whistle."

"How would you torture them?" asked Luke.

"First, I'd make them listen to classical music. Then I'd make them take ballet lessons for a week. Let's see, then I'd make them read the collected works of Jane Austen. I'd top it all off by giving them a sex change operation without anesthesia."

"Such violence, Savannah," I said. "What strange little thoughts roll around in your pretty head."

"If Tom wants to be a coach, let him be a coach," Luke intervened. "Why can't he be what he wants to be?"

"Because he could be a lot more," Savannah insisted, turning toward me. "He's selling himself out to the South for cheap. I'm sorry, Tom. You're a victim of the Southern Disease, boy, and there ain't no known vaccine to save your ass."

"I guess you're going to be hot shit in New York Goddamn City," I said.

"I'm going to be amazing," she said simply.

"Mom still wants you to take that scholarship from Converse College," Luke said. "I heard her talking to Tolitha the other day."

"I'd rather die than stay in South Carolina a day longer than I have to. Do you know what Mama has in store for me? She wants me to marry some lawyer or doctor that I meet in college, then settle down in some teensy South Carolina town and plop out four or five children. If they're boys, she'll expect me to raise them up to be doctors or lawyers. If they're girls, she'll expect me to raise them up to marry doctors or lawyers. Even her dreams smell like death to me. But I'm not buying the program. I'm going to be whatever I want to be. In Colleton, everyone expects you to be a certain way and the whole town makes sure that no one deviates very far from that central idea. The girls are all pretty and perky and the boys all kick ass. No, I'm sick of hiding what I really am, what I feel inside. I'm going to New York where I don't have to be afraid to find out everything there is to know about myself."

"What are you afraid of?" Luke asked as a night heron, shy as a moth, took wing over the marsh.

"I'm afraid if I stay here, I'll end up like Mr. Fruit. Crazy or feeble-minded, begging for sandwiches at the back doors of restaurants and bars. I want to be in a place where if I go crazy for a while it will pass unnoticed. This town has driven me nuts by the sheer effort it's taken to pretend I'm just like everyone else. I've always known I was different. I was born in the South yet I've never been southern a single day in my life. This thing has almost killed me, Tom and Luke. I've been sick, crazy-sick since I was a little girl.

I see things. I hear voices. I have terrible nightmares. Whenever I told Mama about it she said, 'Take two aspirins and don't have any dessert after dinner.' It's been a terrible strain to get this far."

"Why didn't you tell us?" Luke asked.

"What could you have done about it?" she answered.

"We'd have told you to take three aspirins and to skip dessert after dinner," I said.

"Do you know what I see in the water below us?" she said, staring down into the moonlit tide. "There are hundreds of drowned dogs with their eyes open, staring at me."

I looked down into the water and saw only water.

"Yep. Maybe you should move to New York City," I said.

"Shut up, Tom," Luke said, looking at Savannah protectively. "There aren't any dogs down there, poopy-doop. That's just your mind playing tricks on you."

"Sometimes I see the Infant of Prague. You know, that statue Dad brought back from Germany. The infant has pus flowing from his eyeballs and he gestures for me to follow him. Sometimes Mom and Dad are hanging naked from meat hooks, snarling at each other, snapping at each other with fangs and barking like dogs."

"It's hell having a one-forty IQ, isn't it, Savannah," I said.

"Shut up, Tom," Luke said again, more firmly, and I shut up.

Silence fell upon the three of us—an awkward, uncomfortable silence.

"Jesus Christ. This is weird. Pass the bourbon, Luke. I suggest you drink half of it when it passes by you, Savannah. In fact, if I heard those voices and saw all those things, I'd just stay drunk. You know, wake up in the morning and take a nip. Then, just keep nipping until you pass out at night."

"Why don't you become a doctor instead of a coach, Tom?" Luke said. "Our sister's in trouble and is trying to tell us something important and you just sit there and make jokes. We got to try to help her, not laugh at her."

"There's nothing you can do, Luke," she said. "I've lived with it alone for a long time. I tried to get Mama to take me to a psychiatrist in Charleston but she found out they charge forty dollars an hour."

"Forty dollars an hour," I said, whistling. "They'd have to give me a handjob and a box of cigars to be worth forty big ones an hour. Hell, maybe I'll be a psychiatrist. Let's say I work ten hours a day, six days a week. I'll work fifty weeks a year helping people who see their mamas hanging from meat hooks. I'll be pulling down, my God, a hundred twenty thousand dollars a year before taxes. I didn't know you could get rich helping out fruitcakes."

"You're drunk, Tom," Luke said. "I done told you to zipper your lips or I'll throw you in the creek to sober you up."

"You think you could throw me in this creek?" I said, laughing and out of control. "You're talking to *much* man. *Much* man. You're talking to a goddamn college football player now, Luke. Not one of those high school jocks with fuzz on their cheeks."

"Excuse me, poopy-doop," Luke said, pinching Savannah on the cheek. "I've got to teach my baby brother to have respect for his elders."

"Don't hurt him, Luke. He just can't hold his liquor."

"Can't hold my liquor?" I screamed, having a grand time and taking another swig from the bottle. "I can drink any man in this county under the table. Now you sit down, Luke. I don't want to embarrass you in front of the womenfolk."

Luke rose up off the dock and I lifted up unsteadily to meet him. I had that aura of alcoholic invincibility around me but I wove unsteadily as I moved forward to challenge him. Lunging, I tried to get him in a headlock and got a clear glimpse of the Big Dipper as Luke picked me up and threw me somersaulting into the creek. I came up choking and spitting water and heard Savannah's laughter echoing across the marsh.

"You college football players are hell," Luke said to me as I fought the tide and swam back to the bridge.

"You better not have ruined my new sport coat, Luke, or we're going to have a fistfight every day this summer."

"You shouldn't be wearing the sport coat in this heat," Luke said as he jumped into the creek with me. We wrestled in the water and he dunked me several times before I cried uncle.

Pat Conroy

"C'mon, Savannah," Luke called out. "Take off your shoes and let's swim back to the house like we used to do when we were kids."

I removed my shoes and pants and sport coat and passed them up to Savannah. She took off her cotton dress and stood in her panties and bra above us, statuesque and beautiful in the moonlight.

She lifted the bottle of bourbon high in the air and shouted, "Let's make final toasts to our future. First, I'll toast Tom. What do you want out of life, quarterback?"

Floating on my back, I looked up into my sister's moon-struck face and said, "I'm going to be a good ordinary citizen."

"Then let's drink to ordinariness," she said and took a swallow. "And now, Luke, let's toast you."

"I'm a shrimper. I'm going to be steady."

"To steadiness. A toast," she said.

"What about you, New York?" I asked. "Let us give you a toast."

"I plan to write poetry and go wild. I plan to be not only wild but positively sinful. I'm going to get naked and march in parades down Fifth Avenue. I'm going to have affairs with men, women, and animals. I'll buy a parrot and teach it to cuss. Like Dad, I'm going to get it all on film and send it back as home movies."

"Hand me down the bottle," Luke said, swimming toward the bridge. He took the bottle from Savannah and took a drink as he drifted with the tide toward me. "To wildness," he said, drinking, and handed the bottle to me, holding it aloft above the water.

"To Savannah Wingo," I screamed. "The wildest goddamn woman ever to pass through the Holland Tunnel."

"Goodbye, Colleton," she screamed out toward the Atlantic. "Goodbye, South. Goodbye, football. Goodbye, rednecks. Goodbye, Mama. Goodbye, Daddy. And hello, Big Apple."

As I finished the bottle, Savannah executed a perfect front-flip and entered the water with barely a ripple.

And we let the soft tides carry us home.

It was the best summer I would ever have on the island and I prepared myself slowly for the leave-taking. To my surprise, I discovered I did not know how to live without my family gathered around me. Only a few times in my life had I slept away from the sounds of my family sleeping. I was not quite ready to abandon the only life I have ever known or was meant to know up to this time. There was no corrective for growing up and the terror of departure was upon me, insinuating itself in the very rhythms of my tenuous gestures of farewell. I was trying to form the secret words that my heart was screaming out with an inarticulate and soundless passion. An eighteen-year banquet of light and grief was coming to an end and I couldn't stand it and I couldn't tell them what I felt. A family is one of nature's solubles; it dissolves in time like salt in rainwater. It is summer again and silence and heat are the contending kings along the riverbanks. In the paper we read that fire ants have crossed the Savannah River and have established a colony in South Carolina. Near Kiawah Island, Luke hooked and captured his first tarpon after an hour-long fight. The great fish leapt and danced across the waves, powerful as a horse. When we finally got the tarpon into the boat, Luke kissed the fish, then released it in a gesture of both awe and gratitude. Savannah spent the summer painting watercolors and writing poems in imitation of Dylan Thomas. The days ended soundlessly and fireflies disturbed the dusk with their codes of errant light.

I tried to marshal the fragments of wisdom I had learned as an island child and put them in order like some undiscovered archipelago I could return to at will. I counted the dilatory passing of days as though they were beads on a rosary dissolving in my hands. I woke up early each morning and saw my father leave for the shrimp boat. At night, the fireflies floated through the darkness in a shifting accidental zodiac. Tense and self-conscious, we were gentle with each other in the green summering of June.

In my mother's eyes we interpreted a dark text that we translated as a fear of middle age, a loss of purpose in her life. She did not know how to face a world without being a mother. With our new freedom, she lost her sense of definition. We were uneasy about leaving her to face a life with my father alone. She was angry with us and took our growing up as an act of betrayal beyond all powers of forgiveness. Not once that summer would she let us work with our father on the shrimp boat. She demanded that we be full-time children for a last memorial summer. She was thirty-seven years old as her life as a mother was ending and she could not stand the thought of presiding over a house robbed of her children's laughter and tears. We spent almost all of our time with her as the shrimp filled up the creeks again and the cattle egrets, like pillars of fresh salt, formed small colonnades in the fields in the center of the island. Everything was as it had always been, but it was about to change, horribly, irrevocably. We were coming to the moment when all the liturgies of habit would disassemble in a singular, life-transfiguring encounter.

On July nineteenth, my mother celebrated her thirty-seventh birthday, and we gave her a party. Savannah made her a chocolate cake and Luke and I took the boat into town and bought her the largest bottle of Chanel No. 5 that Sarah Poston sold in her dress shop. Mrs. Poston assured us that only women who were "très élégante" wore Chanel. Even though her salesmanship was much better than her French, we bought the perfume and watched as she wrapped the gift in pale lavender paper.

On the night of her birthday, my mother had to blow three times to extinguish all the candles, and as her family teased her, she worried that she was coming down with a hideous lung disease caused by her advancing age. In the gold light of candles, my mother's face glowed with uncommon beauty. When she smiled at me, I felt cleansed in the secret grotto of her highest affection. She kissed me that night and I smelled the Chanel sweetening a small vein in her neck. As she held me, I wanted to cry out with all the wildness and tenderness a boy brought to the task of loving his mother. I wanted to tell her that I understood everything and that I held nothing against either her or my father for our life on the island. But I remained silent, my head against her shoulder, smelling the sweetness of her hair.

That night Luke surprised us all by breaking down while listening to Savannah and me talk about leaving the island at the end of August. Like my mother, he refused to acknowledge that our lives would be different and that our childhood was now unrecallable, a piece of music lost on the continuum of time, ineffable and wordless. Luke trem-

bled when he wept, a soft adagio of suffering, but his sorrow was suffused with strength. With Luke in tears, you
could learn something of the melancholy of kings, the sol-
emnity of a scarred lion banished from a pride. I longed to
hold my brother and feel his face against mine. But I could
not. It was Savannah who took Luke into her arms and
swore to him that nothing would change. Luke belonged
to the island. Savannah and I were simply born on Melrose
Island; we were never a part of it in any vital and essential
way. At least, that was the myth that sustained us, that
nourished our glad dream of voyage beyond the confine-
ments and eclipses of family.

"What's all the boo-hooing about?" my father asked.

"Luke's just sad that we're leaving him," Savannah explained.

"For godsakes, get control of yourself, son," my father
said. "You're a shrimper now, Luke. Shrimpers aren't the
boo-hooing type."

"Quiet, Henry," my mother said, "and leave the boy
alone."

"I sure did raise a sensitive family," my father, isolated
again, answered. "Nothing I hate worse than a sensitive
family."

That night we lay on our backs on the floating dock and
felt the whole river fill up with the grandeur of completion
as it neared the headwaters of the sea. In the scant light of
a new moon, we could see every star that God meant the
naked human eye to see in our part of the world. The Milky
Way was a white river of light above me and I could lift
my hand in front of my face and annihilate half of that river
of stars with the palm of my hand. The tide was dropping
and the fiddler crabs had arisen from their mud caverns
and the males waved their large audacious claws in eerie
harmony. They moved their claws in synchronization with
the tides and stars and winds. They signaled with their
ivory arms that the world was as it was always meant to
be. Thousands of them gestured to God that the tides had
fallen, that the Pegasi shone with the proper magnitude,
that the porpoises were singing of the hunt in the racing
waters, that the moon had been faithful to its covenant.
This movement was a dance, a trust, a ceremony of divine
affirmation. Like a fiddler crab, I lifted my arm and waved

to the militant striding Orion who was walking his unhurried gait in full battle array. His belt was millions of miles
away from my eyes yet seemed closer than the lights of my
house.

On August third I slept again on the dock as a wind rose
in the southeast. By midday the tide was full and when it
turned, the winds kept the tides from receding and a titanic
struggle ensued. The wind wreaked havoc among the orchards and the rows of beans. After lunch, Luke invited
Savannah and me to accompany him to the south end of
the island, where he planned to spend the afternoon fertilizing the pecan grove that had not borne fruit for two
years. I told my brother cheerfully that I did not care if the
pecan trees of Melrose Island did not produce a single nut
in the next fifty years, that I did not intend to walk about
the island in such peculiar weather. Savannah and I stayed
behind with our mother as Luke left the house and walked
the back road through the swamp, the wind at his back.

We listened to a radio station from Georgia and the three
of us sang along in a vain attempt to harmonize whenever
they played a song we favored. My mother's favorite song
of the summer came on and we sang the words loudly,
each of us pretending to croon into invisible microphones
for the pleasure of rapturous crowds. When the song ended,
we applauded each other and took turns bowing deeply at
the waist and throwing kisses to our exalted fans.

We talked to each other as the news interrupted our
recital. The national news shifted indistinguishably into the
local news. The Georgia governor had asked the federal
government for funds to prevent further erosion on Tybee
Beach, and three men had escaped from Reidsville Prison
in central Georgia. They were believed to be armed and
dangerous and heading for Florida. They had killed a guard
at the prison farm during their escape. The Savannah Historical Society had issued a protest over the granting of a
permit to a developer for the building of a hotel in the
historic district. A man was arrested for selling liquor to a
minor in a bar on River Street. My mother's happy voice
and the news of that hour coalesced.

The rain began as the weather forecaster announced that
there was a forty percent chance of rain in the Savannah
area that afternoon.

When the news ended, the sound of the Shirelles came over the radio and my mother squealed and began dancing the Carolina shag with Savannah. Like most high school athletes of my generation, I learned to dive off tackle long before I learned to dance, and I watched their sensuous movements with a feeling of both exhilaration and shame. Some innate shyness had kept me from asking either my sister or my mother to teach me to dance. It embarrassed me to even think of holding their hands. My mother was leading and she spun Savannah around the living room with grace and authority.

What we did not know was that our house was being watched. In happy innocence, my mother danced with my sister as I sang along with the Shirelles and clapped my hands in rhythm to the music. There was thunder over the river but ours was a house of music and dancing and the soft drumming of rain on the roof. We were about to learn that fear is a dark art that requires a perfect teacher. In blood, we were about to sign our names in the indifferent pages of the book of hours. Our perfect teachers had come. But it all began with music.

There was a knock at the front door and we glanced at one another because we had not heard a car approach the house. I shrugged my shoulders and went to answer the door.

I opened the door and felt the cold steel of the gun against my temple. I looked up at the man. He was beardless but I knew his face well. Through the window of time I remembered the cruelty and magnetism of those pale eyes.

"Callanwolde," I said, and I heard my mother scream behind me.

The two other men burst through the back door and again the radio mentioned the three armed men who had escaped from Reidsville Prison and who were believed heading toward Florida. Their names were given. Otis Miller, the one we once called Callanwolde. Floyd Merlin. Randy Thompson. I was overwhelmed by impotence, by fear, by a cowardice so profound that I sank to my knees and cried out in a wordless immolated howl.

"I never forgot you, Lila," the giant said. "All those years in prison and you were the one I remembered. I kept this to remind me of you."

He held up the soiled fragments of the letter my mother had written in Atlanta to my grandfather during the Korean War, the one that had never been delivered to the island.

The fat man had Savannah by the throat and was forcing her toward her bedroom door. Savannah was fighting him and screaming, but he grabbed her roughly by the hair and forced her through the door.

"It's about time we enjoyed ourselves," he said, winking to the others as he slammed the door shut.

"The woman's mine," said Callanwolde, staring at my mother with a primitive hunger so concupiscent that it seemed to poison the air in the room.

"Tom," my mother said, "please help me."

"I can't, Mama," I whispered, but I made a sudden lunge for the gun rack against the far wall.

Callanwolde intercepted me and slapped me to the floor, and as he walked toward my mother with his pistol aimed at her face, he said words I did not understand. "The boy is yours, Randy. He looks pretty good to me."

"Raw meat," Randy said, moving toward me. "Nothing I like better than raw fresh meat."

"Tom," my mother said again, "you've got to help me."

"I can't, Mama," I said, closing my eyes as Randy put a knife to my jugular and Callanwolde shoved my mother through the door and threw her down on the bed where I was conceived.

Randy cut my shirt off from behind and told me to loosen my belt. Not knowing what he wanted, I undid my belt and my pants fell to the floor. I was from rural South Carolina. I did not know a boy could be raped. But my teacher had come to my house.

"Nice. Real nice. What's your name, pretty boy? Tell Randy your name." And he tightened the blade against my throat as I listened to the screams of my mother and sister echo through the house. His breath smelled acrid and metallic. I felt his lips press against the back of my neck. He sucked on my neck and I felt his free hand stroke my genitalia.

"Tell me your name, pretty boy, before I cut your fucking pretty throat," he whispered.

"Tom," I said in a voice I did not recognize.

"You ever had a man before, Tommy?" Randy said, and I heard Savannah weeping in the bedroom. "No, of course not, Tommy. I'll be your first, Tommy. I'll fuck you nice, Tommy, before I cut your throat."

"Please," I said as he grabbed my larynx with his left hand and squeezed so hard I thought I would lose consciousness. I felt the blade along my waist as he cut through my underwear. Then he took my hair and forced me to my knees. I did not know what he was doing until I felt his cock against my ass.

"No," I begged.

He pulled my hair back hard and drew blood on my ass with the pressure of his knife and whispered, "I'll fuck you while you're bleeding to death, Tommy. It don't make no difference to me."

When he entered me I tried to scream but could not. I could give no voice nor utterance to such degradation, to such profuse shame. His cock was enormous and he damaged me as he forced his way inside. I felt a fluid running down my thigh and thought he had come, but it was my own blood running down my thighs. He writhed and forced it deeper inside me as I listened to my mother and sister calling out my name, begging for my intercession.

"Tom, Tom," Savannah cried out in an exhausted voice. "He's hurting me, Tom."

My eyes filled up with tears as he began to ride me hard and whispered, "Tell me you love it, Tommy. Tell me how much you love it."

"No," I whispered.

"Then I'll cut your throat now, Tommy. I'll come inside your asshole while you're bleeding to death. Tell me you love it, Tommy."

"I love it."

"Say it pretty, Tommy."

"I love it," I said prettily.

My humiliation and powerlessness now complete, I felt a quiet shift in my bloodstream as the man groaned and thrust deep inside me. He did not take notice of that subtle moment when a murderous rage shivered through me. I looked up and tried to clear my head of terror. My eyes went around the room and came to rest on the beveled mirror above the mantelpiece. Framed in that mirror, I saw

my brother Luke's face watching from the south windows.
I shook my head and mouthed the word "no." I knew that
all the rifles were in the house and that our best chance lay
in Luke's running for help. When I looked again, Luke was
no longer there.

"Talk to me, Tommy," Randy whispered again. "Talk
me some honey, sweetheart."

Then I heard it through the wind. I recognized the sound
from somewhere out of the past but could not name it
correctly. It was like the cry of a rabbit being lifted from a
field, impaled by a hawk's talons. The wind was blowing
furiously through the trees and the branches beat against
the roof of the house. Again I heard the sound and again
I could neither place it nor say where it was coming from.
Could they hear it? I wondered. I moaned loudly, covering
the sound.

"I like it when you moan, Tommy," Randy Thompson
said. "I like that so much."

"Please. Please," I heard my mother cry out, and I heard
the sound outside in the rain again and this time I knew
it. It was the sound of a wheel turning against an ungreased
axle. It was a sound of late summer during those heady
brawling days when Luke and I began our inexorable preparation for our last football season. It was the sound of the
early August regimen when Luke and I had put on our
pads and cleats and begun the very personal process of
hardening our bodies for the games of September. He and
I would take positions behind the tiger's cage and together
we would push the cage up and down the road until we
dropped from exhaustion. In this seizure of harsh conditioning we pushed ourselves to the outer limits of all human
endurance to make ourselves stronger than all those other
fierce boys who would come charging toward us across the
contested lines of scrimmage. Daily, we hurt ourselves in
our uncompromising effort to hone our bodies with a cruel
discipline of our own invention. We drove that cage up and
down that road until we could not stand without our knees
buckling under our own weight. In the first week, we could
push the tiger's cage only a few yards at a time. By the
time practice began, we could drive it for a quarter of a mile
until we fell in the road, dizzy in the August heat.

Now I could hear Luke's struggle as he pushed the cage

toward the house alone, the wheels digging deep into the wet earth, his movements betrayed by the creaking of the axle of the left wheel.

I cried aloud when the man came inside me, mingling his semen with my blood.

As he rose off me, the knife pressing tighter against my throat, he said, "Now, how do you want to die, Tommy? Which are you more afraid of? The knife or the gun?"

He backed me up against the wall and put his pistol against my head as he held the blade against my groin.

He lifted the blade against my balls and said, "The knife, eh, Tommy? I thought so. I'm gonna cut 'em off, Tommy, and hand them to you. What do you think about that, Tommy? I'm gonna slice you apart a little bit at a time. I just fucked you in the ass, Tommy. I own you now. They're gonna find you with my come up your asshole, Tommy."

I closed my eyes and my arms stretched out wide and his face was almost against mine; as he kissed me and I felt his tongue roll around in my mouth, my right hand came to rest on a piece of cool marble. His eyes remained open as he kissed me, but slowly my fingers wrapped around the neck of the statue of the Infant of Prague my father had stolen from Father Kraus's church in Germany after the war.

Savannah and my mother were crying in their bedrooms.

I heard my mother scream again. "Tom," she cried, and her voice broke my heart.

I heard the wheel move again and then I heard a slight thump against the back door.

Then there was a loud knock at the back door, as though a neighbor had come calling.

"Don't move, Tommy. Don't say a word or you're a dead boy," Randy Thompson whispered to me.

Callanwolde sprinted out of my mother's room, zipping up his pants. My mother was lying naked on her bed, her arm covering her eyes. Callanwolde was joined by my sister's rapist, who came out in his underwear, his fading erection outlined against his briefs. Both of them took positions around the room and pointed their guns toward the door.

"Run, Luke, run," my mother screamed from the bedroom.

Callanwolde opened the door quickly and I saw the cage door slide open.

The man who had just raped and sodomized my mother stood face to face with a Bengal tiger.

Randy Thompson, who had raped me, stood transfixed, his eyes on the entrance of the cage, as Caesar roared out from the semidarkness and moved toward the light of the room.

I saw the tiger lunge out of shadow and a shot rang out as Callanwolde screamed. He staggered backward, screaming, with his face locked in the tiger's jaws. Randy Thompson raised his gun as I brought the marble statue into my hands and gripped it as if it were some sanctified Louisville Slugger. As Caesar tore the face off the man who had raped my mother, portions of Randy Thompson's brain hit the far side of the living room wall. I had nearly decapitated him with the fury of my swing, the taste of his tongue still fresh in my mouth. Straddling him and forgetting the tiger and the third man and the screaming, I kept beating Randy Thompson's face in until it no longer looked like a human face. With cold aim I drove fragments of his skull deep into his brain.

Floyd Merlin was screaming and firing his pistol at the same time, wild careless shots, and blood flowed from a wound near Caesar's shoulders. Callanwolde was moaning softly beneath the weight of the tiger until Caesar swung his paw and tore the man's throat off to the backbone. Floyd Merlin backed up, firing, screaming. All pandemonium was loose in that house, and the smell of death and the sweet odor of brain and the radio playing a song by Jerry Lee Lewis made Floyd Merlin know just before he died that they had chosen wrong when they chose the house of Wingo. Still moving backward he fired his last shot at the tiger and saw me rise up with that statue in my hands. I moved quickly to my left and cut off his retreat to the back door. Savannah had gone to her closet, loaded her shotgun with healthy intent, and came roaring out of that room as the most dangerous woman on earth. The girl Floyd Merlin had raped put the barrel of her shotgun against his groin and pulled the trigger. She cut him in half and his blood and viscera half blinded me as Luke burst past me and grabbed a dining room chair, which he thrust out and stuck in the face of the tiger.

"Freeze," Luke said. "I got to get Caesar back in the cage."

"If Caesar doesn't get back in that cage, I'll blow him to kingdom come," Savannah said, weeping.

The tiger turned, bleeding, and staggered toward Luke. Caesar's jaws were bloody and he was hurt and disoriented. Caesar swung at the chair and broke off a front leg but Luke kept backing him toward the door.

"Easy, boy. Back to the cage, Caesar. You done real good, Caesar."

"Caesar's dying, Luke," my mother said.

"No, Mama. Don't say that. Please don't say that. He saved us. Now we've got to save him."

The tiger left bloody prints on the floor, like grotesque and sudden roses imprinted on fine-grained wood, as he retreated toward the back door. He turned his head once, then struggled toward the safety of his cage. Luke pulled the cage door down and locked it.

Then my family fell apart, broke down, wailed like damaged angels as the wind bore down hard against our house and the radio played on without the slightest trace of pity. We wept hard with the gore of our attackers on our hands and faces, on our walls and furniture and floors. The statue of the infant Jesus lay beside me, covered with blood. In less than a minute we had killed the three men who had brought ruin and havoc to our home, and had established their incumbency in the heedless ordinance of nightmare. In our sleep they would rise from the dust of our terror and rape us a thousand times again. In immortal grandeur they would reassemble their torn bodies and burst into our rooms like evil khans, marauders, and conquerors, and we, again, would smell their breath in ours and feel our clothes ripped away from our bodies. Rape is a crime against sleep and memory; its afterimage imprints itself like an irreversible negative from the camera obscura of dreams. Throughout our lives these three dead and slaughtered men would teach us over and over of the abidingness, the terrible constancy, that accompanies a wound to the spirit. Though our bodies would heal, our souls had sustained a damage

beyond compensation. Violence sends deep roots into the
heart; it has no seasons; it is always ripe, evergreen.

My body shook as I cried and I raised my hands to my
face to cover my eyes and unconsciously covered myself
with Randy Thompson's blood. I could feel his sperm leaking out of me. He had told me something true before he
died; something in me would always belong to him. He
had mortgaged a portion of my boyhood, had stolen my
pure sanction of a world administered by a God who loved
me and who had created heaven and earth as an act of
divine and scrupulous joy. Randy Thompson had defiled
my image of the universe, had instructed me exceedingly
well in the vanity of holding fast to faith in Eden.

For fifteen minutes, we lay on the floor of the slaugh-
terhouse that had always been our home and sanctuary.
Luke was the first to speak.

"I better call the sheriff, Mama."

"Don't you dare," I heard her say in a furious voice.
"We're Wingos. We have too much pride to tell what happened today."

"But we have to, Mama. We've got three dead men in
our living room. We've got to explain that to someone,"
Luke said.

"Those aren't men," she said. "Those are animals. They
are beasts."

She spat on the body of the man who had raped Savannah.

"We've got to get Tom to the doctor, Mama," Luke said.
"He's hurt."

"Where are you hurt, Tom?" she asked, but her voice
was disembodied, figurative, and she spoke in a dispas-
sionate tone as though she were addressing strangers.

"The man raped Tom, Mama. He's bleeding," Luke said.

She laughed, but the laughter was out of place, lunatic,
and said, "A man cannot be raped by another man, Luke."

"Well, no one told it to that guy. I saw him doing something to Tom," Luke said.

"I want these bodies out of here. I want you boys to take
them deep in the woods and bury them so no one will ever
find them. Savannah and I will scrub this house down with
a hose. I don't want there to be a trace of these animals
when your father gets home tonight. Get control of your-

self, Savannah. It's over now. Concentrate on something nice, like shopping for a new dress. And get some clothes on. You're naked in front of your brothers. Tom, you get dressed, too. Right this minute. I want you to haul these carcasses out of here. Stop crying, Savannah. I mean it. Pull yourself together. Think of something pretty—a romantic ride down the Mississippi in a river boat. The music is playing. The wine is flowing and a breeze is cool against your face. A well-heeled gentleman comes out of the moonlight and asks for a waltz. You've seen his face in society quarterlies and you know he comes from one of the richest families in New Orleans. He raises thoroughbred horses and eats only raw oysters and champagne . . ."

"Mama, you're talking crazy," Luke said softly. "Let me call the sheriff and he'll know what to do. I've got to call the vet and see if he can help Caesar."

"You won't call anybody," she said fiercely. "This didn't happen. Do you understand? Do you all understand? This did not happen. Your father would never touch me again if he thought I had sexual intercourse with another man. No fine young man would ever marry Savannah once the word got out that she wasn't a virgin."

"Jesus Christ," I said, incredulous, looking at the naked bodies of my mother and my twin sister. "Dear God, please tell me this is a joke."

"Get dressed, Tom. Now," my mother said. "We've got lots of work to do."

"We've got to tell somebody about this, Mama," Luke pleaded. "We need to get all of you to a doctor. We've got to help Caesar. He saved our lives, Mama. These men were going to kill you."

"I'm thinking of our family's position in this town. We can't do it to Amos and Tolitha. We can't do it to ourselves. I refuse to walk down the street while everyone wonders if I wrote that monster that letter in prison. They'll use that letter against me. They'll say I got what I deserved. But I won't have it. I won't play into their hands."

"Mama," I said, "my asshole is torn up."

"I don't allow language like that used in my house. I simply will not tolerate vulgar talk from my children. I've raised you to be decent and refined citizens."

* * *

Luke and I carried the bodies of the three men to the pickup and stacked them in a grisly heap on the bed of the truck. My mother handed me a Kotex, which I stuffed in my underwear to stop the bleeding. She and Savannah were throwing buckets of soapy water on the wooden floor when we left the house and my mother had started a fire in the back yard where she burned two throw rugs and an easy chair the blood had ruined. She seemed bizarre and vulnerable and crazy as she shouted out orders to us. Caesar, hurt grievously, would not let Luke near the cage to tend to his wounds. Savannah wept and had not said a word since her ordeal had ended.

We buried them in a shallow grave deep in the forest near a tree engulfed by kudzu. We knew the kudzu would cover their graves by next summer and the green roots would twine among their rib cages. I was shy around my brother now, ashamed that he had seen what he had, so we worked in exhausted silence. As the shock of the afternoon wore off, a fatigue so overwhelming as to be sedative entered my body. I sat by the grave and shivered, frail and depleted. Luke had to lift me up and carry me back to the truck.

"I'm sorry they hurt you, Tom," he said. "I'm sorry I didn't get there sooner. I forgot something or I wouldn't have come back to the house. I don't even remember now what I forgot. I saw their footprints in the road."

"Mama's crazy, Luke."

"No, she isn't. She's just afraid. We just got to go along with her."

"She's making it sound like it was our fault or something. No one would blame us. People would feel sorry for us if they knew. They'd help us."

"Mom can't have people going around feeling sorry for her, Tom. You know that. And she never could accept help from anyone, for anything. That's just the way she is. We just got to help each other and help Savannah."

"This isn't right," I said. "Why can't this stupid goddamn family ever do anything right?"

"I don't know. We're just peculiar."

"The whole family just gets raped and we kill the three guys that did it. And I mean we kill them deader than shit,

Luke, with their guts spread all over our house, and she makes us pretend that nothing happened."

"It's peculiar," he repeated.

"It's crazy. It's nuts. It's sick. And because Mom and Dad are crazy that means we're going to be totally fucked up our whole lives and all our children are going to be fucked up and that's the way it's going to be until kingdom come. It's messed Savannah up bad, Luke. What's this going to do to her? Tell me. She's seeing dogs hanging from meat hooks and that's just from living day to day with Mom and Dad. What's going to happen to Savannah?"

"She's going to do whatever she has to do. Just like all the rest of us."

"And me. What's going to happen to me?" I said, beginning to cry again. "I mean, you don't just walk away from a day like this without paying a price. Two hours ago I had a guy humping me, Luke, while he stuck a knife to my throat. I thought I was going to die. I thought he was going to butcher me like a hog in the living room. He kissed me, Luke. Then he was planning to kill me. Can you imagine killing someone you've just kissed?"

"No, I can't imagine that."

"We can't let Mom do this, Luke. It isn't right."

"We already have, Tom. We just buried all the evidence. There would be too much to explain now."

"People would understand, Luke. We've all been in shock."

"In a month, you won't even remember that it happened."

"Luke, I'll remember that it happened if I live to be five hundred."

"It's best not to talk about it. It happened and that's that. I've got to figure out a way to help Caesar."

Caesar was dying in his cage when we returned to the house. His breath was labored and his great yellow and black body was stretched out against the bars. When Luke stroked his head Caesar made no protest. Luke nuzzled his head against the tiger's and stroked the dazzling fur along the spine.

"You were good, Caesar," Luke whispered. "You were so good and we had no right to keep you locked up in this little shitty cage. But you finally got to be a tiger, Caesar.

God, if you didn't prove you were one hell of a tiger, boy. You were pure hell, Caesar, and I'm going to miss you bad. And you were the goddamnedest tiger who ever lived. I swear you were."

Luke lifted his rifle to Caesar's head, and with tears streaming down his face, he put a bullet through the tiger's brain.

As I watched, unable to console my brother, I knew that I would never again see a boy from South Carolina weep over the death of a Bengal tiger.

By the time my father arrived home from the shrimp docks that night, we had buried Caesar, removed all traces of the afternoon's mayhem, and expunged all signs of that singular and life-changing affair. I took the tractor and obscured the tracks of the three men imprinted on the wet earth along the island road. We found the car they had stolen in Georgia and the map with Melrose Island circled in ball-point pen on the front seat. Luke and I rolled the car off the bridge and sank it in the fifteen-foot channel. The house glistened with the fury of my mother's desire to wash every vestige of the men from our home. Her knees bled from her exertions with a wire brush on the oak floor. The statue of the Infant of Prague soaked in a tub of bloody ammonia. Savannah stayed in the shower for over an hour, washing herself obsessively, cleaning the stranger out of her. My mother directed Luke and me as we rearranged the furniture. Nothing was to be like it was that morning. We washed windows, curtains, and scrubbed out bloodstains that had dried in upholstery and the frayed edges of rugs.

My mother had a drink waiting for my father when he entered the house that night and reported that he had caught only forty pounds of shrimp that day. The house smelled like ammonia and cleansing fluid but my father smelled, as he always did, like fish and shrimp and he did not notice. The world held only a single smell for my father and he left a bucket of fish by the sink in the kitchen for Luke and me to clean while he took a shower.

My mother carefully prepared the fish, and during dinner my parents' conversation was so muted I had to fight back an obsessional urge to scream and overturn the dining room table. Savannah stayed in her room and my mother reported casually that she thought Savannah might be coming down with a slight case of the flu. My father detected nothing out of the ordinary. He was exhausted from a long day on the shrimp boat, fighting the wind that had come up strangely from the southeast. I had to summon up a reserve of discipline to keep from telling it all. I do not think the rape affected me as profoundly as my adherence to those laws of concealment and secrecy my mother had put into effect. In the hour it took to finish that meal, I learned that silence could be the most eloquent form of lying. And I never could eat flounder again without thinking of Randy Thompson's blood on my hands or his tongue in my mouth.

Before my father came home, my mother had gathered us together in the living room and extracted a promise from each of us that we would never tell a living soul what had happened to our family that day. In a voice that was both burnt-out and uncompromising, she told us that she would cease being our mother if we broke that promise. She swore that she would never speak to us again if we revealed a single detail of that terrible day. She did not care if we understood her reasons or not. Knowing the nature of small towns, she knew how they pitied and despised their raped women and she would not be counted in their number. We never broke that promise, any of us. We didn't even speak about it to one another. It was a private and binding covenant entered into by a country family remarkable for its stupidity and the protocols of denial it brought to disaster. In silence we would honor our private shame and make it unspeakable.

Only Savannah broke the agreement, but she did it with a wordless and terrible majesty. Three days later, she cut her wrists for the first time.

My mother had raised a daughter who could be silent but could not lie.

When I finished my story, I looked again at Susan Lowenstein across the room. We said nothing at first; then I said, "Do you see why Savannah's children's story made me angry? I don't believe that she doesn't remember that day and I don't want her to write it pretty."

"The whole family might have been killed."

490   *Pat Conroy*

"Maybe that wouldn't have been the worst thing to happen."

"What you've just described is the worst thing I've ever heard happen to a family."

"I thought so, too," I said. "But I was wrong. That was just the warm-up."

"I don't understand, Tom. You mean Savannah and her sickness?"

"No, Lowenstein," I said. "I haven't told you about the moving of the town. I haven't told you about Luke."

23

A coach occupies a high place in a boy's life. It is the one grand component of my arguably useless vocation. If they are lucky, good coaches can become the perfect unobtainable fathers that young boys dream about and rarely find in their own homes. Good coaches shape and exhort and urge. There is something beautiful about watching the process of sport. I have spent almost all the autumns of my life moving crowds of young boys across acres of divided grass. Beneath the sun of late August, I have listened to the chants of calisthenics, watched the initial clumsiness of overgrown boys and the eyes of small boys conquering their fear, and I have monitored the violence of blocking sleds and gang tackling. I can measure my life by the teams I have fielded and I remember by name every player I ever coached. Patiently, I have waited each year for that moment when I had merged all the skills and weaknesses of the boys placed in my care. I have watched for that miraculous synthesis. When it comes I look around my field, I look at my boys, and in a rush of creative omnipotence I want to shout to the sun: "By God, I have created a team."

The boy is precious because he stands on the threshold of his generation and he is always afraid. The coach knows that innocence is always sacred, but fear is not. Through sports a coach can offer a boy a secret way to sneak up on the mystery that is manhood.

I spent my summer with Bernard Woodruff teaching him all the secret ways. Everything I knew about the game of football I taught him in those two-hour sessions in the middle of Central Park. He learned to tackle by tackling me, and he learned to do it well. Bernard was not a gifted athlete, but he was one who did not mind hurting you. He hurt me many times during my practices and I hurt him many more. It took real nerve for a one-hundred-forty-pound boy to throw his body in front of a full-grown man. We played to an audience of great buildings rising out of the city around us.

But our season ended abruptly on the day I taught Bernard the art of pass blocking.

In the park, I lined up against Bernard in the four-point stance of a defensive lineman.

"That tree behind you is the quarterback, Bernard," I said. "If I touch that tree, then I've sacked the quarterback."

He faced me across the grass in full uniform, but I outweighed him by sixty pounds.

"Don't leave your feet. Keep your balance and keep me away from your quarterback," I said.

"I want to play quarterback," he said.

"We're teaching you to appreciate your offensive linemen," I said.

I broke across the line, slapped his helmet with my palm, and knocked him to the ground. I touched the tree and said, "I just made your quarterback mad."

"You just made the offensive lineman mad," he said. "Let's try that again."

This time he put his helmet to my chest when he rose up to meet me. I broke to his left but he kept popping me and retreating slightly, monitoring his center of gravity by flexing his knees and keeping his feet moving. When I tried to sprint by him, he surprised me by diving at my feet and sweeping my legs out from underneath me. I hit the grass hard and had the breath knocked out of me.

"I just made the quarterback happy, huh, Coach Wingo?" Bernard said triumphantly.

"You just hurt the coach," I gasped as I struggled to my feet. "I'm getting too old for this shit. That was terrific, Bernard. You earned the right to play quarterback."

"I whipped your butt on that one, Coach," he crowed. "Why are you limping?"

"I'm limping because I'm hurt," I said as I walked gingerly, testing my left knee.

"The good ones don't worry about little injuries," he teased.

I said, "Who taught you that?"

"You did," he said. "Just run it off, Coach. Like you told me to do when I sprained my ankle."

"You're irritating me, Bernard," I muttered.

"Then let's see you try to touch that tree, Coach," he said, smiling at me with unbearable arrogance.

I lined up across from him again, and with our faces only a foot apart I said, "I'm going to try to kill you this time, Bernard."

Again, he made first contact but I knocked him off balance with my palm again. He recovered and cut off my headlong charge for the tree. I leaned against him and felt him stagger against my weight. I was about to go around him when he surprised me and dove at my ankles. I hit the ground again with Bernard giggling beneath me.

We lay on the ground together, wrestling good-naturedly.

"I think you've become a football player, you little bastard," I said.

"Indeed," I heard a man's voice say behind me.

"Dad!" Bernard said.

I turned and saw Herbert Woodruff observing our impromptu wrestling match with something less than total enchantment. His arms were folded across his chest as primly as two blades in a Swiss Army knife. He possessed the composure and slim elegance of a flamenco dancer and had the dark good looks to match. On his face he wore a cold reserve.

"So this is how your mother allows you to waste the summer," he said sharply to his son. "You look perfectly ridiculous."

Bernard looked miserable and made no attempt to answer his father, who was making a strong point of ignoring me.

"Professor Greenberg just called and said you've skipped two lessons already this week," he said. "He only took you as his student as a special favor to me."

"He's mean," Bernard said.

"He's strict," the man said. "The great teachers are always very demanding. What you lack in talent, Bernard, you must make up for in devotion."

"Hello," I said, interrupting. "I'm Tom Wingo, Mr. Woodruff. I'm Bernard's football coach."

I held out my hand and heard him say, "I don't shake hands." He lifted his long, beautiful hands up to the sunlight and said, "My hands are my life. I'm a violinist."

"Do you want to rub noses instead?" I said cheerfully, hoping to divert his attention from Bernard.

He ignored me and said, "The maid told me you were down here. Go to your room and practice for three hours after you call Professor Greenberg to apologize."

"Football practice isn't over," Bernard said.

"Yes, it is, Bernard," he said. "It's over for the rest of your life. This is another one of you and your mother's little plots."

"Let's call it a day, Bernard," I said. "Run home and practice your violin like your daddy says and maybe we can work something out."

Bernard ran toward Central Park West at a fast trot and I stood alone on the grass with Herbert Woodruff.

"He's a pretty good football player, Mr. Woodruff," I said as we both watched Bernard cross the street through heavy traffic.

Herbert Woodruff turned to me and said, "Who gives a shit?"

"Bernard, for one," I said, controlling my temper with effort. "Your wife asked me to coach Bernard this summer."

"She didn't discuss it with me," he said. "But I guess that's obvious to you by now, Mister . . . What did you say your name was?"

"Wingo. Tom Wingo."

"My wife talks about you frequently," he said. "You're her southern boy, aren't you?"

"I saw you at the Spoleto Festival in Charleston," I said. "You were terrific."

"Yes," he said. "Thank you. Do you know Bach's Chaconne, Mr. Wingo?"

"I don't know very much about music, I'm ashamed to admit," I said.

"A pity," he said. "When I was ten years old, I could perform the Chaconne flawlessly," he said. "Bernard added the Chaconne to his repertoire only this year and his rendering of it is sloppy at best."

"How were you at football at ten?" I asked.

"I've always loathed athletics and all people connected with them, Mr. Wingo," he said. "Bernard knows this well. He probably finds football exotic compared to the concert halls where he grew up."

"I don't think football will cause any permanent damage," I said.

"It could permanently damage his desire to be a violinist," he said.

"Susan said you were displeased when you found out that I was coaching him."

"My wife is sentimental about Bernard," he said. "I am not. I also endured a difficult adolescence, but my parents did not indulge me at all. They believed that discipline is the highest form of love. If Bernard craves physical activity, there is always the Chaconne."

I picked up the football lying on the ground and said, "Why don't you come out here with Bernard sometime and toss the ball around before supper?"

"You have a marvelous sense of humor, Mr. Wingo," he said.

"I'm serious, Mr. Woodruff," I said. "Football is just a passing interest of Bernard's right now, but I bet he'd love it if you'd show some interest in it. It might even hasten the process when he loses interest in sports completely."

"I've already taken steps to hasten that process," he said. "I'm sending him to a music camp in the Adirondacks for the rest of the summer. My wife has allowed you to steal his attention away from his music."

"It's none of my business, sir," I said, "but that's not the way I'd handle it."

"You're perfectly correct, Mr. Wingo," he said with an irritated dignity. "It is not your business."

"If you send him to camp," I said, "he'll never be the violinist you want him to be."

"I'm his father and I assure you he'll be the violinist I want him to be," he said as he turned and walked toward his apartment building.

"I'm his coach," I said to his back. "And you have just created a football player, sir."

The phone was ringing when I returned to my sister's apartment. I was not surprised when I heard Bernard's voice on the phone.

"He threw my uniform away," Bernard said.

"You shouldn't have skipped your violin lessons," I said.

He was silent for a moment, then said, "Have you ever heard my father play the violin, Coach?"

"Sure," I said. "And your mother's taking me to hear him play next week."

"He's one of the fifteen best in the world," Bernard said. "At least, that's what Greenberg says."

"What does that have to do with skipping your music lessons?" I asked.

"I won't even be among the top ten violinists in the camp, Coach Wingo," he said. "Do you understand what I'm trying to say?"

"Yeah, I do," I said. "When do you go to camp?"

"Tomorrow," he said.

"Can I take you to the station?"

"Yeah, that would be great," he said.

The next day we took a cab to Grand Central and I watched his luggage as Bernard bought his train ticket. We walked down to the track where his train was going to arrive. He carried his violin case and I carried his suitcase.

"You've grown this summer," I said as we sat down on a bench.

"Inch and a half," he said. "And I've gained eight pounds."

"I wrote the football coach at Phillips Exeter," I said.

"Why?"

"I told him I'd spent the summer coaching you football,"

I said. "I recommended you as a prospect for his junior varsity team next year."

"My father has forbidden me to play football again," Bernard said.

"I'm sorry," I answered. "I think you could have turned into a hell of a football player."

"You do?" he asked.

"You're a tough kid, Bernard," I said. "When you took me down yesterday, I was trying as hard as I could. I was trying to run over you."

"Tell me that again, Coach," he said.

"Tell you what?"

"Tell me that I'm a tough kid," he said. "No one's ever told me that before."

"You're a damn tough kid, Bernard," I said. "I thought I'd run you into the ground the first week this summer. You surprised me. You took everything I dished out and came back asking for more. Coaches love that."

"You're the best coach I've ever had," he said.

"I'm the only coach you've ever had," I said.

"I meant teacher," Bernard said. "I've had music teachers since I was five. You're the best teacher I've had, Coach Wingo."

The boy moved me and I could not speak for a moment. Finally, I said, "Thanks, Bernard. No one's said that to me in a long time."

"Why were you fired?" Bernard asked.

"I had a nervous breakdown," I said.

He said quickly, "I'm sorry. I had no business asking."

"Sure you did," I said.

"What's it like having a nervous breakdown?" he asked, then said, "I'm sorry. Tell me to shut up."

"It wasn't pleasant," I said, looking for the train.

"Why'd you have it?" he asked, staring at me.

"My brother died, Bernard," I said, turning toward him.

"I'm sorry, I'm really sorry," he said. "Were you close?"

"I worshiped him," I said.

"I'll write a letter," Bernard said.

"To whom?" I asked.

"I'll write a letter saying you're a terrific coach," Bernard said. "You just tell me where to send it."

I smiled. "Don't worry about the letter. But there's one thing I'd like you to do for me, Bernard."

"What's that?" he asked.

"I'd like to hear you play the violin."

"Sure," he said, unsnapping the lock from his violin case. "What would you like to hear?"

"How about the Chaconne?" I asked.

He was playing the Chaconne when his train arrived at the station and he played it beautifully and with a passion that surprised me. When he finished I said to him, "If I could play the violin like that, Bernard, I'd never touch a football."

"What's wrong with doing both?" he asked.

"Nothing," I said. "Write me. I'd like to hear from you next year."

"I will, Coach," he promised as he replaced his violin.

I handed him a sack from Macy's.

"What's this?" he asked.

"A new football," I said. "You'll have to get it blown up at camp. Then find a buddy you can toss it with. And, Bernard, work on being a nice guy. Make friends. Be nice to your teachers. Be thoughtful."

"My father hated you, Coach Wingo," he said.

"But he loves you," I said. "Goodbye, Bernard."

"Thanks for everything, Coach," Bernard Woodruff said, and we embraced on the platform.

When I returned to the apartment I received a phone call from Herbert Woodruff inviting me to dinner after his concert that Saturday night. I did not understand why Herbert wanted someone he hated to dine with him and his friends, but I was from South Carolina and I would never understand how the great city worked.

Susan Lowenstein was already in her seat when I joined her minutes before the concert was to begin. She was dressed in a sleek, long, black gown and leaned over and kissed me when I took my seat. The color black added a touch of the sensual to Susan's shy beauty.

"Tom, you haven't met our friends Madison and Christine Kingsley, have you?" she said as I leaned over and shook hands with one of the most famous playwrights in America and his wife.

"Who else do you know that's famous, Susan?" I whispered. "I want to meet them all so I can brag a lot when I get back down to South Carolina."

"They live on the third floor of our apartment building," she said. "Madison went to prep school with Herbert. By the way, Herbert told me he interrupted you and Bernard in the park."

"He did not seem amused," I said.

"Be cautious around Herbert tonight, Tom," she warned, squeezing my arm. "He can be charming or difficult, but he's impossible to predict."

"I'll be careful," I said. "Were you surprised he invited me, Lowenstein?"

She turned toward me, her black hair loosened, falling onto her white shoulders. Her skin was eggshell-lustered, like the palest chinoiserie. In her office, she disguised her beauty with an efficient, no-nonsense wardrobe. But there was nothing elliptical about her loveliness tonight. On the body of a beautiful woman, black made all colors seem fatuous. Her eyes held that ambiguous melancholy I had grown accustomed to, but now they beheld me in the soft light of a concert hall where she was frontlit in the amplitude of her generous femininity. Her perfume made me dizzy with desire and I felt some shame, but not much, that I was feeling the most wonderful stirrings of lust for my sister's psychiatrist.

"Yes," she said. "I was perfectly shocked. He must have liked you."

Behind the curtain, I could hear the willful soliloquies of instruments being tuned. When the curtain rose to applause, there was Herbert Woodruff, immaculate and stately, acknowledging the crowd and motioning to his ensemble to rise and take an introductory bow.

I had almost forgotten about the existence of the blonde, distressed flutist I had met in Susan's office until I saw her rise along with the other musicians to acknowledge their ovation. I remembered that I had never seen a more beautiful woman, that her name was Monique, that I had lied and told her I was a lawyer, and that Susan thought she was having an affair with Herbert Woodruff. She sat down and I watched her flute rise to her mouth in a silvering, fluid movement. Her lips were full as she took a deep breath and when she exhaled music was born in a happy borealis of sound. With her fingers, her breath, and her lips, Monique brought Vivaldi newly created into the room, and with a passionate, sudden sweep of his arm, Herbert Woodruff answered her in the language of Vivaldi as they shaped together the erotic cousinry between the flute and the violin. Herbert pulled music from his violin as if he were lifting silk from a dressmaker's table. His chin rested on the woman-shaped body of his violin and the music seemed to resonate through his muscle and blood. There was a lucid power in his arms and wrists and during his performance he was part dancer and part athlete. The music blended and coalesced; it asked questions in phrases of honey and milk, then answered them in storm. The chamber group turned the concert hall into a place where butterflies and angels should come to be born. For two hours, we listened to the conversation of well-made instruments. And with Herbert Woodruff, we learned much about the stamina and featureless breadth of a man of genius. Every movement he made with his violin was a provision of sacred order. His was a priestcraft of technique and he moved the audience with the rapture of both his ardor and his restraint. I had never been so jealous of a man in my whole life. Once I had been able to throw a football fifty yards, but not until this moment had my single talent seemed so picayune or cheap to me. Not one member of my family could read a note of music, I thought, as the final sonata by Bach made a dark, flowering sunburst through the concert hall.

We stood and cheered for Herbert Woodruff and the three musicians whose skills had provided the contrast to highlight the transcendence of his gift. As I applauded, I knew that it would always be my burden, not that I lacked genius, but that I was fully aware of it.

There was something off-center and troubling about my inclusion in the intimate circle that gathered for dinner in Herbert Woodruff's apartment. Susan and I rode home in a taxi with the Kingsleys and it was only then that I realized how small and select the gathering would be. Susan was distracted and spent much of her time directing the help in the kitchen. I made drinks for Christine and Madison and was telling them about living in South Carolina when

Herbert walked through the door with Monique on his arm. His sinewy frame glowed in the aftermath of his performance and the adrenaline of center stage still poured through his lighted veins. Often I had seen that overstimulated flow in the joyful exhaustion of an athlete after playing his life's finest game. Herbert, too, was trying to hold fast to the unrepeatable moment; an overlay of ecstasy animated his eyes.

He fixed me with a smile of surprising charm and said, "Southern boy, I'm delighted you could come."

"You were wonderful," I said.

"We've never played that well together," Monique said as Herbert introduced me to her.

"We've met," Monique said, and I knew from her tone, gratefully, that the subject should be dropped.

"Can I fix you a drink?" I asked.

"Scotch on the rocks for me, Tom," Herbert said. "And a glass of white wine for the lovely Monique. Now, while you're making the drinks, Tom, I want to play something just for you. Tell me what you would like to hear. I don't want to retire the Stradivarius for the night just yet."

As I poured the Scotch, I said, "I don't know very much about classical music, Herbert. Anything would be fine with me."

"Our friend Tom is a football coach from South Carolina, Monique," Herbert said, holding his violin beneath his chin.

"I thought he was a lawyer," Monique said.

"I couldn't understand why Bernard was going to hell as a violinist," Herbert continued, "until I found out that Tom was coaching Bernard in the manly art of football."

Madison Kingsley said, "I had no idea that Bernard even knew what a football looked like."

"I think it's nice that Bernard is finally showing some interest in something," Christine Kingsley added.

I felt the evening tense around me but I smiled and handed Monique her glass of white wine and set Herbert's Scotch on the coffee table. The southerner always makes the mistake of believing that he can resurrect the old fluid courtesies and thus make himself invisible at any party imbalanced or endangered by his presence. It was danger I was feeling as I felt Herbert's gaze following me. I realized suddenly that I had erred in accepting Herbert's invitation, but it was too late to do anything but plunge wholeheartedly into the postrecital amusements. I had chameleonlike powers, or so I thought, of sublime and self-effacing mimesis. I fancied myself a heroic listener, a grand appreciator of the wit of others, and I carried with me the southerner's instinctive wisdom of knowing my place. I could make the split-second assessment of that moment when I entered waters out of my depth.

Beneath these misgivings lay a realm of grand feeling. A rare expansiveness had intruded on my consciousness. There had been too many nights alone in Savannah's apartment. Solitude overstretched me when it was force-fed in weekly dosages. The mere sound of human voices in that room, hushed and comfortable, hit my veins and tenderized those suspended carcasses of loneliness the great city always hung next to my heart. And I had the outsider's curiosity about the private utterances of the celebrity at ease above his tossed salad. I wanted to be part of the evening and I would win these folks over by enfolding them in the unrefractive chivalries of my background.

Then Herbert Woodruff played the song "Dixie" on his Stradivarius.

Never had "Dixie" been played so flawlessly or with such ironic intent. Herbert exaggerated his movements to heighten the effect of the satire. When he finished he looked at me with a cunning grin and I saw that Susan had come out of the kitchen into the living room. She looked frightened and angry.

"Well, Tom," Herbert said at last, "what do you think?"

"That Beethoven sure wrote some pretty songs," I said.

In the laughter that followed, Susan ushered us into the dining room, instructing us to take our drinks in with us.

Herbert drained his glass of Scotch and poured himself another before he joined us. He sat at the head of the table with Monique on his left and Christine Kingsley on his right. The food had been expertly arranged on Limoges china. It seemed to have been color-coordinated and was prettier than it was tasty. But the wine was from Bordeaux and hit just the right note on my tongue. To my infinite relief, the evening had regained something of its lost equilibrium. Herbert seemed to have forgotten me as he engaged Monique in a private conversation at his end of the table. Then New York started to do what New York did best and the talk grew animated and testy between Herbert and Madison Kingsley.

Their conversation was irreverent and risqué. Every word seemed well chosen, dewy with spontaneity, mordant and fast on its feet. I laughed a little too hard at Madison's jokey put-downs of other playwrights half as famous as himself. The women spoke briefly, usually bright commentaries or swift summations of major themes the two men had introduced. Despite my best intentions, I found myself memorizing, or trying to, long fragments of conversation between the playwright and the musician. When Herbert talked about giving a benefit performance with Yehudi Menuhin, the whole room grew quiet as he described each subtlety and modulation of that encounter. Herbert was a serious man when he discussed his art. When he finished, Madison Kingsley talked about technical problems he was having in mounting his new play. The two men began to enjoy themselves and their conversation became imperceptibly competitive. They carried the aura of their success well and understood well that they were the ones who were supposed to talk, to dazzle, and to entertain. They were men of substance and distinction and I enjoyed my role of satellite and observer as the meal continued. Once I caught Susan's eye and smiled when she winked at me. I was not ready for the moment when Herbert Woodruff turned mean again.

Madison Kingsley was briefly outlining the plot of his new play, *The Weather in a Dry Season*, about anti-Semitism in Vienna before the last World War. He was explaining the problem of how to dramatize the life of a good man who also happened to be a committed Nazi. Madison was in the middle of a sentence when Herbert interrupted him and directed a question to me.

"Is there a lot of anti-Semitism in Charleston where you live, Tom?" he asked.

"Tons," I said. "But the snobs of Charleston generally don't discriminate, Herbert. They hate just about everybody."

"I just can't imagine living down South," Monique said. "I can't imagine why anyone would do it."

"You kind of get into the habit once you've been born there," I said.

"I've never gotten into the habit of New York," said Christine Kingsley. "And I've never lived anywhere else."

But Herbert was not finished with me, and he said, "What do you do about it, Tom? I mean, when it presents itself. When it rears its ugly head. How do you react when a friend of yours makes a remark that suggests he hates Jews?"

"Herbert," Susan said, laying down her fork. "I want you to quit picking on Tom."

"It's a good question," Madison said. "It's the type of thing I'm trying to resolve in this new play. You see, this character, Horst Workman, is not an anti-Semite even though he is a Nazi. What do you do, Tom?"

Monique said before I could answer, "I always leave the room when I'm confronted with racism of any kind."

"But the subject is Tom," Herbert said. "What does Tom Wingo do? What does our guest, the high school football coach from South Carolina, do?"

"I sometimes do the same thing," I said, looking nervously at Susan. "Or else I leap on them. You know, take them by surprise. Then I throw them on the floor and before any of the other anti-Semites in the room can come to their rescue, I rip out their voice boxes with my teeth and spit them across the room. I'm very hard on anti-Semites."

"That was marvelous, Tom," Christine said kindly. "You deserved that, Herbert."

"Very witty, Tom," Herbert said, clapping his hands in mock applause. "Now that showtime is over, tell us what you really do? I'm truly interested."

"I'm interested in your shutting up, dear," Susan said.

Herbert had leaned forward, his elbows resting on the table, positioning himself like a praying mantis. His eyes had the shining concentration of a predator. I could see nothing at all clearly but I had the dim perception that I had entered an old and melancholy dance between Susan

and Herbert. There was an insatiable quality to Herbert's
maneuvering of the conversation. I was certain that everyone at this table had seen Herbert perform this ritual at
other meals. A violent tension mesmerized the air around
the table as I tried to figure a way to withdraw cordially
from the fray. On Monique's beautiful lips, I saw the beginning of a slight smile as she noticed my discomfiture. I
tried to make sense out of the dramatis personae. Why
would a man bring his mistress to his dinner table and why
would any wife allow it? Why was Herbert moving so deftly
in for the kill? I had committed the unpardonable sin of
coaching his son and befriending his wife, but I was new
to the dance and I knew Herbert was about to teach me all
the steps.

"Cat got your tongue, Tom?" Monique said at last to
break the silence.

"I have to be going, Susan," I said, rising from the
table.

"No, Tom. Please, Tom," Herbert said. "You're taking
this personally. You're a football coach. Just think of this
as an after-dinner sport. The sport of wickedly clever New
Yorkers. We've never had a coach at this table or a southerner, and it's natural for us to want to know what makes
you tick. My wife is Jewish, Tom. Surely you must have
suspected that. Don't you find it charming that she retains
what small Jewish identity she may have once had by
clinging to her rather uneuphonious maiden name? I told
Susan that I suspect you are an anti-Semite. Nothing uncommon about that. The South is chock-full of them, I'm
sure."

"Where are you from, Herbert?" I asked him, resuming
my seat.

"Philadelphia, Tom," he said. "How nice of you to
ask."

"I've had about enough of this, Herbert," Christine said.

"Oh, please, Christine. We must give Madison new material or he'll become dated," Herbert said, laughing.

"I'm not an anti-Semite, Herbert," I said, "but I loathe
all people from Philadelphia."

"Very good, Coach Tom," he said, and he looked truly
pleased with my reply. "I think I may have underesti-

mated our little southern boy. But we come again to the painful question that you've been so adept at avoiding. What do you do when you hear an anti-Semitic remark down South?"

"I do nothing," I said finally. "Just like I do nothing when I'm around people who hate white southerners. I just sit and listen."

"I feel about the South the way I feel about Nazi Germany, Tom," Herbert said. "I think of the South as evil. That's what makes it interesting to me. By the way, I was in the Selma march. I know what the South is like. I put my life on the line to change the South."

I smiled and said, "And we southerners, black and white, will ever be eternally grateful to you, Mr. Woodruff."

"I suggest we change the subject," said Susan, her voice growing shrill and desperate.

"But why, dear?" said Herbert. "It's a fascinating subject and far superior to the chitchat that sustains most dinner parties in New York. Don't you agree? And we owe this to you, Susan. You're the one who discovered little Tom and brought him into our lives; he is a man who provides tension and real hostility—real feelings, as my wife, the psychiatrist, would put it. All of us are feeling real feelings and we owe it all to our friend Tom. Let's face it, the party was a little boring before we got Tom to open up. Who knows the depth of mediocrity we might plumb tonight."

"Make Herbert stop this, Madison," Christine said.

"They're big boys, dear," Madison said, and there was something of the voyeur's secret lust in his face that let me know he had encouraged scenes like this before. "They can stop it themselves."

"Why are you so curious?" Monique asked Herbert without even looking in my direction.

"Because little Tom is fascinating," Herbert answered, and I was beginning to wither beneath the hostility of his gaze. "My wife talks of almost nothing else. She tells me some of his homespun homilies and witticisms, which make him seem like some drawling modern-day Mark Twain. And I like his act. His Tara-like pride. His feistiness."

"Just ignore him, Tom," Susan said in the murderous

climate dimly lit with candles. "Tom is a guest in our home, Herbert, and I want you to leave him alone. You promised me you wouldn't do this."

"You're right, darling," Herbert said. "How insensitive. Tom is up in New York because his sister, the famous redneck feminist poet, tried to kill herself of late while under my wife's indulgent care."

"Excuse me for revealing that information, Tom," Susan said miserably. "Sometimes you make mistakes. One often has the faith one can trust one's own husband."

"Susan," I said, "in the light of the whole evening that seems small potatoes indeed."

"Don't be melodramatic, dear," Herbert said, leaning away from me and toward his wife. "All of us know how proud you are of your literary clientele of scribbling psychotics. My wife is the shrink of choice among artists of distinction in New York, Tom. She drops their names constantly, then pretends it's accidental. All of us find it charming."

"Susan is a marvelous psychiatrist," Monique said. "I know from personal experience."

"You don't need to defend me from Herbert, Monique," Susan said. "Herbert is one of those spouses who waits for a group situation before he attacks and humiliates his wife. It's far more common than you think. I hear of it constantly in therapy. And, Tom, I apologize for the way Herbert is acting. You're my friend and no one can commit a greater crime in Herbert's eyes. His son loved you also."

"I can't believe you two are actually friends," Monique said, flicking her elegant finger in a gesture of dismissal.

"Shut your fucking mouth, Monique," Susan screamed, rising to her feet.

"What?" a stunned Monique said. "I was just expressing an opinion."

"You keep your goddamn mouth shut," Susan said, still screaming. "And, Herbert, if you say one more word to Tom I'm going to fling every goddamn dish on the table at your ugly little head."

"Dear, dear," Herbert said, smiling. "People might think we have marital problems. We don't want to give the wrong impression."

"And, Monique," screamed the outraged Dr. Lowenstein, "get your hand off my husband's cock. That's it. Pull it away discreetly. Pretend you really haven't been giving him a handjob under the table while he's been insulting my friend. I've seen you do that revolting little trick about twenty times now and I'm getting sick of it. That's why I usually try to seat you as far away from him as possible. Because I can stand the fact that you're fucking him in private, but it's too much for me to watch you diddle him in public."

Monique rose out of her chair, first looking at Susan, then at Herbert. Then she staggered out of the room and down the hall. It seemed to me that Herbert had lost control of his dinner party. When he looked at me, I said, "Tide's turned, big boy."

He ignored me and, looking at Susan, said, "You go and apologize to Monique this instant, Susan. How dare you humiliate a g———"

"Go ahead and say it," she yelled. "A guest in our goddamn happy home. I just watched you humiliate Tom in our home. I've watched you do it to every friend I've brought to this house. Neither Christine nor Madison nor I have ever had the guts to stop you because we're afraid you'd turn that ugliness on us. You go in and apologize to that cheap slut."

"I think it's you who should make the appropriate gesture, Susan," he said.

"Are y'all enjoying the party?" I asked Madison and Christine, who were both staring at their plates.

"You can't get up from the table yet, can you, Herbert?" Susan said, laughing. "Tell the people why. I know why, Herbert. Because you've still got a hard-on from her giving you a handjob under the table. Stand up, Herbert. Let everybody see. She handles a flute brilliantly, I'm sure, or anything even remotely shaped like one. Everyone at this table knows you've been having an affair with her for the past two years. Everyone except Tom. We're such a close-knit, supportive little group. So supportive that Christine and Madison entertained you in their house in Barbados last winter."

"We didn't know she would be there, Susan," Madison said.

"We'll talk about this later," Herbert said.

Susan shot back, "We'll talk about it when you end your affair with your flutist."

"A mere dalliance, my dear," he said, regaining his composure. "But I'll put my taste in friends up against your taste in friends any day of the week."

"A small difference, Herbert," Susan said. "Tom and I are not fucking."

"Even you have more taste than that," he said.

"Good God, Herbert," Madison Kingsley moaned.

"Oh, shut up, Madison," Herbert said. "Quit looking so aggrieved and pious. It's not as though you've never seen Susan and me argue before." Then, turning to Susan, "What you love is being Mrs. Herbert Woodruff," he said. "Fame is your one weakness, dear. You see, Tom, I've analyzed my wife's character. She's only attracted to the rich and famous. You're nothing. But your sister. Ah, yes, your sister makes you valuable. But I repeat. You're nothing. Now, Susan, you go apologize to Monique."

"Not until you apologize to Tom," she said.

"I have nothing more to say to your little friend," he said.

I broke the brief silence between them by saying, "I can make Herbert apologize to both of us, Susan."

"You're still here, Tom?" Herbert said. "What a pity. How are you planning to get me to apologize to you?"

"Well," I said, "I was reviewing my options, Herbert. First, I thought I might just kick your ass up and down the stairs. But I rejected that plan. It would prove only that I was the barbarian you take me to be. I would find beating you up personally satisfying, but socially tacky. So I came up with another plan. I think it shows more wit and a lot more culture."

"Herbert has never apologized to anyone for anything," Christine said.

I walked to the sideboard at the end of the room and poured myself a large snifter of cognac.

"To pull this off, I have to be a little drunker," I said.

The cognac went down easily. I felt it light up my bloodstream.

Then I walked out of the dining room and into the living room. I walked quickly past the grand piano and unsnapped the locks that held Herbert Woodruff's Stradivarius. Good, I thought, I'm drunk enough.

"Herbert," I called out, "southern boy has got hold of your fiddle and you best come running."

When the dinner party arrived to join me on the terrace, I was holding the violin out over the edge of the terrace, eight stories above Central Park West.

"That's a Stradivarius, Tom," Madison Kingsley said.

"Yes, I thought I heard that fact mentioned fifty or sixty times tonight," I said cheerfully. "It's a pretty little sucker, isn't it?"

"That's worth three hundred thousand dollars, Wingo," Herbert said, and I thought I noticed a slight catch in his throat.

"Not if I drop it, Herb," I said. "Then it won't be worth a buffalo-head nickel."

"Tom, have you lost your mind?" Susan asked.

"Several times, Susan," I said. "But not this time. Apologize to your wife, Herbert. I love your wife and I think she might be the best friend I've ever made."

"You're just bluffing, Tom," he said, and I could hear some of the power return to his voice.

"I might be," I said. "But it's a powerful bluff, isn't it, asshole?"

I tossed the violin in the air and caught it on the fly, leaning far out over the balcony's edge.

"It's fully insured," Herbert said.

"It might be, Herb. But you'll never own another Stradivarius if I let this one fly."

Christine said, "It's a work of art, Tom."

"Apologize to your wife, creep," I said to Herbert.

"I'm very sorry, Susan," Herbert said. "Now give me my violin, Wingo."

"Not yet, tiger," I said. "Apologize to your nice friends for bringing your girlfriend to Barbados."

"I'm very sorry I did that, Christine and Madison," he said.

"Sincerely, Herb," I continued. "Very sincerely. Take the irony out of your voice or your little fiddle will be bouncing like a beach ball down there among the taxicabs."

"I'm very sorry I did that, Christine and Madison," he said without irony.

"Your apology is accepted with thanks," Christine said.

"That's better, Herbert," I said. "Sincerity becomes you. Now me, Herbert. Apologize for your unforgivable breach of etiquette at the table tonight. I'm sorry that you don't let your wife have friends. That's your business. But you had no right to treat me like that, you possum-breathed cocksucker. None in the world."

He looked at Susan, then at me, and said, "I apologize, Tom."

"Not quite humble enough yet, Herbert," I said sadly. "Let's try to endure the humiliation with a little more grace. One more brief moment of humility, then I'll walk out your front door forever. Otherwise, winos will be using pieces of your fiddle to clean their teeth."

"I'm sorry, Tom. I'm very sorry," he said. Then he added, "And, Susan, I'd mean that even if he wasn't threatening me."

"Good boy, Herb," I said, handing him his violin. "I'm deeply sorry if I've offended you, Susan."

I walked to the front door and rang for the elevator without going through the courteous gestures of leave-taking.

On Central Park West, I was hailing a cab when I heard Susan Lowenstein's voice behind me.

"This is why you're always sad, Susan," I said as she approached me. "And I thought you had it made."

"Have you ever made love to a psychiatrist?" she asked.

"No. Have you ever made love to a football coach?" I asked.

"No," she said, "but I plan to have a different answer tomorrow morning."

And I kissed Susan Lowenstein, who looked beautiful in black, as we stood on the street at the beginning of the most wonderful night I had ever spent in Manhattan.

When we awoke on Sunday morning we made love again and we were good together and sunlight was on my back as we moved together in my sister's bed. Then we slept until ten, entangled in each other's arms.

I rose first and walked to the window in the living room and shouted down to the streets. "I love New York City, I love it. I goddamn love it."

No one even looked up and I walked to the kitchen to fix a perfect omelet for Susan Lowenstein.

"What made you change your mind about New York, Tom?" Susan called from the bedroom.

"Your wicked, sinful body," I yelled back. "Your gorgeous fabulous body and that terrific way it moves has made me see the error of my ways. I've never been in love in New York City before. That's what makes the difference. I feel absolutely great and nothing can make me feel bad today."

She walked into the kitchen and we kissed as bacon sizzled on the stove.

"You kiss good," she whispered.

"After you taste my perfect omelet, Lowenstein," I said, "you'll never leave me. You'll follow me anywhere, begging me to toss beaten eggs into a heated pan."

"Did you enjoy making love to me, Tom?" she asked.

"You must remember, Lowenstein, that I'm Catholic," I said. "I like sex, but only if it's dark and I don't have to talk about it later. I'll feel guilty all day because it was so goddamn fantastic."

"It was fantastic?" she asked.

"Why is that so hard to believe, Susan?"

"Because you were having sex with me," she said. "And I've always received complaints from the men in my life in that department. Also, I'm neurotic and I need a lot of reassurance about sex."

Then the phone rang in the living room and I said, "Ah, what goddamn horror awaits me when I answer that call?"

"Are you going to answer it?" she asked, taking a fork and turning the bacon.

I picked up the receiver and about fell to my knees when I heard my mother say hello.

"Oh, God," I said. "It's you, Mom."

"I'm in New York," my mother said. "I'm about to catch a cab to Savannah's apartment. I want to have a talk with you."

"No," I screamed. "For godsakes, Mom. The place is a wreck and I'm not even dressed yet."

"I'm your mother," she said. "I don't care if you're dressed or not."

"Why are you in New York?" I asked.

"I want to speak to Savannah's psychiatrist," she said.

"Oh, Jesus. You want to speak to Savannah's psychiatrist," I repeated.

"Tell her I just need to put on my pantyhose," Susan whispered from the kitchen door.

"Mom, it's Sunday," I said. "Shrinks all go to their country houses on the weekend. There isn't a psychiatrist left in the city today."

"Excuse me, sir," Susan whispered. "I happen to be a psychiatrist."

"I want to talk to you today, Tom," my mother said. "I've never seen Savannah's apartment and I would very much like to."

"Give me thirty minutes to clean this place up, Mom," I said.

"There's no need to go to any trouble," my mother said.

I heard a rap on the door to the apartment.

"Goodbye, Mom. I'll see you in half an hour."

Susan opened the door and I saw Eddie Detreville standing in the doorway with a bag of fresh croissants.

"Hello, Sallie," he said. "I'm Eddie Detreville, the next-door neighbor. I've heard all about you from Tom and Savannah."

"Hello, Eddie," she answered. "I'm Susan."

I hung up the phone and heard Eddie say, "Nothing I hate worse than cheap heterosexuality, Tom."

When my mother entered the apartment, she kissed me on the cheek, then said, "I smell a woman's perfume."

I closed the door and said, "The man next door is a homosexual, Mom. He was just over here to borrow a cup of sugar."

"How does that explain the perfume?" she asked suspiciously.

"You know how homosexuals are, Mom," I said. "Always flitting around, spraying themselves with perfume, and buying Afghan hounds."

"I know you hate to see me in New York City," she said, walking into the apartment.

"Au contraire, Mama," I said, grateful that she had

dropped the subject of the perfume. "I've been dancing in the streets since I heard the fabulous news. Would you like me to fix you a perfect omelet?"

"I already had breakfast at the St. Regis," she said.

"Did your husband come with you?" I asked from the kitchen. "Or is he off buying Indonesia or something?"

"He knew you wouldn't want to see him," she answered. "He stayed at the hotel."

"A man of insight," I said, bringing her a cup of coffee. "He sees directly into my soul."

"How long will you punish him for what you know to be my sins?" she asked, then said, "The coffee's very good."

"I'll probably forgive him on his deathbed, Mom," I said. "I forgive everybody on their deathbed."

"Even me?" she asked.

"I forgave you a long time ago," I said.

"You most certainly did not," she said. "You've treated me abominably. You're still so angry at me you can hardly look into my eyes."

"I'm not angry just at you, Mom," I said quietly. "I'm angry at everybody. I have this all-consuming, titanic, free-floating rage at everything on the planet."

"I shouldn't have had children," my mother said. "You do everything for them, sacrifice your whole life for their well-being, then they turn on you. I should have had my tubes tied when I was twelve. That's what I'd recommend to any young girl I met."

"Every time you see me, Mama, you look at me like you want some doctor to perform a retroactive abortion," I said, covering my face with my hands. "Oh, let's cut the small talk, Mom. What monstrous reason brings you to New York? What ring of hell are you planning to march me through this time?"

"Do you hear yourself, Tom?" she said. "Who taught you to be so cruel?"

"You did, Mama," I said. "And you also taught me that even though someone destroys your entire life, you can still feel an indestructible love for that person."

"This is supposed to cheer a mother's heart," she said. "Everything you say to me is meant to hurt me."

"My only defense against you, Mama, and I mean the single weapon I bring to the fray, is a bitter honesty."

"I guess it makes no difference to you that I love my children more than anything in the world, does it, Tom?"

"I believe that, Mama," I said. "If I didn't believe that with my whole heart, I would strangle you with my bare hands."

"And you just claimed that you loved me!" she said.

"You're putting words in my mouth again," I said. "I said I forgive you. I did not mention love. In your withered bag of emotions, they're the same thing, Mama. Not in mine."

"You say the cruelest things, Tom," she said, and there were tears in her eyes.

"That was inordinately cruel, Mom," I admitted. "And I apologize for it. But we must admit that we have a history together and that history has made me conscious of the fact that you probably have something hideous up your sleeve."

"Do you mind if I smoke?" she asked, taking a package of Vantages from her purse.

"Of course not," I said. "I don't mind catching lung cancer from my own mother."

"Will you offer me a light?" she asked.

"Mother," I said wearily, "we are perched on the eve of the liberation of all women. It would be gauche of me to light your cigarette when I know you don't even believe that women should be allowed to vote."

"Untrue," she said. "But I'm old-fashioned in other ways. I simply love being a woman. I like to have doors held open for me and a gentleman to hold my chair when I'm being seated. I'm not a bra-burner, nor do I believe in the Equal Rights Amendment. I've always thought women were far superior to men and I never want to do anything to make a man think he could be my equal. Now, please light my cigarette."

I struck a match and she touched my wrist as I lit her cigarette.

"Tell me all about Savannah," she said.

"She looks very becoming in a straitjacket."

"If you wish to become a comedian, Tom—and really, I'd be glad to see you try to hold down any kind of job at all—please let me rent you a concert hall or a nightclub instead of trying out your routines on me."

"Savannah's in very bad shape, Mom," I said. "I've only gotten to see her once since I've been up here. I've told Dr. Lowenstein the stories of Savannah's growing up, filling her in on all the grisly details of our epic childhood."

"And, of course, you felt it necessary to tell about that day on the island," she said.

"Yes, I felt it necessary," I said. "I thought it oddly significant."

"Do you think Dr. Lowenstein can be trusted with that piece of information?" she asked.

I said, "Usually after I tell Dr. Lowenstein some dark secret, it mysteriously appears the very next day in *The New York Times*. Of course she can be trusted, Mom. She's a professional."

"I have too much pride to reveal such a shameful episode to a perfect stranger," my mother said.

"I'm riddled with obsequiousness, Mom," I said. "I like telling total strangers all about it. 'Hi, I'm Tom Wingo. I was buggered by an escaped convict, but then I killed him with a statue of the Christ child.' It establishes immediate intimacy."

My mother studied me dispassionately, then asked, "Have you admitted to Dr. Lowenstein about your own problems, Tom? You're good at revealing all of my family secrets, but I wonder how much you reveal about your own."

"There's nothing to reveal, Mom," I said. "Anybody can see I'm an unhappy, desperate wreck of a man. The details would only bore them."

"Have you told her that Sallie and I had to commit you to the tenth floor of the Medical College last year?"

"No, I haven't," I lied. "I thought I would let Dr. Lowenstein think that I came to my hatred of her profession through my extensive readings, not personal experience."

"I think she needs to know that the stories she's hearing are coming from someone who was committed to an insane asylum," my mother said.

"I prefer to describe it as the psychiatric unit of a teaching college, Mom," I said, closing my eyes. "It does so much more for my self-esteem. Look, Mom, I know it embarrassed you that I spent a week on the tenth floor. It embarrassed me even more. I was depressed. What more can I tell you? I'm still depressed. But I'm getting better. Despite

Sallie and her doctor friend, this summer has been good for me. I've taken stock of my entire life and the life of my family and it's a rare privilege for a man to have that kind of luxury in these grisly times. At rare moments, I'm even starting to like myself again."

"I'm going to tell Dr. Lowenstein that you lied to her about the rape and about everything else you told her," my mother said. "Then I'll tell her they had to send bolts of electricity through your brain just to straighten you out."

"They gave me two electroshock treatments, Mother," I said. "It took me a long time to get my memory back."

"I'm going to tell Dr. Lowenstein that it confused your memory and you started making up stories," my mother said, extinguishing her cigarette.

"Mom," I said, lighting her second cigarette for her, "people are raped in America every day. It wasn't our fault. It was just our turn. Thousands of women are raped in America every day. The men who do it are sickos. Boys get raped in prisons at a hideous rate. It's violent and horrible and it changes you forever. But it doesn't do anyone any good to pretend it didn't happen."

"I wasn't raped," my mother said.

"What?" I said.

"You didn't see what went on in that room," she said, and she began to cry. "He didn't rape me. You have no proof."

"Proof? What proof do I need, Mama? The reason I didn't think you were discussing Bogart films in there is simple. When you busted out of that room naked, I thought you were making a rather strong statement."

My mother cried harder and I passed a handkerchief over to her.

"We showed them, didn't we, Tom?" she said through her tears.

"We sure as hell did, Mama," I said. "We showed the shit out of them."

"It was horrible what he did to me in that room," she said, sobbing.

"The last time I saw that guy alive he was checking out a tiger for halitosis," I said. "I think it spoiled his whole day. He had kudzu growing out of his eyeballs the same night."

"It's odd how things work, Tom," she said. "We'd be dead now if your father hadn't bought that gas station. Having a tiger was the only thing that saved us that day."

"Luke would have found some other way, Mom," I said. "Luke always found a way."

"Not always," she said and paused.

"Will Savannah see me?"

"She doesn't want to see any members of her family right now, Mama," I said. "She's considering whether she should ever see us again or not."

"Do you know it's been three years since she spoke to me?" my mother said.

"She hasn't spoken with me, either," I said. "Same with Dad. We've had some bad things happen in our family, Mom."

"Which makes us exactly like every other family on earth," she said.

"Savannah has also maintained that ours is one of the most screwed-up families in the history of families," I said.

"We can hardly use Savannah as an unbiased arbiter," my mother said. "She's in an insane asylum."

"I think it adds weight to her argument," I said. "Why did you come up to New York, Mama?"

"Because I want both of you to start loving me again, Tom," she said, and her voice broke.

I waited until she regained control of her voice. She seemed brittle and deeply hurt. It was hard for me to believe I could adore someone I distrusted so completely.

"I can do nothing to change the past," she gasped. "I would change every minute of it if I could, but it's not within my power. I don't see any reason to spend the rest of our lives as enemies. I've discovered that I can't stand it that my own children despise me. I want your good will again. I want your love, Tom. I think I deserve it."

"I was angry with you, Mama," I said. "I never stopped loving you. You've taught me that even monsters are people too. That was a joke, Mom."

"It was a bad joke," she said, sniffling.

"I want to be friends with you again, Mom," I said. "I'm not kidding. I need it probably more than you do. I know that everything I say pisses you off. I'll try not to say mean things to you. I mean it. I'll try from this moment to regain my status as a perfectly wonderful son."

"Would you have dinner with us tonight?" my mother asked. "It would mean so much to me."

"Us?" I said. "Oh, God, Mama, you ask so much. Why can't I just start loving you and maintain my undying contempt for your husband. That must not be uncommon in America. I'm a stepson. It's my job to hate my stepfather. It's a literary conceit I picked up somewhere along the trail. You know, Hamlet, Cinderella, all those people."

"Please, Tom," she said. "I'm asking it as a favor. I want you to be friends with my husband."

"Fine, Mom," I said. "It'll be a pleasure to meet you for dinner."

"I've missed you, Tom," she said as she rose to leave.

"I've missed you, too, Mama," I said, and we held each other for a long time, and it was hard to tell who was crying harder as the weight of all the lost years made us desperate to touch each other.

"Don't ever be an asshole again, Mama," I said.

She laughed through tears and said, "I have a perfect right to be an asshole. I'm your mother."

"We've lost some good years, Mama," I said.

"We'll make up for them," she said. "I'm sorry about Luke, Tom. I know that's why you hated me. I cry about Luke every single day of my life."

"Luke gave us something to cry about, Mom," I said.

"Sallie wants you to call her, Tom," she said. "I talked to her just before I left."

"She's going to leave me, Mom," I said. "I've been practicing living without Sallie since I've come to New York."

"I don't think so, Tom," she said. "I think she's been jilted."

"Why didn't she pick up the phone and call me herself?" I asked.

"I don't know, Tom," she said. "She might have been afraid to. She tells me you're starting to sound like the old Tom on the phone and in your letters."

"The old Tom," I said. "I hate the old Tom. I also hate the new Tom."

"I love the old Tom," my mother said. "And the new

Tom is going to have dinner with me and my husband and I love him for it."

"Be patient with me, Mama," I said. "Most of what you say is still going to piss me off."

"If we promise to love each other, Tom, the rest will come soon enough."

"I want your husband to feed me very well, Mom," I said. "I want this reconciliation to cost him a large sum of money. I want his blood pressure to rise and his life expectancy to fall when he gets the check."

"We have reservations at the Four Seasons," she said. "I made reservations for three."

"You dog," I said. "You knew I'd fall for your wicked charms."

I met my mother at the bar of the St. Regis Hotel. She was sitting alone. My mother looked up suddenly and I turned around to see her husband entering the bar. I rose to greet him.

"Hello, Tom," he said. "I'm very grateful you could come."

"I've been a perfect jackass," I said. "I'm sorry."

And I shook hands with my stepfather, Reese Newbury.

24

In late August 1962 I reported early to freshman football practice at the University of South Carolina, becoming the first member of my family ever to matriculate on a college campus. In the histories of families, even these small advances take on monumental dimensions. On the same day I arrived at the university, Luke was shrimping the waters of Colleton in the new shrimp boat he had christened the *Miss Savannah* and was already catching more shrimp than my father. Savannah would not leave for New York until November and she would do it over the strong protests of my parents, who wanted her to stay in Colleton until she had her "head on straight." The pledge of silence had held and I began practice with the guilty knowledge that I was most likely the only boy on the team lucky enough to have been raped by an escaped convict. I became shy in the shower room, fearful that my nakedness would reveal some mark of shame to my teammates. I vowed to myself that I would begin my life again, regain that hell-bent enthusiasm I had lost during the assault on my house, and distinguish myself in every aspect of college life. But already my luck had changed, and college was to teach me that I was one of life's journeymen, eager to excel but lacking the requisite gifts.

In the first week of practice, I was told by my coach that I did not have what it takes to be a college quarterback, and he assigned me to the position of defensive safety, where I was destined to live out the dreams of an athlete. I would return kickoffs and punts on the second unit for three years, and in my senior year, I intercepted four passes and was named to the all-conference second team. But I never threw a single pass or ran a single offensive play from the line of scrimmage. The thresholds of my talents were modest and my desire far exceeded my abilities. I was known as a hustler, and my coaches grew fond of me over the years. When runners burst through the defensive line, I made them remember me. I tackled them with a recklessness, a willed ferocity, not proscribed by minimal talent. Only I knew that this ferocity was the handiwork of terror. I would never lose my visceral fear of the game, but it was a secret I never shared with the world. I turned that fear into an asset and it helped me define myself as I spent a four-year apprenticeship beneath its languid jurisdiction. I played afraid but did not dishonor myself. It was the fear that made me love the sport so much and love myself for turning that fear into an act of ardor, even worship.

Until I went to college I had no conception of how countrified and ingenuous I appeared to others. The boys on the freshman team came from all over America, and with something approaching amazement, I listened to the four boys from New York City talk. I had no idea that such personal assurance, such easy swagger and natural confidence, could accrue so naturally to boys my own age. They were as exotic as Turks and their snappy, rapid-fire speech seemed like some alien, pernicious language to me.

I was so overwhelmed by the newness of college, by the magnitude of the change from island boy to college boy, that I made few alliances in the first year. Light on my feet and vigilant, I kept my own counsel, took it all in, and tried to grow savvy by imitating those glorious, confident southern city boys I admired so extravagantly. The juniors and seniors from Charleston walked like kings, and I tried to copy their elegance of manner, their unself-conscious sophistication, and their deft, civilized wit. My roommate was a boy from Charleston named Boisfeuillet Gailliard, or Bo, as he liked to be called. He reeked of good breeding and inherited privilege. His name sounded like a French meal to me, and one of his Huguenot ancestors had been governor of the colony before the great revolt against King George. I was pleased at my good fortune at drawing such a roommate and my mother had a moment approaching ecstasy when she heard a Wingo had aligned his destiny with a South Carolina Gailliard. I now know Bo was appalled to be saddled with such an undistinguished roommate but he was far too well schooled beneath the colonnades of southern custom ever to impart his discomfiture to me. In fact, after the initial shock, he seemed to take me under his wing as a kind of social reclamation project. He made only one rule, that I could never under any circumstances borrow his clothes. His closet was filled with marvelous suits and sport coats. He seemed stunned by my own negligible wardrobe, but again he said nothing, his eyes merely registering slight surprise when I proudly showed him the blue sport coat my mother had made for my graduation. Bo was happy when he found I played football and asked if I could get his family some complimentary tickets to the Clemson game. I told him I would be happy to and I supplied his family with free tickets for the next four years, long after he had ceased being my roommate. I did not know it then, but with Boisfeuillet Gailliard I was meeting for the first time that indigenous species of southern culture, the natural politician. In that first week, he told me he would be governor of the state when he was forty, and it did not surprise me to see him take the oath of office two years before that projected date. He asked me to be on the lookout for any girl I saw on campus who might be good material for First Lady of the state. I promised I would keep my eyes open. I had not met anyone like Bo Gailliard before. I was a country boy and not yet uncommonly good at sniffing out assholes.

It was Bo who made me want to become a fraternity man and I followed him from frat house to frat house during Rush Week that year, watching him disappear from my side as soon as we entered the smoky, noisy rooms filled with well-dressed Greeks who all seemed like the friendliest people I had ever met. I loved all the fraternities and all the brothers about equally well, but Bo convinced me that SAE was the best and the only one I needed to take seriously. But I ate dinner at all the houses whenever freshmen were invited and laughed at all the jokes and entered every conversation I could and offered my opinions on just about everything under the sun.

When it was time for me to fill out my pledge card, I looked long and hard, then put down the five most popular fraternities on campus as my first choices. The bids were to be placed by the fraternities at five o'clock in the afternoon and there was a huge crowd of boys and girls waiting at the post office when they were delivered. There were screams of joy when some boy or girl would receive a bid from the fraternity or sorority of his or her choice. There was an air of such joy and festivity that I was breathless with anticipation as I kept peeking into the small window of my mail slot.

At seven o'clock I was still there, still checking that empty box, wondering if there had been some terrible mistake. Bo found me there at eight, distraught and edgy, still waiting in the darkened post office.

"I got five bids, but I've been a natural-born SAE as long as I can remember. Come out and I'll buy you a beer to celebrate."

"I don't think so, Bo," I said. "Do they deliver some of the bids tomorrow?"

"Hell, no," he said, laughing. "They'd have kids going crazy if they had to wait until tomorrow."

"I didn't get a bid," I said.

"That doesn't surprise you, does it, Tom?" he said, not unkindly.

"Yes. It surprises me very much," I said.

"Tom, I should have warned you, but I didn't want to hurt your feelings. You became a class joke. Everyone was talking about you."

"Why?" I asked.

"You wore the same sport coat to every single party, every meeting, every activity on campus. Then someone found out your mother had made the coat and everyone went crazy. The girls in some of the sororities thought it was the most adorable thing they had ever heard of, but it sure didn't make you prime Greek material. I mean, who ever heard of a fraternity man walking around in a home-made coat? It would look good in a Norman Rockwell painting, but it doesn't exactly fit the image of any fraternity on campus. Did the Dekes turn you down too?"

"I reckon."

"If you couldn't get in with the Dekes, then there's no chance, Tom. But there are a lot of really sharp guys on campus who don't even want to have anything to do with fraternities, Tom."

"I wish I had been smart enough to be one of them."

"Let me buy you a beer."

"I've got to call home."

I walked to the bank of pay phones near the entrance of the post office and sat in the darkness of the booth to collect my bruised thoughts before I called home. I was overcome with hurt and shame. I tried to analyze my behavior at the dizzying series of parties I had attended. Did I laugh too loud, use bad grammar, or seem too eager to please? I had always taken it for granted that people would like me. It was something I never worried about, but now I worried greatly. If I could just talk to some of the fraternity men and give them the history of the sport coat in my life, I could make them understand and reconsider. But even I understood the futility of such a pitiable gesture. I had simply not understood the nature of the milieu I was attempting to enter. I had tried to join a fraternity and found the Colleton League blocking my way. From my mother, I had learned nothing of the perils of over-reaching.

I called my mother and Savannah answered.

"Hey, Savannah. How are you? This is Tom."

"Hello, college man," she said, her voice still weak and raspy from her ordeal. "I'm fine, Tom. I'm getting better every day. Don't worry. I'm going to make it."

"Is Mom there?" I asked.

"She's in the kitchen."

"I didn't get into a fraternity, Savannah."

"Do you care, Tom?"

"Yeah. I really care. I can't help it, but I do. I liked everybody, Savannah, and thought they were all the nicest bunch of guys I ever met."

"They're creeps, Tom. If they didn't take you, they're nothing but creeps," she said, lowering her voice so my mother couldn't hear.

"I must have done something wrong. I can't figure it out. A lot of guys I didn't think had a chance received bids. College is strange, Savannah."

"I'm sorry. Do you want me to come up this weekend? The scars on my wrists have healed completely."

"No. I just want you to know how much I miss you and Luke, Savannah. I'm not as good without you. The world's not as good."

"You're not without me. Always remember that. Here's Mom."

"I may not tell Mom, Savannah."

"I understand. I love you. Study hard."

"Tom," my mother said. "This was the big day. You must be so excited."

"Well, Mom," I said, "I've been doing a lot of thinking since I've been up here and I've decided not to pledge a fraternity this year. I think I might wait a year or two."

"That doesn't seem like such a good idea to me," she said. "Remember, the boys you meet in your fraternity will be the ones who'll be there to help you in the business world when you graduate."

"That's just it. A fraternity really takes you away from your studies. I've been going to so many parties that I've really been neglecting my schoolwork."

"Now that sounds very mature. I don't really approve, mind you. I think it's better to get set right up in a fraternity the first year, but if you're falling behind . . ."

"Yeah, I flunked a couple of tests last week and the coach called me in to talk about it."

"If you lose your scholarship, you know we can't afford to send you through college, Tom."

"I know, Mom. That's why I think the fraternity might have to wait. I think my studies will have to take priority over my social life for a while."

"Well, you're a man now and can make those decisions for yourself. Savannah is doing so much better, Tom. But I want you to write her a letter and see if you can't talk her out of going to New York. It's too dangerous for a southern girl to walk those streets up there."

"No more dangerous than living on the island, Mom," I said, coming as near to referring to the rape as I ever had with my mother.

"Tell me all about your courses, Tom," she said, changing the subject.

When I hung up the phone I sat in the booth for a minute or two, wondering how I could again face the boys who had voted so overwhelmingly to exclude me. I thought about transferring to a smaller college closer to home. I tried to figure out when I could return to the dormitory so I would not have to face the pity of my classmates who would know I had not received a single bid.

I did not see the girl walk past me and take her place in the phone booth behind mine. I heard her place the coin in the slot and ask the operator if she could make a collect call. Before I could leave the booth, I heard a cry of such pure anguish that it froze me to the spot and I did not move because I did not want the girl to know that anyone had overheard her moment of desolation.

"Oh, Mama," she wept, "not one of them wanted me. Not a single one of them asked me to be in a sorority."

She cried uncontrollably in that booth behind me and I laid my head back and listened to her sobbing.

"They just didn't like me, Mama. They just didn't want me. No, you don't understand, Mama. I didn't do anything to any of them. I was nice, Mama. I was real nice. You know how I am. Oh, Mama, I feel so bad. I feel bad all over."

For ten minutes she talked and wept and listened to her

mother trying to console her. When she hung up she leaned her head against the phone and continued to cry. I leaned around the booth and said, "The same thing happened to me today. You want to go get a Coke?"

She looked up, startled, tears rolling down her cheeks, and said, "I didn't know anybody was in here."

"I just called my mother to tell her the same thing. Only I lied. I didn't have the guts to tell her I didn't get into a single fraternity."

"You didn't get in?" she said, looking at me. "But you're so cute."

I blushed, surprised completely by her candor.

"How about that Coke?" I stammered.

"I'd like to. But I need to wash my face."

"My name's Tom Wingo," I said.

"My name's Sallie Pierson," she said through her tears. "Awfully pleased to meet you."

And that is how I met my wife.

We began our life together at a moment of natural self-pity and defeat that left an inimitable impression on both of us. The rejection chastened me and let me know my proper place in the grand scheme of things. It was the last time I would ever make a move that required bold-ness or a leap of the imagination. I became tentative, sus-picious, and dull. I learned to hold my tongue and mark my trail behind me and to look to the future with a wary eye. Finally, I was robbed of a certain optimism, that reckless acceptance of the world and all it could hand my way that had always been my strength and deliverance. Despite my childhood and the rape, I thought the world was a wonderful place until SAE decided not to include me in its membership.

Of different stuff was Sallie Pierson made. She was the daughter of two mill workers from Pelzer, South Caro-lina, and her rejection was only one in a long series of social catastrophes that had befallen her since she was a small child. It was one measure of her social innocence that she thought a shrimping family was exotic and sub-stantial. She had come to the university on a scholarship that her parents' mill awarded each year to the child of a mill worker with the highest academic average. She had never made a single B in high school and would only make two of them in college. When Sallie Pierson studied, she heard the music of the looms in her head and saw the image of her parents, disfigured by years of exhausting labor so their only daughter would have chances denied to them. On the night we met she told me she wanted to become a medical doctor and then have three children. She had planned her life out like a battle campaign. On our second night together she told me that though she did not want to frighten me, she had decided to marry me. She did not frighten me.

I had never met a girl like Sallie Pierson.

Each night we met at the library and studied together. She took college seriously and passed this seriousness on to me. From seven to ten every evening except Saturdays, we worked at the same desks behind the literature section. She allowed me to write her one love note a night, but that was all. In high school she had learned that dedication to academics had its own special rewards and that they would accrue to us if we were diligent. She never wrote me love notes but she did write down long lists of things she expected from both of us.

Dear Tom:
You will be Phi Beta Kappa, Who's Who in American Colleges and Universities, captain of the football team, and first in your class in the English Department.

Love, Sallie

Dear Sallie [I wrote back and passed the note across her desk]:
What's Phi Beta Kappa?

Love, Tom

Dear Tom:
The only fraternity you can get into, country boy. Now study. No more notes.

Love, Sallie

Like Savannah, Sallie understood the power of writing things down. It was a night of astonishment when we were inducted into Phi Beta Kappa at the same time two years later. I had found, to my surprise, that I was the only boy in my freshman class who had heard of William Faulkner, much less read him. I loved my English courses with a passion and could not believe how lucky I was to be living a life where my job was to read the greatest books ever written. I began a long love affair with the English Department of the University of South Carolina, whose members could not believe a football player could write a standard English sentence without damaging the language. They did not know I had grown up in the same house as a sister who would become the best poet in the American South or that I studied each night for three hours with the girl who had written a single word down on her list of objectives: valedictorian.

My mother was less than enchanted when she found out I was dating a mill town girl and did everything she could to discourage the relationship. She wrote me a series of letters about the kind of woman I should look for when I was shopping around for a wife. I read those letters to Sallie and she agreed with my mother.

"You can't wash a mill village out of your system, Tom," Sallie said. "I'll never be able to give you what some of these other girls can give you."

"And I can't wash the shrimp off my deck either," I answered.

"I like shrimp," she said.

"And I like cotton."

"Let's show them, Tom," she said, kissing me. "Let's you and Sallie show them all. We won't have everything and there'll be some stuff we'll always be lacking, but our kids will have everything. Our kids will have everything in the world."

Those were the words I had been waiting my whole life to hear and I knew the right woman had entered that life.

On the football field I struggled for three years with my own sense of inadequacy. I was surrounded by superb athletes who gave me daily lessons in deficiencies I brought to the game. But I lived in the weight room in the off-season and began building my body with deliberate intent. When I entered the university I weighed one hundred sixty-five pounds. When I left four years later I weighed two hundred ten pounds. As a freshman I bench-pressed one hundred twenty pounds; as a senior, I bench-pressed three hundred twenty. I blocked on the kickoff team and was a third-string defensive back in my sophomore and junior years until Everett Cooper, the kickoff returner, got hurt during the Clemson game my junior year.

When Clemson scored, I heard Coach Bass call my name. And my years in college turned golden.

When I went back to receive the kickoff, no one in the stands except Sallie and Luke and my parents knew my name.

The Clemson kicker approached the ball and I saw that awesome movement of orange helmets downfield and the roar of sixty thousand voices as that ball lifted into pure Carolina sunshine and traveled sixty yards in the air, where I caught it in the end zone and took that son of a bitch where it was supposed to go. "The name, ladies and gentlemen, is Wingo," I screamed as I tucked the ball under my arm and took off up the left-hand side of the field. I was hit on the twenty-five, but spun out of the arms of the tackler, and, cutting back across field, a Clemson player dove and missed me with an arm tackle. I put a move on a defensive back and leapt over two of my teammates who had taken down two Clemson boys. I angled across the entire field until I picked up the blocker I needed and saw the opening I had lofted a prayer to heaven for. When that opening came, I streaked for the open field and felt someone dive for me from behind; I tripped but balanced myself with my left hand, kept my feet, and saw the kicker at their thirty-yard line, the last Clemson player with a chance of keeping me out of their end zone.

But there were sixty thousand people who did not know my name and four people I loved whose voices were urging me along in the stadium called Death Valley, and I had no plans to be tackled by a kicker. I lowered my head and my helmet caught him in the numbers and he melted like snow before the goddamn glance of the Lord, flattened by the only boy on that field who knew Byron's name or a single line of his poetry. Two Clemson players caught me at the five and I gave them a free ride as we tumbled into the end zone at the end of the run that would change my life forever.

The score was thirteen-six and there was a quarter of

football left to play when I heard those sweet words spoken by the announcer. "The run by number forty-three, Tom Wingo, covered one hundred and three yards and sets a new Atlantic Coast Conference record."

I returned to the sidelines and was engulfed by my teammates and coaches. I went past the bench and stood waving like a madman at the place high in the stands where I knew Sallie and Luke and my parents were on their feet cheering for me.

George Lanier kicked the extra point and we were six points behind the Clemson Tigers when we took the field in the fourth quarter.

With two minutes left in the game, we stopped Clemson at their own twenty-yard line. And I heard one of the assistant coaches yell to Coach Bass, "Let Wingo take this punt."

"Wingo," Coach Bass screamed, and I ran up to him.

"Wingo," he said as I adjusted my helmet, "do it again."

I had turned golden that day and Coach Bass had uttered magical, incantatory words and I tried to remember where in my life I had heard that phrase before as I took a position on our thirty-five-yard line, shutting out the extraordinary noise of the crowd. As I watched the center snap the ball to the punter, I remembered that distant sunset when I was three and my mother had walked us out on the dock and brought the moon spinning out from beneath the trees of our island and my sister cried out in a small ecstatic voice, "Oh, Mama, do it again!"

"Do it again," I said as I watched the spiral tower far above the field begin its long descent into the arms of a boy turned golden for a single day in his life.

As I caught the ball I looked upfield.

I took the first marvelous step of the run that would make me the most famous football player in South Carolina for a year I will cherish as long as I live. I caught the ball on our forty-yard line and raced up the right sideline, but all I could see was a movable garden of orange heading my way. Three Clemson players were moving in for the tackle from my left side when I stopped dead and began running the other way, back toward our own goal line, trying to make it to the other side of the field. One

Clemson lineman almost caught me at the seventeen but was cut in half by a vicious block by one of our linebackers, Jim Landon. Two of them were matching me stride for stride when I turned upfield. When I looked up the far sidelines, I saw something amazing happening in front of my eyes. Our blocking had broken down completely after the punt, but each of my teammates trailing the play had watched me reverse my field with eleven Clemson players in healthy pursuit. I was looking down a lane of blockers that stretched for fifty yards downfield. A Clemson player would be about to catch me; then I would see a South Carolina player step between me and the tackler and cut him down at the knees. It was like running inside a colonnade. It was a fine life I was leading that day and I felt like the fastest, sweetest, dandiest boy who ever breathed the clean air of Clemson. When I hit their thirty-yard line running faster than I ever thought I could run, there was not a Clemson player left standing on the field. When I crossed the goal line, I fell to my knees and thanked the God who made me swift for the privilege of feeling like the king of the world for one glorious, unrepeatable day of my young life.

After George Lanier made the extra point and we stopped Clemson's drive on our own twenty-three-yard line and the final whistle blew, I thought I would be killed by the rush of Carolina fans onto the field. I would have died in perfect rapture. A photographer caught the exact moment when Sallie found me in the crowd, leapt into my arms, and kissed me on the mouth while screaming at the same time. That picture was on the front page of every sports section in the state the following morning, even in Pelzer.

At midnight that night, I walked outside Yesterday's restaurant in Five Points where my parents had taken us to dinner and felt diminished when that marvelous day was over.

The following week, bumper stickers appeared on automobiles the length and breadth of South Carolina saying, "Kick it to Wingo, Clemson." Herman Weems of the *Columbia State* newspaper wrote a column about me the following Sunday, calling me the scholar-athlete and the greatest secret weapon in the history of South Carolina football.

"He's not that good a football player," Coach Bass was quoted in the article, "but I'll never convince anybody down at Clemson of that fact."

In the last paragraph, Herman mentioned that I was dating the girl with the highest academic ranking in our class and that she was pretty as a picture to boot. That was Sallie's favorite part of the article.

It was only a few weeks later that I was approached by a contingent of SAEs, including Bo Gailliard, who asked if I would be interested in joining their fraternity. I politely declined, as I did when I was solicited by seven other fraternities that same year. Never has the word *no* held such ethereal beauty for me. The Tri Delts sent a contingent of some of the prettiest and most popular girls in the school to enlist Sallie in their sorority. In a phrase that I loved, Sallie told them they could kiss her mill-town ass.

I would never again have a day of such complete transfiguration. I played good football for the rest of my career at Carolina but I would learn that nature is uncommonly cheap in its allocation of gold. If I had been abundantly talented I would have had many such days. But I knew I was a special and lucky man to have been granted even one. At the lowest point in my college career, I had met the girl I would love for the rest of my life; at the highest, I had scaled the heights of my talent as an athlete and knew for a single day what it felt like to be famous. It didn't feel like much at all and that surprised me.

After graduation, Sallie and I were married in Pelzer with Luke as my best man and Savannah as Sallie's maid of honor. We honeymooned on Melrose Island in the small two-room house that Luke had built for himself on two acres Dad had given him on a point of land near the bridge. Savannah stayed with Mom and Dad for a week and Luke lived on his shrimp boat as I showed Sallie everything I knew about life in the lowcountry.

At night when I lay in Sallie's arms she would whisper to me, "After med school, we'll make pretty babies, Tom. Our job now is to learn to enjoy it."

Together, in that long summer, we repeated the gentlest chapter in the history of the world locked in the sweet embrace of each other's arms. Tenderly, we coaxed out every secret and mystery our bodies had shyly withheld. We made love as though we were putting a long poem together from tongues of rich fire.

When the honeymoon was over, I worked as Luke's striker on the shrimp boat. Sallie and I would rise before dawn and meet Luke down at the shrimp docks. Luke would follow my father's boat and I would make sure the wooden doors went over the sides cleanly without tangling the cables. When we had filled the hold with shrimp and iced them down, I would clean the deck as Luke headed the *Miss Savannah* back toward town. Luke paid me ten cents for every pound of shrimp we brought into the scales and I had money in the bank when I began my life as a teacher and a coach at Colleton High School.

In late August *Saturday Review* published Savannah's first poem in a special issue featuring young poets. It came out on the same day that Luke received notification in the mail that his draft status had been changed to 1-A. Savannah had written an antiwar poem at the very moment that same war had impinged upon the family consciousness.

At our house next evening, Luke asked, "What do you think about this Vietnam stuff, Tom and Sallie?"

"Sallie made me quit ROTC as soon as the war began heating up," I answered, handing Luke a cup of black coffee.

"Dead husbands make lousy fathers," Sallie said. "There's nothing in it for Tom."

"They're not going to let me out of it," said Luke. "I called old Knox Dobbins yesterday down at the draft board and he said they aren't going to defer shrimpers anymore. He said there were too many shrimpers on the river anyhow."

"I guess he found a sure-fire way to thin them out," I said angrily.

"Will they draft you too, Tom?" he asked.

"They don't draft male teachers in rural South Carolina, Luke," I answered. "They just pay us slave wages and hope we never look for real jobs."

"You ever meet up with anybody from Vietnam?" he asked.

534

Pat Conroy

"I met a guy running a Chinese restaurant in Columbia once," I said.

"He was from China, Tom," Sallie said. "It's not the same thing."

"It's the same thing to me," I said.

"Mom says I have to go because we were taught to love America," said Luke.

"We do love America," I said. "What has that got to do with anything?"

"I told her I didn't love America," he said. "I told her I loved Colleton County. The Vietnamese can have the rest of it for all I care. It's the damnedest thing. I'll have to sell the shrimp boat."

"Don't—Tom can run the shrimp boat for you, Luke," Sallie said. "As soon as school is out next summer, he can take the boat out for you and at least keep up the payments."

"Tom went to college so he wouldn't have to run a shrimp boat, Sallie," Luke answered.

"No," I said, "Tom went to college so he could decide to run a shrimp boat or not. I wanted to have a choice, Luke, and I'd consider it an honor to keep your shrimp boat running until you get back."

"I'd appreciate that, Tom," he said simply. "I'd like to know it was back here waiting for me."

"Don't go, Luke," Sallie said. "Tell them you're a conscientious objector. Tell them anything."

"They'll put me in jail, Sallie," he said. "I'd rather die than go to jail."

As our life in Colleton began to unfold in the drowsy fragments of a southern teacher's life, Luke was drawn out of that life to play his small part in the only war America was able to rustle up in our generation. While I was teaching in the classroom and coaching football on the same field where Luke and I had once been co-captains, and Savannah was participating in every antiwar demonstration on the East Coast, Luke was patrolling the rivers of Vietnam, having enlisted as a member of the Navy's most mysterious and elite branch, the SEALs. The Navy was not stupid and they were not about to waste the talents of the strongest and savviest boy who had volunteered in that queasy season of American self-examination. While I was sending boys on downfield blocking drills and Savannah was writing the poems she would include in her first volume, Luke was learning underwater demolition, how to parachute from low-flying aircraft, anti-guerrilla warfare, and how to kill silently when operating behind enemy lines. There was a disturbing apposition to the American lives we were leading, a complex harmony that would be called into play when the world would spin out of control and the stars would align themselves in fabulous and bestial shapes and conspire to take my family into the calms of our weatherless river and cut us up for bait.

"SEAL," Savannah wrote to me when she learned of the naval branch that Luke had joined. "A bad omen, Tom, a very bad omen. A bad word, and a dangerous one in the Wingo family mythology. Do you remember when you wrote me about the Clemson game, the one where you scored the only two touchdowns in your college career? You had a magic word going for you that day. The word was *tiger*. You were playing the Clemson Tigers and the word *tiger* has always been a lucky one for us. But SEAL, Tom. Do you remember what happened to the seal at that circus? Do you remember what tigers do to seals? I think Luke is going into a country of tigers as a seal and it terrifies me, Tom. Poets look at words for signs and symbols. Forgive me, but I don't believe Luke will survive the war."

I followed Luke's war in the letters he wrote me addressed to the coach's office at Colleton High. He wrote other letters to my parents, grandparents, and Savannah—cheerful letters full of pretty lies. In his letters to them he described sunsets over the South China Sea, meals he ate in Saigon, animals he sighted at the edges of jungles, jokes he heard from his friends. In his letters to me he sounded like a drowning man. He described military operations to blow up bridges in North Vietnam, night raids on enemy positions, rescue missions to liberate captured Americans, and ambushes on small supply trails. Once he swam four miles up a river and slit the throat of a village chief who had been consorting with the Viet Cong. He had been the only survivor of a raiding party that had tried to surprise a retreating column of North Vietnamese regulars. His best friend had died in his arms after stepping on a land mine. It was Luke and not the mine that killed him. His friend had begged Luke for the injection of morphine, saying that he would rather die than live like a vegetable without legs or balls. He would have died anyway but he died more quickly because my brother loved him. "I don't dream at night at all, Tom," he wrote me. "It's when I'm awake, when my eyes are wide open, that I live with nightmares. There is only one thing wrong with killing people. It gets so easy. Isn't that terrible?"

Whenever he killed a man, Luke would tell me about it in flat, unemotional prose and ask me to light a candle for the repose of the man's soul whenever I got near the Cathedral in Savannah. We had all been baptized in the Cathedral and it was Luke's favorite place of worship. Before Luke came home, I was lighting thirty-five candles beneath the statue of Our Lady of Perpetual Help and would recite the prayer for the dead in an aura of trembling light for this platoon of unknown men. With the rest of the family he continued to uphold the fiction that he was seeing no action at all. His letters to my parents sounded like a travel agent trying to entice reluctant tourists to an exotic locale in the Orient. He picked orchids in the jungle for my mother, pressed them between the leaves of the Bible my grandfather had given him as a going-away present, and sent the book to her for a Christmas present. The Bible smelled like a buried garden when my mother opened it, and dried orchids, with heads like shy dragons, appeared in hundred-page intervals. My mother wept over the first Christmas Luke had ever missed on the island.

"Dead flowers," my father said. "Luke's become real el cheapo over in Nam."

"My sweet baby boy," my mother said between sobs. "Thank God he's in no danger."

In Colleton I had entered into the teacher's life of sustained regularity. I taught my English students literature and composition for five hours every day, drilling them in the treacherous architecture of English grammar and force-marching them through the thickets of Silas Marner and

Julius Caesar. As a punishment for majoring in English during college, my principal assigned me to teach sophomores my first year in Colleton. Sophomores, sizzling with hormones and beleaguered by bodily changes they barely understood, would sit slack-jawed and comatose as I sang away about the pleasures of the active voice, the perils of "that versus which," or the perfidy of Cassius. I used words like *perfidy* far too much that first unconfident year as a lecturer. I had more in common with a thesaurus than I did with a teacher and the sophomores of Colleton County suffered because of my ineptitude.

At lunch, I would sit in the teachers' lounge. While I ate, I would correct the ghastly papers of my students, who seemed gifted in destroying all vestiges of beauty or grace from the language. After school, I would change into my coaching clothes, loop my whistle around my neck, and coach the junior varsity football team until six in the evening. I would be home by seven o'clock, when I'd begin fixing dinner. Sallie would arrive home later, exhausted from her long commute; she was attending the Medical College of South Carolina in Charleston. We lived in the small house we had rented a block from my grandparents'. Luke had wanted us to live in his house on the island but Sallie had easily assessed my mother's character and decided that Melrose was a one-woman operation. Our house was small but it was located on a creek and we could swim off a dock at high tide. In the mornings I set a crab pot before I left for work and fished for channel bass when they made their run in late September. I chaperoned a sock hop in the lunchroom after a football game on the same night that my sister attended an antiwar rally in Central Park and my brother helped mine the approaches to a North Vietnamese river.

During the Easter holidays, my father and I put the *Miss Savannah* on the rails of the dry dock and pulled her out of the water. We scraped the bottom of barnacles and paint, then put a fresh coat of paint on the blitzed-down wood. I ordered the nets I would need for the summer and we worked on the engine until it purred like a cat when we took the boat into the channel for a trial run.

That summer, I took to the river as a shrimp boat captain
for the first time in my life, a rookie in that hard and sun-
enameled fraternity.

I was tied up next to my father's boat and had to cross
his deck to get to the *Miss Savannah*.

"Good morning, Captain," my father would say.

"Morning, Captain," I would answer.

"Bet you a beer I put more shrimp in the scales than you
do today," he would tease.

"I hate stealing beer from an old man."

"That's too much boat for you, Captain," Dad would
say, looking over at the *Miss Savannah*.

Each summer morning I repeated those unconscious rituals of my childhood when I watched my voluble father,
talking incessantly about his plans to make a million bucks,
as he moved out to intercept the vast swarms of shrimp
efflorescing in the creeks. Only now it was I behind the
wheel—moving the heart-pine vessel through channels I
knew like the ridges of my thumbnail, interpreting the tid-
ings of markers that flashed for a thousand miles along the
inland waterway, and keeping a nervous eye on the depth
recorder whenever I shrimped waters unfamiliar to me. I
would follow my father's boat out each morning and we
would shrimp in tandem.

At sunrise we would have our positions agreed upon and
I would reduce power from 1500 rpm to 900 and listen for
the music of the winch as Ike Brown, the striker I had hired,
began the work of setting the nets and getting them into
the water. When the nets opened underwater, I felt them
drag the boat almost to a halt and I adjusted to the proper
trawling speed of 1½ knots.

That first summer, I caught thirty thousand pounds of
shrimp, paid Ike a good salary, myself a better one, and
made all payments on my brother's boat. When I had to
begin summer football practice on August twentieth, I had
trained Ike Brown to be a captain himself and he had brought
his son, Irvin, aboard as striker. Later, when Luke returned
from overseas, he co-signed the bank note when Ike bought
his own shrimp boat and christened it *Mister Luke*. In the
naming of boats, there is always a sense of honor and sen-
timent at play.

By the time I became a football coach again that August,

Savannah had given her first poetry reading and Luke was about to bring his military career to an end—and get back to the river where he belonged. Invisibly, all the nets were moving in place through the silent channels encircling the shrimper's family.

It was night on the South China Sea and the planes were returning to the carrier after their raids over North Vietnam when the radio control center received an urgent message from a pilot that he was crash landing in a rice paddy less than a mile from the sea. The pilot had given the exact coordinates of his position when he was lost from radio contact. A brief council formed on the bridge of the carrier and a command decision was made that a team be sent ashore to attempt a rescue of the downed pilot.

Lieutenant jg Christopher Blackstock was chosen to lead the mission and when asked by his commanding officer to choose the other members of his team said only a single word: "Wingo."

They were lowered into the sea after dark on a black life raft and paddled beneath a full moon through the three miles of rough water to the beach. The moon was bad luck but they reached the shore without incident, hid the boat beneath a grove of coconut palms, checked their positions, then made their way inland.

It took them an hour to find the plane, which had gone down in the center of a rice field that mirrored the moon in a thousand pools of fresh water. Luke told me later that a rice field was the most beautiful marriage of water and crops he had ever seen.

This rice field inspired both awe and danger as Luke and Lieutenant Blackstock crawled on their bellies along one of the ridges that divided the field into shimmering symmetrical pools. The jet had lost a wing and lay glistening on its side, the high rice reaching up to the fuselage. The rice moved with the wind and reminded Luke of the salt marshes of Carolina, but the smell was more delicate and sensual.

"This was real rice, Tom. Not that Uncle Ben shit. There were some damn good farmers sleeping in that part of the world."

"Did you think the pilot might still be alive?" I asked.

"No, not after we saw the plane," he said.

"Why didn't you turn back and get your butts back to the boat?"

A year later when he was back in Colleton, Luke laughed and said, "We were SEALs, Tom."

"Jerks," I said.

"Blackstock was the best soldier I ever saw, Tom," Luke explained. "I'd have crawled all the way to Hanoi if he'd asked me to."

When they reached the downed jet, Blackstock made a motion for Luke to cover him. Blackstock climbed up the intact wing and peered into the empty cockpit. There was movement in a line of trees a quarter of a mile away and Blackstock dove for the soft watery earth as the first salvo from the AK-47s smashed into the fuselage of the plane. Luke saw five North Vietnamese regulars come running toward them, moving low and fast between the tall sheaves of rice. He waited for the wind to bend the rice again and when it did, he aimed his submachine gun, fired, and watched all five splash heavily into the paddies. Then it seemed as if all of North Vietnam rose up to challenge their return to the sea.

They plunged down an embankment as mortar fire took the damaged plane apart behind them and they sprinted south along a perimeter of solid land as they heard orders shouted in Vietnamese being issued in the darkness. The jet was still receiving most of the incoming fire, and they put as much distance between themselves and the plane as they could before they turned and crawled along one of those straight and vulnerable ridges that divided the rice field into congruent designs. They heard the soldiers moving toward the perimeter and the jet, concentrating their firepower. A hand grenade exploded a hundred yards away.

"There's only about a hundred of them, Luke," Blackstock whispered in Luke's ear.

"For a minute, I thought we were outnumbered," Luke whispered back.

"Poor bastards don't know we're SEALs," he whispered.

"Doesn't seem to bother them much, sir."

"Let's make it to the trees. Then they got to find us in the dark," Blackstock whispered finally.

But while they were lowcrawling toward the looming shadows of the forest the North Vietnamese had overrun the area around the plane and discovered that the Americans had escaped the ambush. Luke heard the sound of men running and of feet splashing through the rice paddies searching for them. But the rice field was vast and its divisions of water and long intersecting footbridges of land made a disciplined search impossible. It was only when a squad of North Vietnamese soldiers came rushing out of the darkness on that same isthmus of land, running headlong and reckless, that Luke and Blackstock instinctively rolled off into opposite sides of the paddy and, lying in water, waited until the men in black were almost on top of them. They killed seven of them in a space of three seconds, then took off, running through the water and high rice with bullets threshing the rice around them. When they reached the tree line, Blackstock rushed for the covering of jungle. Luke heard the single retort of an AK-47 come from the trees, heard Blackstock fire his submachine gun at the point where the shot had been fired, then heard Blackstock fall. Luke came out of that paddy spraying machine-gun fire in all directions. He crouched and fired until his ammunition was spent. He grabbed Blackstock's weapon and continued firing. When he had emptied the second submachine gun, he began lobbing grenades to his left and right. It was ineffective, he agreed later, but he wanted to give the enemy something to occupy their attention.

Weaponless, he lifted Blackstock off the North Vietnamese who had killed him, put Blackstock on his shoulders, and headed for the Pacific Ocean with a large contingent of the enemy forces in serious pursuit. Once he was in the forest, he began walking and listening. Whenever he heard his pursuers, he simply stopped until he no longer heard them. He treated his withdrawal as a long deer hunt and he used the knowledge he had learned from his lifelong association with the white-tailed deer. Movement could kill a deer or save it; it all depended on the wisdom of the choice the deer made when the smell of hunters entered the woods. For an hour Luke hid beneath the roots of a fallen tree that bore a strange fruit he had never seen. He listened to voices, footsteps, heard rifle fire near him and miles away. Again, he lifted Blackstock up on his shoulders

and began carrying the leader of his mission toward the
sound of waves crashing on the beach. It took him three
hours to go half a mile. Luke did not panic. He listened
and made sure that when he moved there was no one
nearby to hear his advance. He was in the country of his
enemy, he reasoned, and they held an enormous advantage
because of their familiarity with the terrain. But the land
was not that much different from coastal South Carolina
and Luke figured that he had learned a thing or two as a
kid. And it was dark and no one could follow a trail in the
dark.

At four in the morning Luke made it to the edge of the
Pacific. He watched a patrol pass him heading north, their
rifles locked and loaded. He let them get three-quarters of
a mile down the beach before he walked in a straight line
to the ocean without looking to his right or left. If someone
saw his bold move to the water, he figured he was a dead
man. But if he waited for daylight he had no chance at all.
He reached the water and hurled Blackstock over a wave
and dove in after him. It took him fifteen minutes to get
past the breakers and into open water. But once he was in
the water, he knew he had entered his element at last and
that no one presently living in North Vietnam could ever
take Luke Wingo in salt water.

When he hit the open sea, he checked the stars and tried
to get his bearings. Then he swam three miles, towing
Lieutenant jg Christopher Blackstock behind him. He was
picked up by an American patrol boat at eleven o'clock the
next morning after being in the water for six and a half
hours.

Luke was called before the admiral of the Pacific Fleet to
give his account. Luke reported that the pilot was not in
the wreckage of his plane and that Lieutenant Blackstock
had confirmed that visually. They did not know if the pilot
was dead, captured, or had bailed out prior to crashing.
Then, they had encountered heavy enemy resistance and
were involved in a fire fight on the way back to the beach.
Lieutenant Blackstock had been killed by rifle fire. Luke
had obeyed his orders and returned to the general staging
area of his mission.

"Sailor," the admiral asked Luke, "why did you bring

Lieutenant Blackstock's body back to the ship with you if you knew he was dead?''

"We learned it during training, Admiral," Luke said.

"Learned what?"

"SEALs don't leave their dead," Luke answered.

When Luke returned to Colleton at the end of his tour of duty, we sat on that same wooden bridge where we had celebrated our graduation from high school. Luke had won a Silver Star and two Bronze Stars.

"Did you learn to hate the North Vietnamese, Luke?" I asked him as I passed the bottle of Wild Turkey to him. "Did you hate the Viet Cong?"

"No," he said, "I admired them, Tom. Those folks are good farmers. Good fishermen, too."

"But they killed your friends. They killed Blackstock."

"When I was in the rice field, Tom," Luke said, "I figured I was the first white man who had ever been to that field. I had come armed with a submachine gun. They were right to try to kill me. I had no business being there."

"Then what were you fighting for?" I asked.

"I was fighting because I live in a country where they put you in jail if you tell them you won't fight. I was earning my right to get back to Colleton," he said. "And I'm never going to leave this island again. I've earned the right to stay here for the rest of my life."

"We're lucky in America," I said. "We don't have to worry about a war on our own soil."

"I don't know, Tom," he said. "The world is a terribly fucked up place."

"Nothing ever happens in Colleton," I said.

"That's what I love about Colleton," he answered. "It's like the whole world is happening for the first time. It's like being born in Eden."

25

Though my parents' marriage could serve as a field manual on the art of misalliance, I thought the mere force of habit had made it indestructible. As I grew older and began raising my own children, I ceased noticing the steady erosion of any respect my mother might once have felt for my father. With her children grown, my mother turned her formidable energies to projects outside her home. By growing up, we had committed the crime of blurring those distinctions by which my mother defined herself; we also provided her manumission from the narrowness of that flawed self-definition. My mother had waited her whole life for that proper moment when her instincts for power and intrigue could be fully tested in the crucible of small-town life. When her time approached, she was not found wanting. With her beauty alone, Lila Wingo could have troubled the licentious dreams of kings. But with her beauty *and* her cunning she could have inspired anarchists and regicides to bring her the heads of a dozen kings, garnished with parsley and roses, on pale blue Wedgwood plates.

Later, we would wonder aloud whether my mother had planned for years to make her spectacular break with the past or had operated with a freestyle genius and seized the opportunity as events unfolded around her. We had long suspected that she was a brilliant woman, but it was only Savannah who was not surprised that my mother would prove to be a bold and unscrupulous one. She never apologized and never explained. She did what she was born to do, and my mother was never one to indulge in sudden flights of honesty or self-examination.

With an impressive command of tactics, she proved herself the designated terrorist of beauty, the queen of the bloodless auto-da-fé, and, in the process, she ate Henry Wingo alive. But the price she paid was high.

In her hour of greatest triumph, when all honors and kudos and riches had accrued to her at last, when she had proven to all that we had underestimated her value and importance, my father went to prison in a last grand gesture to win her admiration and they brought my mother the head of her oldest son on a plate. It would be my mother's destiny to know the dust, and not the savor, of answered prayers.

One day in 1971 I was shrimping with Luke on the ocean side of the Coosaw Flats, heading a little south of east, when the call came in from my mother.

"Captain Wingo. Captain Luke Wingo. Come in Captain. Out," she said.

"Hello, Mama. Out," he said.

"Tell Tom he's about to become a daddy. And congratulations. Out."

"I'll be right there, Mama. Out," I screamed into the radio.

"This also means I'm about to become a grandmother. Out," my mother said.

"Congratulations, Grandma. Out."

"I don't find you amusing, son. Out," my mother said.

"Congratulations, Tom. Out," my father said over the radio.

"Congratulations, Tom," ten other shrimp boat captains radioed in as I struggled to get the nets in and Luke turned the boat toward Colleton.

When we passed the hospital, which sat on the river just south of town, Luke steered the boat close to the river's edge and I dove into the river. I swam to shore, scrambled up the bank, and raced into the maternity ward dripping seawater. A nurse brought me a towel and a hospital bathrobe and I held Sallie's hand until Dr. Keyserling said it was time and they wheeled her away to the delivery room.

That night Jennifer Lynn Wingo was born at 11:25, weighing in at seven pounds, two ounces. Every shrimper on the river sent flowers and every teacher in the high school came to see the baby. My grandfather brought her a white Bible the next morning and filled out her family tree in the middle of the book.

Down the hall from Sallie, my mother found a sick and frightened Isabel Newbury, who had entered the hospital for tests that day after passing blood in her stool. Mrs. Newbury was terrified and could not eat hospital food and my mother began bringing her meals to the hospital whenever she visited Sallie and the baby. It was not until she was transferred to Charleston that the preliminary diagnosis of intestinal cancer was corroborated. It was my mother who drove Mrs. Newbury to Charleston for the tests, and it was my mother who comforted Mrs. Newbury during her terrible ordeal of surgery. Of all my children, my mother always preferred Jennifer, not because she was first born, but because it was her birth that led directly to my mother's great and accidental friendship with Isabel Newbury.

No one could say for sure when the quiet bands of surveyors, with their tapes and transits, invaded our county and began the long study of its metes and bounds. But most agree that it was the same summer that my grandfather, Amos Wingo, had his driver's license suspended by the State Highway Department. Amos had always been a heroically bad driver even as a young man, but as he grew older and his faculties dimmed he became a menace to every living creature who stepped upon a macadam surface in the lowcountry. Because of an uncharacteristic vanity, he refused to wear his eyeglasses, nor did he think he should be held responsible for running red lights he did not see.

"They put them up too high," he explained about the traffic lights. "I'm not bird watching when I drive. I've got my eye on the road and my mind on the Lord."

"You almost ran Mr. Fruit down last week," I said to him. "They said he had to dive off the road to keep from getting hit, Grandpa."

"I didn't see no Mr. Fruit," Amos answered. "He's always been too puny a man to direct traffic anyway. They should only let fat men have that job. Mr. Fruit should specialize now that he's getting older. He should only be allowed to lead parades."

"Patrolman Sasser said he caught you up on the Charleston Highway driving along on the wrong side of the road," I said.

"Sasser!" my grandfather fumed. "I was driving a gasoline-powered automobile before that boy was born. I told that boy I was looking at a field chock-full of cowbirds and that I was appreciating the world God put down here for man to appreciate. Besides, there was nothing coming down the other side of the road, so what's all the fuss about?"

"I ought to just go ahead and put him in a home," my grandmother said. "He's going to kill somebody in that automobile."

"I got the body of a man half my age," my grandfather said, hurt.

My grandmother answered, "We're talking about gray matter, Amos. It's like living with Methuselah, Tom. He can't remember where he puts his teeth at night. I found them in the refrigerator the other day."

"They want you to turn in your license voluntarily, Grandpa," I said.

"There's getting to be too much government in Colleton," my grandfather said. "I never heard of such."

"Will you give me your license, Grandpa?" I asked. "Or else Sasser is going to drive out here to get it."

"I'll consider it directly," he said. "I'll discuss it with the Lord."

"See, Tom?" Tolitha said. "I'm going to have to put him in a home."

After a lengthy discussion of the issue, to no one's astonishment, Jesus allowed that my grandfather should keep his driver's license, but should always wear his glasses. To Amos, the Lord was everything: traffic controller, mediator, and optometrist.

Two days later my grandfather ran over Mr. Fruit on the same corner. Wearing his glasses, my grandfather had turned to observe the team of surveyors who were measuring the boundary lines of the property adjacent to Baitery Street and the Street of Tides. Amos neither saw the red light nor heard Mr. Fruit's frantic toots on the whistle and only when he heard Mr. Fruit crash down on the hood of his 1950 Ford did my grandfather put on the brakes. Mr. Fruit suffered only minor bruises and abrasions but the State Patrol was no longer amused by my grandfather's high jinks behind the wheel of a car.

Patrolman Sasser seized Amos's driver's license on the spot and cut it into pieces with the scissors of a small Swiss Army knife.

"I was driving before you were born, young Sasser," my grandfather complained.

"And I want to live to be an old man just like you, Mr. Wingo," Sasser replied. "But there ain't gonna be anybody alive in this county if I don't get you off the road, sir. Face facts, Mr. Wingo. You are infirm, sir, and a menace to society."

"Infirm!" my grandfather said indignantly as Mr. Fruit wailed in terror and the ambulance rescue squad pulled up with its siren going full blast.

"I'm doing you a favor, Mr. Wingo," Sasser said, "and I'm protecting the public weal."

"Infirm!" my grandfather repeated. "Let's arm-wrestle, Sasser, and we'll see who's infirm and the whole town can be the judge."

"No, sir," said Sasser. "I'm going to the hospital to make sure Mr. Fruit is okay."

My mother, walking down to Long's Pharmacy to fill some prescriptions for the critically ill Isabel Newbury, witnessed the entire confrontation between my grandfather and Patrolman Sasser. She had ducked into Woolworth's as soon as she heard Mr. Fruit scream and saw Amos's Ford screech to a halt. She did not like to be a witness when a Wingo made a horse's ass out of himself in public. Later, we learned that she was the only man or woman on the Street of Tides that day who knew why there were surveying teams the length and breadth of Colleton County.

The following week, Grandpa Wingo wrote a letter to the *Colleton Gazette* complaining of the cavalier treatment he had received at the hands of Patrolman Sasser, his outrage at having his driver's license destroyed in public by a Swiss Army knife, and his intention to prove to both Sasser and Colleton he was not "infirm." He announced that he would water-ski the forty-mile length of the inland waterway between Savannah, Georgia, and Colleton and challenged that "young pup" Sasser to ski alongside him. If he completed the journey, he demanded a public apology from the Highway Department and the immediate reinstatement of his driver's license.

My grandmother promptly began making serious inquiries about the availability of space in nursing homes across the state. But Luke and I took a weekend off to get the Boston Whaler in shape to make the trip. My grandfather was a simple man, but glorious notions had always kept him from being a dull one. Amos had brought the first pair of water skis to the county and, at fifty, was the first man in South Carolina ever to ski barefooted. For ten years, he held the state ski-jump record until a ringer from Cypress Gardens was imported one year for the Water Festival. But he had not skied for ten years when he issued his proclamation in the newspaper.

"You gonna put wheels on those skis, Grandpa?" Luke teased while he loaded a brand-new pair of Head skis into the boat as we were preparing to haul it to Savannah.

"That's what gave folks the idea I was slowing down in the first place," Amos answered. "I should never have put the wheel on the cross."

"I can drive you anywhere you need to go, Amos," my grandmother said. "There's no use proving to the whole world that you're an idiot. They know you can't drive worth a lick, but a lot of them don't know you're soft in the head."

"I need to concentrate more when I drive, Tolitha," my grandfather answered. "I know I make some mistakes behind the wheel, but I was busy listening to the words of the Lord."

"Did the Lord tell you to water-ski up from Savannah?" my grandmother asked.

"Where do you think I got the idea from?" he said.

"Just asking, Amos," my grandmother said. "You take good care of your grandpa, boys."

"We will, Tolitha," I said.

"I got a hundred bucks riding on you, Dad," my father said, slapping Amos on the back.

"I don't approve of betting," Amos admonished his son.

"Who did you bet, Dad?" Luke asked.

"That little son of a bitch Sasser," my father said, whooping. "He says he's going to be waiting at that dock with a new driver's license already made up, Dad, 'cause he don't think you're going to make it as far as Stancil Creek."

"Stancil Creek is just over the border about a mile outside of Savannah," my grandfather said.

"You should have gone to Dr. Keyserling for a checkup," my grandmother said to Amos. To the rest of us she said, "He hasn't had a physical in his whole life."

"You're going to do it, Amos," I heard Sallie say. "I can tell. You're going to do it."

"Feel that arm, Sallie," my grandfather said proudly, flexing his biceps. "The Lord didn't make Wingo men very smart. But he sure made them strong, and he blessed them with mighty fine taste in women."

"I wish He'd given me better taste in men," Tolitha said. "You're making a fool of yourself again, Amos. Lila's too embarrassed to show her face."

"Naw, she's just taking care of Isabel Newbury," my father said. "She's been like a saint since Isabel took sick. I've hardly seen her."

Luke took five twenty-dollar bills from his wallet and handed them to my father. "Here's a hundred bucks, Dad," he said. "A hundred bucks which says that Amos Wingo is going to ski all the way from Savannah to Colleton. Bet anyone you can."

"Your sister called me from New York City last night, boys," Amos said. "She said she was going to put me in one of her poems if I make it."

"You'll look like a fool in a bathing suit, Amos," Tolitha said as we entered the truck.

"Not when I get my brand-new driver's license in my hand, Tolitha," he said. "Then I'll get slicked up and take you for a long ride."

"I'll warn Mr. Fruit," said Tolitha.

These are the moments of surprise and consecration that hold me forever in debt and bondage to the memories I bring to bear from a southern life. I fear emptiness in life, vacuity, boredom, and the hopelessness of a life bereft of action. It is the death-in-life of the middle class that sends a primeval shiver through the nerves and open pores of my soul. If I catch a fish before the sun rises, I have connected myself again to the deep hum of the planet. If I turn on the television because I cannot stand an evening alone with myself or my family, I am admitting my citizenship with the living dead. It is the southern part of me which is most quintessentially and fiercely alive. They are deeply southern memories that surround the lodestar of whatever authenticity I bring to light as a man. Because of our intensity, I belonged to a family with a fatal attraction for the extraordinary gesture. There was always an outrageousness to our response to minor events. Flamboyance and exaggeration were the tail feathers, the jaunty plumage that stretched and flared whenever a Wingo found himself eclipsed in the lampshine of a hostile world. As a family, we were instinctive, not thoughtful. We could never outsmart our adversaries but we could always surprise them with the imaginativeness of our reactions. We functioned best as connoisseurs of hazard and endangerment. We were not truly happy unless we were engaged in our own private war with the rest of the world. Even in my sister's poems, one could always feel the tension of approaching risk. Her poems all sounded as though she had composed them of thin ice and falling rock. They possessed movement, weight, dazzle and craft. Her poetry moved through streams of time, wild and rambunctious, like an old man entering the boundary waters of the Savannah River, planning to water-ski forty miles to prove he was still a man.

"It's going to be a little chillier than we planned, Grandpa," I yelled to him as I fed the towrope out behind the boat. "The sun went behind the clouds and it looks like rain. We can put it off."

"They'll be waiting at the public dock," Amos said, taking the towbar into his hands, getting a good grip.

"Okay," I said. "It's incoming tide all the way, so we don't have to worry as much about sandbars. We're going on a straight line whenever we can and we're going as fast as this boat will take us."

"You think I should just slalom all the way to Colleton?" he asked.

"You're going to need two skis before it's over," I said.

"But I could really show some style when I finished."

"No, Grandpa," I said. "And, remember, I'm going to be tossing you oranges during the trip."

"I've never heard of eating no oranges when you're just out skiing."

"You aren't just out skiing, Grandpa," I said over the engine's idle. "You're going forty miles and you're going to need some fluid in you. Now, you watch for those oranges. If one hits you in the head, we'll be burying you at sea."

"It sounds funny to me," he said.

"You listen to the coach," I said, flashing him a thumbs-up sign. "You ready, old man?"

"Don't call me 'old man,' " he said.

"I won't call you an old man if you're still standing when we hit Colleton," I called out to him as he pointed the skis skyward.

"What'll you call me then, Tom?" he shouted.

"I'll call you one hell of an old man," I screamed as Luke hit the throttle and we headed south along the waterfront where a small crowd had gathered to watch the beginning of my grandfather's trip. They cheered when he lifted out of the water smoothly, and leaving the wake behind the boat, he cut toward them and sprayed them with a sheet of water as he made a dazzling angling turn back toward the boat.

"No tricks," I shouted as he began jumping the sharp rims of the wake and, keeping the line taut, raced out along the water until he was almost even with us in the boat.

"The kid's still got it," he shouted, screaming over the noise of the motor.

He did not settle into the serious business of pacing himself until we turned into Stancil Creek and entered South Carolina waters. Then, he moved behind the boat and let it do most of the work for him. I kept an eye on my grandfather and Luke watched the channel markers as we passed the small islands with their trees arranged on the sunless shores as the water changed from pale jade to a metallic gray. You could feel the sun shopping around for an opening in the massed cumulus, but you could also see the thunderheads, hive-shaped and ominous, gathering darkly to the north.

Behind us, my grandfather stood erect on his skis, his

arms and legs thin and functional, like a set of number-two pencils. There were no soft places on Amos and his body contained that surprising strength one associates with coiled wire. His forearms and triceps strained in graphic bas-relief against the tension of the towrope. His face and neck and arms were dark; his shoulders were shy and pale. As the day darkened and the temperature dropped, his flesh developed a slight bluish color like the tinges of azure in wild birds' eggs. After the tenth mile, he was gaunt and shivering and old. But he was still up and he was wonderful.

"He looks like death warmed over," Luke shouted to me. "Try to get him an orange."

With a pocket knife I cut a quarter-inch hole into the top of an Indian River orange and walked to the stern of the boat. I held it up for him and he nodded that he understood.

I tossed the orange straight up into the air, but I mis-judged the height and it sailed far over his head and Amos almost went down as he tried to leap for it.

"Don't jump, Grandpa," I screamed to him. "Let it come to you."

I wasted three oranges before I got his range and speed figured out and he caught the fourth one like an outfielder leaning over the fence to rob some power hitter of a home run. Luke's arm went up in a gesture of victory when Amos caught it, and Amos sucked that orange dry and emptied it of pulp before he let it drop like bright tissue into the waters behind him. The orange seemed to revive his spirits and he jumped the wake a few times and sat down on his skis while holding the towbar with one hand before we got him calmed down again.

"Mile fifteen," Luke said as we passed the buoy light that marked our entrance into Hanahan Sound.

There are times you can watch the stuff your family is made of, and this was one of those times. In Amos's eyes, we could see the grit and resolution granted in supreme distillation throughout the Wingo gene pool and it made us proud to be the son of his son. At the twenty-mile mark, he was shivering and his deep-set eyes were smoky like ruined aspic. But his skis still cut through the water like blades injuring a pure surface of enamel. He was shivering and exhausted, but he was still up, still moving toward Colleton.

He did not fall until we reached Colleton Sound and the waters were roiled by the approaching storm and we could see lightning scissoring through the clouds to the north.

"He's down," I called to Luke.

"Get in the water with him, Tom," Luke said as he turned the boat in a wide circle and cut the engine to idle as we approached Amos.

I jumped into the water beside him, holding a newly opened orange above my head and taking care that no salt water entered the hole I had just cut.

"How're you doing, Grandpa?" I asked as I swam up to him.

"Sasser's right," Amos answered, and I could hardly hear his voice. "I'm cramping up."

"Where are you cramping, Grandpa?" I said. "Don't worry. Not every water-skier carries his own masseur along with him."

"I'm one big cramp," he said. "I got toes that I never felt before cramping. My teeth are even cramping and they ain't even mine."

"Eat this orange, lie back, and let me work on the body," I said.

"No use," he said. "I've been beaten."

Luke had maneuvered the boat up beside us and I could hear it idling as I began to massage my grandfather's arms and neck.

"He says he's going to quit, Luke," I said.

"No, he isn't," Luke said.

"I'm licked, Luke," Amos said.

"Then you got a big problem, Grandpa," Luke shouted down to Amos.

"How's that, Luke?" my grandfather asked, moaning as my hands worked to soften the knotted muscles in his arms.

"I figure it's a lot easier to ski the ten miles to Colleton than it is to swim them same ten miles," Luke said.

As he said it, he held up his own driver's license and said, "There's one of these waiting for you just a little bit up the river, Grandpa. And I want to see that shit-eating

look on Sasser's young face when we come tearing up that
river."

Amos shouted, "Work on the legs, Tom. And throw me
down another one of those sweet-tasting oranges, Luke. I
swear I never knew an orange could taste so right."

"Take off your skis, Grandpa," I said. "I'm going to massage your feet."

"I've always had the prettiest feet," he said, half delirious.

"Strong feet, too, Grandpa," I whispered. "Strong enough
to go ten miles."

"Think about Jesus walking up to Calvary," Luke said,
his voice blooming from above. "Think if he had just quit,
Grandpa. Where would the world be now? He was strong
when he needed to be. Ask Him to help you."

"He didn't water-ski up to Calvary, boys," my grandfather gasped. "The times were different."

"But he would have if it was necessary, Grandpa," Luke
encouraged. "He'd have done anything to redeem mankind. He didn't quit. That was the whole point. He wouldn't
quit."

"Massage my neck again, Tom," my grandfather said
with his eyes closed and his mouth around the orange. "It's
mighty sore, son."

"Just relax, Grandpa," I said, moving around to massage
his temple and his neck. "Just float with the life jacket and
let all the muscles rest."

"You've always gone three hours on Good Friday," said
Luke. "You've never quit in your life. Tomorrow you can
take the whole family for a ride in the Ford."

"Speak for yourself, Luke," I said as my fingers dug into
my grandfather's shoulders. "Throw down that canteen
and let me give Grandpa some water." He floated in my
arms like a man asleep until he heard Luke say, "Better get
in the boat, Grandpa. You just made Sasser the happiest
man in South Carolina."

"Bring me that towrope, son," he said, his eyes opening
suddenly. "And I don't want to hear no more lip from my
grandsons."

"It's rough water from here on out, Grandpa," I said.

"That'll make it sweeter when you pull me through town,"
he said.

I got back in the boat and played out the towrope again, hand over hand, and fed it out to Amos until the line was taut and seemed to be connected to his navel. When I saw his skis rise up on each side of the rope, I shouted, "Now," and Luke hit the throttle and the boat shot forward through the rough waters. This time Amos came up like a man dying, an altered, quivering man blanched white by spray and exhaustion. He fought the rope, the waves, the storm, himself. The storm broke over us now and it rained so hard Amos dissolved behind us in illusory contours like the shape of a man in a badly focused negative. Lightning slashed at the islands and the thunder indentured the river with an amazing voice of negation. Rainwater flooded my eyes and Luke drove blindly, but with a perfect knowledge of depths and tides, as I watched the dim figure of my grandfather wage war against time and the storm.

"Are we killing him?" I cried out to Luke.

"It'll kill him if he doesn't make it," Luke screamed.

"Down again," I called as I saw Amos take a wave badly and get caught off balance as the next wave struck.

Luke circled the boat once more and I entered the water beside my grandfather, fighting the turbulent waters as I swam up behind him and again began massaging his neck and arms. He cried aloud when my fingers touched those sore muscles along his shoulders and beneath his arms. His coloring was all wrong, like a marlin undermined by the art of taxidermy. His body was limp, drained, and his thoughts rambled as I moved down to work on his legs and feet.

"I think we ought to bring him in the boat," I shouted to Luke as he angled toward us.

"No," my grandfather roared in a whisper. "How far?"

"Seven miles, Grandpa," Luke said.

"How do I look?" he asked.

"You look like hell," I answered.

"You look like a million bucks. Don't listen to Tom," Luke said.

"I'm the coach," I said.

"I taught you how to ski, son," Amos said as he floated on his back, his life jacket bobbing like a cork.

"And you taught me never to ski in weather like this," I said, my hands digging into his tight thighs.

"Then I taught you well," he said, laughing. "I taught you real well, son."

"Then get back in the boat," I ordered. "You gave it your best shot, Grandpa. No one can say you didn't try."

"The Lord wants me to keep going," Amos said.

"Listen to the thunder, Grandpa," I said. "It's saying no."

"It's saying, 'No, don't stop, Amos,' " he answered. "That's what I'm listening to."

"Tom never was good at foreign languages, Grandpa," Luke screamed as he brought the boat around and hauled me up over the side as Grandpa put on his skis again.

"I don't like it, Luke," I said.

"In seven miles, you're gonna love it," he answered as we watched Amos grab hold of the drifting towbar and ready himself for the final run to Colleton.

Luke slammed that throttle forward and again, my grandfather struggled to rise in the rain and white-capped surf, but rise he did, beyond all thresholds of desire or passion. He burned with the appetite of completion. The old lust of sport and competition vitalized his soul, and that was the flame that all the waters of the sky and the Atlantic could not touch as they beat his body senseless.

Two miles before we reached the town, we began to see the cars lining the road beside the river and clogging the boat landing waiting for our arrival. When they saw Amos still up on his skis, the shores erupted with a symphony of car horns and the citizens of Colleton honored Amos's triumph by flashing their headlights in celebration. Amos acknowledged the horns and the lights with a jaunty wave, and as we made the turn at the bend of the river, he started showing off again, doing a few tricks, flashing some of the old style. The noise of the horns was deafening as we passed alongside the Street of Tides, competing well even with the thunder. The bridge was thick with people and umbrellas and a cheer went up as Grandpa passed, waving and preening, beneath the grillwork of the drawbridge. Luke headed toward the public dock, where another crowd was gathered. He raced the boat at full throttle, then turned suddenly back down the river as my grandfather streaked toward shore at breakneck speed, released the towrope as Luke and I headed downriver, and floated magically, like a man walking on water, all the way to the public dock, where my father caught him in his arms.

Luke circled the boat and we witnessed that memorial moment beside the cheering crowd when Amos Wingo received his new driver's license from an impressed and gracious Patrolman Sasser.

We missed the more troubling moment when Amos collapsed in the parking lot and my father had to rush him to the emergency room at the hospital. Dr. Keyserling kept him confined to bed for a day and treated him for both exhaustion and exposure.

A year later Tolitha sent Amos out shopping for a pound of self-rising flour and a bottle of A-1 steak sauce. He had almost made it to the aisle with the steak sauce when he stopped suddenly, gave out with a small cry, and pitched forward into a canned goods display of turnip greens flavored with pork. Amos Wingo was dead when he hit the ground even though Patrolman Sasser tried vainly to revive him with mouth-to-mouth resuscitation. They said that Sasser cried like a baby when the ambulance squad drove off to the hospital with my grandfather's body. But Sasser was only the first in Colleton to weep that night. The whole town knew it had lost something exquisite and irreplaceable. Nothing so affects a small town as the loss of its rarest and finest man. Nothing so affects a southern family as the death of the man who lent it balance and fragility in a world askew with corrupt values. His faith had always been a form of splendid madness and his love affair with the world was a hymn of eloquent praise to the lamb who made him. There would be no more letters to the *Colleton Gazette* with word-by-word transcriptions of the Lord's gossipy chats with Amos. Now those dialogues would be face-to-face as Amos cut the Lord's hair in a mansion sweet with the birdsong of angels. Those were the words of Preacher Turner Ball that rang through the white clapboard church on the day they buried my grandfather.

The South died for me that day, or at least I lost the most resonant and eminent part of it. It lost that blithe magic I associate with earned incongruity. He had caught flies and mosquitoes in jars and set them free in the back yard because he could not bear to kill one of God's creatures.

"They're part of the colony," he had said. "They're part of the design."

His death forced me to acknowledge the secret wisdom that issues naturally from the contemplative life. His was a life of detachment from the material and the temporal. As a boy I was embarrassed by the undiluted ardor he brought to worship. As an adult I would envy forever the simplicity and grandeur of his vision of what it was to be a complete and contributing man. His whole life was a compliance and a donation to an immaculate faith. When I wept at his funeral, it was not because of my own loss. You carry a man like Amos with you, a memory of immortal rose in the garden of the human ego. No, I cried because my children would never know him and I knew that I was not articulate enough in any language to describe the perfect solitude and perfect charity of a man who believed and lived every simple word of the book he sold door to door the length and breadth of the American South. The only word for goodness is goodness, and it is not enough.

Amidst the shouts of "Hallelujah" and "Praise be the Lord" six men with newly made wooden crosses began thumping the bases of the crosses against the wooden floor of the church as a gesture of homage to my grandfather. They drummed the crosses in unison, creating a palsied, unfathomable tattoo, the dark music of crucifixionists. My father rose up with Tolitha leaning against him and he walked his mother down the center aisle, where she faced Amos for the last time. In the open casket, with his hair swept back in a pompadour and a slight bedeviled smile on his face (indelible signature of the undertaker, Winthrop Ogletree), Amos looked like a choirboy gone to seed. A white Bible was opened to the page where Jesus spoke the red words, "I am the Resurrection and the Life." The organist played "Blessed Be the Tie that Binds" and the congregation sang the words as Tolitha leaned down and kissed my grandfather's lips for the last time.

We walked from the church to the cemetery. I held Sallie's hand and Luke walked with my mother. Savannah helped my father with Tolitha. The whole town, black and white, moved in solemn processional silence behind us. The men with the crosses dragged them down the center of the street. Mr. Fruit led the entourage, tooting his whistle with tears streaming down his face. Patrolman Sasser was one of the pallbearers.

We buried him in the paltry light of an overcast day. After they lowered Amos into his grave, Luke, Savannah, and I stayed behind to shovel the dirt ourselves. It took us an hour to get it right. When we had finished we sat beneath the water oak that shaded the Wingo family plot. We cried and we told stories about Amos and his role in our childhood. Our grandfather, in dreamless sleep beneath us, spoke to us from the singing hive of memory. There is an art to farewell, but we were too young to have mastered it. We simply told stories about the man who had cut our hair since we were children and who had fashioned out of his life an incorruptible psalm to the God who made him.

Finally, Savannah said, "I still say, with all due respect, that Grandpa was crazy."

"That's all due respect?" Luke asked.

"Remember, Luke, Grandpa used to talk to Jesus on a daily basis," she said. "That's not what psychiatrists refer to as normal behavior."

"Hell, you talk to dogs and angels on a daily basis," Luke said, angrily. "I think it's a hell of a lot more normal to talk to Jesus."

"That was mean, Luke," said Savannah, her eyes downcast and misty. "I don't want you to make light of my problems. I'm having a very difficult time. I'm always going to have a hard time."

"He didn't mean anything by it, Savannah," I said.

"I shouldn't have come down here," she said. "It's bad for me to be around my family. It's dangerous."

"Why is it dangerous?" I asked. "Is that why we hardly ever see you, Savannah?"

"The dynamic of this family is hideous," she answered. "It's going to catch up to you boys some day just like it caught up with me."

"What are you talking about, Savannah?" Luke asked. "We were just talking so nice about Grandpa and now you have to ruin it by talking about your latest shrink-of-the-month-club bullshit."

"You're next, Luke," she said. "You've got it written all over you."

"Next for what?" he asked.

"Neither of you has faced what really happened in our childhood and because you're both southern males, there's a great chance you'll never face it."

"I apologize for being a southern male, Savannah," Luke said. "What do you want me to be, an Eskimo? A Japanese pearl diver?"

"I want you to look around you and see what's happening, Luke," she said evenly. "You and Tom aren't even aware of what's going on right this minute."

"You've got to excuse us, Savannah," I said, my temper rising congruently with Luke's. "We're just southern males."

"Why do you hate women, Luke?" she asked. "Why don't you ever go out on dates? Why have you never been seriously involved with a woman in your whole life? Have you ever asked yourself these questions?"

"I don't hate women," he said, and there was authentic pain in his voice. "I just don't understand them, honey. I just don't know what they think or why they think it."

"What about you, Tom?" she asked. "How do you feel about women?"

"Me?" I said, "I hate their guts. I think women are the fucking scum of the earth. That's why I married one of them and had three daughters. Hatred was the central driving force behind it all."

"I can understand why you're so defensive," Savannah said in perfect control of herself.

"I'm not being defensive," I disagreed. "Luke and I are reacting to your insufferable piety, Savannah. Every time we see you we have to hear lectures about how we're wasting our lives down here while you're up in New York living a fruitful, self-actualizing, fabulous existence among the most gifted minds of our time."

"That's not true," she said. "I just have a better perspective since I only get home every couple of years. I see things immediately that you can't see because you're so close to them. Have any of you talked to Mom lately?"

"Yeah," Luke said. "Every single day of my life."

"Do you know what she's thinking?" Savannah asked,

ignoring the irony in Luke's voice. "Do you have any idea what she's planning to do?"

"She spends every single waking moment nursing that poor bitch Isabel Newbury," Luke said. "She's usually so exhausted when she gets home that she can barely do anything except fall into bed."

"Sallie looks unhappy, Tom," Savannah said without skipping a beat. "She looks exhausted."

"She's a doctor and a mother, Savannah," I said. "It's tough being one, much less both. Especially when the father teaches school and coaches three sports."

"Well, at least she doesn't have to be a housewife the rest of her life," she said.

"What in the hell do you have against housewives?" I said.

"I was raised by one," Savannah said. "And it almost ruined my life."

"I got knocked around by a shrimper when I was a kid," said Luke, "but I never blamed the shrimp."

"Mom's going to divorce Dad," Savannah said. "That's what she told me last night."

"That's a news bulletin?" Luke said. "How many times in our life has Mom said that?"

"Not many," I replied. "I don't think she's said it more than sixty-eight million times."

"How many times," Luke continued, "did Mom put us in the car, drive off the island, and swear to us that she would never live another night in Henry Wingo's house?"

"Not many," I said again. "That didn't happen but twenty or thirty times when we were kids."

"Where was she going to go?" Savannah asked. "How was she going to feed or clothe us? How was she going to survive without a man? Mom was trapped by the South and it made her a little mean. But I think she's going to leave him this time. She's filing for a divorce next week. She's hired a lawyer and he's drawing up the papers."

"Has she told Dad yet?" I asked.

"No," Savannah answered.

"Hey, first things first, Tom," said Luke.

"Don't you think it's strange that Mom has made this important decision and none of you know about it?" she said. "Doesn't it say something about the way this family communicates?"

"Savannah," said Luke, "why do you always come down to South Carolina just waiting to tell me and Tom how to live our lives? He and I don't breathe a word about how you live your life, but you got a thousand things to say about what we do. We were here saying goodbye to Grandpa and you've got to turn it into a group therapy session. If Mom is going to leave Dad, then that's their business and it'll be up to me and Tom to help get them through the best way we know how. You'll be up in New York, calling us on the telephone, telling us what a shitty job of it we're doing."

"I hate communication, Savannah," I said. "Every time we communicate with you these days we end up fighting. Whenever I find myself communicating with a member of my family, I always find out more than I want to . . . or much less."

"You don't care that Mom is divorcing Dad?" she asked.

"Yes, I care a great deal," I said. "Now that Dad no longer hits me or has an ounce of power over me, I find him merely pathetic. I grew up hating his guts because I was always afraid in his house and because it's difficult to forgive anyone who's robbed you of your childhood. But I have forgiven him, Savannah. I've also forgiven Mom."

"I can't forgive either one of them," said Savannah. "There's too much damage. I have to deal with their mistakes every day."

"They didn't mean nothing by it," Luke said, putting his arm around Savannah and pulling her against his chest. "They were just assholes and they didn't even know how to be good assholes. They just kind of fumbled around at it."

"I didn't mean to jump on you boys so hard," she said. "I'm always afraid this town is going to drag you down to its level."

"It's not a sin to love Colleton," Luke said. "The only real sin is not loving it enough. That's what Grandpa used to say."

"Look where it got him," Savannah said, nodding toward his grave.

"Heaven isn't such a bad place to be," Luke answered.

"You know you don't believe in heaven," she said.

"Yes, I do," he said. "I'm already there, Savannah. That's the big difference between you and me. Colleton's all I've ever wanted and all I've ever needed."

"There's no excitement here, no dazzle, no surge of the crowds, no stimulation," she said.

"What did you think at Grandpa's funeral when those six deacons began pounding their crosses on the floor when you gave your eulogy?" I asked.

"I thought they were nuts," she answered.

"But it was sure stimulating, wasn't it?" Luke said.

"No, it was just nuts," she said. "And it made me want to run out of this town as fast as my two legs could carry me."

"They were just letting everyone know how much they thought about Grandpa, Savannah," Luke said. "They were telling everyone they loved him."

"It might make a good poem," she said, thinking aloud. " 'The Cross-Beaters,' I could call it."

"Did you finish that poem about Grandpa's ski trip yet?" I asked.

"About," she answered. "It still needs work."

"What's taking you so long?" Luke asked.

"You can't rush art," she answered.

"Yeah," I said. "You stupid son of a bitch. You can't rush art."

Savannah ignored us both and rose to her feet and said, "We've got to say goodbye to Grandpa."

"Over there's where we're going to be buried," said Luke, walking to a plot of bare grass. "This plot is for me. Those are for you two and there's even enough room for our wives and children."

"How morbid and depressing, Luke," Savannah said.

"I find it comforting to know where I'll end up after I turn up my toes," Luke said.

"I'm going to be cremated and have my ashes scattered over the tomb of John Keats in Rome," said Savannah.

"A modest request," I said.

"No, little sister," Luke said amiably. "I'm bringing you right down to Colleton and planting your ass right here so I can keep an eye on you."

"How grotesque," she said.

"Let's get back to the house," I suggested. "Most of the fevered brains will have gone by now."

"Bye-bye, Grandpa," Savannah said softly, blowing a kiss downward toward the freshly turned earth. "If it wasn't for you and Tolitha, I don't know what would have happened to us."

"If you ain't in heaven, Grandpa," said Luke as we began walking out of the cemetery, "then it's all bullshit."

I lived in a county without snow or rhododendrons. I lived out my twenties as a coach of both awkward and agile boys. I divided the seasons in the annulling fluency of sports. There was the music of punted footballs spiraling toward clouds in autumn, the squeak of rubber against shining wood as tall boys pivoted toward the basket in winter, and the crack of Hillerich and Bradsby ash bats against baseballs in late spring. Coaching was not a mislaid passion. At its best, it was the art of giving meaning to a boy's childhood. I was not the best of coaches, but I was not a harmful one either. I figured greatly in no boy's nightmare. Never once did I defeat those awesomely disciplined football teams of the great John McKissick of Summerville. He was a maker of dynasties and I was a coach limited in purview and scope. I had neither a quarrel with nor addiction to winning. I had played on teams that had done both and though winning was better, it lacked that brittle sublimity, that slight wisdom one took from a game in which you played with all your heart and your effort fell short. I taught my boys that losing well was a gift, but that winning well was the stuff of authentic manhood. Losing, I told them, was good for your sense of proportion.

I tried to live well in that county without snow or rhododendrons. I took up bird watching, became an amateur butterfly collector, set gill nets for the annual run of shad, and collected Bach and Carolina beach music. I became one of those anonymous Americans who tries to keep his mind sharp and inquisitive while performing all the humiliating rituals of the middle class. I subscribed to five magazines at the teacher discount rate: *The New Yorker*, *Gourmet*, *Newsweek*, *The Atlantic*, and *The New Republic*. I thought my choices of magazines indicated a thoughtful, liberal man with a variety of interests. It never once occurred to me that those carefully considered choices revealed the irrefutable fact that I was both a joke and a cliché of my times. Savannah would send me boxes of books she had bought from Barnes & Noble. She believed I had traded in my mind when I decided to remain in the South. She had a grocer's faith in books; they could be handed out like Green Stamps and were redeemable for a variety of useful gifts. I know Savannah worried about me and the fatal attraction I had for the conventional and the safe. I think she was wrong about me; my disease was much stranger. I brought to my adult life a nostalgia for a lost childhood. I longed to raise my children in a South stolen from me by my mother and father. What I wanted most was a life of vigorous quality. I had some knowledge to pass on to my children and it had nothing to do with great cities. Savannah did not understand that I had a burning need to be a decent man and nothing more. When I died, I wanted Sallie to say when she kissed me for the last time, "I chose the right man." It was the one fire that sustained me, the one idea I consigned as first principle of my life as a man. That I failed, I think, had less to do with me than with the raw obliquity of circumstance. When I chose to return to Colleton, I had no idea, and I would have laughed had it been suggested, that Colleton would cease to be an incorporated township in South Carolina. I was about to learn much about my century. I would like none of it.

Three weeks after my grandfather's funeral, I saw my father's truck parked outside my house when I returned from football practice. He had a bumper sticker on the back of his truck picturing a peace symbol followed by these words: "This is the footprint of the American chicken." He was sitting in the living room talking to Sallie when I entered the house. Jennifer was sitting in my father's lap and Sallie was changing Lucy's diapers on the couch.

"Hi, Dad," I said. "Can I fix you a drink?"

"Sure, son. Anything you've got is fine with me."

Sallie came into the kitchen when I made the drinks and I said, "You want me to fix you one, Sallie, or do you want to wait until we get these tigers to bed?"

"Something's happened," Sallie whispered. "He was crying just a minute ago."

"My father? Crying?" I said in a low voice. "That's impossible. Only human beings cry when they become emotionally upset. My father was born without emotions like some people are born without little fingers."

"You be nice to him, Tom," she said. "You be real nice. I'm going to take the girls over to Tolitha's house. He wants to talk to you alone."

"Let us go somewhere, Sallie," I said. "It's easier for us."

"He needs to talk now," she answered, and she went to gather up the children.

When I returned to the living room, I found my father sitting with his head resting on the back of the armchair. He was breathing heavily and more distraught than I had ever seen him. He looked like he was strapped to an electric chair. His hands shivered and his knuckles were purple.

"How's the team coming along?" he asked as I handed him his drink.

"They're doing real well, Dad," I answered. "I think we have a real good chance against Georgetown."

"Can I talk to you, son?" he asked.

"Sure, Dad."

"Your mother moved out on me a couple of days ago," he said, and each word came hard. "I didn't think much of it at first. I mean, we have our ups and downs just like all couples, but we usually patch it up pretty quick. But I got served with papers by the sheriff today. She wants a divorce."

"I'm sorry, Dad," I said.

"Has she spoken to you about it?" he asked. "Did you know this was coming?"

"Savannah told me something about it after Grandpa's funeral," I said. "I didn't think too much about it, Dad."

"Why didn't you tell me, son?" he said in a wounded voice. "I could have bought her some flowers or taken her to a fancy restaurant in Charleston."

"I didn't think it was any of my business," I said. "I thought it had to be worked out by the two of you."

"None of your business!" he shouted. "I'm your father and she's your mother. If it's not your goddamn business, then whose is it? What in the hell am I gonna do if she leaves me, Tom? Can you tell me that? What good is my goddamn life without your mother? Why in the hell do you think I worked so hard all my life? I wanted to give her all the things she always dreamed of. Not everything worked out like I hoped it would, but I always gave it the old college try."

"You did try," I said. "No one can ever deny that."

"If I had hit paydirt just once, she'd never have left me," he said. "You have no idea how your mother loves money."

"I have some idea, Dad," I said.

"That's why she'll be back," he said. "She doesn't know what it is to make a living and she sure as hell is too old to learn how at this late stage in the game."

"Mom's a very bright woman," I said. "If she left you, Dad, I promise you she has a plan."

"She can have all the plans in the world," he said, "but she doesn't have any of the cash dough to carry out those plans. Why did she do it, son? Please help me, son. Why did she go and do that?"

He put his face in his enormous hands and wept so violently that tears rolled between his fingers and down the back of his hands and wrists. He came apart as if he had thrown a piston in one of the valves of his heart. It was not grief I was witnessing; it was the agony of a man who knew he would have to pay in full the dues of his ungentle tyranny. He had to account for a thirty-year reign of mild terror and he brought to the task no talent for contrition.

"I treated her like a queen," he said. "That was my problem. I was too goddamn nice to her. I gave her everything she wanted. I let her put on airs and pretend she was something she never was. I went along with everything when I should have just run a tighter ship."

"You knocked her around, Dad," I said, "just like you knocked us around."

He tried to answer but could not talk. Great sobs broke out of him like waves breaking against an endangered beach. For a moment I almost pitied him until I remembered my eighteen-year apprenticeship in his guild of storm. Cry for my mother, Dad, I wanted to say to him. Weep for my brother and sister. Shed a tear for me, Dad. There were not enough tears in his body to absolve the thoughtless crimes he committed as both husband and father. I could grant no amnesty to the man who did not touch me as a child except when he was backhanding me to the floor. But I was astonished when he could finally speak and said, "I never laid a hand on your mother and I never once touched my children."

"What?" I screamed at him, and again he sobbed out of control.

When he quieted down, I knelt beside his chair and I whispered, "This is what makes me crazy in this family, Dad. I don't care that you hit us. I really don't. That's over and there's nothing any of us can do about it. But I can't stand it when I state a simple fact about this family's history and I'm told by you or Mom that it didn't happen. But you've got to know, Dad, and I'm saying this as a son who loves you, that you were a shit to Mom and a shit to your kids. Not all the time. Not every day. Not every month. But we never knew what would set you off. We never knew when your temper would explode and we'd have the strongest shrimper on the river knocking us around the house. So we learned to be quiet, Dad. We learned to tiptoe around you. We learned how to be afraid without making a sound. And Mom was a loyal wife to you, Dad. She would never let us tell a soul that you were hitting us. Most of the time, she was like you and would simply tell us it didn't happen the way we remembered it."

"You're a liar, Tom," he said suddenly. "You're a god-damn liar and you've let your mother poison you against me. I was too good. I was too good and that was my only mistake."

I grabbed his right arm, unbuttoned his sleeve, and rolled his shirt up to his elbow. I turned his arm palm side up, and I traced a scar, talon-shaped and purple with damaged skin, imprinted in the rolled muscle of his forearm. I stared at that arm with great tenderness. Enormous labor had shaped his arms into objects of lyrical beauty. The veins in his arm protruded like the roots of great trees along eroded banks. He had taken to wearing hats and long-sleeved shirts on the shrimp boat because he knew my mother admired the white pallor of men who did not work with their hands. My father's hands were rough and stained with grease.

You could take a razor blade and cut the moon of callus below his thumb and go a quarter of an inch before you drew blood. These hands had beaten me, but they had also worked for me, and I was a teacher because of them.

"How did you get this scar, Dad?" I asked. "Your son, the liar, your son who loves you, wants to know how you got this scar on your arm."

"How should I know?" he said. "I'm a shrimper. I've got scars all over my body."

"I'm sorry, Dad," I said. "That's not good enough."

"What are you trying to do to me, Tom?" he said.

"You can't change the way you are if you can't admit to the way you've been, Dad. Think about it. Where did you get that scar? I'll help you. Savannah and I are sitting at the dining room table. It's our tenth birthday. There's a cake on the table. No, I'm sorry. There are two cakes. Mom always made sure we each had our own cake."

"I don't know anything you're talking about," he said. "I should have gone to see Luke. You're trying to make me think I'm a rotten person."

"I just asked you where you got that scar, Dad," I said. "You called me a liar and I'm trying to let you know that I remember every single detail of how you got that scar. I've had nightmares about that scar."

"So kill me. I don't remember. It's not a crime not to remember something," he shouted.

"Sometimes, it is a crime, Dad," I said. "And now I want you to let me tell you about that night. It's important, Dad. It's just one night out of ten thousand, but it will help you get some small perspective on why Mom might be leaving you now."

"I didn't ask for no perspective," he whined. "I asked for some help."

"That's what I'm giving you," I said, and I began my story as my father wept in his outsized hands.

It began as it always did, without warning or time to withdraw. My father had left the dinner table early and was watching the *Ed Sullivan Show* on television. He was at the end of a bad shrimping season and that always made him dangerous and unpredictable. He had not spoken during dinner and he took a bottle of bourbon with him to the living room. But nothing in his carriage implied menace. Even his silence could be benign and ascribed to physical exhaustion rather than a secret consolidation of rage. My mother lit the ten candles on each of our cakes and Savannah clapped her hands in delight and said, "We're in double figures now, Tom. We'll have two numbers from now until we're a hundred."

"Come to the table, Henry," my mother said. "The kids are about to blow out the candles."

Had they argued the night before? Was there a fight between them left unfinished? I do not know, nor does it matter.

"Henry, did you hear me?" my mother said again, walking toward the living room. "It's time to sing 'Happy Birthday' to Savannah and Tom."

My father did not move from his chair or make any sign that he had heard my mother's voice.

"Let it drop, Mama," I prayed behind the small fires of ten candles.

"Get up and help your children celebrate their birthday," she ordered as she walked over and turned the television set off.

I could not see his eyes, but I saw his shoulders stiffen and saw him lift the drink to his lips and empty the glass.

"Don't you ever do that again, Lila," he said. "I was watching that program."

"You'll make your children think you don't love them enough to even wish them Happy Birthday."

"I'll make you wish you were never born if you don't switch that TV back on," he said, his voice without affect or inflection.

"It's all right, Mama," said Savannah. "Turn the television back on. Please, Mama."

"I will not," my mother said. "Your father can watch all the TV he wants after we cut the cake."

Now, with all the engines of their intricate discord throbbing, the vibrations heartfelt in a ten-year-old bloodstream, I watched with powerless eyes as my father rose lion-eyed in the dumb sterility of his defeated life and shoved my mother toward the television set. He grabbed her hair and forced her to her knees as his children cried out in the keepsake light of birthday candles.

"Turn on the TV set, Lila," he said. "And never tell me what to do in my own house again. This is my house and I just let you live in it."

"No," she said.

He smashed her face against the picture tube and I was amazed it did not break with the impact.

"No," she said again with blood running out of both nostrils.

"Do it, Mama," I screamed.

Savannah ran to the television set, fought her way around them, and once again Ed Sullivan's voice filled the room.

"She turned it on," my mother gasped. "I didn't."

My father reached down and turned the set off again. There was a constrained terrible grief in that silence.

"I told you to turn it on, Lila," he said. "You're setting a bad example for the boys. They've got to learn that a woman is supposed to respect a man in his own home."

Savannah turned the television set on again, but this time she turned the volume up too loud and Ed Sullivan entered our house screaming. My father backhanded my sister and she fell across the coffee table and rolled into a fetal position on the rug.

My mother ran to Savannah and the two of them wept in each other's arms as my father moved slowly and deliberately toward them. He was hovering over them when six quick shots from a .38 revolver destroyed the television set in a spectacular explosion of wood and glass.

I turned and saw Luke standing by our bedroom door, calmly reloading the pistol as smoke spiraled upward out of the barrel of the gun.

"The television's broken," Luke said. "Now you can sing 'Happy Birthday' to your kids."

My father began moving slowly toward Luke, his eyes pale and brutal and glistening with a dull animal shine. He approached Luke as archfiend, hitter of sons, wife-beater, lucid with seething, prowling fury. But Luke had reloaded the gun and snapped the chamber shut and aimed at my father's heart.

"What makes a man act like you?" Luke asked. "Why would anyone so big hit his wife or little girl? Why are you so mean?"

My father kept moving toward Luke, who retreated toward the kitchen, the gun still aimed at my father's chest. The noise I heard was the single merged voice of my mother and sister and myself screaming out in mortal steadfast horror.

When my father took hold of Luke's wrist and wrenched the gun from his grasp, he hit Luke's face with his fist. Luke went to his knees but my father lifted him up by the hair and hit his semiconscious son once again.

I found myself on my father's back with his left ear between my teeth. He roared and I felt myself being flung across the kitchen counter and landed on top of the stove. I rolled off to the floor and looked up to see my mother raking his face with her fingernails. I ran between them, tried to separate them, and heard him punching her face. I pounded against his stomach and chest, felt him slapping my head, was dazzled by the voices and noise and potent light when I looked up and saw the butcher knife, which my mother was going to use to cut my birthday cake, come out of the light. A jet of blood hit my face and blinded my eyes and I did not know if it was my mother or father who had been stabbed. Savannah was screaming and I was screaming and my mother was shouting for us to get out of the house, but I could not clear my eyes, could not find my bearings while blinded with one of my parents' blood as I clawed at my eyes with my hands.

Luke pulled me toward the door and through a red haze I saw my father staggering back against his own bedroom door with blood spurting from a wound in his forearm. My mother held the bloody knife in her hands and she was telling my father that she would plunge it into his heart if he ever touched one of us again. Luke shoved me and Savannah out the front door and told us to run for the truck.

"If you see Dad coming out of the house, run for the woods," he said, sprinting back for my mother.

Together, Savanah and I stumbled toward the truck, our voices rising together in a single high-pitched wail of anguish. Later, I would find out that Savannah thought I had been stabbed in the face with the butcher knife. My father's blood covered my entire face like a grotesque, sanguinary mask. My hands looked like sponges from an operating table.

In the light coming from the house, I watched as Luke and my mother broke from the front door together. Behind them, reeling and moaning with an eerie unsteadiness, my father filled the doorway as my mother entered the cab of the truck. Luke vaulted into the flatbed as my mother hunted for the keys in her purse.

"Hurry, Mama," Luke cried. "He's coming."

My father lurched toward us across the grass, losing blood with every step he took, but coming with malevolent stubbornness as my mother fumbled with a set of keys. "He's almost here, Mama," Savannah screamed as the engine turned over and coughed, then exploded into life as we shot out of the yard and away from that staggering, bleeding man.

As we raced down the dirt road leading toward the bridge, my mother swore to us, "We'll never go back, kids. I promise you that much. We'll never go back to him. What kind of mother would I be if I let my children grow up with that kind of man?"

For two days we stayed with Tolitha and Amos; then we returned to our life on the island. Before we returned, my mother gathered her children together and told us we were never to mention to anyone what happened that night. She told us that the greatest virtue in the world was family loyalty and only the finest people, the very best, possessed it. On the night we returned, my parents were unusually affectionate with each other. It was almost six months before he hit her again or laid a hand on any of his children.

"To this day," I said to my weeping father, "I always thought you would have killed the four of us if you had made it to the truck."

"It's not true," he said miserably. "Not a single word of it is true. How can you say such a thing about your own father?"

"I find it rather easy to say, Dad," I said.

"I don't remember any of that," he said. "If it happened, I must have been drunk. I must not have known what I was doing. I must have been drunk out of my mind. I admit I wasn't the best at holding my liquor."

"Savannah doesn't remember it either, Dad," I said. "I asked her about it once. Luke won't talk about it with me."

"So it could just be your imagination playing tricks on you, son," he said. "Yeah. That's it. You've always loved to make up stories about people. I bet you and your mother got together and cooked this one up to tell the judge, didn't you?"

"How did you get the scar, Dad?" I asked.

"I told you I'm a shrimper," he answered. "I do dangerous work. It could have been the winch, or the time the cables snapped . . ."

"It was a butcher knife," I said evenly. "And what about the television set, Dad? Do you remember having to buy a new TV set? Since we were a dumb-ass southern family who would rather starve than live for twenty-four hours without a TV set, we replaced that ruined set rather quickly. In fact, I think there was a new one already there when we returned to the house. Nor was there any sign of blood or violence or discord. As always, we just went on and pretended nothing had happened."

"Well, maybe that's what we should do now, son," he said. "Pretend that nothing happened, even though nothing I can say will make you believe me."

"But something has happened now," I said. "Finally, you are going to have to face the kind of man you've been because Mom has left you. We can't pretend that didn't happen, can we? The family has finally come to a moment that we can't pretend isn't real."

"Why do you hate me so much?" he asked, and there were tears again.

"It's easy to hate a man who beat you when you were a little kid, Dad," I said softly. "But I only hate you when I'm forced to remember those things."

"If I did those things, I'm sorry, Tom," he said, looking up at me. "I honestly don't remember any of them. I don't know what I can do to make it up to you."

"You can start by giving me a great amount of money, preferably in twenties," I said.

He looked up at me, puzzled, and I said, "A mere attempt

at humor, father dear. Now what would you like me to do for you? What can I do to help you? One thing I know, Dad, is that you can't help being a southern asshole. You were to the manner born."

"Could you talk to her and see what she wants?" he said. "Tell her I'll do anything if she comes back. Anything she wants, she's got. And that's a promise."

"What if she just doesn't want to come back?" I asked.

"Then what would I do?" he asked. "What would I be without your mother?"

"You'd still be the best shrimper on the river," I said. "You'd still own the prettiest island in the world."

"But I'd have lost the prettiest woman in the world," he said.

"There's no doubt about that. But you've been working hard on losing her for a long time now. Where is she? I'll go talk to her."

"She's where she always is," he said. "She's taking care of that Newbury bitch. I'll never understand why your mother is so goddamn nice to the one woman in this town who always treated her like shit."

"I understand it perfectly," I said. "Mom's been waiting her whole life for Isabel Newbury to need her."

"But I need her," he whined.

"Did you ever tell her that, Dad?" I asked.

"I didn't have to," he said. "I married her."

"Oh, I see," I said. "Crude of me to ask such an obvious question."

He began crying again and I watched him without interference, thinking that grief might be the one emotion which could prove the redemption of Henry Wingo. Also, there was a cold part of me that thought my family deserved every single one of those tears and that they had been a goddamn long time in the coming.

When he controlled himself again he said, "You know that Tolitha left your grandfather when I was a little boy?"

"Yes," I said.

"I never learned how a husband was supposed to treat a wife," he said. "I thought Tolitha had left Amos because my father was weak. He never seemed like much of a man to me. I didn't want that to happen to me."

THE PRINCE OF TIDES 577

"My mother didn't leave my father," I said, leaning closer to him. "So I learned how to treat a wife by watching how you treated Mom. I learned that it's normal for a man to beat his wife, Dad. I learned that it's normal for a man to beat his children, to brutalize his whole family anytime he felt like it, because he was stronger than any of them and because they couldn't fight back and had no place to go. I learned everything there was to know about being a man from you, Dad, and I want to thank you for that. Because it made me want to be a man like your father, Amos. I want to be weak and gentle and kind to every creature on this earth. And, Dad, I would rather be dead than be the kind of man you taught me to be."

"You think you're better than me," he said. "Your mother always thought she was better than me too, even though her parents made hillbillies look high class."

"I don't think I'm better than you," I said. "I think I'm nicer than you, Dad."

"I should have gone to talk to Luke," he said. "I should never have come here. Luke would never had said such terrible things about his own father."

"And he wouldn't have agreed to go talk to Mom, either," I said.

"You'll still talk to her?" he asked.

"Yep," I said. "I see a chance for you to learn something for the first time in your life. Who would have thought the old mountain gorilla would cry when his wife left him? And even if Mom leaves you, I see a chance for you to become a good father out of all this. And I wouldn't mind having a father for the first time in my life."

"I don't like to ask people for anything," he said.

"That makes it very difficult to give you anything, Dad," I answered.

"Hey," he said, "don't forget it was me who gave you the gift of life."

I roared. "Thanks tons," I said.

26

I stood on the verandah of the Newbury mansion watching the moonlight ignite the marsh like some dream of altered gold. Reese Newbury answered my knock at the door and the moonlight did something quite different to his face. He had softened around the edges since I last had stood at his doorway. The pouches beneath his eyes had the look of exhausted luggage. But his eyes returned that same raw glitter of uncommon control. Those eyes were still the source of tremendous power in the leavened, pale-white body.

"I need to talk with my mother, Mr. Newbury," I said.

He squinted in the light of porches and moons before he recognized me. "She's been an angel, Tom. I don't know what we would have done without her. Your mother's an incredible woman, son. I hope you know that."

"Yes, sir, I've always known that," I said. "Would you tell her I'm down here?"

"Come in. Please come in," he said, and I followed him into the hushed entranceway of the house.

"She's with Isabel," he whispered. "She barely leaves her side, even to eat. The doctor says it won't be long now. The cancer has spread all . . ."

He could not go on and he strangled on the words he was about to utter. As he fought for control, I could hear great clocks spooning out moments with metallic strokes, their long blades cutting through the silks of time. All the clocks struck nine as we stood in semidarkness and the somber tolling of every clock in every room of the house disowned the hour in the dumbstruck language of bells. I wondered if it was just in the house of the dying that you became so acutely aware of the presence of clocks.

"Why don't you wait in my study upstairs," he said. "It's private and you and your mother can talk."

"I know where it is," I said as I followed him up the carpeted staircase.

As I sat in his study, I wondered if he had brought me to this room on purpose. But then, I figured that Reese Newbury had performed so many execrable acts in his life that he probably did not even remember slapping a twelve-year-old kid who had fought with his son. There were the same sterile rows of unread books and the map of the county studded with pins marking the land in his possession.

My mother entered the room and whispered, "Isabel would like to see you, Tom. She's so pleased you came for a visit. Isn't that sweet?"

Why Isabel Newbury would be pleased was a bright mystery to me, but my mother seemed delighted that Isabel even knew I inhabited the same planet she did. My mother held my hand and led me down the quiet darkened hallway.

"It's right here," my mother said, forgetting that I once helped cart a two-hundred-pound loggerhead turtle up to this very room.

But whatever ill feelings I harbored for Isabel Newbury vanished when I saw her cruelly wasted form propped up against a bank of pillows in her bed. I could hate somebody for my whole life and still pray they did not die like this. Her body had surrendered to a pearly withering. She shone with fever. There was a muscadine smell of death in the room, medicine and flowers and cologne distilled into a fragrance of bad wine.

"Your mother has been the only one, Tom," she said. "All the others are afraid to see me."

"That's just not so, Isabel," my mother said. "I just do what any friend would do. And you've got more cards and flowers than anyone could ever imagine."

"I was mean to you and your family, Tom," she said, the words coming slowly. "I've apologized to your mother a hundred times."

"I've told you there's nothing to apologize for, Isabel," my mother said quickly. "I always considered you one of

my good friends. We were both just busy raising our own
families and didn't get to see much of each other."

"Your apology is accepted, Mrs. Newbury," I said. "And
it's gracious of you to make it."

"Tom, how rude!" my mother said.

"Thank you for accepting it," Mrs. Newbury said. "I've
been lying here for the past couple of weeks thinking about
my life. There are some things I did that I can't understand.
I don't know who the person was that did those things.
She doesn't seem related to me at all. It's a shame you have
to be dying to know all this."

"Shoot, who says you're dying, Isabel?" my mother said.
"I still say you're going to beat this thing and then go on
a long cruise with Reese."

"The only cruise I'll be taking is down to Ogletree's
Funeral Home," she answered.

"Don't talk like that, Isabel," my mother said, hiding her
face in her hands. "Don't talk about giving up. I want you
to fight it."

"Dying's just the final phase of life. We all go through
it, Lila," Mrs. Newbury said. "It sure hasn't been my favorite phase. I'll grant you that."

"How is Todd, Mrs. Newbury?" I asked.

"Todd?" she said. "Todd is like he's always been. Selfish,
spoiled. He married a sweet girl. A Lee from Virginia. He
spends his spare time bullying her. He's only been to see
me twice since I've been ill. But he phones once a month
whether it's convenient or not."

"He was down here last weekend, Tom," my mother
said to me. "You could tell his mother's illness just breaks
his heart. He loves you so much, Isabel. He's like so many
men. He just doesn't know how to express it."

"He expresses it eloquently," she said. "He doesn't come
to see me."

"You're getting tired," my mother said. "Say good night
to Tom and I'll tuck you in for the night."

"Could you please get me some more ice water, Lila
dear?" she said, motioning to the pitcher on her nightstand.
"I'm so thirsty."

"I'll be right back," said my mother.

As we heard my mother's footsteps on the staircase, Isabel Newbury turned her dying, wasted eyes on me and said the words that would change my life forever.

"My husband is in love with your mother, Tom," she said. "And I approve."

"What?" I whispered, stunned.

"Reese needs taking care of. He simply would not be able to survive alone," she said, as matter-of-factly as if she were discussing a change in the weather.

"And your mother has been so kind to me," she added. "I've come to love her very much."

"Well, isn't that grand?" I said. "Did you ever consider my father?"

"She's told me all about your father," she said. "I imagine you hate your father as much as she does."

"No ma'am," I said. "And I like him a million times more than I like Reese Newbury."

"It's been platonic," she said. "I assure you of that. Your mother is probably not even aware of it."

"Mrs. Newbury, how could you let a woman into your husband's bed who couldn't get into your fucking cookbook?" I asked.

"I don't approve of vulgarity," she said, weak-voiced and edgy.

"You have the nerve to call me vulgar, Mrs. Newbury?" I said. "You, who pimps for her husband on her deathbed."

"I'm simply looking after my affairs," she said. "I thought you should know. I didn't wish this to come as a complete surprise."

"Yeah, I hate surprises," I said. "Does my mother know any of this?"

"No," she said. "Reese and I have discussed it. We discuss everything."

"Then tell Reese that he and my mother will marry over my dead body," I said. "There's a lot I can take in this world, but one of them is not being Reese Newbury's stepson. And the next is being Todd Newbury's step-brother. What's wrong with you? You've been shitting all over my family since I was born. Is this the ultimate gambit? Is this your final gesture of contempt?"

Together we heard my mother approaching the door again.

Mrs. Newbury put a finger to her lips as my mother entered the room and poured a glass of ice water for her.

"Did you have a nice chat while I was gone?" my mother asked. "I've told Isabel all about you, Tom. She says that she's never met a mother any prouder of her children and I guess that's true. My children have always been my whole life to me."

"Thanks for coming by, Tom," Mrs. Newbury said, shaking my hand. "Please come back and visit soon."

"I hope you start feeling better, Mrs. Newbury," I said formally. "Please let me know if there's anything I can do for you. Good night, ma'am."

My mother and I sat opposite each other in the study while I considered the infinite possibilities I had of making a grinning ass out of myself. If my mother and Reese Newbury were signing valentines to each other over the recumbent body of his dying wife, then that was no business of mine, especially when the same wife seemed to be charmed by her generous, self-effacing role of matchmaker.

"Why isn't she in the hospital, Mom?" I said, avoiding all issues for a moment. "She's obviously dying."

"She wants to die in the house where all her forebears have died," my mother said. "She made the decision that she wants to die in her own bed."

"What kind of cancer does she have?" I asked.

"It's spread all over her body," my mother said. "She began with cancer of the rectum."

"Please, Mom," I said. "Even God doesn't have that good a sense of humor."

"That's one of the cruelest things I've ever heard anyone say," my mother said, rising to make sure no one was listening at the door. "Isabel Newbury and I are very close friends, Tom, and I'll not have you being disrespectful about her. She's been very hurt that her best friends have practically abandoned her during her ordeal. Oh, they'll come by once or twice a month and stay for an hour, but she can see how anxious they are to leave her bedside."

"What's truly surprising, Mom," I said, "is that Lila Wingo, one of her worst enemies, is looking after her every single day and almost every night, too."

"I've always said that bygones should be bygones. I've

never been one to hold a grudge. This has all been so hard on poor Reese. He's been so upset."

"Good," I said. "I'm delighted he's upset. I've always thought you could measure the depth of your humanity by just how much you could hate Reese Newbury."

"He's a greatly misunderstood man," she said.

"I think he's very well understood, Mom," I said. "Now if he gets rectal cancer, we'll know that God indeed has a divine plan worked out for all of us."

"I won't have you talking ugly about the Newburys again, Tom," she said furiously. "I mean that. They're my closest friends in Colleton now. I know that must seem strange to you, but they've been almost pathetically grateful for the help I've been able to give them. Now, I've never been one to accept any gratitude for just doing my neighborly duty. I've always given freely of myself and asked for nothing in return. But since I've been helping them out, I've realized how profoundly lonely Reese and Isabel are. I mean that. They have no true friends as you and I understand the term. They just have people who want to be around them to take advantage of their money and social position. Of course, being the sophisticated couple they are, they can spot a phony a mile away."

"I bet they can. Mirrors must drive them crazy," I said. "Mom, I came here because Dad came to the house tonight."

"I know that's why you came," she said. "I've been expecting you, Tom."

"He says he's sorry and he'll do anything if you come back home," I said, feeling strange using the awkward phrases of my father.

"I've wasted too many years of my life with your father," she said. "Do you realize I never even loved him when we first got married?"

"He was served papers today, Mom," I said. "I think those papers convinced him you were serious."

"Reese and Isabel have let me use a little house they own over on Lanier Street. They're not even charging me rent. Isn't that the sweetest thing?" she said.

"About Dad," I said. "What do you want me to tell him, Mom?"

"Tell him," she said, rising up to her full height, "tell

him that I'm sorry I ever met him and sorry I conceived children with him and it'll be the happiest day of my life when I'm free of him forever."

I said, "Are you sure you don't want to phrase that more strongly?"

"What right have you to disapprove of my decision?" she said. "You used to beg me to divorce your father. What's changed for you?"

"He's become pathetic to me, Mom," I answered. "I can't help it. Every time I see him he strikes the deepest chord of pity in me. He has that unsurpassable aura of failure around him that he's never been able to shake. He doesn't even seem like my father to me. It's more like he's some crippled disfigured uncle that I visit once or twice a year on holidays."

"So you don't think I should leave him?" she asked.

"I think you should do exactly what you want to do," I said as our eyes met. "I think you should do what will make you happy, Mama."

"Do you really believe that?"

"Probably not, but they sound like the words I should say," I said.

"Then I have your full support?" she asked.

"You both have my full support," I said.

"Then you'll agree to testify for me in court?"

"No, I will testify for neither of you in court," I said.

"That's what you consider full support?" she asked, one side of her face obscured by the shadow of the lamp.

"Mama," I said, "I want you to listen to something. I've been damaged enough by this family. I've been hurt enough by growing up with you and Dad as my parents. But I'm an adult now, and if you don't mind, I'd like to see you two end this marriage without any of my blood being sprinkled about the venue of the divorce. You and Dad are old enough to get a divorce without involving your children. I encourage you to do so."

"You won't testify that he beat me when you were a child?" she asked.

"No, I'll say I don't remember those times," I said.

"I can understand why you might not remember those times," she said furiously. "Because they usually occurred when I was trying to pull him off you or Luke."

"Mama, I know those things happened," I said. "What I'm telling you is to try to protect us from it just this once more. It will be bad for us if we have to testify for or against either of you."

"Well, I don't need you," she said. "Savannah has already said she'll testify in court if I need her. She says I've been one of the most abused and exploited women she's ever known and she'll do anything to help me start a new life."

"I'm sorry I can't help you, Mom," I said. "But someone's got to be there to help Dad pick up the pieces when you're gone."

"Just like I had to pick up the pieces when he beat your face in when you were just a little boy," she said.

"Mom," I asked, "why do you blame me for the fact that Henry Wingo is my father? Why do you hold that against me?"

"I'll only hold one thing against you," my mother said. "I will always hold it against you that the one time I asked you for help, you refused to give it to me. I have a chance to be happy now for the first time in my life and you will not help me to achieve that happiness."

"Mrs. Newbury told me just now that Mr. Newbury is in love with you, Mom," I said, closing my eyes.

"She's half delirious now," she said. "She's saying things, crazy things, all kinds of things that just aren't making sense. But that's the cancer in her. Reese and I just laugh when she starts to say those things to us. We don't pay it a bit of mind."

"Whatever you do is your own business," I said. "And anything that makes you happy will make me happy. I promise you that. But I'd like you to promise me that you won't screw Dad in the process."

"I only want what I deserve," she said. "What I've earned from the marriage."

"That's what I'm afraid of," I said. "Mom, as I've been sitting here talking to you, my eyes keep moving to that map above your head. I saw it years ago when you brought me over here to apologize after my fight with Todd Newbury. Todd told me that the green pins marked the property that Reese Newbury owned and the red pins marked the property that he was trying to own. There's all kinds of rumors going around that the federal government is coming into Colleton with a big project. Land speculators are everywhere. Folks might make a lot of money."

"I don't understand what you're talking about, Tom," she said coolly.

"It looks from all the green pins in that map of Colleton County that Reese has succeeded in buying up most of the county," I said.

"Everyone knows he's the largest landowner in Colleton," she said with a strange misplaced pride.

"Tell Reese I think it's a bit tacky for him to put a green pin on our island before he owns it, Mom," I said, pointing to the map. "And I find it troublesome that you're talking about giving away our island before it's even legally yours. Because if you get the island, Mama, it means Reese Newbury has to steal it for you. And we know, Mama, that in this town he can do it. He's got more toadies around him than a country pond and half of them are the judges in this town."

"I don't care a single thing for that island," she said. "I almost died of loneliness out there and I'll be glad never to step foot on it again."

"Dad only knew how to abuse power," I said. "I don't want you to make that same mistake."

"My only mistake in life is that I've been far too kind to everyone," she said.

"That's funny," I replied. "That's what Dad said."

"In my case," she said, "it happens to be true."

"Mom," I said, rising to go, "for what it's worth, I think you're doing the right thing. He was never the proper man for you."

"I think I could have been the First Lady," she said, apropos of nothing at all.

"What?" I answered.

"I simply feel that I have all the qualities that would make a dignified and worthy First Lady of our country. I think I would have been an asset as the helpmate of the president or perhaps a governor. I have a real talent for entertaining that no one knows about. And I love to meet the people who count. I sometimes think of all I could have been if I hadn't met your father in Atlanta that day."

"I'm not going to take sides in this, Mama," I said as I moved toward the door. "I know that both of you will probably hate me for it, but that's the way I'm going to play it."

"You're a loser, Tom," my mother said sadly as we kissed farewell. "You're a loser just like your father. For years, I fooled myself and said that you were the most like me. You had such potential."

"Who's most like you now?" I asked.

"Luke," she said. "He fights for what he wants. He's a born fighter, just like his mother."

Having finished my business, I rose to leave, and my mother said, "Please don't repeat what Isabel told you tonight, Tom. No one should be held accountable for what they say when they're dying."

"I won't say anything, Mama," I promised as we walked to the door.

I kissed my mother in the front hallway and then held her at arm's length and studied her. Her beauty touched me deeply. It made me proud to be her son. It caused me to worry about her future.

"Look," she said, and she took me into the living room and whispered. "There are eight museum-quality pieces in this living room. Eight!"

"It makes it kind of hard to relax in here, doesn't it?" I said.

"I'm worried about your father," she said, suddenly. "I'm afraid he'll hurt me if I go through with the divorce."

"He won't hurt you, Mom," I said. "I promise you that."

"How can you be so sure?" she asked.

"Because Luke and I would kill him if he ever laid a hand on you," I said. "You don't ever have to worry about that again, Mama. Luke and I aren't little boys anymore."

But my mother was not listening to me. Her eyes were shining with pleasure and they engaged in a slow inventory of all the items in the living room.

"Do you want to try to guess which of the eight pieces are museum quality, Tom?" she asked as I left the Newbury house.

Isabel Newbury died in her sleep after a period of intense suffering. My mother sat with the family at the funeral.

My father contested the divorce on the novel grounds

that he was a Catholic and that the Catholic Church did
not believe in divorce. The sovereign state of South Carolina, however, did. Savannah arrived from New York the
day before the trial to prepare for her role as my mother's
star witness.

Savannah wept during her entire testimony, as did Lila
and Henry Wingo. Judge Cavender was a long-time business associate of Reese Newbury's. There was sadness but
there were no surprises during the trial. My mother and
father drifted by each other in the corridors of the courthouse without the slightest sign of recognition passing between them. Already, they had begun the cold business of
dissolving into strangers when the other came into view.
Their history was like a child found murdered in the snow.
The trial was a deathwatch, an abstraction, and the em-
blems of their disaffection were their three children who
watched in agony as they sundered the marriage that we
all agreed was terrible. Henry Wingo's fists and temper
were nothing before the fluent contempt that the law accorded to husbands who abused their wives. On the witness stand, my father whined and lied and tried to flatter
the judge. He was very human and his performance broke
my heart. My mother was lovely and controlled and decent.
But there was something artificial and unpersuaded in her
voice. She seemed to deliver her lines to a secret listener
at the window instead of directing her statements to the
lawyers or Judge Cavender.

The judge immediately granted the divorce after all the
testimony was heard. Then he divided the property. Henry
Wingo retained possession of the shrimp boat, the house
and furniture on the island, all monies in savings and checking accounts, all motor vehicles and farm equipment, and
all liquid assets of any kind. My father was not required to
pay a penny of alimony, nor would he be held responsible
for any debts my mother had accrued since she had moved
out of my father's house. Just when it seemed the judge
had left my mother destitute, he issued the final and most
amazing portion of the settlement.

He granted to my mother sole and exclusive possession
of Melrose Island.

A year later my mother married Reese Newbury in a
private ceremony conducted by the governor of South Car-

olina. The same week she attended her first session as a member in good standing of the Colleton League.

On the morning of her remarriage, my father guided his shrimp boat out beyond the three-mile limit and turned south toward Florida. For six months we did not hear a word from him until Luke received a postcard from Key West. He said he was catching a ton of shrimp and had finally figured out a way to make some real money. He did not mention our mother or let us know when we might see him again. He was on the high seas, west of Jamaica, when agents of the federal government finally announced their plans for Colleton County.

In Columbia, at a news conference in the governor's mansion attended by Reese Newbury and my mother, the United States Atomic Energy Commission announced that its new production plants were to be designed, built, and operated by the Y. G. Mewshaw Company of Baltimore, Maryland, and would be located within the designated borders of Colleton County, South Carolina. The entire county would be acquired for the site, which would be known henceforth as the Colleton River Project. The purpose of these new plants would be the manufacture of materials that could be used either for the production of nuclear weapons or as fuels essential for the operation of nuclear power plants. The Congress of the United States had appropriated $875 million to start construction.

A spokesman for the commission said the site had been selected after an exhaustive study of more than three hundred sites around the continental United States. He also emphasized that to make way for the plants and the required safety zone, it would be imperative for about thirty-four hundred families to relocate in the next year and a half. The federal and state agricultural agencies were organizing to give assistance to the families forced to relocate. With the moving of the town of Colleton, it was the first time in the history of the republic that an incorporated community had been taken over by the federal government. The plants would be operational within three years and pretty Colleton would lead the world in the production of plutonium and would produce more hydrogen bombs than any place outside of the Soviet Union.

"I don't mind giving up my hometown to save my country from the Russian Communists," Reese Newbury said before the television cameras.

The government ballyhooed the project as the largest, most expensive enterprise ever undertaken by the federal government south of the Mason-Dixon Line. It would bring billions of dollars into the economy of lower South Carolina and would provide jobs from Charleston to Savannah. By right of eminent domain, the United States government claimed all land within the borders of Colleton County, which they emphasized was the poorest and most sparsely populated county in the state. The government would send agents to the county to appraise the worth of the land and to purchase it from the property owners at its fair market value. The government commissioned a special appeals court to adjudicate disputes between the appraisers and the landowners. The government also promised to move any houses at government expense to any piece of property within two hundred miles of Colleton.

Since it was recognized that Colleton had some historical significance, the government wanted to keep as much of the town intact as possible and had begun to clear four thousand acres in southern Charleston County. The town would be called New Colleton and the land would be free to the disenfranchised citizens of "old" Colleton. The newspapers around the state began to speak of Colleton in the past tense. Editorials applauded the government's decision to locate such a huge complex in South Carolina and praised the people of Colleton for their sacrifice in the interest of national defense. Every politician in the state threw his fervent support behind the project. It was a time of the most bilious platitudes and embroidered lies. The mayor of Colleton supported the Colleton River Project fully. So did the city council. So did every local government official in the county. Reese Newbury had tipped off each of them before the announcement was made and all of them had speculated heavily in tracts of available land throughout the county.

There were town meetings with furious exchanges between town officials and private citizens but the awful machinery of government had been set in motion and we could not even slow the pace of the juggernaut as it rolled across our county. Natives of Colleton wrote letters of protest to newspapers and their congressman. But everyone in power could see past the temporal loss of a pretty backwater town to the time when Colleton County would support a teeming array of skilled workers and scientists. Only eighty-two hundred people would lose their homes in the displacement and the government was promising to be both solicitous and generous in helping the people of Colleton make the transition. There was no vote, no referendum, no private poll of the citizenry. We had awakened one morning to find out that our town would vanish without a trace in the dunes of memory. There was no way to reverse the decision since we were denied any redress of grievance if we refused to accept the government's basic premise—that Colleton had to be moved in the sacrosanct name of progress.

The government held one meeting and one meeting only to explain to the people of Colleton how the diaspora would work. It was held in the gynmasium of the high school in the debilitating heat of August. The crowd overflowed out into the street and loudspeakers were set up so the people who stood outside could hear. A federal agent who worked for the Atomic Energy Commission would deliver the speech and answer all questions. His name was Patrick Flaherty and he was slim, handsome, and tidy of manner. He gave the appearance of being untouchable and fastidious. He spoke with an unaccented atonal voice. In the province of law, he represented government, science, the strangers who were entering the county in staunchless floods, and all the disfigured mottoes and brutalized language used to soften the fact that they were killing our town.

Patrick Flaherty was the perfect manifestation of the modern American man. I listened in amazement as he began to speak, anesthetized by his heroic, unblemishable command of every cliché in the language. His tongue was a hermitage for banality. Every movement he made and every word he spoke was buttery with condescension. He was the quintessential organization man and all his i's were dotted and all his sentences were diagrammed by a portentous vacuity. Clean and supple and lacking in all vestiges of compassion, Patrick Flaherty stood before us as an eyesore on our aberrant, hallucinating century. His voice flooded the gymnasium with a whole lottery of statistics. It was a coppery, inanimate voice and all the words seemed dusted with bright and deadly motes of silica. In silence, we listened as he explained how our town was going to be moved house by house and brick by brick.

Then he said, in closing, "I want to say that I think the people of Colleton are the luckiest people in the United States. You have a chance to prove your patriotism to the whole world and you're doing it with the knowledge that America will be safer because of your sacrifice. America needs plutonium and it needs nuclear submarines and it needs MIRV missiles because America loves peace. You can spell plutonium P-E-A-C-E. We know that many of you are sorry to leave your homes, and, believe me, there's no one involved in this project who doesn't feel for you good folks. It gets me right here in the gut. I can tell you that much. But we know that as much as you love Colleton, you love America even more. And, folks, if you think you love Colleton, just wait and see what we have in store for you in New Colleton. A new fire station, courthouse, police station, schools, parks. We promise that New Colleton will be one of the most beautiful communities in America when we're finished. If you love the old ancestral home, then we'll be glad to move it up to New Colleton at our expense. We're here to make you folks happy. Because when America needed a hand, you folks stood up for America by saying yes to the 'Atoms for Peace' program of the Atomic Energy Commission. I think all of you should get up and give yourselves a standing ovation."

No one moved. There was not a sound in the gymnasium except for that of Patrick Flaherty clapping alone.

Unnerved by the silence, Flaherty asked if there was anyone in Colleton who had something to say to his fellow citizens.

My brother Luke rose up beside me and walked the full length of that gymnasium with the eyes of the town upon him. He created a field of disturbance in his passage. He moved with a supple intensity and his face wore the dark, lacquered expressiveness of a sublime wound to the spirit. When he stood before the microphone, he did not acknowledge the presence of the politicians behind him. He gave no sign of recognition to his mother, who sat on the raised platform with the other guests of honor. Carefully, he spread out three sheets of yellow paper on the rostrum before him. Then he spoke.

"When I fought in Asia, they sent me to Japan for R and R. I visited two cities there—Hiroshima and Nagasaki. I talked to folks lucky enough to have seen Atoms for Peace in action. I talked to people who had been present in those cities when those two bombs were dropped in 1945. One man showed me a picture of a baby girl being eaten by a starving dog in the ruins. I saw women with hideous scars. I went to a museum in Hiroshima and it made me sick to my stomach to be an American. Plutonium has nothing to do with peace. It is a code word for the Apocalypse, for the Beast of Zion. It will do for the whole world what it's now doing for Colleton alone. Soon they will turn our beautiful town into a place dedicated to the destruction of the universe. And I have not heard a single man or woman from this town say 'No.' I keep asking myself, 'How many sheep can one town produce?' I keep asking myself, 'Where are the lions? Where are they sleeping?'

"Since the announcement by the federal government that they were going to steal my town, I've done what any southerner would do: I've turned to the Bible for solace and strength. I've tried to find in the Bible some message that would give me comfort during this time of distress. I've looked to the story of Sodom and Gomorrah to see if I could find some comparison between those two wicked cities and Colleton. Now, I admit to you I found nothing. Colleton is a town of gardens and pleasure boats and church bells on Sunday. It is not evil in any way that I can judge evil. Its only fault that I can see is that it produced people who didn't love her enough, people who would sell her to strangers for thirty pieces of silver. So I kept reading the Bible, hoping to find a message from God that would grant me succor during the wrath of the Philistines. Because, if I don't try to save the one town in the world I truly love, then I want God to turn me into a pillar of salt because I did not look back. I would rather be a lifeless pillar of salt in Colleton than a Judas Iscariot covered with gold and the blood of his hometown anywhere else in the world."

As Luke spoke, you could feel the voiceless conscience of the town rising from the dead. You could hear the mur-

mur of insurgency purling through the humming crowd.
His voice set off a chime of coalition resonating through
the breasts of every man, woman, and child who could be
touched by a passionate cry of home. The very gentleness
of his voice was an indictment against the lethargy that had
fallen on the town like some insensible dust. When he
invoked the name of Iscariot you could feel the hardening,
the unhiving, and the exhilarated clarity that rises from the
fires of dissent.

"I could not find what I wanted from the Bible until I
started over at the beginning. Then I heard God speaking
to me in a voice I could understand and obey. Many of you
believe in the literal interpretation of the Bible. I also believe
in the literal interpretation of God's Word. But all of us
know there are two kinds of ways that God speaks to us
in the Bible and we have to distinguish between the two
of them. There are books of revelation and books of prophecy. The books of revelation are those that tell us about
historical occurrences like the birth of Jesus, his crucifixion
and death on the cross. The Book of Revelation itself is a
work of prophecy in which the evangelist predicts the Final
Judgment and the coming of the Four Horsemen of the
Apocalypse. None of these things have come to pass, but
we know they will come to pass because it is written in the
name of the Lord.

"It was while I was reading the story of the Creation that
it came to me like a vision. Genesis is not a book of revelation, but a book of prophecy. I think it foretells what will
happen in the future, not what has happened in the past.
And is it so difficult for those who've grown up by the
Colleton River and known the beauty of the seasons and
the marshes—is it so difficult for us to imagine that we are
still in Paradise, that we have yet to be denied the Garden
of Eden? That Adam and Eve are still waiting to be born
and that you and I are living in Paradise without even
knowing it?

"You know that Jesus loved to speak in parables in the
Bible. Is it possible that the Book of Genesis is simply another parable, God's way of warning us of the dangers of
the world by telling us a story? And if you can agree with
me for just a moment that Genesis might be a parable,
consider this: When Eve reaches up and touches the for-

bidden fruit and loses Paradise and is driven from the perfect happiness of Eden, is it possible that God is speaking to us today here in Colleton? What is it that will destroy our perfect home? What is it that will drive us out of Paradise and into unknown lands? What is it that will take away from us everything we have known and loved and thanked God for every single day of our lives?

"I have read Genesis, my friends and neighbors, and I think I know the answer. I have prayed to God for wisdom and I think he has granted that wisdom to me.

"Genesis is a parable and it is God trying to reach down through the ages to warn the people of Colleton and all the people of the world of the one thing that can destroy Paradise for all of us.

"It was not an apple that Eve touched," he said, and he paused. "I think that the forbidden fruit is plutonium."

Lucy Emerson, the bank teller, jumped to her feet at the top of the bleachers behind me and shouted, "Amen, brother."

And the crowd let out with a roar of solidarity.

Patrick Flaherty walked up to the podium and tried to take the microphone from Luke. Luke's words were picked up by the mike as he said, "Sit down, sciencehead. I ain't finished yet."

The crowd was restless now, weightless in the sunlight and altered by the power of the spoken word.

Luke continued: "I think that we have in Colleton what everyone else is looking for. I think it's a town worth fighting for. I even think it's a town worth dying for. I've been surprised, my friends, that we have let strangers into our midst who have promised to destroy our town, to remove our houses, to unbury our dead. I thought we were southerners and that our love of the land was what made us different from all other Americans. Then I remembered it was southerners and citizens of Colleton who were the ones who brought the strangers to our town and sold Colleton down the river for a fistful of money."

He turned and faced my mother and the politicians and the businessmen on the platform.

He made a gesture of dismissal with his arm and said, "These are the new southerners whose hearts and souls are for sale, who can be bought with the money of strangers.

They can go live in New Colleton or they can go straight
to hell. They are not brothers and sisters of mine. They are
not part of the South I love.

"I have a single suggestion. I make it out of desperation
because they are already clearing trees on the island where
I was born. Let us remember who we are—the descendants
of men who once shook the world because they would not
surrender their rights to the federal government. Our forebears died at Bull Run and Antietam and Chancellorsville.
I think they fought for a bad reason and I want no man as
my slave. But neither do I wish to be a slave to any man,
nor will I allow any man to banish me from the land that
God gave me at birth. They tell me that Luke Wingo will
have to be packed and out of Colleton County in one year
or be subject to punishment by the law of the land."

He paused a moment, then said in an even, cold-blooded
voice, "I promise you this: Luke Wingo ain't going. And I
promise you that they'll have to come and throw me off
this land and Luke Wingo promises that it ain't gonna be
easy.

"I've talked with most of you and I know you don't like
it. But they're playing with your thoughts and telling you
it's your patriotic duty to go like cringing dogs across the
bridge into strange lands. They know you're southern and
they think you're stupid, and you are stupid if you go
without a fight. They tell you that these bombs and subs
and missiles will be used to kill Russians. There isn't one
person in this gym who's ever seen a Russian. What would
you do if a damn Russian came to your house tonight and
said, 'We're going to move every single person in this town
forty miles up the road and tear down your schools and
churches and divide your families and desecrate the graves
of your loved ones.' There would be dead Russians lying
all over this county, and you and I know that with our
hearts. They might as well send me to Russia as send me
to New Colleton. I don't know no New Colleton."

"Tell us what to do, Luke," a voice called out.

"Tell us, Luke," other voices called.

"I don't know what to do," he said to the voices. "But
I've got a few suggestions. I don't know if they'd work or
not, but we could try. Tomorrow, let's get a petition going
to recall every elected official in this county. Let's throw

the greedy bastards out. Then let's pass a law forbidding all new federal construction in the county. They'll have laws to counter our measures, of course. And the full weight of all the law of the land and the state will be brought to bear upon us.

"If they persist, then I would like to suggest that Colleton County draw up a Bill of Secession from the state of South Carolina. And in the light of history, no state should understand the urge to secede any more than South Carolina. Let us take our destinies into our own hands and declare that Colleton County be free in perpetuity from the manufacture of plutonium. Let us proclaim, if necessary, that Colleton is a sovereign state. Let us give the federal government thirty days in which to cease and desist in the building of the Colleton River Project and the dispossession of the people from their land. Let us shout the words of Thomas Jefferson in the Declaration of Independence. Let us shout those words as they come to our doors: 'Whenever any form of government becomes destructive of these ends—life, liberty, and the pursuit of happiness—it is the right of the people to alter or to abolish it, and to institute new government.' If they refuse to listen to us, then I believe a state of war should be declared. We would be defeated easily. But we could walk away from our homes with some sense of honor. In a hundred years, they'd sing songs celebrating our courage. We'd teach them the power of saying no.

"If the agents of the federal government continue to come to your houses and continue the forced removal of all the citizens of Colleton, then I say to all of you, the friends and neighbors I have known all my life: Fight them. Fight them.

"When they come to your door, wear a green armband to let them know you're one of us. This'll be the uniform of our discontent. Ask them kindly to leave your property. If they refuse, put a gun in their faces. Then ask them again. If they still refuse, put a bullet through their foot.

"I once read that when the concept of common law first began in England, the king himself was not allowed to cross the threshold of the poorest peasant's house without permission. I'm claiming for all of us that the king shall not cross our thresholds. The son of a bitch just wasn't invited."

*   *   *

Sheriff Lucas approached Luke from the rear and snapped a handcuff around Luke's wrist. The sheriff and two deputies pushed Luke roughly toward the door and the meeting adjourned without a sound from the thousand people who had packed the gymnasium. There was bad blood and sedition rising in the silence, but not enough.

Luke was booked and fingerprinted and charged with making terroristic threats against federal and state officials. He was also charged with urging seditious acts against the state of South Carolina. Luke said that he no longer recognized the authority of the state or federal government and considered himself a prisoner of war in the current hostilities between Colleton and the United States. He gave his name, rank, and serial number and, citing the treaties of the Geneva Convention concerning the handling of prisoners of war, refused to answer all other questions.

The *Charleston News and Courier* printed an ironic article the next day, reporting that the Colleton sheriff had to break up the first secessionist meeting in South Carolina in over a hundred years. There were no recall petitions passed in the shops along the Street of Tides and there were no green armbands worn in defiance of the Colleton River Project. Only one man had taken Luke's words to heart and he was already imprisoned in a cell overlooking the river.

Luke's war had begun.

With some reluctance, I accompanied my mother when she went to visit Luke in jail the following evening. She took my arm as we walked toward town with the pale lights blooming in the dining room windows. The mansions that had once seemed eternal to me now seemed as fragile and effaceable as love letters written in snow. A bulldozer was parked beneath a streetlight, articulating the fate of Colleton in its hunched, stubby silence. It seemed part insect, part samurai, and it had the dirt of my town bleeding along its gums. As my mother and I walked in silence, I could feel the soft linens of my family unraveling in my hands. The streets were rain-sweetened and we could smell the gardens burning with long streamers of wisteria and disciplined medallions of roses, and I thought, What will happen to these gardens? I ached with a sense of ineffable loss.

I hurt because I could not say a single kind word to my mother. If I had been enough of a man, I would have taken my mother in my arms and told her I understood completely. But when you are dealing with Tom Wingo, it is a given that he will always find a way to cheapen and debase any virtues a confident manhood might provide. There was a spurious shine to my manhood, like the gleaming artillery of a county that surrendered without a fight.

Before we walked into the jail, my mother squeezed my hand and said, "Please support me on this, Tom. I know you're mad with me now, but I'm afraid of what Luke might do. I know him better than anyone, Tom. Luke has been looking for a cause he could die for his whole life, and I'm afraid he thinks he's found it. If we don't stop him now, we're going to lose him."

The room was divided into eight equal parts as it flowed into Luke's cell. Luke was staring out toward the river when the sheriff left us to talk outside his cell door. The moon rummaged through his hair and the light and the shadow of the bars turned his face into something as deliberately spaced as an octave of a piano. The light housed itself in the muscles along his neck and shoulders and as I studied him, I knew that I would never see a more beautiful body on a man. His muscles were long and fine and layered along his bones in perfect articulation and symmetry. His aura was one of cold substantiality. You could smell his fury or you could read it in the graffiti of his stressed shoulders. He did not look around to greet us.

"Hello, Luke," my mother said uncertainly.

"Hey, Mama," he said, his eyes affixed on the shining river.

"You're awfully mad at me, aren't you, Luke?" she said, trying to make light of it.

"Yeah, Mama," he said. "How long did you know about it? When did Newbury let you in on the big piece of news? When did you plan to steal the only thing Dad ever owned?"

"I earned the right to own that island," she said. "I bled for that piece of land."

"You stole it fair and square," Luke said. "Just don't expect your children to love you for it."

"There's nothing you can do about it," she said. "The island's gone. Colleton's gone. We've all got to start over."

"How do you start over, Mama?" he said to the river. "How do you start over when you can't look back? What happens to a man when he looks back over his shoulder to see where he came from, to see what he is, and all he sees is a sign that says, 'Keep Out'?"

"Who wrote that speech for you?" my mother asked. "The one you gave last night."

"I did," he said. "No one else thinks like I do."

"Thank God that other people have more sense," she said. "But who helped you write it? You can tell me."

"Mom, all my life you've thought I was stupid," he said. "I've never understood it. You convinced me of it, too. I always felt dumb in school and dumb when I was around Tom and Savannah. I just see things differently from most folks. I've got a different angle of vision. Most people are smart about a hundred things. I'm just smart about four or five things. You're right about one thing. I didn't make up that part about Genesis being a book of prophecy. I heard Amos give that sermon in that little church of his before he died. I liked that sermon a lot."

"And you're telling me that Amos thought that plutonium was the forbidden fruit?" my mother asked in an acidulous voice.

"Naw, I changed that part," Luke said. "Amos thought air conditioning was the forbidden fruit. It just didn't fit with what I wanted to say."

"The government knows best," my mother said, softening. "It needs this plant for national defense."

"Since when does the government know best, Mama?" Luke said in a tired and daunted voice. "Knows best about what? You told me that when I went to Vietnam. The same damn thing. So, I went around killing peasants, Mama, nothing but peasants so poor it would make you cry. I killed their buffalo, their wives and kids—I killed anything that moved in front of me. I even killed a couple of soldiers, Mama, but not many. I did it all because my government knew best. I'm standing here before you, Mama, to tell you that government don't know shit. Government is mean. No matter what kind it is. I've figured it out for myself. If they feed a poor man it's because they think that poor man might rise up and cut their throats. All this talk about Russia. You know what I think about Russia? I think it's shit.

I think America is shit, too. The government in Nam I helped defend was shit. The North Vietnamese is shit. You know why I fought in Vietnam, Mama? Because if I didn't, they'da put me in jail. That's a hell of a choice, isn't it? That's why I pay taxes, too. Because if I don't, they'll throw me in jail. And now if I want to go back to the place I was born, my wonderful government will throw my ass in jail. And yesterday, I speak words from the Declaration of Independence, and my fabulous government tosses me in jail."

"You can't fight the law, son," my mother said.

"Who says I can't? I fought the Viet Cong. Tell me why I can't fight the law."

"Luke, you assume that you can make the world exactly as you want it to be," my mother said, her head leaning against the bars of his cell. "You're so rigid and stubborn and . . ."

"Stupid, Mama?" he said, walking over to face us through the bars. "I know that's what you think."

"No, stupid isn't the word I was hunting for, Luke," she said. "The word is pure. But your purity never leads to wisdom. It only makes you fall in love with lost causes."

"I don't consider this a lost cause," he said. "I'm just saying no. I've got a right to say no. I'm a goddamn American. I fought a war so I could say no. I earned that simple right. My country fought a shitty war in a shitty country and I said yes to that. But the reason they told us we were fighting was to preserve the rights of people to choose how they wanted to live. They told us that over and over again. Of course, they were lying. But I chose to believe it. I didn't fight that war thinking my own government would then take my own home away from me. I would have fought for the Viet Cong if I ever once thought that. Savannah and Tom said no to the war. I fought so they could say that. Because, Mama, you're right. I'm stupid. I believed everything I was taught about America. There's no one who loves this country more than me. Nobody. Only it's not the whole country. I don't give a shit about Idaho or South Dakota. Never been there. My county is my home. It's what I can see from this window. It's only about forty square miles of the planet Earth. But it's what I love and what I fought for."

"And it's what you'll leave, Luke," my mother said. "Did you hear about poor Mr. Eustis? He refused to let the agents look at his farm today up by the Kiawah River. It seems he took your speech seriously last night. Old man Jones tried the same thing and he just lives in a trailer. They've both got warrants out for their arrest now."

"Mama, I ain't leaving my house when I get out of here," Luke said fiercely.

"You're just talking to hear yourself talk, Luke," she said. "If you try to remain on the island, they'll just come and take you like they're going to do to Eustis and Jones."

"I ain't poor Eustis and I ain't old Jones," Luke said.

"You were raised to be a law-abiding citizen," my mother said.

"Where I was raised doesn't exist anymore," he said. "Your husband and the goddamn politicians conspired to give my home away."

"Reese did not conspire to do anything and I resent your implying that about my husband," she said.

"He's been buying up land for years, Mama," said Luke, "and forcing poor farmers out of the county. He knew about this a long time ago. The county population has been dropping for ten years because he's been pushing people off their land. He married you so he could have the last large piece of land he couldn't buy outright."

My mother put her hand through the bars and slapped Luke hard across the face.

"He married me because he worships the ground I walk on," she said, enraged. "And even if my children haven't noticed, I'm worth every bit of that worship."

"You are, Mama," Luke said quietly. "I've always believed that. I've always believed that you were wonderful and was always sorry that you and Daddy were so unhappy. I'm glad that you're happy now and I understand that you just did what you had to do. Now I want you to understand that I've got to do things my own way too. I've thought this all out very carefully. I ain't thought about nothing else since the announcement."

"What do you think you can do, Luke?" my mother asked.

"I think I can stop them," he answered.

"You're nuts, Luke," I said, uttering my first words of

the evening. "I made a deal with the sheriff. He'll let you go if you'll agree to go up to the state mental hospital and turn yourself in for observation for two weeks. I think you should do it."

"Why, Tom?" he asked.

"Because you're talking crazy, Luke," I said. "There's nothing you can do about any of this. It's a fait accompli. It's finished and you've got to think about starting a new life."

"Everyone tells me there's nothing I can do," he said. "Human beings just love to roll over on their backs like puppies."

"What are you planning to do?" I asked.

"Register a small protest," he answered, his hair cottony in the moonlight.

"It won't do any good," I said.

"That's true, Tom," he said, smiling. "So what?"

"Then why are you doing it?" I said desperately.

"So I can live with myself," Luke said. "Why don't you come with me, Tom? The two of us could give them a run for their money. No one knows these woods and waters better than we do. We could make the Viet Cong look like rookies."

"I've got a family," I said angrily. "Or hadn't you noticed? I'm in a different situation than you."

"You're right," he said. "Your situation is different."

"I don't like your tone of voice when you say that," I said.

"It don't change a thing," he answered. "You know, Tom, I think you had more promise than any of us. But somewhere along the line you turned from something into not much. And you've got a good chance of turning into nothing, nothing at all. A man's only got so many yeses inside him before he uses them all up."

I shouted at him, "I'm saying no to you."

"No, little brother," he said. "You're just saying yes to them."

"You can't stop the government, Luke," my mother said.

Luke turned his sad, luminous eyes toward her; they were like the eyes of an obedient panther.

He said, "I know, Mama. But I think I can be a worthy opponent."

27

And worthy opponent Luke Wingo became.

I speak now not as witness but as the troubled gleaner of threads and fragments. I listened well and consolidated the hazes of rumor and innuendo in the single year it took to dissolve my town and family. I kept the inventory of ruin up to date. Comely was the town by the curving river that they dismantled in a year's time. Beautiful was Colleton in her last spring as she flung azaleas like a girl throwing rice at a desperate wedding. In dazzling profusion, Colleton ripened in a gauze of sweet gardens and the town ached beneath a canopy of promissory fragrance. Blue herons steepled out of marsh grass, agile in their ethereal stillness. A family of otters flowed through whitecaps in the wreck near the bridge and all the dead trees along the river were busy with shy rookeries of egrets. Ospreys brought quivering trout to the fledglings in their hatlike nests high atop telephone poles. Porpoises danced in the channels. The shrimp moved into the creeks to spawn.

But there was no shrimp fleet to meet them and not a single net interrupted their passage in countless billions toward the swaying acreage of marsh.

The waters of Colleton, because of security, were made off-limits to shrimpers and fishermen. It was the spring that the town began to move.

I watched them move the great mansions on the Street of Tides. Hundreds of men with jacks and pulleys and vast inclined planes loosed the great houses from their foundations and with all the cunning and mystery of physics, slid and coaxed those houses toward huge waiting barges in the river. Battened down with steel cable, houses began to move upstream toward Charleston. I saw my mother's house floating above the tide, looking like the wedding cake of a good king. She and Reese Newbury stood on their verandah, waving to people on the shore. They poured champagne into fine crystal, toasted the town, and threw their glasses into the tawny waters. The bridge opened and my mother and her new house and new husband floated miraculously between the spans in a river suddenly alive with an armada of white-pillared mansions. In the next weeks you could not look down toward the river without seeing a familiar house moving with strange dignity above the marsh, sailing out of the majestic past.

The highways also became clogged with the traffic of vast trucks moving houses to various destinations around South Carolina. I was startled one day to see a house pass me and I did not realize until several minutes after it had traveled by that I had witnessed the maiden voyage of my grandmother's house. The steeple of the Baptist church, looking like some great recumbent missile, went by me only minutes later. I took photographs with my Minolta and sent them to Savannah, who wrote a long poem about the unmaking of her town. Through the aperture of my camera, I watched them move the Episcopal church in its entirety. It moved through the twilight so gracefully that it seemed airborne. I photographed the sweating laborers who excavated the boxes of the dead and deported them in plastic bags to new grassless cemeteries along the interstate highway between Charleston and Columbia. If a building could not be moved or sold, it was destroyed and sold for scrap. Stray dogs were shot by hunters with special licenses. Cats were trapped and drowned by the public dock. Tomato plants sprang up wild and useless. Watermelons and cantaloupes rotted on vines in fields beside abandoned cabins. They dynamited the schoolhouse and the courthouse. They tore down every store along the Street of Tides. By September 1, the town of Colleton was as extinct as Pompeii or Herculaneum.

For the land they expropriated, the government paid out a total of $98,967,000. My mother was paid $2,225,000 for the loss of Melrose Island.

Alert to the nuances of feeling in her divided family, my mother prepared four cashier's checks, each one made out for the sum of one hundred thousand dollars. Savannah and I accepted the checks gratefully. Savannah no longer was imprisoned in the despised role of starving artist. The money paid off Sallie's medical school loans and enabled us to buy our house on Sullivans Island. My father had not been seen since the day of my mother's marriage to Reese Newbury, so she deposited the check in a savings account until my father showed up to collect his portion.

Luke set the check afire before my mother's eyes, and as she wept he reminded her that he was Luke Wingo, a river boy from Colleton, and she had raised him to understand that a river boy could not be bought at any price.

In June, the foreman of the project had sent a demolition crew out to Melrose Island to destroy the house where I had grown up. A twelve-man crew, three trucks, and two bulldozers were sent to complete the job. When one of the crew took a crowbar to the front door, a shot was fired from the forest, splintering the wood two inches above his head. Rifle fire began spraying the yard. Three bullets punctured tires on the three trucks and the crew ran down the island road toward town.

When they were gone, Luke walked out of the forest, and using Molotov cocktails he had hidden in the barn, he blew up the three trucks and the two bulldozers that had been sent by strangers to pull down his house.

It had begun now in earnest.

The next day, the crew returned, accompanied by a battalion of National Guardsmen who made a sweep through the woods around the house before signaling that it was all clear for the demolition to commence. From a tree across the river, Luke watched them raze the house where we had grown up. Later, he told me it was like watching his entire family die right before his eyes.

So, my town became a designated ruin, but unlike the virile and eternal remnants of older civilizations, Colleton was left with no subterranean sign of its former existence. They stripped the earth of even a memory of a town. The site of Colleton was plowed under and white pines were planted under the auspices of the United States Department of Agriculture. Each day, six thousand workers with special decals on their cars and trucks streamed across the bridges that led to the construction sites. By October 1, access to Colleton County was forever closed to any citizen not employed by the Atomic Energy Commission. Aircraft were forbidden by the Civil Aeronautics Board from making flights over the classified areas. Work was progressing rapidly on the four separate construction sites around the county.

The governor of South Carolina made the announcement that all citizens of Colleton had been successfully relocated in other towns and cities around the state and that the Colleton River Project would be fully operational in three years.

We, the people of Colleton, left like sheep, docile and banished to unspeakable newly created towns without the dark resonance of memory to sustain us. We walked the Carolina earth without the wisdom and accumulated suffering of our forebears to instruct us in times of danger or folly. Set adrift, we floated into the driftless suburbs at the edge of cities. We left not like a defeated tribe, but like one brushed with the black veils and garments of extinction. Singly and in pairs, we left that archipelago of green islands that had been spared the worst disfigurements and indemnities of our times. As a town, we had made the error of staying small—and there is no more unforgivable crime in America.

Wordlessly, we did what they commanded us to do. They praised us for our selflessness. They broke us with their generosity. They scattered us and sent us to live among strangers. We crawled across those bridges on our knees, whimpering with gratitude for every crumb of praise they threw in the dirt for us to lap up with our tongues. We were Americans, we were southerners, and, God help us, we were heroically and irrevocably stupid and compliant. The meek may yet inherit the earth, but they will not inherit Colleton.

Only one of us stayed behind to register a small protest. Luke had sold his shrimp boat to a shrimper from Saint Augustine and began to prepare a base of operations from which he would try to slow the progress of the construction. He planned a small rear-guard action that would prove nettlesome to the Mewshaw Company and its workers. But his dreams of insurrection began to grow after his first triumphs. His missions against the project grew more and more bold. The more he dared, the more he achieved. He fashioned a dangerous equation from his early successes.

The chief of security discerned during the first month of the construction phase of the project that four tons of dynamite were missing from the main construction site on the western edge of the county. The dynamite, he felt, had been removed slowly, over a long period of time. The automobiles of sixty construction workers had their tires slashed in the dirt parking lot near the main construction site. Ten bulldozers were destroyed by fire in a single night. The trailer of the chief engineer was dynamited. Four guard dogs were shot and killed as they patrolled the perimeter of the construction grounds.

Someone was in the woods and he was armed and dangerous and the construction workers were getting edgy as they crossed the bridges each morning for work.

It was during this time that my father made his grand re-entry into one of the obscure harbors of South Carolina. While shrimping in Key West, he was approached by a well-dressed man who wore an Accutron watch and a diamond ring and asked my father if he was interested in making some real money. Three days later, my father was on his way to Jamaica, where he had a rendezvous at a swank bar in Montego Bay with a partner of the man with the diamond. My father did not fail to notice that the second man also wore a diamond the size of a lima bean on his left pinkie. Henry Wingo had been waiting his whole life to meet guys who were rich and tasteless enough to cover their hands with women's jewels. He never learned their last names; he trusted their sense of style.

"Class," my father would say later. "Just pure class."

Two Jamaicans loaded my father's shrimp boat down with fifteen hundred pounds of top-grade marijuana, which my father knew about, and fourteen kilos of pure heroin, which they failed to mention to him. One of the Jamaicans made his living as a busboy in a resort hotel but loaded shipments of marijuana whenever the opportunity arose. The other Jamaican, Victor Paramore, worked as an informant for the U.S. Treasury Department, and he was the first witness called to testify when my father's case came up on the docket in Charleston. When my father landed at a point between Kiawah and Seabrook islands, most of the narcotics agents in our part of the world arrived for his landing party. It was to prove my father's last attempt at mastering the nuances of venture capitalism.

When my father went to court, he offered no defense for himself and did not choose to have a lawyer represent him. What he had done was dead wrong, he told the judge, and he had no excuses for his actions nor would he make any. He deserved full punishment under the law for his crime because it had brought shame on him and his family. He received a ten-year sentence and was fined ten thousand dollars.

My mother paid the fine with the money she had set aside for my father from the sale of the island. In a space of one year I had faced my brother and my father as prisoners.

But by the time my father went to prison in Atlanta I had little hope that I would ever see my brother Luke alive again.

"Think bigger. Think bigger," Luke would tell himself as he roamed the county by night. He was the last remaining citizen of the town of Colleton, and he promised himself he would give them a run for their money before they caught up with him.

One thing worked greatly in his favor during the first months of his rebellion. The government was not sure that Luke was the saboteur in the forests. He was the main suspect, of course, but no one had seen him to make a positive identification. Like the Viet Cong he had come to admire so much, Luke owned those long morning hours after midnight when he filled the lives of ill-paid guards with dread. He moved only at night in his displaced country, avoiding the patrol boats in the rivers and the cruising police cars along the abandoned roads. As the weeks passed, a terrible sense of priesthood obsessed him as he walked through the memorized woods of his childhood. He heard voices and began to see the faces of his family materialize in the branches of trees. All the hallucinations—or visions, as he preferred to call them—were brimming with applause

and consent for the efficacy of his mission, his sacred walk-
about in the war zone where he served as a liberation army
of one. It worried him when he began to talk to himself.

But he was the almsman of a valuable birthright in these
first weeks of his war against the state and he was secure
in his unconferrable knowledge of all the mysteries of the
lowcountry. They were hunting a native son who had
appropriated all the secrets the rivers could articulate in
a single lifetime. He surveyed the vast estate of that terrain
he vowed to keep open. He circumnavigated the entire
county by foot and by small sailboat. He noted the flow
of traffic in the rivers and across the bridges, and the number of railcars bringing in loads of coal across the two trestles in the north of the county. He established a safe house
in Savannah and one in Brunswick, Georgia. After each
strike, he would leave Colleton for three weeks until the
men who hunted him grew tired of following cold trails.
All over the sea islands, in abandoned wells or buried beneath the foundations of houses, he hid contraband, weapons, and food.

His first acts were simple vandalism, but of a high order.
He had developed good habits over the years, and he studied his job and grew more skillful at it. He examined both
his mistakes and his small victories, gathering data for future operations, amending his techniques, then perfecting
them. The isolation, the self-containment, and the fierce
necessity for concentration made him both cautious and
formidable. In the deep woods near the great swamps, he
hunted the white-tailed deer with a bow and arrow, marveling at his capacity for stillness as he waited in trees above
salt licks. He felt green and magic and his heart was glad
for trees and deer and islands. He hunted with the astonishment of one who had retreated a thousand years, stepped
back into the clean and timeless realms when tribes of
Yemassee had stalked deer in the same way. Luke was
grateful to the animals who sustained him and he knew
why primitive men had worshiped deer as gods and painted
them on the walls of caves as an act of ecstasy and prayer.
He had never felt so startlingly alive, so authentic, or so
necessary. Always he had visions, but they possessed the
supple intensity of dreams. He slept during the day and
sang in his sleep. Search planes and helicopters hunted for

him as he slept. He dreamed of things dazzling and miraculous and was happy when he awoke to starlight that the dreams did not fade but retained their shape in frescoes inked in light and blood across the sky. He burned with a revolutionary zeal. Ideas rose out of him, streamed through his hair like wildflowers.

In some ways, he felt as if he was the last sane man in America. He recited the statistics of Hiroshima and Nagasaki to himself whenever he felt doubts about his calling. If he could prevent the construction of a thousand nuclear weapons, he could in theory be responsible for saving a hundred million human lives. He began to listen to the passionate counsel of a single voice within him whose tone was urgent and committed. This voice set down laws of behavior, established long-range goals, and initiated guerrilla actions. Luke thought it was his own conscience speaking, and he listened to it in a kind of rapture as he wandered alive and free in a stateless state, discovering with pleasure that an enlightened banditry came easily to him. He stole supplies, an occasional fast boat, rifles, and ammunition. His was an uncompromising advocacy of a beloved, endangered land. It was not his fault if that vision was enlarging to include not only Colleton but all of a wonderful planet.

Often he would enter into the surreal devastated town of Colleton itself, walking through the expunged streets and naming aloud each family who once lived on each acre of overgrown earth. He drifted through the ruptured wasteland of cemeteries and felt the small wounds in the bulldozed earth where his townsmen had once been interred. He walked down the Street of Tides, forever silenced of commerce or the murmuring of neighbors, forever bereft of the dark, glorious aromas of coffee or the polite skirmishing of traffic. Luke could feel the vital presence of the town beneath him. He felt it straining to rise out of the earth full born, healthy and blooming with the buoyant aura of resurrection. Dreaming again, he thought he could hear the town screaming at him, reciting the long elegies of its aggrievement, singing out an anthem of subversion and loss, demanding restitution, hoarse from reciting the powerful litanies of extinction. In moonlight, he moved toward our grandmother's house and was furious when he could not find that half-acre of land beside the river. All landmarks had been effaced and not until he found the water oak where he, Savannah, and I had carved our names one Easter Sunday was he certain he had found the right spot. Crabgrass and kudzu were growing in the scarred earth where Tolitha and Amos once lived. He walked back toward the floating dock and tripped on something in the high grass. Reaching back, he knew what it was going to be, and he lifted my grandfather's cross up on his shoulder and as an act of homage he took that cross back to the Street of Tides and walked the length and breadth of that street in happy remembrance of his grandfather. He felt the weight of that cross cutting into his shoulder, felt the wood printing the truth of its undamaged grain in his flesh, marking him, wounding him, reminding him of the righteousness of his mission.

As he walked the street with the cross on his back, all the voices came roaring out of the air at him, urging him on, their river boy, their lowcountryman, their champion. They cheered as he swore that he would not allow this to happen, that he was not resigned to the death of the town he loved the most. He swore to himself, to those thrilling and partisan voices, to the river and his slain town, that he would make his message known, that he would breathe into this violated soil the new life of towns, that he would raise Colleton like Lazarus up from the pillaged earth.

"They will know me," Luke screamed. "They will learn my name. They will respect me. And I'll make them build this town exactly like it was."

He stopped himself and the voices left him. He laid the cross down in the dirt and he felt the melodies of liberation pouring through him. He began to dance down the Street of Tides, spinning and shouting. He would stop suddenly and say, "Right here. I'm going to put up Mr. Danner's men's clothing shop. And next to it is Mr. Schein's food store and right next to that will be Sarah Poston's dress shop and Bitty Wall's florist and Woolworth's five-and-dime."

He could feel the earth tremble as he passed and he could feel those old proud stores struggling to be reborn. He could hear the whole town gathered on the roofs of once visible stores cheering him on. In his mind, he re-created the street exactly as he remembered it. When he left the Street of Tides that night, he looked back and saw all the stores lit up and the Christmas ornaments strung out across the streets and a boy putting letters on the marquee of the Breeze Theater and Mr. Luther sweeping the front of his store with a broom and Sheriff Lucas coming out of Harry's Restaurant after a meal, loosening his belt and belching.

He had become, at last, he thought, an essential man, a man risen in spring, a man on fire.

He looked back with pride at the town he had created.

He heard something behind him. He whirled around and drew his pistol.

Then he heard it again. It was a whistle.

He saw the figure of a man moving toward him along the river with unutterable joy.

Mr. Fruit.

In March he made his small skirmish official, expanded its nature into full-fledged guerrilla warfare by an act purely symbolic to him but not to the state. At three A.M. on the morning of March fourteenth, four jury-rigged but immensely powerful bombs blew out the four bridges that connected the northern and eastern frontiers of Colleton to the mainland. An hour later, two more bombs wiped out the two railroad trestles that brought the freight trains of the Southern Railway into the county.

One of these trains, delivering a vast load of coal to the construction site, came roaring out of the night from Charleston twenty minutes after the trestle had been destroyed. The chief engineer took the long trestle at full throttle and the train was airborne for sixty yards before it crashed spectacularly into the black waters of the Little Carolina River. The engineer and three crewmen were killed instantly and first blood had been drawn in the war the newspapers soon called the War of Colleton Secession.

Luke wrote a letter to fifteen newspapers around the state of South Carolina declaring the land around Colleton in a forty-mile radius—an area that included thirty sea islands and forty-seven thousand acres of mainland—free from the manufacture of plutonium. He apologized to the families of the four men who lost their lives in the train crash and said he would do anything in the world to bring those men back to life. His task was to preserve human life, not destroy or forfeit it. The letter was a shorter version of the speech he had delivered to the citizens of Colleton on the night Patrick Flaherty told them how their town would be dismantled. He issued a manifesto declaring that the portion of land formerly known as Colleton County was hereby a sovereign state with himself as governor, high sheriff, commander of the armed forces, and, until he could recruit a population, its lone citizen. The federal government had decreed that the land belonged to the people of the United States and Luke agreed, but the manner of governance was at issue. This new state, one-twentieth the size of Rhode Island, was to be called Colleton. He gave the federal government thirty days in which to cease and desist in the building of the Colleton River Project and to return all lands stolen from the people of Colleton in their dispossession. If the government failed to cancel the project, the state of Colleton would formally secede from the Union and war would be declared. All construction workers would be considered members of an invading army of occupation and would be the target of hostile fire.

Luke also asked for volunteers to serve in a force of irregulars to patrol the borders of Colleton against incursion by federal agents. He ordered that they enter the new territory alone, wearing green armbands for identification, and establish listening points and outposts the length and breadth of the disenfranchised county. When there were enough of them dispersed through the swamps and forests, he would make contact and they would begin to operate as a small army. But at first, each man or woman would operate alone in a guerrilla action to stop the flow of materials and to halt the building of the plant.

The letter was front-page news across the state. There was a picture of Luke and me holding a huge trophy aloft when we won the state football championship our senior year and a picture of Savannah taken from the jacket of *The Shrimper's Daughter*. The National Guard was given the job of protecting all the bridges entering the county and work began immediately to repair the damaged bridges and trestles. Security was tightened at the camp and a warrant for Luke's arrest was issued. I think I met every cop and law enforcement officer in South Carolina after the letter appeared. Luke was considered armed, dangerous, and probably insane. There were hysterical editorials in leading newspapers and Senator Ernest Hollings was quoted as saying in the *News and Courier*, "The boy may be crazy, but there sure ain't many bridges leading out to Colleton anymore." The KA chapter of the University of South Carolina gave a green armband party to raise money for disabled children. One letter to the editor appeared in the *Columbia State* calling Luke Wingo "the last of the great South Carolinians."

Three weeks after Luke's letter appeared, a seventy-year-old man named Lucius Tuttle, a former fur trapper, was seized and arrested in the area near the main construction site of the Colleton River Project. The *News and Courier* reported the incident but did not disclose the fact that the man was apprehended wearing a green armband and that he resisted arrest by holding off twenty deputies with rifle fire until his ammunition gave out. Ten women, all members of Women Strike for Peace, lay down in front of a bus carrying construction men to their work. They all wore green armbands and were chanting "No more nukes" as they were led off to jail.

In conservative circles in the state, Luke was considered a murderer and a crackpot. But there were some men and women, admittedly few, who looked upon him as the ultimate environmentalist—the only man in the history of the republic who had come up with a reasonably sane response to the chilling grotesqueries of the nuclear age. At the very moment that the public's perception of Luke's insurgency was changing, the federal government was becoming deadly serious about terminating Luke's war against the state. As a guerrilla he had proven himself formidable and cunning, but as a symbol it was feared he could jeopardize the entire Colleton River Project. Luke had become a hazard, an explicit public relations dilemma. By taking out the six bridges, Luke had demonstrated a refined tactical sense behind his genius for disruption. FBI agents began flocking into Colleton County and a Special Forces team from Fort Bragg, North Carolina, trained in anti-insurgency warfare began to make night sweeps of the islands. Luke assessed the time he had left by the prestige of those they sent to stop him. He began noticing the increasing number of reconnaissance flights over the marshes. The Coast Guard increased its patrols on the river. Their engagement was an act of homage to him. He appreciated the quality of the men commissioned to apprehend him and bring him to justice, and although they brought extraordinary skills to the matter of his interdiction, he had brought to his campaign a lifetime's head start in his familiarity with and mastery of the terrain.

I learned to identify an FBI agent from a distance of a hundred yards or more and these sightings were always error-free. Their markings were as distinctive as an eastern diamondback's. They had all watched too many movies and read too many books about how fabulous their investigative powers were. They believed all the happy horseshit that the FBI fed in liberal doses to its own agents. I've always hated men firm of jaw and handshake who look like they're imitating the style of B-grade actors. All FBI agents appeared to have shopped for the same colorless suits off the same rack at the same cheap men's stores. Their badges were the most attractive part of their wardrobes. I was interviewed by a dozen of them the first year of Luke's engagement in the woods of Colleton and it gave me small pleasure. I could be inordinately offensive when talking with men who might one day kill my brother. The FBI considered me hostile and this estimation could cheer me up on bad days.

It was almost a year before J. William Covington was assigned to Luke's case. He appeared during a spring football practice as I was trying to install a new veer offense to take advantage of a quarterback who ran like a deer but also passed like one. Bob Marks, the line coach I had just hired fresh out of The Citadel, spotted Covington sitting in his government-issue Chevrolet as we ran the team through wind sprints at the end of practice.

"More fuzz, Tom," he said.

"Next year, I think I'm going to pay my taxes," I said, walking toward the car.

He got out of the car when he saw me approach. J. William was exemplary of the breed. If he had been stark naked dancing through a field of lilies, you could still make a positive identification of him as an FBI agent.

"Excuse me, sir," I said to him. "We don't let Hare Krishnas pass out literature on the football field. The airport is fifteen miles west of here."

He laughed and it surprised me that his laughter sounded genuine. "I heard you had a sense of humor," he said, extending his hand.

"That's not true," I answered. "You heard I was a wise-ass."

"In your file, you are described as being uncooperative," he said. "My name is J. William Covington. My friends call me Cov."

"What do your enemies call you?" I asked.

"Covington."

"It's a pleasure to meet you, Covington," I said. "Now, to continue with my career of noncooperation, I'll tell you everything I know. I don't know where Luke is hiding. I have not heard a single word from my brother. He has not written, called, or wired. I am not supplying him with food or shelter or aid of any kind. And, no, I will not help you with your investigation in any way."

"I would like to help Luke get out of this, Tom," Covington said. "I like everything I hear about Luke. I think I can work a deal with the prosecutor's office where we can plea-bargain a sentence of only three to five years."

"The four men who were killed on the train?" I asked.

"It's obvious he didn't know that train was coming then," he said. "When your family lived in Colleton, no train ever used that trestle at night. I call that involuntary manslaughter."

"He could get more than five years for taking out the bridges," I said. "Why would the prosecutor go along with that?"

"Because I can convince the prosecutor that by working out a deal, he might be able to save all the bridges in the southern part of the county," said Covington.

"Why are you saying this to me?" I asked. "I don't see how I can help you."

"Because I've read Luke's file very carefully, Tom," he said. "And there are three people who could find Luke if they put their mind to it. There is your father, who, as you know, is currently indisposed."

"Indisposed," I said. "I like the way you use the language, Covington."

"The other two are you and your sister. She writes excellent poetry. I'm a big fan of hers," he said.

"She'll be thrilled," I said.

"Can I count on your help?" he asked.

"No, you can't, Cov," I said. "You didn't hear me the first time. I won't help in your investigation in any way."

"The Mewshaw Company's offering a twenty-five-thousand-dollar reward to anyone who can neutralize your brother," Covington said. "Do I need to translate the word *neutralize* for you? They are starting to put guys in that county who are more than a match for your brother. Two Green Berets who both received the Congressional Medal of Honor are in the county right now, hunting him. They may not get him tomorrow or the next day, Tom, but eventually someone's going to kill Luke. I'd like to prevent that. I admire your brother very much. I would like to save his life, Tom. I can't do it without your help."

"So far, Mr. Covington," I said, "you're the first person from the Federal Bureau of Investigation who has not pissed me off. This, however, makes me very nervous. Why did you decide to become an FBI agent? And why, for godsakes, do you call yourself J. William?"

"My first name is Jasper," he said. "I would rather die than have anybody call me by my first name. My wife came up with the idea for J. William, since I work for an organization founded by a J. Edgar. She thought there might be some subliminal value whenever a promotion was in order. I joined the FBI because I was a lousy athlete, and like most lousy athletes, I suffered through a painful high school experience and had doubts about my manhood. We FBI agents suffer no doubts about our manhood."

"You give good answers, Jasper," I said. "Unlike your associates, you're giving out small intimations that I'm dealing with something vaguely human."

"I studied your file carefully," he said. "I knew if we did not establish some basis for trust you would not cooperate with me at all."

"I didn't say I trusted you, Jasper," I answered. "And I already told you that I would not cooperate."

"That's not true," he said. "Because you're talking to the only man in the world who is interested in saving your brother's life instead of killing him."

I studied J. William Covington's face. It was a handsome, sentient, chivalrous face, the kind that inspired a titanic distrust in me. He met my gaze with candor—another mark against him. His eyes were clear and untroubled.

"I think I can find my brother for you, Jasper," I said. "But I want the deal in writing."

"You'll have the deal in writing and you'll have my word that everyone will go along with that deal," he said.

"I'll do it, but I'll never like or trust you, Jasper," I said. "And I don't like your suit."

"I'm not interested in finding out the name of your tailor either," he answered, pointing to my khakis and sweat shirt.

When school was out, Savannah flew down to Charleston and we spent several days gathering supplies and making plans for our expedition into our lost county. At night, Sallie, Savannah, and I would study the nautical chart of the county, a Mercator projection at a scale 1:80,000 at latitude 32°15'. The rivers and creeks were covered with small precise numbers giving the depth in soundings of feet at mean low water. Our fingers moved through marshes and channels and the long, flat geography of our childhood. We tried to put ourselves in Luke's place and see the world as he was now seeing it. I thought he must be living in the Savannah River Swamp south of the county, making his brief forays of sabotage and disruption at night, then skipping back into the impenetrable swamp before dawn.

Savannah disagreed. She thought that Luke had a single refuge within the county where he based his operations and that it was a place we all knew. She reminded me that Luke was a creature of habit and she didn't believe he would wage a war to liberate Colleton without being able to live there.

"You'd make a shitty guerrilla," I said.

I also told her that they were hunting Luke with bloodhounds over the length and breadth of the islands and it seemed unlikely to me that those dogs would not have discovered a base camp.

"Then it must be a place they don't know about, Tom," Savannah said. "A place that only Luke knows about."

"They know about every place Luke knows about, Savannah," I said. "You can buy this same map at any port in the United States. America is nothing if not well mapped."

"If it's so well mapped, why can't they find Luke?" she asked.

"He's taken great care to hide himself well," I said, looking at the map.

"What is that place you told me about in college, Tom?" Sallie said. "Your daddy used to fish there or something."

"Marsh Hen Island," Savannah and I both shouted simultaneously.

When my father was a boy he had been hunting marsh hens in the vast marshes along the Upper Estill River. One of his friends was paddling his small bateau through the marsh grass at high tide, flushing the birds from their hiding places in the lush spartina. He had killed a dozen birds when he saw a modest clump of low-growing trees rise out of the marsh. The water had turned as they paddled toward the small unmarked island and they barely made it to land before they realized they would have to wait for the next tide till they could return to the main channel. They were thirteen miles from the nearest habitation and they had discovered, by accident, one of those secret sanctuaries that provide a sense of rapture and anchorage to a small boy. It was a quarter-acre of uncharted land, a cluster of palmettos and one spindly oak. They had happened upon a failed island marooned in an endless expanse of salt marsh, almost invisible from either land or river. They cleaned the marsh hens and soaked them in seawater. They pitched their tent, made a fire and sautéed onions in three tablespoons of bacon fat, then rolled the birds in flour and fried them until they turned dark as chocolate. They added water to the pan and simmered them slowly until they were tender. They lifted clams out of the exposed mudflats and ate them raw while waiting for the birds to cook. Both boys were convinced they had come to a place where no man had been before them. They claimed the land for themselves and my father and his friends carved their names into the trunk of the oak. Before they left on the next tide, they christened their discovery Marsh Hen Island.

Once, after my grandmother had left Amos and moved to Atlanta, my father ran away from home and his friends found him on Marsh Hen, crying for his lost mother. When the cobia and shad entered the rivers each spring to spawn, my father would spend a week on his island, fishing and crabbing and camping out beneath the stars. I was seven when he first took his three children with him on his annual fishing trip. By then, he had built a small hut to escape the rain. Using a live eel, I caught a thirty-pound cobia that first season, and we set a gill net for shad in the river. For a week, we lived on the steaks of cobia barbecued over a slow fire and pale sacs of shad roe covered with strips of thick bacon. Whenever I thought of my father's retreat from the world, I envisioned great feasts of seafood and my father's laughter when he navigated his boat through acres of dense marsh as the tides lifted us up to that inconsequential piece of land that cut us off from the rest of the planet. It was only after my father discovered that his camp had been used by other fishermen that he ceased his annual pilgrimage to Marsh Hen Island. When it was no longer secret, the island lost its aura of magic—and hence its value. By permitting the incursion of strangers, Marsh Hen Island had betrayed its discoverer. In the bill of particulars of my father's philosophy, a place could be inviolable only once. He never visited the island again, and sensing something genuine in our father's disillusionment, neither had his children.

But Savannah and I knew you could live a whole lifetime in Colleton County, spend all your leisure time fishing and crabbing in the most obscure creeks and tributaries, and never once even imagine the existence of that heart-shaped fritter of land embedded like a sapphire in the dead center of the largest salt marsh north of Glynn County, Georgia. The only other people who shared this piece of earned intelligence were my father, my brother, and those anonymous fishermen whose innocent footprints undermined the numinous rarity of my father's secret hermitage.

On the map, in a thirty-mile swathe of marshland, I marked an X at the spot where I thought Marsh Hen Island might be. I knew it was a misnomer even to call it an island; it was a piece of retreating land in the process of being overwhelmed by the marsh.

On the night before we left for Colleton, I read a bedtime story to the three girls and tucked them in. Sallie left for the late shift at the hospital and Savannah and I made drinks and took them out to the front porch. The lights of Charleston were wreathed across the harbor in the soft haze. My mother had eaten dinner with us that evening and the tension had been unbearable. She blamed my father and us for Luke's defection. She told us that Reese had offered to hire the finest lawyers in South Carolina for Luke's defense and was furious when Savannah hinted that such an arrangement might not meet with Luke's approval. My mother could not recognize that Reese Newbury had mastered the abstruse art of humiliation by kindness. We took no pleasure in the fact that our mother was crying when she left the house.

"I think Mom will be the real tragic figure in all this, no matter what happens to Luke," Savannah said as we stared out toward Fort Sumter.

"She deserves to be," I said. "She didn't act in good faith."

"You don't know how difficult it is to be a woman," Savannah said sharply. "After the life she led, anything she does is fine with me."

"Then why do you act like you hate her guts when she's around you, Savannah?" I asked. "Why can't you speak a civil word to her or make her feel genuinely loved for even a single moment when she's in your presence?"

"Because she's my mother and it's a natural law and a sign of mental health when any woman can summon enough strength to hate her mother," she answered. "My analyst says it's an important stage for me to work through."

"Your analyst!" I said. "How many shrinks, analysts, therapists, and meatballs have you been to since you left South Carolina?"

"I'm trying to have a life, Tom," she said, hurt. "You have no right to undermine my therapy."

"Has there ever been anyone who lived in New York City who didn't see a therapist?" I asked. "I mean, there must have been some poor schnook who changed planes at La Guardia who didn't have time to make it to the Upper East Side for a fifty-minute session."

"You need a therapist more than anybody I ever met," she said. "If you could only hear your voice. If you only knew how angry you sound."

"I don't know how to deal with someone I love who has all the answers," I said. "Mom has all the answers and you have all the answers and it seems like an endemic disease with all the women in this family. Don't you ever find yourself plagued with doubts?"

"Yes," she said. "I have great doubts about you, Tom. I've got serious doubts about the choices you've made in your life. I don't see any direction to your life. I see no ambition, no desire to change and take chances. I see you floating along, slightly detached from your wife and children, slightly alienated from your job, not knowing what you want or where you want to go."

"That's what makes me an American, Savannah," I said. "There's nothing rare about that."

"You come home after coaching, make yourself a drink, and sit in front of the television set until you're tired enough or drunk enough to go to sleep," she said. "You don't read books, you don't have conversations, you only vegetate."

"I'm having a conversation right now," I said. "This is why I hate conversations."

"You hate looking at yourself, Tom," said Savannah, reaching over and squeezing my arm.

"You're smack in the middle of living an unexamined life and it's going to catch up to you. That's what I'm worried about."

"Why do you force an admission of insanity and unhappiness out of everyone you meet?" I asked. "Why is craziness the only response to the world you recognize as valid?"

"I've heard rumors about people who are mentally healthy, but I've never met any members of the tribe up close," she answered. "They're like Incas. You can read about them and study their ruins but you can never interview any of them personally to see what makes them tick."

"Savannah," I said, "they're going to kill Luke if we don't find him. And if they kill Luke, I don't know what's going to happen to me."

"Then we'll find him and bring him back," she said.

"They've hired men to hunt him down like he was a deer or something," I said.

She said, "I'm more afraid for them than I am for Luke. You and I both know how capable he is in the woods.

Everything's always worked out for Luke. I think if he'd failed just once, he wouldn't be out there now. If we'd gotten caught when we rescued the porpoise. If we hadn't been able to put the loggerhead in the Newbury's bed. If Luke hadn't been able to swim with the body of his CO out of North Vietnam. He always has faith that it'll work out for him and he's always been right."

"But this is senseless," I said. "He has no chance of achieving anything."

"He's certainly gotten their attention, Tom," she said. "Do you think about him often?"

"I try not to," I said. "I try not to think about Luke or Dad at all. There are times when I pretend that neither one of them has ever been a part of my life."

"The old Mom technique," Savannah said, laughing. "Truth is only what you choose to remember."

"I write to Dad once a week. It's like writing a pen pal from Estonia, some stranger I never met. He writes very loving and very intelligent letters in return. How can I relate to a loving father? It's even more difficult to relate to an intelligent one. We've almost established a friendship through the mail. Yet when I think of our childhood, I feel the greatest tenderness and gratitude toward Mom. I fill up absolutely with love for her and yet I can hardly bear to be around her now. The thing with Luke is killing her and I can't help her with it at all."

"Why are you so mad at Luke?"

"Because I think he's an idiot," I said. "Because I think he is egomaniacal, inflexible, and selfish. But there's something else, Savannah, that I don't understand. I've envied him his freedom to step out in the full fury of his beliefs armed with a passion that I'll never know or feel. I'm jealous that Luke can alarm the whole countryside by that cold, unknowable rapture he brings to every article of his simple goddamn faith. The reason I need to stop him, Savannah, is because, in the deepest part of me, I believe in the rectitude of his private war with the world. Because I believe it so deeply, his sense of engagement is a constant reminder of how much I've surrendered. I've been tamed by mortgages, car payments, lesson plans, children, and a wife with more compelling dreams and ambitions than my own. I'm living out my life in a bedroom community watching the seven o'clock news and doing the daily crossword puzzle while my brother eats raw fish and wages a war of resistance against an army of occupation who stole the only home we ever knew. I'm not a fanatic or a saboteur, I tell myself. I'm a good citizen, I tell myself. I have duties and responsibilities, I tell myself. But Luke has proven something to me. I'm not a man of principle, I'm not a man of faith, and I'm not a man of action. I have the soul of a collaborator. A Vichy government has set up headquarters in that soul. I've become exactly the kind of man I hate more than anything in the world. I keep a nice lawn and I've never gotten a speeding ticket."

"I think of Luke as a modern-day equivalent of Don Quixote," Savannah said. "I want to write a long poem about all this."

"I'm sure he thinks of himself in exactly the same terms," I said. "But I don't see how it's helped him or anyone else at all. Four men are dead because of Luke and no matter how hard I try to rationalize it, murder just doesn't appeal to me."

"He didn't murder those men," she said. "That was an accident."

"Would you like to explain that to their wives and children?" I asked.

"You're a sentimentalist, Tom," Savannah said.

"I imagine their wives and children are, too," I said.

"Luke is not a murderer," Savannah said to me.

"Then what the hell is he, Savannah?"

"He's an artist and a completely free man," she answered. "Two things you'll never understand."

We had waited for a calm night and a moon that would help us navigate. At the Charleston marina, Sallie kissed both me and Savannah and wished us good luck as we embarked for Colleton.

"Bring Luke back safely," Sallie said. "Tell him that he's deeply loved by a great many people and that the girls need an uncle."

"I will, Sallie," I said, holding her. "I don't know how long we're going to be."

"You've got all summer," she replied. "My mama's coming down tomorrow to help with the kids. Lila's going to take them up to Pawleys Island next month. I'll be working my ass off saving lives and doing good for humanity."

"Say a prayer for us, Sallie," Savannah said as I started the engine and moved the boat out into the Ashley River. "And say one for Luke."

"I thought you didn't believe in God," I said to Savannah as we moved slowly past the Coast Guard base at the end of the Charleston peninsula.

"I don't," Savannah answered, "but I believe in Luke and he believes in God and I always believe in God when I truly need him."

"Situational faith," I said.

"You got it, buster," she answered happily. "Isn't this wonderful, Tom? We're in another adventure together. It's just like the time we went to Miami to rescue the white porpoise. We're going to find Luke. I can feel it. I can feel it in my bones. Look up above us, Tom."

I looked in the direction she was pointing in the sky and said, "Orion, the Hunter."

"No," she answered. "I've got to teach you to think like a poet, Tom. That's the reflection of Luke hiding in the lowcountry."

"Savannah, I might puke if you keep referring to Luke as the subject of your future poems," I said. "We're not in the middle of a poem. This is a journey—a last chance to save our brother."

"It's an odyssey," she said, teasing me.

"There's a difference between life and art, Savannah," I said as we moved out into Charleston Harbor.

"You're wrong," she said. "You've always been wrong about that."

I guided the boat past the lights of Mount Pleasant, the solitary shadows of Fort Sumter, the lights of my house on Sullivans Island, past lighthouses and the low-throttled murmur of the harbor pilot's boat rendezvousing with a freighter from Panama. As I moved the boat through the breakwaters, with James Island on my starboard side, moonlight infused the tassels of sea oats shimmering on the tide-stuck dunes. The waves, inlaid with phosphorus and plankton, fell in soft wings against the bow. The sea flittered and the air was strange as milk. The raw smell of childbirth rose out of the marsh as we approached the windless sea on a night without small craft advisories for five hundred miles. We left the lassitude of barrier islands and entered the soft eye of the Atlantic freckled with stars, and the moon lay against the waters in a stole of bright ermine.

I headed the boat straight out toward the Gulf Stream, out toward Bermuda, east toward Africa, until I could no longer see the lights of South Carolina behind me. Then I turned the boat due south and set a course toward the country of my birth and said a prayer that I could deliver my brother from the tyranny of an absolute vision. I prayed that I could teach him the art of compromise and genuflection to higher authority. I prayed that I could teach him not to be Luke, that I could tame him and make him more like Tom.

Savannah and I held hands as I urged the boat toward Colleton and the wind lifted my sister's hair like a veil. For two hours, I watched the stars and the compass until I saw the blinking green channel marker that indicated the entrance to Colleton Sound. As trespassers, we entered the forbidden waters where we had first drawn breath during the hurricane of 1944.

It was just after midnight at mean low tide when we dropped anchor on the leeward side of Kenesaw Island and waited for the tides to change again. We reckoned we would need at least two feet of rising water to make the approach to Marsh Hen Island. When the tide did change, we could feel the boat strain against the anchor line. At three in the morning, I started the motor and slowly began to navigate through the most obscure creeks in the county. The hum of the boat seemed an obscene intervention in the complete silence that engulfed us. It took us an hour before we reached the vast stretch of salt marsh that held Marsh Hen Island in its secret center. I tried three small creeks that led to dead ends. I had to return to the river to get my bearings, then start out again. We followed two more inconsequential ribbons of water that ambled off into the great marsh with the same result. As we traveled below the marsh, the spartina formed impenetrable walls of grass on both sides of us, making it impossible to get our true heading. It was not until full high tide with the sun rising in the east and at our moment of profoundest despair that we ran into a creek I thought we had explored before and almost ran aground on the island we were searching for.

As I lifted the motor out of the water, Savannah sprang onto the bow and stepped out onto dry land. I locked the motor in place and heard Savannah say in the darkness behind me, "He's been here, Tom. Jesus Christ, has he been here."

"We need to hide the boat, Savannah," I said. "We can't let them spot us from the air."

"He's made it easy for us," she answered.

Beneath the wind-stunted oak and the dense grove of palmettos, Savannah stood at the center of Luke's base of operations. He had placed camouflage netting in the trees and beneath the netting had erected a large waterproof tent. We found boxes of dynamite covered with oilskin and drums of gasoline. There were rifles, boxes of ammunition, and cases of she-crab soup manufactured by the Blue Channel Corporation. There was a small sailboat and a small bateau with an eight horsepower engine. Savannah found thirty-one gallon jugs filled with fresh water.

Luke had restored the small fishing lodge my father had built. He had put on a new roof and replaced the floorboards that had rotted away. His sleeping bag was in the corner and there was a wooden chair and table in the middle of the room. A half-empty bottle of Wild Turkey stood on the table beside a place setting for one. Beside the plate was a copy of *The Shrimper's Daughter* inscribed to Luke.

"Luke always did have good taste in literature," said Savannah.

"I'm surprised he's not reading Chairman Mao's Little Red Book," I said.

"He doesn't need to," she said. "He's living it."

We unloaded the boat quickly, then dragged it into the camouflaged tent. Dawn approached through the marsh in curling foils of gold. The tide kept rising, erasing the deep scar in the soft earth left by the keel of the boat. We placed our own sleeping bags beside Luke's and I brewed us coffee on a Coleman stove when the sun had fully risen.

"He hasn't been here in a while," I said.

"Where would you have looked if he hadn't been here?" Savannah asked.

"I don't know," I answered. "This seemed like it had to

be the place. Colleton is a lousy place to run a guerrilla war. It's too easy to get trapped on one of these islands."

"He seems to be doing all right," she said.

"The FBI agent, Covington, told me that they thought they had him captured last week. They had him cornered up above the site of the town and had a hundred men and six bloodhounds trying to flush him out of the woods."

"How did he get away?" she asked.

"It was nighttime. He doesn't fart unless the sun is down. Covington thinks they didn't move fast enough. He thinks Luke made it to the marsh, crawled to the river, and then let the tides take him. They had boats positioned in the river, but he avoided them."

"Good for him. I always love movies where the good guy gets away," she said.

"There's some dispute about who the good guys really are," I said. "He set off a stick of dynamite in the darkness when it appeared they were getting too close. It unnerved the dogs and made the pursuers edgy."

"Did he hurt anyone?" she asked.

"He turned a cottonwood tree into pick-up sticks, but miraculously, no one was injured," I said.

"What are you going to say to Luke when he comes here, Tom?" she said as I handed her a cup of coffee. "Since you know he believes in what he's doing, since you know he thinks he's doing both the moral and the correct thing, the only thing that means anything to him, what are you going to tell him to make him give up the fight?"

"I'm going to describe in great detail how upset you and I are going to be at his funeral. I'm going to talk about the wife he's not met and the children he's not going to have and the life he'll forfeit if he persists in this senseless bullshit," I said.

"Luke's never even had a girlfriend," said Savannah. "I don't see how all this talk of a wife, a roaring fire, a pair of slippers, and a couple of towheaded kids is going to flush him out of these woods. To some of us, Tom, the middle-class life in America is a death sentence."

"You mean my life's a death sentence, Savannah?" I said.

"It would be for me, Tom," she said. "And I think it might be for Luke. Look, I'm not trying to hurt your feelings . . ."

"Thank God, Savannah," I said. "I can't even imagine

the brutality if you actually set out to hurt my feelings. But we Americans who're living out our middle-class death sentences and are dull and desensitized survive and we don't hurt easily."

"Touchy, touchy," she said.

"I reserve the right to be touchy when someone refers to me as the living dead," I said.

"It's not my fault that you're unhappy with your life," she said.

"It's your condescension I find so difficult to bear, Savannah," I said. "It's that maddening air of superiority you assume when you discuss the various choices we've all made. It's the New York disease you've picked up while congratulating other emigrants from small towns who've wended their joyous way to Manhattan."

"I have to be honest with you," she said. "The best and the brightest southerners I know all have found themselves in New York City. The South requires that you give up too much of what you really are to even consider living here."

"I don't want to talk about it," I said.

"Of course you don't, Tom," she answered. "The subject must be very painful to you."

"It's not painful at all," I shot back. "I just can't bear your aura of self-congratulation. I find you full of shit on this subject and I find you a bit mean."

"How am I mean?"

"You enjoy telling me that I'm wasting my life," I said.

"I don't enjoy that, Tom," she said quietly. "It hurts me very much to say that. I just want you and Luke to have everything in the world, to be open to everything, not to let them steal your souls and make southerners out of you."

"See that sun, Savannah?" I said, pointing across the marsh. "That's a Carolina sun and it southern-fried the three of us, and I don't care how long you live in New York, that stuff just don't wash out."

"We're talking about something else now," Savannah said. "I worry that the South will bleed out all that's rare about you. I'm afraid it will kill Luke because he's been seduced by a vision of the South as some fatal paradise."

"When Luke comes, Savannah," I said, "please help me talk him into going back with us. Don't let him talk you into seeing his point of view. He makes a powerful case and it's romantic as hell. Luke's a terrific fanatic. He glows with this goddamn romantic inner light and his eyes get funny and he doesn't want to entertain opposing arguments. The poet in you is going to love the guerrilla in Luke."

"I'm here to help you, Tom," she said. "I'm here to help bring Luke back home."

"He's going to tell you that he *is* at home," I said.

"He'll have a hell of a point, won't he, Tom?" Savannah said, reaching for the coffee pot.

"He sure will, Savannah," I admitted.

"I won't play my role of New York critic anymore," she said. "That's a promise."

"And I won't play redneck anymore," I said. "That's also a promise."

We shook hands and began the long business of waiting for Luke.

For a week Savannah and I lived alone in the center of the great salt marsh. We spent the time renewing those fragile, tenuous bonds that are both the conundrum and the glory of facing the world as twins. By day, we remained hidden inside the hut and we passed the time telling and retelling the stories of our life as a family. We told every story we could remember about our early childhood and we tried to assess the damages and the strengths we brought to our adult life after being raised by Henry and Lila Wingo. Our life in the house by the river had been dangerous and harmful, yet both of us had found it somehow magnificent. It had produced extraordinary and somewhat strange children. The house had been the breeding ground of madness, poetry, courage, and an ineffable loyalty. Our childhood had been harsh but also relentlessly interesting. Though we could draw up passionate indictments against both of our parents, their particularity had indemnified our souls against the wages of tedium and ennui. To our surprise, Savannah and I agreed that we had been born to the worst possible parents but we would have it no other way. On Marsh Hen Island while waiting for Luke, I think we began to forgive our parents for being exactly what they were meant to be. We would begin our talks with memories of brutality or treachery and end them by affirming over and over again our troubled but authentic love of Henry and Lila. At last, we were old enough to forgive them for not having been born perfect.

At night, Savannah and I would take turns hurling the cast net into the rising tides. I would watch her toss the net, see the wide spread of its circular shadow as it billowed out in a perfect circle, and hear the weights splash against the dark waters like the entry of some great unseen fish. Shrimp danced across the top of the water in skittering thousands. We caught more shrimp than we could ever eat. I cooked fabulous meals and we took infinite pleasure in eating them. I caught a ten-pound sea bass and stuffed it with shrimp and fresh crabmeat, then cooked it over slow coals. At breakfast, I mulled shrimp in bacon fat, made red-eye gravy, and poured the shrimp and gravy over a plate of grits.

Before we went to bed, we would sit beneath the stars drinking French wines as Savannah recited from memory every poem she had ever written. Most of them were love songs to the lowcountry and she did honor to the language as her words floated above the marsh like butterflies, silver-winged and distracted, feeding on secret nectars born of time and starlight and winds from the Atlantic. When she wrote her poetry about the Carolinas, Savannah brought instant authority to her words by the correct naming of things. Her poems were full of tanagers and grosbeaks, not just birds. She had carried from this land a vast treasury of exact names to her task. She praised hummingbird moths for the happy genius of their mimicry, lavished affection on mockingbirds for their virtuosity, could name every conceivable variety of marine life a shrimp net could sweep from a river channel, and knew thirty discrete varieties of carnations and roses. Her knowledge of the lowcountry was innate and showy. It had accrued to her naturally like the lightening of a beachcomber's hair in summer. In her poetry, she flung roses into the burning tides of our shared history. When there were no roses to be thrown, she brought forward the disturbed angels of nightmare who sang the canticles of knives and the blue vulnerable veins in her pale wrists. As with all the fine women poets of our century, her own screams and wounds sustained the imperishable beauty of her art.

Sitting in the darkness, she would recite some of her poems with tears streaming down her face.

"Don't recite the ones that make you sad, Savannah," I said, holding her.

"They're the only ones that are worth a damn," she answered.

"You ought to write poems about a totally wonderful subject, one that would bring joy and happiness to all the world," I advised her. "You ought to write poems about me."

"I'm writing some New York poems," she said.

"There's a real upbeat topic," I said.

"No more Mr. Redneck," she warned. "You promised. Is it because I love New York so much that you hate it?"

"I don't know, Savannah," I said, listening to the cicadas singing to each other from island to island. "I grew up in a town of six thousand people and I wasn't even the most interesting person in that town. Hell, I wasn't even the most interesting person in my own family. I wasn't prepared for a city of eight million people. I've gone into phone booths up there and dialed up operators who had better personalities than I have. I don't like cities that roar down at me, 'You ain't shit, Wingo,' when I'm just on my way to get a pastrami sandwich. There's too much of too much up there, Savannah. I can adapt myself to anything, I think, except the titanic and the colossal. This doesn't make me a bad person."

"But it's such a predictable response for a provincial," she said. "That's what worries me. You've never been predictable."

"Untrue, beloved sister," I said. "You must remember our mutually shared roots. Our father is a southern cliché. Our mother is a southern cliché honed to the point of either genius or parody. Luke is a southern cliché. Hell, Luke has goddamn seceded from the Union. I'm a total cliché. There are no ideas in the South, just barbecue. I got my feet nailed to the red clay but I get to eat all the barbecue I want. You got the wings, Savannah. And it's been one of life's pleasures to see you take to the fucking sky."

"But the cost, Tom?" she said.

"Think of the cost if you'd stayed in Colleton," I said.

"I'd be dead," she said. "The South kills women like me."

"That's why we ship you ol' gals up to Manhattan," I said. "It cuts down on burial costs."

"The first poem in the New York cycle is called 'Etude: Sheridan Square,' " she announced, and her voice again tossed anapests into the night.

During the day we kept out of sight and Savannah worked obsessively on her journal. She recorded every story I told about our childhood and it was at this time I first became aware of huge, unbridgeable gaps in her memory of our life in Colleton. Repression was both a great theme and a burden of her life. Her madness was a ruthless censor; it was not content only to ruin the quality of her daily life in New York, but it also effaced the past and replaced it with the white baffled noise of forgetfulness. Her journals preserved the particulars of her life. She filled them with hard facts and nothing else. They were her rose windows into the past. Writing in her journals was but one other technique Savannah had devised to save her own life.

Each Christmas since I had left college, Savannah had sent me one of the same beautiful leather journals she used herself and encouraged me to record the details of my life every day. The trim brown volumes lined a shelf above my desk at home, remarkable only because I had never made a single entry or written down a random thought. In my own book of life, for reasons unclear to me, I never broke the vow of silence. I owned an accusatory shelf of journals that revealed nothing at all about my interior existence. I had a gift for self-criticism, yet I thought there was the most unforgivable vainglory in the history of my own deficiencies. Knowing that I could cheerfully tally my faults all day long did not diminish the fact that I could never erase that special sense of self-congratulation I would bring to the task. I told myself I would write in my journals only when I had something interesting and original to say. I did not wish merely to be the biographer of my own failure. I wanted to say something. Those empty volumes were an eloquent metaphor of my life as a man. I lived with the terrible knowledge that one day I would be an old man still waiting for my real life to start. Already, I pitied that old man.

On the sixth night we spent on the island, we bathed in the creek when the tide rushed in at midnight. We swam out into the marsh and soaped down our naked bodies, feeling the tide move through our hair. The water was moon-ruled and brilliant. Aloud, we wondered how long we could afford to wait for Luke before we had to return to Charleston for supplies. We dried off in the hut and poured ourselves a glass of cognac before we went to sleep. Savannah sprayed the inside of the hut with insecticide and I passed the bottle of bug repellent to her after I had slicked my own body down. The mosquitoes had kept this from being a perfect vacation. We gave enough blood to the mosquitoes that week to satisfy the demands of a small chapter of the Red Cross. Savannah decided the world would be a finer place if mosquitoes tasted as good as shrimp and could be harvested by a boat pulling a net. A cool wind was rising out of the west as we went to sleep.

I awoke with a rifle barrel against my throat. Then a pencil point of light blinded me as I lifted up out of my sleeping bag.

Then I heard Luke laughing.

"Che Guevara, I presume," I said.

"Luke!" Savannah screamed, and they struggled to find each other in the darkness.

Their two shadows embraced in the moonlight and they spun in circles on the wooden floor, sending the wooden chair clattering into the wall.

"I'm so glad I didn't kill you two," Luke shouted. "You surprised me."

"We're delighted you didn't kill us, Luke," said Savannah.

"Kill us!" I said. "Jesus Christ. Why would you even think of killing us?"

"They find this place, little brother," he answered, "and there's no more time on the big clock. I didn't even think you two little poots would remember this place."

"We've come to talk you into going back with us, Luke," Savannah said.

"Not even you talk that good, sugar-peeps," Luke said.

We moved out under the stars and we watched him pull his kayak to the shelter of the tent. Savannah brought out the bottle of Wild Turkey and she poured him a glassful as we sat on the small porch smelling the wind as it came through the marsh. For ten minutes none of us said a single word as we all tried to marshal both our arguments and our declarations of love for one another. I wanted to say the words that would save my brother's life but I was not certain what those words were. My tongue lay like a stone in my mouth. My head was full of ferocities, assertions, and absolute demands spinning out of control in orbits of collision. All the preludes of silence were dangerous and electric.

"You're looking good, Luke," said Savannah, at last. "Revolution seems to agree with you."

Luke laughed and said, "I'm not much of a revolutionary. You're talking to the whole army of the revolution right here. I need to work a little bit on recruitment."

"What are you trying to prove, Luke?" I asked.

"I don't know, Tom," he answered. "I think I'm trying to prove that there's one human being left on earth who's not a sheep. That's how it started out anyway. I was so goddamn angry at Mom and the town and the government that I got caught up in the procedures of it all and couldn't see my way out of it. Once I blew out the bridges and those guys on the train were killed, there wasn't any turning back. Now I spend most of my time hiding from them."

"Have you thought about giving up?" Savannah asked.

"No," he answered. "They need to know that their project has attracted some loyal opposition. I don't regret anything I've done except for the death of those men. I just wish I could have been more effective."

"They've got guys out hunting you all over these islands, Luke," I said.

"I've seen them," he said.

"I hear they're good," I said. "They've got two ex-Green Berets who like to eat babies with their morning coffee out in the woods looking for you."

"They don't know the terrain," he said. "It makes it hard on them. I've thought about hunting them down and killing them but I've got no quarrel with them."

"You've got no quarrel with men who've been hired to kill you?" Savannah said.

"It's just their job," he replied. "Just like mine used to be shrimping. How're Mom and Dad getting along?"

"Dad's making license plates to repay his debt to society," I said. "Mom is somewhat embarrassed when she goes to the post office to find her oldest son's photograph on wanted posters up on the wall, but she's a Newbury now and she's farting through silk and there's always a hint of caviar on her breath."

"They're both worried sick about you, Luke," said Savannah. "They want you to give it up and come back with us."

"It was all perfectly clear to me when I started this thing," he said. "I thought it was the right thing to do. I thought it was the only sane response a person could have. I did what came natural to me. I find it hard to think I acted like a complete asshole. Do you know I have enough stolen dynamite on this island to blow up half of Charleston? But I can't even get close enough to the building site now to blow up a workman's lunch pail. They've nearly caught me the last three times I tried. I blew up a kennel full of guard dogs a month ago."

"Jesus!" I said. "No more Mr. Nice Guy, huh, Luke?"

"Dogs are a serious threat, Tom," he said. "They hunt me with dogs."

"You've got all the environmentalists behind you," Savannah said. "They don't approve of your tactics, but they all agreed that your protest was what mobilized them to action."

"All the members of the Sierra Club and the Audubon Society wear green armbands to their meetings," I said.

"La-di-da," he answered. "I've studied this carefully. I know that both of you think I've never opened a book in my whole life, but I've looked at these issues carefully. Whenever Big Money goes up against the Environment, Big Money always wins. It's an American law, like the right

of free assembly. Someone is going to make millions of
dollars manufacturing plutonium in this county and that's
the only fact that makes any difference at all. Someone will
make millions of dollars turning that plutonium into nuclear
weapons. I can't tolerate the thought of those weapons,
Tom and Savannah. It's not in me to do it. All the politicians
and all the generals and all the soldiers and all the civilians
who make the weapons aren't human beings to me. I don't
care if anybody agrees with me or not. This is the way I'm
made up. I'm talking of the only part of me that means
anything to me at all. That they would give away Colleton
is one thing. I could abide that. I really could. If they were
providing six thousand jobs and put people to work growing tomatoes or oysters or gardenias. Hell, I could make
that sacrifice. If it was a steel mill or a chemical company,
I wouldn't like it much, but I could adjust. But to desecrate
the memory of Colleton for plutonium. I'm sorry. I can't
swing with the program."

"Most people think you're crazy, Luke," I said. "They
think you're a murderer and that you're insane."

"I have terrible headaches, Tom," he said. "That's the
only thing wrong with me."

"I have migraines too," I said. "But I haven't killed four
people."

"That wasn't my plan," he said. "That train was not
scheduled."

"You're still wanted for murder," I said.

"They build hydrogen bombs and call me a murderer,"
he said, taking a long pull on the bourbon. "The world is
fucked, Tom and Savannah."

"It's not your job to stop the world from building hydrogen bombs," Savannah said.

"Then whose job is it, Savannah?" he asked.

"Your whole outlook is too simple," I said.

"Teach me how to be complex," he answered. "What
I'm doing makes very little sense to me, Tom. But what
you and everyone else are doing makes no sense at all."

"Where did this amazing moral sensitivity come from?"
I asked. "Why wasn't it in operation during the Vietnam
War when you merrily went on search-and-destroy missions and got pissed off at Savannah and me for marching
in antiwar demonstrations?"

"They told us we were fighting so the Vietnamese could be free. That seemed like a fine idea to me. I didn't see one thing wrong with it. I didn't know I was fighting so they could steal my house when I got back."

"Why didn't you just protest nonviolently against the building of the Colleton River Project?" Savannah asked.

"I thought this would be more likely to get their attention, Savannah," he said. "I thought it would be more effective. I also thought I was good enough to run the sons of bitches clean out of the county. I underestimated them and over-estimated myself. I haven't done shit to even slow them up."

"Knocking out those bridges slowed the hell out of them," I said. "I promise you that much, son. You re-routed a bunch of trucks in your career."

"But you don't understand," he said. "I thought I could shut the whole operation down."

"How?" Savannah asked.

"Because I could see it," he answered. "I could actually visualize the whole thing. In my whole life if I could see something in my own mind, I could make it happen. Before we went to get the white porpoise, I had made that trip a hundred times in my mind. When we were down there in Miami, there wasn't one thing that happened that surprised me."

"The whole thing surprised me," Savannah said. "I couldn't believe it was me coming up the coastal highway lying on top of a porpoise."

"I thought I could make the construction workers so afraid of me that they wouldn't set foot in Colleton," Luke said.

"You did, Luke," I said. "They're terrified of you but they've got families to feed."

"It all makes more sense when I'm out here alone," he smiled. "I can talk myself into anything. Do y'all remember when Mama read us *The Diary of Anne Frank* when we were kids?"

"She should never have read us that book," I said. "Savannah had nightmares about Nazis breaking down the door for years."

"Do you remember when Savannah made us go see Mrs. Regenstein after we read that book?" he asked.

"I don't remember that at all, Luke," said Savannah.

"Neither do I," I said. "We were little kids when Mom read us that book."

"Mrs. Regenstein was a refugee from Germany living with Aaron Greenberg and his family. She'd lost her whole family in a concentration camp."

"She showed us her tattoo," I said, remembering.

"Not a tattoo, Tom," Luke said. "She showed us the number they put on her forearm at the concentration camp."

"What's the point of the story, Luke?" I asked.

"No point," he said. "It was the first time I realized about Savannah's greatness."

"Do tell me all about it, Luke," Savannah said, hugging him. "I love stories where I'm a figure of grandeur."

"Do you stock vomit bags in your rebel camp?" I asked.

"After Mama read about Anne Frank, Savannah spent three days fixing up a hiding place in the barn. She put up food and water and everything. She even fixed up this little bulletin board, so some other kid could paste up pictures out of magazines like Anne Frank did."

"How ridiculous," I said.

"Yes," Luke agreed. "But it was a gesture, Tom. It was something. Most of Europe did nothing when they heard about the Jews. We had a sister who was eight years old who fixed up a place in our barn in case it happened again. But that isn't the story I remembered the most."

"I'm sure I did something outrageously heroic," Savannah said, enjoying herself.

"No, you did something nice," he said. "You made Tom and me go with you when you went to visit Mrs. Regenstein. She always scared me because she spoke English with such a thick accent and I didn't want to go. But you made us both go, Savannah. Tom and I were standing behind you when Mrs. Regenstein answered the door. She said, 'Guten Morgen, Kinder,' when she saw us. Her glasses were thick and she was very thin. Do you remember what you said to her that day, Savannah?"

"I don't even remember that day, Luke," Savannah said.

"You said, 'We'll hide you,' " he said. "You said, 'You'll never have to worry about the Nazis coming to Colleton, Mrs. Regenstein, because my brothers and I are here and we'll hide you. We've fixed up a nice place in the barn and we'll bring you food and magazines.' "

"What did Mrs. Regenstein do that day, Luke?" Savannah asked.

"She fell apart, Savannah," Luke said. "She cried like I've never seen a woman cry before. You thought you had done something terribly wrong and you started to apologize. Mrs. Goldberg came to the door and calmed Mrs. Regenstein down. Mrs. Goldberg gave us some milk and cookies before we left. Mrs. Goldberg loved our butts after that day."

"I knew I was a wonderful kid," Savannah said. "Thanks for telling that story, Luke."

"I can tell you thirty more where you were a perfect shit, Savannah," I said.

"Who invited him to this island?" Savannah asked, pointing to me.

"It sure wasn't me," Luke said.

"We came with a proposition, Luke," I said. "The forces of evil are willing to make a deal."

"Don't tell me," he said sadly. "If I come to the peace table, they'll let me keep the whole state of South Carolina."

"I don't think we're very far apart," I said. "They sent a guy named Covington."

For two days in a world refreshed with the presence of Luke, a secret world lacquered with an argentine shine to the fragrant, palm-scented mornings, we let Luke tell the story of his modest rebellion against his country. A sense of injustice had brought him armed and vengeful to roam his purloined homeland. His failure to change a single thing had transformed his engagement into an addiction. Because he had failed so nakedly, he could not withdraw from his own call to arms. He had become the first victim of his own unappeasable bravado. At first, he thought he had returned to Colleton because he was the only man of principle our town had produced. But in the long solitude of his private struggle he had come to realize that his own contentious vanity had made a defiant affair of honor out of a simple political decision. He did not know how to disengage from the struggle and there were times when he still felt he was doing the only thing a man of his instincts could be expected to do. Luke did not feel that he had been wrong; he felt only that he had acted alone and that was his most grievous crime.

His voice was like a page of music as he told his story.
He told of his slow wanderings through the razed county,
his encounters with armed guards, his disappearances to
his two safe houses in Georgia after a successful raid, his
patient theft of dynamite from the construction site, and
the dangers he faced every time he took a boat out on the
river. From the Viet Cong he had learned to reach an ac-
cordance with darkness and the efficacy of patience in dealing with a numerically superior enemy. He recounted his
long surveillance of the four bridges he had taken out on
the northern frontier of the county. He could not believe
how poorly guarded those bridges were or how easy it was
to set powerful time bombs to go off simultaneously at two
A.M. and still be back at Marsh Hen Island before the sun
rose. He had improved security on the bridges leading to
the county immeasurably, he told us, but the death of the
men on the train had changed the nature of his protest.
Once he had drawn first blood, his war against the property
of the state lost all its moral resonance. If he had to kill,
then he wished he had not wasted the killings.

"I should've shot the three chief engineers from the
Mewshaw Company who are directing the project. I watched
each one of them through cross hairs and I thought about
putting them down. Then I would think about all their
wives and children feeling like shit when they heard that
Daddy got a bullet through his eye and I just set the rifle
down. I found myself running the stupidest, shittiest guerrilla war I ever heard tell of. I can't even get the indigenous
population to support me because there ain't no indigenous
population. They've got scars in the earth where houses
used to be. So I blew up a few tractors and trucks and I
scared the living hell out of a few Pinkerton guards. My
one victory, if you can call it that, is that they haven't caught
me yet. But Lord, brother and sister, they sure have tried
like hell."

He did not feel defeated, only stalemated. The metaphors
that had sustained him in the early days of his dispute had
lost their freshness and potency. In solitude, he had discovered he brought no philosophical bedrock to dissent.
He had brought passion to the islands but no consistent
system of belief. His thoughts were conflicting, romantic,
querulous, and intemperate. He could not force his century

to make sense and he could find no place for himself within it. He had tried to conduct himself as an honorable man, a man who could not be bought or sold, and woke up one morning to find himself a man with a price on his head. In his deepest self, he did not understand why every American did not join him on the islands when they heard about the nature of his disenchantment with the government. He thought he understood the American soul and learned that he could not even sound the depths of his own. He had never known that the selling of one's own land and birthright for money was the sport of kings in America. Our parents had raised us to believe that southerners held the land in highest esteem. It was the land and our veneration of the land that made us distinct, and defined our fabulous separateness from other Americans. Luke had made one mistake, he thought. He had believed in the sublimity of the southern way; he hadn't just mouthed the words.

"When I first came out here I thought of myself as the last southerner," he said. "But lately I've just thought of myself as the last southern asshole."

"We've got a gene pool like Loch Ness, Luke," said Savannah. "We're all gonna have monsters rising to the surface before it's over."

"If you no longer believe in what you're doing," I asked, "then why in the hell are you still out here playing war games?"

"Because no matter how wrong I am, Tom," he said, "I'm not quite as wrong as they are. And my being out here reminds them that the stealing of a town can prove hazardous to your health. I've even thought about an attack on the construction camp in broad daylight. I'd kill the armed guards first, then I'd try to put down twenty or thirty of the construction workers. I know how to fight a war like this. I just don't have the heart to fight it like it's supposed to be fought."

"They'd have landed the Marines if you killed that many people," I said.

"Acting alone, I lack the courage to kill innocent people," he said. "I could only kill the innocent in Vietnam when I had the strongest country in the world backing me up. I realized early that unless you're willing to kill the innocent, you can't win. You can't even be noticed."

"You never were very good at compromise, Luke," I said.

"Compromise!" he said. "Where was the goddamn compromise? They didn't tell us that they would build the plant at one end of the county and we could continue to live where we'd lived our whole lives. They said, 'Leave, fuckers, leave!' And I understood why they had to do that, Tom. If they ever have an accident in that plant, then everything downstream, every shrimp, octopus, and horseshoe crab, is going to glow in the dark for two hundred years. They mess up one time and they could kill every form of sea life within a fifty-mile radius. They could make a desert out of this entire salt marsh."

"When did you become a radical?" Savannah asked. "Was it Vietnam?"

"I'm not a goddamn radical, Savannah," he said with fierce conviction. "I hate radicals of every kind whether they call themselves liberals or conservatives. I don't give a damn about politics and I hate politicians and demonstrators in any form."

"Wrong, Luke, honey," said Savannah. "You're the best demonstrator I've ever seen."

He spoke of his frequent returns to Melrose Island when he would wander through the overgrown yard where our house and barn used to be. One night he had slept on the spot where our bedroom had been. He had taken honey from abandoned hives that the wrecking crews had left behind when they destroyed the house. In our mother's garden, he had picked azaleas and roses and dahlias and placed them on the tiger's unmarked grave. On the south side of the island he killed with his bow and arrow a wild boar rooting for pecans.

On the second night, he told of his return to the site of the town and his extraordinary vision of the town rising miraculously out of the earth. With fear and wonder, he told of the increasing frequency of the monologues he conducted with himself. These meditations of solitude frightened him, yet they endowed him with a renewed sense of purpose and clarity. He recalled his difficulty in finding the location of our grandparents' homesite and tripping over Amos's cross in the darkness and bearing it down the Street of Tides beneath the strange light of a penumbrous moon. Then he called for all the stores in the town to arise and saw their struggle to be reborn before his eyes. The town had risen in the fury of extinction and he had seen it with his own eyes. Then he had turned and seen Mr. Fruit coming down the street toward him, wild and outcast, still performing his exotic lunatic dance on the street corner where he had spent his entire life. Mr. Fruit was blowing his whistle and directing phantom traffic in the wordless simplicity and grandeur of his art. But when Mr. Fruit materialized, the resurrected town vanished into an altered mirage of nightmare and dust.

"The town was there for a moment," Luke said in awe. "I don't know how to explain it. For a moment I could smell fresh paint and coffee and heard the voices of shopkeepers and the sound of their brooms against the sidewalks. It was all so beautiful and real."

Savannah took Luke's hand and kissed it softly, then said, "You don't have to explain it to me, Luke. I've been seeing things like that my whole life."

"But I'm not crazy," Luke protested. "This was all right there in front of me. I saw the stores. There were sale signs in the window. I could even hear the macaw say 'good morning' in the shoe shop. The traffic lights were all working. You've got to believe me. This wasn't a dream."

"I know it wasn't a dream," Savannah said. "It was just a nice little hallucination. I'm the Queen of Hallucinations. I can tell you all about them."

"You're saying I'm crazy," Luke said. "You've always been the crazy one, Savannah."

"No, Luke," she said. "I'm just the only one that knew it."

"But this was religious," Luke said. "I felt like I'd been touched by God and He was allowing me to glimpse the future if I remained true to my mission."

"You've been out in the woods alone way too long," I said.

"But I didn't dream up Mr. Fruit," Luke said.

"That's the strangest part of your hallucination," Savannah said.

"No. He was there. They forgot about Mr. Fruit when they moved the town. He must have gotten scared when they started knocking the houses down. He hid out in the forest and lived the best he could. He was half starved and dressed in rags when I found him at his corner directing traffic. How are you going to explain to a man like Mr. Fruit about plutonium and right of eminent domain? He was half dead from malnutrition when I found him. I got him to a Catholic mission in Savannah even though it was hell to pull him off that street corner and get him into that boat. They sent Mr. Fruit to the state mental hospital up in Milledgeville. No one would listen when I explained he just needed a new street corner where he could get comfortable. But you had to grow up in Colleton to understand Mr. Fruit. No one would listen. I couldn't make them understand the importance of Mr. Fruit in the grand scheme of things."

Savannah said, "You need help too. Just like Mr. Fruit. You're just as much a victim of them moving the town as he was."

"My seeing the town was a moment of clarity, Savannah," Luke said. "When you sit down to write a poem you must be able to see a poem hidden somewhere on a blank page. I saw our town on a piece of dark earth. I'm talking about imagination, not insanity."

"You need to go back with us," Savannah said. "It's time for you to start a life."

He buried his face in his enormous hands. There was a bestial, primitive quality to his grief. His face was lionesque and kingly but he had the soft, startled eyes of a fallow deer.

"The FBI agent, Covington, Tom," he asked, "do you trust him?"

"I trust him as much as I can trust any man who's hunting my brother," I said.

"He said I'd get three years in prison?" Luke asked.

"He said you'd get three to five years," I said. "That's the deal he worked out."

"Maybe I can room with Dad," he said.

"He wants you to come in, too," Savannah said. "He's very worried. So is Mom."

"Maybe in about five years we can have a family reunion," Luke said.

"Let's hold it at Auschwitz," said Savannah.

"Tell Covington I'll give myself up at the Charleston Bridge,

Tom," Luke said. "I'd like to surrender to an officer of the National Guard. I'd like to surrender as a soldier."

"Why don't you just go back with us tonight?" I said. "I could call Covington from our house."

"I'd like to spend a couple of nights out here alone," Luke said. "I'd like to say goodbye to Colleton. I'll meet them at the Charleston Bridge on Friday."

"The tide is coming in, Savannah," I said. "We need to start soon."

"Let me stay with you, Luke," she said worriedly. "I'm afraid to leave you here alone."

"I can take care of myself, little sister," Luke said. "I'll be fine. Tom's right. If you don't catch the tide in the next hour, you'll never make it out tonight."

Luke helped me drag my boat to the water. He embraced Savannah and held her for a long time as she wept against his chest.

Then he turned to me.

I broke down as soon as he touched me.

"It's over now, Tom," he said, holding me. "In three years we'll laugh like hell about this. It all turned to shit, but we can change it back into something wonderful. I'll get out and we'll buy us a big shrimp boat and we'll catch more goddamn shrimp than anyone on the East Coast. We'll be famous and clean out bars of sailors and drink our liquor neat."

Savannah and I got into the boat and Luke pushed us off into the tide. Savannah blew him kisses and we left him enkindled in the papery light of a fine moon. We left him and turned into the comely boulevards of the great salt marsh as we left our home county for the last time in our lives. As I steered the boat through the narrow channel, I tossed a small prayer toward the river. It was a prayer of gratitude. Though God had burdened me with strange and wounded parents, he had granted me the presence of the most extraordinary brother and sister to balance the hand. I could not have made the journey without them. Nor would I have chosen to make it.

On the way to his rendezvous at the Charleston Bridge, Luke made a last sentimental visit to the island where we had grown up in a small white house by the Colleton River. He was standing on the foundation of that house when he was killed by a single rifle shot by one of the ex-Green Berets who had been commissioned to hunt him down in Colleton County. J. William Covington delivered the news to my house on Sullivans Island on the Saturday after Luke failed to surrender to Colonel Bryson Kelleher at the Charleston Bridge.

After the funeral, Savannah and I took Luke's body far out beyond the three-mile limit and buried him at sea, in the Gulf Stream that he loved. When we put the weighted coffin overboard, Savannah read a poem she had written as a last farewell to Luke. She called the poem "The Prince of Tides."

When she had finished we returned to Charleston knowing that we had the rest of our lives to learn how to live without Luke. We had years to learn how to fall apart at the seams and to do it prettily.

EPILOGUE

There are last things to say.

I took my time telling Luke's story to Susan Lowenstein and all the words came hard. But it was easier telling it to a woman I loved and one who whispered every day that she loved me. She had awakened something in me that had slumbered far too long. Not only did I feel passion again, I felt the return of hope and a clearance of all storm warnings in the danger zones of memory.

I had spent the summer writing love songs to my daughters and love letters to my wife. I missed my daughters terribly and the mere mention of their names could wound me. But they could not cast me out of their lives, and it

was Sallie I thought I had lost forever. My letters to Sallie
had one repeating theme: No one understood better than
I the reason she had to find love outside our home. In my
grief and bitterness I had turned my own wife into a stranger, a trespasser, and, most cruelly of all, a widow presiding
over a house of purest sorrow. The island boy, Tom Wingo,
had cut himself off from all who loved him and set himself
adrift in the sea lanes of a long and dreamless attrition. I
told Sallie that her affair with Dr. Cleveland had taught me
that I could still hurt in those same places laid waste by the
death of my brother. It had stopped my long slide into self-
pity and I could feel the fighter in me struggling for recognition once again. Now I knew that deliverance often
requires the kiss of Judas as prelude; there are times when
betrayal can be an act of love in itself. I had thrown Sallie
out of my heart and Jack Cleveland had welcomed her into
his. I didn't like it, but I told Sallie that I understood it
perfectly. Her letters back to me were the letters of a hurt
and bewildered woman. She needed time, she said, and I
gave her time and waited for her decision. It never once
occurred to me that the decision would be mine or that I
would ever feel any emotion other than joy when leaving
New York City.

In the last two weeks of August, Susan Lowenstein rented
a cabin on the coast of Maine and I told her of Luke's death
as I watched a much wilder and colder Atlantic assault the
wild, indifferent cliffs. I told her everything and how I could
not place a value on any life that did not include my brother.
In that country cleansed beneath vast linens of snow each
winter, I praised my brother's spirit and mourned his death
in the fierce green beauty of a Maine summer. I told her
all the bleak, unornamental stanzas of both my allegiance
and my grief. I could not measure the cost of loving a family
so deeply and with such cold fury.

When I spoke of burying Luke at sea, Susan Lowenstein
held me in her arms and stroked my hair and dried my
tears. It was not as Savannah's psychiatrist that she heard
my story of Luke but as my lover, my companion and best
friend. For two weeks we made love as though we had
been waiting our whole lives to fall into each other's arms.
Each day we would walk for miles by the sea, pick wildflowers and blackberries, and dig for clams, until she would

turn toward me, slide her nails across my back, and whisper, "Let's go back to the house and make love and tell each other everything in the world." It was a pleasure telling Susan Lowenstein everything in the world.

On our last night in Maine we huddled together on a rock with a blanket over our shoulders. The moon laid a sheet of silver across the ocean and the sky was starry and clear.

"Aren't you looking forward to getting back to the city, Tom?" she said, kissing my cheek. "I'm tired of all this peace, quiet, beauty, great food, and terrific sex."

I laughed and said, "If we stay together, Lowenstein, will I have to become Jewish?"

"Of course not," she answered. "Herbert's not Jewish."

"Look, I don't mind," I said. "Everyone in my family's doing it. Don't forget about Renata."

"Hasn't this been a nice look at what our life could be like together?" she said. "A preview of coming attractions."

I did not answer at first and the images of my wife and children bloomed in the darkness, vivid as fireflies. "Before I met you, I was in a deep sleep. I was a dead man and didn't even know it. Should I call you Susan now, Lowenstein?"

She answered, "No. I love the way you say 'Lowenstein,' especially when we're making love. I feel beautiful again, Tom. I feel absolutely gorgeous."

I waited for a moment, then said, "I need to see Savannah when we get back."

"It's time," she agreed. "For both of you."

"I need to tell her some things," I said. "I need to tell everyone some things."

"I'm afraid of what's going to happen when Sallie calls and wants you back."

"How do you know she'll want me back?" I asked.

"I've sampled the merchandise," she whispered. "I can't wait to get back to the house so we can take off our clothes and tell each other everything in the world."

"Lowenstein," I said, as I turned to kiss her, "you've got a lot to learn about the outdoors."

And I began unbuttoning her shirt.

* * *

Savannah looked surprised to see me when an orderly led her into the visitors' lounge. She seemed uncomfortable when she kissed me, but she held me tightly for a moment and said, "They let you in."

"Lowenstein's letting you out for the day," I said. "I'm going to be held strictly accountable if you do a half-gainer with twist off the Empire State Building."

"I'll try to control myself," she said, and she almost smiled.

I took her to the Museum of Modern Art, where they were having an exhibit of Alfred Stieglitz's photographs and Georgia O'Keeffe's art. We spoke very little the first hour we were together, but wandered through the galleries side by side. Too much time and blood summered in the marshes of our shared past. We had lost years to the piracies of a ruthless fate and neither of us wished to speak too quickly.

Her first question caught me off guard.

"You know about Renata Halpern?" she asked as we studied a photograph of a New York street scene.

"Yep," I said.

"It made sense to me at the time," she said. "I wasn't in very good shape."

"You needed an escape," I said. "Anyone can understand that. Especially me."

"Do you?" she said, and there was a touch of anger in her voice. "You stayed in the South."

"Do you know what the South is to me?" I said back to her.

"No," she said, but my sister was lying.

"It's soul food, Savannah. I can't help it. It's what I am."

"It's mean and cheap and backward," she said. "The southern life is a death sentence."

I turned away from a photograph of a young and beautiful Georgia O'Keeffe and said, "I know that's how you feel, Savannah. We've had this conversation a thousand times."

She took my hand and squeezed it. "You sold yourself short. You could've been more than a teacher and a coach."

I returned the squeeze and said, "Listen to me, Savannah. There's no word in the language I revere more than *teacher*. None. My heart sings when a kid refers to me as his teacher and it always has. I've honored myself and the entire family of man by becoming one."

Savannah looked at me and said, "Then why aren't you happy, Tom?"

"For the same reason you're not," I said.

We walked into the Monet room and sat down on a bench in the center of the gallery and studied the large canvases filled with lilies and pondwater. It was Savannah's favorite place in the world and she always came here to lift her spirits.

"Lowenstein's going to let you go home soon," I said.

"I think I'm ready," she answered.

"If you ever decide to go away again, let me help you do it, Savannah."

"I may still need to stay away from all of you for a very long time," she said.

"I can love you no matter what you do," I said. "But I can't bear to think of a world without you."

"Sometimes I think the world would be better off without me," she said, and the sadness in her voice touched a deep place within me.

"We haven't mentioned Luke's name to each other since he died," I said, taking my sister's hand.

She leaned her head against my shoulder and her voice was exhausted and fearful as she said, "Not yet, Tom. Please."

"It's time," I said. "We loved Luke so much we forgot how much we love each other."

"Something came apart in me," she said, almost strangling. "Something unfixable."

"I know what can fix it," I said, and I pointed to the dreaming, immemorial flowers of Monet floating in the cool waters of Giverny. Savannah looked up at the huge painting in her favorite room in Manhattan as I said, "Your art can fix it. You can write beautiful poems about our brother. You're the only one who can bring Luke back to us."

She began crying but I could feel her relief. "But he's dead, Tom."

"That's because you haven't written about him since he died," I said. "Do with Luke what Monet did with flowers.

Use your art. Give him back to us. Let the whole world love Luke Wingo."

Late that afternoon, the phone call from Sallie came, the one that Susan Lowenstein had come to fear, the one that I had come to fear. She started to speak but her voice broke.

"What's wrong, Sallie?" I asked.

"He was having an affair with two other women, Tom," she said. "I was planning to leave you and have him move in with me and the girls and he was screwing two other goddamn women."

"It was his collection of British motorcycles," I said. "The meerschaum pipes were harmless affectations, but when a doctor starts collecting motorcycles, it's a sign of something askew in the male ego."

"I loved him, Tom," she said. "I won't lie to you about it."

"Your taste in men has always been a little suspect," I said.

She said, "I feel used, violated, and disgusting. I didn't know how to conduct an affair. It was all new to me and I'm sure I made a perfect ass out of myself."

"You did fine, Sallie," I said. "No one knows how to do it right."

"He was horrible when I confronted him about the other women," she said. "He said some terrible things to me."

"Do you want me to beat him up?" I asked.

"No," she said, "of course not. Why?"

"I'd like to beat him up," I said. "I'd let you watch."

"He said I was too old for him ever to consider marrying," she said. "One of his girlfriends was nineteen."

"Depth was never one of his big problems."

"What about us, Tom?" she said. "Where do we go from here? Your letters have been beautiful, but if I were you, I'd never forgive me."

"I've got to tell you about Lowenstein, Sallie," I said.

I waited for Lowenstein to come out of her office. I was trying to think of the proper words when I saw her come down the stairs of the brownstone. She saw me across the street, leaning against a lamppost. Her beauty moved me, as it always did, but it was her kindness that was breaking my heart as she approached me. When I tried to speak, the tears came. No one had invented the proper way to say goodbye to Lowenstein. She saw it and she screamed as she ran across the street. "No, no, Tom. No. It's not fair."

She dropped her briefcase on the sidewalk and threw her arms around my neck. Her briefcase snapped open and papers fluttered down the sidewalk and beneath a row of cars. She wiped a tear from my face and kissed another one away.

"We knew this day would come. We talked about it. One of the things I love about you, Tom, is you're the kind of man who'll always go back to his family. But goddamn her anyway. Goddamn Sallie for loving you before I did."

Her words cut through me and I cried harder, resting my head on her shoulder. She stroked my head and said, "I've got to find me a nice Jewish boy. You goys are killing me." And through tears, Lowenstein and I roared with laughter.

She was sitting in a chair in her apartment, staring out the window onto Bleecker Street. Her hair was discolored and her flesh was bleached and puffy. She did not turn around when I entered the room. I had packed my bags the night before and they were sitting by the kitchen door. From a florist on Eighth Avenue, I had bought her a gardenia bush in full flower. I cut off a single gardenia, walked over to her, and placed it in my sister's hair.

Then I asked her the old question, "What was your family life like, Savannah?"

"Hiroshima," she answered.

"And what has life been like since you left that wonderful family?"

"Nagasaki," she said, still not turning to face me.

"Name the poem you wrote in honor of your family," I said.

" 'The History of Auschwitz,' " she said, and I thought she was about to smile.

"Here's the really important question," I said, leaning down over her and smelling the gardenia in her hair. "Whom do you love more than anyone in the world?"

She pulled my head down against her face and her tears and she whispered, "I love my brother, Tom Wingo. My fabulous goddamn twin. I'm so sorry for everything."

"It's all right, Savannah," I said. "We've made it back to each other. We've got lots of time to try our hands at restoring the ruins."

"Hold me, Tom," she said, "hold me tight."

When I was ready to leave her apartment, I brought my bags into the hallway where Eddie Detreville was waiting to help me with my luggage. I embraced Eddie, kissed him on the cheek, and told him I had rarely known such a generous and loving man. Then I turned to say goodbye to my sister. She looked up at me from her chair, appraising me, and she said, "Do you think you and I are survivors, Tom?"

"I think I am. I'm not sure about you," I said.

"Survival. So that's the gift our family gave to you."

I kissed her, held her, then walked toward the door. I lifted my luggage and said to Savannah, "Yeah. But the family gave you something far greater."

"Ha!" she said bitterly. "What's that?"

"Genius," I said. "It gave you genius."

That night Susan Lowenstein took me high above the city where we ate a final meal at Windows on the World. The sun had already set when we arrived and there was only a last hint of ruby julienned through the clouds massed along the horizon. Beneath us, the city was laid out in a noiseless place setting of fire and crystal. New York was never the same city no matter how many times you saw it or from what angle. Nothing in God's world was as beautiful as Manhattan Island seen from above at night.

Over wine I asked, "What do you feel like eating tonight, Lowenstein?"

In silence, she watched me for a moment, then said, "I plan to order a perfectly lousy meal. I don't want to have anything like a wonderful meal on the night you say goodbye to me forever."

"I'm going back to South Carolina, Lowenstein," I said, reaching over and squeezing her hand. "That's where I belong."

"You could belong anywhere you wanted to," she said,

turning her eyes out toward the city. "You just chose not to belong here."

"Why are you making it so hard for us to part as friends?" I asked.

"Because I want you to stay with me, Tom," she said. "I think you love me and I'm certain I love you and I think we have a chance to make each other happy for the rest of our lives."

"I couldn't make anybody happy for the rest of their life," I said.

"Everything you say is only an excuse to leave me," she said, snatching up the menu suddenly and studying it carefully so our eyes did not have to meet.

Then she said, "What's the worst thing on this menu? That's what I want to order."

"Someone recommended pig's anus tartare," I said.

"Do not even try to make me laugh tonight," she said, her face hidden by the menu. "This is the night you're leaving me for another woman."

"The other woman happens to be my wife," I said.

"Why did you let it go so far between us," she said, "if you knew, in the end, you'd return to Sallie?"

"I didn't know that," I said. "I thought we might be together forever."

"What happened?"

"My character rose to the surface," I said. "I didn't have the courage to leave my wife and children to make a new life with you. It's just not in me. You'll have to forgive me, Lowenstein. One part of me wants you more than anything else in the world. The other part of me is terrified of any major change in my life. That's the strongest part."

"But you love me, Tom," she said.

"I didn't know it was possible to be in love with two women at the same time."

"Yet you chose Sallie."

"I chose to honor my own history," I said. "If I were a braver man, I could do it."

"What could I do to make you stay?" she asked me fiercely. "Tell me, please. I don't know how to beg, but I'll try to learn the words and all the steps. Help me with them, please."

I closed my eyes and took both her hands in mine and

said, "Have me born in New York City. Take away my past. Take away everything I've known and loved. Make it so I never met Sallie and that we never had children with each other. Make it that I don't love Sallie."

She smiled and said, "I thought I could make you stay if I made you feel guilty enough, if I made you feel responsible for me."

"A shameless breed, you shrinks."

"If it doesn't work out between you and Sallie," she said, then stopped in midsentence.

"Then you'll find me barking like a dog outside your building on Central Park West," I said. "I find it strange, Lowenstein, that at this very moment I love you more than I ever remember loving Sallie."

"Then stay with me, Tom."

"I've got to try to make something beautiful out of the ruins, Lowenstein," I said, looking into her eyes. "I don't know if I'll succeed, but I've got to try. That's what I told Savannah when I saw her this afternoon."

"Speaking of ruins, Herbert called today," she said as she waved off a waiter who had come to take our order. "He's begging me to give him another chance. He even claimed he broke off his affair with Monique."

"You wouldn't happen to have Monique's phone number handy, would you?" I asked.

"That's not even humorous by your slapstick standards," she said.

"This atmosphere seems heavy enough to be made of titanium. I thought I'd lighten it a bit."

"I don't want to lighten it," she said. "I'm perfectly miserable and I have a right to wallow in that misery."

"I like the thought of Herbert begging, Lowenstein," I said. "It must become him so."

"He doesn't do it very well," she said. "I've told him about our affair. He finds it unimaginable that I'm consorting with someone like you."

"Tell the son of a bitch about my elephantine genitalia," I said, slightly irritated. "Or my wicked use of the Chinese basket trick during intercourse."

"I told him that we were wonderful in bed together," she said, abstractedly gazing out toward the city. "I told him that we sizzle."

"Sizzle," I said. "You make us sound like two New York strips."

"It's terrible how much I've come to enjoy hurting him," she said. "Have you told Sallie about us, Tom?"

"Yes," I said.

"Then you used me, Tom," she said.

"Yes," I said. "I used you, Susan, but not before I started loving you."

"If you liked me enough, Tom . . ."

"No, Lowenstein. I adore you. You've changed my life. I've felt like a whole man again. An attractive man. A sensual one. You've made me face it all and you made me think I was doing it to help my sister."

"So this is how the story ends," she said.

"I believe so, Lowenstein," I answered.

"Then let's make our last night perfect," she said, kissing my hand, then slowly kissing each one of my fingers as the building swayed in a strong wind from the north.

After dinner we went to the Rainbow Room in Rockefeller Center and we toasted each other with champagne. I kissed her with all the city below us and the Atlantic moving its tides into the Hudson and my sister, at home again, sleeping in her apartment on Grove Street. We checked into the Plaza for the night and stayed awake all night talking, making love, then talking again. Since we had no plans to make, there were only eight hours in the world left for us. But I had made my refusal. I had said no.

When I said goodbye at La Guardia, I kissed her once and began walking rapidly to the gate without looking back. But she called my name and I turned and heard her say, "Tom, remember the dream I had about you and me dancing in the snow storm?"

"I'll never forget it," I said.

Now Susan was crying and leaving her was a killing thing again when she said, "Promise me this, Coach. When you get back to South Carolina, dream one for me. Dream one for Lowenstein."

A year after my New York summer, I drove to Atlanta alone to pick up my father on the day he was released from the federal penitentiary. I wanted to give him some time to compose himself before he had to face the abundant, guilty love of a damaged family who did not know how to welcome him home. None of us knew what his life would be like now that he had lost so much time and his own vigor. He was thinner and his face was sallow and jowly. I was with him when he picked up his personal possessions and the warden signed his papers of release. The warden said the prison would miss him and that it needed more prisoners like Henry Wingo.

"The only thing I ever did right," my father said. "I made a great jailbird."

We took in a Braves game at the stadium and spent the night at the Hyatt Regency. The next day, we left early and took the back roads to Charleston, driving slowly, taking time to know each other again, trying to find the right words, the safe words, painfully avoiding the wrong subjects.

My father looked older, but so did I. In his face, I saw Luke's face. In my face, as he shyly studied me, I knew he must have seen my mother's face. My face hurt him now but neither one of us could help that. We talked about sports and coaching. The long, clean seasons of football, basketball, and baseball that divided all the years of our lives and provided this father and son with the only language of love allowed to pass between them.

"The Braves are only four games out of first, Dad," I said as we crossed the Savannah River.

"Niekro's got to get hot for them to have any kind of a chance at all. No one in the major leagues can touch his knuckleball when he's got it dancing good," Dad answered, but beneath the answer I heard the inarticulate cry, the heartbreaking cry of the father's clumsy effort to force up all the strength of love he could summon for a child. I heard it and it was enough.

"Are you gonna have a good team this year?" he asked.

"I think we might surprise some people," I said. "Maybe you can help me coach the linemen."

"I'd like that," he said.

Savannah had arrived from New York when we drove up into the back yard on Sullivans Island. My children poured out of the house and shyly approached their grandfather.

"Be careful, girls," I said. "He hits."

"No, I don't, kids. Come here and kiss your grandpa," he said in a beaten, tired voice, and I was sorry I said what I did.

Sallie came to the door, slim and dark-haired, tanned and serious. She ran up to my father, threw her arms around him, and tears were streaming down her face as he turned her round and round and buried his face against her shoulder.

"Welcome home, Dad," she said.

Then Savannah came out of the house. And there was something I cannot explain that I felt as they ran to each other and where I felt it was in the deepest part of me, an untouched place that trembled with something instinctual and rooted in the provenance of the species—unnamable, yet I knew it could be named if it could be felt. It was not Savannah's tears or my father's tears that caused this resonance, this fierce interior music of blood and wildness and identity. It was the beauty and fear of kinship, the ineffable ties of family, that sounded a blazing terror and an awe-struck love inside of me. There was my father, the source of all these lives, the source of all these tears, crying now, crying hard and without shame. The tears were water, salt water, and I could see the ocean behind him, could smell it, could taste my own tears, the sea and hurt within me leaking out into the sunlight and my children crying to see me cry. The story of my family was the story of salt water, of boats and shrimp, of tears and storm.

And my twin, my beautiful, damaged sister, her scarred wrists around my father's neck, her eyes dimmed by a lifetime of visions and laying hold to a language strong enough to make these visions clear, to turn nightmare and horror into the astonishing lyrics that burned into the consciousness of her time, to turn sorrow into a life-giving beauty. And my wife, who had married into this family and who had to grow tolerant of a large cast of family demons, who did it because she loved me, even though I was incapable of responding to love from a woman, that I could never make her feel loved or needed or wanted even though that's what I wanted to give her more than anything else in the world. And my children, three daughters, whom I could love with some perfect love that seemed unrelated to me, because I wanted so badly to make them unlike me in any way, because I wanted to make sure they would never have a childhood like mine, that they would never be struck by me, that they would never fear the approach of their father. With them, I tried to re-create my own childhood as I dreamed it should have been. With them, I tried to change the world.

In the late afternoon we loaded the station wagon with a beer cooler and a picnic basket and drove toward Charleston. We turned off at the shrimp dock at Shem Creek and I parked the car in sight of the only shrimp boat still at the docks.

"You know how to work one of those things?" I asked my father, pointing toward the shrimp boat.

"Naw," he said, "but I bet I could learn fast."

"It's registered under the name of Captain Henry Wingo," I said. "It's a homecoming gift from Mom."

"I can't accept that," he said.

"You wrote that you wanted to get back on the river," I said. "Mom wanted to make a gesture. I think it's a nice one."

"It's a fine boat," my father said. "They catching many shrimp this season?"

"The good ones are," I said. "It's a month before I have to start football practice, Dad. I'll work as your striker until you can hire one."

"I'll pay you six cents on the pound," he said.

"The hell you will, you cheap son of a bitch," I said. "You'll pay me ten cents on the pound. The price of labor has gone up."

He smiled and said, "Tell your mother thanks."

"She wants to see you," I said.

"I don't know about that," he said.

"You've got all the time in the world, Dad," I said. "Now, I want you to take us up the Wando River."

We entered the main channel of Charleston Harbor an hour before sunset and the bells of St. Michael's Church rang clearly through the shimmering light and the humid perfumed air of the old city. My father steered the shrimp boat beneath the enormous iron vertebrae of the two Cooper River bridges and we passed a white freighter loaded with cargo from the docks of North Charleston moving out to sea. All of us waved and the invisible captain sounded his horn in greeting. We made a starboard turn into the Wando River and the tide was so high that my father did not have to refer to the navigational charts a single time. We went for a mile until we neared a vast marsh in the round curve of the river and there was not a house in sight.

"It's about time, Tom," Sallie said, coming into the wheel house.

"Time for what?" my father asked.

"A homecoming surprise for you and Savannah," Sallie said, checking her watch.

"Tell us, Mama," my children said.

"No," she answered, "then it won't be a surprise."

We swam in the warm opaque waters, diving in deep from the shrimp boat's bow. After swimming, we ate dinner from the picnic basket and toasted my father's homecoming with champagne. Savannah approached my father and I watched them as they walked to the front of the boat holding hands.

I tried to think of something to say, a summing up, but I could think of nothing. I had taught myself to listen to the black sounds of the heart and learned some things that would serve me well. I had come to this moment with my family safely around me and I prayed that they would always be safe and that I would be contented with what I had. I am southern made and southern broken, Lord, but I beseech you to let me keep what I have. Lord, I am a teacher and a coach. That is all and it is enough. But the black sounds, the black sounds, Lord. When they toll within me, I am seized with a capacity for homage and wonder. I hear them and want to put my dreams to music. When they come I can feel an angel burning in my eye like a rose, and canticles of the most meticulous praise rise out of the clear submarine depths of secret ambient ecstasy.

The white porpoise comes to me at night, singing in the river of time, with a thousand dolphins in radiant attendance, bringing charismatic greetings from the Prince of Tides, calling out our name: Wingo, Wingo, Wingo. It is enough, Lord. It is enough.

"It's time, Tom," Sallie said, lifting up to kiss me on the lips.

The whole family gathered on the bow of the boat to watch day come to an end.

The sun, red and enormous, began to sink into the western sky and simultaneously the moon began to rise on the other side of the river with its own glorious shade of red, coming up out of the trees like a russet firebird. The sun and the moon seemed to acknowledge each other and they moved in both apposition and concordance in a breathtaking dance of light across the oaks and palms.

My father watched it and I thought he would cry again. He had returned to the sea from prison and his heart was a lowcountry heart. The children were screaming, pointing to the sun, then turning to look at the rising moon, calling to the sun, then to the moon.

My father said, "It'll be good shrimping tomorrow."

Savannah came up beside me and put her arm around my waist. We walked to the back of the boat.

"A terrific surprise, Tom," she said.

"I thought you'd like it," I answered.

"Susan sends her love," Savannah said. "She's dating a lawyer now."

"She wrote me about it," I said. "You're looking good, Savannah."

"I'm going to make it, Tom," she said. Then, looking at the sun and the moon again, she added, "Wholeness, Tom. It all comes back. It's all a circle."

She turned around, and facing the moon, which was higher now and silvering, she lifted herself up on her toes, raised her arms into the air, and cried out in a brittle yet defiant voice, "Oh, Mama, do it again!"

With those words of Savannah's, that should be the end of it, but it is not.

Each night, when practice is over and I'm driving home through the streets of Charleston, I ride with the top down on my Volkswagen convertible. It is always dark and the air is crisp with autumn and the wind is rushing through my hair. At the top of the bridge with the stars shining above the harbor, I look to the north and wish again that there were two lives apportioned to every man and woman. Behind me the city of Charleston simmers in the cold elixirs of its own incalculable beauty and before me my wife and children are waiting for me to arrive home. It is in their eyes that I acknowledge my real life, my destiny. But it is the secret life that sustains me now, and as I reach the top of that bridge I say it in a whisper, I say it as a prayer, as regret, and as praise. I can't tell you why I do it or what it means, but each night when I drive toward my southern home and my southern life, I whisper these words: "Lowenstein, Lowenstein."

A SELECTION OF NOVELS
AVAILABLE FROM BANTAM BOOKS

☐	40385 0	BREAK AND ENTER	Colin Harrison	£3.99
☐	17490 8	THE WATER IS WIDE	Pat Conroy	£2.99
☐	17489 4	THE GREAT SANTINI	Pat Conroy	£3.99
☐	17557 2	THE LORDS OF DISCIPLINE	Pat Conroy	£3.95
☐	17510 6	A GREAT DELIVERANCE	Elizabeth George	£2.99
☐	17511 4	PAYMENT IN BLOOD	Elizabeth George	£3.99
☐	17606 4	MOTIVE TO MURDER	Georgina Lloyd	£2.99
☐	17605 6	ONE WAS NOT ENOUGH	Georgina Lloyd	£2.99
☐	17602 1	SEARCH THE SHADOWS	Barbara Michaels	£2.99
☐	17599 8	SHATTERED SILK	Barbara Michaels	£2.99
☐	17694 3	SMOKE AND MIRRORS	Barbara Michaels	£3.99
☐	17204 2	THE SICILIAN	Mario Puzo	£3.95
☐	17524 6	THE SPY IN QUESTION	Tim Sebastian	£3.50
☐	40055 X	SPY SHADOW	Tim Sebastian	£3.99
☐	17493 2	FAVOURITE SON	Steve Sohmer	£3.99
☐	17697 8	THE BLOODING	Joseph Wambaugh	£3.99
☐	17555 6	ECHOES IN THE DARKNESS	Joseph Wambaugh	£3.99
☐	40154 8	LOVE OR HONOUR	Joan Barthel	£3.99